THE
DISCOVERIE
of WITCHCRAFT
by REGINALD SCOT: with
an introduction by the
Rev. Montague Summers

DOVER PUBLICATIONS, INC.
NEW YORK

This Dover edition, first published in 1972, is an unabridged and unaltered republication of the work originally published in Great Britain by John Rodker in 1930.

International Standard Book Number: 0-486-22880-0
Library of Congress Catalog Card Number: 72-79958

Manufactured in the United States of America
Dover Publications, Inc.
180 Varick Street
New York, N. Y. 10014

CONTENTS

Contents

Contents

Contents

Contents

Contents

Contents

Contents

Contents

Contents

INTRODUCTION

ACOMMON tradition, to say nothing of vulgar ignorance, has always assumed and confidently affirmed that the most prominent and responsible, as he was the most highly-placed, figure in the history of English witchcraft is King James I, whose accession from Scotland to the English throne revived and fearfully energized a furious and long unbated flood of prosecutions, a veritable *hexenhetze* not merely favoured but preached and actively directed by the new monarch himself. The chaste beams " of that bright *Occidental Star,* Queen *Elizabeth,*" had, we are assured, long since dispelled the thick and palpable clouds of darkness of so dangerous and superstitious a delusion. Witchcraft was no more accredited by her enlightened subjects; the fires set to consume the sorcerer and the satanist had long died down; it was the luckless advent of James that fanned the expiring embers into an infuriate flame, that literally sent thousands of crazy gaffers and doting beldames to torture and the stake.

In the first place, as the error is so obstinate and continues so widely to persist, it may not be impertinent parenthetically to remark that burning at the stake was never in England the punishment for a convicted witch, who had murdered by her evil arts. In England the penalty was the gallows tree; and although in Scotland and upon the Continent death by fire was almost universally the doom of the devil's votary, no single instance throughout the centuries can be quoted to show that within the confines of English jurisdiction a witch was burned. At the same time this terrible punishment was by no means unknown to English law; it was the reward of any woman who had committed either high treason (an attempt, direct or indirect upon the life of the sovran) or petty treason (the murder of a husband by a wife, the murder of a master or a mistress by a servant); for these crimes a wife or a female servant was sentenced to the stake. Thus on 10 May, 1652, Evelyn notes in his *Diary:* " Passing by Smithfield I saw a miserable creature burning who had murdered her husband." It is true that although the law made no such provision of clemency, culprits were generally first strangled at the stake by the executioner. Tennyson's grandmother saw a young widow who had killed her husband, on her way to be strangled and burned. This would be about 1760. On 18 March, 1789, Christian Bowman (*alias* Murphy) was hanged and burned at a stake at the Old Bailey for high treason "in feloniously and traitorously counterfeiting the Silver Coin of the Realm." Actually she was hanging forty minutes before the faggots were fired. The law was altered by 30 George III, c. 48 (1790), which provided that after 5 June, 1790, women under this sentence should be hanged. The exact method of execution is, however, a detail. The gross and peccant error prevails.

Even writers of some authority and some research have declared that although before the reign of James I the English trials for witchcraft "had been characterized rather by folly than ferocity, the new rule was marked by ferocious folly"; that under the Stuart king there commenced a dark and bloody period in the annals of this horrid superstition. Thus Professor G. L. Burr, *A Witch-Hunter in the Book-Shops,* after the studies of a quarter of a century quite mistakenly writes: "Fitting it is to begin with that new edition of his *Dæmonologie* with which the royal inquisitor, James of Scotland, celebrated his accession to the English throne. It was but a prelude to that new and sharper statute against witches which in that same year of 1603 disgraced the English statute-book. It was the real beginning of the persecution, not only in England, but in these transatlantic colonies." It is not altogether surprising then that this fallacy should be echoed and re-echoed again; that G. M. Trevelyan should write: "The sceptical Elizabeth, perhaps with some pity for her sex, had refused to yield when the pamphlet press called on the Government to enact fiercer laws 'not suffering a witch to live.' The outburst came with the accession of a Scottish king, who, though he rejected the best part of the spirit of Knox, was crazed beyond his English subjects with the witch-mania of Scotland and the Continent. His first Parliament created new death-laws; at once the judges and magistrates, the constables and the mob, began to hunt up the oldest and ugliest spinster who lived with her geese on the common or tottered about the village street muttering the inaudible soliloquies of second childhood." All this is, of course, so far as historical accuracy is concerned, entirely in keeping with the remaining pages of *England under the Stuarts,* but in no detail whatsoever can this misconception and misjudgement be borne out by the facts.

In the first place, under Elizabeth, anno 1563, a new Act was passed against witchcraft, and hereby death was the penalty for all who "use, practise, or exercise invocations or conjurations of evil and wicked spirits to or for any intent or purpose," a wide clause which certainly included and was meant to touch "wise women" and "white witches," that is to say, those who evoked and raised infernal, or at least mystic and equivocal, spirits, not for harming and bale, but to cure diseases of men and salve cattle, to resolve inquiries as to the future estate of the consultant or to reveal hidden treasure, ends not in themselves directly mischievous and malign. Moreover, the same statute decreed death for all who practised any art or craft of witchcraft whereby a person was killed. If any "witchcraft, enchantment, charm, or sorcery" injured (although not mortally) any human being or did damage to goods and chattels, the witch was to be punished with a year's imprisonment and a quarterly exposure in the pillory (no light sentence) for the first offence; with death for a second offence. Imprisonment and the pillory were likewise prescribed for any who should seek by art magic to discover hidden treasure or to trace stolen property, or who should thus procure unlawful love or "hurt or destroy any person in his or her body, member, or goods." A second offence in this kind was visited with lifelong incarceration, a duress without let or remittance.

It is plain that the provisions of the Elizabethan law were strictly rigid and inflexible, whilst the large number of presentments and indictments at sessions with the judgements recorded are ample evidence that the penalties were exacted to the uttermost, that the enactments were carried out with unflinching and merciless severity.

In the first year of King James' reign in England was passed the statute of 1604, which remained upon the books until 1736, and now we may well expect to find a bloody and revengeful code of Draconian terrors, a pandect breathing a barbarous and awesome malevolence. Far otherwise are the simple facts. In the main tenor, even to its phraseology, the statute of James I follows that of Elizabeth. Death as before is the penalty for the invocation or conjuration of evil spirits, for any purpose of whatsoever kind; but a clause is added making it a capital offence to "consult, covenant with, entertain, employ, feed, or reward" any such familiar, and to dig up any dead body or to use any member of a corpse for purposes of sorcery also merits the gallows. Any deed of black magic which harms but does not kill is to be punished with death on the first offence (not on the second offence as under Elizabeth); and death is substituted for lifelong imprisonment as the penalty for the confection of evil love charms, for the hurting and maiming of persons and cattle, for the practice of treasure-troving and working other spells or of malice prepense reciting hell's lurries and infernal incantations.

If one dispassionately compares and contrasts the two statutes there is little increase in severity. Since death was the reward for the evocation of a demon as under Elizabeth, assuredly the same fate was deserved by one who not merely called upon but maintained, fed, and rewarded any such diabolical agent of mischief. Unhallowed exhumation of the dead had not been specifically touched upon by the Elizabethan law, but such hideous disinterments did occur, and who would deny that the hags who desecrated cemeteries and sepulchres to use the mortal remains of those laid to sleep in the Lord for purposes of foulest sorcery were not deserving of the extremest penalty? These horrors were of no infrequent occurrence. The learned and judicious Nicolas Remy, in the Second Book and Third Chapter of his *Demonolatry*, tells us that "Witches make Evil Use of Human Corpses," and he relates among many other instances that in October 1586, at Dieuze, Anna Ruffa confessed she had assisted a witch named Lolla to dig up a corpse, which they burned to concoct a potion mingled with its charred ashes, Marie Schneider at Metzeresch disinterred an infant to utilize the grease and fat of the body; whilst the women Nichel and Besskers scraped up two corpses from the common cemetery to cut off the arms from the elbow that they might make "Hands of Glory." The admired Guazzo in his *Compendium Maleficarum* (1608) relates at length (Book II, Chapter 2) how *Witches use Human Corpses for the Murder of Men.*

In the fetid state of the common prisons, mere dens of misery and disease, during the sixteenth and seventeenth centuries, when jail fever annually carried off its toll of hundreds, and prisoners, owing to the loathsomeness of their dungeons, often died even before trial, a lifelong incarceration was equivalent to a capital sentence, and that this should have been actually pronounced from the bench was no very great change and no very great hardship. In 1579, the 4th, 5th, and 6th of July, when the Assizes were being held at Oxford, there arose such a stench and such an infection from the prisoners, that, as Webster tells us in his *Displaying of Supposed Witchcraft,* chapter xii, "The Jurors died presently: shortly after died Sir *Robert Bell*, Lord Chief Baron, Sir *Robert de Olie*, Sir *William Babington*, Mr *Weneman*, Mr *De Olie*, High Sheriff, Mr *Davers*, Mr *Farcurt*, Mr *Kirle*, Mr *Pheteplace*, Mr *Greenwood*, Mr *Foster*, Serjeant *Baram*, Mr *Stevens*, &c. There died in Oxford 300. persons, and sickned there but died in other places 200. and odd." So great was the terror that some explanation was devised to cover the scandal, but there could be no gainsaying the facts.

It is to be concluded then that, so far as severer measures prevailed, there was actually and in practice only one change in the law, namely, the infliction of the death penalty for the first, instead of the second, operation of witchcraft that maimed and injured the body even without actual loss of life.

How then, it is not impertinent to inquire, did this vulgar prejudice against King James I arise? Whence comes it that in past days the less informed and to-day the ignorant have regarded him as a monomaniacal persecutor, who, arriving from Scotland, stirred up a veritable tempest of intolerance and immanity, harrying to the death multitudes whose only crimes were decrepitude, dotage and senility?

Probably the answer is not far to seek. Imprimis, the Scottish legislation "Anentis Witchcraft," first passed by the ninth Parliament of Queen Mary in 1563, was eagerly and vehemently enforced and continuously urged by the clergy, whose pulpit denunciations of the accursed folk filled every heart with panic and dismay. In 1590 occurred one of the most famous cases in the whole annals of witchcraft, the trial of Geillis Duncan, Agnes Sampson, John Fian, Barbara Napier, Euphemia McCalyan, and the North Berwick coven. Over seventy persons were implicated in this affair, and we know that there was a deep-laid and widespread conspiracy, high treason being mingled with the sorcery. The brain which contrived and the hidden hand which directed these plots were those of Francis Stewart, Earl of Bothwell, who was aiming at the throne. James, naturally, was intensely interested in the confessions of the criminals, and he attended their examinations in person, himself asking them nimble questions and receiving their depositions, which touched him so nearly.

Again, after he had occupied the English throne for some nine years, there took place the well-known Lancashire trials, when nineteen persons were arraigned, of whom eight were acquitted. Ten were hanged, and one, Margaret Pearson, was sentenced to the pillory. Perhaps, because of its romantic setting, and because of the masterpiece of that great novelist, Harrison Ainsworth, a fine piece of writing which made its first appearance in serial form in the *Sunday Times* of 1848, and was issued by Colburn in three volumes, 1849, not to mention Thomas Potts' *The Wonderfvl Discoverie of Witches In the Covntie of Lancaster*, published in 1613, this affair has attained a celebrity in the annals of English witchcraft which seems out of all proportion to its actual importance. It is true that in 1633-4 the Pendle tradition was notoriously revived, that there was a recrudescence of the most resounding scandals when young Robinson set the whole county aflame with his lies, and seventeen suspected persons were tried and condemned, only to be reprieved by King Charles I. Combining the two incidents for dramatic purposes, Heywood and Brome produced their " Well Received Comedy" *The Late Lancashire Witches* at the Globe in 1634, and Shadwell used the same material for his *The Lancashire Witches* given at Dorset Garden in the autumn of 1681. Although they may have been, as Dryden tartly remarked, "without Doubt the most *insipid* Jades that ever flew upon a stage," the play remained popular until well-nigh the middle of the eighteenth century, and as late as 1782 Charles Dibdin's pantomime, *The Lancashire Witches; or, The Distresses of Harlequin,* was having a vast winter success at the Circus.

By such adventitious literary circumstance the tradition crystallized; and be it noted it was always to the reign of James I that the events were romantically referred.

Moreover, King James' authorship of a famous treatise, *Dæmonologie, in Forme of a Dialogue, Divided into three Bookes,* Edinburgh, 1597 (re-issued in London, 1603), has been taken to prove that the royal scribe was the most furious of persecutors, who not content with his own active labours, industriously compiled a manual for the use and guidance of other inquisitors, since had not his zeal blazed to madness he would assuredly never have penned such a piece. The book was certainly inspired by the notorious case of the North Berwick coven, as also by many subsequent trials which followed fast during the next seven years; but it is a great mistake to suppose that either in scope, authority, or importance the *Dæmonologie* is for a moment to be compared with the classic volumes of Boguet, Remy or De Lancre. In England the work, as was natural, attained a certain influence and was employed by many officials as a text-book of the subject. But it added nothing new either in exposition or in argument. As Gardiner has well said, James "had only echoed opinions which were accepted freely by the multitude, and were tacitly admitted without inquiry by the first intellects of the day." In reading this shrewd dialogue one is often surprised by the moderation and reserve with which the author states his case. It has been observed that "some of the talk is rank folly and (quite unconsciously) profane to loot. . . . Perhaps we might sum up the matter by saying that the

xxii

treatise is able rather than profound. It is rather ' the small clack of a Pistolet ' than ' the rummishing shot of a Cannon.' "

It is not improbable that the reputation of King James as a hunter and harrier of witches may in the first place be due to Bishop Hutchinson, who in his *Historical Essay Concerning Witch-craft*, Chapter xiv, certainly gives it as his opinion that James was a " Mover and Director " in these matters. However, Hutchinson was careful to speak with reserve; but the many following writers who repeated and enlarged upon his words unfortunately forgot the reserve, and surmise became assertion.

Mr. L'Estrange Ewen, who has examined the public records and the gaol delivery rolls with singular care and the most laborious exactitude, does not hesitate to say that " So far as can be estimated from existing records, there were more trials in forty-two years of the reign of Elizabeth than during the entire [seventeenth] century."

The *Dæmonologie* of King James was, in fact, largely directed " *against the damnable opinions of two principally in an age, whereof the one called* SCOT *an Englishman, is not ashamed in publike print to deny that ther can be such a thing as Witch-craft: and so mainteines the old error of the Sadducees, in denying of spirits. The other called* VVIERVS, *a German Phisition, sets out a publick apologie for al these craftes-folkes, whereby, procuring for their impunitie, he plainely bewrayes himselfe to have bene one of that profession.*"

Reginald Scot was the son of Richard, the youngest of the three sons of Sir John Scot who died in 1533. Richard Scot married Mary, daughter of George Whetenall, whose father was Sheriff of Kent in 1527, and whose family had long resided at Hextall's Place, near Maidstone. Of Richard Scot little is known, but he certainly died before December, 1554, since his decease is mentioned in the will of his brother Sir Reginald, who died on the 16th of that month. By this will Sir Reginald, failing his own issue (which did not occur), left his real estate " unto Rainolde Scotte, son and heire of my brother Richard Scotte dec^d." Mary, the widow of Richard Scott, married *en secondes noces* Fulke Onslow, Clerk of the Parliaments, whom she predeceased on 8th October, 1582, and was buried in Hatfield Church, Herts.

Reginald Scot was born in or before 1538, and, if we may accept the statement of Anthony à Wood in the *Athenae Oxonienses*, " at about 17 years of age was sent to *Oxon*, particularly, as it seems, to *Hart* hall, where several of his Country-men and name studied in the latter end of K. *Hen*. 8 and in the reign of *Ed. 6.* &c. Afterwards he retired to his native County [Kent] without the honour of a degree, and settled at *Smeeth*, where he found great incouragement in his studies from his kinsman Sir *Thos. Scot*. About which time taking to himself a Wife, he gave himself up solely to solid reading, to the perusing of obscure authors that had by the generality of Scholars been neglected, and at times of leisure to husbandry and gardening."

Hart Hall was originally nothing more than a boarding-house for scholars of the University, which passed into the hands of one Elias de Hertford, whence it derived its name, *Aula Ceruina*. This would have been between 1261 and 1284. In the fourteenth century the Hall was tenanted by a body of scholars supported by Glastonbury Abbey, and at the dissolution a pension of £16 13s. 4d. was paid to the University for the support of five scholars at Hart Hall. After many vicissitudes into which it is hardly necessary to enter, Hart Hall, in 1740, under the famous Dr. Newton, who as Hearne maliciously wrote, was "commonly said to be Founder-mad," became Hertford College. This institution, however, collapsed on the death of the fourth Principal, Dr. Bernard Hodgson, and presently the University closed the building. In 1874 was founded the present Hertford College, which may be said to include Hart Hall, Arthur Hall, Black Hall, and Cat Hall, which four Hospices were comprised within the limits of the present buildings that take the name from the senior and most important. Among distinguished alumni of Hart Hall were Selden, Bishop Ken, and Sir Henry Wotton, although in fact the two latter merely resided here whilst waiting for vacancies at New College. Charles James Fox was a Gentleman Commoner of the College (Hart Hall) from 1764–1765 during the tutorship of Newcome, afterwards Archbishop of Armagh.

The "right worshipfull" Sir Thomas Scot, the kinsman who gave Reginald Scot great encouragement in his studies, and to whom with four others *The Discouerie of Witchcraft* is dedicated, was the son and successor of Sir Reginald, who died on the 16th October, 1554. He was a man of considerable intelligence and won no small repute by his energies on behalf of the shire. He was deputy-lieutenant of his county, sheriff of Kent in 1576, and foremost in the local movements of the day. Thus amongst other activities he was a Commissioner for drain-ing and improving Romney Marsh, and a little later Super-intendent of the reconstruction of Dover Harbour, concerning which business several of his letters may be found in the State Calendars. By his first wife, Emmeline Kempe, he was the father of seventeen children. He died on the 30th December,

1594, and this event was celebrated in various copies of verses more distinguished for piety than poetry. It is probable that Sir Thomas bore the expenses of his cousin, Reginald, at Hart Hall.

On the 11th of October, 1568, the following entry occurs in the Registers of Brabourne: " Mr. Reignold Scott and Jane Cobbe were maryed the xi^{th} of October 1568." The Cobbes were an old yeoman family long resident at Cobbe's Place in the adjoining parish of Aldington. The only issue (that survived) of this marriage was a daughter, Elizabeth, afterwards married to Sackville Turnor. In 1602 this lady is said to be " 28 et amplius."

In 1574 Reginald Scot published his first work, *A Perfect Platforme of a Hoppe-Garden*, which is said to be the earliest treatise that advocates the culture of the hop in England, and wherein the whole subject is thoroughly discussed in a practical manner. A second edition was called for in 1576, and a third in 1578. " From these we can date the commencements of hop-harvests in Kent."

According to the Inquisition *post mortem* of Lady Winifred Rainsford, which was taken on 20th March, 1575, Sir Thomas Scot and his brothers are declared to be co-heirs with Reginald of the lands held by the deceased lady in gavelkind, the sons having one half, and Reginald the other. This moiety he subsequently appears to have lost, as there is no mention of such property in his will, whilst he disposes of the lands " Lyinge in Aldington . . . Ruckinge . . . and Sellenge" to his second wife, Alice, and his lands in Romney Marsh and the lease of Brabourne Rectory to his daughter, Elizabeth Turnor.

When Reginald Scot's first wife died and when he remarried are facts which have been unascertained, but it is certain that his second marriage could not have taken place at earliest before the winter of 1584. Moreover, nothing beyond the few particulars which may be gathered from Scot's will are known concerning this lady. Her christian name was Alice; she was a widow with a daughter by her former husband; she possessed some land, either in her own right or inherited from her first husband. Scot bequeaths " to my daughter in Lawe Marie Collyar six poundes thirteene shillings four pence to be bestowed in app[ar]ell," but whether Collier was the name of Mary's husband, or whether she was unmarried and her mother was thus Alice Collier is not to be decided. Scot's will was made on the 15th September, 1599, and proved on the following 22nd November. A copy (not the original document) is preserved in the Principal Registry of the Probate,

Divorce, and Admiralty Division of the High Court of Justice, whence it was printed by Dr. Brinsley Nicholson. To this is appended a document stating that Alicia Scott, relicta, and Elizabetha Turnor, als Scott, filia naturalis et legitima, had contended before certain functionaries, who are named, concerning the provisions of the will of which probate was granted on 22nd November, 1599, as aforesaid. The subject of the dispute is not recorded.

With regard to further details of Scot's life, we know that he was collector of subsidies for the lathe of Shepway in 1586–87, an office which brought him a salary of forty shillings. In the documents he is twice termed *armiger,* that is to say Esquire. Thomas Ady in his *A Candle in the Dark,* 1656 (reissued as *A Perfect Discovery of Witches,* 1661), a book which endorses the opinions of and frequently refers to *The Discouerie of Witchcraft,* tells us (p. 87) that Scot " was a student in the laws and learned in the *Roman* Laws." Moreover, Scot's last will and testament, made, ordained, and written " wth myne owne hande," is drawn up in exactest legal phraseology by one who had been completely trained and exercised in the law. The Rev. Joseph Hunter is certainly correct when in his *Chorus Vatum* he states that Scot was made a Justice of the Peace, and the magistracy may safely be held to have been conferred at some date between 1578 and 1584.

The Dedications to the *Hoppe Garden* and to the *Discouerie* are addressed to judges of the Ecclesiastical and Civil Courts, whilst the legal aspect of the latter book is so marked that in the editions of 1651 and 1665 it is especially said to contain matters " very necessary to be known for the undeceiving of Judges, Justices, and Juries," particularly " before they pass Sentence upon Poor, Miserable, and Ignorant People." Scot assisted when Margaret Symons of Brencheley was tried at the Rochester assizes on the 3rd July, 1581, and he was obviously present in some official capacity. He himself had examined several witnesses and cross-questioned the accused woman, who was found not guilty.

Reginald Scot died on the 9th October, 1599, at Smeeth; and, according to Anthony à Wood, " was buried among his Ancestors in the Church " there. Other chroniclers say that he was interred at the side of and adjacent to Sir Thomas Scot's tomb in Brabourne Church, which monument, according to Philipot in his Kent Notes (*Harl. MS.* 3917, fol. 78a) he himself erected.

It has been asked how Scot came " to inquire into and

write so strongly against witchcraft"? But the answer is assuredly simple. Here we have a man of legal training, an active man in his own circuit, a man full of little businesses and yet of leisure to give to "solid reading" and "the perusing of obscure authors," a man who had a great reputation in his own circles as a scholar and a bibliophile, above all a man of intensely sceptical turn of mind. The general opinion of the day was greatly exercised by the subject of witchcraft. Pierre Le Loyer, in his *IIII Livres des Spectres* (1586), a second edition of which appeared in 1605, and which was that year translated into English (from the *editio princeps*) by one Z. Jones, speaks of the great hold the problems of the supernatural had over the minds of men in every walk and rank. "Of all the common and familiar subjects of conversation that are entered upon in company of things remote from nature and cut off from the senses, there is none so ready to hand, none so usual, as that of visions of Spirits, and whether that said of them is true. It is the topic that people most readily discuss and on which they linger the longest because of the abundance of examples, the subject being fine and pleasing and the discussion the least tedious that can be found."

Witchcraft in particular was not merely a matter for speculation, but it was a dangerous charge constantly brought at the assizes, an offence which, although yet argued and even disputed, carried in generality the penalty of death. Reginald Scot had, as we have seen, interested himself in the trial of the Kentish witch, Margaret Symons, but undoubtedly his main inspiration for inditing his *Discouerie* was the trial of the witches of S. Osyth's, just as a century and a quarter later the case of Jane Wenham of Walkern, Herts, suggested to Dr. Francis Hutchinson his *Historical Essay concerning Witchcraft*, 1718.

S. Osyth's or S. Oses is a hamlet to the north-east of Chelmsford, a district long infested by covens of witches. This gang was discovered almost as it might appear by accident when Grace Thurlow, "a poor and needie woman," laid information before the magistrate concerning one Ursley Kemp, *alias* Gray. When the accused was committed on ample evidence to the assizes she appeared before Justice Brian Darcy, a man of sound common sense and vigour, who, having straitly examined her, soon perceived that he had to deal with no ordinary malice and malignancy. He probed the black business to the very heart. Eventually he caught in his kiddle some sixteen persons all found to be deeply involved, of whom thirteen, as it was proved beyond all question, were held to be guilty of murder owing to their sorceries. It is uncertain how many paid the penalty of their crimes, but according to some accounts the thirteen were executed. Scot briefly notes: "At S. Osses 17. or 18. witches cōdemned at once," but his accuracy in this, as in other particulars, may be doubted. A full account of the whole case, which resounded throughout England and was long remembered, may be found in Montague Summers' *The Geography of Witchcraft*.

That Reginald Scot's *The Discouerie of Witchcraft* is both historically and as a literary curiosity a book of the greatest value and interest, no one, I suppose, would dispute or deny. Elizabethan drama and poetry are informed and as it were saturated by the supernatural. The demonology and ghost-lore of the time are ever sensibly felt, not as a mere fantastical or mythical convention, but as a very real and deeply conceived spiritual background. The ghost, one of the most important figures of the Elizabethan theatre, soon flung off his Senecan cerements and became a vivid phantom, a thing of terror and awe, a spectre that might stand by the side of anyone of the audience in the lonely watches of the night, that might chill with fear any wayfarer upon his solitary path. It were superfluous to mention the ghosts of Shakespeare, and it is allowed by all scholars that Scot's *Discouerie* was one of Shakespeare's source-books. One would need to give a lengthy catalogue even barely to name the plays by Shakespeare and other dramatists wherein magicians and witches play a leading part, wherein the dark mysteries of the warlock and the midnight hag are exhibited to the spectators. *Macbeth; The Witch; The Witch of Edmonton, A known True Story; The Late Lancashire Witches;* Jonson's *Masque of Queens,* and a score beside will be readily remembered. I have dealt with the whole subject in "The Witch in Dramatic Literature," the final chapter of my *History of Witchcraft*.

There have been named as the three principal source-books for Elizabethan spiritualism: King James' *Dæmonologie*; the translation (1572) by R. H. of Lavater's *De Spectris* as *Of ghostes and spirites walking by nyght;* and Scot's *A Discourse upon diuels and spirits* which concludes the *Discouerie*. In one restricted sense this is true; but it should be remarked that although these volumes were no doubt prominent, men of culture and learning were drinking an accurate knowledge from less narrow channels, from the *Malleus Maleficarum,* from Nider and Lorenzo Anania, from Bodin and Paul Grilland.

It must steadily be borne in mind that the turbidity of a pseudo-intellectual revolt had attempted—of necessity all in vain —to sweep away and obliterate the eternal landmarks of truth.

That complex code of obfuscated contradictions, yet universally subscribed to by the clergy of the Established Church and as universally scouted, " Articles agreed upon by the Archbishops and Bishops of both Provinces and the Whole Clergy in the Convocation holden at London in the year 1562," had, amongst other impious rejections of divine revelation, declared (XXII) that " The Romish Doctrine concerning Purgatory . . . is a fond thing vainly invented, and grounded upon no warranty of Scripture but rather repugnant to the Word of God." Men were bewildered and bemused. The old familiar facts of life and death were gone, and who was to teach them these new toys and trumperies? It would, I suppose, have been as impossible to have obtained in the days of Elizabeth a consonant consensus of opinion from the Anglican bishops and clergy with regard to the estate of the soul after death as it were bootless to make such inquiry as to the " mind " of the Church of England in these matters to-day.

And so some men wisely but tacitly continued to hold fast the earlier doctrine, and some flung themselves into rank infidelity. Amongst the latter we number Reginald Scot.

Unlike our modernists, Scot scarce dared exhibit himself as a complete agnostic. " Truelie I denie not that there are witches," he ingenuously cries in his Epistle " To the Readers," and forthwith expends some five hundred and sixty pages to prove that witches and all their works are but spleenful fantasy or cozenage and a chouse.

In *A discourse of divels and spirits*, Chapter XXXII, we have: " This is mine opinion concerning this present argument. First that divels are spirits, and no bodies. . . . And that the divell, whether he be manie or one (for by the waie you shall understand, that he is so spoken of in the scriptures, as though there were but one, and sometimes as though one were manie legions, the sense whereof I have alreadie declared according to *Calvins* opinion, he is a creature made by God, and that for vengance, as it is written in *Eccl.* 39. verse 28 : and of himselfe naught, though emploied by God to necessarie and good purposes." These may seem to be very discreet and tempered words, but they are of purpose smoky and obscure, so it is no easy matter to catch their precise drift. Which is precisely the intention of the writer. That they are flatly contradicting of the Scriptures is plain enough, for, to quote only two passages from many in the Gospels : " And he healed many that were sick of divers diseases, and cast out many devils ; and suffered not the devils to speak, because they knew him " (S. Mark i. 34, A.V.) :

"And unclean spirits, when they saw him, fell down before him, and cried, saying, Thou art the Son of God" (S. Mark iii. 11, A.V.). But perhaps the writers of the Gospels boasted a "holie ignorance," a phrase some mad fanatic used of S. Paul, words echoed with delight by Scot. Yet we might at once without wasting further thought very well realize that if Calvin's opinion is to be quoted the Bible will be as flouted and contemned as by the veriest Modernist of them all. Calvin (*Discourse of divels and spirits*, XXXI) denied "corporall assaults" of the devil, or "his attempts upon our bodies." Yet it is written: "One of the multitude answered and said, Master, I have brought unto thee my son, which hath a dumb spirit; And wheresoever he taketh him, he teaseth him: and he foameth, and gnasheth with his teeth, and pineth away: . . . When Jesus saw that the people came running together, he rebuked the foul spirit, saying unto him, Thou dumb and deaf spirit, I charge thee, come out of him, and enter no more into him. And the spirit cried, and rent him sore, and came out of him: and he was as one dead; insomuch that many said, He is dead. But Jesus took him by the hand, and lifted him up; and he arose" (S. Mark ix, A.V.).

It has been poised that the fatal flaw in Scot's argument is comprised in the following circumstance. Whilst allowing the existence of evil spirits, he tells us that we know nothing about them and their activities, yet it is most certain that they can neither appear to men, traffic with any person, nor affect mankind in any way, that they do not produce the phenomena and performances ascribed to their agency. Hence these marvellous happenings are the result of chance, are legerdemain and prestidigitation, or fraud and concerted delusion. Accordingly we find that many chapters of the *Discouerie* are concerned with common jugglers' tricks, *To cut halfe your nose asunder, and to heale it againe presentlie without anie salve; To put a ring through your cheeks;* (xiii, 23); with more of the same kind which, however ingenious and interesting, are utterly impenitent and inconsequent in any serious sense.

De non apparentibus et non existentibus eadem est lex says the old apophthegm. But this hardly applies here. Upon a careful investigation it appears that the flaw in Scot's argument is not that admitting the existence of evil spirits he declared that we know nothing of them or in relation to them save that they do not and cannot intermingle with the affairs of men, a sufficiently illogical position, but rather that although for caution's sake covering his atheism with the thinnest veneer, in fact he wholly and essentially denies the supernatural.

Accordingly we are not surprised to encounter a heap of irrelevant matter in his treatise. Surely the first chapter of his Eighth Book is a clear announcement of atheism : *That miracles are ceased.* Need we then be surprised at his tedious railing against popery; his citation of poetical authorities; his scoffing recitation of old wives' charms; his excerpts from the Psalms and from the Rituale; his sneering quotation from old lectionaries of the legenda of S. Margaret and S. Katherine, and *how S. Martine conjured the divell?* Yet the treatise is valuable; it gives us the complete armoury of the atheist. But, Good Lord! what feeble rusted weapons!

The catalogue of authorities, the two hundred and twenty-four " forren authors " and twenty-three English " used in this Booke," when Bale is jumbled with S. Jerome and Chaucer with Ovid and Vergil, may appear a formidable array, but so far as I have tested them the citations are at second-hand, divorced from their context, and not patent of the meaning Scot ascribes and infers.

The treatise is built upon Weyer, a disciple of Cornelius Agrippa. But Weyer was more sensible than Scot. He at least recognized that Satan and the demons have extensive powers; that they may and do interfere with the welfare of mankind; and he was convinced that persons such as Faust were indeed warlocks, well versed in black arts and damnable crafts, deserving a supreme punishment. He argued, it is true, that many of the feats ascribed to witches were pure fantasy; that the miserable creatures were inveigled and deluded by the arch-fiend. Hysteria, hallucination, account for much; but there is a horrid foundation of fact, of evil and sorcery.

So far we may perhaps allow, although I must subscribe to Casaubon, that the intention of Weyer " was not so much to favour *women*, as the *Devil* himself, with whom, it is to be feared, that he was too well acquainted."

Of Scot a cautious and circumstantial investigator has written : " In 1584 there came from the press his *Discouerie of Witchcraft*, a subject which he seems to have studied, and concerning which he had in a somewhat desultory fashion been collecting notes for a long period. It is obvious that the immediate occasion of publication was the S. Osees affair, and the greater part of the *Discouerie* was most certainly written in 1583, in some haste, no doubt, to strike lustily whilst the iron was hot. For years before he put pen to paper he had been investigating on his account alleged cases of Witchcraft, attending trials, closely questioning magistrates and divines. His mind was naturally sceptical, and in religion he would be now-a-days a pseudo-scientific modernist. That is to say, he was utterly without imagination, a very dull, narrow, and ineffective little soul. When he has exposed certain egregious impostures of contemporary date, enlarged upon card tricks and prestidigitation at inordinate length, attributed the appearance of Samuel in the cave of Endor to ventriloquism, and more than hinted that possession in the New Testament merely means disease, this myopic squireen deems that the matter is settled once and for all. It is true that he gives us an ample bibliography, over two hundred Latin and a couple of dozen English titles, but he came to the subject with a deeply prejudiced mind and was determined not to find in any author other than what he sought. Had he dared, Scot would have openly denied the supernatural, of that there can be no doubt; and to-day he might have shone in the company of Mr. Clodd and Mr. McCabe."

This is temperately and fairly stated. One can hardly suppose that any could wish seriously to echo Scot's sophistries as philosophical arguments. None the less, as has already been remarked, *The Discouerie of Witchcraft* remains, and will remain, a work of the greatest historical and literary interest, an original with which every student of Elizabethan literature must needs be familiar and well-acquaint.

MONTAGUE SUMMERS.

In Festo B.M.V. uulgo Del Conforto : 1930.

A BIBLIOGRAPHICAL NOTE UPON SCOT'S "DISCOUERIE"

The discouerie / of witchcraft, / Wherein the lewde dealing of witches / *and witchmongers is notablie detected, the* / knauerie of coniurors, the im- / pietie of inchan- / *tors, the follie of soothsaiers, the impudent fals-* / hood of cousenors, the infidelitie of atheists, / *the pestilent practises of Pythonists, the* / curiositie of figure casters, the va- / *nitie of dreamers, the begger-* / lie art of Alcu- / mystrie, / The abhomination of idolatrie, the hor- / *rible art of poisoning, the vertue and power of* / naturall magike, and all the conueiances / *of Legierdemaine and iuggling are deciphered:* / and many other things opened, which / *haue long lien hidden, howbeit* / verie neces- / sarie to / be knowne. / Heerevnto is added a treatise vpon the / *nature and substance of spirits and diuels,* / &c.: all latelie written / *by Reginald Scot* / Esquire. / 1. Iohn. 4, 1. / *Beleeue not euerie spirit, but trie the spirits, whether they are* / *of God; for manie false prophets are gone* / out into the world, &c. / 1584.

Editio princeps. Black letter. Not entered in the Stationers' Regis- ters. The name of the printer appears only at the end of the book, without date or place of address;—"Imprinted at London by / *William Brome.* Although usually described (*e.g.* by Graesse) as a quarto the signatures are in eights.

Cole, as quoted in Bliss's edition of the *Athenae Oxonienses* says: "See a full account of this curious book, as Mr. Oldys calls it, in his *British Librarian,* p. 213. All the copies of the first edit., 1584, that could be found were burnt by order of K. James I, an author on the other side of the question."—Vid. *Hist. Dictionary,* sub voce "Scot."

["*Reginaldus Scotus, Anglus, tractatum de Incantamentis* scripsit, in quo plerasque traditiones de Magia Melancholiae, & morbis variis, aut artibus histrionicis adscribit."] "Hunc in Anglia publica auctoritate combustum, sibi autem nunquam fuisse visum refert Thomasius de crimine magiae 83." *Vide* [J.V.] Vogt., *Cat. Libr. rar.,* p. 617 [1713].

The book in question, to which a somewhat inaccurate reference was here made, is a quarto:] "Theses inaugurales de crimine magiae, quas in Academia Regia Fridericiana praeside D. Christiano Thomasio pro licentia summos in utroque jure honores et doctoralia privilegia legitime consequendi—solemni eruditorum disquisitioni submittit M. Joannes Reiche, ampliss. ordinis Philosoph. Adjunctus ad. d. 12 Novembr. CIƆIƆCCI. Halae Magd. etc." Reiche refers to an earlier authority, "Gisberti Voetii Theologiae in Acad. Ultrajectina Pro- fessoris Selectarum Disputationum Theologicarum. Pars tertia . . . Ultrajecti, Ex Officina Johannis à Waesberge, Anno CIƆIƆCLIX." On p. 564 is the following account of Scot: "*Reginaldus Scot* nobilis Anglus magiae crimen aperte negavit, & ex professo oppugnavit, omnes ejus mirables effectus aut ad melancoliam, aliosve naturales morbos, aut ad artem, industriam, & agilitatem hominum figmentis & prae- stigiis suis illudentium, aut ad stolidas imaginationes, dictorum magorum referens. Ejus liber tit. *Discoverie of Withcraft* [*sic*] in Anglia combustus est; quem nominatim etiam perstringit Sereniss. Magnae Briantniae [*sic*] *Rex Jacobus in Daemonologia*, eumque tangit diffusissimae eruditionis Theologus *Johannes Raynoldus, in cens. lib. Apocryph. tom. 2 praelect.* 169. In eundem, sed innominatum calamum strinxit eximius & subacti judicii Theologus, *Guilelm. Perkinsus in tractatu de Bascanologia. Pars libri* istius *Reginaldi Scot elenctica* (nam reliqua in editione Anglicana conjurationes continebat,) in Belgicum idioma translata est, ante annos aliquot Lugd. Batav. per Thomam Basson: ex illius libri lectione, seu fonte perenni, non pauci ab illo tempore docti & indocti in Belgio fluctuare, & de Magia σκεωτικιζειν ac λιβερτινιζειν, (ut Libertinis & Semilibertinis infesta est patria nostra) quin eo ignorantiae saepe prolabi, ut non inique illis applicari potuerit, quod Sereniss. *Rex Jacobus in Daemonologiâ* subdito suo Reginaldo Scot: *esse quasi novos Sadducæos:* cum omnes diabolorum operationes & apparitiones suaviter exsibilant: tanquam anicularum, aut superstitionis meticulosæ phantasmata ac fabellas. Sunt & alii sed pessimi magiæ patroni, qui ad Deum & divina charismata seu gratias gratis datas, aut ad angelos bonos, operationes magicas referunt."

Although no contemporary English accounts of or references to the burning of Scot's book have, I believe, as yet been traced, there can be no doubt that the *Discouerie* was indeed publicly consigned to the flames by the common hangman. Not a few treatises, known and unknown, were ordered to be thus officially destroyed during the reign of James I, and no record of these holocausts was preserved. It seems certain that, as Gisbert Voet tells us, the king would have been particularly eager to obliterate and exterminate a volume so prejudicial to his own royal dignity both as a theologian and an author. It is probable that the great rarity of the first edition is in no small measure due to this destruction of all such copies as were found.

The translation of Scot of which Voet makes mention is a Dutch version made and edited by Thomas Basson, an English stationer resident at Leyden. The book is a duodecimo, 1609. The dedication, dated 10th January of that year, is to the Curators of the University and to the burgomasters of the town. The work was originally undertaken at the request of the professorial boards of law and history. A second and corrected edition, published by G. Basson, son of Thomas Basson, was printed at Leyden in 1637. The dedication is dated 8th May, 1637, Amsterdam. Dr. W. N. du Rieu, Librarian of the University of Leyden, informed Dr. Brinsley Nicholson that the omissions consisted of "some formulæ of malediction and other matters which would more interest English readers."

In 1651 was produced a new edition of the *Discouerie*, a quarto, which again was not entered in the Stationers' Registers. There are three issues with three slightly different title-pages. The first has—LONDON / Printed by *Richard Cotes.* 1651. The second has—*Printed by* R. C. *and are to be sold by* Giles Calvert, *dwelling at the* / *Black Spread-Eagle at the West-end of* Pauls. 1651. On both title-pages these words are separated by a rule from the rest. Otherwise they are identical, even to the misprint "superstious." The third issue has below the rule: *London* / Printed by E. [not R.] Cotes and are to be sold by Thomas Williams at the / Bible in *Little Britain* 1654. / "SCOTS" is here printed without the apostrophe; "men," "women," "children," and "treatise" have

xxxiv

capital initials; on both occasions "Devils" is given, not "Divels"; and on the last line but one above the rule ends "De-" not "Divels." The misprint "superstious" is duly corrected. It is plain that Thomas Williams had acquired Calvert's remainder, or at least the set-up type, and. then issued the sheets, prefixing a new title-page of his own, printed by E. Cotes.

SCOT'S / Discovery of VVitchcraft: / Proving / The common opinions of Witches con- / tracting with Divels, Spirits, or Familiars; and / their power to kill, torment, and consume the bodies of / men women, and children, or other creatures by diseases / or otherwise; their flying in the Air, &c. To be but imaginary / Erronious conceptions and novelties; / WHEREIN ALSO, / The lewde unchristian practises of Witchmongers, upon aged / melancholy, ignorant, and superstious people in extorting con- / fessions, by inhumane terrors and tortures is notably detected. /

ALSO {
The knavery and confederacy of Conjurors.
The impious blasphemy of Inchanters.
The imposture of Soothsayers, and Infidelity of Atheists.
The delusion of Pythonists, Figure-casters, Astrologers, and vanity of Dreamers.
The fruitlesse beggerly art of Alchimistry.
The horrible art of Poisoning and all the tricks and conveyances of juggling and Liegerdemain are fully deciphered.
}

With many other things opened that have long lain hidden: though / very necessary to be known for the undeceiving of Judges, Justices, / and Juries, and for the preservation of poor, aged, deformed, ignorant / people; frequently taken, arraigned, condemned and executed for / Witches, when according to a right understanding, and a good / conscience, Physick, Food, and necessaries should be / administered to them. / Whereunto is added, a treatise upon the nature, and substance of Spirits and Divels, / &c. all written and published in *Anno* 1584. by *Reginald Scot*, Esquire. / [rule] / *LONDON*, / Printed by *Richard Cotes*. 1651. / [rule] /.

Again without entry in the Stationers' Registers there was issued, in 1665, the third edition of the *Discouerie*. This is a folio, measuring 10¼ inches by 6⅛ inches, although actually the sheets are in sixes. No doubt the occasion of this reprint was the famous trial at Bury S. Edmunds in March, 1665, when Amy Duny and Rose Cullender, two widows of Lowestoft, were indicted for witches. Sir Thomas Browne, being a "person of great knowledge," was desired by the court to give his opinion, "and he was clearly of opinion that the persons were bewitched." The accused were condemned to death and were duly hanged on Monday, 17th March. The presiding judge was Sir Matthew Hale, chief baron of the exchequer.

For the edition of 1665 the title-page was elaborately re-written.

THE / Discovery of Witchcraft: / *PROVING*, / That the Compacts and Contracts of WITCHES / with *Devils* and all *Infernal Spirits* or *Familiars*, are but / Erroneous Novelties and Imaginary Conceptions. / *Also discovering*, How far their power extendeth, in Killing, Tormenting, / Consuming, or Curing the bodies of Men, Women, Children, or Animals, / by Charms, Philtres, Periapts, Pentacles, Curses, and Conjurations. / *WHEREIN LIKEWISE* / The Unchristian Practices and

Inhumane Dealings of / *Searchers* and *Witch-tryers* upon *Aged, Melancholy,* and *Superstitious* / people, in extorting Confessions by Terrors and Tortures, / and in devising false Marks and Symptoms, are notably Detected. / And the Knavery of Juglers, Conjurers, Charmers, Soothsayers, Figure-Casters, / *Dreamers, Alchymists* and *Philterers;* with many other things / that have long lain hidden, fully Opened and Deciphered. / *ALL WHICH* / Are very necessary to be known for the undeceiving of *Judges, Justices,* / and *Jurors,* before they pass Sentence upon Poor, Miserable and Ignorant People; / who are frequently Arraigned, Condemned, and Executed for *Witches* and *Wizzards.* / *IN SIXTEEN BOOKS.* / [rule] / By REGINALD SCOT *Esquire.* / [rule] / Whereunto is added / An excellent Discourse of the *Nature* and *Substance* / OF / DEVILS and SPIRITS, / *IN TWO BOOKS*: / The *First* by the aforesaid *Author:* The *Second* now / added in this *Third Edition,* as Succedaneous to the *former,* / and conducing to the compleating of the *Whole Work:* / With *Nine Chapters* at the beginning of the *Fifteenth. Book* / of the DISCOVERY. / [rule] / *LONDON:* / Printed for *A. Clark,* and are to be sold by *Dixy Page* at the *Turks-Head* / in *Cornhill* near the *Royall Exchange,* 1665. / [double rule] /.

It were merest conjection to inquire who may have been the author of this second book of the "Discourse on Devils and Spirits." But it is certainly important to remark that this tractate is entirely at variance with the preceding chapters and the whole tenor of Scot's work. It is indeed nothing more or less than a brief necromantic manual giving explicit directions *How to raise up the Ghost of one that hath hanged himself; How to Conescrate all manner of Circles, Fumigations, Fire, Magical Garments, and Utensills; How to Conjure the Spirit* Balkin *the Master of* Luridan; with other runes, charms, and discourses such as might have found a fitting place in Barrett's *Magus.* Anything more contrary to Scot and more antidotal could not well be conceived.

It is interesting to note that on Monday, 12th August, 1667, Pepys has: "to my bookseller's, and did buy Scott's Discourse of Witches." On Saturday, 24th November, 1666, he had set himself "to read the late printed discourse of witches by a member of Gresham College," that is to say, Glanvil's *Philosophical Considerations touching Witches and Witchcraft,* published in 1666 and reissued in 1667. It is better known in its later and augmented form, *Saducismus Triumphatus,* 1681. Pepys writes: "the discourse being well writ, in good stile, but methinks not very convincing." When on Monday, 15th June, 1663, he dined at the Trinity House, "Both at and after dinner we had great discourses of the nature and power of spirits, and whether they can animate dead bodies; in all which, as of the general appearance of spirits, my Lord Sandwich is very scepticall. He says the greatest warrants that ever he had to believe any, is the present appearing of the Devil in Wiltshire, much of late talked of, who beats a drum up and down. There are books of it, and, they say, very true; but my Lord observes, that though he do answer to any tune that you will play to him upon another drum, yet one tune he tried to play and could not; which makes him suspect the whole; and I think it is a good argument." The reference is, of course, to the famous haunting by an invisible drummer of the house of Mr. Mompesson at Tedworth, Wilts.

The Whig dramatist Thomas Shadwell in his notorious play *The*

Lancashire Witches, And Tegue o Divelly The Irish Priest, produced at the Duke's Theatre in the autumn of 1681, has made some use of the *Discouerie of Witches* and even reproduces Scot's very words, just as an earlier poet, Middleton, had exactly conveyed certain striking phrases from Scot's pages in his drama *The Witch.*

In 1886 a reprint of the first edition of 1584 of the *Discouerie of Witches* was issued *curâ* Dr. Brinsley Nicholson, who furnished an Introduction and excursuses: 250 copies only were done, and a list is given of seventy-four original subscribers. The book is now not easily to be procured.

THE DISCOVERIE / of / WITCHCRAFT / BY / REGINALD SCOT, Esquire / BEING A REPRINT OF THE FIRST EDITION / PUBLISHED IN 1584 / EDITED / *WITH EXPLANATORY NOTES, GLOSSARY, AND INTRODUCTION* / BY / BRINSLEY NICHOLSON, M.D. / DEPUTY INSPECTOR GENERAL / [fleuron] / LONDON / ELLIOT STOCK, 62 PATERNOSTER ROW, E.C. / [rule] / 1886. /

¶ *Note:* The spelling of this present edition is that of the edition of 1584.

THE

DISCOVERIE

OF

WITCHCRAFT

*

BOOKE I.

*

CHAPTER I.

An impeachment of Witches power in meteors and elementarie bodies tending to the rebuke of such as attribute too much unto them.

THE fables of Witchcraft have taken so fast hold and deepe root in the heart of man, that fewe or none can (nowadaies) with patience indure the hand and correction of God. For if any adversitie, greefe, sicknesse, losse of children, corne, cattell, or libertie happen unto them; by & by they exclaime uppon witches. As though there were no God in Israel   Job. 5. that ordereth all things according to his will; punishing both just and unjust with greefs, plagues, and afflictions in maner and forme as he thinketh good: but that certeine old women heere on earth, called witches, must needs be the contrivers of all mens calamities, and as though they themselves were innocents, and had deserved no such punishments. Insomuch as they sticke not to ride and go to such, as either are injuriouslie tearmed witches, or else are willing so to be accounted, seeking at their hands comfort and remedie in time of their tribulation, contrarie to Gods will and commandement in that behalfe,   Matth. 11. who bids us resort to him in all our necessities.

Such faithlesse people (I saie) are also persuaded, that neither haile nor snowe, thunder nor lightening, raine nor tempestuous winds come from the heavens at the commandement of God: but are raised by the cunning and power of witches and conjurers; insomuch as a clap of thunder, or a gale of wind is no sooner heard, but either they run to ring bels, or crie out to burne witches; or else burne consecrated things, hoping by the smoke thereof, to drive the divell out of the aire, as though spirits could be fraied awaie with such externall toies: howbeit, these are right inchantments, as *Brentius* affirmeth.   *In concione.*

Psal. 25.
Psal. 83.
Eccles. 43.
Luke. 8.
Matth. 8.
Mark. 4, 41.
Luke. 8, 14.
Psal. 170.
Job. 38, 22.

Eccles. 43.

Leviti. 26.
verse. 3. 4.

Psal. 78, 23.

Nahum. 1.

But certeinlie, it is neither a witch, nor divell, but a glorious God that maketh the thunder. I have read in the scriptures, that God maketh the blustering tempests and whirlewinds: and I find that it is the Lord that altogither dealeth with them, and that they blowe according to his will. But let me see anie of them all rebuke and still the sea in time of tempest, as Christ did; or raise the stormie wind, as God did with his word; and I will beleeve in them. Hath anie witch or conjurer, or anie creature entred into the treasures of the snowe; or seene the secret places of the haile, which GOD hath prepared against the daie of trouble, battell, and warre? I for my part also thinke with Jesus Sirach, that at Gods onelie commandement the snowe falleth; and that the wind bloweth according to his will, who onelie maketh all stormes to cease; and who (if we keepe his ordinances) will send us raine in due season, and make the land to bring forth hir increase, and the trees of the field to give their fruit.

But little thinke our witchmongers, that the Lord commandeth the clouds above, or openeth the doores of heaven, as *David* affirmeth; or that the Lord goeth forth in the tempests and stormes, as the Prophet *Nahum* reporteth: but rather that witches and conjurers are then about their businesse.

The *Martionists* acknowledged one God the authour of good things, and another the ordeiner of evill: but these make the divell a whole god, to create things of nothing, to knowe mens cogitations, and to doo that which God never did; as, to transubstantiate men into beasts, &c. Which thing if divels could doo, yet followeth it not, that witches have such power. But if all the divels in hell were dead, and all the witches in *England* burnt or hanged; I warrant you we should not faile to have raine, haile and tempests, as now we have: according to the appointment and will of God, and according to the constitution of the elements, and the course of the planets, wherein God hath set a perfect and perpetuall order.

Job. 26, 8.
Job. 37.
Psalme. 135.
Jer. 10 & 15.
Ose. 13.

Psa. 39, &c.

In epist. ad
Jo. Wierum.

Exod. 13.
Isai. 66.
Ps. 18, 11. 19.
August. 3. de
sancta Trinit.

Mar. 4, 41.

I am also well assured, that if all the old women in the world were witches; and all the priests, conjurers: we should not have a drop of raine, nor a blast of wind the more or the lesse for them. For the Lord hath bound the waters in the clouds, and hath set bounds about the waters, untill the daie and night come to an end: yea it is God that raiseth the winds and stilleth them: and he saith to the raine and snowe; Be upon the earth, and it falleth. The wind of the Lord, and not the wind of witches, shall destroie the treasures of their plesant vessels, and drie up the fountaines; saith *Oseas*. Let us also learne and confesse with the Prophet *David*, that we our selves are the causes of our afflictions; and not exclaime upon witches, when we should call upon God for mercie.

The Imperiall lawe (saith *Brentius*) condemneth them to death that trouble and infect the aire: but I affirme (saith he) that it is neither in the power of witch not divell so to doo, but in God onelie. Though (besides *Bodin*, and all the popish writers in generall) it please *Daænus, Hyperius, Hemingius, Erastus,* &c. to conclude otherwise. The clouds are called the pillers of Gods tents, Gods chariots, and his pavillions. And if it be so, what witch or divell can make maisteries therof? S. *Augustine* saith, *Non est putandum istis transgressoribus angelis servire hanc rerum visibilium materiem, sed soli Deo:* We must not thinke that these visible things are at the commandement of the angels that fell, but are obedient to the onelie God.

Finallie, if witches could accomplish these things; what needed it seeme so strange to the people, when Christ by miracle commanded both seas and winds, &c. For it is written; Who is this? for both wind and sea obeie him.

CHAPTER II.

The inconvenience growing by mens credulitie herein, with a reproofe of some churchmen, which are inclined to the common conceived opinion of witches omnipotencie, and a familiar example thereof.

BUT the world is now so bewitched and over-run with this fond error, that even where a man shuld seeke comfort and counsell, there shall hee be sent (in case of necessitie) from God to the divell; and from the Physician, to the coosening witch, who will not sticke to take upon hir, by wordes to heale the lame (which was proper onelie to Christ; and to them whom he assisted with his divine power) yea, with hir familiar & charmes she will take upon hir to cure the blind: though in the tenth of S. *Johns* Gospell it be written, that the divell cannot open the eies of the blind. And they attaine such credit as I have heard (to my greefe) some of the ministerie affirme, that they have had in their parish at one instant, xvii. or xviii. witches: meaning such as could worke miracles supernaturallie. Whereby they manifested as well their infidelitie and ignorance, in conceiving Gods word; as their negligence and error in instructing their flocks. For they themselves might understand, and also teach their parishoners, that God onelie worketh great woonders; and that it is he which sendeth such punishments to the wicked, and such trials to the elect: according to the saieng of the Prophet *Haggai*, I smote you with blasting and mildeaw, and with haile, in all the labours of your hands; and yet you turned not unto me, saith the Lord. And therefore saith the same Prophet in another place; You have sowen much, and bring in little. And both in *Joel* and *Leviticus*, the like phrases and proofes are used and made. But more shalbe said of this hereafter.

    S. *Paule* fore-sawe the blindnesse and obstinacie, both of these blind shepheards, and also of their scabbed sheepe, when he said; They will not suffer wholsome doctrine, but having their eares itching, shall get them a heape of teachers after their own lusts; and shall turne their eares from the truth, and shall be given to fables. And in the latter time some shall depart from the faith, and shall give heed to spirits of errors, and doctrines of divels, which speake lies (as witches and conjurers doo) but cast thou awaie such prophane and old wives fables. In which sense Basil saith; Who so giveth heed to inchanters, hearkeneth to a fabulous and frivolous thing. But I will rehearse an example whereof I my selfe am not onelie *Oculatus testis*, but have examined the cause, and am to justifie the truth of my report: not bicause I would disgrace the ministers that are godlie, but to confirme my former assertion, that this absurd error is growne into the place, which should be able to expell all such ridiculous follie and impietie.

    At the assises holden at *Rochester*, Anno 1581, one *Margaret Simons*, the wife of *John Simons*, of *Brenchlie* in *Kent*, was araigned for witchcraft, at the instigation and complaint of divers fond and malicious persons; and speciallie by the meanes of one *John Ferrall* vicar of that parish: with whom I talked about that matter, and found him both fondlie assotted in the cause, and enviouslie bent towards hir: and (which is worse) as unable to make a good account of his faith, as shee whom he accused. That which he, for his part, laid to the poore womans charge, was this.

    His sonne (being an ungratious boie, and prentise to one *Robert Scotchford* clothier, dwelling in that parish of *Brenchlie*) passed on a daie by hir house; at whome by chance hir little dog barked. Which thing the boie taking in evill part, drewe his knife, & pursued him therewith even to hir doore: whom she rebuked with some such words as the boie disdained, & yet neverthelesse would not be persuaded to depart in a long time. At the last he returned to his maisters house, and within five or six daies fell sicke. Then was called to mind the fraie betwixt the dog and the boie: insomuch as the vicar (who thought himselfe

Margin notes:
Joh. 10, 21.

Psal. 72, &
136.
Jeremie, 5.
Hag. 2, 28.

Idem. cap. 1,
6.
Joel. 1.
Leviti. 26.

2 Tim. 4, 34.

1 Tim. 4. 1.

A storie of
Margaret
Simons, a
supposed
witch.

so privileged, as he little mistrusted that God would visit his children with sicknes) did so calculate; as he found, partlie through his owne judgement, and partlie (as he himselfe told me) by the relation of other witches, that his said sonne was by hir bewitched. Yea, he also told me, that this his sonne (being as it were past all cure) received perfect health at the hands of another witch.

He proceeded yet further against hir, affirming, that alwaies in his parish church, when he desired to read most plainelie, his voice so failed him, as he could scant be heard at all. Which hee could impute, he said, to nothing else, but to hir inchantment. When I advertised the poore woman hereof, as being desirous to heare what she could saie for hir selfe; she told me, that in verie deed his voice did much faile him, speciallie when he strained himselfe to speake lowdest. How beit, she said that at all times his voice was hoarse and lowe: which thing I perceived to be true. But sir, said she, you shall understand, that this our vicar is diseased with such a kind of hoarsenesse, as divers of our neighbors in this parish, not long since, doubted that he had the French pox; & in that respect utterly refused to communicate with him: untill such time as (being therunto injoined by M. D. *Lewen* the Ordinarie) he had brought frō *London* a certificat, under the hands of two physicians, that his hoarsenes proceeded from a disease in the lungs. Which certificat he published in the church, in the presence of the whole congregation: and by this meanes hee was cured, or rather excused of the shame of his disease. And this I knowe to be true by the relation of divers honest men of that parish. And truelie, if one of the Jurie had not beene wiser than the other, she had beene condemned thereupon, and upon other as ridiculous matters as this. For the name of a witch is so odious, and hir power so feared among the common people, that if the honestest bodie living chance to be arraigned therupon, she shall hardlie escape condemnation.

CHAPTER III.

Who they be that are called witches, with a manifest declaration of the cause that mooveth men so commonlie to thinke, and witches themselves to beleeve that they can hurt children, cattell, &c. with words and imaginations: and of coosening witches.

ONE sort of such as are said to bee witches, are women which be commonly old, lame, bleare-eied, pale, fowle, and full of wrinkles; poore, sullen, superstitious, and papists; or such as knowe no religion: in whose drousie minds the divell hath goten a fine seat; so as, what mischeefe, mischance, calamitie, or slaughter is brought to passe, they are easilie persuaded the same is doone by themselves; imprinting in their minds an earnest and constant imagination hereof. They are leane and deformed, shewing melancholie in their faces, to the horror of all that see them. They are doting, scolds, mad, divelish; and not much differing from them that are thought to be possessed with spirits; so firme and stedfast in their opinions, as whosoever shall onelie have respect to the constancie of their words uttered, would easilie beleeve they were true indeed.

Cardan. de var. rerum.

These miserable wretches are so odious unto all their neighbors, and so feared, as few dare offend them, or denie them anie thing they aske: whereby they take upon them; yea, and sometimes thinke, that they can doo such things as are beyond the abilitie of humane nature. These go from house to house, and from doore to doore for a pot full of milke, yest, drinke, pottage, or some such releefe; without the which they could hardlie live: neither obtaining for their service and paines, nor by their art, nor yet at the divels hands (with whome they are said to make a perfect and visible bargaine) either beautie, monie, promotion, welth, worship, pleasure, honor, knowledge, learning, or anie other benefit whatsoever.

It falleth out many times, that neither their necessities, nor their expectation is answered or served, in those places where they beg or borrowe; but rather their lewdnesse is by their neighbors reprooved. And further, in tract of time the witch waxeth odious and tedious to hir neighbors; and they againe are despised and despited of hir: so as sometimes she cursseth one, and sometimes another; and that from the maister of the house, his wife, children, cattell, &c. to the little pig that lieth in the stie. Thus in processe of time they have all displeased hir, and she hath wished evill lucke unto them all; perhaps with cursses and imprecations made in forme. Doubtlesse (at length) some of hir neighbors die, or fall sicke; or some of their children are visited with diseases that vex them strangelie: as apoplexies, epilepsies, convulsions, hot fevei ;, wormes, &c. Which by ignorant parents are supposed to be the vengeance of witches. Yea and their opinions and conceits are confirmed and maintained by unskilfull physicians: according to the common saieng; *Inscitiæ pallium maleficium* & *incantatio*, Witchcraft and inchantment is the cloke of ignorance: whereas indeed evill humors, & not strange words, witches, or spirits are the causes of such diseases. Also some of their cattell perish, either by disease or mischance. Then they, upon whom such adversities fall, weighing the fame that goeth upon this woman (hir words, displeasure, and cursses meeting so justlie with their misfortune) doo not onelie conceive, but also are resolved, that all their mishaps are brought to passe by hir onelie meanes.

The witch on the other side exspecting hir neighbours mischances, and seeing things sometimes come to passe according to hir wishes, cursses, and incantations (for *Bodin* himselfe confesseth, that not above two in a hundred of their witchings or wishings take effect) being called before a Justice, by due examination of the circumstances is driven to see hir imprecations and desires, and hir neighbors harmes and losses to concurre, and as it were to take effect: and so confesseth that she (as a goddes) hath brought such things to passe. Wherein, not onelie she, but the accuser, and also the Justice are fowlie deceived and abused; as being thorough hir confession and other circumstances persuaded (to the injurie of Gods glorie) that she hath doone, or can doo that which is proper onelie to God himselfe.

I. Bodin. li. 2. de dæmono: cap. 8.

Another sort of witches there are, which be absolutelie cooseners. These take upon them, either for glorie, fame, or gaine, to doo anie thing, which God or the divell can doo: either for foretelling of things to come, bewraieng of secrets, curing of maladies, or working of miracles. But of these I will talke more at large heereafter.

CHAPTER IV.

What miraculous actions are imputed to witches by witchmongers, papists, and poets.

ALTHOUGH it be quite against the haire, and contrarie to the divels will, contrarie to the witches oth, promise, and homage, and contrarie to all reason, that witches should helpe anie thing that is bewitched; but rather set forward their maisters businesse: yet we read *In malleo maleficarum*, of three sorts of witches; and the same is affirmed by all the writers heereupon, new and old. One sort (they say) can hurt and not helpe, the second can helpe and not hurt, the third can both helpe and hurt. And among the hurtfull witches he saith there is one sort more beastlie than any kind of beasts, saving woolves: for these usuallie devoure and eate yong children and infants of their owne kind. These be they (saith he) that raise haile, tempests, and hurtfull

Mal. Malef. par. 2. quæst. 1. cap. 2.

weather; as lightening, thunder, &c. These be they that procure barrennesse in man, woman, and beast. These can throwe children into waters, as they walke with their mothers, and not be seene. These can make horsses kicke, till they cast the riders. These can passe from place to place in the aire invisible. These can so alter the mind of judges, that they can have no power to hurt them. These can procure to themselves and to others, taciturnitie and insensibilitie in their torments. These can bring trembling to the hands, and strike terror into the minds of them that apprehend them. These can manifest unto others, things hidden and lost, and foreshew things to come; and see them as though they were present. These can alter mens minds to inordinate love or hate. These can kill whom they list with lightening and thunder. These can take awaie mans courage, and the power of generation. These can make a woman miscar ie in childbirth, and destroie the child in the mothers wombe, without any sensible meanes either inwardlie or outwardlie applied. These can with their looks kill either man or beast.

All these things are avowed by *James Sprenger* and *Henrie Institor In malleo maleficarum*, to be true, & confirmed by *Nider*, and the inquisitor *Cumanus;* and also by *Danæus, Hyperius, Hemingius*, and multiplied by *Bodinus*, and frier *Bartholomæus Spineus*. But bicause I will in no wise abridge the authoritie of their power, you shall have also the testimonies of manie other grave authors in this behalfe; as followeth.

Ovid. lib. metamorphoseôn 7.
Danæus in dialog.
Psellus in operatione dæm.
Virg. in Damo Hora. epod. 5.
Tibul. de fascinat.
lib. 1. *eleg.* 2.
Ovid. epist. 4.
Lex. 12.
Tabularum.
Mal. Malef.
Lucā. de bello civili. lib. 6.
Virg. eclog. 8.
Ovid. de remedio amoris. lib. 1.
Hyperius.
Erastus.
Rich. Gal. in his horrible treatise.
Hemingius.
Bar. Spineus.
Bryan Darcy Confessio Windesor.
Virgil.
Aeneid. 4.
C. Manlius astrol. lib. 1.
Mal. Malef. part. 2. *quæst* 1. *cap.* 14.
1. *Cor.* 9, 9.

And first *Ovid* affirmeth, that they can raise and suppresse lightening and thunder, raine and haile, clouds and winds, tempests and earthquakes. Others doo write, that they can pull downe the moone and the starres. Some write that with wishing they can send needles into the livers of their enimies. Some that they can transferre corne in the blade from one place to another. Some, that they can cure diseases supernaturallie, flie in the aire, and danse with divels. Some write, that they can plaie the part of *Succubus*, and contract themselves to *Incubus;* and so yoong prophets are upon them begotten, &c. Som saie they can transubstantiate themselves and others, and take the forms and shapes of asses, woolves, ferrets, cowes, apes, horsses, dogs, &c. Some say they can keepe divels and spirits in the likenesse of todes and cats.

They can raise spirits (as others affirme) drie up springs, turne the course of running waters, inhibit the sunne, and staie both day and night, changing the one into the other. They can go in and out at awger holes, & saile in an egge shell, a cockle or muscle shell, through and under the tempestuous seas. They can go invisible, and deprive men of their privities, and otherwise of the act and use of venerie. They can bring soules out of the graves. They can teare snakes in peeces with words, and with looks kill lambes. But in this case a man may saie, that *Miranda canunt sed non credenda Poetæ*. They can also bring to passe, that chearne as long as you list, your butter will not come; especiallie, if either the maids have eaten up the creame; or the goodwife have sold the butter before in the market. Whereof I have had some triall, although there may be true and naturall causes to hinder the common course thereof: as for example. Put a little sope or sugar into your chearne of creame, and there will never come anie butter, chearne as long as you list. But *M. Mal.* saith, that there is not so little a village, where manie women are not that bewitch, infect, and kill kine, and drie up the milke: alledging for the strengthening of that assertion, the saieing of the Apostle, *Nunquid Deo cura est de bobus?* Dooth God take anie care of oxen?

CHAPTER V.

A confutation of the common conceived opinion of witches and witchcraft, and how detest-
able a sinne it is to repaire to them for counsell or helpe in time of affliction.

BUT whatsoever is reported or conceived of such maner of witchcrafts, I
dare avow to be false and fabulous (coosinage, dotage, and poisoning
excepted:) neither is there any mention made of these kind of witches in
the Bible. If Christ had knowne them, he would not have pretermitted to invaie
against their presumption, in taking upon them his office: as, to heale and cure
diseases; and to worke such miraculous and supernaturall things, as whereby he
himselfe was speciallie knowne, beleeved, and published to be God; his actions
and cures consisting (in order and effect) according to the power of our witchmoongers imputed to witches. Howbeit, if there be any in these daies afflicted
in such strange sort, as Christs cures and patients are described in the new testament to have beene: we flie from trusting in God to trusting in witches, who doo
not onelie in their coosening art take on them the office of Christ in this behalfe;
but use his verie phrase of speech to such idolaters, as com to seeke divine
assistance at their hands, saieng; Go thy waies, thy sonne or thy daughter, &c.
shall doo well, and be whole.   John. 5: 6.

    It will not suffice to dissuade a witchmonger from his credulitie, that he seeth   Mark. 5. 34.
the sequele and event to fall out manie times contrarie to their assertion; but in
such case (to his greater condemnation) he seeketh further to witches of greater
fame. If all faile, he will rather thinke he came an houre too late; than that he
went a mile too far. Trulie I for my part cannot perceive what is to go a whoring   To go to
after strange gods, if this be not. He that looketh upon his neighbors wife, and   witches, &c.
lusteth after hir, hath committed adulterie. And truelie, he that in hart and by   is idolatrie.
argument mainteineth the sacrifice of the masse to be propitiatorie for the quicke
and the dead, is an idolater; as also he that alloweth and commendeth creeping
to the crosse, and such like idolatrous actions, although he bend not his corporall
knees.

    In like manner I say, he that attributeth to a witch, such divine power, as dulie
and onelie apperteineth unto GOD (which all witchmongers doo) is in hart a
blasphemer, an idolater, and full of grosse impietie, although he neither go nor
send to hir for assistance.

CHAPTER VI.

A further confutation of witches miraculous and omnipotent power, by invincible reasons and
authorities, with dissuasions from such fond credulitie.

IF witches could doo anie such miraculous things, as these and other which
are imputed to them, they might doo them againe and againe, at anie time
or place, or at anie mans desire: for the divell is as strong at one time as at
another, as busie by daie as by night, and readie enough to doo all mischeefe,
and careth not whom he abuseth. And in so much as it is confessed, by the most
part of witchmoongers themselves, that he knoweth not the cogitation of mans
heart, he should (me thinks) sometimes appeere unto honest and credible
persons, in such grosse and corporall forme, as it is said he dooth unto witches:
which you shall never heare to be justified by one sufficient witnesse. For the
divell indeed entreth into the mind, and that waie seeketh mans confusion.

7

The art alwaies presupposeth the power; so as, if they saie they can doo this or that, they must shew how and by what meanes they doo it; as neither the witches, nor the witchmoongers are able to doo. For to everie action is required the facultie and abilitie of the agent or dooer; the aptnes of the patient or subject; and a convenient and possible application. Now the witches are mortall, and their power dependeth upon the analogie and consonancie of their minds and bodies; but with their minds they can but will and understand; and with their bodies they can doo no more, but as the bounds and ends of terrene sense will suffer: and therefore their power extendeth not to doo such miracles, as surmounteth their owne sense, and the understanding of others which are wiser than they; so as here wanteth the vertue and power of the efficient. And in reason, there can be no more vertue in the thing caused, than in the cause, or that which proceedeth of or from the benefit of the cause. And we see, that ignorant and impotent women, or witches, are the causes of incantations and charmes; wherein we shall perceive there is none effect, if we will credit our owne experience and sense unabused, the rules of philosophie, or the word of God. For alas! What an unapt instrument is a toothles, old, impotent, and unweldie woman to flie in the aier? Truelie, the divell little needs such instruments to bring his purposes to passe.

Aristot. de anima. lib. 2. Acts. 8.

It is strange, that we should suppose, that such persons can worke such feates: and it is more strange, that we will imagine that to be possible to be doone by a witch, which to nature and sense is impossible; speciallie when our neighbours life dependeth upon our credulitie therein; and when we may see the defect of abilitie, which alwaies is an impediment both to the act, and also to the presumption thereof. And bicause there is nothing possible in lawe, that in nature is impossible; therefore the judge dooth not attend or regard what the accused man saith; or yet would doo: but what is prooved to have beene committed, and naturallie falleth in mans power and will to doo. For the lawe saith, that To will a thing unpossible, is a signe of a mad man, or of a foole, upon whom no sentence or judgement taketh hold. Furthermore, what Jurie will condemne, or what Judge will give sentence or judgement against one for killing a man at *Berwicke;* when they themselves, and manie other sawe that man at *London,* that verie daie, wherein the murther was committed; yea though the partie confesse himself guiltie therein, and twentie witnesses depose the same? But in this case also I saie the judge is not to weigh their testimonie, which is weakened by lawe; and the judges authoritie is to supplie the imperfection of the case, and to mainteine the right and equitie of the same.

Why shuld not the divell be as readie to helpe a theefe reallie as a witch?

L. multum. l. si quis alteri, vel sibi.

Seeing therefore that some other things might naturallie be the occasion and cause of such calamities as witches are supposed to bring; let not us that professe the Gospell and knowledge of Christ, be bewitched to beleeve that they doo such things, as are in nature impossible, and in sense and reason incredible. If they saie it is doone through the divels helpe, who can work miracles; whie doo not theeves bring their busines to passe miraculouslie, with whom the divell is as conversant as with the other? Such mischeefes as are imputed to witches, happen where no witches are; yea and continue when witches are hanged and burnt: whie then should we attribute such effect to that cause, which being taken awaie, happeneth neverthelesse?

An objection answered.

CHAPTER VII.

By what meanes the name of witches becommeth so famous, and how diverslie people be opinioned concerning them and their actions.

SURELIE the naturall power of man or woman cannot be so inlarged, as to doo anie thing beyond the power and vertue given and ingraffed by God. But it is the will and mind of man, which is vitiated and depraved by the divell: neither dooth God permit anie more, than that which the naturall order appointed by him dooth require. Which naturall order is nothing else, but the ordinarie power of God, powred into everie creature, according to his state and condition. But hereof more shall be said in the title of witches confessions. Howbeit you shall understand, that few or none are throughlie persuaded, resolved, or satisfied, that witches can indeed accomplish all these impossibilities: but some one is bewitched in one point, and some is coosened in another, untill in fine, all these impossibilities, and manie mo, are by severall persons affirmed to be true. Miracles are ceased.

And this I have also noted, that when anie one is coosened with a coosening toie of witchcraft, and maketh report thereof accordinglie verifieng a matter most impossible and false as it were upon his owne knowledge, as being overtaken with some kind of illusion or other (which illusions are right inchantments) even the selfe-same man will deride the like lie proceeding out of another mans mouth, as a fabulous matter unworthie of credit. It is also to be woondered, how men (that have seene some part of witches coosenages detected, and see also therein the impossibilitie of their owne presumptions, & the follie and falsehood of the witches confessions) will not suspect, but remaine unsatisfied, or rather obstinatelie defend the residue of witches supernaturall actions: like as when a juggler hath discovered the slight and illusion of his principall feats, one would fondlie continue to thinke, that his other petie juggling knacks of legierdemaine are done by the helpe of a familiar: and according to the follie of some papists, who seeing and confessing the popes absurd religion, in the erection and maintenance of idolatrie and superstition, speciallie in images, pardons, and relikes of saints, will yet persevere to thinke, that the rest of his doctrine and trumperie is holie and good. *(The opinions of people concerning witchcraft are diverse and inconstant.)*

Finallie, manie mainteine and crie out for the execution of witches, that particularlie beleeve never a whit of that which is imputed unto them; if they be therein privatelie dealt withall, and substantiallie opposed and tried in argument.

CHAPTER VIII.

Causes that moove as well witches themselves as others to thinke that they can worke impossibilities, with answers to certeine objections: where also their punishment by lawe is touched.

CARDANUS writeth, that the cause of such credulitie consisteth in three points; to wit, in the imagination of the melancholike, in the constancie of them that are corrupt therewith, and in the deceipt of the Judges; who being inquisitors themselves against heretikes and witches, did both accuse and condemne them, having for their labour the spoile of their goods. So as these inquisitors added manie fables hereunto, least they should seeme to have doone injurie to the poore wretches, in condemning and executing them for none offense. But sithens (saith he) the springing up of *Luthers* sect, these priests have tended more diligentlie upon the execution of them; bicause more wealth is to be caught from them: insomuch as now they deale so looselie *(Card. de var. rerum. lib.* 15. *cap.* 80.)*

with witches (through distrust of gaines) that all is seene to be malice, follie, or avarice that hath beene practised against them. And whosoever shall search into this cause, or read the cheefe writers hereupon, shall find his words true.

An objection
answered.

It will be objected, that we here in *England* are not now directed by the popes lawes; and so by consequence our witches not troubled or convented by the inquisitors *Hæreticæ pravitatis.* I answer, that in times past here in *England,* as in other nations, this order of discipline hath beene in force and use; although now some part of old rigor be qualified by two severall statutes made in the fift of *Elizabeth,* and xxxiii of *Henrie* the eight. Nevertheles the estimation of the omnipotencie of their words and charmes seemeth in those statutes to be some-what mainteined, as a matter hitherto generallie received; and not yet so looked into, as that it is refuted and decided. But how wiselie so ever the Parlement house hath dealt therin, or how mercifullie soever the prince beholdeth the cause: if a poore old woman, supposed to be a witch, be by the civill or canon lawe convented; I doubt, some canon will be found in force, not onelie to give scope to the tormentor, but also to the hangman, to exercise their offices upon hir. And most certaine it is, that in what point soever anie of these extremities, which I shall rehearse unto you, be mitigated, it is thorough the goodnesse of the Queenes Majestie, and hir excellent magistrates placed among us. For as touching the opinion of our writers therein in our age; yea in our owne countrie, you shall see it doth not onlie agree with forren crueltie, but surmounteth it farre. If you read a foolish pamphlet dedicated to the lord *Darcy* by *W. W.* 1582. you shall see that he affirmeth, that all those tortures are farre too light, and their rigor too mild; and that in that respect he impudentlie exclameth against our magistrates, who suffer them to be but hanged, when murtherers, *&* such malefactors be so used, which deserve not the hundreth part of their punishments. But if you will see more follie and lewdnes comprised in one lewd booke, I commend you to *Ri. Ga.* a *Windsor* man; who being a mad man hath written according to his frantike humor: the reading wherof may satisfie a wise man, how mad all these witchmoongers dealings be in this behalfe.

W. W. his
booke, prin-
ted in Anno
Dom. 1582.

CHAPTER IX.

A conclusion of the first booke, wherein is fore-shewed the tyrannicall crueltie of witch-mongers and inquisitors, with a request to the reader to peruse the same.

AND bicause it may appeare unto the world what trecherous and faithlesse dealing, what extreame and intollerable tyrannie, what grosse and fond absurdities, what unnaturall *&* uncivil discourtisie, what cancred and spitefull malice, what outragious and barbarous crueltie, what lewd and false packing, what cunning and craftie intercepting, what bald and peevish inter-pretations, what abhominable and divelish inventions, and what flat and plaine knaverie is practised against these old women; I will set downe the whole order of the inquisition, to the everlasting, inexcusable, and apparent shame of all witchmoongers. Neither will I insert anie private or doubtful dealings of theirs; or such as they can either denie to be usuall, or justlie cavill at; but such as are published and renewed in all ages, since the commensement of poperie estab-lished by lawes, practised by inquisitors, privileged by princes, commended by doctors, confirmed by popes, councels, decrees, and canons; and finallie be left of all witch moongers; to wit, by such as attribute to old women, and such like creatures, the power of the Creator. I praie you therefore, though it be tedious *&* intollerable (as you would be heard in your miserable calamities) so heare with compassion, their accusations, examinations, matters given in evidence, confessions, presumptions, interrogatories, conjurations, cautions, crimes, tortures and condemnations, devised and practised usuallie against them.

BOOKE II.

CHAPTER I.

What testimonies and witnesses are allowed to give evidence against reputed witches, by the report & allowance of the inquisitors themselves, and such as are speciall writers heerein.

EXCOMMUNICAT persons, partakers of the falt, infants, wicked servants, and runnawaies are to be admitted to beare witnesse against their dames in this mater of witchcraft: bicause (saith *Bodin* the champion of witchmoongers) none that be honest are able to detect them. Heretikes also and witches shall be received to accuse, but not to excuse a witch. And finallie, the testimonie of all infamous persons in this case is good and allowed. Yea, one lewd person (saith *Bodin*) may be received to accuse and condemne a thousand suspected witches. And although by lawe, a capitall enimie may be challenged; yet *James Sprenger*, and *Henrie Institor*, (from whom *Bodin*, and all the writers that ever I have read, doo receive their light, authorities and arguments) saie (upon this point of lawe) that The poore frendlesse old woman must proove, that hir capitall enimie would have killed hir, and that hee hath both assalted & wounded hir; otherwise she pleadeth all in vaine. If the judge aske hir, whether she have anie capitall enimies; and she rehearse other, and forget hir accuser; or else answer that he was hir capitall enimie, but now she hopeth he is not so: such a one is nevertheles admitted for a witnes. And though by lawe, single witnesses are not admittable; yet if one depose she hath bewitched hir cow; another, hir sow; and the third, hir butter: these saith (saith *M. Mal.* and *Bodin*) are no single witnesses; bicause they agree that she is a witch.

Mal. Malef. quest. 5. pa. 3. I. Bod. lib. 4. cap. 2, de dæmon.

Arch. in C. alle. accusatus. in §. lz. super. verba.
I. Bod. lib. 4. cap. 1. de dæmon.
Mal. Malef. quest. 56. pa. 3, & quæ. 5, part. 3. Ibidem.

Que. 7. act 2.

CHAPTER II.

The order of examination of witches by the inquisitors.

WOMEN suspected to be witches, after their apprehension may not be suffered to go home, or to other places, to seek suerties: for then (saith *Bodin*) the people would be woorse willing to accuse them; for feare least at their returne home, they worke revenge upon them. In which respect *Bodin* commendeth much the *Scottish* custome and order in this behalfe: where (he saith) a hollowe peece of wood or a chest is placed in the church, into the which any bodie may freelie cast a little scroll of paper, wherein may be conteined the name of the witch, the time, place, and fact, &c. And the same chest being locked with three severall locks, is opened everie fifteenth daie by three inquisitors or officers appointed for that purpose; which keepe three severall kaies. And thus the accuser need not be knowne, nor shamed with the reproch of slander or malice to his poore neighbour.

The Scottish custõe of accusing a witch.

Item, there must be great persuasions used to all men, women, and children, to accuse old women of witchcraft.

Item, there may alwaies be promised impunitie and favour to witches, that confesse and detect others; and for the contrarie, there may be threatnings and violence practised and used.

Item, the little children of witches, which will not confesse, must be attached; who (if they be craftilie handled saith *Bodin*) will confesse against their owne mothers.

Item, witches must be examined as suddenlie, and as unawares as is possible: the which will so amaze them, that they will confesse any thing, supposing the divell hath forsaken them; wheras if they should first be cōmitted to prison, the divell would temper with them, and informe them what to doo.

Item, the inquisitor, judge, or examiner, must begin with small matters first.

Item, they must be examined, whether their parents were witches or no: for witches (as these Doctors suppose) come by propagation. And *Bodin* setteth downe this principle in witchcraft, to wit, *Si saga sit mater, sic etiam est filia:* howbeit the lawe forbiddeth it, *Ob sanguinis reverentiam.*

I. Bod. lib. de dæmon. 4. cap. 4. L. parentes de testibus.

Item, the examiner must looke stedfastlie upon their eies: for they cannot looke directlie upon a mans face (as *Bodin* affirmeth in one place, although in another he saith, that they kill and destroie both men and beasts with their lookes.)

Item, she must be examined of all accusations, presumptions, and faults, at one instant; least sathan should afterwards dissuade hir from confession.

Item, a witch may not be put in prison alone, least the divell dissuade hir from confession, through promises of her indemnitie. For (saith *Bodin*) some that have beene in the gaole have prooved to flie awaie, as they were woont to doo when they met with *Diana* and *Minerva*, &c.: and so brake their owne necks against the stone walles.

Item, if anie denie hir owne confession made without torture, she is neverthelesse by that confession to be condemned, as in anie other crime.

Item, the judges must seeme to put on a pittifull countenance and to mone them; saieng, that It was not they, but the divell that committed the murther, and that he compelled them to doo it; and must make them beleeve that they thinke them to be innocents.

Item, if they will confesse nothing but upon the racke or torture; their apparell must be changed, and everie haire in their bodie must be shaven off with a sharpe razor.

K. Childeberts cruell devise.
P. Grillandus.

Item, if they have charmes for taciturnitie, so as they feele not the common tortures, and therefore confesse nothing: then some sharpe instrument must be thrust betwixt everie naile of their fingers and toes: which (as *Bodin* saith) was king *Childeberts* devise, and is to this daie of all others the most effectuall. For by meanes of that extreme paine, they will (saith he) confesse anie thing.

Item, *Paulus Grillandus*, being an old dooer in these matters, wisheth that when witches sleepe, and feele no paine upon the torture, *Domine labia mea aperies* should be said, and so (saith he) both the torments will be felt, and the truth will be uttered: *Et sic ars deluditur arte.*

A subtill and divelish devise.

Item, *Bodin* saith, that at the time of examination, there should be a semblance of great a doo, to the terrifieing of the witch: and that a number of instruments, gieves, manacles, ropes, halters, fetters, &c. be prepared, brought foorth, and laid before the examinate: and also that some be procured to make a most horrible and lamentable crie, in the place of torture, as though he or she were upon the racke, or in the tormentors hands: so as the examinate may heare it whiles she is examined, before she hir selfe be brought into the prison; and perhaps (saith he) she will by this meanes confesse the matter.

Item, there must be subborned some craftie spie, that may seeme to be a prisoner with hir in the like case; who perhaps may in conference undermine hir, and so bewraie and discover hir.

Item, if she will not yet confesse, she must be told that she is detected, and accused by other of hir companions; although in truth there be no such matter: and so perhaps she will confesse, the rather to be revenged upon hir adversaries and accusers.

Chapter III.

Matters of evidence against witches.

IF an old woman threaten or touch one being in health, who dieth shortlie after; or else is infected with the leprosie, apoplexie, or anie other strange disease: it is (saith *Bodin*) a permanent fact, and such an evidence, as condemnation or death must insue, without further proofe; if anie bodie have mistrusted hir, or said before that she was a witch.

Item, if anie come in, or depart out of the chamber or house, the doores being shut; it is an apparent and sufficient evidence to a witches condemnation, without further triall: which thing *Bodin* never sawe. If he can shew me that feat, I will subscribe to his follie. For Christ after his resurrection used the same: not as a ridiculous toie, that everie witch might accomplish; but as a speciall miracle, to strengthen the faith of the elect.

Item, if a woman bewitch anie bodies eies, she is to be executed without further proofe.

Item, if anie inchant or bewitch mens beasts, or corne, or flie in the aire, or make a dog speake, or cut off anie mans members, and unite them againe to men or childrens bodies; it is sufficient proofe to condemnation.

Item, presumptions and conjectures are sufficient proofes against witches.

Item, if three witnesses doo but saie, Such a woman is a witch; then is it a cleere case that she is to be executed with death. Which matter *Bodin* saith is not onelie certeine by the canon and civill lawes, but by the opinion of pope *Innocent,* the wisest pope (as he saith) that ever was. *Bar. Spineus, &, I. Bod. de dæmon. lib. 2. cap. 2.*

Item, the complaint of anie one man of credit is sufficient to bring a poore woman to the racke or pullie. *Alexander. L. ubi numerus de testibus. I. Bod. de dæmon. lib. 2. cap. 2.*

Item, a condemned or infamous persons testimonie is good and allowable in matters of witchcraft.

Item, a witch is not to be delivered, though she endure all the tortures, and confesse nothing; as all other are in anie criminall cases.

Item, though in other cases the depositions of manie women at one instant are disabled, as insufficient in lawe; bicause of the imbecillitie and frailtie of their nature or sex: yet in this matter, one woman, though she be a partie, either accuser or accused, and be also infamous and impudent (for such are *Bodins* words) yea and alreadie condemned; she may neverthelesse serve to accuse and condemne a witch.

Item, a witnesse uncited, and offering himselfe in this case is to be heard, and in none other.

Item, a capitall enimie (if the enimitie be pretended to growe by meanes of witchcraft) may object against a witch; and none exception is to be had or made against him.

Item, although the proofe of perjurie may put backe a witnesse in all other causes; yet in this, a perjured person is a good and lawfull witnesse. *Par. in L. post. legatum. 9. his, de iis quibus ut indig. Alex. cap. 72. L. 2. &c.*

Item, the proctors and advocats in this case are compelled to be witnesses against their clients, as in none other case they are to be constrained there unto.

Item, none can give evidence against witches, touching their assemblies, but witches onelie: bicause (as *Bodin* saith) none other can doo it. Howbeit, *Ri. Ga.* writeth, that he came to the God speed, and with his sword and buckler killed the divell; or at the least he wounded him so sore, that he made him stinke of brimstone. *In his foolish pamphlet of the execution of Windsor witches.*

Item, *Bodin* saith, that bicause this is an extraordinarie matter; there must heerein be extraordinarie dealing: and all maner of waies are to be used, direct and indirect.

CHAPTER IV.

Confessions of witches, whereby they are condemned.

I. Bod. lib. 4.
cap. 3.
Is there anie
probabilitie
that such
would con-
tinue
witches?
Idem Ibid.
Joan. An. ad
speculat. tit.
de litis con-
test. part. 2.
L. non. alie-
num eodem.
L. de ætat. 5.
nihil eodem.
&c.
I. Bod. de dæ-
mono. lib. 4.
cap. 3.

SOME witches confesse (saith *Bodin*) that are desirous to die; not for glorie, but for despaire: bicause they are tormented in their life time. But these may not be spared (saith he) although the lawe dooth excuse them.

The best and surest confession is at shrift, to hir ghostlie father.

Item, if she confesse manie things that are false, and one thing that may be true; she is to be taken and executed upon that confession.

Item, she is not so guiltie that confesseth a falshood or lie, and denieth a truth; as she that answereth by circumstance.

Item, an equivocall or doubtfull answer is taken for a confession against a witch.

Item, *Bodin* reporteth, that one confessed that he went out, or rather up into the aire, and was transported manie miles to the fairies danse, onelie bicause he would spie unto what place his wife went to hagging, and how she behaved hir selfe. Whereupon was much a doo among the inquisitors and lawyers, to dis- cusse whether he should be executed with his wife or no. But it was concluded that he must die, bicause he bewraied not his wife: the which he forbare to doo, *Propter reverentiam honoris & familiæ.*

Item, if a woman confesse freelie herein, before question be made; and yet afterward denie it: she is neverthelesse to be burned.

Item, they affirme that this extremitie is herein used, bicause not one among a thousand witches is detected. And yet it is affirmed by *Sprenger*, in *M. Mal.* that there is not so little a parish, but there are manie witches knowne to be therein.

CHAPTER V.

Presumptions, whereby witches are condemned.

I. Bod. de dæ-
mono. lib. 4.
cap. 4.

IF anie womans child chance to die at hir hand, so as no bodie knoweth how; it may not be thought or presumed that the mother killed it, except she be supposed a witch: and in that case it is otherwise, for she must upon that presumption be executed; except she can proove the negative or contrarie.

Item, if the child of a woman that is suspected to be a witch, be lacking or gone from hir; it is to be presumed, that she hath sacrificed it to the divell: except she can proove the negative or contrarie.

Item, though in other persons, certeine points of their confessions may be thought erronious, and imputed to error: yet (in witches causes) all oversights, imperfections, and escapes must be adjudged impious and malicious, and tend to hir confusion and condemnation.

Item, though a theefe be not said in lawe to be infamous in any other matter than in theft; yet a witch defamed of witchcraft is said to be defiled with all maner of faults and infamies universallie, though she were not condemned; but (as I said) defamed with the name of a witch. For rumors and reports are sufficient (saith *Bodin*) to condemne a witch.

I. Bod. de dæ-
mono. lib. 4.
cap. 4.

Item, if any man, woman, or child doo saie, that such a one is a witch; it is a most vehement suspicion (saith *Bodin*) and sufficient to bring hir to the racke: though in all other cases it be directlie against lawe.

14

Item, in presumptions and suspicions against a witch, the common brute or voice of the people cannot erre.

Item, if a woman, when she is apprehended, crie out, or saie; I am undoone; Save my life; I will tell you how the matter standeth, &c: she is thereupon most vehementlie to be suspected and condemned to die.

Item, though a conjurer be not to be condemned for curing the diseased by vertue of his art: yet must a witch die for the like case.

Item, the behaviour, looks, becks, and countenance of a woman, are sufficient signes, whereby to presume she is a witch: for alwais they looke downe to the ground, and dare not looke a man full in the face.

Item, if their parents were thought to be witches, then is it certeinlie to be presumed that they are so: but it is not so to be thought of whoores.

Item, it is a vehement presumption if she cannot weepe, at the time of hir examination: and yet *Bodin* saith, that a witch may shed three drops out of hir right eie.

Item, it is not onelie a vehement suspicion, and presumption, but an evident proofe of a witch, if any man or beast die suddenlie where she hath beene seene latelie; although hir witching stuffe be not found or espied.

Item, if any bodie use familiaritie or companie with a witch convicted; it is a sufficient presumption against that person to be adjudged a witch.

Item, that evidence that may serve to bring in any other person to examination, may serve to bring a witch to her condemnation.

Item, herein judgment must be pronounced & executed (as *Bodin* saith) without order, and not like to the orderlie proceeding and forme of judgement in other crimes.

Item, a witch may not be brought to the torture suddenlie, or before long examination, least she go awaie scotfree: for they feele no torments, and therefore care not for the same (as *Bodin* affirmeth.)

Item, little children may be had to the torture at the first dash; but so may it not be doone with old women: as is aforesaid.

Item, if she have anie privie marke under hir arme pokes, under hir haire, under hir lip, or in hir buttocke, or in hir privities: it is a presumption sufficient for the judge to proceed and give sentence of death upon hir.

The onlie pitie they shew to a poore woman in this case, is; that though she be accused to have slaine anie bodie with her inchantments; yet if she can bring foorth the partie alive, she shall not be put to death. Whereat I marvell, in as much as they can bring the divell in any bodies likenesse and representation.

Item, their lawe saith, that an uncerteine presumption is sufficient, when a certeine presumption faileth.

L. decurionè de pænis. Panorm. & Felin. in C. veniens. 1. de testib. parsi causa. 15. 4. Lib. 4. numero. 12. usq; a 18.

L. 5. de adult. §. gl. & Bart. c. venerabilis de electio. &c. I. Bod. de dæmono. lib. 4. cap. 4.

Idem Ibid.

Cap. præterea cum glos. extra de test. Panormit. in C. vener. col. 2. eodem, &c.

CHAPTER VI.

Particular Interogatories used by the inquisitors against witches.

I NEEDE not staie to confute such parciall and horrible dealings, being so apparentlie impious, and full of tyrannie which except I should have so manifestlie detected, even with their owne writings and assertions, few or none would have beleeved. But for brevities sake I will passe over the same; supposing that the citing of such absurdities may stand for a sufficient confutation thereof. Now therefore I will proceed to a more particular order and maner of examinations, &c: used by the inquisitors, and allowed for the most part throughout all nations.

First the witch must be demanded, why she touched such a child, or such a cow, &c: and afterward the same child or cow fell sicke or lame, &c.

Mal. malef. super, interrog.

Item, why hir two kine give more milke than hir neighbors. And the note before mentioned is heere againe set downe, to be speciallie observed of all men: to wit; that Though a witch cannot weepe, yet she may speake with a crieng voice. Which assertion of weeping is false, and contrarie to the saieng of *Seneca, Cato,* and manie others; which affirme, that A woman weepeth when she meaneth most deceipt: and therefore saith *M. Mal.* she must be well looked unto, otherwise she will put spettle privilie upon hir cheeks, and seeme to weepe: which rule also *Bodin* saith is infallible. But alas that teares should be thought sufficient to excuse or condemne in so great a cause, and so weightie a triall! I am sure that the woorst sort of the children of Israel wept bitterlie: yea, if there were any witches at all in Israel, they wept. For it is written, that all the children of Israel wept. Finallie, if there be any witches in hell, I am sure they weepe: for there is weeping, wailing, and gnashing of teeth.

But God knoweth, many an honest matrone cannot sometimes in the heavines of her heart shed teares; the which oftentimes are more readie and common with craftie queanes and strumpets, than with sober women. For we read of two kinds of teares in a womans eie, the one of true greefe, the other of deceipt. And it is written, that *Dediscere flere fœminam est mendacium:* which argueth, that they lie which say, that wicked women cannot weepe. But let these tormentors take heed, that the teares in this case which runne downe the widowes cheeks, with their crie spoken of by Jesus Sirach, be not heard above. But lo what learned, godlie, and lawfull meanes these popish inquisitors have invented for the triall of true or false teares.

Seneca in tragæd. Mal. malef. part. 3. quæst 15. act. 10.

Num. 11, 4. 1. Sam. 11, 4. 2. Sa. 15, 23. Mat. 8. & 13. & 22. & 24. & 25. Luke. 3. &c.

Seneca in tragæd.

Eccl. 35, 15.

CHAPTER VII.

The inquisitors triall of weeping by conjuration.

I CONJURE thee by the amorous teares, which Jesus Christ our Saviour shed upon the crosse for the salvation of the world; and by the most earnest and burning teares of his mother the most glorious virgine *Marie,* sprinkled upon his wounds late in the evening; and by all the teares, which everie saint and elect vessell of God hath powred out heere in the world, and from whose eies he hath wiped awaie all teares; that if thou be without fault, thou maist powre downe teares aboundantlie; and if thou be guiltie, that thou weepe in no wise: In the name of the father, of the sonne, and of the holie ghost; Amen. And note (saith he) that the more you conjure, the lesse she weepeth.

Triall of teares.

Mal. malef. quæ. 15, pa. 3.

CHAPTER VIII.

Certaine cautions against witches, and of their tortures to procure confession.

BUT to manifest their further follies, I will recite some of their cautions, which are published by the ancient inquisitors, for perpetuall lessons to their successors: as followeth.

The first caution is that, which was last rehearsed concerning weeping; the which (say they) is an infallible note.

Secondlie, the judge must beware she touch no part of him, speciallie of his bare; and that he alwaies weare about his necke conjured salt, palme, herbes, and waxe halowed: which (say they) are not onelie approoved to be good by the witches confessions; but also by the use of the Romish church, which halloweth them onelie for that purpose.

Ja. Sprenger.
H. Institor.

Item, she must come to hir arreignement backward, to wit, with hir taile to the judges face, who must make manie crosses, at the time of hir approaching to the barre. And least we should condemne that for superstition, they prevent us with a figure, and tell us, that the same superstition may not seeme superstitious unto us. But this resembleth the persuasion of a theefe, that dissuadeth his sonne from stealing; and neverthelesse telleth him that he may picke or cut a pursse, and rob by the high waie.

Mal. malef.
pa. 3, quæ. 15.

Prolepsis or
Præoccupation.

One other caution is, that she must be shaven, so as there remaine not one haire about hir: for sometimes they keepe secrets for taciturnitie, and for other purposes also in their haire, in their privities, and betweene their skinne and their flesh. For which cause I marvell they flea them not: for one of their witches would not burne, being in the middest of the flame, as *M. Mal.* reporteth; untill a charme written in a little scroll was espied to be hidden betweene hir skin and flesh, and taken awaie. And this is so gravelie and faithfullie set downe by the inquisitors themselves, that one may beleeve it if he list, though indeed it be a verie lie. The like lie citeth *Bodin*, of a witch that could not be strangled by the executioner, doo what he could. But it is most true, that the inquisitor *Cumanus* in one yeare did shave one and fourtie poore women, and burnt them all when he had done.

Mal. malef.

John. Bod.
Anno. 1485 a
knave inqui-
sitor.

Another caution is, that at the time and place of torture, the hallowed things aforesaid, with the seaven words spoken on the crosse, be hanged about the witches necke; and the length of Christ in waxe be knit about hir bare naked bodie, with relikes of saints, &c. All which stuffe (saie they) will so worke within and upon them, as when they are racked and tortured, they can hardlie staie or hold themselves from confession. In which case I doubt not but that pope, which blasphemed Christ, and curssed his mother for a pecocke, and curssed God with great despights for a peece of porke, with lesse compulsion would have renounced the trinitie, and have worshipped the divell upon his knees.

Q. 16. de tem-
pore & modo
interrog.

Blasphemous
pope Julie, of
that name
the third.

Another caution is, that after she hath beene racked, and hath passed over all tortures devised for that purpose; and after that she hath beene compelled to drinke holie water, she be conveied againe to the place of torture: and that in the middest of hir torments, hir accusations be read unto hir; and that the witnesses (if they will) be brought face to face unto hir: and finallie, that she be asked, whether for triall of hir innocencie she will have judgement, *Candentis ferri*, which is; To carrie a certeine weight of burning iron in hir bare hand. But that may not (saie they) in anie wise be granted. For both *M. Mal.* and *Bodin* also affirme, that manie things may be promised, but nothing need be performed: for whie, they have authoritie to promise, but no commission to performe the same.

Mal. malef.
par. 3, quæ. 16.

Another caution is, that the judge take heed, that when she once beginneth to confesse, he cut not off hir examination, but continue it night and daie. For many-times, whiles they go to dinner, she returneth to hir vomit.

Another caution is, that after the witch hath confessed the annoieing of men and beasts, she be asked how long she hath had *Incubus*, when she renounced the faith, and made the reall league, and what that league is, &c. And this is indeede the cheefe cause of all their incredible and impossible confessions: for upon the racke, when they have once begunne to lie, they will saie what the tormentor list.

The last caution is, that if she will not confesse, she be had to some strong castle or gaole. And after certeine daies, the gaolor must make hir beleeve he goeth foorth into some farre countrie: and then some of hir freends must come in to hir, and promise hir, that if she will confesse to them, they will suffer hir to escape out of prison: which they may well doo, the keeper being from home. And this waie (saith *M. Mal.*) hath served, when all other meanes have failed.

Mal. malef.
par. 3, quæ. 16.
act. 11.

And in this place it may not be omitted, that above all other times, they confesse upon fridaies. Now saith *James Sprenger*, and *Henrie Institor*, we must saie all, to wit: If she confesse nothing, she should be dismissed by lawe; and yet by order she may in no wise be bailed, but must be put into close prison, and there be talked withall by some craftie person (those are the words) and in the meane while there must be some eves-dropers with pen and inke behind the wall, to hearken and note what she confesseth: or else some of hir old companions and acquaintance may come in and talke with hir of old matters, and so by eves-droppers be also bewraied; so as there shall be no end of torture before she have confessed what they will.

CHAPTER IX.

The fifteene crimes laid to the charge of witches, by witchmongers; speciallie by Bodin, in Dæmonomania.

THEY denie God, and all religion.
     Answere. Then let them die therefore, or at the least be used like infidels, or apostataes.
They cursse, blaspheme, and provoke God with all despite.
Answere. Then let them have the law expressed in *Levit.* 24. and *Deut.* 13. & 17.
     They give their faith to the divell, and they worship and offer sacrifice unto him.
Ans. Let such also be judged by the same lawe.
They doo solemnelie vow and promise all their progenie unto the divell.
Ans. This promise proceedeth from an unsound mind, and is not to be regarded; bicause they cannot performe it, neither will it be prooved true. Howbeit, if it be done by anie that is sound of mind, let the cursse of *Jeremie*, 32. 36. light upon them, to wit, the sword, famine and pestilence.
They sacrifice their owne children to the divell before baptisme, holding them up in the aire unto him, and then thrust a needle into their braines.
Ans. If this be true, I maintaine them not herein: but there is a lawe to judge them by. Howbeit, it is so contrarie to sense and nature, that it were follie to beleeve it; either upon *Bodins* bare word, or else upon his presumptions; speciallie when so small commoditie and so great danger and inconvenience insueth to the witches thereby.
They burne their children when they have sacrificed them.
Ans. Then let them have such punishment, as they that offered their children unto *Moloch: Levit.* 20. But these be meere devises of witchmoongers and inquisitors, that with extreame tortures have wroong such confessions from them; or else with false reports have beelied them; or by flatterie & faire words and promises have woon it at their hands, at the length.
They sweare to the divell to bring as manie into that societie as they can.
Ans. This is false, and so prooved elsewhere.
They sweare by the name of the divell.
Ans. I never heard anie such oth, neither have we warrant to kill them that so doo sweare; though indeed it be verie lewd and impious.
They use incestuous adulterie with spirits.
Ans. This is a stale ridiculous lie, as is prooved apparentlie hereafter.
They boile infants (after they have murthered them unbaptised) untill their flesh be made potable.
Ans. This is untrue, incredible, and impossible.
They eate the flesh and drinke the bloud of men and children openlie.
Ans. Then are they kin to the *Anthropophagi* and *Canibals*. But I beleeve never

an honest man in *England* nor in *France*, will affirme that he hath seene any of these persons, that are said to be witches, do so; if they shuld, I beleeve it would poison them.

They kill men with poison.

Ans. Let them be hanged for their labour.

They kill mens cattell.

Ans. Then let an action of trespasse be brought against them for so dooing.

They bewitch mens corne, and bring hunger and barrennes into the countrie; they ride and flie in the aire, bring stormes, make tempests, &c.

Ans. Then will I worship them as gods; for those be not the works of man nor yet of witch: as I have elsewhere prooved at large.

They use venerie with a divell called *Incubus*, even when they lie in bed with their husbands, and have children by them, which become the best witches.

Ans. This is the last lie, verie ridiculous, and confuted by me elsewhere.

CHAPTER X.

A refutation of the former surmised crimes patched togither by Bodin, and the onelie waie to escape the inquisitors hands.

IF more ridiculous or abhominable crimes could have beene invented, these poore women (whose cheefe fault is that they are scolds) should have beene charged with them.

In this libell you dooe see is conteined all that witches are charged with; and all that also, which anie witchmoonger surmiseth, or in malice imputeth unto witches power and practise.

Some of these crimes may not onelie be in the power and will of a witch, but may be accomplished by naturall meanes: and therefore by them the matter in question is not decided, to wit; Whether a witch can worke woonders supernaturallie? For manie a knave and whore dooth more commonlie put in execution those lewd actions, than such as are called witches, and are hanged for their labour.

The question or matter in controversie: that is to say, the proposition or theme.

Some of these crimes also laid unto witches charge, are by me denied, and by them cannot be prooved to be true, or committed, by any one witch. Othersome of these crimes likewise are so absurd, supernaturall, and impossible, that they are derided almost of all men, and as false, fond, and fabulous reports condemned: insomuch as the very witchmoongers themselves are ashamed to heare of them.

If part be untrue, why may not the residue be thought false? For all these things are laid to their charge at one instant, even by the greatest doctors and patrones of the sect of witchmongers, producing as manie proofs for witches supernaturall and impossible actions, as for the other. So as, if one part of their accusation be false, the other part deserveth no credit. If all be true that is alledged of their dooings, why should we beleeve in Christ, bicause of his miracles, when a witch dooth as great wonders as ever he did?

But it will be said by some; As for those absurd and popish writers, they are not in all their allegations, touching these matters, to be credited. But I assure you, that even all sorts of writers heerein (for the most part) the very doctors of the church to the schoolemen, protestants and papists, learned and unlearned, poets and historiographers, Jewes, Christians, or Gentiles agree in these impossible and ridiculous matters. Yea and these writers, out of whome I gather most absurdities, are of the best credit and authoritie of all writers in this matter. The reason is, bicause it was never throughlie looked into; but everie fable credited; and the word (Witch) named so often in scripture.

A gen. error.

The onelie
way for
witches to
avoid the
inquisitors
hands.

They that have seene further of the inquisitors orders and customes, saie also; that There is no waie in the world for these poore women to escape the inquisitors hands, and so consequentlie burning: but to gild their hands with monie, wherby oftentimes they take pitie upon them, and deliver them, as sufficientlie purged. For they have authoritie to exchange the punishment of the bodie with the punishment of the pursse, applieng the same to the office of their inquisition: whereby they reape such profit, as a number of these seelie women paie them yeerelie pensions, to the end they may not be punished againe.

<hr />

CHAPTER XI.

The opinion of Cornelius Agrippa concerning witches, of his pleading for a poore woman accused of witchcraft, and how he convinced the inquisitors.

CORNELIUS AGRIPPA saith, that while he was in *Italie*, manie inquisitors in the dutchie of *Millen* troubled divers most honest & noble matrones, privilie wringing much monie from them, untill their knaverie was detected. Further he saith, that being an advocate or councellor in the Commonwelth of *Maestright* in *Brabant*, he had sore contention with an inquisitor, who through unjust accusations drew a poore woman of the countrie into his butcherie, and to an unfit place; not so much to examine hir, as to torment hir. Whom when *C. Agrippa* had undertaken to defend, declaring that in the things doone, there was no proofe, no signe or token that could cause hir to be tormented; the inquisitor stoutlie denieng it, said; One thing there is, which is proofe and matter sufficient: for hir mother was in times past burned for a witch. Now when *Agrippa* replied, affirming that this article was impertinent, and ought to be refused by the judge, as being the deed of another; alledging to the inquisitor, reasons and lawe for the same: he replied againe that this was true, bicause they used to sacrifice their children to the divell, as soone as they were borne; and also bicause they usuallie conceived by spirits transformed into mans shape, and that thereby witchcraft was naturallie ingraffed into this child, as a disease that commeth by inheritance.

A bitter
invective
against a
cruell
inquisitor.

C. Agrippa replieng against the inquisitors follie & superstitious blindnesse, said; O thou wicked preest! Is this thy divinitie? Doost thou use to drawe poore guiltlesse women to the racke by these forged devises? Doost thou with such sentences judge others to be heretikes, thou being a more heretike than either *Faustus* or *Donatus*? Be it as thou saiest, dooest thou not frustrate the grace of Gods ordinance; namelie baptisme? Are the words in batisme spoken in vaine? Or shall the divell remaine in the child, or it in the power of the divell, being there and then consecrated to Christ Jesus, in the name of the father, the sonne, and the holie ghost? And if thou defend their false opinions, which affirm, that spirits accompanieng with women, can ingender; yet dotest thou more than anie of them, which never beleeved that anie of those divels, togither with their stolne seed, doo put part of that their seed or nature into the creature. But though indeed we be borne the children of the divell and damnation, yet in baptisme, through grace in Christ, sathan is cast out, and we are made new creatures in the Lord, from whome none can be separated by another mans deed. The inquisitor being hereat offended, threatened the advocate to proceed against him, as a supporter of heretikes or witches; yet neverthelesse he ceased not to defend the seelie woman, and through the power of the lawe he delivered hir from the clawes of the bloodie moonke, who with hir accusers, were condemned in a great summe of monie to the charter of the church of *Mentz*, and remained infamous after that time almost to all men.

20

But by the waie you must understand, that this was but a petie inquisitor, and had not so large a commission as *Cumanus*, *Sprenger*, and such other had; nor yet as the *Spanish* inquisitors at this daie have. For these will admit no advocats now unto the poore soules, except the tormentor or hangman may be called an advocate. You may read the summe of this inquisition in few words set out by M. *John Fox* in the Acts and monuments. For witches and heretikes are among the inquisitors of like reputation; saving that the extremitie is greater against witches, bicause through their simplicitie, they may the more boldlie tyrannize upon them, and triumph over them.

John Fox in the acts and monuments.

CHAPTER XII.

What the feare of death and feeling of torments may force one to doo, and that it is no marvell though witches condemne themselves by their owne confessions so tyrannicallie extorted.

HE that readeth the ecclesiasticall histories, or remembreth the persecutions in Queene *Maries* time, shall find, that manie good men have fallen for feare of persecution, and returned unto the Lord againe. What marvell then, though a poore woman, such a one as is described elsewhere, & tormented as is declared in these latter leaves, be made to confesse such absurd and false impossibilities; when flesh and bloud is unable to endure such triall? Or how can she in the middest of such horrible tortures and torments, promise unto hir selfe constancie; or forbeare to confesse anie thing? Or what availeth it hir, to persevere in the deniall of such matters, as are laid to her charge unjustlie; when on the one side there is never anie end of hir torments; on the other side, if she continue in hir assertion, they saie she hath charmes for taciturnitie or silence?

Peter the apostle renounced, curssed, and forsware his maister and our Saviour Jesus Christ, for feare of a wenches manaces; or rather at a question demanded by hir, wherein he was not so circumvented, as these poore witches are, which be not examined by girles, but by cunning inquisitors, who having the spoile of their goods, and bringing with them into the place of judgement minds to maintaine their bloudie purpose, spare no maner of allurements, thretenings, nor torments, untill they have wroong out of them all that, which either maketh to their owne desire, or serveth to the others destruction.

Peters apostacie & renouncing of Christ.

Peter (I saie) in the presence of his Lord and maister Christ, who had instructed him in true knowledge manie yeares, being forewarned, not passing foure or five houres before, and having made a reall league and a faithfull promise to the contrarie, without anie other compulsion than (as hath beene said) by a question proposed by a girle, against his conscience, forsooke, thrise denied, and abandoned his said maister: and yet he was a man illuminated, and placed in dignitie aloft, and neerer to Christ by manie degrees, than the witch, whose fall could not be so great as *Peters;* because she never ascended halfe so manie steps. A pastors declination is much more abhominable that the going astraie of anie of his sheepe: as an ambassadors conspiracie is more odious than the falsehood of a common person: or as a capteins treason is more mischeevous than a private soldiers mutinie. If you saie, *Peter* repented; I answer that the witch dooth so likewise sometimes, and I see not in that case, but mercie may be emploied upon hir. It were a mightie temptation to a seelie old woman, that a visible divell (being in shape so ugglie, as *Danæus* and others saie he is) should assalt hir in maner and forme as is supposed, or rather avowed; speciallie when there is promise made that none shall be tempted above their strength. The poore old witch is commonlie unlearned, unwarned, and unprovided of

Danæus in dialog.

1 Cor. 10.

21

counsell and freendship, void of judgement and discretion to moderate hir life and communication, hir kind and gender more weake and fraile than the masculine, and much more subject to melancholie; hir bringing up and companie is so base, that nothing is to be looked for in hir speciallie of these extraordinarie qualities; hir age also is commonlie such, as maketh her decrepite, which is a disease that mooveth them to these follies.

Finallie, Christ did cleerelie remit *Peter*, though his offense were committed both against his divine and humane person: yea afterwards he did put him in trust to feed his sheepe, and shewed great countenance, freendship and love unto him. And therefore I see not, but we may shew compassion upon these poore soules; if they shew themselves sorrowfull for their misconceipts and wicked imaginations.

BOOKE III.

Chapter I.

The witches bargaine with the divell, according to M. Mal. Bodin, Nider, Danæus, Psellus, Erastus, Hemingius, Cumanus, Aquinas, Bartholomæus, Spineus, &c.

THAT which in this matter of witchcraft hath abused so manie, and seemeth both so horrible and intollerable, is a plaine bargaine, that (they saie) is made betwixt the divell and the witch. And manie of great learning conceive it to be a matter of truth, and in their writings publish it accordinglie: the which (by Gods grace) shall be prooved as vaine and false as the rest.

The order of their bargaine or profession is double; the one solemne and publike; the other secret and private. That which is called solemne or publike, is where witches come togither at certeine assemblies, at the times prefixed, and doo not onelie see the divell in visible forme; but confer and talke familiarlie with him. In which conference the divell exhorteth them to observe their fidelitie unto him, promising them long life and prosperitie. Then the witches assembled, commend a new disciple (whom they call a novice) unto him: and if the divell find that yoong witch apt and forward in renunciation of christian faith, in despising anie of the seven sacraments, in treading upon crosses, in spetting at the time of the elevation, in breaking their fast on fasting daies, and fasting on sundaies; then the divell giveth foorth his hand, and the novice joining hand in hand with him, promiseth to observe and keepe all the divels commandements.

The double bargane of witches with the divell.

This done, the divell beginneth to be more bold with hir, telling hir plainlie, that all this will not serve his turne; and therefore requireth homage at hir hands: yea he also telleth hir, that she must grant him both hir bodie and soule to be tormented in everlasting fire: which she yeeldeth unto. Then he chargeth hir, to procure as manie men, women, and children also, as she can, to enter into this societie. Then he teacheth them to make ointments of the bowels and members of children, whereby they ride in the aire, and accomplish all their desires. So as, if there be anie children unbaptised, or not garded with the signe of the crosse, or orizons; then the witches may and doo catch them from their mothers sides in the night, or out of their cradles, or otherwise kill them with their ceremonies; and after buriall steale them out of their graves, and seeth them in a caldron, untill their flesh be made potable. Of the thickest whereof they make ointments, whereby they ride in the aire; but the thinner potion they put into flaggons, whereof whosoever drinketh, observing certeine ceremonies, immediatlie becommeth a maister or rather a mistresse in that practise and facultie.

Mal. malef. de modo professionis.

CHAPTER II.

The order of the witches homage done (as it is written by lewd inquisitors and peevish witchmoongers) to the divell in person; of their songs and danses, and namelie of La volta, and of other ceremonies, also of their excourses.

Homage of witches to the divell.

SOMETIMES their homage with their oth and bargaine is received for a certeine terme of yeares; sometimes for ever. Sometimes it consisteth in the deniall of the whole faith, sometimes in part. The first is, when the soule is absolutelie yeelded to the divell and hell fier: the other is, when they have but bargained to observe certeine ceremonies and statutes of the church; as to conceale faults at shrift, to fast on sundaies, &c. And this is doone either by oth, protestation of words, or by obligation in writing, sometimes sealed with wax, sometimes signed with bloud, sometimes by kissing the divels bare buttocks; as did a Doctor called *Edlin*, who as (*Bodin* saith) was burned for witch-craft.

Bar. Spineus, cap. I. in novo Mal. malef.

You must also understand, that after they have delicatlie banketted with the divell and the ladie of the fairies; and have eaten up a fat oxe, and emptied a butt of malmesie, and a binne of bread at some noble mans house, in the dead of the night, nothing is missed of all this in the morning. For the ladie *Sibylla*, *Minerva*, or *Diana* with a golden rod striketh the vessell & the binne, and they are fullie replenished againe. Yea, she causeth the bullocks bones to be brought and laid togither upon the hide, and lappeth the foure ends thereof togither, laieng her golden rod thereon; and then riseth up the bullocke againe in his former estate and condition; and yet at their returne home they are like to starve for hunger; as *Spineus* saith. And this must be an infallible rule, that everie fortnight, or at the least everie moneth, each witch must kill one child at the least for hir part.

Idem Ibid.

I. Bod. de dæmon. lib. 2, cap. 4.

And here some of *Monsieur Bodins* lies may be inserted, who saith that at these magicall assemblies, the witches never faile to danse; and in their danse they sing these words; Har, har, divell divell, danse here, danse here, plaie here, plaie here, *Sabbath, sabbath*. And whiles they sing and danse, everie one hath a broome in hir hand, and holdeth it up aloft. Item he saith, that these night-walking or rather night-dansing witches, brought out of *Italie* into *France*, that danse, which is called *La volta*.

Mal. malef.

A part of their league is, to scrape off the oile, which is received in extreame follie (unction I should have said). But if that be so dangerous, they which socke the corps had neede to take great care, that they rub not off the oile, which divers other waies may also be thrust out of the forehead; and then I perceive all the vertue thereof is gone, and farewell it. But I marvell how they take on to preserve the water powred on them in baptisme, which I take to be largelie of as great force as the other; and yet I thinke is commonlie wiped and washed off, within foure and twentie houres after baptisme: but this agreeth with the residue of their follie.

Grillandus. de sort. 10. vol. tract.

And this is to be noted, that the inquisitors affirme, that during the whole time of the witches excourse, the divell occupieth the roome and place of the witch, in so perfect a similitude, as hir husband in his bed, neither by feeling, speech, nor countenance can discerne hir from his wife. Yea the wife departeth out of her husbands armes insensiblie, and leaveth the divell in hir roome visiblie. Wherein their incredulitie is incredible, who will have a verie bodie in the feined plaie, and a phantasticall bodie in the true bed: and yet (forsooth) at the name of Jesus, or at the signe of the crosse, all these bodilie witches (they saie) vanish awaie.

CHAPTER III.

How witches are summoned to appeere before the divell, of their riding in the aire, of their accompts, of their conference with the divell, of his supplies, and their conference, of their farewell and sacrifices: according to Danæus, Psellus, &c.

HITHERTO, for the most part, are the verie words conteined in *M. Mal.* or *Bodin,* or rather in both; or else in the new *M. Mal.* or at the least-wise of some writer or other, that mainteineth the almightie power of witches. But *Danæus* saith, the divell oftentimes in the likenes of a sumner, meeteth them at markets and faires, and warneth them to appeere in their assemblies, at a certeine houre in the night, that he may understand whom they have slaine, and how they have profited. If they be lame, he saith the divell delivereth them a staffe, to conveie them thither invisiblie through the aire; and that then they fall a dansing and singing of bawdie songs, wherein he leadeth the danse himselfe. Which danse, and other conferencies being ended, he supplieth their wants of powders and roots to intoxicate withall; and giveth to everie novice a marke, either with his teeth or with his clawes, and so they kisse the divels bare buttocks, and depart: not forgetting every daie afterwards to offer to him, dogs, cats, hens, or bloud of their owne. And all this dooth *Danæus* report as a troth, and as it were upon his owne knowledge. And yet else-where he saieth; In these matters they doo but dreame, and doo not those things indeed, which they confesse through their distemperature, growing of their melancholike humor: and therefore (saith he) these things, which they report of themselves, are but meere illusions.

Psellus addeth hereunto, that certeine magicall heretikes, to wit; the *Eutychians,* assemblie themselves everie good fridaie at night; and putting out the candles, doo commit incestuous adulterie, the father with the daughter, the sister with the brother, and the sonne with the mother; and the ninth moneth they returne and are delivered; and cutting their children in peeces, fill their pots with their bloud; then burne they the carcases, and mingle the ashes therewith, and so preserve the same for magicall purposes. *Cardanus* writeth (though in mine opinion not verie probablie) that these excources, dansings, &c: had their beginning from certeine heretikes called *Dulcini,* who devised those feasts of *Bacchus* which are named *Orgia,* whereunto these kind of people openlie assembled; and beginning with riot, ended with this follie. Which feasts being prohibited, they nevertheles hanted them secretlie; and when they could not doo so, then did they it in cogitation onelie, and even to this daie (saith he) there remaineth a certeine image or resemblance thereof among our melancholike women.

Danæus in dialog. cap. 4.

Ide. Ibidem.
Idem. in dialog. cap. 3.

Card. lib. de var. rerum. 15. cap. 80.

CHAPTER IV.

That there can no reall league be made with the divell the first author of the league, and the weake proofes of the adversaries for the same.

IF the league be untrue, as are the residue of their confessions, the witch-mongers arguments fall to the ground: for all the writers herein hold this bargaine for certeine, good, and granted, and as their onelie maxime. But surelie the indentures, conteining those covenants, are sealed with butter; and the labels are but bables. What firme bargaine can be made betwixt a carnall bodie and a spirituall? Let any wise or honest man tell me, that either hath beene a partie, or a witnesse; and I will beleeve him. But by what authoritie, proofe, or testimonie; and upon what ground all this geere standeth, if you read *M. Mal.* you shall find, to the shame of the reporters (who doo so varie in their tales, and are at such contrarietie:) and to the reproch of the beleevers of such absurd lies.

For the beginning of the credit hereof, resteth upon the confession of a baggage yoong fellow condemned to be burnt for witchcraft; who said to the inquisitors, of likelihood to prolong his life, (if at leastwise the storie be true, which is taken out of *Nider;*) If I wist (quoth he) that I might obteine pardon, I would discover all that I knowe of witchcraft. The which condition being accepted, and pardon promised (partlie in hope thereof, and partlie to be rid of his wife) he said as followeth.

The novice or yoong disciple goeth to some church, togither with the mistresse of that profession, upon a sundaie morning, before the conjuration of holie water, & there the said novice renounceth the faith, promiseth obedience in observing, or rather omitting of ceremonies in meetings, and such other follies; and finallie, that they doo homage to their yoong maister the divell, as they covenanted.

But this is notable in that storie, that this yoong witch, doubting that his wives examination would bewraie his knaverie, told the inquisitor; that in truth his wife was guiltie as well as he, but she will never, I am sure (quoth he) though she should be burned a thousand times, confesse any of these circumstances.

And this is in no wise to be forgotten, that notwithstanding his contrition, his confession, and his accusation of his owne wife (contrarie to the inquisitors promise and oth) he and his wife were both burned at a stake, being the first discoverers of this notable league, whereupon the fable of witchcraft is mainteined; and whereby such other confessions have beene from the like persons, since that time, extorted and augmented.

CHAPTER V.

Of the private league, a notable tale of Bodins concerning a French ladie, with a confutation.

THE maner of their private league is said to be, when the divell invisible, and sometimes visible, in the middest of the people talketh with them privatelie; promising, that if they will followe his counsell, he will supplie all their necessities, and make all their endevors prosperous: and so beginneth with small matters: whereunto they consent privilie, and come not into the fairies assemblie.

And in this case (mee thinks) the divell sometimes, in such externall or corporall shape, should meete with some that would not consent to his motions (except you will saie he knoweth their cogitations) and so should be bewraied. They also (except they were idiots) would spie him, and forsake him for breach of covenants. But these bargaines, and these assemblies doo all the writers hereupon mainteine: and *Bodin* confirmeth them with a hundred and odd lies; among the number whereof I will (for diverse causes) recite one.

There was (saith he) a noble Gentlewoman at *Lions,* that being in bed with a lover of hirs, suddenlie in the night arose up, and lighted a candle: which when she had done, she tooke a box of ointment, wherewith she annointed her bodie; and after a few words spoken, she was carried awaie. Hir bedfellow seeing the order hereof, lept out of his bed, tooke the candle in his hand, and
26

sought for the ladie round about the chamber, and in everie corner thereof. But though he could not find hir, yet did he find hir box of ointment: and being desirous to know the vertue thereof, besmeered himselfe therewith, even as he perceived hir to have done before. And although he were not so superstitious, as to use anie words to helpe him forward in his busines, yet by the vertue of that ointment (saith *Bodin*) he was immediatlie conveied to *Lorreine*, into the assemblie of witches. Which when he sawe, he was abashed, and said; In the name of God, what make I heere? And upon those words the whole assemblie vanished awaie, and left him there alone starke naked; and so was he faine to returne to *Lions*. But he had so good a conscience (for you may perceive by the first part of the historie, he was a verie honest man) that he accused his true lover for a witch, and caused hir to be burned. But as for his adulterie, neither *M. Mal.* nor *Bodin* doo once so much as speake in the dispraise thereof.

This agreeth not with their interpreta-tion, that saie, this is onlie done by vertue of the legue: nor yet to them that referre it unto words: quoth nota.

It appeareth throughout all *Bodins* booke, that he is sore offended with *Cornelius Agrippa*, and the rather (as I suppose) bicause the said *C. Agrippa* re-canted that which *Bodin* mainteineth, who thinketh he could worke wonders by magicke, and speciallie by his blacke dog. It should seeme he had prettie skill in the art of divination. For though he wrote before *Bodin* manie a yeare, yet uttereth he these words in his booke *De vanitate scientiarum:* A certeine French protonotarie (saith he) a lewd fellow and a coosener, hath written a certeine fable or miracle done at *Lions*, &c. What *Bodin* is, I knowe not, otherwise than by report; but I am certeine this his tale is a fond fable: and *Bodin* saith it was performed at *Lions;* and this man (as I understand) by profession is a civill lawier.

C. Agrippa, cap. 51.

CHAPTER VI.

A disproofe of their assemblies, and of their bargaine.

THAT the joining of hands with the divell, the kissing of his bare buttocks, and his scratching and biting of them, are absurd lies; everie one having the gift of reason may plainlie perceive: in so much as it is manifest unto us by the word of God, that a spirit hath no flesh, bones, nor sinewes, whereof hands, buttocks, claws, teeth, and lips doo consist. For admit that the constitu-tion of a divels bodie (as *Tatian* and other affirme) consisteth in spirituall con-gelations, as of fier and aire; yet it cannot be perceived of mortall creatures. What credible witnesse is there brought at anie time, of this their corporall, visible, and incredible bargaine; saving the confession of some person diseased both in bodie and mind, wilfullie made, or injuriouslie constrained? It is mervell that no penitent witch that forsaketh hir trade, confesseth not these things without compulsion. Mee thinketh their covenant made at baptisme with God, before good witnesses, sanctified with the word, confirmed with his promises, and established with his sacraments, should be of more force than that which they make with the divell, which no bodie seeth or knoweth. For God deceiveth none, with whom he bargaineth; neither dooth he mocke or disappoint them, although he danse not among them.

Tatianus contra Græcos.

Their oth, to procure into their league and fellowship as manie as they can (whereby everie one witch, as *Bodin* affirmeth, augmenteth the number of fiftie) bewraieth greatlie their indirect dealing. Hereof I have made triall, as also of the residue of their coosening devices; and have beene with the best, or rather the woorst of them, to see what might be gathered out of their counsels; and have cunninglie treated with them thereabouts; and further, have sent cer-teine old persons to indent with them, to be admitted into their societie. But as well by their excuses and delaies, as by other circumstances, I have tried and found all their trade to be meere coosening.

The author speaketh upon due proofe and triall.

I praie you what bargaine have they made with the divell, that with their angrie lookes beewitch lambs, children, &c? Is it not confessed, that it is naturall, though it be a lie? What bargaine maketh the soothsaier, which hath his severall kinds of witchcraft and divination expressed in the scripture? Or is it not granted that they make none? How chanceth it that we heare not of this bargaine in the scriptures?

<hr />

CHAPTER VII.

A confutation of the objection concerning witches confessions.

IT is confessed (saie some by the waie of objection) even of these women themselves, that they doo these and such other horrible things, as deserveth death, with all extremitie, &c. Whereunto I answer, that whosoever consideratelie beholdeth their confessions, shall perceive all to be vaine, idle, false, inconstant, and of no weight; except their contempt and ignorance in religion; which is rather the fault of the negligent pastor, than of the simple woman.

Confession compulsorie; as by Hispanicall inquisition: Looke Mal. malef. & Jo. Bodin. Confession persuasorie; as by flatterie: Looke Bry. Darcie against Ursu. Kempe. John. Bod. Mal. Malef.

First, if their confession be made by compulsion, of force or authoritie, or by persuasion, and under colour of freendship, it is not to be regarded; bicause the extremitie of threts and tortures provokes it; or the qualitie of faire words and allurements constraines it. If it be voluntarie, manie circumstances must be considered, to wit; whether she appeach not hir selfe to overthrow hir neighbour, which manie times happeneth through their cankered and malicious melancholike humor: then; whether in that same melancholike mood and frentike humor, she desire not the abridgment of hir owne daies. Which thing *Aristotle* saith dooth oftentimes happen unto persons subject to melancholike passions: and (as *Bodin* and *Sprenger* saie) to these old women called witches, which manie times (as they affirme) refuse to live; thretning the judges, that if they may not be burned, they will laie hands upon themselves, and so make them guiltie of their damnation.

L. absent de poenis. L. 2. cum glos. de iis, qui ante sentent, mortui sunt, sibi necem consciscentes.

I my selfe have knowne, that where such a one could not prevaile, to be accepted as a sufficient witnesse against himselfe, he presentlie went and threw himselfe into a pond of water, where he was drowned. But the lawe saith; *Volenti mori non est habenda fides,* that is; His word is not to be credited that is desirous to die. Also sometimes (as else-where I have prooved) they confesse that whereof they were never guiltie; supposing that they did that which they did not, by meanes of certeine circumstances. And as they sometimes confesse impossibilities, as that they flie in the aire, transubstantiate themselves, raise tempests, transfer or remoove corne, &c: so doo they also (I saie) confesse voluntarilie, that which no man could proove, and that which no man would ghesse, nor yet beleeve, except he were as mad as they; so as they bring death wilfullie upon themselves: which argueth an unsound mind.

If they confesse that, which hath beene indeed committed by them, as poisoning, or anie other kind of murther, which falleth into the power of such persons to accomplish; I stand not to defend their cause. Howbeit, I would wish that even in that case there be not too rash credit given, nor too hastie proceedings used against them: but that the causes, properties, and circumstances

Absurdities in witches confessions.

of everie thing be dulie considered, and diligentlie examined. For you shall understand, that as sometimes they confesse they have murthered their neighbours with a wish, sometimes with a word, sometimes with a looke, &c: so they confesse, that with the delivering of an apple, or some such thing, to a woman with child, they have killed the child in the mothers wombe, when nothing was added thereunto, which naturallie could be noisome or hurtfull.

In like maner they confesse, that with a touch of their bare hand, they sometimes kill a man being in perfect health and strength of bodie; when all his garments are betwixt their hand and his flesh.

But if this their confession be examined by divinitie, philosophie, physicke, lawe or conscience, it will be found false and insufficient. First, for that the working of miracles is ceased. Secondlie, no reason can be yeelded for a thing so farre beyond all reason. Thirdlie, no receipt can be of such efficacie, as when the same is touched with a bare hand, from whence the veines have passage through the bodie unto the hart, it should not annoie the poisoner; and yet re-teine vertue and force enough, to pearse through so manie garments and the verie flesh incurablie, to the place of death in another person. *Cui argumento* (saith *Bodin*) *nescio quid responderi possit.* Fourthlie, no lawe will admit such a confession, as yeeldeth unto impossibilities, against the which there is never any lawe provided; otherwise it would not serve a mans turne, to plead and proove that he was at *Berwicke* that daie, that he is accused to have doone a murther in *Canturburie;* for it might be said he was conveied to *Berwicke,* and backe againe by inchantment. Fiftlie, he is not by conscience to be executed, which hath no sound mind nor perfect judgement. And yet forsooth we read, that one mother *Stile* did kill one *Saddocke* with a touch on the shoulder, for not keeping promise with hir for an old cloake, to make hir a safegard; and that she was hanged for hir labour.

J. Bod. de dæmon. lib. 2. cap. 8.

In a little pamphlet of the acts and hanging of foure witches, in anno. 1579.

CHAPTER VIII.

What follie it were for witches to enter into such desperate perill, and to endure such intoller-able tortures for no gaine or commoditie, and how it comes to passe that witches are overthrowne by their confessions.

ALAS! if they were so subtill, as witchmongers make them to be, they would espie that it were meere follie for them, not onelie to make a bar-gaine with the divell to throw their soules into hell fire, but their bodies to the tortures of temporall fire and death, for the accomplishment of nothing that might benefit themselves at all: but they would at the leastwise indent with the divell, both to inrich them, and also to enoble them; and finallie to endue them with all worldlie felicitie and pleasure: which is furthest from them of all other. Yea, if they were sensible, they would saie to the divell; Whie should I hearken to you, when you will deceive me? Did you not promise my neigh-bour mother *Dutton* to save and rescue hir; and yet lo she is hanged? Surelie this would appose the divell verie sore. And it is a woonder, that none, from the beginning of the world, till this daie, hath made this and such like objections, whereto the divell could never make answer. But were it not more madnes for them to serve the divell, under these conditions; and yet to endure whippings with iron rods at the divels hands; which (as the witchmongers write) are so set on, that the print of the lashes remaine upon the witches bodie ever after, even so long as she hath a daie to live?

John Bod.

But these old women being daunted with authoritie, circumvented with guile, constrained by force, compelled by feare, induced by error, and deceived by ignorance, doo fall into such rash credulitie, and so are brought unto these absurd confessions. Whose error of mind and blindnes of will dependeth upon the disease and infirmitie of nature: and therefore their actions in that case are the more to be borne withall; bicause they, being destitute of reason, can have no consent. For, *Delictum sine consensu non potest committi, neque injuria sine animo injuriandi;* that is, There can be no sinne without consent, nor injurie com-mitted without a mind to doo wrong. Yet the lawe saith further, that A purpose

L. si per erro-rem jurisd. omni cum inde.

C. sed hoc d.
de publ. &c.
Bal. in leg.
&c.

reteined in mind, dooth nothing to the privat or publike hurt of anie man; and much more that an impossible purpose is unpunishable. *Sanæ mentis voluntas, voluntas rei possibilis est;* A sound mind willeth nothing but that which is possible.

CHAPTER IX.

How melancholie abuseth old women, and of the effects thereof by sundrie examples.

IF anie man advisedlie marke their words, actions, cogitations, and gestures, he shall perceive that melancholie abounding in their head, and occupieng their braine, hath deprived or rather depraved their judgements, and all their senses: I meane not of coosening witches, but of poore melancholike women, which are themselves deceived. For you shall understand, that the force which melancholie hath, and the effects that it worketh in the bodie of a man, or rather of a woman, are almost incredible. For as some of these melancholike persons imagine, they are witches and by witchcraft can worke woonders, and doo what they list: so doo other, troubled with this disease, imagine manie strange, incredible, and impossible things. Some, that they are monarchs and princes, and that all other men are their subjects: some, that they are brute beasts: some, that they be urinals or earthen pots, greatlie fearing to be broken: some, that everie one that meeteth them, will conveie them to the gallowes; and yet in the end hang themselves. One thought, that *Atlas,* whome the poets feigne to hold up heaven with his shoulders, would be wearie, and let the skie fall upon him: another would spend a whole daie upon a stage, imagining that he both heard and saw interludes, and therewith made himselfe great sport. One *Theophilus* a physician, otherwise sound inough of mind (as it is said) imagined that he heard and sawe musicians continuallie plaieng on instruments, in a certeine place of his house. One *Bessus,* that had killed his father, was notablie detected; by imagining that a swallowe upraided him therewith: so as he himselfe thereby revealed the murther.

But the notablest example heereof is, of one that was in great perplexitie, imagining that his nose was as big as a house; insomuch as no freend nor physician could deliver him from this conceipt, nor yet either ease his greefe, or satisfie his fansie in that behalfe: till at the last, a physician more expert in this humor than the rest, used this devise following. First, when he was to come in at the chamber doore being wide open, he suddenlie staied and withdrew himselfe; so as he would not in any wise approch neerer than the doore. The melancholike person musing heereat, asked him the cause why he so demeaned himselfe? Who answered him in this maner: ' Sir, your nose is so great, that I can hardlie enter into your chamber but I shall touch it, and consequentlie hurt it. Lo (quoth he) this is the man that must doo me good; the residue of my freends flatter me, and would hide mine infirmitie from me. Well (said the physician) I will cure you, but you must be content to indure a little paine in the dressing: which he promised patientlie to susteine, and conceived certeine hope of his recoverie. Then entred the physician into the chamber, creeping close by the walles, seeming to feare the touching and hurting of his nose. Then did he blindfold him, which being doone, he caught him by the nose with a paire of pinsors, and threw downe into a tub, which he had placed before his patient, a great quantitie of bloud, with manie peeces of bullocks livers, which he had conveied into the chamber, whilest the others eies were bound up, and then gave him libertie to see and behold the same. He having doone thus againe twoo or three times, the melancholike humor was so qualified, that the mans mind being satisfied, his greefe was eased, and his disease cured.

Thrasibulus, otherwise called *Thrasillus,* being sore oppressed with this melan-

Of one that
through
melancholie
was induced
to thinke
that he had a
nose as big
as a house,
&c.

cholike humor, imagined, that all the ships, which arrived at port *Pyræus*, were his: insomuch as he would number them, and command the mariners to lanch, &c: triumphing at their safe returnes, and moorning for their misfortunes. The *Italian*, whom we called here in *England*, the Monarch, was possessed with the like spirit or conceipt. *Danæus* himselfe reporteth, that he sawe one, that affirmed constantlie that he was a cocke: and saith that through melancholie, such were alienated from themselves.

Danæus in dialog. cap. 3.

Now, if the fansie of a melancholike person may be occupied in causes which are both false and impossible; why should an old witch be thought free from such fantasies, who (as the learned philosophers and physicians saie) upon the stopping of their monethlie melancholike flux or issue of bloud, in their age must needs increase therein, as (through their weaknesse both of bodie and braine) the aptest persons to meete with such melancholike imaginations: with whome their imaginations remaine, even when their senses are gone. Which *Bodin* laboureth to disproove, therein shewing himselfe as good a physician, as else-where a divine.

J. Baptist. P. N. cap. 2.
Card. de var. rerum.
J. Wier. de prestigiis dæmonum, &c.
Aristotle.
John. Bod.

But if they may imagine, that they can transforme their owne bodies, which neverthelesse remaineth in the former shape: how much more credible is it, that they may falselie suppose they can hurt and infeeble other mens bodies; or which is lesse, hinder the comming of butter? &c. But what is it that they will not imagine, and consequentlie confesse that they can doo; speciallie being so earnestlie persuaded thereunto, so sorelie tormented, so craftilie examined, with such promises of favour, as wherby they imagine, that they shall ever after live in great credit & welth? &c.

If you read the executions doone upon witches, either in times past in other countries, or latelie in this land; you shall see such impossibilities confessed, as none, having his right wits, will beleeve. Among other like false confessions, we read that there was a witch confessed at the time of her death or execution, that she had raised all the tempests, and procured all the frosts and hard weather that happened in the winter 1565: and that manie grave and wise men beleeved hir.

Ant. Houin.

CHAPTER X.

That voluntarie confessions may be untrulie made, to the undooing of the confessors, and of the strange operation of melancholie, prooved by a familiar and late example.

BUT that it may appeere, that even voluntarie confession (in this case) may be untrulie made, though it tend to the destruction of the confessor; and that melancholie may moove imaginations to that effect: I will cite a notable instance concerning this matter, the parties themselves being yet alive, and dwelling in the parish of *Sellenge* in *Kent*, and the matter not long sithence in this sort performed.

One *Ade Davie*, the wife of *Simon Davie*, husbandman, being reputed a right honest bodie, and being of good parentage, grew suddenlie (as hir husband informed mee, and as it is well knowne in these parts) to be somewhat pensive and more sad than in times past. Which thing though it greeved him, yet he was loth to make it so appeere, as either his wife might be troubled or discontented therewith, or his neighbours informed thereof; least ill husbandrie should be laid to his charge (which in these quarters is much abhorred). But when she grew from pensivenes, to some perturbation of mind; so as hir accustomed rest began in the night season to be withdrawne from hir, through sighing and secret lamentation; and that, not without teares, hee could not but demand the cause of hir conceipt and extraordinarie moorning. But although at that time

A Kentish storie of a late accident.

she covered the same, acknowledging nothing to be amisse with hir: soone after notwithstanding she fell downe before him on hir knees, desiring him to forgive hir, for she had greevouslie offended (as she said) both God & him. Hir poore husband being abashed at this hir behaviour, comforted hir, as he could; asking hir the cause of hir trouble & greefe: who told him, that she had, (contrarie to Gods lawe) & to the offense of all good christians, to the injurie of him, & speciallie to the losse of hir owne soule, bargained and given hir soule to the divell, to be delivered unto him within short space. Whereunto hir husband answered, saieng; Wife, be of good cheere, this thy bargaine is void and of none effect: for thou hast sold that which is none of thine to sell; sith it belongeth to Christ, who hath bought it, and deerelie paid for it, even with his bloud, which he shed upon the crosse; so as the divell hath no interest in thee. After this, with like submission, teares, and penitence, she said unto him; Oh husband, I have yet committed another fault, and doone you more injurie: for I have bewitched you and your children. Be content (quoth he) by the grace of God, Jesus Christ shall unwitch us: for none evill can happen to them that feare God.

And (as trulie as the Lord liveth) this was the tenor of his words unto me, which I knowe is true, as proceeding from unfeigned lips, and from one that feareth God. Now when the time approched that the divell should come, and take possession of the woman, according to his bargaine, he watched and praied earnestlie, and caused his wife to read psalmes and praiers for mercie at Gods hands: and suddenlie about midnight, there was a great rumbling beelowe under his chamber windowe, which amazed them exceedinglie. For they conceived, that the divell was beelowe, though he had no power to come up, bicause of their fervent praiers.

He that noteth this womans first and second confession, freelie and voluntarilie made, how everie thing concurred that might serve to adde credit thereunto, and yeeld matter for hir condemnation, would not thinke, but that if *Bodin* were foreman of hir inquest, he would crie; Guiltie: & would hasten execution upon hir; who would have said as much before any judge in the world, if she had beene examined; and have confessed no lesse, if she had beene arraigned therupon. But God knoweth, she was innocent of anie these crimes: howbeit she was brought lowe and pressed downe with the weight of this humor, so as both hir rest and sleepe were taken awaie from hir; & hir fansies troubled and disquieted with despaire, and such other cogitations as grew by occasion thereof. And yet I beleeve, if any mishap had insued to hir husband, or his children; few witchmongers would have judged otherwise, but that she had bewitched them. And she (for hir part) so constantlie persuaded hir selfe to be a witch, that she judged hir selfe worthie of death; insomuch as being reteined in hir chamber, she sawe not anie one carrieng a faggot to the fier, but she would saie it was to make a fier to burne hir for witcherie. But God knoweth she had bewitched none, neither insued there anie hurt unto anie, by hir imagination, but unto hir selfe.

And as for the rumbling, it was by occasion of a sheepe, which was flawed, and hoong by the wals, so as a dog came and devoured it; whereby grew the noise which I before mentioned: and she being now recovered, remaineth a right honest woman, far from such impietie, and shamed of hir imaginations, which she perceiveth to have growne through melancholie.

Note the christian comfort of the husbad to his wife.

Confutation.

A comicall catastrophe.

CHAPTER XI.

The strange and divers effects of melancholie, and how the same humor abounding in witches, or rather old women, filleth them full of mervellous imaginations, and that their confessions are not to be credited.

BUT in truth, this melancholike humor (as the best physicians affirme) is the cause of all their strange, impossible, and incredible confessions: which are so fond, that I woonder how anie man can be abused thereby. Howbeit, these affections, though they appeare in the mind of man, yet are they bred in the bodie, and proceed from this humor, which is the verie dregs of bloud, nourishing and feeding those places, from whence proceed feares, cogitations, superstitions, fastings, labours, and such like. *H. Card. de var. rerum. cap. 8. Jo. Wierus de præst. lib. 6. cap. 8.*

This maketh sufferance of torments, and (as some saie) foresight of things to come, and preserveth health, as being cold and drie: it maketh men subject to leanenesse, and to the quartane ague. They that are vexed therewith, are destroiers of themselves, stout to suffer injuries, fearefull to offer violence; except the humor be hot. They learne strange toongs with small industrie (as *Aristotle* and others affirme). *Aristotle de somnio. H. Card. lib. 8 de var. rer.*

If our witches phantasies were not corrupted, nor their wils confounded with this humor, they would not so voluntarilie and readilie confesse that which calleth their life in question; whereof they could never otherwise be convicted. *J. Bodin* with his lawyers physicke reasoneth contrarilie; as though melancholie were furthest of all from those old women, whom we call witches: deriding the most famous and noble physician *John Wier* for his opinion in that behalfe. But bicause I am no physician, I will set a physician to him; namelie *Erastus*, who hath these words, to wit, that These witches, through their corrupt phantasie abounding with melancholike humors, by reason of their old age, doo dreame and imagine they hurt those things which they neither could nor doo hurt; and so thinke they knowe an art, which they neither have learned nor yet understand. *Jo. Bod. contra Jo. Wierum.*

But whie should there be more credit given to witches, when they saie they have made a reall bargaine with the divell, killed a cow, bewitched butter, infeebled a child, forespoken hir neighbour, &c: than when she confesseth that she transubstantiateth hir selfe, maketh it raine or haile, flieth in the aire, goeth invisible, transferreth corne in the grasse from one field to another? &c. If you thinke that in the one their confessions be sound, whie should you saie that they are corrupt in the other; the confession of all these things being made at one instant, and affirmed with like constancie, or rather audacitie? But you see the one to be impossible, and therefore you thinke thereby, that their confessions are vaine and false. The other you thinke may be doone, and see them confesse it, and therefore you conclude, *A posse ad esse;* as being persuaded it is so, bicause you thinke it may be so. But I saie, both with the divines, and philosophers, that that which is imagined of witchcraft, hath no truth of action; or being besides their imagination, the which (for the most part) is occupied in false causes. For whosoever desireth to bring to passe an impossible thing, hath a vaine, an idle, and a childish persuasion, bred by an unsound mind: for *Sanæ mentis voluntas, voluntas rei possibilis est;* The will of a sound mind, is the desire of a possible thing. *August. lib. de Trinit. 3. Idem. de civit. Dei. Idem. de civit. Dei. Clemens. recogn. 3. Iamblichus. Jo. Wierus. Cardanus. Pampia. &c.*

Chapter XII.

A confutation of witches confessions, especiallie concerning their league.

An objection.

The
resolution.

BUT it is objected, that witches confesse they renounce the faith, and as their confession must be true (or else they would not make it:) so must their fault be worthie of death, or else they should not be executed. Whereunto I answer as before; that their confessions are extorted, or else proceed from an unsound mind. Yea I saie further, that we our selves, which are sound of mind, and yet seeke anie other waie of salvation than Christ Jesus, or breake his commandements, or walke not in his steps with a livelie faith, &c: doo not onlie renounce the faith, but God himselfe: and therefore they (in confessing that they forsake God, and imbrace sathan) doo that which we all should doo. As touching that horrible part of their confession, in the league which tendeth to the killing of their owne and others children, the seething of them, and the making of their potion or pottage, and the effects thereof; their good fridaies meeting, being the daie of their deliverance, their incests, with their returne at the end of nine moneths, when commonlie women be neither able to go that journie, nor to returne, &c; it is so horrible, unnaturall, unlikelie, and unpossible; that if I should behold such things with mine eies, I should rather thinke my selfe dreaming, dronken, or some waie deprived of my senses; than give credit to so horrible and filthie matters.

A forged
miracle.

How hath the oile or pottage of a sodden child such vertue, as that a staffe annointed therewith, can carrie folke in the aire? Their potable liquor, which (they saie) maketh maisters of that facultie, is it not ridiculous? And is it not, by the opinion of all philosophers, physicians, and divines, void of such vertue, as is imputed thereunto?

Their not fasting on fridaies, and their fasting on sundaies, their spetting at the time of elevation, their refusall of holie water, their despising of superstitious crosses, &c: which are all good steps to true christianitie, helpe me to confute the residue of their confessions.

Chapter XIII.

A confutation of witches confessions, concerning making of tempests and raine: of the naturall cause of raine, and that witches or divels have no power to doo such things.

AND to speake more generallie of all the impossible actions referred unto them, as also of their false confessions; I saie, that there is none which acknowledgeth God to be onlie omnipotent, and the onlie worker of all miracles, nor anie other indued with meane sense, but will denie that the elements are obedient to witches, and at their commandement; or that they may at their pleasure send raine, haile, tempests, thunder, lightening; when she being but an old doting woman, casteth a flint stone over hir left shoulder, towards the west, or hurleth a little sea sand up into the element, or wetteth a broome sprig in water, and sprinkleth the same in the aire; or diggeth a pit in the earth, and putting water therein, stirreth it about with hir finger; or boileth hogs bristles, or laieth sticks acrosse upon a banke, where never a drop of water is; or burieth sage till it be rotten: all which things are confessed by witches, and affirmed by writers to be the meanes that witches use to moove extraordinarie tempests and raine, &c.

The waies
that witches
use to make
raine, &c.
*Nider. Mal.
Malef. J.
Bod. Frier
Barth.
Heming.
Danæus,* &c.

34

We read in *M. Maleficarum*, that a little girle walking abroad with hir father in his land, heard him complaine of drought, wishing for raine, &c. Whie father (quoth the child) I can make it raine or haile, when and where I list? He asked where she learned it. She said, of hir mother, who forbad hir to tell anie bodie thereof. He asked hir how hir mother taught hir? She answered, that hir mother committed hir to a maister, who would at anie time doo anie thing for hir. Whie then (said he) make it raine but onlie in my field. And so she went to the streame, and threw up water in hir maisters name, and made it raine presentlie. And proceeding further with hir father, she made it haile in another field, at hir fathers request. Hereupon he accused his wife, and caused hir to be burned; and then he new christened his child againe: which circumstance is common among papists and witchmongers. And howsoever the first part hereof was prooved, there is no doubt but the latter part was throughlie executed. If they could indeed bring these things to passe at their pleasure, then might they also be impediments unto the course of all other naturall things, and ordinances appointed by God: as, to cause it to hold up, when it should raine; and to make midnight, of high noone: and by those meanes (I saie) the divine power should beecome servile to the will of a witch, so as we could neither eat nor drinke but by their permission.

Mal. Malef. par. 2. quæ. 1. cap. 12.

He that can lie, can steale; as he that can worke can plaie.

Me thinks *Seneca* might satisfie these credulous or rather idolatrous people, that runne a whorehunting, either in bodie or phansie, after these witches, beleeving all that is attributed unto them, to the derogation of Gods glorie. He saith, that the rude people, and our ignorant predecessors did beleeve, that raine and showers might be procured and staied by witches charmes and inchantments: of which kind of things that there can nothing be wrought, it is so manifest, that we need not go to anie philosophers schoole, to learne the confutation thereof.

But *Jeremie*, by the word of God, dooth utterlie confound all that which may be devised for the maintenance of that foolish opinion, saieng; Are there any among the gods of the gentiles, that sendeth raine, or giveth showers from heaven? Art not thou the selfe same our Lord God? We will trust in thee, for thou dooest and makest all these things. I may therefore with *Brentius* boldlie saie, that It is neither in the power of witches nor divels, to accomplish that matter; but in God onelie. For when exhalations are drawne and lifted up from out of the earth, by the power of the sunne, into the middle region of the aire, the coldnes thereof constreineth and thickeneth those vapours; which being beecome clouds, are dissolved againe by the heate of the sunne, wherby raine or haile is ingendred; raine, if by the waie the drops be not frosen and made haile. These circumstances being considered with the course of the whole scripture, it can neither be in the power of witch or divell to procure raine, or faire weather.

Jere. 16, 22. *Dii gentium dæmonia,* The gods of the gentiles are divels.

The naturall generations of haile and raine.

And whereas the storie of *Job* in this case is alledged against me (wherein a witch is not once named) I have particularlie answered it else-where. And therefore thus much onelie I say heere; that Even there, where it pleased God (as *Calvine* saith) to set downe circumstances for the instruction of our grosse capacities, which are not able to conceive of spirituall communication, or heavenlie affaires; the divell desireth God to stretch out his hand, and touch all that *Job* hath. And though he seemeth to grant sathans desire, yet God himselfe sent fire from heaven, &c. Where, it is to be gathered, that although God, said, He is in thine hand: it was the Lords hand that punished *Job*, and not the hand of the divell, who said not, Give me leave to plague him; but, Laie thine hand upon him. And when *Job* continued faithfull notwithstanding all his afflictions, in his children, bodie and goods; the divell is said to come againe to God, and to saie as before, to wit: Now stretch out thine hand, and touch his bones and his flesh. Which argueth as well that he could not doo it, as that he himselfe did it not before. And be it here remembred, that *M. Mal.* and the residue of the witchmongers denie, that there were any witches in *Jobs* time. But see more hereof elsewhere.

Job 1, 11.

Ib. verse 16.

Job 2, 5.

Mal. Malef. pa. 1, quæ. 2.

35

CHAPTER XIV.

What would ensue, if witches confessions or witchmongers opinions were true, concerning the effects of witchcraft, inchantments, &c.

IF it were true that witches confesse, or that all writers write, or that witchmongers report, or that fooles beleeve, we should never have butter in the chearne, nor cow in the close, nor corne in the field, nor faire weather abroad, nor health within doores. Or if that which is conteined in M. Mal. *Bodin, &c*: or in the pamphlets late set foorth in English, of witches executions, shuld be true in those things that witches are said to confesse, what creature could live in securitie? Or what needed such preparation of warres, or such trouble, or charge in that behalfe? No prince should be able to reigne or live in the land. For (as *Danæus* saith) that one *Martine* a witch killed the emperour of *Germanie* with witchcraft: so would our witches (if they could) destroie all our magistrates. One old witch might overthrowe an armie roiall: and then what needed we any guns, or wild fire, or any other instruments of warre? A witch might supplie all wants, and accomplish a princes will in this behalfe, even without charge or bloudshed of his people.

If it be objected, that witches worke by the divell, and christian princes are not to deale that way; I answer, that few princes disposed to battell would make conscience therin, speciallie such as take unjust wars in hand, using other helpes, devises, & engines as unlawfull and divelish as that; in whose campe there is neither the rule of religion or christian order observed: insomuch as ravishments, murthers, blasphemies and thefts are there most commonlie and freelie committed. So that the divell is more feared, and better served in their camps, than God almightie.

But admit that souldiers would be scrupulous herein, the pope hath authoritie to dispense therewith; as in like case he hath doone, by the testimonie of his owne authors and friends. Admit also, that throughout all christendome, warres were justly mainteined, and religion dulie observed in their camps; yet would the Turke and other infidels cut our throtes, or at least one anothers throte, with the helpe of their witches; for they would make no conscience thereof.

CHAPTER XV.

Examples of forren nations, who in their warres used the assistance of witches; of eybiting witches in Ireland, of two archers that shot with familiars.

IN the warres between the kings of *Denmarke* and *Sueveland, 1563.* the *Danes* doo write, that the king of *Sueveland* caried about with him in his campe, foure old witches, who with their charms so qualified the *Danes*, as they were thereby disabled to annoie their enimies: insomuch as, if they had taken in hand anie enterprise, they were so infeebled by those witches, as they could performe nothing. And although this could have no credit at the first, yet in the end, one of these witches was taken prisoner, and confessed the whole matter; so as (saith he) the threds, the line, and the characters were found in the high waie and water plashes.

The *Irishmen* addict themselves wonderfullie to the credit and practise hereof; insomuch as they affirme, that not onelie their children, but their cattell, are (as they call it) eybitten, when they fall suddenlie sicke, and terme one sort of their witches eybiters; onelie in that respect: yea and they will not sticke to affirme, that they can rime either man or beast to death. Also the West *Indians* and *Muscovits* doo the like: and the *Hunnes* (as *Gregorie Turonensis* writeth) used the helpe of witches in time of war.

I find another storie written in *M. Mal.* repeated by *Bodin;* that one souldier called *Pumher,* dailie through witchcraft killed with his bowe and arrowes three of the enimies, as they stood peeping over the walles of a castell besieged: so as in the end he killed them all quite, saving one. The triall of the archers sinister dealing, and a proofe thereof expressed, is; for that he never lightly failed when he shot, and for that he killed them by three a daie; and had shot three arrowes into a rood. This was he that shot at a pennie on his sonnes head, and made readie another arrow, to have slaine the duke *Remgrave* that commanded it. And doubtlesse, bicause of his singular dexteritie in shooting, he was reputed a witch, as dooing that which others could not doo, nor thinke to be in the power of man to doo: though indeed no miracle, no witchcraft, no impossibilitie nor difficultie consisted therein.

Pumher an archer.

But this latter storie I can requite with a familiar example. For at Towne *Malling* in kent, one of Q. *Maries* justices, upon the complaint of many wise men, and a few foolish boies, laid an archer by the heeles; bicause he shot so neere the white at buts. For he was informed and persuaded, that the poore man plaied with a flie, otherwise called a divell or familiar. And bicause he was certified that the archer aforesaid shot better than the common shooting, which he before had heard of or seene, he conceived it could not be in Gods name, but by inchantment: whereby this archer (as he supposed by abusing the Queenes liege people) gained some one daie two or three shillings, to the detriment of the commonwealth, and to his owne inriching. And therefore the archer was severelie punished, to the great encouragement of archers, and to the wise example of justice; but speciallie to the overthrowe of witchcraft. And now againe to our matter.

A skilfull archer punished by an unskilfull Justice.

CHAPTER XVI.

Authorities condemning the fantasticall confessions of witches, and how a popish doctor taketh upon him to disproove the same.

CERTEINE generall councels, by their decrees, have condemned the confessions and erronious credulitie of witches, to be vaine, fantasticall and fabulous. And even those, which are parcell of their league, wherupon our witchmongers doo so build, to wit; their night walkings and meetings with *Herodias,* and the *Pagan* gods: at which time they should passe so farre in so little a space on cockhorsse; their transubstantiation, their eating of children, and their pulling of them from their mothers sides, their entring into mens houses, through chinks and little holes, where a flie can scarselie wring out, and the disquieting of the inhabitants, *&c:* all which are not onelie said by a generall councell to be meere fantasticall, and imaginations in dreames; but so affirmed by the ancient writers. The words of the councell are these; It may not be omitted, that certeine wicked women following sathans provocations, being seduced by the illusion of divels, beleeve and professe, that in the night times they ride abroad with *Diana,* the goddesse of the *Pagans,* or else with *Herodias,* with an innumerable multitude, upon certeine beasts, and passe over manie countries and nations, in the silence of the night, and doo whatsoever those fairies or ladies command, *&c.* And it followeth even there; Let all ministers therefore in their severall cures, preach to Gods people, so as they may knowe all these things to be false, *&c.* It followeth in the same councell; Therefore,

Concil. Acquirens in decret. 26. quæ. 5. can. episcopi. August. de spiritu & anima cap. 8. Franc. Ponzivib. tract. de lam. numero 49. Grillandus de sort. numero. 6.

whosoever beleeveth that any creature may be either created by them, or else changed into better or worsse, or be any way transformed into any other kind or likenes of any, but of the creator himselfe, is assuredlie an infidell, and woorsse than a *Pagan*.

In histor. vel vita sancti Germani.

And if this be credible, then all these their bargaines and assemblies, &c: are incredible, which are onelie ratified by certeine foolish and extorted confessions; and by a fable of S. *Germane*, who watched the fairies or witches, being at a reere banket, and through his holinesse staied them, till he sent to the houses of those neighbours, which seemed to be there, and found them all in bed; and so tried, that these were divels in the likenesse of those women. Which if it were as true, as it is false, it might serve well to confute this their meeting and night-walking. For if the divels be onlie present in the likenesse of witches, then is that false, which is attributed to witches in this behalfe.

Novus. Mal. Mal. in quæ. de strigib. cap. 21. 22. 23, &c.

But bicause the old hammar of *Sprenger* and *Institor*, in their old *Malleo Maleficarum*, was insufficient to knocke downe this councell; a yoong beetle-head called Frier *Bartholomæus Spineus* hath made a new leaden beetle, to beate downe the councell, and to kill these old women. Wherein he counterfeiting *Aesops* asse, claweth the pope with his heeles: affirming upon his credit, that the councell is false and erronious; bicause the doctrine swarveth from the popish church, and is not authenticall but apocryphall; saieng (though untrulie) that that councell was not called by the commandement and pleasure of the pope, nor ratified by his authoritie, which (saith he) is sufficient to disanull all councels. For surelie (saith this frier, which at this instant is a cheefe inquisitor) if the words of this councell were to be admitted, both I, and all my predecessors had published notorious lies, and committed manie injurious executions; whereby the popes themselves also might justlie be detected of error, contrarie to the catholike beleefe in that behalfe. Marrie he saith, that although the words and direct sense of this councell be quite contrarie to truth and his opinion; yet he will make an exposition thereof, that shall somewhat mitigate the lewdnes of the same; and this he saith is not onlie allowable to doo, but also meritorious. Marke the mans words, and judge his meaning.

Bar. Spineus. Mal. Malef. cap. 23. in quæ. de strigib.

CHAPTER XVII.

Witchmongers reasons, to proove that witches can worke wonders, Bodins tale of a Friseland preest transported, that imaginations, proceeding of melancholie doo cause illusions.

Mal. Malef. pa. 1, cap. 3. Guli. Parisi.

OLD *M. Maleficarum* also saith, that the councels and doctors were all deceived heerein, and alledging authoritie therfore, confuteth that opinion by a notable reason, called *Petitio principii*, or rather, *Ignotum per ignotius*, in this maner: They can put changlings in the place of other children; *Ergo* they can transferre and transforme themselves and others, &c: according to their confession in that behalfe. Item he saith, and *Bodin* justifieth it, that a preest in *Friseland* was corporallie transferred into a farre countrie, as witnessed another preest of *Oberdorf* his companion, who saw him aloft in the aire: *Ergo* saith *M. Mal.* they have all beene deceived hitherto, to the great impunitie of horrible witches. Wherein he opposeth his follie against God and his church, against the truth, and against all possibilitie. But surelie it is almost incredible, how imagination shall abuse such as are subject unto melancholie; so as they shall beleeve they see, heare, and doo that, which never was nor shall be; as is partlie declared, if you read *Galen De locis affectis*, and may more plainelie appeere also if you read *Aristotle De somnio*.

August. de spiritu & anima.

And thereof S. *Augustine* saith well, that he is too much a foole and a blockhead, that supposeth those things to be doone indeed, and corporallie, which

38

are by such persons phantasticallie imagined : which phantasticall illusions do as well agree and accord (as *Algerus* saith) with magicall deceipts, as the veritie accompanieth divine holinesse.

Lib. 1. *cap.* 7. *de eucharist.*

Chapter XVIII.

That the confession of witches is insufficient in civill and common lawe to take awaie life. What the sounder divines, and decrees of councels determine in this case.

ALAS! what creature being sound in state of mind, would (without compulsion) make such maner of confessions as they do; or would, for a trifle, or nothing, make a perfect bargaine with the divell for hir soule, to be yeelded up unto his tortures and everlasting flames, and that within a verie short time; speciallie being through age most commonlie unlike to live one whole yeare? The terror of hell fire must needs be to them diverslie manifested, and much more terrible; bicause of their weaknesse, nature, and kind, than to any other : as it would appeere, if a witch were but asked, Whether she would be contented to be hanged one yeare hence, upon condition hir displesure might be wreked upon hir enimie presentlie. As for theeves, & such other, they think not to go to hell fire; but are either persuaded there is no hell, or that their crime deserveth it not, or else that they have time enough to repent : so as, no doubt, if they were perfectlie resolved heereof, they would never make such adventures. Neither doo I thinke, that for any summe of monie, they would make so direct a bargaine to go to hell fire. Now then I conclude, that confession in this behalf is insufficient to take awaie the life of any body; or to atteine such credit, as to be beleeved without further proofe. For as *Augustine* and *Isidore*, with the rest of the sounder divines saie, that these prestigious things, which are wrought by witches are fantasticall : so doo the sounder decrees of councels and canons agree, that in that case, there is no place for criminall action. And the lawe saith, that The confession of such persons as are illuded, must needs be erronious, and therefore is not to be admitted : for, *Confessio debet tenere verum* & *possibile.* But these things are opposite both to lawe and nature, and therfore it followeth not; Bicause these witches confesse so, *Ergo* it is so. For the confession differeth from the act, or from the possibilitie of the act. And whatsoever is contrarie to nature faileth in his principles, and therefore is naturallie impossible.

The lawe also saith, *In criminalibus regulariter non statur soli confessioni rei,* In criminall cases or touching life, we must not absolutelie stand to the confession of the accused partie : but in these matters proofes must be brought more cleare than the light it selfe. And in this crime no bodie must be condemned upon presumptions. And where it is objected and urged, that Since God onelie knoweth the thoughts, therefore there is none other waie of proofe but by confession : It is answered thus in the lawe, to wit : Their confession in this case conteineth an outward act, and the same impossible both in lawe and nature, and also unlikelie to be true; and therefore *Quod verisimile non est, attendi non debet.* So as, though their confessions may be worthie of punishment, as whereby they shew a will to commit such mischeefe, yet not worthie of credit, as that they have such power. For, *Si factum absit, soláque opinione laborent, é stultorum genere sunt;* If they confesse a fact performed but in opinion, they are to be reputed among the number of fooles. Neither may any man be by lawe condemned for criminall causes, upon presumptions, nor yet by single witnesses : neither at the accusation of a capitall enimie, who indeed is not to be admitted to give evidence in this case; though it please *M. Mal.* and *Bodin* to affirme the contrarie. But beyond all equitie, these inquisitors have shifts and devises enow, to plague and kill

It is not likelie they would so doo : *Ergo* a lie.

August. de civit. Dei. Isidor. lib. (8. cap. 9) Etymol. 26. quæ. 5. ca. nec mirum. Ponzivibius de lamiis, volum. 10. L. error, & L. cum post. c. de juris & facti ignor. ac in L. de ætat. §. item de interrog. actiõ. Per glos. Bal. & alios in L. 1. c. de confes. glos. nec. in 6. § ad leg. Aquil L. Neracius. §. fin. Ut per Bald. & August. in L. I. c. de confess, &c. Extra. de presump. literas. Per Bald. in d. leg. &c. Extra. de test cum literis. Mal. Malef. pa. 3 quæst. 5. cap. 11.

*Mal. Malef.
quæst.* 14.
pa. 1.

*C. de malef. L.
nullus. L.
nemo & L.
culpa.* and
*affirmed by
Mal. malef.*

*Mal. malef.
quæst.* 17.

these poore soules: for (they say) their fault is greatest of all others; bicause of their carnall copulation with the divell, and therefore they are to be punished as heretikes, foure maner of waies: to wit; with excommunication, deprivation, losse of goods, and also with death.

And indeede they find lawe, and provide meanes thereby to mainteine this their bloudie humor. For it is written in their popish canons, that As for these kind of heretikes, how much soever they repent and returne to the faith, they may not be reteined alive, or kept in perpetuall prison; but be put to extreame death. Yea, *M. Mal.* writeth, that A witches sinne is the sinne against the Holie-ghost; to wit, irremissible: yea further, that it is greater than the sinne of the angels that fell. In which respect I wonder, that *Moses* delivered not three tables to the children of Israell; or at the leastwise, that he exhibited not commandements for it. It is not credible that the greatest should be included in the lesse, &c.

But when these witchmongers are convinced in the objection concerning their confessions; so as thereby their tyrannicall arguments cannot prevaile, to imbrue the magistrates hands in so much bloud as their appetite requireth: they fall to accusing them of other crimes, that the world might thinke they had some colour to mainteine their malicious furie against them.

CHAPTER XIX.

Of foure capitall crimes objected against witches, all fullie answered and confuted as frivolous.

1. Idolatrie,
confuted.

FIRST therefore they laie to their charge idolatrie. But alas without all reason: for such are properlie knowne to us to be idolaters, as doo externall worship to idols or strange gods. The furthest point that idolatrie can be stretched unto, is, that they, which are culpable therein, are such as hope for and seeke salvation at the hands of idols, or of anie other than God; or fix their whole mind and love upon anie creature, so as the power of God be neglected and contemned thereby. But witches neither seeke nor beleeve to have salvation at the hands of divels, but by them they are onlie deceived; the instruments of their phantasie being corrupted, and so infatuated, that they suppose, confesse, and saie they can doo that, which is as farre beyond their power and nature to doo, as to kill a man at *Yorke* before noone, when they have beene seene at *London* in that morning, &c. But if these latter idolaters, whose idolatrie is spirituall, and committed onelie in mind, should be punished by death; then should everie covetous man, or other, that setteth his affection anie waie too much upon an earthlie creature, be executed, and yet perchance the witch might escape scot-free.

2. Apostasie,
confuted.

Secondlie, apostasie is laid to their charge, whereby it is inferred, that they are worthie to die. But apostasie is, where anie of sound judgement forsake the gospell, learned and well knowne unto them; and doo not onelie imbrace impietie and infidelitie; but oppugne and resist the truth erstwhile by them professed. But alas these poore women go not about to defend anie impietie, but after good admonition repent.

3. Seducing
of the
people,
confuted.

Thirdlie, they would have them executed for seducing the people. But God knoweth they have small store of Rhetorike or art to seduce; except to tell a tale of Robin good-fellow be to deceive and seduce. Neither may their age or sex admit that opinion or accusation to be just: for they themselves are poore seduced soules. I for my part (as else-where I have said) have prooved this point to be false in most apparent sort.

40

Fourthlie, as touching the accusation, which all the writers use herein against them for their carnall copulation with *Incubus:* the follie of mens credulitie is as much to be woondered at and derided, as the others vaine and impossible confessions. For the divell is a spirit, and hath neither flesh nor bones, which were to be used in the performance of this action. And since he also lacketh all instruments, substance, and seed ingendred of bloud; it were follie to staie overlong in the confutation of that, which is not in the nature of things. And yet must I saie somewhat heerein, bicause the opinion hereof is so stronglie and universallie received, and the fables hereupon so innumerable; wherby *M. Mal. Bodin, Hemingius, Hyperius, Danæus, Erastus,* and others that take upon them to write heerein, are so abused, or rather seeke to abuse others; as I woonder at their fond credulitie in this behalfe. For they affirme undoubtedlie, that the divell plaieth *Succubus* to the man, and carrieth from him the seed of generation, which he delivereth as *Incubus* to the woman, who manie times that waie is gotten with child; which will verie naturallie (they saie) become a witch, and such a one they affirme *Merline* was.

4. Carnall copulation with Incubus, confuted.

How the divell plaieth Succubus and Incubus.

CHAPTER XX.

A request to such readers as loath to heare or read filthie and bawdie matters (which of necessitie are heere to be inserted) to passe over eight chapters.

BUT in so much as I am driven (for the more manifest bewraieng and displaieng of this most filthie and horrible error) to staine my paper with writing thereon certeine of their beastlie and bawdie assertions and examples, whereby they confirme this their doctrine (being my selfe both ashamed, and loth once to thinke upon such filthinesse, although it be to the condemnation thereof) I must intreat you that are the readers hereof, whose chaste eares cannot well endure to heare of such abhominable lecheries, as are gathered out of the bookes of those witchmongers (although doctors of divinitie, and otherwise of great authoritie and estimation) to turne over a few leaves, wherein (I saie) I have like a groome thrust their bawdie stuffe (even that which I my selfe loath) as into a stinking corner: howbeit, none otherwise, I hope, but that the other parts of my writing shall remaine sweet, and this also covered as close as may be.

A perorati to the readers.

BOOKE IV.

Chapter I.

Of witchmongers opinions concerning evill spirits, how they frame themselves in more excellent sort than God made us.

Mal. malef.
par. 2. cap. 4.
quæst. 1.

JAMES SPRENGER and *Henrie Institor*, in *M. Mal.* agreing with *Bodin, Barth. Spineus, Danæus, Erastus, Hemingius,* and the rest, doo make a bawdie discourse; labouring to proove by a foolish kind of philosophie, that evill spirits cannot onlie take earthlie forms and shapes of men; but also counterfeit hearing, seeing, &c: and likewise, that they can eate and devoure meats, and also reteine, digest, and avoid the same: and finallie, use diverse kinds of activities, but speciallie excell in the use and art of venerie. For *M. Mal.* saith, that

If his bodilie
eies were out,
he would see
but ilfavored-
lie.

The eies and eares of the mind are farre more subtill than bodilie eies or carnal eares. Yea it is there affirmed, that as they take bodies and the likenesse of members; so they take minds and similitudes of their operations. But by the way, I would have them answer this question. Our minds and soules are spirituall things. If our corporall eares be stopped, what can they heare or conceive of anie externall wisedome? And truelie, a man of such a constitution of bodie, as they imagine of these spirits, which make themselves, &c: were of farre more excellent substance, &c: than the bodies of them that God made in paradise; and so the divels workmanship should exceed the handie worke of God the father and creator of all things.

Chapter II.

Of bawdie Incubus and Succubus, and whether the action of venerie may be performed betweene witches and divels, and when witches first yeelded to Incubus.

Nider in
fornicario.
T. Brabant in
lib. de apib.

HERETOFORE (they saie) *Incubus* was faine to ravish women against their will, untill Anno. 1400: but now since that time witches consent willinglie to their desires: in so much as some one witch exerciseth that trade of lecherie with *Incubus* twentie or thirtie yeares togither; as was confessed by fourtie and eight witches burned at *Ravenspurge*. But what goodlie fellowes

In. sen. dist. 4,
art. 4.

Incubus begetteth upon these witches, is prooved by *Thomas of Aquine, Bodin, M. Mal. Hyperius,* &c.

Gen. 6, 4.

This is prooved first by the divels cunning, in discerning the difference of the seed which falleth from men. Secondlie, by his understanding of the aptnes of the women for the receipt of such seed. Thirdlie by his knowledge of the constellations, which are freendlie to such corporall effects. And lastlie, by the excellent complexion of such as the divell maketh choice of, to beget such notable personages upon, as are the causes of the greatnesse and excellencie of the child thus begotten.

Mal. malef.
par. 2. quæ. 1.
August. de
doctrina Christ.

And to proove that such bawdie dooings betwixt the divell and witches is not fained, S. *Augustine* is alledged, who saith, that All superstitious arts had their beginning of the pestiferous societie betwixt the divell and man. Wherein he

42

saith truelie; for that in paradise, betwixt the divell and man, all wickednes was so contrived, that man ever since hath studied wicked arts: yea and the divell will be sure to be at the middle and at both ends of everie mischeefe. But that the divell ingendreth with a woman, in maner and forme as is supposed, and naturallie begetteth the wicked, neither is it true, nor *Augustines* meaning in this place.

Howbeit *M. Mal.* proceedeth, affirming that All witches take their beginning from such filthie actions, wherein the divell, in likenes of a prettie wench, lieth prostitute as *Succubus* to the man, and reteining his nature and seede, conveieth it unto the witch, to whome he delivereth it as *Incubus*. Wherein also is refuted the opinion of them that hold a spirit to be unpalpable. *M. Mal.* saith, There can be rendred no infallible rule, though a probable distinction may be set downe, whether *Incubus* in the act of venerie doo alwaies powre seed out of his assumed bodie. And this is the distinction; Either she is old and barren or yoong and pregnant. If she be barren, then dooth *Incubus* use hir without decision of seed; bicause such seed should serve for no purpose. And the divell avoideth superfluitie as much as he may; and yet for hir pleasure and condemnation togither, he goeth to worke with hir. But by the waie, if the divell were so compendious, what should he need to use such circumstances, even in these verie actions, as to make these assemblies, conventicles, ceremonies, &c: when he hath alreadie bought their bodies, and bargained for their soules? Or what reason had he, to make them kill so manie infants, by whom he rather loseth than gaineth any thing; bicause they are, so farre as either he or we knowe, in better case than we of riper yeares by reason of their innocencie? Well, if she be not past children, then stealeth he seed awaie (as hath beene said) from some wicked man being about that lecherous busines, and therewith getteth yoong witches upon the old.

*Mal. malef.
quæ.* I. *par.* I.

And note, that they affirme that this businesse is better accomplished with seed thus gathered, than that which is shed in dremes, through superfluitie of humors: bicause that is gathered from the vertue of the seed generative. And if it be said that the seed will wax cold by the waie, and so lose his naturall heate, and consequentlie the vertue: *M. Mal. Danæus*, and the rest doo answere, that the divell can so carrie it, as no heate shall go from it, &c.

*Mal. malef.
par.* I. *quæ.* I.
*Danæus in
dialog. de
sortiariis.
Ja. Sprenger
in Mal. male.*

Furthermore, old witches are sworne to procure as manie yoong virgins for *Incubus* as they can, whereby in time they growe to be excellent bawds: but in this case the preest plaieth *Incubus*. For you shall find, that confession to a preest, and namelie this word *Benedicite*, driveth *Incubus* awaie, when *Ave Maries*, crosses, and all other charmes faile.

CHAPTER III.

Of the divels visible & invisible dealing with witches in the waie of lecherie.

BUT as touching the divels visible or invisible execution of lecherie, it is written, that to such witches, as before have made a visible legue with the preest, (the divell I should saie) there is no necessitie that *Incubus* should appeere invisible: marrie to the standers by hee is for the most part invisible. For proofe hereof *James Sprenger* and *Institor* affirme, that Manie times witches are seene in the fields, and woods, prostituting themselves uncovered and naked up to the navill, wagging and mooving their members in everie part, according to the disposition of one being about that act of concupiscence, and yet nothing seene of the beholders upon hir; saving that after such a convenient time as is required about such a peece of worke, a blacke vapor of the length and bignesse of a man, hath beene seene as it were to depart from hir, and to ascend from

This was
doone at
Ravenspurge.

Mal. Malef.

that place. Neverthelesse, manie times the husband seeth *Incubus* making him cuckhold, in the likenesse of a man, and sometimes striketh off his head with his sword: but bicause the bodie is nothing but aire, it closeth togither againe: so as, although the goodwife be some times hurt thereby; yet she maketh him beleeve he is mad or possessed, & that he dooth he knoweth not what. For she hath more pleasure and delight (they say) with *Incubus* that waie, than with anie mortall man: whereby you may perceive that spirits are palpable.

CHAPTER IV.

That the power of generation is both outwardlie and inwardlie impeached by witches, and of divers that had their genitals taken from them by witches, and by the same meanes againe restored.

THEY also affirme, that the vertue of generation is impeached by witches, both inwardlie, and outwardlie: for intrinsecallie they represse the courage, and they stop the passage of the mans seed, so as it may not descend to the vessels of generation: also they hurt extrinsecallie, with images, hearbs, &c. And to proove this true, you shall heare certeine stories out of *M. Mal.* worthie to be noted.

Mal. Malef.
cap. 6. *quæ.* 1.
pa. 2.

A yoong priest at *Mespurge* in the diocese of *Constance* was bewitched so as he had no power to occupie any other or mo women than one; and to be delivered out of that thraldom, sought to flie into another countrie, where he might use that preestlie occupation more freelie. But all in vaine; for evermore he was brought as far backward by night, as he went forward in the daie before; sometimes by land, sometimes in the aire, as though he flew. And if this be not true, I am sure that *James Sprenger* dooth lie.

For the further confirmation of our beleefe in *Incubus*, *M. Mal.* citeth a storie of a notable matter executed at *Ravenspurge*, as true and as cleanlie as the rest. A yoong man lieng with a wench in that towne (saith he) was faine to leave his instruments of venerie behind him, by meanes of that prestigious art of witchcraft: so as in that place nothing could be seene or felt but his plaine bodie. This yoong man was willed by another witch, to go to hir whom he suspected, and by faire or fowle meanes to require hir helpe: who soone after meeting with hir, intreated hir faire, but that was in vaine; and therefore he caught hir by the throte, and with a towell strangled hir, saieng: Restore me my toole, or thou shalt die for it: so as she being swolne and blacke in the face, and through his boisterous handling readie to die, said; Let me go, and I will helpe thee. And whilest he was loosing the towell, she put hir hand into his codpeece, and touched the place; saieng; Now hast thou thy desire: and even at that instant he felt himselfe restored.

Ja. Sprenger.
in Mal. malef.
par. 2. *quæ.* 1.

Item, a reverend father, for his life, holinesse, and knowledge notorious, being a frier of the order and companie of *Spire*, reported, that a yoong man at shrift made lamentable moane unto him for the like losse: but his gravitie suffered him not to beleeve lightlie any such reports, and therefore made the yoong man untrusse his codpeece point, and sawe the complaint to be true and just. Whereupon he advised or rather injoined the youth to go to the witch whome he suspected, and with flattering words to intreat hir, to be so good unto him, as to restore him his instrument: which by that meanes he obteined, and soone after returned to shew himselfe thankfull; and told the holie father of his good successe in that behalfe: but he so beleeved him, as he would needs be *Oculatus testis*, and made him pull downe his breeches, and so was satisfied of the troth and certaintie thereof.

44

Another yoong man being in that verie taking, went to a witch for the resti-tution thereof, who brought him to a tree, where she shewed him a nest, and bad him clime up and take it. And being in the top of the tree, he tooke out a mightie great one, and shewed the same to hir, asking hir if he might not have the same. Naie (quoth she) that is our parish preests toole, but take anie other which thou wilt. And it is there affirmed, that some have found 20. and some 30. of them in one nest, being there preserved with provender, as it were at the racke and manger, with this note, wherein there is no contradiction (for all must be true that is written against witches) that If a witch deprive one of his privi-ties, it is done onlie by prestigious meanes, so as the senses are but illuded. Marie by the divell it is reallie taken awaie, and in like sort restored. These are no jestes, for they be written by them that were and are judges upon the lives and deaths of those persons.

Mal. malef. cap. 7. *par.* 2. *quæst.* 1.

Note.

CHAPTER V.

Of bishop Sylvanus his leacherie opened and covered againe, how maides having yellow haire are most combred with Incubus, how maried men are bewitched to use other mens wives, and to refuse their own.

YOU shall read in the legend, how in the night time *Incubus* came to a ladies bed side, and made hot loove unto hir: whereat she being offended, cried out so lowd, that companie came and found him under hir bed in the likenesse of the holie bishop *Sylvanus*, which holie man was much defamed therebie, untill at the length this infamie was purged by the confession of a divell made at S. *Jeroms* toombe. Oh excellent peece of witchcraft or cousening wrought by *Sylvanus!* Item, S. *Christine* would needes take unto hir another maides *Incubus*, and lie in hir roome: and the storie saith, that she was shrewdlie accloied. But she was a shrew indeed, that would needes change beds with hir fellow, that was troubled everie night with *Incubus*, and deale with him hir selfe. But here the inquisitors note maie not be forgotten, to wit: that Maides having yellow haire are most molested with this spirit. Also it is written in the Legend, of S. *Barnard*, that a pretie wench that had had the use of *Incubus* his bodie by the space of six or seven yeares in *Aquitania* (being beelike wearie of him for that he waxed old) would needes go to S. *Barnard* another while. But *Incubus* told hir, that if she would so forsake him, being so long hir true loover, he would be revenged upon hir, *&*c. But befall what would, she went to S. *Barnard*, who tooke hir his staffe, and bad her laie it in the bed besides hir. And indeed the divell fearing the bedstaffe, or that S. *Barnard* laie there himselfe, durst not approch into hir chamber that night: what he did afterwards, I am uncerteine. Marrie you may find other circumstances hereof, and manie other like bawdie lies in the golden Legend. But here againe we maie not forget the inquisitors note, to wit; that manie are so bewitched that they cannot use their owne wives: but anie other bodies they maie well enough away withall. Which witch-craft is practised among manie bad husbands, for whom it were a good excuse to saie they were bewitched.

In vita Hie-ronym.

Saincts as holie and chaste as horsses & mares.

Maides having yellow haire.

Mal. Malef. par. 2. *quæ.* 2. *cap.* 2.

CHAPTER VI.

How to procure the dissolving of bewitched love, also to enforce a man (how proper so ever he be) to love an old hag: and of a bawdie tricke of a priest in Gelderland.

THE priests saie, that the best cure for a woman thus molested, next to confession, is excommunication. But to procure the dissolving of bewitched and constrained love, the partie bewitched must make a jakes of the lovers shooe. And to enforce a man, how proper so ever he be, to love an old hag, she giveth unto him to eate (among other meates) hir owne doong: and this waie one old witch made three abbats of one house successivelie to die for hir love as she hir selfe confessed, by the report of *M. Mal.* In *Gelderland* a priest persuaded a sicke woman that she was bewitched; and except he might sing a masse upon hir bellie, she could not be holpen. Whereunto she consented, and laie naked on the altar whilest he sang masse, to the satisfieng of his lust; but not to the release of hir greefe. Other cures I will speake of in other places more civill. Howbeit, certaine miraculous cures, both full of bawderie and lies, must either have place here, or none at all.

Of a bawdie priest in Gelderland.

CHAPTER VII.

Of divers saincts and holie persons, which were exceeding bawdie and lecherous, and by certeine miraculous meanes became chaste.

CASSIANUS writeth, that S. *Syren* being of bodie verie lecherous, and of mind woonderfull religious, fasted and praied; to the end his bodie might be reduced miraculouslie to chastitie. At length came an angell unto him by night, and cut out of his flesh certeine kernels, which were the sparkes of concupiscence; so as afterwards he never had anie more motions of the flesh. It is also reported, that the abbat *Equicius* being naturallie as unchast as the other, fell to his beads so devoutlie for recoverie of honestie, that there came an angell unto him in an apparition, that seemed to geld him; and after that (forsooth) he was as chaste as though he had had never a stone in his breech; and before that time being a ruler over monkes, he became afterwards a governour over nunnes. Even as it is said *Helias* the holie monke gathered thirtie virgins into a monasterie, over whom he ruled and reigned by the space of two yeares, and grew so proud and hot in the codpeece, that he was faine to forsake his holie house, and flie to a desert, where he fasted and praied two daies, saieng; Lord quench my hot lecherous humors, or kill me. Whereupon in the night following, there came unto him three angels, and demanded of him why he forsooke his charge: but the holie man was ashamed to tell them. Howbeit they asked him further, saieng; Wilt thou returne to these damsels, if we free thee from all concupiscence? Yea (quoth he) with all my heart. And when they had sworne him solemnelie so to doo, they tooke him up, & gelded him; and one of them holding his hands, and another his feete, the third cut out his stones. But the storie saith it was not so ended, but in a vision. Which I beleeve, because within five daies he returned to his minions, who pitiouslie moorned for him all this while, and joyfullie embraced his sweete companie at his returne. The like storie dooth *Nider* write of *Thomas*, whome two angels cured of that lecherous disease; by putting about him a girdle, which they brought downe with them from heaven.

In coll. patrum.

Gregor. lib. 1. dial. 2.

In vitis patrum. Heraclides in paradiso.

Nider in fornicario.

CHAPTER VIII.

Certeine popish and magicall cures, for them that are bewitched in their privities.

FOR direct cure to such as are bewitched in the privie members, the first and speciall is confession: then follow in a row, holie water, and those ceremoniall trumperies, *Ave Maries*, and all maner of crossings; which are all said to be wholesome, except the witchcraft be perpetuall, and in that case the wife maie have a divorse of course.

Item, the eating of a haggister or pie helpeth one bewitched in that member. *Aliter.*
Item, the smoke of the tooth of a dead man. *Aliter.*
Item, to annoint a mans bodie over with the gall of a crow. *Aliter.*
Item, to fill a quill with quicke silver, and laie the same under the cushine, where such a one sitteth, or else to put it under the threshold of the doore of the house or chamber where he dwelleth.
Item, to spet into your owne bosome, if you be so bewitched, is verie good. *Aliter.*
Item, to pisse through a wedding ring. If you would know who is hurt in his *Aliter.* privities by witchcraft; and who otherwise is therein diseased, *Hostiensis* answereth: but so, as I am ashamed to english it: and therefore have here set downe his experiment in Latine; *Quando virga nullatenùs movetur, & nunquam potuit cognoscere; hoc est signum frigiditatis: sed quando movetur & erigitur, perficere autem non potest, est signum maleficii.*
But Sir *Th. Moore* hath such a cure in this matter, as I am ashamed to write, S. Thomas either in Latine or English: for in filthie bawderie it passeth all the tales that Moores, ever I heard. But that is rather a medicine to procure generation, than the medicinable cure of witchcraft, though it serve both turnes. receipt, &c.
Item, when ones instrument of venerie is bewitched, certeine characters must *Aliter.* be written in virgine parchment, celebrated and holied by a popish priest; and thereon also must the 141. Psalme be written, and bound *Ad viri fascinati coxam.*
Item, one *Katharine Loe* (having a husband not so readilie disposed that waie *Aliter.* as she wished him to be) made a waxen image to the likenes of hir husbands bewitched member, and offered it up at S. *Anthonies* altar; so as, through the holinesse of the masse it might be sanctified, to be more couragious, and of better disposition and abilitie, &c.

CHAPTER IX.

A strange cure done to one that was molested with Incubus.

NOW being wearied with the rehearsall of so manie lecheries most horri- *Jaso.* ble, and very filthie and fabulous actions and passions of witches, together *Pratensis* with the spirit *Incubus*, I will end with a true storie taken out of *Jason* *de cerebri* *Pratensis*, which though it be rude, yet is it not altogither so uncleane as the rest. *morbo*, ca. 16.
There came (saith he) of late a masse priest unto me, making pitious moane, and saieng, that if I holpt him not, he should be undoone, and utterlie overthrowne; so great was his infirmitie: for (saith he) I was woont to be faire and fat, and of an excellent complexion; and lo how I looke, being now a verie ghost consisting of skinne and bone, &c. What is the matter (quoth *Jason?*) I will shew you sir, said the priest. There commeth unto mee, almost everie night, a certeine woman, unknowne unto me, and lieth so heavie upon my brest, that I cannot fetch my breath, neither have anie power to crie, neither doo my hands

serve me to shoove hir awaie, nor my feete to go from hir. I smiled (quoth *Jason*) and told him that he was vexed with a disease called *Incubus*, or the mare; and the residue was phantasie and vaine imagination. Naie (said the priest) it cannot be so: for by our blessed ladie, I tell you nothing but that with waking I saw hir when she commeth upon me, and strive to repell hir; but I am so infeebled that I cannot: and for remedie I have runne about from place to place, but no helpe that I could get. At length I went to an old frier that was counted an od fellow; and thought to have had help at his hands, but the divell a whit had I of him; saving that for remedie he willed me to praie to God; whome I am sure I wearied with my tedious praiers long before. Then went I unto an old woman (quoth the priest) who was said to be a cunning witch: and she willed me, that the next morning, about the dawning of the daie, I should pisse, and immediatlie should cover the pispot, or stop it with my right netherstocke, and before night the witch should come to visit me. And although (quoth he) the respect of mine orders somewhat terrified me from the execution of hir advise; yet my necessities diverse waies, and speciallie my paines moved me to make triall of hir words. And by the masse (quoth the priest) hir prophesie fell out as sure as a club. For a witch came to my house, and complained of a greefe in hir bladder, and that she could not pisse. But I could neither by faire nor fowle meanes obteine at hir hands, that she would leave molesting me by night; but she keepeth hir old custome, determining by these filthie meanes to dispatch me. I could hardlie (saith *Jason*) reclaime him from this mad humor; but by that time he had beene with me three or foure times, he began to comfort himselfe, and at last perceiving it, he acknowledged his disease, and recovered the same.

The priest
is opinion-
ative in the
error of his
phantasia.

The priest
recovered.

Chapter x.

A confutation of all the former follies touching Incubus, which by examples and proofes of like stuffe is shewed to be flat knaverie, wherein the carnall copulation with spirits is overthrowne.

THUS are lecheries covered with the cloke of *Incubus* and witchcraft, contrarie to nature and veritie: and with these fables is mainteined an opinion, that men have beene begotten without carnall copulation (as *Hyperius* and others write that *Merlin* was, An. 440.) speciallie to excuse and mainteine the knaveries and lecheries of idle priests and bawdie monkes; and to cover the shame of their lovers and concubines.

Merlin
begotten of
Incubus.

And alas, when great learned men have beene so abused, with the imagination of *Incubus* his carnall societie with women, misconstruing the scriptures, to wit, the place in *Genesis* 6. to the seducing of manie others; it is the lesse woonder, that this error hath passed so generallie among the common people.

But to use few words herein, I hope you understand that they affirme and saie, that *Incubus* is a spirit; and I trust you know that a spirit hath no flesh nor bones, &c: and that he neither dooth eate nor drinke. In deede your grandams maides were woont to set a boll of milke before him and his cousine Robin goodfellow, for grinding of malt or mustard, and sweeping the house at midnight: and you have also heard that he would chafe exceedingly, if the maid or goodwife of the house, having compassion of his nakednes, laid anie clothes for him, beesides his messe of white bread and milke, which was his standing fee. For in that case he saith; What have we here? Hemton hamten, here will I never more tread nor stampen.

But to proceed in this confutation. Where there is no meate eaten, there can be no seed which thereof is ingendred : although it be granted, that Robin could both eate and drinke, as being a cousening idle frier, or some such roge, that wanted nothing either belonging to lecherie or knaverie, &c. Item, where the genitall members want, there can be no lust of the flesh : neither dooth nature give anie desire of generation, where there is no propagation or succession required. And as spirits cannot be greeved with hunger, so can they not be inflamed with lustes. And if men should live ever, what needed succession or heires? For that is but an ordinance of God, to supplie the place, the number, the world, the time, and speciallie to accomplish his will. But the power of generation consisteth not onlie in members, but chieflie of vitall spirits, and of the hart : which spirits are never in such a bodie as *Incubus* hath, being but a bodie assumed, as they themselves saie. And yet the most part of writers herein affirme, that it is a palpable and visible bodie ; though all be phansies and fables that are written hereupon.

Quia humor spermaticus ex succo alimentari provenit.

Ad facultatem generandi tam interna quàm externa organa requiruntur.

CHAPTER XI.

That Incubus is a naturall disease, with remedies for the same, besides magicall cures herewithall expressed.

BUT in truth, this *Incubus* is a bodilie disease (as hath beene said) although it extend unto the trouble of the mind : which of some is called The mare, oppressing manie in their sleepe so sore, as they are not able to call for helpe, or stir themselves under the burthen of that heavie humor, which is ingendred of a thicke vapor proceeding from the cruditie and rawnesse in the stomach : which ascending up into the head oppresseth the braine, in so much as manie are much infeebled therebie, as being nightlie haunted therewith. They are most troubled with this disease, that being subject thereunto, lie right upward : so as, to turne and lie on the one side, is present remedie. Likewise, if anie heare the groning of the partie, speake unto him, so as he wake him, he is presentlie releeved. Howbeit, there are magicall cures for it, as for example.

What Incubus is, & who be most troubled therwith.

> *S. George, S. George, our ladies knight,*
> *He walkt by daie, so did he by night :*
> *Untill such time as he hir found,*
> *He hir beat and he hir bound,*
> *Untill hir troth she to him plight,*
> *She would not come to hir that night.*

Whereas S. *George* our ladies knight, was named three times S. *George.*

Item, hang a stone over the afflicted persons bed, which stone hath naturallie such a hole in it, as wherein a string may be put through it, and so be hanged over the diseased or bewitched partie ; be it man, woman, or horsse.

Item, you shall read in *M. Malefic.* that excommunication is verie notable, and better than any charme for this purpose. There are also other verses and charmes for this disease devised, which is the common cloke for the ignorance of bad physicians. But *Leonard Fuchsius* in his first booke, and 31. chapter, dooth not onelie describe this disease, and the causes of it ; but also setteth downe verie learnedlie the cure thereof, to the utter confusion of the witchmongers follie in this behalfe. *Hyperius* being much bewitched and blinded in this matter of witchcraft, hoovering about the interpretation of *Genesis* 6. from whence the opinion of *Incubus* and *Succubus* is extorted, *Viderunt filii Dei filias hominum, quòd elegantes essent, acceperunt sibi in uxores ex omnibus, quas elegerant, &c:* seemeth to

M. malefic. par. 2. quæ. 2. cap. 1. col. 2.

Leon. Fuchsius de curandi ratione.

mainteine upon heare-saie, that absurd opinion; and yet in the end is driven to conclude thus, to wit: Of the evill spirits *Incubus* and *Succubus* there can be no firme reason or proofe brought out of scriptures, using these verie words; *Hæc ut probabilia dicta sunto, quandoquidem scripturarum præsidio hac in causa destituimur.* As if he should saie, Take this as spoken probablie; to wit, by humane reason, bicause we are destitute of scriptures to mainteine the goodnesse of the cause.

Tertullian and *Sulpicius Severus* doo interpret *Filios Dei* in that place to be angels, or evill spirits, and to have beene enamored with the beautie of those wenches; and finallie, begat giants by them. Which is throughlie confuted by *Chrysostome*, *Hom.* 22. in *Gen:* but speciallie by the circumstance of the text.

Tertull. in libro de habitu muliebri. Sulp. Sever. in epitome hist. sacr.

CHAPTER XII.

The censure of G. Chaucer, upon the knaverie of Incubus

NOW will I (after all this long discourse of abhominable cloked knaveries) here conclude with certeine of *G. Chaucers* verses, who as he smelt out the absurdities of poperie, so found he the priests knaverie in this matter of *Incubus,* and (as the time would suffer him) he derided their follie and falshood in this wise:

Geffr. Chau. in the beginning of the wife of Baths tale.

> *For now the great charitie and praiers*
> *Of limitors and other holie friers,*
> *That searchen everie land and everie streame*
> *As thicke as motes in the sunne beame,*
> *Blissing halles, kitchens, chambers & bowers,*
> *Cities, borroghes, castels and hie towers,*
> *Thropes, barnes, shepens, and dairies,*
> *This maketh that there beene now no fairies;*
> *For there as woont to walken was an elfe,*
> *There walketh now the limitor himselfe,*
> *In undermeales, and in mornings,*
> *And saith his mattens and his holie things*
> *As he goeth in his limitatiowne,*
> *Women may go safelie up and downe,*
> *In everie bush, and under everie tree,*
> *There nis none other Incubus but hee, &c.*

BOOKE V.

Chapter i.

Of transformations, ridiculous examples brought by the adversaries for the confirmation of their foolish doctrine.

NOW that I may with the verie absurdities, conteined in their owne authors, and even in their principall doctors and last writers, confound them that mainteine the transubstantiations of witches; I will shew you certeine proper stuffe, which *Bodin* (their cheefe champion of this age) hath gathered out of *M. Mal.* and others, whereby he laboureth to establish this impossible, incredible, and supernaturall, or rather unnaturall doctrine of transubstantiation. *J. Bod. lib. 2. de dæmon. cap. 6.*

First, as touching the divell (*Bodin* saith) that he dooth most properlie and commonlie transforme himselfe into a gote, confirming that opinion by the 33. and 34. of *Esaie:* where there is no one title sounding to anie such purpose. Howbeit, he sometimes alloweth the divell the shape of a blacke Moore, and as he saith he used to appeare to *Mawd Cruse*, *Kate Darey*, and *Jone Harviller*. But I mervell, whether the divell createth himselfe, when he appeareth in the likenesse of a man; or whether God createth him, when the divell wisheth it. As for witches, he saith they speciallie transubstantiate themselves into wolves, and them whom they bewitch into asses: though else-where they differ somewhat herein from himselfe. But though he affirme, that it may be naturallie brought to passe, that a girle shall become a boie; and that anie female may be turned into the male: yet he saith the same hath no affinitie with *Lycanthropia;* wherein he saith also, that men are wholie transformed, and citeth infinite examples hereof. *J. Bodin abuseth scripture to proove a lie.* *Pudendis tunc primùm erumpentibus.*

First, that one *Garner* in the shape of a woolfe killed a girle of the age of twelve yeares, and did eat up hir armes and legges, and carried the rest home to his wife. Item, that *Peter Burget*, and *Michael Werdon*, having turned themselves with an ointment into woolves, killed, and finallie did eate up an infinite number of people. Which lie *Wierus* dooth sufficientlie confute. But untill you see and read that, consider whether *Peter* could eate rawe flesh without surfetting, speciallie flesh of his owne kind. Item, that there was an arrowe shot into a woolves thigh, who afterwards being turned into his former shape of a man, was found in his bed, with the arrowe in his thigh, which the archer that shot it knew verie well. Item, that another being *Lycanthropus* in the forme of a woolfe, had his woolves feet cut off, and in a moment he became a man without hands or feete. *Jo. Wier. lib. 6. de mag. ca. 12.*

He accuseth also one of the mightiest princes in christendome, even of late daies, to be one of those kind of witches (so as he could, when he list, turne himselfe to a woolfe) affirming that he was espied and oftentimes seene to performe that villanie; bicause he would be counted the king of all witches. He saith that this transubstantiation is most common in *Greece*, and through out all *Asia*, as merchant strangers have reported to him. For *Anno Domini.* 1542, when *Sultan Solimon* reigned, there was such force and multitude of these kind of woolves in *Constantinople*, that the emperour drave togither in one flocke 150. of them, which departed out of the citie in the presence of all the people. *J. Bodinus mendaciorum heluo.*

To persuade us the more throughlie heerein, he saith, that in *Livonia*, yearelie (about the end of December) a certeine knave or divell warneth all the witches A warme season to swim in.

I mervell
that they
forsake not
the divell,
who punish-
eth them so
sore: ywis
they get not
so much at
his hands.

in the countrie to come to a certeine place: if they faile, the divell commeth
and whippeth them with an iron rod; so as the print of his lashes remaine upon
their bodies for ever. The capteine witch leadeth the waie through a great
poole of water: manie millians of witches swim after. They are no sooner passed
through that water, but they are all transformed into woolves, and flie upon
and devoure both men, women, cattell, &c. After twelve daies they returne
through the same water, and so receive humane shape againe.

Item, that there was one *Bajanus* a *Jew*, being the sonne of *Simeon*, which
could, when he list, turne himselfe into a woolfe; and by that meanes could
escape the force and danger of a whole armie of men. Which thing (saith *Bodin*)
is woonderfull: but yet (saith he) it is much more marvelous, that men will not
beleeve it. For manie poets affirme it; yea, and if you looke well into the matter
(saith he) you shall find it easie to doo. Item, he saith, that as naturall woolves

Leviti. 16.
[26, 22].
Deut. 32.
[v. 24].

persecute beasts; so doo these magicall woolves devoure men, women, and
children. And yet God saith to the people (I trowe) and not to the cattell of
Israell: If you observe not my commandements, I will send among you the beasts
of the feeld, which shall devoure both you and your cattell. Item, I will send
the teeth of beasts upon you. Where is *Bodins* distinction now become? He never
saith, I will send witches in the likenes of wolves, &c: to devoure you or your
cattell. Nevertheles, *Bodin* saith it is a cleare case: for the matter was disputed
upon before pope *Leo* the seventh, and by him all these matters were judged
possible: and at that time (saith he) were the transformations of *Lucian* and
Apuleius made canonicall.

Stasus a
witch could
not be ap-
prehended
and why?
J. Bodin.
Mal. malef.

Furthermore, he saith, that through this art they are so cunning that no man
can apprehend them, but when they are a sleepe. Item, he nameth another
witch, that (as *M. Mal.* saith) could not be caught, bicause he would transforme
himselfe into a mouse, and runne into everie little hole, till at length he was
killed comming out of the hole of a jamme in a windowe: which indeed is as
possible, as a camell to go through a needels eie. Item, he saith, that diverse

John. Bodin.
Mal. malef.
Barth. Spin.
&c.
Mal. malef.
part. 3.

witches at *Vernon* turned themselves into cats, and both committed and received
much hurt. But at *Argentine* there was a wonderfull matter done, by three
witches of great wealth, who transforming themselves into three cats, assalted
a faggot-maker: who having hurt them all with a faggot sticke, was like to have
beene put to death. But he was miraculouslie delivered, and they worthilie
punished; as the storie saith, from whence *Bodin* had it.

An error
about Ly-
canthropia.

After a great manie other such beastlie fables, he inveieth against such
physicians, as saie that *Lycanthropia* is a disease, and not a transformation. Item,
he mainteineth, as sacred and true, all *Homers* fables of *Circes* and *Ulysses* his
companions: inveieng against *Chrysostome*, who rightlie interpreteth *Homers*
meaning to be, that *Ulysses* his people were by the harlot *Circes* made in their
brutish maners to resemble swine.

But least some poets fables might be thought lies (whereby the witchmongers
arguments should quaile) he mainteineth for true the most part of *Ovids Metamorphôsis*, and the greatest absurdities and impossibilities in all that booke:
marie he thinketh some one tale therein may be fained. Finallie, he confirmeth all these toies by the storie of *Nabuchadnez-zar*. And bicause (saith he)
Nabuchadnez-zar continued seven yeres in the shape of a beast, therefore may
witches remaine so long in the forme of a beast; having in all the meane time,
the shape, haire, voice, strength, agilitie, swiftnes, food and excrements of beasts,

August. lib. 8
de civit. Dei.
cap. 18.
Idem. lib. de
spiritu &
anima, cap. 26.

and yet reserve the minds and soules of women or men. Howbeit, S. *Augustine*
(whether to confute or confirme that opinion judge you) saith; *Non est credendum,
humanum corpus dæmonum arte vel potestate in bestialia lineamenta converti posse:* We
may not beleeve that a mans bodie may be altered into the lineaments of a beast
by the divels art or power. Item, *Bodin* saith, that the reason whie witches are
most commonlie turned into woolves, is; bicause they usuallie eate children, as
woolves eate cattell. Item, that the cause whie other are truelie turned into
asses, is; for that such have beene desirous to understand the secrets of witches.

Ironia.

Whie witches are turned into cats, he alledgeth no reason, and therefore (to
helpe him foorth with that paraphrase) I saie, that witches are curst queanes,

and manie times scratch one another, or their neighbours by the faces; and therefore perchance are turned into cats. But I have put twentie of these witchmongers to silence with this one question; to wit, Whether a witch that can turne a woman into a cat, &c: can also turne a cat into a woman?

Chapter II.

Absurd reasons brought by Bodin, and such others, for confirmation of transformations.

THESE Examples, and reasons might put us in doubt, that everie asse, woolfe, or cat that we see, were a man, a woman, or a child. I marvell that no man useth this distinction in the definition of a man. But to what end should one dispute against these creations and recreations; when *Bodin* washeth away all our arguments with one word, confessing that none can create any thing but God; acknowledging also the force of the canons, and imbracing the opinions of such divines, as write against him in this behalfe? Yea he dooth now (contrarie to himselfe elsewhere) affirme, that the divell cannot alter his forme. And lo, this is his distinction, *Non essentialis forma (id est ratio) sed figura solùm permutatur:* The essentiall forme (to wit, reason) is not changed, but the shape or figure. And thereby he prooveth it easie enough to create men or beasts with life, so as they remaine without reason. Howbeit, I thinke it is an easier matter, to turne *Bodins* reason into the reason of an asse, than his bodie into the shape of a sheepe: which he saith is an easie matter; bicause *Lots* wife was turned into a stone by the divell. Whereby he sheweth his grosse ignorance. As though God that commanded *Lot* upon paine of death not to looke backe, who also destroied the citie of *Sodome* at that instant, had not also turned hir into a salt stone. And as though all this while God had beene the divels drudge, to go about this businesse all the night before, and when a miracle should be wrought, the divell must be faine to doo it himselfe.

> *J. Bod. lib. 2. de mag. dæmon. cap. 6.*

> *Gen. 19, 24. & 26. & 27.*

Item, he affirmeth, that these kind of transfigurations are more common with them in the west parts of the world, than with us here in the east. Howbeit, this note is given withall; that that is ment of the second persons, and not of the first: to wit, of the bewitched, and not of the witches. For they can transforme themselves in everie part of the world, whether it be east, west, north, or south. Marrie he saith, that spirits and divels vex men most in the north countries, as *Norway, Finland, &c:* and in the westerne ilands, as in the west *India:* but among the heathen speciallie, and wheresoever Christ is not preached. And that is true, though not in so foolish, grosse, and corporall a sense as *Bodin* taketh it. One notable instance of a witches cunning in this behalfe touched by *Bodin* in the chapter aforesaid, I thought good in this place to repeat: he taketh it out of *M. Mal.* which tale was delivered to *Sprenger* by a knight of the Rhods, being of the order of S. *Jones* at *Jerusalem;* and it followeth thus.

> *J. Bod. lib. de dæmon. 2. cap. 20. M. Mal. pa. 1. quæ. 9.*

> *John. Bodin. lib. de dæmon. 2. cap 1.*

> *Mal. malefic. par. 2. quæ. 2. cap. 4.*

CHAPTER III.

Of a man turned into an asse, and returned againe into a man by one of Bodins witches: S. Augustines opinion thereof.

I T happened in the city of *Salamin*, in the kingdome of *Cyprus* (wherein is a good haven) that a ship loaden with merchandize staied there for a short space. In the meane time many of the souldiers and mariners went to shoare, to provide fresh victuals. Among which number, a certaine English man being a sturdie yoong fellowe, went to a womans house, a little waie out of the citie, and not farre from the sea side, to see whether she had anie egs to sell. Who perceiving him to be a lustie yoong fellowe, a stranger, and farre from his countrie (so as upon the losse of him there would be the lesse misse or inquirie) she considered with hir selfe how to destroie him; and willed him to staie there awhile, whilest she went to fetch a few egs for him. But she tarried long, so as the yoong man called unto hir, desiring hir to make hast: for he told hir that the tide would be spent, and by that meanes his ship would be gone, and leave him behind. Howbeit, after some detracting of time, she brought him a few egs, willing him to returne to hir, if his ship were gone when he came. The young fellowe returned towards his ship; but before he went aboord, hee would needs eate an eg or twaine to satisfie his hunger, and within short space he became dumb and out of his wits (as he afterwards said). When he would have entred into the ship, the mariners beat him backe with a cudgell, saieng; What a murren lacks the asse? Whither the divell will this asse? The asse or yoong man (I cannot tell by which name I should terme him) being many times repelled, and understanding their words that called him asse, considering that he could speake never a word, and yet could understand everie bodie; he thought that he was bewitched by the woman, at whose house he was. And therefore, when by no means he could get into the boate, but was driven to tarrie and see hir departure; being also beaten from place to place, as an asse; he remembred the witches words, and the words of his owne fellowes that called him asse, and returned to the witches house, in whose service hee remained by the space of three yeares, dooing nothing with his hands all that while, but carried such burthens as she laied on his backe; having onelie this comfort, that although he were reputed an asse among strangers and beasts, yet that both this witch, and all other witches knew him to be a man.

After three yeares were passed over, in a morning betimes he went to towne before his dame; who upon some occasion (of like to make water) staied a little behind. In the meane time being neere to a church, he heard a little saccaring bell ring to the elevation of a morrowe masse, and not daring to go into the church, least he should have beene beaten and driven out with cudgels, in great devotion he fell downe in the churchyard, upon the knees of his hinder legs, and did lift his forefeet over his head, as the preest doth hold the sacrament at the elevation. Which prodigious sight when certeine merchants of Genua espied, and with woonder beheld; anon commeth the witch with a cudgell in hir hand, beating foorth the asse. And bicause (as it hath beene said) such kinds of witch-crafts are verie usuall in those parts; the merchants aforesaid made such meanes, as both the asse and the witch were attached by the judge. And she being examined and set upon the racke, confessed the whole matter, and promised, that if she might have libertie to go home, she would restore him to his old shape; and being dismissed, she did accordinglie. So as notwithstanding they apprehended hir againe, and burned hir: and the young man returned into his countrie with a joifull and merrie hart.

Upon the advantage of this storie M. *Mal.* *Bodin,* and the residue of the witch-mongers triumph; and speciallie bicause S. *Augustine* subscribeth thereunto; or at the least to the verie like. Which I must confesse I find too common in his

What the divel shuld the witch meane to make chois of the English man?

A strange metamor-phôsis of bodie, but not of mind

Note the devotion of the asse.

August. lib. 18. de civi. Dei. cap. 17 & 18.

books, insomuch as I judge them rather to be foisted in by some fond papist or witchmonger, than so learned a mans dooings. The best is, that he himselfe is no eie-witnesse to any of those his tales; but speaketh onelie by report; wherein he uttereth these words: to wit, that It were a point of great incivilitie, &c: to discredit so manie and so certeine reports. And in that respect he justifieth the corporall transfigurations of *Ulysses* his mates, throgh the witchcraft of *Circes:* and that foolish fable of *Præstantius* his father, who (he saith) did eate provender and haie among other horsses, being himselfe turned into an horsse. Yea he verifieth the starkest lie that ever was invented, of the two alewives that used to transforme all their ghests into horsses, and to sell them awaie at markets and faires. And therefore I saie with *Cardanus,* that how much *Augustin* saith he hath seen with his eies, so much I am content to beleeve. Howbeit S. *Augustin* concludeth against *Bodin.* For he affirmeth these transubstantiations to be but fantasticall, and that they are not according to the veritie, but according to the appearance. And yet I cannot allow of such appearances made by witches, or yet by divels: for I find no such power given by God to any creature. And I would wit of S. *Augustine,* where they became, whom *Bodins* transformed woolves devoured. But

At the alps in Arcadia.

Card. de Var. rerum. lib. 15. cap. 80. August. Lib. de civit. Dei.

—————————————————*ô quàm*
Credula mens hominis, & erectæ fabulis aures!

    Good Lord! how light of credit is
    the wavering mind of man!
    How unto tales and lies his eares
    attentive all they can?

Englished by Abraham Fleming.

Generall councels, and the popes canons, which *Bodin* so regardeth, doo condemne and pronounce his opinions in this behalfe to be absurd; and the residue of the witchmongers, with himselfe in the number, to be woorsse than infidels. And these are the verie words of the canons, which else-where I have more largelie repeated; Whosoever beleeveth, that anie creature can be made or changed into better or woorsse, or transformed into anie other shape, or into anie other similitude, by anie other than by God himselfe the creator of all things, without all doubt is an infidell, and woorsse than a pagan. And therewithall this reason is rendered, to wit: bicause they attribute that to a creature, which onelie belongeth to God the creator of all things.

Canon. quæ. 5. episcopi ex con. acquir. &c.

Chapter IV.

A summarie of the former fable, with a refutation thereof, after due examination of the same.

CONCERNING the veritie or probabilitie of this enterlude, betwixt *Bodin, M. Mal.* the witch, the asse, the masse, the merchants, the inquisitors, the tormentors, &c: First I woonder at the miracle of transubstantiation: Secondlie at the impudencie of *Bodin* and *James Sprenger,* for affirming so grosse a lie, devised beelike by the knight of the *Rhodes,* to make a foole of *Sprenger,* and an asse of *Bodin:* Thirdlie, that the asse had no more wit than to kneele downe and hold up his forefeete to a peece of starch or flowre, which neither would, nor could, nor did helpe him: Fourthlie, that the masse could not reforme that which the witch transformed: Fiftlie, that the merchants, the inquisitors, and the tormentors, could not either severallie or jointlie doo it, but referre the matter to the witches courtesie and good pleasure.

But where was the yoong mans owne shape all these three yeares, wherein he was made an asse? It is a certeine and a generall rule, that two substantiall formes cannot be in one subject *Simul & semel,* both at once: which is confessed

His shape was in the woods: where else should it be?

Mal. malef.
par. 1. quæ. 2.

by themselves. The forme of the beast occupied some place in the aire and so I thinke should the forme of a man doo also. For to bring the bodie of a man, without feeling, into such a thin airie nature, as that it can neither be seene nor felt, it may well be unlikelie, but it is verie impossible : for the aire is inconstant, and continueth not in one place. So as this airie creature would soone be carried into another region : as else-where I have largelie prooved. But indeed our bodies are visible, sensitive, and passive, and are indued with manie other excellent properties, which all the divels in hell are not able to alter : neither can one haire of our head perish, or fall awaie, or be transformed, without the speciall providence of God almightie.

In my discourse of spirits and divels, being the 17 booke of this volume.

But to proceed unto the probabilitie of this storie. What lucke was it, that this yoong fellow of *England*, landing so latelie in those parts, and that old woman of *Cyprus*, being both of so base a condition, should both understand one anothers communication; *England* and *Cyprus* being so manie hundred miles distant, and their languages so farre differing? I am sure in these daies, wherein trafficke is more used, and learning in more price; few yong or old mariners in this realme can either speake or understand the language spoken at *Salamin* in *Cyprus*, which is a kind of *Greeke;* and as few old women there can speake our language. But *Bodin* will saie; You heare, that at the inquisitors commandement, and through the tormentors correction, she promised to restore him to his owne shape : and so she did, as being thereunto compelled. I answer, that as the whole storie is an impious fable; so this assertion is false, and disagreeable to their owne doctrine, which mainteineth, that the witch dooth nothing but by the permission and leave of God. For if she could doo or undoo such a thing at hir owne pleasure, or at the commandement of the inquisitors, or for feare of the tormentors, or for love of the partie, or for remorse of conscience : then is it not either by the extraordinarie leave, nor yet by the like direction of God; except you will make him a confederate with old witches. I for my part woonder most, how they can turne and tosse a mans bodie so, and make it smaller and greater, to wit, like a mowse, or like an asse, &c : and the man all this while to

Dan. in
dialog. cap. 3.
August. lib.
de civit. Dei.
cap. 17. 18.

feele no paine. And I am not alone in this maze : for *Danæus* a special mainteiner of their follies saith, that although *Augustine* and *Apuleius* doo write verie crediblie of these matters; yet will he never beleeve, that witches can change men into other formes; as asses, apes, woolves, beares, mice, &c.

CHAPTER V.

That the bodie of a man cannot be turned into the bodie of a beast by a witch, is prooved by strong reasons, scriptures, and authorities.

Hermes Trismeg. in suo Periandro.

BUT was this man an asse all this while? Or was this asse a man? *Bodin* saith (his reason onelie reserved) he was trulie transubstantiated into an asse; so as there must be no part of a man, but reason remaining in this asse. And yet *Hermes Trismegistus* thinketh he hath good authoritie and reason to saie; *Aliud corpus quàm humanum non capere animam humanam; nec fas esse in corpus animæ ratione carentis animam rationalem corruere;* that is; An humane soule cannot receive anie other than an humane bodie, nor yet canne light into a bodie that wanteth reason of mind. But S. *James* saith; the bodie without the spirit is dead. And surelie, when the soule is departed from the bodie, the life of man is dissolved : and therefore *Paule* wished to be dissolved, when he would have beene with Christ. The bodie of man is subject to divers kinds of agues, sicknesses, and infirmities, whereunto an asses bodie is not inclined : and mans bodie must be fed with bread, &c : and not with hay. *Bodins* asseheaded man must either eate haie, or nothing : as appeareth in the storie. Mans bodie also

Jam. 2, 26.

Phili. 1, 23.

is subject unto death, and hath his daies numbred. If this fellowe had died in the meane time, as his houre might have beene come, for anie thing the divels, the witch, or *Bodin* knew; I mervell then what would have become of this asse, or how the witch could have restored him to shape, or whether he should have risen at the daie of judgement in an asses bodie and shape. For *Paule* saith, that that verie bodie which is sowne and buried a naturall bodie, is raised a spirituall bodie. The life of Jesus is made manifest in our mortall flesh, and not in the flesh of an asse.

1 Cor. 15. 44.

God hath endued everie man and everie thing with his proper nature, substance, forme, qualities, and gifts, and directeth their waies. As for the waies of an asse, he taketh no such care: howbeit, they have also their properties and substance severall to themselves. For there is one flesh (saith *Paule*) of men, another flesh of beasts, another of fishes, another of birds. And therefore it is absolutelie against the ordinance of God (who hath made me a man) that I should flie like a bird, or swim like a fish, or creepe like a worme, or become an asse in shape: insomuch as if God would give me leave, I cannot doo it; for it were contrarie to his owne order and decree, and to the constitution of anie bodie which he hath made. Yea the spirits themselves have their lawes and limits prescribed, beyond the which they cannot passe one haires breadth; otherwise God should be contrarie to himselfe: which is farre from him. Neither is Gods omnipotencie hereby qualified, but the divels impotencie manifested, who hath none other power, but that which God from the beginning hath appointed unto him, consonant to his nature and substance. He may well be restreined from his power and will, but beyond the same he cannot passe, as being Gods minister, no further but in that which he hath from the beginning enabled him to doo: which is, that he being a spirit, may with Gods leave and ordinance viciat and corrupt the spirit and will of man: wherein he is verie diligent.

1. Cor. 15, 39.

Psal. 119.

What a beastlie assertion is it, that a man, whom GOD hath made according to his owne similitude and likenes, should be by a witch turned into a beast? What an impietie is it to affirme, that an asses bodie is the temple of the Holy-ghost? Or an asse to be the child of God, and God to be his father; as it is said of man? Which *Paule* to the *Corinthians* so divinelie confuteth, who saith, that Our bodies are the members of Christ. In the which we are to glorifie God: for the bodie is for the Lord, and the Lord is for the bodie. Surelie he meaneth not for an asses bodie, as by this time I hope appeareth: in such wise as *Bodin*, may go hide him for shame; especiallie when he shall understand, that even into these our bodies, which God hath framed after his owne likenesse, he hath also brethed that spirit, which *Bodin* saith is now remaining within an asses bodie, which God hath so subjected in such servilitie under the foote of man; Of whom God is so mindfull, that he hath made him little lower than angels, yea than himselfe, and crowned him with glorie and worship, and made him to have dominion over the workes of his hands, as having put all things under his feete, all sheepe and oxen, yea woolves, asses, and all other beasts of the field, the foules of the aire, the fishes of the sea, &c. *Bodins* poet, *Ovid*, whose *Metamorphôsis*, make so much for him, saith to the overthrow of this phantasticall imagination:

1. Cor. 6, 19.
verse. 15, &c.
verse. 2.
verse. 13.

Psalm. 8.
verses 5, 6,
7, 8.

> *Os homini sublime dedit, cælúmque videre*
> *Jussit, & erectos ad sydera tollere vultus.*

The effect of which verses is this;

> *The Lord did set mans face so hie,*
> *That he the heavens might behold,*
> *And looke up to the starrie skie,*
> *To see his woonders manifold.*

Now, if a witch or a divell can so alter the shape of a man, as contrarilie to make him looke downe to hell, like a beast; Gods works should not onelie be defaced and disgraced, but his ordinance should be woonderfullie altered, and thereby confounded.

57

CHAPTER VI.

The witchmongers objections, concerning Nabuchadnez-zar answered, and their errour concerning Lycanthropia confuted.

Their
ground-
worke is
as sure as
to hold a
quick eele
by the
taile.
Dan. 4.

MALLEUS MALEFICARUM, *Bodin*, and manie other of them that mainteine witchcraft, triumph upon the storie of *Nabuchadnez-zar;* as though *Circes* had transformed him with hir sorceries into an oxe, as she did others into swine, &c. I answer, that he was neither in bodie nor shape transformed at all, according to their grosse imagination; as appeareth both by the plaine words of the text, and also by the opinions of the best interpretors thereof: but that he was, for his beastlie government and conditions, throwne out of his kingdome and banished for a time, and driven to hide himselfe in the wildernesse, there in exile to lead his life in beastlie sort, among beasts of the field, and fowles of the aire (for by the waie I tell you it appeareth by the text, that he was rather turned into the shape of a fowle than of a beast) untill he rejecting his beastlie conditions, was upon his repentance and amendment called home, and restored unto his kingdome. Howbeit, this (by their confession) was neither divels nor witches dooing; but a miracle wrought by God, whom alone I acknowledge to be able to bring to passe such workes at his pleasure. Wherein I would know what our witchmongers have gained.

*Cor. Agrip.
de vanit.
scient. cap.* 44.

I am not ignorant that some write, that after the death of *Nabuchadnez-zar,* his sonne *Eilumorodath* gave his bodie to the ravens to be devoured, least afterwards his father should arise from death, who of a beast became a man againe. But this tale is meeter to have place in the *Cabalisticall* art, to wit: among unwritten verities than here. To conclude, I saie that the transformations, which these witchmongers doo so rave and rage upon, is (as all the learned sort of physicians affirme) a disease proceeding partlie from melancholie, wherebie manie suppose themselves to be woolves, or such ravening beasts. For *Lycanthropia* is of the ancient physicians called *Lupina melancholia,* or *Lupina insania.* *J. Wierus* declareth verie learnedlie, the cause, the circumstance, and the cure of this disease. I have written the more herein; bicause hereby great princes and potentates, as well as poore women and innocents, have beene defamed and accounted among the number of witches.

*Paul. Aegi-
net. li.* 3. *c.* 16.
Aetius. lib. 6.
cap. 11.
*J. Wier, de
præst. dæm.
lib.* 4. *cap.* 23.

CHAPTER VII.

A speciall objection answered concerning transportations, with the consent of diverse writers thereupon.

Matth. 4, 8.
Luk. 3, 9.

FOR the maintenance of witches transportations, they object the words of the Gospell, where the divell is said to take up Christ, and to set him on a pinnacle of the temple, and on a mountaine, &c. Which if he had doone in maner and forme as they suppose, it followeth not therefore that witches could doo the like; nor yet that the divell would doo it for them at their pleasure; for they know not their thoughts, neither can otherwise communicate with them. But I answer, that if it were so grosselie to be understood, as they

Answer to
the former
objection.

imagine it, yet should it make nothing to their purpose. For I hope they will not saie, that Christ had made anie ointments, or entred into anie league with the divell, and by vertue thereof was transported from out of the wildernes, unto the top of the temple of Jerusalem; or that the divell could have maisteries

58

over his bodie, whose soule he could never laie hold upon; especiallie when he might (with a becke of his finger) have called unto him, and have had the assistance of manie legions of angels. Neither (as I thinke) will they presume to make Christ partaker of the divels purpose and sinne in that behalfe. If they saie; This was an action wrought by the speciall providence of God, and by his appointment, that the scripture might be fulfilled: then what gaine our witchmongers by this place? First, for that they maie not produce a particular example to prove so generall an argument. And againe, if it were by Gods speciall providence and appointment; then why should it not be doone by the hand of God, as it was in the storie of *Job?* Or if it were Gods speciall purpose and pleasure, that there should be so extraordinarie a matter brought to passe by the hand of the divell; could not God have given to the wicked angell extraordinarie power, and cloathed him with extraordinarie shape; whereby he might be made an instrument able to accomplish that matter, as he did to his angell that carried *Abacuck* to *Daniell*, and to them that he sent to destroie *Sodome?* But you shall understand, that this was doone in a vision, and not in veritie of action. So as they have a verie cold pull of this place, which is the speciall peece of scripture alledged of them for their transportations.

Heare therefore what *Calvine* saith in his commentarie upon that place, in these words; The question is, whether Christ were carried aloft indeed, or whether it were but in a vision? Manie affirme verie obstinatlie, that his bodie was trulie and reallie as they saie taken up: bicause they thinke it too great an indignitie for Christ to be made subject to sathans illusions. But this objection is easilie washed awaie. For it is no absurditie to grant all this to be wrought through Gods permission, or Christes voluntarie subjection: so long as we yeeld not to thinke that he suffered these temptations inwardlie, that is to saie, in mind or soule. And that which is afterwards set downe by the Evangelist, where the divell shewed him all the kingdoms of the world, and the glorie of the same, and that to be doone (as it is said in *Luke*) in the twinkling of an eie, dooth more agree with a vision than with a reall action. So farre are the verie words of *Calvine*. Which differ not one syllable nor five words from that which I had written herein, before I looked for his opinion in the matter. And this I hope will be sufficient to overthrow the assertions of them that laie the ground of their transportations and flieng in the aire hereupon.

He that will saie, that these words; to wit, that Christ was taken up, *&c*: can hardlie be applied to a vision, let him turne to the prophesie of *Ezechiell*, and see the selfe-same words used in a vision: saving that where Christ is said to be taken up by the divell, *Ezechiell* is taken up, and lifted up, and carried by the spirit of God, and yet in a vision. But they have lesse reason that build upon this sandie rocke, the supernaturall frame of transubstantiation; as almost all our witching writers doo. For *Sprenger & Institor* saie, that the divell in the likenesse of a falcon caught him up. *Danæus* saith, it was in the similitude of a man; others saie, of an angell painted with wings; others, invisiblie: *Ergo* the divell can take (saie they) what shape he list. But though some may cavill upon the divels transforming of himselfe; yet, that either divell or witch can transforme or transubstantiat others, there is no tittle nor colour in the scriptures to helpe them. If there were authoritie for it, and that it were past all peradventure, lo, what an easie matter it is to resubstantiate an asse into a man. For *Bodin* saith upon the word of *Apuleius*, that if the asse eate new roses, anise, or baie leaves out of spring water, it will presentlie returne him into a man. Which thing *Sprenger* saith maie be doone, by washing the asse in faire water: yea he sheweth an instance, where, by drinking of water an asse was turned into a man.

Matt. 26, 53.

Job. 1, 11.
Job. 2, 5.

J. Calvine in harmon. E- vang. in Matth. 4. & *Luk.* 4.

Ezec. 3, 12. and 14.

Mal. malef.

J. Bod. lib. de dæm. 3. *cap.* 5.

In Mal. mal.

CHAPTER VIII.

The witchmongers objection concerning the historie of Job answered.

THESE witchmongers, for lacke of better arguments, doo manie times object *Job* against me; although there be never a word in that storie, which either maketh for them, or against me: in so much as there is not the name of a witch mentioned in the whole booke. But (I praie you) what witchmonger now seeing one so afflicted as *Job*, would not saie he were bewitched, as *Job* never saith? For first there came a messenger unto him, and said; Thy oxen were plowing, and thy asses were feeding in their places, and the *Sabeans* came violentlie and tooke them; yea they have slaine thy servants with the edge of the sword; but I onelie am escaped to tell thee. And whilest he was yet speaking, another came, and said; The fier of God is fallen from the heaven, & hath burnt up thy sheepe and thy servants, and devoured them; but I onlie am escaped to tell thee. And while he was yet speaking, another came, and said; The *Chaldæans* set out their bands, and fell upon thy camels, and have taken them, and have slaine thy servants with the edge of the sword; but I onelie am escaped alone to tell thee. And whilest he was yet speaking, came another, and said; Thy sonnes and thy daughters were eating and drinking wine in their elder brothers house, and behold there came a great wind from beyond the wildernesse, and smote the foure corners of the house, which fell upon thy children, and they are dead; and I onlie am escaped alone to tell thee. Besides all this, he was smitten with biles, from the sole of his foote to the crowne of his head. If anie man in these daies called *Job* should be by the appointment or hand of God thus handled, as this *Job* was; I warrant you that all the old women in the countrie would be called *Coram nobis:* warrants would be sent out on everie side, publike and private inquirie made what old women latelie resorted to *Jobs* house, or to anie of those places, where these misfortunes fell. If anie poore old woman had chanced within two or three moneths to have borrowed a curtsie of seasing, or to have fetcht from thence a pot of milke, or had she required some almes, and not obteined it at *Jobs* hand; there had beene argument enough to have brought hir to confusion: and to be more certeine to have the right witch apprehended, figures must have beene cast, the sive and sheares must have beene set on worke; yea rather than the witch should escape, a conjuror must have earned a little monie, a circle must have beene made, and a divell raised to tell the truth: mother *Bungie* must have been gon unto, and after she had learned hir name, whom *Job* most suspected, she would have confirmed the suspicion with artificiall accusations: in the end, some woman or other must have beene hanged for it. But as *Job* said; *Dominus dedit:* so said he not; *Diabolus vel Lamia sed Dominus abstulit.* Which agreeth with the tenor of the text, where it is written, that the divell at everie of *Jobs* afflictions desired God to laie his hand upon him. Insomuch as *Job* imputed no part of his calamitie unto divels, witches, nor yet unto conjurors, or their inchantments; as we have learned now to doo. Neither sinned he, or did God any wrong, when he laid it to his charge: but we dishonour God greatlie, when we attribute either the power or proprietie of God the creator unto a creature.

Calvine said; We derogate much from Gods glorie and omnipotencie, when we saie he dooth but give sathan leave to doo it: which is (saith he) to mocke Gods justice; and so fond an assertion, that if asses could speake, they would speake more wiselie than so. For a temporall judge saith not to the hangman; I give thee leave to hang this offender, but commandeth him to doo it. But the mainteiners of witches omnipotencie, saie; Doo you not see how reallie and palpablie the divell tempted and plagued *Job*? I answer first, that there is no corporall or visible divell named nor seene in any part of that circumstance; secondlie, that it was the hand of God that did it; thirdlie, that as there is no

Marginal notes:

Job. 1, 14.
verse 15.,

verse, 16.

verse, 17.

verse, 18.

verse, 19.

Ibid. ca. 2.
vers. 7.

*J. Calvin in
Job. cap.* 1.
21.

*J. Calvin. in
Job, cap.* 2.
Sermon. 8.
*Muscul. in
loc. comm.
Idem, ibidem.*

communitie betweene the person of a witch, and the person of a divell, so was there not any conference or practise betwixt them in this case.

And as touching the communication betwixt God and the divell, behold what *Calvine* saith, writing or rather preaching of purpose upon that place, wheruppon they thinke they have so great advantage; When sathan is said to appeere before God, it is not doone in some place certeine, but the scripture speaketh so to applie it selfe to our rudenes. Certeinlie the divell in this and such like cases is an instrument to worke Gods will, and not his owne: and therefore it is an ignorant and an ungodlie saieng (as *Calvine* judgeth it) to affirme, that God dooth but permit and suffer the divell. For if sathan were so at his owne libertie (saith he) we should be overwhelmed at a sudden. And doubtlesse, if he had power to hurt the bodie, there were no waie to resist: for he would come invisiblie upon us, and knocke us on the heads; yea hee would watch the best and dispatch them, whilest they were about some wicked act. If they saie; God commandeth him, no bodie impugneth them: but that God should give him leave, I saie with *Calvine*, that the divell is not in such favour with God, as to obteine any such request at his hands.

J. Calvine in his sermon upon Job.

And whereas by our witchmongers opinions and arguments, the witch procureth the divell, and the divell asketh leave of God to plague whom the witch is disposed: there is not (as I have said) any such corporall communication betweene the divell and a witch, as witchmongers imagine. Neither is God mooved at all at sathans sute, who hath no such favour or grace with him, as to obteine any thing at his hands.

J. Calvine in Job. cap. 1. sermon. 5.

But *M. Mal.* and his friends denie, that there were any witches in *Jobs* time: yea the witchmongers are content to saie, that there were none found to exercise this art in Christs time, from his birth to his death, even by the space of thirtie three yeares. If there had beene anie (saie they) they should have beene there spoken of. As touching the authoritie of the booke of *Job*, there is no question but that it is verie canonicall and authentike. Howbeit, manie writers, both of the Jewes and others, are of opinion, that *Moses* was the author of this booke; and that he did set it as a looking glasse before the people: to the intent the children of *Abraham* (of whose race he himselfe came) might knowe, that God shewed favour to others that were not of the same line, and be ashamed of their wickednesse: seeing an uncircumcised Painime had so well demeaned himselfe. Upon which argument *Calvine* (though he had written upon the same) saith, that Forsomuch as it is uncerteine, whether it were *Res gesta* or *Exempli gratia*, we must leave it in suspense. Nevertheless (saith he) let us take that which is out of all doubt; namelie, that the Holy-ghost hath indited the booke, to the end that the Jewes should knowe that God hath had a people alwaies to serve him throughout the world, even of such as were no Jewes, nor segregated from other nations.

Mal. malef. pa. 1. quæst. 1. Idem part 1. quæst. 4.

Note what is said touching the booke of Job.

Howbeit, I for my part denie not the veritie of the storie; though indeed I must confesse, that I thinke there was no such corporall enterlude betweene God, the divell, and *Job*, as they imagine: neither anie such reall presence and communication as the witchmongers conceive and mainteine; who are so grosse herein, that they doo not onlie beleeve, but publish so palpable absurdities concerning such reall actions betwixt the divell and man, as a wise man would be ashamed to read, but much more to credit: as that S. *Dunstan* lead the divell about the house by the nose with a paire of pinsors or tongs, and made him rore so lowd, as the place roong thereof, &c: with a thousand the like fables, without which neither the art of poperie nor of witchcraft could stand. But you may see more of this matter else-where, where in few words (which I thought good here to omit, least I should seeme to use too manie repetitions) I answer effectuallie to their cavils about this place.

In legenda aurea.

CHAPTER IX.

What severall sorts of witches are mentioned in the scriptures, and how the word witch is there applied.

BUT what sorts of witches so ever *M. Mal.* or *Bodin* saie there are; *Moses* spake onlie of foure kinds of impious couseners or witches (whereof our witchmongers old women which danse with the fairies, &c; are none.) The first were *Præstigiatores Pharaonis*, which (as all divines, both Hebrues and others conclude) were but couseners and jugglers, deceiving the kings eies with illusions and sleights; and making false things to appeare as true: which nevertheles our witches cannot doo. The second is *Mecasapha*, which is she that destroieth with poison. The third are such as use sundrie kinds of divinations, and hereunto perteine these words, *Kasam*, *Onen*, *Ob*, *Idoni*. The fourth is *Habar*, to wit: when magicians, or rather such, as would be reputed cunning therein, mumble certeine secret words, wherin is thought to be great efficacie.

1. Præstigiatores Pharaonis.
2. Mecasapha.
3. Kasam. Onen. Ob. Idoni.
4. Habar.

These are all couseners and abusers of the people in their severall kinds. But bicause they are all termed of our translators by the name of witches in the Bible: therefore the lies of *M. Mal.* and *Bodin*, and all our old wives tales are applied unto these names, and easilie beleeved of the common people, who have never hitherto beene instructed in the understanding of these words. In which respect, I will (by Gods grace) shew you (concerning the signification of them) the opinion of the most learned in our age; speciallie of *Johannes Wierus*; who though hee himselfe were singularlie learned in the toongs, yet for his satisfaction and full resolution in the same, he sent for the judgement of *Andræas Massius*, the most famous *Hebrician* in the world, and had it in such sense and order, as I meane to set downe unto you. And yet I give you this note by the waie, that witchcraft or inchantment is diverslie taken in the scriptures; somtimes nothing tending to such end as it is commonlie thought to doo. For in 1 *Samuell*, 15, 23. it is all one with rebellion. *Jesabell* for hir idolatrous life is called a witch. Also in the new testament, even S. *Paule* saith the *Galathians* are bewitched, bicause they were seduced and lead from the true understanding of the scriptures.

Note. 1. Sa. 15, 23. 2. Re. 9, 22. Gal. 3, 1.

Item sometimes it is taken in good part; as the magicians that came to worship and offer to Christ: and also where *Daniell* is said to be an inchanter, yea a principall inchanter: which title being given him in divers places of that storie, he never seemeth to refuse or dislike; but rather intreateth for the pardon and qualification of the rigor towards other inchanters, which were meere couseners indeed: as appeareth in the second chapter of *Daniell*, where you may see that the king espied their fetches.

Matth. 2, 1. Daniel. 4. Dan. 2, 8.

Sometimes such are called conjurors, as being but roges, and lewd people, would use the name of Jesus to worke miracles, whereby, though they being faithlesse could worke nothing; yet is their practise condemned by the name of conjuration. Sometimes jugglers are called witches. Sometimes also they are called sorcerers, that impugne the gospell of Christ, and seduce others with violent persuasions. Sometimes a murtherer with poison is called a witch. Sometimes they are so termed by the verie signification of their names; as *Elimas*, which signifieth a sorcerer. Sometimes bicause they studie curious and vaine arts. Sometimes it is taken for woonding or greeving of the hart. Yea the verie word *Magus*, which is Latine for a magician, is translated a witch; and yet it was hertofore alwaies taken in the good part. And at this daie it is indifferent to saie in the English toong; She is a witch; or, She is a wise woman.

Actes. 19. Gen. 4, 18. Exod. 7, 13, &c. Acts. 13. Exod. 22, &c. Acts. 13. Acts. 19. Canticles of Salomon. cap. 4. verse. 9.

Sometimes observers of dreames, sometimes soothsaiers, sometimes the observers of the flieng of foules, of the meeting of todes, the falling of salt, &c are called witches. Sometimes he or she is called a witch, that take upon them

Deut. 18, 2. Jerem. 27. Acts. 8.

either for gaine or glorie, to doo miracles; and yet can doo nothing. Sometimes they are called witches in common speech, that are old, lame, curst, or melancholike, as a nickname. But as for our old women, that are said to hurt children with their eies, or lambs with their lookes, or that pull downe the moone out of heaven, or make so foolish a bargaine, or doo such homage to the divell; you shall not read in the bible of any such witches, or of any such actions imputed to them.

BOOKE VI.

CHAPTER I

The exposition of this Hebrue word Chasaph, wherein is answered the objection conteined in Exodus 22. to wit: Thou shalt not suffer a witch to live, and of Simon Magus. Acts. 8.

CHASAPH, being an Hebrue word, is Latined *Veneficium*, and is in English, poisoning, or witchcraft; if you will so have it. The Hebrue sentence written in *Exodus*, 22. is by the 70. interpretors translated thus into Greeke, Φάρμακὸυς ὄυκ ἔπιζεώσετε, which in Latine is, *Veneficos (sive) veneficas non retinebitis in vita*, in English, You shall not suffer anie poisoners, or (as it is translated) witches to live. The which sentence *Josephus* an Hebrue borne, and a man of great estimation, learning and fame, interpreteth in this wise; Let none of the children of Israel have any poison that is deadlie, or prepared to anie hurtfull use. If anie be apprehended with such stuffe, let him be put to death, and suffer that which he meant to doo to them, for whom he prepared it. The *Rabbins* exposition agree heerewithall. *Lex Cornelia* differeth not from this sense, to wit, that he must suffer death, which either maketh, selleth, or hath anie poison, to the intent to kill anie man. This word is found in these places following: *Exodus.* 22, 18. *Deut.* 18, 10. 2 *Sam.* 9, 22. *Dan.* 2, 2. 2 *Chr.* 33, 6. *Esay.* 47, 9, 12. *Malach*, 3, 5. *Jerem.* 27, 9, *Mich.* 5, 2. *Nah.* 3, 4. *bis.* Howbeit, in all our English translations, *Chasaph* is translated, witchcraft.

    And bicause I will avoid prolixitie and contention both at once, I will admit that *Veneficæ* were such witches, as with their poisons did much hurt among the children of Israell; and I will not denie that there remaine such untill this daie, bewitching men, and making them beleeve, that by vertue of words, and certeine ceremonies, they bring to passe such mischeefes, and intoxications, as they indeed accomplish by poisons. And this abuse in cousenage of people, together with the taking of Gods name in vaine, in manie places of the scripture is reprooved, especiallie by the name of witchcraft, even where no poisons are. According to the sense which S. *Paule* useth to the *Galathians* in these words, where he sheweth plainelie, that the true signification of witchcraft is cousenage; O ye foolish *Galathians* (saith he) who hath bewitched you? to wit, cousened or abused you, making you beleeve a thing which is neither so nor so. Whereby he meaneth not to aske of them, who have with charmes, *&c*: or with poisons deprived them of their health, life, cattell, or children, *&c*: but who hath abused or cousened them, to make them beleeve lies. This phrase is also used by *Job.* 15. But that we may be throughlie resolved of the true meaning of this phrase used by *Paule, Gal.* 3. let us examine the description of a notable witch called *Simon Magus*, made by S. *Luke*; There was (saith he) in the citie of *Samaria*, a certeine man called *Simon*, which used witchcraft, and bewitched the people of *Samaria*, saieng that he himself was some great man. I demand, in what other thing here do we see anie witchcraft, than that he abused the people, making them beleeve he could worke miracles, whereas in truth he could doo no such thing; as manifestlie may appeare in the 13. and 19. verses of the same chapter: where he wondered at the miracles wrought by the apostles, and would have purchased with monie the power of the Holy-ghost to worke wonders.

    It will be said, the people had reason to beleeve him, bicause it is written, that he of long time had bewitched them with sorceries. But let the bewitched

Joseph. in Judæorum antiquitat.

Gal. 3, 1.

Job. 15, 12.

Acts. 8, 9.

Acts. 8, 11.

64

Galathians be a warning both to the bewitched *Samaritans*, and to all other that are cousened or bewitched through false doctrine, or legierdemaine; least while they attend to such fables and lies, they be brought into ignorance, and so in time be led with them awaie from God. And finallie, let us all abandon such witches and couseners, as with *Simon Magus* set themselves in the place of God, boasting that they can doo miracles, expound dreames, foretell things to come, raise the dead, &c: which are the workes of the Holy-ghost, who onlie searcheth the heart and reines, and onelie worketh great wonders, which are now staied and accomplished in Christ, in whome who so stedfastlie beleeveth shall not need to be by such means resolved or confirmed in his doctrine and gospell. And as for the unfaithfull, they shall have none other miracle shewed unto them, but the signe of *Jonas* the prophet.

    And therefore I saie, whatsoever they be that with *Simon Magus* take upon them to worke such wonders, by soothsaieng, sorcerie, or witchcraft, are but liers, deceivers, and couseners, according to *Syrachs* saieng; Sorcerie, witchcraft, soothsaieng, and dreames, are but vanitie, and the lawe shalbe fulfilled without such lies. God commanded the people, that they should not regard them that wrought with spirits, nor soothsaiers: for the estimation that was attributed unto them, offended God.

1. Reg. 9, 39.
Matth. 9. 4.
12. 25. 22.
Acts. 1, 24.
& 15, 8.
Rom. 8, 27.
Mark. 2.
Luk. 6, 17. &
11. & 9.
Joh. 1 & 2.
& 6. & 13.
Apoc. 2. & 3.
Luk. 11, 29.
Eccl. 34, 5.
Eccl. 34, 8.
Levi. 19, 31.

CHAPTER II.

The place of Deuteronomie expounded, wherin are recited all kind of witches; also their opinions confuted, which hold that they can worke such miracles as are imputed unto them.

THE greatest and most common objection is, that if there were not some, which could worke such miraculous or supernaturall feats, by themselves, or by their divels, it should not have beene said; Let none be found among you, that maketh his sonne or his daughter to go through the fier, or that useth witchcraft, or is a regarder of times, or a marker of the flieng of fowles, or a sorcerer, or a charmer, or that counselleth with spirits, or a soothsaier, or that asketh counsell of the dead, or (as some translate it) that raiseth the dead. But as there is no one place in the scripture that saith they can worke miracles, so it shalbe easie to proove, that these were all couseners, everie one abusing the people in his severall kind; and are accurssed of God. Not that they can doo all such things indeed, as there is expressed; but for that they take upon them to be the mightie power of God, and to doo that which is the onelie worke of him, seducing the people, and blaspheming the name of God, who will not give his glorie to anie creature, being himselfe the king of glorie and omnipotencie.

Deut. 18. 10.
11.

    First I aske, what miracle was wrought by their passing through the fier? Trulie it cannot be prooved that anie effect followed; but that the people were bewitched, to suppose their sinnes to be purged thereby; as the *Spaniards* thinke of scourging and whipping themselves. So as Gods power was imputed to that action, and so forbidden as an idolatrous sorcerie. What woonders worketh the regarder of times? What other divell dealeth he withall, than with the spirit of superstition? Doth he not deceive himselfe and others, and therefore is worthilie condemned for a witch? What spirit useth he, which marketh the flieng of fowles? Nevertheles, he is here condemned as a practiser of witchcraft; bicause he couseneth the people, and taketh upon him to be a prophet; impiouslie referring Gods certeine ordinances to the flittering fethers and uncerteine waies of a bird. The like effects produceth sorcerie, charming, consultation with spirits, soothsaieng, and consulting with the dead: in everie of the which Gods power is obscured, his glorie defaced, and his commandement infringed.

Esay. 42, 8.
Ps. 24. 8. 10.

And to proove that these soothsaiers and witches are but lieng mates and couseners; note these words pronounced by God himselfe, even in the selfe same place to the children of Israell: Although the Gentiles suffered themselves to be abused, so as they gave eare to these sorcerers, &c: he would not suffer them so, but would raise them a prophet, who should speake the truth. As if he should saie; The other are but lieng and cousening mates, deceitfull and undermining merchants, whose abuses I will make knowne to my people. And that everie one maie be resolved herein, let the last sentence of this precept be well weighed; to wit, Let none be found among you, that asketh counsell of (or raiseth the dead.)

First you know the soules of the righteous are in the hands of God, and resting with *Lazarus* in *Abrahams* bosome, doo sleepe in Jesus Christ. And from that sleepe, man shall not be raised, till the heavens be no more: according to this of *David*; Wilt thou shew woonders among the dead? Nay, the Lord saith, The living shall not be taught by the dead, but by the living. As for the unrighteous, they are in hell, where is no redemption; neither is there anie passage from heaven to earth, but by God and his angels. As touching the resurrection and restauration of the bodie, read *John.* 5. and you shall manifestlie see, that it is the onelie worke of the father, who hath given the power thereof to the sonne, and to none other, &c. *Dominus percutit,* & *ipse medetur: Ego occidam,* & *ego vive-faciam.* And in manie other places it is written, that God giveth life and beeing to all. Although *Plato,* with his maister *Socrates,* the cheefe pillers of these vanities, say, that one *Pamphilus* was called up out of hel, who when he cam among the people, told manie incredible tales concerning infernall actions. But herein I take up the proverbe; *Amicus Plato, amicus Socrates, sed major amica veritas.*

So as this last precept, or last part thereof, extending to that which neither can be done by witch nor divell, maie well expound the other parts and points therof. For it is not ment hereby, that they can doo such things indeed; but that they make men beleeve they doo them, and thereby cousen the people, and take upon them the office of God, and therewithall also blaspheme his holie name, and take it in vaine; as by the words of charmes and conjurations doo appeare, which you shall see, if you looke into these words, *Habar* and *Idoni.*

In like manner I saie you may see, that by the prohibition of divinations by augurie, and of soothsaiengs, &c, who are witches, and can indeed doo nothing but lie and cousen the people, the lawe of God condemneth them not, for that they can worke miracles, but bicause they saie they can doo that which per-teineth to God, and for cousenage, &c. Concerning other points of witchcraft conteined therein, and bicause some cannot otherwise be satisfied, I will alledge under one sentence, the decretals, the mind of S. *Augustine,* the councell *Aurelian,* and the determination of *Paris,* to wit: Who so observeth, or giveth heed unto soothsaiengs, divinations, witchcraft, &c, or doth give credit to anie such, he renounceth christianitie, and shalbe counted a pagane, & an enemie to God; yea and he erreth both in faith and philosophie. And the reason is therewithall expressed in the canon, to wit; Bicause hereby is attributed to a creature, that which perteineth to God onelie and alone. So as, under this one sentence (Thou shalt not suffer a poisoner or a witch to live) is forbidden both murther and witchcraft; the murther consisting in poison; the witchcraft in cousenage or blasphemie.

Deut. 18, 14.

Sap. 3, 1.
Luk. 16, 23.
Job. 14, 12.
Psal. 88, 10.
Deut. 18, 11.
Luk. 16. 29.
31.
Luk. 16, 22.
Joh. 5, 21.

Ose. 6.
Acts. 17. 25.
28.
Tim. 6, 13.

26. quæ. 7.
non. obser.
fact. 1398.
act. 17.
August. de
spirit. & ani-
ma. cap. 28.

CHAPTER III.

That women have used poisoning in all ages more than men, and of the inconvenience of poisoning.

AS women in all ages have beene counted most apt to conceive witchcraft, and the divels speciall instruments therin, and the onelie or cheefe practisers therof: so also it appeareth, that they have been the first inventers, and the greatest practisers of poisoning, and more naturallie addicted and given thereunto than men: according to the saieng of *Quintilian*; *Latrocinium facilius in viro, veneficium in fæmina credam.* From whom *Plinie* differeth nothing in opinion, when he saith, *Scientiam fæminarum in veneficiis prævalere.* To be short, *Augustine, Livie, Valerius, Diodorus,* and manie other agree, that women were the first inventers and practisers of the art of poisoning. As for the rest of their cunning, in what estimation it was had, may appeare by these verses of *Horace,* wherein he doth not onelie declare the vanitie of witchcraft, but also expoundeth the other words, wherewithall we are now in hand.

Plin. lib. 25. cap. 2.

> *Somnia, terrores magicos, miracula, sagas,*
> *Nocturnos lemures, portentáq; Thessala rides:*

> *These dreames and terrors magicall,*
>   *these miracles and witches,*
> *Night-walking sprites, or Thessal bugs,*
>   *esteeme them not twoo rushes.*

Here *Horace* (you see) contemneth as ridiculous, all our witches cunning: marrie herein he comprehendeth not their poisoning art, which hereby he onelie seemed to thinke hurtfull. *Pythagoras* and *Democritus* give us the names of a great manie magicall hearbs and stones, whereof now, both the vertue, and the things themselves also are unknowne: as *Marmaritin,* whereby spirits might be raised: *Archimedon,* which would make one bewraie in his sleepe, all the secrets in his heart: *Adincantida, Calicia, Mevais, Chirocineta, &c:* which had all their severall vertues, or rather poisons. But all these now are worne out of knowledge: marrie in their steed we have hogs turd and chervill, as the onelie thing whereby our witches worke miracles.

Trulie this poisoning art called *Veneficium,* of all others is most abhominable; as whereby murthers maie be committed, where no suspicion maie be gathered, nor anie resistance can be made; the strong cannot avoid the weake, the wise cannot prevent the foolish, the godlie cannot be preserved from the hands of the wicked; children maie hereby kill their parents, the servant the maister, the wife hir husband, so privilie, so inevitablie, and so incurablie, that of all other it hath beene thought the most odious kind of murther; according to the saieng of *Ovid:*

> ————————*non hospes ab hospite tutus,*
> *Non socer à genero, fratrum quóq; gratia rara est:*
> *Imminet exitio vir conjugis, illa mariti,*
> *Lurida terribiles miscent aconita novercæ,*
> *Filius ante diem patrios inquirit in annos.*

Ovid. metamorph. lib. 1.

> ————*The travelling ghest opprest*
> *Dooth stand in danger of his host,*
>   *the host eke of his ghest:*
> *The father of his sonne in lawe,*
>   *yea rare is seene to rest*

Englished by Abraham Fleming.

Twixt brethren love and amitie,
  and kindnesse void of strife;
The husband seekes the goodwifes death,
  and his againe the wife.
Ungentle stepdames grizlie poi-
  son temper and doo give:
The sonne too soone dooth aske how long
  his father is to live.

The monke that poisoned king *John,* was a right *Veneficus;* to wit, both a witch and a murtherer: for he killed the king with poison, and persuaded the people with lies, that he had doone a good and a meritorious act: and doubt-lesse, manie were so bewitched, as they thought he did verie well therein. *Antonius Sabellicus* writeth of a horrible poisoning murther, committed by women at *Rome,* where were executed (after due conviction) 170. women at one time; besides 20. women of that consort, who were poisoned with that poison which they had prepared for others.

Aeneid. 4.
lib. 4.

CHAPTER IV.

Of divers poisoning practises, otherwise called veneficia, committed in Italie, Genua, Millen, Wittenberge, also how they were discovered and executed.

Veneficæ
in Italie.

ANOTHER practise, not unlike to that mentioned in the former chapter, was doone in *Cassalis* at *Salassia* in *Italie,* Anno 1536. where 40. *Veneficæ* or witches being of one confederacie, renewed a plague which was then almost ceased, besmeering with an ointment and a pouder, the posts and doores of mens houses; so as thereby whole families were poisoned: and of that stuffe they had prepared above 40. crocks for that purpose. Herewithall they con-veied inheritances as it pleased them, till at length they killed the brother and onelie sonne of one *Necus* (as lightlie none died in the house but the maisters and their children) which was much noted; and therewithall that one *Andro-gina* haunted the houses, speciallie of them that died: and she being suspected, apprehended, and examined, confessed the fact, conspiracie, and circumstance, as hath beene shewed. The like villanie was afterwards practised at *Genua,* and execution was doone upon the offenders. At *Millen* there was another like attempt that tooke none effect. This art consisteth as well in poisoning of cattell as of men: and that which is doone by poisons unto cattell, towards their de-struction, is as commonlie attributed to witches charms as the other. And I doubt not, but some that would be thought cunning in incantations, and to doo miracles, have experience in this behalf. For it is written by divers authors, that if wolves doong be hidden in the mangers, racks, or else in the hedges about the pastures, where cattell go (through the antipathie of the nature of the woolfe and other cattell) all the beasts that savour the same doo not onlie forbeare to eate, but run about as though they were mad, or (as they say) bewitched.

Veneficæ
in Genua
& Millen.

Of a but-
cher a right
veneficall
which

But *Wierus* telleth a notable storie of a *Veneficus,* or destroier of cattell, which I thought meete heere to repeat. There was (saith he) in the dukedome of *Wittingberge,* not farre from *Tubing,* a butcher, anno 1564. that bargained with the towne for all their hides which were of sterven cattell, called in these parts *Morts.* He with poison privilie killed in great numbers, their bullocks, sheepe, swine, &c: and by his bargaine of the hides and tallowe he grew infinitlie rich. And at last being suspected, was examined, confessed the matter and maner thereof, and was put to death with hot tongs, wherewith his flesh was pulled from his bones. We for our parts would have killed five poore women, before we would suspect one rich butcher.

Chapter v.

A great objection answered concerning this kind of witchcraft called Veneficium.

IT is objected, that if *Veneficium* were comprehended under the title of man-slaughter, it had beene a vaine repetition, and a disordered course under-taken by *Moses*, to set foorth a lawe against *Veneficas* severallie. But it might suffice to answer any reasonable christian, that such was the pleasure of the Holie-ghost, to institute a particular article herof, as of a thing more odious, wicked and dangerous, than any other kind of murther. But he that shall read the lawe of *Moses*, or the testament of Christ himselfe, shall find this kind of repetition and reiteration of the law most common. For as it is written *Exod.* 22, 21. Thou shalt not greeve nor afflict a stranger, for thou wast a stranger in the land of *Aegypt*: so are the same words found repeated in *Levit.* 19, 33.   Levit. 19, 33. Polling and shaving of heads and beards is forbidden in *Deut.* 27, which was before prohibited in 22. It is written in *Exodus* the 20. Thou shalt not steale: and it is repeated in *Leviticus* 19. and in *Deut.* 5. Murther is generallie for-bidden in *Exod.* 20. and likewise in 22. and repeated in *Num.* 35. But the aptest example is, that magicke is forbidden in three severall places, to wit, once in *Levit.* 19. and twise in *Levit.* 20. For the which a man might as well cavill with the Holie-ghost as for the other.

Chapter vi.

In what kind of confections that witchcraft, which is called Venificium, consisteth:
of love cups, and the same confuted by poets.

AS touching this kind of witchcraft, the principall part thereof consisteth in certeine confections prepared by lewd people to procure love; which indeed are meere poisons, bereaving some of the benefit of the braine, and so of the sense and understanding of the mind. And from some it taketh awaie life, & that is more common than the other. These be called *Philtra*, or *Pocula amatoria*, or *Venenosa pocula*, or *Hippomanes*; which bad and blind physicians rather practise, than witches or conjurers, &c. But of what value these bables are, towards the end why they are provided, may appeere by the opinions of poets themselves, from whence was derived the estimation of that stuffe. And first you shall heare what *Ovid* saith, who wrote of the verie art of love, and that so cunninglie and feelinglie, that he is reputed the speciall doctor in that science:

> *Fallitur Æmonias si quis decurrit ad artes,*
> *Dátq; quod à teneri fronte revellit equi.*
> *Non facient ut vivat amor Medeides herbæ,*
> *Mistáq; cum magicis mersa venena sonis.*
> *Phasias Æsonidem, Circe tenuisset Ulyssem,*
> *Si modò servari carmine posset amor:*
> *Nec data profuerint pallentia philtra puellis,*
> *Philtra nocent animis, vímq; furoris habent.*

Ovid. lib. 2.
de arte
amandi.

> *Who so dooth run to Hæmon arts,*
>   *I dub him for a dolt,*
> *And giveth that which he dooth plucke*
>   *from forhead of a colt:*

Englished by
Abraham
Fleming.

> Medeas herbs will not procure
>   that love shall lasting live,
> Nor steeped poison mixed with ma-
>   gicke charms the same can give.
> The witch Medea had full fast
>   held Jason for hir owne,
> So had the grand witch Circe too
>   Ulysses, if alone
> With charms mainteind & kept might be
>   the love of twaine in one.

Philtra, slibbersaw-ces to pro-cure love.

> No slibbersawces given to maids,
>   to make them pale and wan,
> Will helpe: such slibbersawces marre
>   the minds of maid and man,
> And have in them a furious force
>   of phrensie now and than.

Ovid. lib. de remedio amoris, 1.

> Viderit Aemoniæ si quis mala pabula terræ,
> Et magicas artes posse juvare putat.

Ab. Fleming.

> If any thinke that evill herbs
>   in Hæmon land which be,
> Or witchcraft able is to helpe,
>   let him make proofe and see.

These verses precedent doo shew, that *Ovid* knew that those beggerlie sorceries might rather kill one, or make him starke mad, than doo him good towards the atteinement of his pleasure or love; and therefore, he giveth this counsell to them that are amorous in such hot maner, that either they must enjoy their love, or else needs die; saieng:

> Sit procul omne nefas, ut ameris amabilis esto:

Englished by Abraham Fleming.

> Farre off be all unlawfull meanes
>   thou amiable bee,
> Loving I meane, that she with love
>   may quite the love of thee.

CHAPTER VII.

It is proved by more credible writers, that love cups rather ingender death through venome, than love by art: and with what toies they destroie cattell, and procure love.

Hieronym. in Ruff. Plin. lib. 25. cap 3. Joseph lib. 11. de Judæorum antiquit. Aristot. lib. 8. de natura animal. cap. 24. Jo. Wier. de venef. cap. 40.

BUT bicause there is no hold nor trust to these poets, who saie and unsaie, dallieng with these causes; so as indeed the wise may perceive they have them in derision: let us see what other graver authors speake hereof. *Eusebius Cæsariensis* writeth, that the poet *Lucretius* was killed with one of those lovers poisoned cups. *Hierome* reporteth that one *Livia* herewith killed hir husband, whome she too much hated; and *Lucilla* killed hirs, whome she too much loved. *Calisthenes* killed *Lucius Lucullus* the emperor with a love pot, as *Plutarch* and *Cornelius Nepos* saie. *Plinie* & *Josephus* report, that *Cæsonia* killed hir husband *Caligula Amatorio poculo* with a lovers cup, which was indeed starke poison. *Aristotle* saith, that all which is beleeved touching the efficacie of these matters, is lies and old wives tales. He that will read more arguments and histories concerning these poisons, let him looke in *J. Wier De Veneficiis.*

70

The toies, which are said to procure love, and are exhibited in their poison looving cups, are these: the haire growing in the nethermost part of a woolves taile, a woolves yard, a little fish called *Remora*, the braine of a cat, of a newt, or of a lizzard: the bone of a greene frog, the flesh thereof being consumed with pismers or ants; the left bone whereof ingendereth (as they saie) love; the bone on the right side, hate. Also it is said, that a frogs bones, the flesh being eaten off round about with ants, whereof some will swim, and some will sinke: those that sinke, being hanged up in a white linnen cloth, ingender love, but if a man be touched therewith, hate is bred thereby. Another experiment is thereof, with yoong swalowes, whereof one brood or nest being taken and buried in a crocke under the ground, till they be starved up; they that be found open mouthed, serve to engender love; they whose mouthes are shut, serve to procure hate. Besides these, manie other follies there be to this purpose proposed to the simple; as namelie, the garments of the dead, candels that burne before a dead corps, and needels wherwith dead bodies are sowne or sockt into their sheetes: and diverse other things, which for the reverence of the reader, and in respect of the uncleane speach to be used in the description thereof, I omit; which (if you read *Dioscorides*, or diverse other learned physicians) you maie see at large. In the meane while, he that desireth to see more experiments concerning this matter, let him read *Leonardus Vairus de fascino*, now this present yeare 1583. newlie published; wherein (with an incestuous mouth) he affirmeth directlie, that Christ and his apostles were *Venefici*; verie fondlie prosecuting that argument, and with as much popish follie as may be; labouring to proove it lawful to charme and inchant vermine, &c.

Toies to mocke apes.

Dioscorid. de materia medicin.
L. Vairus de fascin. lib. 2. cap. 11. prope finem.

CHAPTER VIII.

John Bodin triumphing against John Wier is overtaken with false Greeke & false interpretation thereof.

MONSIEUR BODIN triumpheth over doctor *Wier* herein, pronouncing a heavie sentence upon him; bicause he referreth this word to poison. But he reigneth or rather rideth over him, and much more for speaking false Greeke; affirming that he calleth *Veneficos Φαρμακένους*, which is as true as the rest of his reports and fables of witches miracles conteined in his bookes of divelish devises. For in truth he hath no such word, but saith they are called *Φαρμακένεις*, whereas he should have said *Φαρμακεῖς*, the true accent being omitted, and *ἔν* being interposed, which should have beene left out. Which is nothing to the substance of the matter, but must needs be the Printers fault.

J. Bodin.

But *Bodin* reasoneth in this wise, *Φαρμακεῖς* is sometimes put for *Magos* or *Præstigiatores*: *Ergo* in the translation of the *Septuaginta*, it is so to be taken. Wherein he manifesteth his bad Logicke, more than the others ill Greeke. For it is well knowne to the learned in this toong, that the usuall and proper signification of this word, with all his derivations and compounds doo signifie *Veneficos*, Poisoners by medicine. Which when it is most usuall and proper, why should the translators take it in a signification lesse usuall, and nothing proper. Thus therefore he reasoneth and concludeth with his new found Logicke, and old fond Greeke; Sometimes it signifieth so, though unproperlie, or rather metaphoricallie; *Ergo* in that place it is so to be taken, when another fitter word might have beene used. Which argument being vaine, agreeth well with his other vaine actions. The *Septuaginta* had beene verie destitute of words, if no proper word could have beene found for this purpose. But where they have occasion to speake of witchcraft in their translations, they use *Magian, Maggagian*, &c: and therfore belike they see some difference betwixt them and the other, and knew some cause that mooved them to use the word *Φαρμακεία, Veneficium*.

71

BOOKE VII.

CHAPTER I.

Of the Hebrue word Ob, what it signifieth where it is found, of Pythonisses called Ventriloquæ, who they be, and what their practises are, experience and examples thereof shewed.

THIS word *Ob*, is translated *Pytho*, or *Pythonicus spiritus*: *Deutre.* 18. *Isaie.* 19. 1. *Sam.* 28. 2. *Reg.* 23. &c: sometime, though unproperlie, *Magus* as 2. *Sam.* 33. But *Ob* signifieth most properlie a bottle, and is used in this place, bicause the *Pythonists* spake hollowe; as in the bottome of their bellies, whereby they are aptlie in Latine called *Ventriloqui*: of which sort was *Elizabeth Barton*, the holie maid of *Kent*, &c. These are such as take upon them to give oracles, to tell where things lost are become, and finallie to appeach others of mischeefs, which they themselves most commonlie have brought to passe: whereby many times they overthrowe the good fame of honest women, and of such others of their neighbors, with whome they are displeased. For triall hereof, letting passe a hundred cousenages that I could recite at this time, I will begin with a true storie of a wench, practising hir diabolicall witchcraft, and ventriloquie An. 1574. at *Westwell* in *Kent*, within six miles where I dwell, taken and noted by twoo ministers and preachers of Gods word, foure substantiall yeomen, and three women of good fame & reputation, whose names are after written.

The holie maid of Kent a ventriloqua.

Mildred, the base daughter of *Alice Norrington*, and now servant to *William Sponer* of *Westwell* in the countie of *Kent*, being of the age of seventeene yeares, was possessed with sathan in the night and daie aforesaid. About two of the clocke in the afternoone of the same day, there came to the same *Sponers* house *Roger Newman* minister of *Westwell*, *John Brainford* minister of *Kenington*, with others, whose names are underwritten, who made their praiers unto God, to assist them in that needfull case; and then commanded sathan in the name of the eternall God, and of his sonne Jesus Christ, to speake with such a voice as they might understand, and to declare from whence he came. But he would not speake, but rored and cried mightilie. And though we did command him manie times, in the name of God, and of his sonne Jesus Christ, and in his mightie power to speake; yet he would not: untill he had gon through all his delaies, as roring, crieng, striving, and gnashing of teeth; and otherwhile with mowing, and other terrible countenances, and was so strong in the maid, that foure men could scarse hold hir downe. And this continued by the space almost of two houres. So sometimes we charged him earnestlie to speake; and againe praieng unto GOD that he would assist us, at the last he spake, but verie strangelie; and that was thus; He comes, he comes: and that oftentimes he repeated; and He goes, he goes. And then we charged him to tell us who sent him. And he said; I laie in her waie like a log, and I made hir runne like fier, but I could not hurt hir. And whie so, said we? Bicause God kept hir, said he. When camest thou to her, said we? To night in her bed, said he. Then we charged him as before, to tell what he was, and who sent him, and what his name was. At the first he said, The divell, the divell. Then we charged him as before. Then he rored and cried as before, and spake terrible words; I will kill hir, I will kill hir; I will teare hir in peeces, I will teare hir in peeces. We said, Thou shalt not hurt hir. He said, I will kill you all. We said, Thou shalt hurt none of us all. Then we charged him as before. Then he said, You will give me no rest. Wee said, Thou shalt have none here, for thou must have no rest within the servants of God: but tell us in the name of God what thou art, and who sent thee. Then he said he would teare hir in peeces. We said, Thou shalt

An. Domi. 1574. Octob. 13.

Confer this storie with the woman of Endor, 1. Sam. 28. and see whether the same might not be accomplished by this devise

not hurt hir. Then he said againe he would kill us all. We said againe, Thou shalt hurt none of us all, for we are the servants of God. And we charged him as before. And he said againe, Will you give me no rest? We said, Thou shalt have none here, neither shalt thou rest in hir, for thou hast no right in hir, sith Jesus Christ hath redeemed hir with his bloud, and she belongeth to him; and therefore tell us thy name, and who sent thee? He said his name was sathan. We said, Who sent thee? He said, Old *Alice*, old *Alice*. Which old *Alice*, said we? Old *Alice*, said he. Where dwelleth she, said we? In *Westwell* streete, said he. We said, How long hast thou beene with hir? These twentie yeares, said he. We asked him where she did keepe him? In two bottels, said he. Where be they, said we? In the backside of hir house, said he. In what place, said we? Under the wall, said he. Where is the other? In *Kenington*. In what place, said we? In the ground, said he. Then we asked him, what she did give him. He said, hir will, hir will. What did shee bid thee doo, said we? He said, Kill hir maid. Wherefore did she bid thee kill hir, said we? Bicause she did not love hir, said he. We said; How long is it ago, since she sent thee to hir? More than a yeare, said he. Where was that, said we? At hir masters, said he. Which masters, said we? At hir master *Brainfords* at *Kenington*, said he. How oft wert thou there, said we? Manie times, said he. Where first, said we? In the garden, said he: Where the second time? In the hall: Where the third time? In hir bed: Where the fourth time? In the field: Where the fift time? In the court: Where the sixt time? In the water, where I cast hir into the mote: Where the seventh time. In hir bed. We asked him againe, where else? He said, in *Westwell*. Where there, said we? In the vicarige, said he. Where there? In the loft. How camest thou to hir, said we? In the likenesse of two birds, said he. Who sent thee to that place, said we? Old *Alice*, said he. What other spirits were with thee there, said we? My servant, said he. What is his name, said we? He said, little divell. What is thy name, said we? Sathan, said he. What dooth old *Alice* call thee, said we? Partener, said he. What dooth she give thee, said we? Hir will, said he. How manie hast thou killed for hir, said we? Three, said he. Who are they, said we? A man and his child, said he. What were their names, said we? The childs name was *Edward*, said he: what more than *Edward*, said we? *Edward Ager*, said he. What was the mans name, said we? *Richard*, said he. What more, said we? *Richard Ager*, said he. Where dwelt the man and the child, said we? At *Dig* at *Dig*, said he. This *Richard Ager* of *Dig*, was a Gentleman of xl. pounds land by the yeare, a verie honest man, but would often saie he was bewitched, and languished long before he died. Whom else hast thou killed for hir, said we? *Woltons* wife said he. Where did she dwell? In *Westwell*, said he. What else hast thou doone for hir said we? What she would have me, said he. What is that said we? To fetch hir meat, drinke, and corne, said he. Where hadst thou it, said we? In everie house, said he. Name the houses, said we? At *Petmans*, at *Farmes*, at *Millens*, at *Fullers*, and in everie house. After this we commanded sathan in the name of Jesus Christ to depart from hir, and never to trouble hir anie more, nor anie man else. Then he said he would go, he would go: but he went not. Then we commanded him as before with some more words. Then he said, I go, I go; and so he departed. Then said the maid, He is gone, Lord have mercie upon me, for he would have killed me. And then we kneeled downe and gave God thanks with the maiden; praieng that God would keepe hir from sathans power, and assist hir with his grace. And noting this in a peece of paper, we departed. Sathans voice did differ much from the maids voice, and all that he spake, was in his owne name. *Subscribed thus*:

Witnesses to this, that heard and
sawe this whole matter, as followeth:

Roger Newman, vi- car of Westwell. John Brainford, vi- car of Kenington. Thomas Tailor. Henrie Tailors wife.	John Tailor. Thomas French- borns wife. William Spooner. John Frenchborne, and his wife.

CHAPTER II.

How the lewd practise of the Pythonist of Westwell came to light, and by whome she was examined; and that all hir diabolicall speach was but ventriloquie and plaine cousenage, which is prooved by hir owne confession.

Matt. 24, 44
2. Thes. 2, 9.

IT is written, that in the latter daies there shalbe shewed strange illusions, &c: in so much as (if it were possible) the verie elect shal be deceived: howbeit, S. *Paule* saith, they shalbe lieng and false woonders. Neverthelesse, this sentence, and such like, have beene often laid in my dish, and are urged by diverse writers, to approve the miraculous working of witches, whereof I will treat more largelie in another place. Howbeit, by the waie I must confesse, that I take that sentence to be spoken of Anti-christ, to wit: the pope, who miraculouslie, contrarie to nature, philosophie, and all divinitie, being of birth and calling base, in learning grosse; in valure, beautie, or activitie most commonlie a verie lubber, hath placed himselfe in the most loftie and delicate seate, putting almost all christian princes heads, not onelie under his girdle, but under his foote, &c.

Surelie, the tragedie of this *Pythonist* is not inferior to a thousand stories, which will hardlie be blotted out of the memorie and credit either of the common people, or else of the learned. How hardlie will this storie suffer discredit, having testimonie of such authoritie? How could mother *Alice* escape condemnation and hanging, being arreigned upon this evidence; when a poore woman hath beene cast away, upon a cousening oracle, or rather a false lie, devised by *Feats* the juggler, through the malicious instigation of some of hir adversaries?

The ventriloqua of Westwell discovered.

But how cunninglie soever this last cited certificat be penned, or what shew soever it carrieth of truth and plaine dealing, there may be found conteined therein matter enough to detect the cousening knaverie therof. And yet diverse have been deepelie deceived therewith, and can hardlie be removed from the credit thereof, and without great disdaine cannot endure to heare the reproofe thereof. And know you this by the waie, that heretofore Robin goodfellow, and Hob gobblin were as terrible, and also as credible to the people, as hags and witches be now: and in time to come, a witch will be as much derided and contemned, and as plainlie perceived, as the illusion and knaverie of Robin goodfellow. And in truth, they that mainteine walking spirits, with their transformation, &c: have no reason to denie Robin goodfellow, upon whom there hath gone as manie and as credible tales, as upon witches; saving that it hath not pleased the translators of the Bible, to call spirits by the name of Robin goodfellow, as they have termed divinors, soothsaiers, poisoners, and couseners by the name of witches.

The Pythonist of westwell convicted by hir owne confession.

But to make short worke with the confutation of this bastardlie queanes enterprise, & cousenage; you shall understand, that upon the brute of hir divinitie and miraculous transes, she was convented before M. *Thomas Wotton* of *Bocton Malherbe*, a man of great worship and wisedome, and for deciding and ordering of matters in this commonwealth, of rare and singular dexteritie; through whose discreet handling of the matter, with the assistance & aid of M. *George Darrell* esquire, being also a right good and discreet Justice of the same limit, the fraud was found, the coosenage confessed, and she received condigne punishment. Neither was hir confession woone, according to the forme of the Spanish inquisition; to wit, through extremitie of tortures, nor yet by guile or flatterie, nor by presumptions; but through wise and perfect triall of everie circumstance the illusion was manifestlie disclosed; not so (I say) as witches are commonlie convinced and condemned; to wit, through malicious accusations, by ghesses, presumptions, and extorted confessions, contrarie to sense and possibilitie, and for such actions as they can shew no triall nor example before the wise, either by direct or indirect meanes; but after due triall she shewed hir feats, illusions, and transes, with the residue of all hir miraculous works, in the presence of divers gentlemen and gentlewomen of great worship and credit, at *Bocton Malherbe*, in the house of the aforesaid M. *Wotton*. Now compare this wench with the witch of *Endor*, & you shall see that both the cousenages may be doone by one art.

CHAPTER III.

Bodins stuffe concerning the Pythonist of Endor, with a true storie of a counterfeit Dutchman.

UPON the like tales dooth *Bodin* build his doctrine, calling them *Atheists* that will not beleeve him, adding to this kind of witchcraft, the miraculous works of diverse maidens, that would spue pins, clowts, &c: as one *Agnes Brigs*, and *Rachell Pinder* of London did, till the miracles were detected, and they set to open penance. Others he citeth of that sort, the which were bound by divels with garters, or some such like stuffe to posts, &c: with knots that could not be undone, which is an *Aegyptians* juggling or cousening feat. And of such foolish lies joined with bawdie tales, his whole booke consisteth; wherein I warrant you there are no fewer than twoo hundreth fables, and as manie impossibilities. And as these two wenches, with the maiden of *Westwell*, were detected of cousenage; so likewise a Dutchman at *Maidstone* long after he had accomplished such knaveries, to the astonishment of a great number of good men, was revealed to be a cousening knave; although his miracles were imprinted and published at *London*: anno 1572. with this title before the booke, as followeth.

J. Bodin. lib. de dæmon. 3. cap. 2.

A verie wonderfull and strange mi-
racle of God, shewed upon a Dutchman of the age of
23. yeares, which was possessed of ten divels, and was by Gods mightie providence dis-
possessed of them againe, the 27.
of Januarie last past, 1572.

UNTO this the Maior of *Maidstone*, with diverse of his brethren subscribed, chieflie by the persuasion of *Nicasius Vander Schuere*, the minister of the Dutch church there, *John Stikelbow*, whome (as it is there said) God made the instrument to cast out the divels, and foure other credible persons of the Dutch church. The historie is so strange, & so cunninglie performed, that had not his knaverie afterwards brought him into suspicion, he should have gone awaie unsuspected of this fraud. A great manie other such miracles have beene latelie printed, whereof diverse have beene bewraied: all the residue doubtles, if triall had beene made, would have beene found like unto these. But some are more finelie handled than othersome. Some have more advantage by the simplicitie of the audience, some by the majestie and countenance of the confederates; as namelie, that cousening of the holie maid of *Kent*. Some escape utterlie unsuspected, some are prevented by death; so as that waie their examination is untaken. Some are weakelie examined: but the most part are so reverenced, as they which suspect them, are rather called to their answers, than the others.

CHAPTER IV.

*Of the great oracle of Apollo the Pythonist, and how men of all sorts have been deceived,
and that even the apostles have mistaken the nature of spirits, with an unanswerable
argument, that spirits can take no shapes.*

The am-
phibolo-
gies of
oracles.

WITH this kind of witchcraft, *Apollo* and his oracles abused and cousened
the whole world : which idoll was so famous, that I need not stand long
in the description thereof. The princes and monarchs of the earth reposed no small confidence therein : the preests, which lived thereupon, were so
cunning, as they also overtooke almost all the godlie and learned men of that
age, partlie with their doubtfull answers ; as that which was made unto *Pyrrhus*,
in these words, *Aio te Aeacida Romanos vincere posse*, and to *Cræsus* his ambas-
sadours in these words, *Si Cræsus arma Persis inferat, magnum imperium evertat*;
and otherwise thus, *Cræsus Halin penetrans, magnam subvertet opum vim:* or thus,
Cræsus perdet Halin, trangressus plurima regna, &c: partlie through confederacie,
whereby they knew mens errands yer they came, and partlie by cunning, as
promising victorie upon the sacrificing of some person of such account, as

The sub-
tiltie of
oracles.

victorie should rather be neglected, than the murther accomplished. And if it
were, yet should there be such conditions annexed thereunto, as alwaies remained unto them a starting hole, and matter enough to cavill upon ; as that
the partie sacrificed must be a virgin, no bastard, &c. Furthermore, of two
things onelie proposed, and where yea or naie onelie dooth answer the question, it is an even laie, that an idiot shall conjecture right. So as, if things fell
out contrarie, the fault was alwaies in the interpretor, and not in the oracle
or the prophet. But what mervell, (I saie) though the multitude and common
people have beene abused herein ; since lawiers, philosophers, physicians,
astronomers, divines, generall councels, and princes have with great negligence
and ignorance been deceived and seduced hereby, as swallowing up and de-
vouring an inveterate opinion, received of their elders, without due examination
of the circumstance?

Howbeit, the godlie and learned fathers (as it appeereth) have alwaies had a
speciall care and respect, that they attributed not unto God such divelish devises ; but referred them to him, who indeed is the inventer and author thereof,
though not the personall executioner, in maner and forme as they supposed :
so as the matter of faith was not thereby by them impeached. But who can assure

John. 20, 9.

himselfe not to be deceived in matters concerning spirits, when the apostles
themselves were so far from knowing them, as even after the resurrection of
Christ, having heard him preach and expound the scriptures, all his life time,
they shewed themselves not onelie ignorant therein, but also to have misconceived thereof? Did not the apostle *Thomas* thinke that Christ himselfe had
beene a spirit ; until Christ told him plainelie, that a spirit was no such creature,
as had flesh and bones, the which (he said) *Thomas* might see to be in him?
And for the further certifieng and satisfieng of his mind, he commended unto
him his hands to be seene, and his sides to be felt. *Thomas*, if the answer be
true that some make hereunto, to wit: that spirits take formes and shapes of
bodies at their pleasure, might have answered Christ, and remaining unsatisfied
might have said ; Oh sir, what do you tell me that spirits have no flesh and
bones? Why they can take shapes and formes, and so perchance have you doone.
Which argument all the witchmongers in the world shall never be able to
answere.

Some of them that mainteine the creation, the transformation, the transportation, and transubstantiation of witches, object that spirits are not palpable,
though visible, and answer the place by me before cited : so as the feeling and
not the seeing should satisfie *Thomas*. But he that shall well weigh the text and
the circumstances thereof, shall perceive, that the fault of *Thomas* his incredulitie

was secondlie bewraied, and condemned, in that he would not trust his owne eies, nor the view taken by his fellow apostles, who might have beene thought too credulous in this case, if spirits could take shapes at their pleasure. Jesus saith to him; Bicause thou hast seene (and not, bicause thou hast felt) thou beleevest. Item he saith; Blessed are they that beleeve and see not (and not, they that beleeve and feele not.) Whereby he noteth that our corporall eies may discerne betwixt a spirit and a naturall bodie; reprooving him, bicause he so much relied upon his externall senses, in cases where faith should have prevailed; & here, in a matter of faith revealed in the word, would not credit the miracle which was exhibited unto him in most naturall and sensible sort.   John. 20, 29.

Howbeit, *Erastus* saith, and so dooth *Hyperius, Hemingius, Danæus, M. Mal. Bodin,* &c. that evill spirits eate, drinke, and keepe companie with men, and that they can take palpable formes of bodies, producing examples thereof, to wit: *Spectrum Germanicum seu Augustanum,* and the angell whose feet *Lot* washed; as though bicause God can indue his messengers with bodies at his pleasure, therefore the divell and everie spirit can doo the like. How the eleven apostles were in this case deceived, appeareth in *Luke.* 24. and in *Mark.* 16. as also in *Matth.* 14. where the apostles and disciples were all deceived, taking Christ to be a spirit, when he walked on the sea. And why might they not be deceived herein, as well as in that they thought Christ had spoken of a temporall kingdome, when he preached of the kingdome of heaven? Which thing they also much misconceived; as likewise when he did bid them beware of the leven of the Pharisies, they understood that he spake of materiall bread.   Erast. fol. 62.   Luk. 24, 27. Mark. 16, 14. Mat. 14, 16.   Matth. 20. Matt. 16, 11.

CHAPTER V.

Why Apollo was called Pytho whereof those witches were called Pythonists: Gregorie his letter to the divell.

BUT to returne to our oracle of *Apollo* at *Delphos,* who was called *Pytho,* for that *Apollo* slue a serpent so called, whereof the *Pythonists* take their name: I praie you consider well of this tale, which I will trulie rehearse out of the ecclesiasticall historie, written by *Eusebius,* wherein you shall see the absurditie of the opinion, the cousenage of these oraclers, and the deceived mind or vaine opinion of so great a doctor bewraied and deciphered altogither as followeth.   Euseb. lib. 7. cap. 25.

Gregorie Neocæsariensis in his jornie and waie to passe over the *Alpes,* came to the temple of *Apollo*: where *Apollos* priest living richlie upon the revenues and benefit proceeding from that idoll, did give great intertainement unto *Gregorie,* and made him good cheare. But after *Gregorie* was gone, *Apollo* waxed dumbe, so as the priests gaines decaied: for the idoll growing into contempt, the pilgrimage ceased. The spirit taking compassion upon the priests case, and upon his greefe of mind in this behalfe, appeared unto him, and told him flatlie, that his late ghest *Gregorie* was the cause of all his miserie. For (saith the divell) he hath banished me, so that I cannot returne without a speciall licence or pasport from him. It was no need to bid the priest make hast, for immediatlie he tooke post horsses, and galloped after *Gregorie,* till at length he overtooke him, and then expostulated with him for this discourtesie profered in recompense of his good cheare; and said, that if he would not be so good unto him, as to write his letter to the divell in his behalfe, he should be utterlie undone. To be short, his importunitie was such, that he obtained *Gregorie* his letter to the divell, who wrote unto him in maner and forme following, word for word: *Permitto tibi redire in locum tuum,* & *agere quæ consuevisti*; which is in English; I am content thou returne into thy place, and doo as thou wast woont. Immediatlie upon the receipt of this letter, the idoll spake as before. And here is to be noted, that as well in this, as in the execution of all their other oracles and cousenages, the answers were never given *Ex tempore*, or in that daie wherein the question was demanded, because forsooth they expected a vision (as they said) to be given the night following, whereby the cousenage might the more easilie be wrought.

CHAPTER VI.

Apollo, who was called Pytho, compared to the Rood of grace: Gregories letter to the divell confuted.

WHAT need manie words to confute this fable? For if *Gregorie* had beene an honest man, he would never have willinglie permitted, that the people should have beene further cousened with such a lieng spirit: or if he had beene halfe so holie as *Eusebius* maketh him, he would not have consented or yeelded to so lewd a request of the priest, nor have written such an impious letter, no not though good might have come thereof. And therefore as well by the impossibilitie and follie conteined therein, as of the impietie (whereof I dare excuse *Gregorie*) you maie perceive it to be a lie. Me thinks they which still mainteine that the divell made answer in the idoll of *Apollo*, &c: maie have sufficient persuasion to revoke their erronious opinions: in that it appeareth in record, that such men as were skilfull in augurie, did take upon them to give oracles at *Delphos*, in the place of *Apollo*: of which number *Tisanius* the sonne of *Antiochus* was one. But vaine is the answer of idols. Our Rood of grace, with the helpe of little S. *Rumball*, was not inferior to the idoll of *Apollo*: for these could not onlie worke externall miracles, but manifest the internall thoughts of the hart, I beleeve with more livelie shew, both of humanitie and also of divinitie, than the other. As if you read M. *Lamberts* booke of the perambulation of *Kent*, it shall partlie appeare. But if you talke with them that have beene beholders thereof, you will be satisfied herein. And yet in the blind time of poperie, no man might (under paine of damnation) nor without danger of death, suspect the fraud. Naie, what papists will yet confesse they were idols, though the wiers that made their eies gogle, the pins that fastened them to the postes to make them seeme heavie, were seene and burnt together with the images themselves, the knaverie of the priests bewraied, and everie circumstance thereof detected and manifested?

CHAPTER VII.

How diverse great clarkes and good authors have beene abused in this matter of spirits through false reports, and by meanes of their credulitie have published lies, which are confuted by Aristotle and the scriptures.

PLUTARCH, *Livie*, and *Valerius Maximus*, with manie other grave authors, being abused with false reports, write that in times past beasts spake, and that images could have spoken and wept, and did let fall drops of blood, yea and could walk from place to place: which they saie was doone by procuration of spirits. But I rather thinke with *Aristotle*, that it was brought to passe *Hominum & sacerdotum deceptionibus*, to wit: by the cousening art of craftie
78

knaves and priests. And therefore let us follow *Esaies* advise, who saith; When they shall saie unto you, Enquire of them that have a spirit of divination, and at the soothsaiers, which whisper and mumble in your eares to deceive you, &c: enquire at your owne God, &c. And so let us doo. And here you see they are such as runne into corners, and cousen the people with lies, &c. For if they could doo as they saie, they could not aptlie be called liers, neither need they go into corners to whisper, &c.

Esai. 8, 19.

CHAPTER VIII.

Of the witch of Endor, and whether she accomplished the raising of Samuel truelie, or by deceipt: the opinion of some divines hereupon.

THE woman of *Endor* is comprised under this word *Ob*: for she is called *Pythonissa*. It is written in 2. *Sam. cap.* 28. that she raised up *Samuel* from death, and the other words of the text are stronglie placed, to inforce his verie resurrection. The mind and opinion of Jesus Syrach evidentlie appeareth to be, that *Samuel* in person was raised out from his grave, as if you read *Eccl.* 46. 19, 20. you shall plainlie perceive. Howbeit he disputeth not there, whether the storie be true or false, but onlie citeth certaine verses of the 1. booke of *Samuel cap.* 18. simplie, according to the letter, persuading maners and the imitation of our vertuous predecessors, and repeating the examples of diverse excellent men; namelie of *Samuel*: even as the text it selfe urgeth the matter, according to the deceived mind and imagination of *Saule*, and his servants. And therefore in truth, *Sirach* spake there according to the opinion of *Saule*, which so supposed, otherwise it is neither heresie nor treason to saie he was deceived.

2. Sam. 28.

He that weigheth well that place, and looketh into it advisedlie, shall see that *Samuel* was not raised from the dead; but that it was an illusion or cousenage practised by the witch. For the soules of the righteous are in the hands of God: according to that which *Chrysostome* saith; Soules are in a certeine place expecting judgement, and cannot remove from thence. Neither is it Gods will, that the living should be taught by the dead. Which things are confirmed and approved by the example of *Lazarus* and *Dives*: where it appeareth according to *Deut.* 18. that he will not have the living taught by the dead, but will have us sticke to his word, wherein his will and testament is declared. In deed *Lyra* and *Dionysius* incline greatlie to the letter. And *Lyra* saith, that as when *Balaam* would have raised a divell, God interposed himselfe: so did he in this case bring up *Samuell*, when the witch would have raised hir divell. Which is a probable interpretation. But yet they dare not stand to that opinion, least they should impeach S. *Augustines* credit, who (they confesse) remained in judgement and opinion (without contradiction of the church) that *Samuell* was not raised. For he saith directlie, that *Samuell* himselfe was not called up. And indeed, if he were raised, it was either willinglie, or perforce: if it were willinglie, his sinne had beene equall with the witches.

Sap. 3.
Ps. 92. & 97.
*Chrysost.
homilia.* 21.
in Matth.
· Luke. 16.

*August. lib.
quæ. vet. et
novi testam.
quæst.* 27.
Item, part. 2.
cap. 26.
Item. quæ. 5.
*nec mirum
ad Simplician.
lib.* 2. 93.
*ad Dulcitium.
quæ.* 6.
Item. lib. 2.
de doct. chri.

And *Peter Martyr* (me thinks) saith more to the purpose, in these words, to wit: This must have beene doone by Gods good will, or perforce of art magicke: it could not be doone by his good will, bicause he forbad it; nor by art, bicause witches have no power over the godlie. Where it is answered by some, that the commandement was onlie to prohibit the Jewes to aske counsell of the dead, and so no fault in *Samuell* to give counsell. We may as well excuse our neighbours wife, for consenting to our filthie desires, bicause it is onlie written in the decalog; Thou shalt not desire thy neighbours wife. But indeed *Samuell* was directlie forbidden to answer *Saule* before he died: and therefore it was not likelie that God would appoint him, when he was dead, to doo it.

Deut. 18.
Exodus. 20.

Chapter IX.

That Samuel was not raised indeed, and how Bodin and all papists dote herein, and that
soules cannot be raised by witchcraft.

FURTHERMORE, it is not likelie that God would answer *Saule* by dead
Samuell, when he would not answer him by living *Samuell*: and most
unlikelie of all, that God would answer him by a divell, that denied to doo
it by a prophet. That he was not brought up perforce, the whole course of the
scripture witnesseth, and prooveth; as also our owne reason may give us to
understand. For what quiet rest could the soules of the elect enjoy or possesse
in *Abrahams* bosome, if they were to be plucked from thence at a witches call and
commandement? But so should the divell have power in heaven, where he is
unworthie to have anie place himselfe, and therefore unmeete to command
others.

Manie other of the fathers are flatlie against the raising up of *Samuell*: namelie,
Tertullian in his booke *De anima*, *Justine Martyr In explicatione*, *quæ*. 25. *Rabanus In
epistolis ad Bonas. Abat*, *Origen In historia de Bileamo*, &c. Some other dote exceedinglie herein, as namelie *Bodin*, and all the papists in generall: also *Rabbi Sedias
Haias*, & also all the Hebrues, saving *R. David Kimhi*, which is the best writer of
all the *Rabbins*: though never a good of them all. But *Bodin*, in maintenance
therof, falleth into manie absurdities, prooving by the small faults that *Saule* had
committed, that he was an elect: for the greatest matter (saith he) laid unto his
charge, is the reserving of the *Amalekits* cattell, &c. He was an elect, &c: confirming his opinion with manie ridiculous fables, & with this argument, to wit:
His fault was too little to deserve damnation; for *Paule* would not have the incestuous man punished too sore, that his soule might be saved. *Justine Martyr* in
another place was not onlie deceived in the actuall raising up of *Samuels* soule,
but affirmed that all the soules of the prophets and just men are subject to the
power of witches. And yet were the Heathen much more fond herein, who (as
Lactantius affirmeth) boasted that they could call up the soules of the dead, and
yet did thinke that their soules died with their bodies. Whereby is to be seene,
how alwaies the world hath beene abused in the matters of witchcraft & conjuration. The Necromancers affirme, that the spirit of anie man may be called
up, or recalled (as they terme it) before one yeare be past after their departure
from the bodie. Which *C. Agrippa* in his booke *De occulta philosophia* saith, may
be doone by certeine naturall forces and bonds. And therefore corpses in times
past were accompanied and watched with lights, sprinkled with holie water,
perfumed with incense, and purged with praier all the while they were above
ground: otherwise the serpent (as the Maisters of the Hebrues saie) would devoure them, as the food appointed to him by God: *Gen.* 3. alledging also this
place; We shall not all sleepe, but we shall be changed, bicause manie shall remaine for perpetuall meate to the serpent: whereupon riseth the contention
betweene him and *Michaell*, concerning the bodie of *Moses*; wherein scripture is
alledged. I confesse that *Augustine*, and the residue of the doctors, that denie the
raising of *Samuell*, conclude, that the divell was fetcht up in his likenesse: from
whose opinions (with reverence) I hope I may dissent.

*J. Bod. lib. de
dæm* 2. *cap.* 3.

1. Samu. 28.

1. Cor. 5.
*J. Martyr in
colloquio
cum Tripho-
ne Judæo.*

Lact. lib. 7.
cap. 13.

Jud. vers. 9.

CHAPTER X.

That neither the divell nor Samuell was raised, but that it was a meere cousenage, according to the guise of our Pythonists.

AGAINE, if the divell appeared, and not *Samuell:* whie is it said in *Eccle.* that he slept? for the divell neither sleepeth nor dieth. But in truth we may gather, that it was neither the divell in person, nor *Samuell:* but a circumstance is here described, according to the deceived opinion and imagination of *Saule.* Howbeit *Augustine* saith, that both these sides may easilie be defended. But we shall not need to fetch an exposition so farre off: for indeed (me thinkes) it is *Longè petita;* nor to descend so lowe as hell, to fetch up a divell to expound this place. For it is ridiculous (as *Pompanacius* saith) to leave manifest things, and such as by naturall reason may be prooved, to seeke unknowne things, which by no likeliehood can be conceived, nor tried by anie rule of reason. But in so much as we have libertie by S. *Augustines* rule, in such places of scripture as seeme to conteine either contrarietie or absurditie, to varie from the letter, and to make a godlie construction agreeable to the word; let us confesse that *Samuell* was not raised (for that were repugnant to the word) and see whether this illusion may not be contrived by the art and cunning of the woman, without anie of these supernaturall devices: for I could cite a hundred papisticall and cousening practises, as difficult as this, and as cleanlie handled. And it is to be surelie thought, if it had beene a divell, the text would have noted it in some place of the storie: as it dooth not. But *Bodin* helpeth me exceedinglie in this point, wherein he forsaketh (he saith) *Augustine, Tertullian,* and *D. Kimhi* himselfe, who saie it was the divell that was raised up: which (saith *Bodin*) could not be; for that in the same communication betweene *Saule* and *Samuell,* the name of *Jehovah* is five times repeated, of which the name the divell cannot abide the hearing.

Pompanacius lib. de ineant. cap. 2.

J. Bod. lib. de dæm. 2. cap. 3.

CHAPTER XI.

The objection of the witchmongers concerning this place fullie answered, and what circumstances are to be considered for the understanding of this storie, which is plainelie opened from the beginning of the 28. chap. of the 1. Samuel, to the 12. verse.

WHERE such a supernaturall miracle is wrought, no doubt it is a testimonie of truth; as *Peter Martyr* affirmeth. And in this case it should have beene a witnesse of lies: for (saith he) a matter of such weight cannot be attributed unto the divell, but it is the mightie power of God that dooth accomplish it. And if it laie in a witches power to call up a divell, yet it lieth not in a witches power to worke such miracles: for God will not give his power and glorie to anie creature. To understand this place, we must diligentlie examine the circumstance thereof. It was well knowne that *Saule,* before he resorted to the witch, was in despaire of the mercies and goodnes of God; partlie for that *Samuell* told him long before, that he should be overthrowne and *David* should have his place; and partlie bicause God before had refused to answer him, either by *Samuell* when he lived, or by anie other prophet, or by *Urim* or *Thumim, &c.* And if you desire to see this matter discussed, turne to the first of *Samuell,* the 28. chapter, and conferre my words therewith.

Saule seeing the host of the *Philistines* come upon him (which thing could not be

P. Martyr in comment. in Sam. 28. verse. 9.

Isai. 42. 1. Sam. 28.

unknown to all the people) fainted, bicause he sawe their strength, and his owne weaknesse, and speciallie that he was forsaken: so as being now straught of mind, desperate, and a verie foole, he goeth to certeine of his servants, that sawe in what taking he was, and asked them for a woman that had a familiar spirit, and they told him by and by that there dwelt one at *Endor*. By the waie you shall understand, that both *Saule* and his servants ment such a one as could by hir spirit raise up *Samuell*, or any other that was dead and buried. Wherein you see they were deceived, though it were true, that she tooke upon hir so to doo. To what use then served hir familiar spirit, which you conceive she had, bicause *Saules* servants said so? Surelie, as they were deceived and abused in part, so doubtlesse were they in the rest. For to what purpose (I saie) should hir familiar serve, if not for such intents as they reported, and she undertooke? I thinke you will grant that *Saules* men never sawe hir familiar: for I never heard any yet of credit saie, that he was so much in the witches favour, as to see hir divell; although indeed we read among the popish trumperie, that S. *Cicilie* had an angell to hir familiar, and that she could shew him to whom she would, and that she might aske and have what she or hir friend list: as appeareth in the lesson read in the popish church on saint *Ciciles* daie. Well, I perceive the woman of *Endors* spirit was a counterfeit, and kept belike in hir closet at *Endor*, or in the bottle, with mother *Alices* divell at *Westwell*, and are now bewraied and fled togither to *Limbo patrum*, &c. And though *Saule* were bewitched and blinded in the matter; yet doubtlesse a wise man wold have perchance espied her knaverie. Me thinks *Saule* was brought to this witch, much after the maner that doctor *Burcot* was brought to *Feats*, who sold maister Doctor a familiar, wherby he thought to have wrought miracles, or rather to have gained good store of monie. This fellowe by the name of *Feats* was a jugler, by the name of *Hilles* a witch or conjurer, everie waie a cousener: his qualities and feats were to me and manie other well knowne and detected. And yet the opinion conceived of him was most strange and woonderfull; even with such and in such cases, as it greeveth me to thinke of; speciallie bicause his knaverie and cousenage reached to the shedding of innocent bloud. But now forsooth *Saule* covereth himselfe with a net; and bicause he would not be knowne, he put on other garments. But to bring that matter to passe, he must have beene cut shorter by the head and shoulders, for by so much he was higher than any of the people. And therfore whatsoever face the craftie quene did set upon it, she knew him well enough. And for further proofe thereof, you may understand, that the princes of the Jewes were much conversant with the people. And it appeereth manifestlie, that *Saule* dwelt verie neere to *Endor*, so as she should the rather knowe him; for in the evening he went from his lodging unto hir house: neither should it seeme that she was gone to bed when he came. But bicause that may be uncerteine, you may see in the processe of the text, that in a peece of the night he went from his house to hirs, and with much adoo intreated her to consent to his request. She finished hir conjuration, so as both *Saules* part, the witches part, and also *Samuels* part was plaied: and after the solemnization therof, a calfe was killed, a batch of bread baked, and a supper made readie and eaten up; and after all this, he went home the same night: and had need so to doo, for he had some businesse the next daie. By these and manie other circumstances it may bee gathered, that she dissembled, in saieng she knew him not, and consequentlie counterfaited, and made a foole of him in all the rest.

It appeereth there, that he, with a couple of his men, went to hir by night, and said; Conjecture unto me by thy familiar spirit, and bring me up whom I shall name unto thee. The godlie learned knowe that this was not in the power of the witch of *Endor*, but in the God of heaven onelie to accomplish. Howbeit, *Saule* was bewitched so to suppose: and yet is he more simple that will be overtaken with the devises of our old witches, which are produced to resemble hir. And why should we thinke, that GOD would rather permit the witch to raise *Samuel*, than that *Dives* could obteine *Lazarus* to come out of *Abrahams* bosome, upon more likelie and more reasonable conditions? Well now dooth this strumpet (according to the guise of our cousening witches and conjurers) make

82

1. Sam. 28, 7.

S. Ciciles familiar.

D. Burcot. Feats.

1. Sam. 28, 8.

1. Sa. 10, 23.

Ibidem.

Ibidem.

the matter strange unto *Saule*, saieng that he came to take hir in a snare, &c.   1. Sam. 28, 9.
But witches seldome make this objection, saving when they mistrust that he
which commeth to them will espie their jugling: for otherwise, where the witchmonger is simple and easie to be abused, the witch will be as easie to be intreated, and nothing dangerous of hir cunning; as you see this witch was soone
persuaded (notwithstanding that objection) bicause she perceived and sawe that
Saule was affraid and out of his wits. And therfore she said unto him; Whom   1. Sa. 28. 12.
shall I raise up? As though she could have brought unto him *Abraham*, *Isaac*, or
Jacob; who cannot heare us, therefore cannot rise at our call. For it is written;
Looke thou downe from heaven and behold us, &c: as for *Abraham* he is ignorant   Isa. 63,15. 16.
of us, and Israel knoweth us not.

CHAPTER XII.

The 12. 13. & 14. *verses of* 1. *Samuel* 28. *expounded: wherin is shewed that Saule was*
cousened and abused by the witch, and that Samuel was not raised, is prooved by the
witches owne talke.

T HE manner and circumstance of their communication, or of his conjuration, is not verbatim set downe and expressed in the text; but the effect
thereof breeflie touched: yet will I shew you the common order of their
conjuration, and speciallie of hirs at this time used. When *Saule* had told hir,   The maner
that he would have *Samuel* brought up to him, she departed from his presence   of the witch
into hir closet, where doubtles she had hir familiar; to wit, some lewd craftie   of Endors
preest, and made *Saule* stand at the doore like a foole (as it were with his finger   cousening
in a hole) to heare the cousening answers, but not to see the cousening handling   of Saule.
thereof, and the couterfetting of the matter. And so goeth she to worke, using
ordinarie words of conjuration, of which there are sundrie varieties and formes
(whereof I shall have occasion to repeat some in another place) as you see the
juglers (which be inferior conjurors) speake certeine strange words of course to
lead awaie the eie from espieng the maner of their conveiance, whilest they may
induce the mind to conceive and suppose that he dealeth with spirits; saieng,
Hay, fortune furie, nunq; credo, passe, passe, when come you sirra. So belike after many
such words spoken, she saith to hir selfe; Lo now the matter is brought to passe,
for I see woonderfull things. So as *Saule* hearing these words, longed to knowe   1. Sa. 28, 13.
all, and asked hir what she sawe. Whereby you may know that *Saule* sawe
nothing, but stood without like a mome, whilest she plaied hir part in hir
closet: as may most evidentlie appeere by the 21. verse of this chapter where it is   1. Sa. 28, 21.
said; Then the woman came out unto *Saule*. Howbeit, a little before she cunninglie counterfaited that she sawe *Samuel*, and thereby knew it was *Saule* that
was come unto hir. Whereby all the world may perceive the cousening, and hir
dissimulation. For by that which hath beene before said, it must needs be that
she knew him. And (I praie you) why should she not have suspected aswell him
to be *Saule* before, when in expresse words he required hir to bring unto him
Samuel, as now, when *Samuel* appeered unto hir?

    Well, to the question before proposed by *Saule*, she answereth and lieth, that   1. Sa. 28, 4.
she saw angels or gods ascending up out of the earth. Then proceedeth she with
her inchanting phrases and words of course: so as thereby *Saule* gathereth and
supposeth that she hath raised a man. For otherwise his question dependeth
not upon any thing before spoken. For when she hath said; I sawe angels
ascending, &c: the next word he saith is; What fashion is he of? Which (I saie)
hangeth not upon hir last expressed words. And to this she answered not
directlie, that it was *Samuel*; but that it was an old man lapped in a mantell: as
though she knew not him that was the most notorious man in Israell, that had

beene her neighbour by the space of manie yeeres, and upon whom (while he lived) everie eie was fixed, and whom also she knew within lesse than a quarter of an houre before, as by whose meanes also she came acquainted with *Saule*.

1. Sa. 28, 12.

Read the text and see.

But she describeth his personage, and the apparell which he did usuallie weare when he lived: which if they were both buried togither, were consumed and rotten, or devoured with wormes before that time. Belike he had a new mantell made him in heaven: and yet they saie Tailors are skantie there, for that their consciences are so large here. In this countrie, men give awaie their garments when they die: if *Samuel* had so doone, hee could not have borrowed it againe; for of likeliehood it would have beene worne out in that space, except the donee had beene a better husband than I: for the testator was dead (as it is supposed) two yeares before.

CHAPTER XIII.

The residue of 1. *Sam.* 28. *expounded: wherin is declared how cunninglie this witch brought Saule resolutelie to beleeve that she raised Samuel, what words are used to colour the cousenage, and how all might also be wrought by ventriloquie.*

1. Sa. 28, 15.
Ibidem.

NOW commeth in *Samuel* to plaie his part: but I am persuaded it was performed in the person of the witch hir selfe, or of hir confederate. He saith to *Saule*; Why has thou disquieted me, to bring me up? As though without guile or packing it had beene *Samuel* himselfe. *Saule* answered that he was in great distresse: for the *Philistines* made warre upon him. Whereby the witch, or hir confederate priest might easilie conjecture that his heart failed, and direct the oracle or prophesie accordinglie: especiallie understanding by his present talke, and also by former prophesies and dooings that were past, that God had forsaken him, and that his people were declining from him. For when *Jonathan*

1. Sam. 13, 5.
1. Sa. 13, 15.

(a little before) overthrew the *Philistines*, being thirtie thousand chariots and six thousand horssemen; *Saule* could not assemble above six hundred souldiers.

Then said *Samuel* (which some suppose was sathan, and as I thinke was the witch, with a confederate; for what need so farre fetches, as to fetch a divell supernaturallie out of hell, when the illusion may be here by naturall meanes deciphered? And if you note the words well, you shall perceive the phrase not to come out of a spirituall mouth of a divell, but from a lieng corporall toong of a cousener, that careth neither for God nor the divell, frō whence issueth such advise and communication, as greatlie disagreeth from sathans nature and pur-

1. Sam. 28.
16. 17.

pose. For thus (I saie) the said *Samuel* speaketh: Wherefore dooest thou aske me, seeing the Lord is gone from thee, and is thine enemie? Even the Lord hath doon

1. Sa. 15, 28.

unto him as he spake by mine hand: for the Lord will rent thy kingdome out of thine hand, and give it to thy neighbour *David*, bicause thou obeiedst not the voice of the Lord, &c. This (I say) is no phrase of a divell, but of a cousener, which knew before what *Samuel* had prophesied concerning *Saules* destruction. For it is the divels condition, to allure the people unto wickednes, and not in this sort to admonish, warne, and rebuke them for evill. And the popish writers confes, that the divell would have beene gone at the first naming of God. If it bee said, that it was at Gods speciall commandement and will, that *Samuel* or the divell should be raised, to propound this admonition, to the profit of all posteritie: I answer, that then he would rather have doone it by some of his living prophets, and that sathan had not beene so fit an instrument for that purpose. After this falleth the witch (I would saie *Samuel*) into the veine of prophesieng,

1. Sa. 28, 17.
18.

and speaketh to *Saule* on this wise; The Lord will rent thy kingdome out of thine hand, and give it to thy neighbor *David*, bicause thou obeiedst not the voice of

84

the Lord, nor executedst his fierse wrath upon the *Amalekites*: therefore hath the   Ibid.
Lord doone this unto thee this daie. Moreover, the Lord shall deliver thee into   19.
the hands of the *Philistines*, and to morrowe shalt thou and thy sonnes be with
me, and the Lord shall give the host of Israel into the hands of the *Philistines*.
What could *Samuel* have said more?

Me thinks the divell would have used another order, encouraging *Saule* rather
than rebuking him for his evill. The divell is craftier than to leave such an admonition to all posterities, as should be prejudiciall unto his kingdome, and also
be void of all impietie. But so divine a sentence maketh much for the maintenance of the witches credit, and to the advancement of hir gaines. Howbeit,
concerning the veritie of this prophesie, there be many disputable questions:
first, whether the battell were fought the next daie; secondlie, whether all his
sonnes were killed with him; item, whether they went to heaven or hell togither,
as being with *Samuel*, they must be in heaven, and being with sathan, they must
be in hell. But although everie part of this prophesie were false, as that all his
sonnes were not slaine (*Ishbosheth* living and reigning in Israel two yeares after
Saules death) and that the battell was not on the morrow, and that wicked *Saule*,   2. Reg. 4.
after that he had killed himselfe, was not with good *Samuel*; yet this witch did
give a shrewd gesse to the sequele. Which whether it were true or false, perteins
not to my purpose; and therfore I will omit it. But as touching the opinion of
them that saie it was the divell, bicause that such things came to passe; I would
faine knowe of them where they learne that divels foreknow things to come. If
they saie he gesseth onelie upon probabilities, the witch may also doo the like.
But here I may not forget the decrees, which conclude, that *Samuel* appeered not   *Canon.* 26.
unto *Saule*; but that the historiographer set foorth *Saules* mind and *Samuels*   *quæst. cap.* 5.
estate, and certeine things which were said & seene, omitting whether they were   *nec mirum.*
true or false; and further, that it were a great offense for a man to beleeve the
bare words of the storie. And if this exposition like you not, I can easilie frame
my selfe to the opinion of some of great learning, expounding this place, and that
with great probabilitie, in this sort; to wit, that this *Pythonist* being *Ventriloqua*;
that is, Speaking as it were from the bottome of hir bellie, did cast hir selfe into a
transe, and so abused *Saule*, answering to *Saule* in *Samuels* name, in hir counterfeit
hollow voice: as the wench of *Westwell* spake, whose historie I have rehearsed   Right Ven-
before at large, in pag. 127 and this is right *Ventriloquie*.   triloquie.

CHAPTER XIV.

Opinions of some learned men, that Samuel was indeed raised, not by the witches art or
power, but by the speciall miracle of God, that there are no such visions in these our daies,
& that our witches cannot doo the like.

AIAS and *Sadaias* write, that when the woman sawe the miracle indeed,
and more than she looked for, or was woont to doo; she began to crie out,
that this was a vision indeed, and a true one, not doone by hir art, but by
the power of God. Which exposition is far more probable than our late writers
judgements hereupon, and agreeth with the exposition of diverse good divines.
Gelasius saith, it was the verie spirit of *Samuel*: and where he suffered himself to
be worshipped, it was but in civill salutation and courtesie; and that God did
interpose *Samuel*, as he did *Elias* to the messenger of *Ochosias*, when he sent to   J. Bodin &
Belzebub the god of *Acharon*. And here is to be noted, that the witchmongers are   L. vairus
set up in this point: for the papists saie, that it cannot be a divell, bicause   differ
Jehovah is thrise or five times named in the storie. Upon this peece of scripture   herein.
arguments are daielie devised, to proove and mainteine the miraculous actions of
witchcraft, and the raising of the dead by conjurations. And yet if it were true,

that *Samuel* himselfe were raised, or the divell in his likenesse; and that the witch of *Endor* by hir art and cunning did it, &c: it maketh rather to the disproofe than to the proofe of our witches, which can neither do that kind of miracle, or any other, in any such place or companie, where their jugling and cousenage may be seen and laid open. And I challenge them all (even upon the adventure of my life) to shew one peece of a miracle, such as Christ did trulie, or such as they suppose this witch did diabolicallie, be it not with art nor confederacie, whereby some colour thereof may be made; neither are there any such visions in these daies shewed.

A bold, discreet, and faithfull challenge.

Heretofore God did send his visible angels to men: but now we heare not of such apparitions, neither are they necessarie. Indeed it pleased God heretofore, by the hand of *Moses* and his prophets, and speciallie by his sonne Christ and his apostles, to worke great miracles, for the establishing of the faith: but now whatsoever is necessarie for our salvation, is conteined in the word of God: our faith is alredie confirmed, and our church established by miracles; so as now to seeke for them, is a point of infidelitie. Which the papists (if you note it) are greatlie touched withall, as in their lieng legends appeareth. But in truth, our miracles are knaveries most commonlie, and speciallie of priests, whereof I could cite a thousand. If you read the storie of Bell and the dragon, you shall find a cousening miracle of some antiquitie. If you will see newer devises, read *Wierus, Cardanus, Baleus*, and speciallie *Lavaterns*, &c. There have been some walking spirits in these parts so conjured not long since, as afterwards they little delighted to make anie more apparitions.

At Canturburie by Rich. Lee esquire, & others, anno. 1573. At Rie by maister Gaymor & others, anno. 1577.

Chapter xv.

Of vaine apparitions, how people have beene brought to feare bugges, which is partlie reformed by preaching of the gospell, the true effect of Christes miracles.

BUT certeinlie, some one knave in a white sheete hath cousened and abused manie thousands that waie; speciallie when Robin good-fellow kept such a coile in the countrie. But you shall understand, that these bugs speciallie are spied and feared of sicke folke, children, women, and cowards, which through weaknesse of mind and bodie, are shaken with vaine dreames and continuall feare. The *Scythians*, being a stout and a warlike nation (as divers writers report) never see anie vaine sights or spirits. It is a common saieng; A lion feareth no bugs. But in our childhood our mothers maids have so terrified us with an ouglie divell having hornes on his head, fier in his mouth, and a taile in his breech, eies like a bason, fanges like a dog, clawes like a beare, a skin like a Niger, and a voice roring like a lion, whereby we start and are afraid when we heare one crie Bough: and they have so fraied us with bull beggers, spirits, witches, urchens, elves, hags, fairies, satyrs, pans, faunes, sylens, kit with the cansticke, tritons, centaurs, dwarfes, giants, imps, calcars, conjurors, nymphes, changlings, *Incubus*, Robin good-fellowe, the spoorne, the mare, the man in the oke, the hell waine, the fierdrake, the puckle, Tom thombe, hob gobblin, Tom tumbler, boneles, and such other bugs, that we are afraid of our owne shadowes: in so much as some never feare the divell, but in a darke night; and then a polled sheepe is a perillous beast, and manie times is taken for our fathers soule, speciallie in a churchyard, where a right hardie man heretofore scant durst passe by night, but his haire would stand upright. For right grave writers report, that spirits most often and speciallie take the shape of women appearing to monks, &c: and of beasts, dogs, swine, horsses, gotes, cats, hairs; of fowles, as crowes, night owles, and shreeke owles; but they delight most in the likenes of snakes and dragons. Well, thanks be to God, this wretched and cowardlie in-

J. Wier. lib. 3. cap. 8. Theodor. Bizantius. Lavat. de spect. & lemurib. Cardan. de var. rerum Peucer. &c.

Lavat. de spect.

fidelitie, since the preaching of the gospell, is in part forgotten: and doubtles, the rest of those illusions will in short time (by Gods grace) bé detected and vanish awaie.

Divers writers report, that in *Germanie*, since *Luthers* time, spirits and divels have not personallie appeared, as in times past they were woont to doo. This argument is taken in hand of the ancient fathers, to proove the determination and ceasing of oracles. For in times past (saith *Athanasius*) divels in vaine shapes did intricate men with their illusions, hiding themselves in waters, stones, woods, &c. But now that the word of GOD hath appeared, those sights, spirits, and mockeries of images are ceased. Truelie, if all such oracles, as that of *Apollo*, &c (before the comming of Christ) had beene true, and doone according to the report, which hath beene brought through divers ages, and from farre countries unto us, without preestlie fraud or guile, so as the spirits of prophesie, and working of miracles, had beene inserted into an idoll, as hath beene supposed: yet we christians may conceive, that Christs coming was not so fruteles and prejudiciall in this point unto us, as to take awaie his spirit of prophesie and divination from out of the mouth of his elect people, and good prophets, giving no answers of anie thing to come by them, nor by *Urim* nor *Thumim*, as he was woont, &c. And yet to leave the divell in the mouth of a witch, or an idoll to prophesie or worke miracles, &c: to the hinderance of his glorious gospell, to the discountenance of his church, and to the furtherance of infidelitie and false religion, whereas the working of miracles was the onelie, or at least the most speciall meanes that mooved men to beleeve in Christ: as appeareth in sundrie places of the gospell, and speciallie in *John*, where it is written, that a great multitude followed him, bicause they sawe his miracles which he did, &c. Naie, is it not written, that Jesus was approoved by God among the Jewes, with miracles, wonders and signes, &c? And yet, if we conferre the miracles wrought by Christ, and those that are imputed to witches; witches miracles shall appeare more common, and nothing inferior unto his.

Car. de var. rerum.
J. Wier. de præst. dæmon. &c.
Athanas. de humanitate verbi.

The true end of miracles.

John 2.
Act. 2. 2.
John. 5.

CHAPTER XVI.

Witches miracles compared to Christs, that God is the creator of all things, of Apollo, and of his names and portraiture.

IF this witch of *Endor* had performed that, which manie conceive of the matter, it might have beene compared with the raising up of *Lazarus*. I praie you, is not the converting of water into milke, as hard a matter as the turning of water into wine? And yet, as you may read in the gospell, that Christ did the one, as his first miracle; so may you read in *M. Mal.* and in *Bodin*, that witches can easilie doo the other: yea, and that which is a great deale more, of water they can make butter. But to avoid all cavils, and least there should appeare more matter in Christs miracle, than the others, you shall find in *M. Mal.* that they can change water into wine: and what is it to attribute to a creature, the power and worke of the creator, if this be not? Christ saith, *Opera quæ ego facio nemo potest facere.* Creation of substance was never granted to man nor angell; *Ergo* neither to witch nor divell: for God is the onlie giver of life and being, and by him all things are made, visible and invisible.

An ironicall collation.

Mal. malef. par. 2. quæ. 1. cap. 14.
Acts. 17.
Tim. 6, 13.
Col. 1, 16.
Athanas. symbol.

Finallie, this woman of *Endor* is in the scripture called *Pythonissa*: whereby it may appeare that she was but a verie cousener. For *Pytho* himselfe, whereof *Pythonissa* is derived, was a counterfet. And the originall storie of *Apollo*, who was called *Pytho*, bicause he killed a serpent of that name, is but a poeticall fable. For the poets saie he was the god of musicke, physicke, poetrie, and

Apollo
Pytho the
uncased.

shooting. In heaven he is called *Sol,* in earth *Liber pater,* in hell *Apollo.* He flor-
isheth alwaies with perpetuall youth, and therefore he is painted without a
beard : his picture was kept as an oracle-giver : and the preests that attended
thereon at *Delphos* were couseners, and called *Pythonists* of *Pytho,* as papists of
Papa; and afterwards all women that used that trade, were named *Pythonissæ,* as
was this woman of *Endor.* But bicause it concerneth this matter, I will breefelie
note the opinions of divers learned men, and certeine other proofes, which I find
in the scripture touching the ceasing of miracles, prophesies and oracles.

BOOKE VIII.

CHAPTER I.

That miracles are ceased.

ALTHOUGH in times past, it pleased God, extraordinarilie to shew miracles amongest his people, for the strengthening of their faith in the Messias; and againe at his comming to confirme their faith by his wonderfull dooings, and his speciall graces and gifts bestowed by him upon the apostles, &c: yet we ordinarilie read in the scriptures, that it is the Lord that worketh great wonders. Yea *David* saith, that among the dead (as in this case of *Samuel*) God himselfe sheweth no wonders. I find also that God will not give his glorie and power to a creature. *Nichodemus* being a Pharisie could saie, that no man could do such miracles as Christ did, except God were with him, according to the saieng of the prophet to those gods and idols, which tooke on them the power of God; Doo either good or ill if you can, &c. So as the prophet knew and taught thereby, that none but God could worke miracles. Infinite places for this purpose might be brought out of the scripture, which for brevitie I omit and overslip.

    S. *Augustine*, among other reasons, whereby he prooveth the ceasing of miracles, saith; Now blind flesh dooth not open the eies of the blind by the miracle of God, but the eies of our hart are opened by the word of God. Now is not our dead carcase raised any more up by miracle, but our dead bodies be still in the grave, and our soules are raised to life by Christ. Now the eares of the deafe are not opened by miracle, but they which had their eares shut before, have them now opened to their salvation. The miraculous healing of the sicke, by annointing, spoken of by S. *James*, is objected by manie, speciallie by the papists, for the maintenance of their sacrament of extreame unction: which is apishlie and vainelie used in the Romish church, as though that miraculous gift had continuance till this daie: wherein you shall see what *Calvine* speaketh in his institutions. The grace of healing (saith he) spoken of by S. *James*, is vanished awaie, as also the other miracles, which the Lord would have shewed onelie for a time, that he might make the new preaching of the gospell mervellous for ever. Why (saith he) doo not these (meaning miraclemongers) appoint some *Siloah* to swim in, whereinto at certeine ordinarie recourses of times sicke folke maie plunge themselves? Why doo they not lie a long upon the dead, bicause *Paule* raised up a dead child by that meanes? Verelie (saith he) *James* in the miracle to annoint, spake for that time, whiles the church still enjoied such blessings of God. Item, he saith, that the Lord is present with his in all ages; and so often as need is, he helpeth their sicknesses, no lesse than in old time. But he dooth not so utter his manifest powers, nor distributeth miracles, as by the hands of the apostles, bicause the gift was but for a time. *Calvine* even there concludeth thus; They saie such vertues or miracles remaine, but experience saith naie. And see how they agree among themselves. *Danæus* saith, that neither witch nor divell can worke miracles. *Giles Alley* saith directlie, that witches worke miracles. *Calvine* saith they are all ceased. All witchmongers saie they continue. But some affirme, that popish miracles are vanished and gone awaie: howbeit witches miracles remaine in full force. So as S. *Loy* is out of credit for a horsseleach, Maister *T.* and mother *Bungie* remaine in estimation for prophets: naie Hobgoblin and Robin goodfellow are contemned among yoong children, and mother *Alice* and mother *Bungie* are feared among old fooles. The estimation of these continue, bicause the matter hath not beene called in question: the credit of the

Psal. 136. 4.
Psal. 72. 18.
Psal. 88. 10.

Isai. 42.
John 3, 2.
Ibid. 7, 16.
In annotat. in Johan. 3.
Isai. 45.

August. de verbis Dom. secundum Matth. sermone. 18.

James. 5, 14.

J. Calvin. Institut. lib. 4. *cap.* 19. *sect.* 18.

Idem. ibid. sect. 19,
Isai. 9. 7.

Acts. 20, 10.
Idem. ibid. nempe J. Calvine.

other decaieth, bicause the matter hath beene looked into. Whereof I saie no more, but that S. *Anthonies* blisse will helpe your pig, whensoever mother *Bungie* dooth hurt it with hir cursse. And therefore we are warned by the word of God, in anie wise not to feare their cursses. But let all the witchmongers, and speciallie the miraclemongers in the world answer me to this supposition; Put case that a woman of credit, or else a woman-witch should saie unto them, that she is a true prophet of the Lord, and that he revealeth those secret mysteries unto hir, whereby she detecteth the lewd acts and imaginations of the wicked, and that by him she worketh miracles, and prophesieth, &c: I thinke they must either yeeld, or confesse that miracles are ceased. But such things (saith *Cardane*) as seeme miraculous, are cheeflie doone by deceipt, legierdemaine, or confederacie; or else they maie be doone, and yet seeme unpossible, or else things are said to be done, and never were nor can be doone.

Prov. 51.

H. Card. de miracul.

Chapter II.

That the gift of prophesie is ceased.

THAT witches, nor the woman of *Endor*, nor yet hir familiar or divell can tell what is to come, may plainelie appeare by the words of the prophet, who saith; Shew what things are to come, and we will saie you are gods indeed. According to that which *Salomon* saith; Who can tell a man what shall happen him under the sunne? Marrie that can I (saith the witch of *Endor* to *Saule*.) But I will rather beleeve *Paule* and *Peter*, which saie, that prophesie is the gift of God, and no worldlie thing. Then a cousening queane, that taketh upon hir to doo all things, and can doo nothing but beguile men: up steppeth also mother *Bungie*, and she can tell you where your horsse or your asse is bestowed, or anie thing that you have lost is become, as *Samuell* could; and what you have doone in all your age past, as Christ did to the woman of *Sichar* at *Jacobs* well; yea and what your errand is, before you speake, as *Elizæus* did.

Peter Martyr saith, that onelie God and man knoweth the heart of man, and therefore, that the divell must be secluded, alledging these places; *Solus Deus est scrutator cordium*, Onelie God is the searcher of hearts. And, *Nemo scit quæ sunt hominis, nisi spiritus hominis qui est in eo*, None knoweth the things of man, but the spirit of man which is within him. And *Salomon* saith, *Tu solus nosti cogitationes hominum*, Thou onelie knowest the thoughts of men. And *Jeremie* saith in the person of God, *Ego Deus scrutans corda & renes*, I am God searching hearts and reines. Also *Matthew* saith of Christ, *Jesus autem videns cogitationes eorum*, And Jesus seeing their thoughts, who in scripture is called the searcher and knowerof the thoughts in the heart: as appeareth in *Acts*, 1. & 15. *Rom.* 8. *Matth.* 9. 12. & 22. *Marke.* 2. *Luke.* 6, & 7. & 11. *John* 1. 2. 6. & 13. *Apoc.* 2. & 3. and in other places infinite.

The same *Peter Martyr* also saith, that the divell maie suspect, but not know our thoughts: for if he should know our thoughts, he should understand our faith; which if he did, he would never assalt us with one temptation. Indeed we read that *Samuel* could tell where things lost were straied, &c: but we see that gift also ceased by the comming of Christ, according to the saieng of *Paule*; At sundrie times, and in diverse maners God spake in the old times by our fathers the prophets, in these last daies he hath spoken unto us by his sonne, &c. And therefore I saie that gift of prophesie, wherewith God in times past endued his people, is also ceased, and counterfeits and couseners are come in their places, according to this saieng of *Peter*: There were false prophets among the people, even as there shalbe false teachers among you, &c. And thinke not that so notable a gift should be taken from the beloved and elect people of God, and committed to mother *Bungie*, and such like of hir profession.

Isai. 41.

1. Sam. 28.
Rom. 12.
1. Cor. 12.
1. Pet. 1.

John. 4.

P. Martyr.
loc. com. 9.
sect. 17.

P. Martyr.
in loc. comm.

Hebr. 1, 8.
& 2.

2. Pet. 2. 1.

The words of the prophet *Zacharie* are plaine, touching the ceasing both of the good and bad prophet, to wit: I will cause the prophets and uncleane spirits to depart out of the land, and when anie shall yet prophesie, his parents shall saie to him; Thou shalt not live, for thou speakest lies in the name of the Lord: and his parents shall thrust him through when he prophesieth, &c. No, no: the fore-telling of things to come, is the onelie worke of God, who disposeth all things sweetlie, of whose counsell there hath never yet beene anie man. And to know our labours, the times and moments God hath placed in his owne power. Also *Phavorinus* saith, that if these cold prophets or oraclers tell thee prosperitie, and deceive thee, thou art made a miser through vaine expectation: if they tell thee of adversitie, &c: and lie, thou art made a miser through vaine feare. And therefore I saie, we maie as well looke to heare prophesies at the tabernacle, in the bush, of the cherubin, among the clouds, from the angels, within the arke, or out of the flame, &c: as to expect an oracle of a prophet in these daies.

But put the case, that one in our common wealth should step up and saie he were a prophet (as manie frentike persons doo) who would beleeve him, or not thinke rather that he were a lewd person? See the statutes *Elizab.* 5. whether there be not lawes made against them, condemning their arrogancie and cousen-age: see also the canon lawes to the same effect.

Zach. 13.

J. Chrysost. in evang. Johan. hom. 18. Pet. Blest. epist. 49.

Canon. de malef. & mathemat.

CHAPTER III.

That Oracles are ceased.

TOUCHING oracles, which for the most part were idols of silver, gold, wood, stones, &c: within whose bodies some saie uncleane spirites hid themselves, and gave answers: as some others saie, that exhalations rising out of the ground, inspire their minds, whereby their priests gave out oracles; so as spirits and winds rose up out of that soile, and indued those men with the gift of prophesie of things to come, though in truth they were all devises to cousen the people, and for the profit of preests, who received the idols answers over night, and delivered them backe to the idolaters the next morning: you shall understand, that although it had beene so as it is supposed; yet by the reasons and proofes before rehearsed, they should now cease: and whatsoever hath affinitie with such miraculous actions, as witchcraft, conjuration, &c: is knocked on the head, and nailed on the crosse with Christ, who hath broken the power of divels, and satisfied Gods justice, who also hath troden them under his feete, & subdued them, &c. At whose comming the prophet *Zacharie* saith, that the Lord will cut the names of idols out of the land, and they shall be no more remembered; and he will then cause the prophets and uncleane spirits to depart out of the land. It is also written; I will cut off thine inchanters out of thine hand, and thou shalt have no more soothsaiers. And indeed the gospell of Christ hath so laid open their knaverie, &c: that since the preaching thereof, their combes are cut, and few that are wise regard them. And if ever these prophesies came to take effect, it must be upon the coming of Christ, whereat you see the divels were troubled and fainted, when they met him, saieng, or rather ex-claming upon him on this wise; *Fili Dei cur venisti nos cruciare ante tempus?* O thou sonne of God, whie commest thou to molest us (or confound us) before our time appointed? Which he indeed prevented, and now remaineth he our defender and keeper from his clawes. So as now you see here is no roome left for such ghests.

Howbeit, you shall heare the opinion of others, that have beene as much de-ceived as your selves in this matter: and yet are driven to confesse, that GOD hath constituted his sonne to beat downe the power of divels, and to satisfie Gods

Thucidid. lib. 2. Cicer. de di-vin. lib. 2.

Zach. 13, 2.

Mich. 5, 12.

justice, and to heale our wound received by the fall of *Adam*, according to Gods

Gen. 3.
promise in *Genesis*. 3. The seed of the woman shall tread downe the serpent, or

Euseb. lib. 5.
cap. 1.
the divell. *Eusebius* (in his fift booke *De prædicatione Evangelii*, the title whereof is
this, that the power of divels is taken awaie by the comming of Christ) saith; All
answers made by divels, all soothsaiengs and divinations of men are gon and

Idem. Ibid.
Porphyr. in
lib. contra
christ. relig.
vanished awaie. Item he citeth *Porphyrie* in his booke against christian religion,
wherein these words are rehearsed; It is no mervell, though the plague be so hot
in this citie: for ever since Jesus hath beene worshipped, we can obteine nothing
that good is at the hands of our gods. And of this defection and ceasing of

Cic. de divin.
lib. 2.
J. Chrysost.
de laud.
Paul. hom. 4.
oracles writeth *Cicero* long before, and that to have happened also before his
time. Howbeit, *Chrysostome* living long since *Cicero*, saith, that *Apollo* was forced
to grant, that so long as anie relike of a martyr was held to his nose, he could not
make anie answer or oracle. So as one may perceive, that the heathen were
wiser in this behalfe than manie christians, who in times past were called
Oppugnatores incantamentorum, as the English princes are called *Defensores fidei*.
Plutarch calleth *Bœotia* (as we call bablers) by the name of manie words, bicause
of the multitude of oracles there, which now (saith he) are like to a spring or
fountaine which is dried up. If anie one remained, I would ride five hundred
miles to see it: but in the whole world there is not one to be seene at this houre;
popish cousenages excepted.

Porphyr.
writeth
verses in
Apollos name,
of the death
of Apollo :
cited by J.
Bod. fol. 5.
But *Plutarch* saith, that the cause of this defection of oracles, was the divels
death, whose life he held to be determinable and mortall, saieng they died for
verie age; and that the divining preests were blowne up with a whirlewind, and
soonke with an earthquake. Others imputed it to the site or the place of the
planets, which when they passed over them, carried awaie that art with them,
and by revolution may returne, &c. *Eusebius* also citeth out of him the storie of
Pan, which bicause it is to this purpose, I will insert the same; and since it men-
tioneth the divels death, you may beleeve it if you list: for I will not, as being
assured that he is reserved alive to punish the wicked, and such as impute unto
those idols the power of almightie God.

<hr>

Chapter IV.

*A tale written by manie grave authors, and beleeved by manie wise men of the divels death.
An other storie written by papists, and beleeved of all catholikes, approoving the divels
honestie, conscience, and courtesie.*

PLUTARCH saith, that his countriman *Epotherses* told him, that as he
passed by sea into *Italie*, manie passengers being in his bote, in an evening,
when they were about the ilands *Echinadæ*, the wind quite ceased: and the
ship driving with the tide, was brought at last to *Paxe*. And whilest some slept,
and others quaft, and othersome were awake (perhaps in as ill case as the rest)
after supper suddenlie a voice was heard calling, *Thamus*; in such sort as everie

Thamus
having little
to doo,
thought to
plaie with
his compa-
nie, whom
he might
easilie
overtake
with such
a jest.
man marvelled. This *Thamus* was a pilot, borne in *Aegypt*, unknowne to manie
that were in the ship. Wherefore being twise called, he answered nothing; but
the third time he answered: and the other with a lowder voice commanded him,
that when he came to *Palodes*, he should tell them that the great God *Pan* was
departed. Whereat everie one was astonied (as *Epitherses* affirmed.) And being
in consultation what were best to doo, *Thamus* concluded, that if the wind were
hie, they must passe by with silence; but if the weather were calme, he must
utter that which he had heard. But when they came to *Palodes*, and the wether
calme, *Thamus* looking out toward the land, cried alowd, that the great god *Pan*
was deceased: and immediatlie there followed a lamentable noise of a multitude
of people, as it were with great woonder and admiration. And bicause there

were manie in the ship, they said the fame thereof was speedilie brought to *Rome*, and *Thamus* sent for by *Tiberius* the Emperour, who gave such credit thereto, that he diligentlie inquired and asked, who that *Pan* was. The learned men about him supposed, that *Pan* was he who was the sonne of *Mercurie* and *Penelope*, &c. *Eusebius* saith, that this chanced in the time of *Tiberius* the Emperor, when Christ expelled all divels, &c.

Paulus Marsus, in his notes upon *Ovids Fasti*, saith, that this voice was heard out of *Paxe*, that verie night that Christ suffered, in the yeare of *Tiberius* the nineteenth. Surelie, this was a merrie jest devised by *Thamus*, who with some confederate thought to make sport with the passengers, who were some asleepe, and some droonke, and some other at plaie, &c: whiles the first voice was used. And at the second voice, to wit, when he should deliver his message, he being an old pilot, knew where some noise was usuall, by meanes of some eccho in the sea, and thought he would (to the astonishment of them) accomplish his devise, if the wether prooved calme. Whereby may appeare, that he would in other cases of tempests, &c: rather attend to more serious busines, than to that ridiculous matter. For whie else should he not doo his errand in rough wether, as well as in calme? Or what need he tell the divell thereof, when the divell told it him before, and with much more expedition could have done the errand himselfe? *A detection of Thamus his knaverie.*

But you shall read in the Legend a fable, an oracle I would saie, more authentike. For many will say that this as a prophane storie, and not so canonicall as those which are verefied by the popes authoritie: and thus it is written. A woman in hir travell sent hir sister to *Diana*, which was the divell in an idoll (as all those oracles are said to be) and willed hir to make hir praiers, or rather a request, to knowe of hir safe deliverie: which thing she did. But the divell answered; Why praiest thou to me? I cannot helpe thee, but go praie to *Andrew* the apostle, and he may helpe thy sister, &c. Lo, this was not onelie a gentle, but a godlie divell, pittieng the womans case, who revealing his owne disabilitie, enabled S. *Andrew* more. I knowe some protestants will saie, that the divell, to mainteine idolatrie, &c: referred the maid to S. *Andrew*. But what answer will the papists make, who thinke it great pietie to praie unto saints, and so by consequence honest courtesie in the divell, to send hir to S. *Andrew*, who wold not faile to serve hir turne, &c. *Legend. aur. in vita sancti Andreæ. fol.* 39.

A gentle and a god-lie divell.

CHAPTER V.

The judgments of the ancient fathers touching oracles, and their abolishment, and that they be now transferred from Delphos to Rome.

THE opinions of the fathers, that oracles are ceased by the cōming of Christ, you shall find in these places following, to wit: *Justinus In dialogis adversus Judæos, Athanasius De humanitate verbi, Augustine De civitate Dei, Eusebius Lib.* 7. *cap.* 6, Item *lib.* 5. *cap.* 1. 8. *Rupertus In Joan. lib.* 10. 12. *Plutarch De abolitione oraculorum, Plinie lib.* 30. *natural. historiæ.* Finallie, *Athanasius* concludes, that in times past there were oracles in *Delphos, Bœotia, Lycia*, and other places: but now since Christ is preached to all men, this madnesse is ceased. So as you see, that whatsoever estimation in times past, the ancient fathers conceived (by heeresaie) of those miraculous matters of idols and oracles, &c: they themselves refuse now, not onelie to beare witnesse of; but also affirme, that ever since Christs comming their mouthes have beene stopped. *Athanas. de human. verbi. fol.* 55 & 64.

For the ceasing of the knaveries and cousening devises of preests, I see no authoritie of scripture or ancient father, but rather the contrarie; to wit, that there shall be strange illusions shewed by them, even till the end. And truelie, whosoever knoweth and noteth the order and devises of and in popish pilgrimages, shall see both the oracles & their conclusions remaining, and as it were transferred from *Delphos* to *Rome*, where that adulterous generation continuallie seeketh a signe, though they have *Moses* & the prophets, yea even Christ & his apostles also, &c.

Chapter vi.

Where and wherein couseners, witches, and preests were woont to give oracles, and to worke their feats.

THESE cousening oracles, or rather oraclers used (I saie) to exercise their feats and to doo their miracles most commonly in maids, in beasts, in images, in dens, in cloisters, in darke holes, in trees, in churches or church-yards, &c: where preests, moonks, and friers had laid their plots, and made their confederacies aforehand, to beguile the world, to gaine monie, and to adde credit to their profession. This practise began in the okes of *Dodona*, in the which was a wood, the trees thereof (they saie) could speake. And this was doone by a knave in a hollowe tree, that seemed sound unto the simple people. This wood was in *Molossus* a part of *Greece*, called *Epyrus*, and it was named *Dodonas* oracles. There were manie oracles in *Aegypt*; namelie, of *Hercules*, of *Apollo*, of *Minerva*, of *Diana*, of *Mars*, of *Jupiter*, and of the oxe *Apys*, who was the sonne of *Jupiter*, but his image was worshipped in the likenesse of an oxe. *Latona*, who was the mother of *Apollo*, was an oracle in the citie of *Bute*. The preests of *Apollo*, who alwaies counterfaited furie and madnesse, gave oracles in the temple called *Clarius*, within the citie of *Colophon* in *Greece*. At *Thebes* in *Bœotia* and also in *Lœbadia*, *Trophonius* was the cheefe oracle. At *Memphis* a cow, at *Corinth* an oxe called *Mineus*, in *Arsinoe* a crocodile, in *Athens* a prophet called *Amphiaraus*, who indeed died at *Thebes*, where they saie the earth opened, & swallowed him up quicke. At *Delphos* was the great temple of *Apollo*, where divels gave oracles by maides (as some saie) though indeed it was doone by preests. It was built upon *Parnassus* hill in *Greece*. And the defenders of oracles saie, that even as rivers oftentimes are diverted to another course; so likewise the spirit, which inspired the cheefe prophets, may for a time be silent, and revive againe by revolution.

Demetrius saith, that the spirits, which attended on oracles, waxed wearie of the peoples curiositie and importunitie, and for shame forsooke the temple. But as one that of late hath written against prophesies saith; It is no marvell, that when the familiars that speake in trunks were repelled from their harbour for feare of discoverie, the blocks almightie lost their senses. For these are all gone now, and their knaverie is espied; so as they can no longer abuse the world with such bables. But whereas these great doctors suppose, that the cause of their dispatch was the comming of Christ; if they meane that the divell died, so soone as he was borne, or that then he gave over his occupation: they are deceived. For the popish church hath made a continuall practise hereof, partlie for their owne private profit, lucre, and gaine; and partly to be had in estimation of the world, and in admiration among the simple. But indeed, men that have learned Christ, and beene conversant in his word, have discovered and shaken off the vanitie and abhomination heereof. But if those doctors had lived till this daie, they would have said and written, that oracles had ceased, or rather beene driven out of *England* in the time of K. *Henrie* the eight, and of Queene *Elizabeth* his daughter; who have doone so much in that behalfe, as at this houre they are not onlie all gone, but forgotten here in this English nation, where they swarmed as thicke as they did in *Bœotia*, or in any other place in the world. But the credit they had, depended not upon their desart, but upon the credulitie of others. Now therefore I will conclude and make an end of this matter, with the opinion and saieng of the prophet; Vaine is the answer of idols. For they have eies and see not, eares and heare not, mouthes and speake not, &c: and let them shew what is to come, and I will saie they are gods indeed.

Strabo Geog. lib. 16.
J. Wier. li. 1. *de præs. dæm. cap.* 12.

H. Haw. in his defen-sative against prophesies.

In whose daies oracles ceased in England.

Zach. 10.
Isai. 44.

94

BOOKE IX.

Chapter I.

The Hebrue word Kasam expounded, and how farre a Christian may conjecture of things to come.

KASAM (as *John Wierus* upon his owne knowledge affirmeth, and upon the word of *Andræas Masius* reporteth) differeth little in signification from the former word *Ob:* betokening *Vaticinari*, which is, To prophesie, and is most commonlie taken in evill part; as in *Deut.* 18. *Jerem.* 27. &c: howbeit, sometime in good part, as in *Esaie* 3. verse. 2. To foretell things to come upon probable conjectures, so as therein we reach no further than becommeth humane capacitie, is not (in mine opinion) unlawfull, but rather a commendable manifestation of wisedome and judgment, the good gifts and notable blessings of GOD, for the which we ought to be thankfull; as also to yeeld due honour and praise unto him, for the noble order which he hath appointed in nature: praieng him to lighten our hearts with the beames of his wisedome, that we may more and more profit in the true knowledge of the workemanship of his hands. But some are so nise, that they condemne generallie all sorts of divinations, denieng those things that in nature have manifest causes, and are so framed, as they forshew things to come, and in that shew admonish us of things after to insue, exhibiting signes of unknowne and future matters to be judged upon, by the order, lawe, and course of nature proposed unto us by God.

    And some on the other side are so bewitched with follie, as they attribute to creatures that estimation, which rightlie and truelie apperteineth to God the creator of all things; affirming that the publike and private destinies of all humane matters, and whatsoever a man would knowe of things come or gone, is manifested to us in the heavens: so as by the starres and planets all things might be knowne. These would also, that nothing should be taken in hand or gone about, without the favourable aspect of the planets. By which, and other the like devises they deprave and prophane the ancient and commendable observations of our forfathers: as did *Colebrasus*, who taught, that all mans life was governed by the seven planets; and yet a christian, and condemned for heresie. But let us so farre foorth imbrace and allow this philosophie and prophesieng, as the word of God giveth us leave, and commendeth the same unto us.

J. Wier. lib. de præst. dæmon.

All divinations are not condemnable.

Colebrasus erronious & impious opinion.

Chapter II.

Proofes by the old and new testament, that certaine observations of the weather are lawfull.

WHEN God by his word and wisedome had made the heavens, and placed the starres in the firmament, he said; Let them be for signes, and for seasons, and for daies, and yeares. When he created the rainebowe in the clouds, he said it should be for a signe and token unto us. Which we find true, not onelie of the floud past, but also of shewers to come. And therefore according to Jesus *Sirachs* advise, let us behold it, and praise him that made it.

Psalm. 13.
Jerem. 54.
Gen. 1.
Ezech. 1.
Gen. 9.

Ecclus. 43.
Ps. 19 & 50.

Ecclus. 43.
Baruch. 3.

Luk. 12, 24.

Matt. 16. 2,
3.

The prophet *David* saith; The heavens declare the glorie of God, and the firmament sheweth his handie worke: daie unto daie uttereth the same, and night
unto night teacheth knowledge. It is also written that by the commandement of
the holie one the starres are placed, and continue in their order, & faile not in
their watch. It should appeare, that Christ himselfe did not altogither neglect
the course & order of the heavens, in that he said; When you see a cloud rise out
of the west, streight waie you saie a shewer commeth: and so it is. And when you
see the southwind blowe; you saie it will be hot, and so it commeth to passe.
Againe, when it is evening, you saie faire weather, for the skie is red: and in the
morning you saie, to daie shalbe a tempest, for the skie is red and lowring.
Wherein as he noteth that these things doo trulie come to passe, according to
ancient observation, and to the rule astonomicall: so doth he also by other
words following admonish us, that in attending too much to those observations,
we neglect not speciallie to follow our christian vocation.

Lactant.
contra
astrologos.

Peucer. de
astrol. pag.
383.

The physician is commended unto us, and allowed in the scriptures: but so to
put trust in him, as to neglect & distrust God, is severelie forbidden and re-
proved. Surelie it is most necessarie for us to know and observe diverse rules
astrologicall; otherwise we could not with oportunitie dispatch our ordinarie
affaires. And yet *Lactantius* condemneth and recounteth it among the number of
witchcrafts: from whose censure *Calvine* doth not much varie. The poore husbandman perceiveth that the increase of the moone maketh plants and living
creatures frutefull: so as in the full moone they are in best strength, decaieng
in the wane, and in the conjunction doo utterlie wither and vade. Which when
by observation, use and practise they have once learned, they distribute their
businesse accordinglie; as their times and seasons to sowe, to plant, to proine, to
let their cattell bloud, to cut, &c.

<hr>

CHAPTER III.

*That certeine observations are indifferent, certeine ridiculous, and certeine impious, whence
that cunning is derived of Apollo, and of Aruspices.*

The ridicu-
lous art of
nativitie-
casting.

Julius
Maternus
his most
impious
opinion.

Bodinus.
Danæus.
Erastus.
Hemingius.
Mal. malef.
Thom. Aqui-
nas, &c.

I KNOW not whether to disallow or discommend the curious observation
used by our elders, who conjectured upon nativities: so as, if *Saturne* and *Mercurie* were opposite in anie brute signe, a man then borne should be dumbe or
stammer much; whereas it is dailie seene, that children naturallie imitate their
parents conditions in that behalfe. Also they have noted, that one borne in the
spring of the moone, shalbe healthie; in that time of the wane, when the moone
is utterlie decaied, the child then borne cannot live; and in the conjunction, it
cannot long continue.

But I am sure the opinion of *Julius Maternus* is most impious, who writeth, that
he which is borne when *Saturne* is in *Leone*, shall live long, and after his death shall
go to heaven presentlie. And so is this of *Albumazar*, who saith, that whosoever
praieth to God, when the moone is in *Capite draconis*, shalbe heard, and obteine
his praier. Furthermore, to plaie the cold prophet, as to recount it good or bad
lucke, when salt or wine falleth on the table, or is shed, &c: or to prognosticate
that ghests approch to your house, upon the chattering of pies or haggisters,
wherof there can be yeelded no probable reason, is altogither vanitie and superstition: as hereafter shalbe more largelie shewed. But to make simple people
beleeve, that a man or woman can foretell good or evill fortune, is mere witchcraft or cousenage. For God is the onlie searcher of the heart, and delivereth not
his counsell to so lewd reprobates. I know diverse writers affirme, that witches
foretell things, as prompted by a reall divell; and that he againe learneth it out
of the prophesies written in the scriptures, and by other nimble sleights, wherein
he passeth anie other creature earthlie; and that the same divell, or some of his

fellowes runnes or flies as farre as *Rochester*, to mother *Bungie*; or to *Canturburie* to M. *T*; or to *Delphos*, to *Apollo*; or to *Aesculapius*, in *Pargamo*; or to some other idoll or witch, and there by waie of oracle answers all questions, through his understanding of the prophesies conteined in the old testament, especiallie in *Daniel* and *Esaie*; whereby the divell knew of the translation of the monarchie from *Babylon* to *Græcia*, &c. But either they have learned this of some oracle or witch; or else I know not where the divell they find it. Marrie certeine it is, that herein they shew themselves to be witches and fond divinors; for they find no such thing written in Gods word.

Of the idoll called *Apollo*, I have somewhat already spoken in the former title of *Ob* or *Pytho*; and some occasion I shall have to speake thereof hereafter; and therfore at this time it shall suffice to tell you, that the credit gained thereunto, was by the craft and cunning of the priests, which tended thereupon; who with their counterfeit miracles so bewitched the people, as they thought such vertue to have beene conteined in the bodies of those idols, as God hath not promised to anie of his angels, or elect people. For it is said, that if *Apollo* were in a chafe, he would sweat: if he had remorse to the afflicted, and could not help them, he would shed teares, which I beleeve might have beene wiped awaie with that handkerchiefe, that wiped and dried the Rood of graces face, being in like perplexities. Even as another sort of witching priests called *Aruspices*, prophesied victorie to *Alexander*, bicause an eagle lighted on his head: which eagle might (I beleeve) be cooped or caged with *Mahomets* dove, that picked peason out of his eare.

Apollos passions.

CHAPTER IV.

The predictions of soothsaiers and lewd priests, the prognostications of astronomers and physicians allowable, divine prophesies holie and good.

THE cousening tricks of oracling priests and monkes, are and have beene speciallie most abhominable. The superstitious observations of sensles augurors and soothsaiers (contrarie to philosophie, and without authoritie of scripture) are verie ungodlie and ridiculous. Howbeit, I reject not the prognostications of astronomers, nor the conjectures or forewarnings of physicians, nor yet the interpretations of philosophers; although in respect of the divine prophesies conteined in holie scriptures, they are not to be weighed or regarded. For the end of these and the other is not onlie farre differing; but whereas these conteine onlie the word and will of God, with the other are mingled most horrible lies and cousenages. For though there may be many of them learned and godlie, yet lurke there in corners of the same profession, a great number of counterfets and couseners. *J. Bodin* putteth this difference betweene divine prophets and inchantors; to wit, the one saith alwaies true, the others words (proceeding from the divell) are alwaies false; or for one truth they tell a hundred lies. And then why maie not everie witch be thought as cunning as *Apollo*? And why not everie counterfet cousener as good a witch as mother *Bungie*? For it is ods, but they will hit the truth once in a hundred divinations as well as the best.

What prophesies allowable.

J. Bod. lib. de dæm. lib. 1. cap. 4.

Chapter v.

The diversitie of true prophets, of Urim, and of the propheticall use of the twelve precious stones conteined therein, of the divine voice called Eccho.

Diverse degrees of prophesie.

2. Reg. 2.

IT should appeare, that even of holie prophets there were diverse sorts. For *David* and *Salomon*, although in their psalmes and parables are conteined most excellent mysteries, and notable allegories: yet they were not indued with that degree of prophesie, that *Elie* and *Elisha* were, &c. For as often as it is said, that God spake to *David* or *Salomon*, it is meant to be done by the prophets. For *Nathan* or *Gad* were the messengers and prophets to reveale Gods will to *David*. And *Ahiam* the *Silonite* was sent from God to *Salomon*. Item, the spirit of prophesie, which *Elias* had, was doubled upon *Elisha*. Also some prophets prophesied all their lives, some had but one vision, and some had more, according to Gods pleasure; yea some prophesied unto the people of such things as came not to passe, and that was where Gods wrath was pacified by repentance. But these prophets were alwaies reputed among the people to be wise and godlie; whereas the heathen prophets were evermore knowne and said to be mad and foolish: as it is written both of the prophets of *Sibylla*, and also of *Apollo;* and at this daie also in the *Indies*, &c.

J. Bodin.

Joseph. de antiquit.

Josue filius Levi. lib. Pirkeaboth.

But that anie of these extraordinarie gifts remaine at this daie, *Bodin*, nor anie witchmonger in the world shall never be able to proove: though he in his booke of divelish madnesse would make men beleeve it. For these were miraculouslie mainteined by God among the Jewes, who were instructed by them of all such things as should come to passe; or else informed by *Urim:* so as the preests by the brightnes of the twelve pretious stones conteined therein, could prognosticate or expound anie thing. Which brightnes and vertue ceased (as *Josephus* reporteth) two hundred yeares before he was borne. So as since that time, no answers were yelded thereby of Gods will and pleasure. Neverthelesse, the Hebrues write, that there hath beene ever since that time, a divine voice heard among them, which in Latine is called *Filia vocis*, in Greeke ἠχώ, in English The daughter of speech.

Chapter vi.

Of prophesies conditionall: whereof the prophesies in the old testament doo intreate, and by whom they were published; witchmongers aunswers to the objections against witches supernaturall actions.

Prophesies conditio-nall.

CHRIST and his apostles prophesied of the calamities and afflictions, which shall greeve and disturbe the church of God in this life: also of the last daie, and of the signes and tokens that shall be shewed before that daie: and finallie of all things, which are requisite for us to foreknowe. Howbeit, such is the mercie of God, that all prophesies, threatnings, plagues, and punishments are annexed to conditions of repentance: as on the other side, corporall blessings are tied under the condition of the crosse and castigation. So as by them the mysteries of our salvation being discovered unto us, we are not to seeke new signes and miracles; but to attend to the doctrine of the apostles, who preached Christ exhibited and crucified for our sinnes, his resurrection, ascension, and thereby the redemption of as manie as beleeve, &c.

The subject of the pro-phesies of the old testa-ment.

The prophesies in the old testament treat of the continuance, the governe-ment, and the difference of estates: of the distinction of the four monarchies, of their order, decaie, and instauration; of the changes and ruines of the king-

98

domes of *Juda, Israel, Aegypt, Persia, Græcia*, &c: and speciallie of the comming of our Saviour Jesus Christ; and how he should be borne of a virgine, and where, of his tribe, passion, resurrection, &c. These prophesies were published by Gods speciall and peculiar prophets, endued with his particular and excellent gifts, according to his promise; I will raise them up a prophet out of the midst of their brethren, I will put my words in his mouth, &c. Which though it were speciallie spoken of Christ, yet was it also spoken of those particular prophets, which were placed among them by God to declare his will; which were also figures of Christ the prophet himselfe. Now, if prophesie be an extraordinarie gift of God, and a thing peculiar to himselfe, as without whose speciall assistance no creature can be a prophet, or shew what is to come; whie should we beleeve, that those lewd persons can performe by divinations and miracles that which is not in humane but in divine power to accomplish?

    Howbeit, when I denie that witches can ride in the aire, and the miraculous circumstance thereof: by and by it is objected unto me, that *Enoch* and *Elie* were rapt into heaven bodilie; and that *Abacuke* was carried in the aire, to feed *Daniel:* and so falselie oppose a divels or a witches power against the vertue of the Holy-ghost. If I deride the poets opinions, saieng, that witches cannot *Cælo deducere lunam*, fetch the moone from heaven, &c: they tell me that at *Joshuas* battell the sunne staied, and at the passion of Christ there was palpable darknes. If I denie their cunning in the exposition of dreames, advising them to remember *Jeremies* counsell, not to followe or credit the expositors of dreames; they hit me in the teeth with *Daniel* and *Joseph:* for that the one of them expounded *Pharao* the *Persian* kings, the other *Nabuchadnez-zar* the *Aegyptian* kings dreame. If I saie with *Salomon*, that the dead knowe nothing, and that the dead knowe us not, neither are remooveable out of *Abrahams* bosome, &c: they produce the storie of *Samuel:* wherein, I saie, they set the power of a creature as high as the creator. If I saie, that these witches cannot transubstantiate themselves, nor others into beasts, &c. they cite the storie of *Nabuchadnez-zar;* as though indeed he were made a materiall beast, and that also by witchcraft; and strengthen that their assertion with the fables of *Circe* and *Ulysses* his companions, &c.

2. Reg. 2. 13.

Eccles. 9. 5.

1. Sam. 28.

CHAPTER VII.

What were the miracles expressed in the old testament, and what are they in the new testament: and that we are not now to looke for anie more miracles.

THE miracles expressed in the old testament were manie, but the end of them all was one, though they were divers and differing in shew: as where the sacrifices of *Moses, Elias*, and *Salomon*, being abundantlie wet were burnt with fier from heaven, &c. The varietie of toongs at the building of *Babylon*, *Isaachs* birth of *Sarah* being by nature past children, the passage through the red sea, *Daniels* foretelling of the foure monarchies, in the fourth whereof he apparantlie foresheweth the comming of the Lord. All these, and manie other, which are expressed in the old testament, were mercifull instructions and notable miracles to strengthen the faith of Gods people in their Messias. If you had gone to *Delphos, Apollo* would have made you beleeve with his amphibologicall answers, that he could have foretold you all these things.

Gen. 11, 6.
Gen. 21.
Dan. 11.

    The miracles wrought by Christ were the raising up of the dead (which manie would impute to the woman of *Endor*, and also to our witches and conjurors) the restoring of the lame to lims, the blind to sight, the dumbe to speach, and finallie the healing of all diseases; which manie beleeve our witches can doo; yea, and as they themselves will take it upon them. As for casting out of divels (which was another kind of miracles usuall with Christ) witches and conjurors are said

A summe of Christs miracles.

Matt. 12. 25.

to be as good thereat as ever he was : and yet, if you will beleeve Christs words, it cannot be so. For he saith; Everie kingdome divided against it selfe, shall be brought to naught, &c. If sathan cast out sathan, he is divided, &c: and his kingdome shall not endure, &c.

Peters chaines fell off in prison, so did *Richard Gallisies* fetters at *Windsor :* marrie the prison doores opened not to *Richard*, as they did to *Peter. Helias* by speciall grace obtained raine, our witches can make it raine, when they list, &c. But sithens Christ did these miracles, and manie more, and all to confirme his truth, and strengthen our faith, and finallie for the conversion of the people (as appeareth in *John*. 6. 7, and 12 : in so much as he vehementlie reprooved such, as upon

Luk. 10, 13.

the sight of them would not beleeve, saieng; Wo be to thee *Chorazin*, wo be to thee *Bethsaida*. If the miracles had beene doone in *Tyre* and *Sidon*, which have beene doone in you, they had a great while ago repented, &c. Let us settle and acquiet our faith in Christ, and beleeving all his wonderous works, let us reject these old wives fables, as lieng vanities : whereof you may find in the golden legend, *M. Mal.* and speciallie in *Bodin* miraculous stuffe, enough to checke all the miracles expressed in the old and new testament; which are of more credit with manie bewitched people, than the true miracles of Christ himselfe. Insomuch as they stand in more awe of the manacies of a witch, than of all the threatnings and cursses pronounced by God, and expressed in his word. And thus much touching the word *Kasam*.

BOOKE X.

CHAPTER I.

The interpretation of this Hebrue word Onen, of the vanitie of dreames, and divinations thereupon.

ONEN differeth not much from *Kasam*, but that it is extended to the interpretation of dreames. And as for dreames, whatsoever credit is attributed unto them, proceedeth of follie: and they are fooles that trust in them, for whie they have deceived many. In which respect the Prophet giveth us good warning, not to followe nor hearken to the expositors of dreames, for they come through the multitude of busines. And therefore those witches, that make men beleeve they can prophesie upon dreames, as knowing the interpretation of them, and either for monie or glorie abuse men & women therby, are meere couseners, and worthie of great punishment: as are such witchmongers, as beleeving them, attribute unto them such divine power as onelie belongeth to God: as appeereth in *Jeremie* the Prophet.

Ecclus. 24.
Jerem. 27.
Eccle. 5.

Jerem. 23.
25. 26. 27.
Read the
words.

CHAPTER II.

Of divine, naturall, and casuall dreames, with their differing causes and effects.

MACROBIUS recounteth five differences of images, or rather imaginations, exhibited unto them that sleepe, which for the most part doo signifie somewhat in admonition. There be also many subdivisions made hereof, which I thinke needlesse to reherse. In *Jasper Peucer* they are to be seene, with the causes and occasions of dreames. There were woont to be delivered from God himselfe or his angels, certeine dreames and visions unto the prophets and holie fathers: according to the saieng of *Joel*; I will powre my spirit upon all flesh, your yoong men shall dreame dreames, and your old men shall see visions. These kind of dreames (I say) were the admonishments and forewarnings of God to his people: as that of *Joseph*, to abide with *Marie* his wife, after she was conceived by the Holie-ghost, as also to conveie our Saviour Christ into *Aegypt*, &c: the interpretation whereof are the peculiar gifts of God, which *Joseph* the patriarch, and *Daniel* the prophet had most speciallie.

Peucer in
*divinat. ex
somniis.*

Joel. 2.

Matth. 1. 20.

Matth. 2, 13.

Gen. 39. &
40. & 41.
Dani. 2.

As for physicall conjectures upon dreames, the scriptures improove them not: for by them the physicians manie times doo understand the state of their patients bodies. For some of them come by meanes of choler, flegme, melancholie, or bloud; and some by love, surfet, hunger, thirst, &c. *Gallen* and *Boetius* were said to deale with divels, bicause they told so justlie their patients dreames, or rather by their dreames their speciall diseases. Howbeit, physicall dreames are naturall, and the cause of them dwelleth in the nature of man. For they are the inward actions of the mind in the spirits of the braine, whilest the bodie is occupied with sleepe: for as touching the mind it selfe, it never sleepeth. These dreames varie, according to the difference of humors and vapors. There are also casuall dreames, which (as *Salomon* saith) some through the multitude of

Eccles. 5.

businesse. For as a looking glasse sheweth the image or figure thereunto opposite: so in dreames, the phantasie & imagination informes the understanding of
such things as haunt the outward sense. Whereupon the poet saith:

Somnia ne cures, nam mens humana quod optat,
Dum vigilat sperans, per somnum cernit id ipsum:

Englished by
Abraham
Fleming.

Regard no dreames, for why the mind
Of that in sleepe a view dooth take,
Which it dooth wish and hope to find,
At such time as it is awake.

CHAPTER III.

The opinion of divers old writers touching dreames, and how they varie in noting the causes
thereof.

A dissonan-
cie in
opinions
about
dreames.

SYNESIUS, *Themistius, Democritus,* and others grounding themselves
upon examples that chance hath sometimes verified, persuade men, that
nothing is dreamed in vaine: affirming that the hevenlie influencies doo
bring foorth divers formes in corporall matters; and of the same influencies,
visions and dreames are printed in the fantasticall power, which is instrumentall,
with a celestiall disposition meete to bring foorth some effect, especiallie in
sleepe, when the mind (being free from bodilie cares) may more liberallie
receive the heavenlie influencies, wherby many things are knowne to them sleeping in dreames, which they that wake cannot see. *Plato* attributeth them to the
formes and ingendred knowledges of the soule; *Avicen* to the last intelligence that
moveth the moone, through the light that lighteneth the fantasie in sleepe;
Aristotle to the phantasticall sense; *Averroës* to the imaginative; *Albert* to the
influence of superior bodies.

CHAPTER IV.

Against interpretors of dreames, of the ordinarie cause of dreames, Hemingius his opinion
of diabolicall dreames, the interpretation of dreames ceased.

THERE are bookes carried about concerning this matter, under the name
of *Abraham,* who (as *Philo In lib. gigantum* saith) was the first inventor of the
exposition of dreames: and so likewise of *Salomon* and *Daniel.* But *Cicero In*
lib. de divinatione confuteth the vanitie and follie of them that give credit to
dreames. And as for the interpretors of dreames, as they knowe not before the
dreame, nor yet after, any certeintie; yet when any thing afterwards happeneth,
then they applie the dreame to that which hath chanced.
    Certeinlie men never lightlie faile to dreame by night, of that which they
meditate by daie: and by daie they see divers and sundrie things, and conceive
them severallie in their minds. Then those mixed conceits being laid up in the
closset of the memorie, strive togither; which, bicause the phantasie cannot discerne nor discusse, some certeine thing gathered of manie conceits is bred and
contrived in one togither. And therefore in mine opinion, it is time vainelie

emploied, to studie about the interpretation of dreames. He that list to see the follie and vanitie thereof, maie read a vaine treatise, set out by *Thomas Hill* Londoner, 1568.

The pleasant art of the interpretation of dreames. *N. Hemin. in admonitionib. de superstitionib. magicis vitādis.*

Lastlie, there are diabolicall dreames, which *Nicolaus Hemingius* divideth into three sortes. The first is, when the divell immediatlie of himselfe (he meaneth corporallie) offereth anie matter of dreame. Secondlie, when the divell sheweth revelations to them that have made request upon him therefore. Thirdlie, when magicians by art bring to passe, that other men dreame what they will. Assuredlie these, and so all the rest (as they maie be used) are verie magicall and divelish dreames. For although we maie receive comfort of mind by those, which are called divine dreames, and health of bodie through physicall dreames; yet if we take upon us to use the office of God in the revelation or rather the interpretation of them; or if we attribute unto them miraculous effects (now when we see the gifts of prophesie, and of interpretation of dreames, and also the operation of miracles are ceased, which were speciall and peculiar gifts of God, to confirme the truth of the word, and to establish his people in the faith of the Messias, who is now exhibited unto us both in the testament, and also in the bloud of our Saviour Jesus Christ) we are bewitched, and both abuse and offend the majestie of God, and also seduce, delude and cousen all such as by our persuasion, and their owne light beleefe, give us credit.

The end & use of prophesie, interpretatiō of dreames, operation of miracles, &c.

CHAPTER V.

That neither witches, nor anie other, can either by words or hearbs, thrust into the mind of a sleeping man, what cogitations or dreames they list; and whence magicall dreames come.

I GRANT there maie be hearbs and stones found and knowne to the physicians, which maie procure dreames; and other hearbs and stones, &c: to make one bewraie all the secrets of his mind, when his bodie sleepeth, or at least wise to procure speech in sleepe. But that witches or magicians have power by words, herbs, or imprecations to thrust into the mind or conscience of man, what it shall please them, by vertue of their charmes, hearbs, stones, or familiars, &c: according to the opinion of *Hemingius*, I denie: though therewithall I confesse, that the divell both by daie and also by night, travelleth to seduce man, and to lead him from God; yea and that no waie more than this, where he placeth himselfe as God in the minds of them that are so credulous, to attribute unto him, or unto witches, that which is onlie in the office, nature, and power of God to accomplish.

Seeke for such stuffe in my booke of Hartumim.

Doth not *Daniel* the prophet saie, even in this case; It is the Lord onelie that knoweth such secrets, as in the exposition of dreames is required? And doth not *Joseph* repeat those verie words to *Pharaos* officers, who consulted with him therein? Examples of divine dreames you maie find a great number in the scripture, such (I meane) as it pleased God to reveale his pleasure by. Of physicall dreames we maie both read in authors, and see in our owne experience dailie, or rather nightly. Such dreams also as are casuall, they are likewise usuall, and come (as hath beene said) through the multitude of affaires and businesse. Those which in these daies are called magicall or diabolicall dreames, maie rather be called melancholicall. For out of that blacke vapor in sleepe, through dreames, appeareth (as *Aristotle* saith) some horrible thing; and as it were the image of an ouglie divell: sometimes also other terrible visions, imaginations, counsels, and practises. As where we read of a certeine man, that dreamed there appeared one unto him that required him to throwe himselfe into a deepe pit, and that he should reape great benefit thereby at Gods hands. So as the miserable wretch giving credit thereunto, performed the matter, and killed himselfe.

Dan. 2.

Gen. 11, 8.
Gen. 37, & 11.
Isai. 11.
Dan. 2.

Aristot. de somnio.

Now I confesse, that the interpretation or execution of that dreame was indeed diabolicall: but the dreame was casuall, derived from the heavie and blacke humor of melancholie.

CHAPTER VI.

How men have beene bewitched, cousened or abused by dreames to dig and search for monie.

Such would be imbarked in the ship of fooles.

HOW manie have beene bewitched with dreames, and thereby made to consume themselves with digging and searching for monie, &c: whereof they, or some other have drempt? I my selfe could manifest as having, knowne how wise men have beene that waie abused by verie simple persons, even where no dreame hath beene met withall, but waking dreames. And this hath beene used heretofore, as one of the finest cousening feates: in so much as there is a verie formall art thereof devised, with manie excellent superstitions and ceremonies thereunto belonging, which I will set downe as breeflie as maie be.

An english proverbe.

Albeit that here in *England*, this proverbe hath beene current; to wit, Dreames proove contrarie: according to the answer of the priests boy to his master, who told his said boy that he drempt he kissed his taile: Yea maister (saith he) but dreames proove contrarie, you must kisse mine.

CHAPTER VII.

The art and order to be used in digging for monie, revealed by dreames, how to procure pleasant dreames, of morning and midnight dreames.

Note this superstitious dotage.

THERE must be made upon a hazell wand three crosses, and certeine words both blasphemous and impious must be said over it, and hereunto must be added certeine characters, & barbarous names. And whilest the treasure is a digging, there must be read the psalmes, *De profundis, Missa, Misereatur nostri, Requiem, Pater noster, Ave Maria, Et ne nos inducas in tentationem, sed libera nos à malo, Amen. A porta inferi credo videre bona,* &c. *Expectate Dominum, Requiem æternam.* And then a certeine praier. And if the time of digging be neglected, the divell will carie all the treasure awaie. See other more absolute conjurations for this purpose, in the word *Iidoni* following.

J. Bap. Neap. in natural. mag. lib. 2. cap. 26. fol. 83. & 84.

You shall find in *Johannes Baptista Neapolitanus*, diverse receipts by hearbes and potions, to procure pleasant or fearefull dreames; and perfumes also to that effect; who affirmeth, that dreames in the dead of the night are commonlie preposterous and monstrous; and in the morning when the grosse humors be spent, there happen more pleasant and certeine dreames, the bloud being more pure than at other times: the reason whereof is there expressed.

CHAPTER VIII.

Sundrie receipts and ointments, made and used for the transportation of witches, and other miraculous effects: an instance therof reported and credited by some that are learned.

IT shall not be amisse here in this place to repeate an ointment greatlie to this purpose, rehearsed by the foresaid *John Bapt. Neap.* wherein although he maie be overtaken and cousened by an old witch, and made not onelie to beleeve, but also to report a false tale; yet bicause it greatlie overthroweth the opinion of *M. Mal. Bodin,* and such other, as write so absolutelie in maintenance of witches transportations, I will set downe his words in this behalfe. The receipt is as followeth.

℞. The fat of yoong children, and seeth it with water in a brasen vessell, reserving the thickest of that which remaineth boiled in the bottome, which they laie up and keepe, untill occasion serveth to use it. They put hereunto *Eleoselinum, Aconitum, Frondes populeas,* and Soote.

Confections or receipts for the miraculous transportation of witches.

Another receipt to the same purpose.

℞. *Sium, acarum vulgare, pentaphyllon,* the bloud of a flitter-mouse, *solanum somniferum,* & *oleum.* They stampe all these togither, and then they rubbe all parts of their bodies exceedinglie, till they looke red, and be verie hot, so as the pores may be opened, and their flesh soluble and loose. They joine herewithall either fat, or oile in steed thereof, that the force of the ointment maie the rather pearse inwardly, and so be more effectuall. By this means (saith he) in a moone light night they seeme to be carried in the aire, to feasting, singing, dansing, kissing, culling, and other acts of venerie, with such youthes as they love and desire most: for the force (saith he) of their imagination is so vehement, that almost all that part of the braine, wherein the memorie consisteth, is full of such conceipts. And whereas they are naturallie prone to beleeve anie thing; so doo they receive such impressions and stedfast imaginations into their minds, as even their spirits are altered thereby; not thinking upon anie thing else, either by daie or by night. And this helpeth them forward in their imaginations, that their usuall food is none other commonlie but beets, rootes, nuts, beanes, peaze, &c.

Now (saith he) when I considered throughlie hereof, remaining doubtfull of the matter, there fell into my hands a witch, who of hir owne accord did promise me to fetch me an errand out of hand from farre countries, and willed all them, whome I had brought to witnesse the matter, to depart out of the chamber. And when she had undressed hir selfe, and froted hir bodie with certeine ointments (which action we beheld through a chinke or little hole of the doore) she fell downe thorough the force of those soporiferous or sleepie ointments into a most sound and heavie sleepe: so as we did breake open the doore, and did beate hir exceedinglie; but the force of hir sleepe was such, as it tooke awaie from hir the sense of feeling: and we departed for a time. Now when hir strength and powers were wearie and decaied, shee awoke of hir owne accord, and began to speake manie vaine and doting words, affirming that she had passed over both seas and mountaines; delivering to us manie untrue and false reports: we earnestlie denied them, she impudentlie affirmed them. This (saith he) will not so come to passe with everie one, but onlie with old women that are melancholike, whose nature is extreame cold, and their evaporation small; and they both perceive and remember what they see in that case and taking of theirs.

Vetule, quas à strigis similitudine, striges vocant, quæq; noctu puerulorum sanguinem in cunis cubantium exsorbent.

CHAPTER IX.

A confutation of the former follies, as well concerning ointments, dreames, &c. as also of the
assemblie of witches, and of their consultations and bankets at sundrie places, and all in
dreames.

B UT if it be true that S. *Augustine* saith, and manie other writers, that
witches nightwalkings are but phantasies and dreames: then all the reportes
of their bargaine, transporting, and meetings with *Diana, Minerva, &c*: are
but fables; and then do they lie that mainteine those actions to be doone in deed
and veritie, which in truth are doone no waie. It were marvell on the one side
(if those things happened in dreames, which neverthelesse the witches affirme to
be otherwise) that when those witches awake, they neither consider nor remember that they were in a dreame. It were marvell that their ointments, by the
physicians opinions having no force at all to that effect, as they confesse which
are inquisitors, should have such operation. It were marvell that their ointments
cannot be found anie where, saving onelie in the inquisitors bookes. It were
marvell, that when a stranger is annointed therewith, they have sometimes, and
yet not alwaies, the like operation as with witches; which all the inquisitors
confesse.

But to this last, frier *Bartholomæus* saith, that the witches themselves, before they
annoint themselves, do heare in the night time a great noise of minstrels, which
flie over them, with the ladie of the fairies, and then they addresse themselves to
their journie. But then I marvell againe, that no bodie else heareth nor seeth this
troope of minstrels, especiallie riding in a moone light night. It is marvell that
they that thinke this to be but in a dreame, can be persuaded that all the rest is
anie other than dreames. It is marvell that in dreames, witches of old acquaintance meet so just togither, and conclude upon murthers, and receive ointments,
roots, powders, &c: (as witchmongers report they doo, and as they make the
witches confesse) and yet lie at home fast asleepe. It is marvell that such preparation is made for them (as *Sprenger, Bartholomew*, and *Bodin* report) as well in
noble mens houses, as in alehouses; and that they come in dreames, and eate up
their meate: and the alewife speciallie is not wearied with them for non paiment
of their score, or false paiment; to wit, with imaginarie monie, which they saie is
not substantiall, and that they talke not afterwards about the reckoning, and so
discover the matter. And it is most marvell of all, that the hostesse, &c: dooth
not sit among them, and take part of their good cheere. For so it is, that if any
part of these their meetings and league be true, it is as true and as certeinlie
prooved and confessed, that at some alehouse, or sometime at some Gentlemans
house, there is continuall preparation made monethlie for this assemblie: as
appeereth in S. *Germans* storie.

Barthol. Spi-
næus, q. de
strigib. c. 31.

Bar. Spin. qu.
de strigib. c.
30.

New matter
& worthie
to be mar-
velled at.

Legend. aur.
in vita S.
Germani.

CHAPTER X.

That most part of prophesies in the old testament were revealed in dreames, that we are not
now to looke for such revelations, of some who have drempt of that which hath come to
passe, that dreames proove contrarie, Nabuchadnez-zars rule to knowe a true expositor of
dreames.

I T is held and mainteined by divers, and gathered out of the 12. of *Numbers*,
that all which was written or spoken by the prophets, among the children of
Israel (*Moses* excepted) was propounded to them by dreames. And indeed it
is manifest, that manie things, which are thought by the unlearned to have

beene reallie finished, have beene onlie performed by dreams and visions. As where *Salomon* required of God the gift of wisdome: that was (I say) in a dreame; and also where he received promise of the continuance of the kingdome of Israel in his line. So was *Esais* vision in the 6. of his prophesie: as also that of *Ezechiel* the 12. Finallie, where *Jeremie* was commanded to hide his girdle in the clift of a rocke at the river *Euphrates* in *Babylon;* and that after certeine daies, it did there putrifie, it must needs be in a dreame; for *Jeremie* was never (or at leastwise not then) at *Babylon.* We that are christians must not now slumber and dreame, but watch and praie, and meditate upon our salvation in Christ both daie and night. And if we expect revelations in our dreams, now, when Christ is come, we shall deceive our selves: for in him are fulfilled all dreames and prophesies. Howbeit, *Bodin* holdeth that dreames and visions continue till this daie, in as miraculous maner as ever they did.

    If you read *Artemidorus*, you shall read manie stories of such as drempt of things that afterwards cam to passe. But he might have cited a thousand for one that fell out contrarie: for as for such dreamers among the Jews themselves, as had not extraordinarie visions miraculouslie exhibited unto them by God, they were counted couseners, as may appeere by these words of the prophet *Zacharie;* Surelie the idols have spoken vanitie, and the soothsaiers have seene a lie, and the dreamers have told a vaine thing. According to *Salomons* saieng; In the multitude of dreames and vanities are manie words. It appeereth in *Jeremie* 23. that the false prophets, whilest they illuded the people with lies, counterfetting the true prophets, used to crie out; Dreames, dreames; We have dreamed a dreame, &c. Finallie, *Nabuchadnez-zar* teacheth all men to knowe a true expositor of dreames; to wit, such a one as hath his revelation from GOD. For he can (as *Daniel* did) repeate your dreame before you discover it: which thing if anie expounder of dreames can doo at this daie, I will beleeve him.

Marginal notes:
- 1. Re. 3, 5, 15.
- 1. Reg. 9. Isai. 6. Ezech. 12. Jerem. 13.
- *J. Bodin. lib. de dæmon. 1. cap. 5.*
- Zach. 10, 2.
- Eccles. 5, 6. Jerem. 23.
- Daniel. 2.

BOOKE XI.

Chapter i.

*The Hebrue word Nahas expounded, of the art of augurie, who invented it, how slovenlie a
science it is: the multitude of sacrifices and sacrificers of the heathen, and the causes thereof.*

N AHAS, is To observe the flieng of birds, & comprehendeth all such other
observations, where men do ghesse upon uncerteine toies. It is found in
Deut. 18. and in 2. *Chron.* 33. and else-where. Of this art of augurie
Tyresias the king of the *Thebans* is said to be the first inventor: but *Tages* first
published the discipline thereof, being but a little boie; as *Cicero* reporteth out
of the bookes of the *Hetruscans* themselves. Some points of this art are more high
and profound than some others, and yet are they more homelie and slovenlie
than the rest; as namelie, the divination upon the entrailes of beasts, which the
Gentiles in their sacrifices speciallie observed. Insomuch as *Marcus Varro*, seeing
the absurditie thereof, said that these gods were not onlie idle, but verie slovens,
that used so to hide their secrets and counsels in the guts and bowels of beasts.

The slo-
venlie art
of augurie.

How vainlie, absurdlie, and superstitiouslie the heathen used this kind of
divination in their sacrifices, is manifested by their actions & ceremonies in that
behalfe practised, as well in times past, as at this houre. The *Aegyptians* had 666.
severall sorts and kinds of sacrifices; the *Romans* had almost as manie; the
Græcians had not so few as they; the *Persians* and the *Medes* were not behind
them; the *Indies* and other nations have at this instant their sacrifices full of
varietie, and more full of barbarous impietie. For in sundrie places, these offer
sacrifices to the divell, hoping thereby to moove him to lenitie: yea, these commonlie sacrifice such of their enimies, as they have taken in warre: as we read
that the Gentiles in ancient time did offer sacrifice, to appease the wrath and
indignation of their feigned gods.

Chapter ii.

Of the Jewes sacrifice to Moloch, a discourse thereupon, and of Purgatorie.

2. Re. 23, 10.
2. Chr. 33.
Jerem. 7.

T HE *Jewes* used one kind of diabolical sacrifice, never taught them by
Moses, namelie, to offer their children to *Moloch*, making their sonnes and
their daughters to runne through the fire; supposing such grace and efficacie to have beene in that action, as other witches affirme to be in charmes
and words. And therfore among other points of witchcraft, this is speciallie
and namelie forbidden by *Moses*. We read of no more miracles wrought hereby,
than by any other kind of witchcraft in the old or new testament expressed. It
was no ceremonie appointed by God, no figure of Christ: perhaps it might be a
sacrament or rather a figure of purgatorie, the which place was not remembred
by *Moses*. Neither was there anie sacrifice appointed by the lawe for the releefe
of the Israelites soules that there should be tormented. Which without all doubt
should not have beene omitted, if any such place of purgatorie had beene then,
as the Pope hath latelie devised for his private and speciall lucre. This sacri-
108

Deut. 18, 10.
Levi, 18, 21.
Id. cap. 20. 2.
An invin-
cible argu-
ment
against
purgatorie.

ficing to *Moloch* (as some affirme) was usuall among the Gentiles, from whence the Jewes brought it into Israel : and there (of likeliehood) the *Eutichists* learned the abhomination in that behalfe.

CHAPTER III.

The Canibals crueltie, of popish sacrifices exceeding in tyrannie the Jewes or Gentiles.

THE incivilitie and cruell sacrifices of popish preests do yet exceed both the Jew and the Gentile : for these take upon them to sacrifice Christ himselfe. And to make their tyrannie the more apparent, they are not contented to have killed him once, but dailie and hourelie torment him with new deaths ; yea they are not ashamed to sweare, that with their carnall hands they teare his humane substance, breaking it into small gobbets ; and with their external teeth chew his flesh and bones, contrarie to divine or humane nature ; and contrarie to the prophesie, which saith ; There shall not a bone of him be broken. Finallie, in the end of their sacrifice (as they say) they eate him up rawe, and swallow downe into their guts everie member and parcell of him : and last of all, that they conveie him into the place where they bestowe the residue of all that which they have devoured that daie. And this same barbarous impietie exceedeth the crueltie of all others : for all the Gentiles consumed their sacrifices with fier, which they thought to be holie.

Against the papists abhominable and blasphemous sacrifice of the masse.

Psal. 34, 20.

CHAPTER IV.

The superstition of the heathen about the element of fier, and how it grew in such reverence among them, of their corruptions, and that they had some inkling of the godlie fathers dooings in that behalfe.

AS touching the element of fier, & the superstition therof about those businesses, you shall understand, that manie superstitious people and nations have received, reverenced, & reserved fier, as the most holy thing among their sacrifices : insomuch (I saie) as they have worshipped it among their gods, calling it *Orimasda* (to wit) holie fier, and divine light. The Greekes called it ἑσίαν, the Romans *Vesta*, which is, The fier of the Lord. Surelie they had heard of the fier that came downe from heaven, and consumed the oblations of the fathers ; and they understood it to be God himselfe. For there came to the heathen, the bare names of things, from the doctrine of the godlie fathers and patriarchs, and those so obscured with fables, and corrupted with lies, so overwhelmed with superstitions, and disguised with ceremonies, that it is hard to judge from whence they came. Some cause thereof (I suppose) was partlie the translations of governements, whereby one nation learned follie of another ; and partlie blind devotion, without knowledge of Gods word : but speciallie the want of grace, which they sought not for, according to Gods commandement and will. And that the Gentiles had some inkling of the godlie fathers dooings, may diverslie appeare. Doo not the *Muscovits* and *Indian* prophets at this daie, like apes, imitate *Esaie?* Bicause he went naked certeine yeares, they forsooth counterfet madnes, and drinke potions for that purpose ; thinking that whatsoever they saie in their madnes, will certeinelie come to passe. But hereof is more largelie discoursed before in the word *Kasam.*

The Gymnosophists of India their apish imitation of Esaie.

CHAPTER V.

Of the Romane sacrifices: of the estimation they had of augurie, of the lawe of the twelve tables.

THE *Romans*, even after they were growne to great civilitie, and enjoied a most flourishing state and commonwealth, would sometimes sacrifice themselves, sometimes their children, sometimes their friends, &c: consuming the same with fier, which they thought holie. Such estimation (I saie) was attributed to this art of divination upon the entrails of beasts, &c: at *Rome*, as the cheefe princes themselves exercised the same; namelie, *Romulus, Fabius Maximus*, &c: in so much as there was a decree made there, by the whole senate, that six of the cheefe magistrats sonnes should from time to time be put foorth, to learne the mysterie of these arts of augurie and divination, at *Hetruria*, where the cunning and knowledge thereof most abounded. When they came home well informed and instructed in this art, their estimation and dignitie was such, as they were accounted, reputed, and taken to be the interpretors of the gods, or rather betweene the gods and them. No high preest, nor anie other great officer was elected, but these did either absolutelie nominate them, or else did exhibit the names of two, whereof the senate must choose the one.

The lawe of the twelve tables.

In their ancient lawes were written these words : *Prodigia & portenta ad Hetruscos aruspices (si senatus jusserit) deferunto, Hetruriæq; principes disciplinam discunto. Quibus divis decreverunt, procuranto, iisdem fulgara & ostenta pianto, auspicia servanto, auguri parento:* the effect of which words is this; Let all prodigious and portentous matters be carried to the soothsaiers of *Hetruria*, at the will and commandement of the senat; and let the yoong princes be sent to *Hetruria*, there to learne that discipline, or to be instructed in that art and knowledge. Let there be alwaies some solicitor, to learne with what gods they have decreed or determined their matters, and let sacrifices be made unto them in times of lightening, or at anie strange or supernaturall shew. Let all such conjecturing tokens be observed; whatsoever the soothsaier commandeth, let it be religiouslie obeied.

CHAPTER VI.

Colleges of augurors, their office, their number, the signification of augurie, that the practisers of that art were couseners, their profession, their places of exercise, their apparrell, their superstition.

ROMULUS erected three colleges or centuries of those kinds of soothsaiers, which onelie (and none other) should have authoritie to expound the minds and admonishments of the gods. Afterwards that number was augmented to five, and after that to nine: for they must needs be od. In the end, they increased so fast, that they were feine to make a decree for staie from the further proceeding in those erections: like to our statute of *Mortmaine*. Howbeit, *Silla* (contrarie to all orders and constitutions before made) increased that number to foure and twentie.

Magna charta. Hen. 3. 36. 7 *Ed.* 1. 15. *Ri.* 2. 5.

And though *Augurium* be most properlie that divination, which is gathered by birds; yet bicause this word *Nahas* comprehendeth all other kinds of divination, as *Extispicium, aruspicium*, &c: which is as well the ghessing upon the entrailes of beasts, as divers other waies: omitting physiognomie and palmestrie, and such like, for the tediousnes and follie thereof; I will speake a little of such arts, as were above measure regarded of our elders: neither mind I to discover the whole circumstance, but to refute the vanitie thereof, and speciallie of the professors of them, which are and alwaies have beene cousening arts, and in them conteined both speciall and severall kinds of witchcrafts. For the maisters of these faculties have ever taken upon them to occupie the place and name of God; blasphemouslie ascribing unto themselves his omnipotent power, to foretell, &c: whereas, in truth, they could or can doo nothing, but make a shew of that which is not.

One matter, to bewraie their counsening, is; that they could never worke nor foreshew anie thing to the poore or inferior sort of people: for portentous shewes (saie they) alwaies concerned great estates. Such matters as touched the baser sort, were inferior causes; which the superstition of the people themselves would not neglect to learne. Howbeit, the professors of this art descended not so lowe, as to communicate with them: for they were preests (which in all ages and nations have beene jollie fellowes) whose office was, to tell what should come to passe, either touching good lucke, or bad fortune; to expound the minds, admonitions, warnings and threatnings of the gods, to foreshew calamities, &c: which might be (by their sacrifices and common contrition) remooved and qualified. And before their entrance into that action, they had manie observations, which they executed verie superstitiouslie; pretending that everie bird and beast, &c, should be sent from the gods as foreshewes of somewhat. And therefore first they used to choose a cleare daie, and faire wether to doo their busines in: for the which their place was certeinelie assigned, as well in *Rome* as in *Hetruria*, wherein they observed everie quarter of the element, which waie to looke, and which way to stand, &c. Their apparell was verie preestlike, of fashion altered from all others, speciallie at the time of their praiers, wherein they might not omit a word nor a syllable: in respect whereof one read the service, and all the residue repeated it after him, in the maner of a procession.

A manifest
discoverie
of augurors
cousenage.

CHAPTER VII.

The times and seasons to exercise augurie, the maner and order thereof, of the ceremonies thereunto belonging.

NO lesse regard was there had of the times of their practise in that ministerie: for they must beginne at midnight, and end at noone, not travelling therein in the decaie of the day, but in the increase of the same; neither in the sixt or seventh houre of the daie, nor yet after the moneth of August; bicause then yoong birds flie about, and are diseased, and unperfect, mounting their fethers, and flieng out of the countrie: so as no certeine ghesse is to be made of the gods purposes by them at those seasons. But in their due times they standing with a bowed wand in their hand, their face toward the east, &c: in the top of an high tower, the weather being cleare, watch for birds, noting from whence they came, and whether they flie, and in what sort they wag their wings, &c.

Note the
superstitious
ceremonies
or augurors.

CHAPTER VIII.

Upon what signes and tokens augorors did prognosticate, observations touching the inward and outward parts of beasts, with notes of beasts behaviour in the slaughterhouse.

THESE kind of witches, whom we have now in hand, did also prognosticate good or bad lucke, according to the soundnes or imperfection of the
entrailes of beasts; or according to the superfluities or infirmities of nature;
or according to the abundance of humors unnecessarie, appearing in the inward
parts and bowels of the beasts sacrificed. For as touching the outward parts, it
was alwaies provided and foreseene, that they should be without blemish. And
yet there were manie tokens and notes to be taken of the externall actions of
those beasts, at the time of sacrifice : as if they would not quietlie be brought to
the place of execution, but must be forceablie hailed; or if they brake loose; or
if by hap, cunning, or strength they withstood the first blowe; or if after the
butchers blowe, they leaped up, rored, stood fast; or being fallen, kicked, or
would not quietlie die, or bled not well; or if anie ill newes had beene heard, or
anie ill sight seene at the time of slaughter or sacrifice : which were all significa-
tions of ill lucke and unhappie successe. On the other side, if the slaughterman
performed his office well, so as the beast had beene well chosen, not infected,
but whole and sound, and in the end faire killed; all had beene safe : for then
the gods smiled.

*Observa-
tions in the
art auguri-
ficall.*

CHAPTER IX.

A confutation of augurie, Plato his reverend opinion thereof, of contrarie events, and false predictions.

BUT what credit is to be attributed to such toies and chances, which grow
not of nature, but are gathered by the superstition of the interpretors? As
for birds, who is so ignorant that conceiveth not, that one flieth one waie,
another another waie, about their private necessities? And yet are the other
divinations more vaine and foolish. Howbeit, *Plato* thinketh a commonwealth
cannot stand without this art, and numbereth it among the liberall sciences.
These fellowes promised *Pompeie*, *Cassius*, and *Cæsar*, that none of them should
die before they were old, and that in their owne houses, and in great honor;
and yet they all died cleane contrarilie. Howbeit doubtles, the heathen in this
point were not so much to be blamed, as the sacrificing papists : for they were
directed hereunto without the knowledge of Gods promises; neither knew they
the end why such ceremonies and sacrifices were instituted; but onelie understood by an uncerteine and slender report, that God was woont to send good or
ill successe to the children of Israell, and to the old patriarchs and fathers, upon
his acceptance or disallowance of their sacrifices and oblations. But men in all
ages have beene so desirous to know the effect of their purposes, the sequele of
things to come, and to see the end of their feare and hope : that a seelie witch,
which had learned anie thing in the art of cousenage, may make a great manie
jollie fooles.

*Plato in
Phædro, in
Timeo, in
lib. de
Republ.
Wherein
the papists
are more
blame wor-
thie than
the heathen.*

CHAPTER X.

The cousening art of sortilege or lotarie, practised especiallie by Aegyptian vagabonds, of allowed lots, of Pythagoras his lot, &c.

THE counterfeit *Aegyptians*, which were indeed cousening vagabonds, prac- Sortilege
tising the art called *Sortilegium*, had no small credit among the multitude: or lotshare.
howbeit, their divinations were as was their fast and loose, and as the
witches cures and hurtes, & as the soothsaiers answers, and as the conjurors
raisings up of spirits, and as *Apollos* or the Rood of graces oracles, and as the
jugglers knacks of legierdemaine, and as the papists exorcismes, and as the
witches charmes, and as the counterfeit visions, and as the couseners knaveries.
Hereupon it was said; *Non inveniatur inter vos menahas*, that is *Sortilegus*, which
were like to these Aegyptian couseners. As for other lots, they were used, and
that lawfullie; as appeareth by *Jonas* and others that were holie men, and as
may be seene among all commonwelths, for the deciding of diverse contro-
versies, &c: wherein thy neighbour is not misused, nor God anie waie offended.
But in truth I thinke, bicause of the cousenage that so easilie may be used
herein, God forbad it in the commonwealth of the Jewes, though in the good
use thereof it was allowed in matters of great weight; as appeareth both in the   Levit. 16.
old and new testament; and that as well in doubtfull cases and distributions,   Num. 33.
   & 36.
as in elections and inheritances, and pacification of variances. I omit to speake   Josu. 14.
anie thing of the lots comprised in verses, concerning the lucke ensuing, either   1. Chron. 24.
   & 26.
of *Virgil*, *Homer*, or anie other, wherein fortune is gathered by the sudden turning   Prover. 18.
unto them: bicause it is a childish and ridiculous toie, and like unto childrens   Jonas. 1.
plaie at *Primus secundus*, or the game called The philosophers table: but herein I   Acts. 1.
will referre you to the bable it selfe, or else to *Bodin*, or to some such sober writer
thereupon; of whome there is no want.

    There is a lot also called *Pythagoras* lot, which (some saie) *Aristotle* beleeved: Of Pytha-
and that is, where the characters of letters have certeine proper numbers;   goras lot.
whereby they divine (through the proper names of men) so as the numbers of
each letters being gathered in a summe, and put togither, give victorie to them
whose summe is the greater; whether the question be of warre, life, matrimonie,
victorie, &c: even as the unequall number of vowels in proper names portendeth
lacke of sight, halting, &c: which the godfathers and godmothers might easilie
prevent, if the case stood so.

CHAPTER XI.

Of the Cabalisticall art, consisting of traditions and unwritten verities learned without booke, and of the division thereof.

HERE is place also for the Cabalisticall art, consisting of unwritten verities, which the Jewes doo beleeve and brag that God himselfe gave to
Moses in the mount *Sinai*; and afterwards was taught onelie with livelie
voice, by degrees of succession, without writing, untill the time of *Esdras*: even
as the scholers of *Archippus* did use wit and memorie in steed of bookes. They   The art
divide this in twaine; the one expoundeth with philosophicall reason the secrets   Cabalisticall
   divided.
of the lawe and the bible, where (they saie) that *Salomon* was verie cunning;
bicause it is written in the Hebrew stories, that he disputed from the Cedar of
Libanus, even to the Hisop, and also of birds, beasts, &c. The other is as it were

a symbolicall divinitie of the highest contemplation, of the divine and angelike vertues, of holie names and signes; wherein the letters, numbers, figures, things and armes, the prickes over the letters, the lines, the points, and the accents doo all signifie verie profound things and great secrets. By these arts the Atheists suppose *Moses* wrote all his miracles, and that hereby they have power over angels and divels, as also to doo miracles: yea and that hereby all the miracles that either anie of the prophets, or Christ himselfe wrought, were accomplished.

C. Agrippa lib. de vanit. scient.

But *C. Agrippa* having searched to the bottome of this art, saith it is nothing but superstition and follie. Otherwise you maie be sure Christ would not have hidden it from his church. For this cause the Jewes were so skilfull in the names of God. But there is none other name in heaven or earth, in which we might be saved, but Jesus: neither is that meant by his bare name, but by his vertue and goodnes towards us. These Cabalists doo further brag, that they are able

The blasphemie of the Cabalists.

hereby, not onelie to find out and know the unspeakeable mysteries of God; but also the secrets which are above scripture; whereby also they take upon them to prophesie, and to worke miracles: yea hereby they can make what they list to be scripture; as *Valeria Proba* did picke certeine verses out of *Virgil* alluding them to Christ. And therefore these their revolutions are nothing but allegoricall games, which idle men busied in letters, points, and numbers (which the Hebrew toong easilie suffereth) devise, to delude and cousen the simple and ignorant. And this they call Alphabetarie or Arythmanticall divinitie, which Christ shewed to his apostles onelie, and which *Paule* saith he speaketh but among perfect men; and being high mysteries are not to be committed unto writing, and so made popular. There is no man that readeth anie thing of this *Cabalisticall* art, but must needs think upon the popes cunning practises in this

In colcil. Trident.

behalfe, who hath *In scrinio pectoris*, not onelie the exposition of all lawes, both divine and humane, but also authoritie to adde thereunto, or to drawe back therefrom at his pleasure: and this may he lawfullie doo even with the scriptures, either by addition or substraction, after his owne pontificall liking. As for example: he hath added the Apocrypha (whereunto he might as well have

[C. of Trent 1550.]

joined S. *Augustines* works, or the course of the civill lawe, &c:) Againe, he hath diminished from the decalog or ten commandements, not one or two words, but a whole precept, namelie the second, which it hath pleased him to dash out with his pen: and trulie he might as well by the same authoritie have rased out of the testament S. *Markes* gospell.

Chapter XII.

When, how, and in what sort sacrifices were first ordained, and how they were prophaned, and how the pope corrupteth the sacraments of Christ.

Gen. 2. 17.

AT the first God manifested to our father *Adam*, by the prohibition of the apple, that he would have man live under a lawe, in obedience and submission; and not to wander like a beast without order or discipline. And

Gen. 3. 6.
Gen. 3. 15.

after man had transgressed, and deserved thereby Gods heavie displeasure; yet his mercie prevailed; and taking compassion upon man, he promised the Messias, who should be borne of a woman, and breake the serpents head; declaring by evident testimonies, that his pleasure was that man should be restored to favour and grace, through Christ: and binding the minds of men to this promise, and to be fixed upon their Messias, established figures and ceremonies wherewith to nourish their faith, and confirmed the same with miracles, prohibiting and excluding all mans devises in that behalfe. And upon his pro-

Levit. 12. 3. &c.

mise renewed, he injoined (I say) and erected a new forme of worship, whereby he would have his promises constantlie beheld, faithfullie beleeved, and reve-

114

rentlie regarded. He ordeined six sorts of divine sacrifices; three propitiatorie, not as meriting remission of sinnes, but as figures of Christs propitiation: the other three were of thanksgiving. These sacrifices were full of ceremonies, they were powdered with consecrated salt, and kindled with fier, which was preserved in the tabernacle of the Lord: which fier (some thinke) was sent downe from heaven. GOD himselfe commanded these rites and ceremonies to our forefathers, *Noah, Abraham, Isaac, Jacob,* &c: promising therein both the amplification of their families, and also their Messias. But in tract of time (I saie) wantonnesse, negligence, and contempt, through the instigation of the divell, abolished this institution of GOD: so as in the end, God himselfe was forgotten among them, and they became pagans & heathens, devising their owne waies, untill everie countrie had devised and erected both new sacrifices, and also new gods particular unto themselves. Whose example the pope followeth, in prophaning of Christs sacraments, disguising them with his devises and superstitious ceremonies; contriving and comprehending therein the follie of all nations: the which bicause little children doo now perceive and scorne, I will passe over; and returne to the Gentiles, whome I cannot excuse of cousenage, superstition, nor yet of vanitie in this behalfe. For if God suffered false prophets among the children of Israell, being Gods peculiar people, and hypocrits in the church of Christ; no marvell if there were such people amongst the heathen, which neither professed nor knew him.

A gird at the pope for his saw-cinesse in Gods matters.

CHAPTER XIII.

Of the objects whereupon the augurors used to prognosticate, with certeine cautions and notes.

THE Gentiles, which treat of this matter, repeat an innumerable multitude of objects, whereupon they prognosticate good or bad lucke. And a great matter is made of neezing, wherein the number of neezings & the time therof is greatlie noted; the tingling in the finger, the elbowe, the toe, the knee, &c: are singular notes also to be observed in this art; though speciallie heerin are marked the flieng of fowles, and meeting of beasts; with this generall caution, that the object or matter whereon men divine, must be sudden and unlooked for: which regard, children and some old fooles have to the gathering primrose, true loves, and foure leaved grasse; Item the person unto whome such an object offereth it selfe unawares; Item the intention of the divinor, whereby the object which is met, is referred to augurie; Item the houre in which the object is without foreknowledge upon the sudden met withall; and so foorth.

Plinie reporteth that griphes flie alwaies to the place of slaughter, two or three daies before the battell is fought; which was seene and tried at the battell of *Troie:* and in respect thereof, the griph was allowed to be the cheefe bird of augurie. But among the innumerable number of the portentous beasts, fowles, serpents, and other creatures, the tode is the most excellent object, whose ouglie deformitie signifieth sweete and amiable fortune: in respect whereof some superstitious witches preserve todes for their familiars. And some one of good credit (whome I could name) having convented the witches themselves, hath starved diverse of their divels, which they kept in boxes in the likenesse of todes.

Plin. lib. natural. hist. 10. cap. 6.

Arist. in auguriis.

Plutarch Chironæus saith, that the place and site of the signes that we receive by augurie, are speciallie to be noted: for if we receive them on the left side, good lucke; if on the right side, ill lucke insueth: bicause terrene and mortall things are opposite & contrarie to divine and heavenlie things; for that which the gods deliver with the right hand, falleth to our left side; and so contrariwise.

Plutarch doteth by his leave, for all his learning.

CHAPTER XIV.

The division of augurie, persons admittable into the colleges of augurie, of their superstition.

Aug. Niphus de fiauguriis, lib. 1.

THE latter divinors in these mysteries, have divided their soothsaiengs into twelve superstitions: as *Augustinus Niphus* termeth them. The first is prosperitie; the second, ill lucke, as when one goeth out of his house, and seeth an unluckie beast lieng on the right side of his waie; the third is destinie; the fourth is fortune; the fift is ill hap, as when an infortunate beast feedeth on the right side of your waie; the sixt is utilitie; the seventh is hurt; the eight is called a cautell, as when a beast followeth one, and staieth at any side, not passing beyond him, which is a signe of good lucke; the ninth is infelicite, and that is contrarie to the eight, as when the beast passeth before one; the tenth is perfection; the eleventh is imperfection; the twelfe is conclusiin. Thus farre he.

Who were not admittable into the college of augurors among the Romans.

Among the *Romans* none could be received into the college of augurors that had a bile, or had beene bitten with a dog, &c: and at the times of their exercise, even at noone daies, they lighted candels. From whence the papists conveie unto their church, those points of infidelitie. Finallie, their observations were so infinite and ridiculous, that there flew not a sparkle out of the fier, but it betokened somewhat.

CHAPTER XV.

Of the common peoples fond and superstitious collections and observations.

O vaine follie and foolish vanitie!

AMONGST us there be manie women, and effeminat men (marie papists alwaies, as by their superstition may appeere) that make great divinations upon the shedding of salt, wine, &c: and for the observation of daies, and houres use as great withcraft as in anie thing. For if one chance to take a fall from a horsse, either in a slipperie or stumbling waie, he will note the daie and houre, and count that time unluckch for a journie. Otherwise, he that receiveth a mischance, wil consider whether he met not a cat, or a hare, when he went first out of his doores in the morning; or stumbled not at the threshhold at his going out; or put not on his shirt the wrong side outwards; or his left shoo on his right foote, which *Augustus Cæsar* reputed for the woorst lucke that might befall. But above all other nations (as *Martinus de Arles* witnesseth) the *Spaniards* are most superstitious herein; & of *Spaine*, the people of the province of *Lusitania* is the most fond. For one will saie; I had a dreame to night, or a crowe croked upon my house, or an owle flew by me and screeched (which augurie *Lucius Silla* tooke of his death) or a cocke crew contrarie to his houre. Another saith; The moone is at the prime; another, that the sun rose in a cloud and looked pale, or a starre shot and shined in the aire, or a strange cat came into the house, or a hen fell from the top of the house.

Martin. de Arles in tract. de superst. contra maleficta. Appian. de bello civili.

Augurificall toies.

Many will go to bed againe, if they neeze before their shooes be on their feet; some will hold fast their left thombe in their right hand when they hickot; or else will hold their chinne with their right hand whiles a gospell is soong. It is thought verie ill lucke of some, that a child, or anie other living-creature, should passe betweene two friends as they walke together; for they say it portendeth a division of freendship. Among the papists themselves, if any hunters, as they were a hunting, chanced to meet a frier or a preest; they thought it so ill lucke, as they would couple up their hounds, and go home, being in despaire of any further sport that daie. Marrie if they had used venerie with a beggar, they should win all the monie they plaied for that daie at dice. The like follie is to be imputed unto them, that observe (as true or probable) old verses, wherein can be no reasonable cause of such effects; which are brought to passe onlie by Gods power, and at his pleasure. Of this sort be these that follow:

> *Vincenti festo si sol radiet memor esto,*
>
> > Remember on S. Vincents daie,
> > If that the sunne his beames displaie.

Englished by Abraham Fleming.

> *Clara dies Pauli bona tempora denotat anni,*
>
> > If Paule th'apostles daie be cleare,
> > It dooth foreshew a luckie yeare.

By Ab. Fleming.

> *Si sol splendescat Maria purificante,*
> *Major erit glacies post festum quàm fuit ante,*
>
> > If Maries purifieng daie,
> > Be cleare and bright with sunnie raie,
> > Then frost and cold shalbe much more,
> > After the feast than was before.

By Ab. Fleming.

> *Serò rubens cœlum cras indicat esse serenum,*
> *Si manè rubescit, ventus vel pluvia crescit.*
>
> > The skie being red at evening,
> > Foreshewes a faire and cleare morning;
> > But if the morning riseth red,
> > Of wind or raine we shalbe sped.

By Ab. Fleming.

Some sticke a needle or a buckle into a certeine tree, neere to the cathedrall church of S. *Christopher*, or of some other saint; hoping thereby to be delivered that yeare from the headach. Item maids forsooth hang some of their haire before the image of S. *Urbane*, bicause they would have the rest of their haire grow long and be yellow. Item, women with child runne to church, and tie their girdles or shoo latchets about a bell, and strike upon the same thrise, thinking that the sound thereof hasteth their good deliverie. But sithence these things beginne to touch the vanities and superstitions of incantations, I will referre you thither, where you shall see of that stuffe abundance; beginning at the word *Habar*.

Seeke more hereof in the word Habar.

CHAPTER XVI.

How old writers varie about the matter, the manor and the meanes, whereby things augurificall are mooved.

THEOPHRASTUS and *Themistius* affirme, that whatsoever happeneth unto man suddenlie and by chance, commeth from the providence of God. So as *Themistius* gathereth, that men in that respect prophesie, when they speake what commeth in their braine, upon the sudden; though not knowing or understanding what they saie. And that seeing God hath a care for us, it agreeth with reason (as *Theophrastus* saith) that he shew us by some meane whatsoever shall happen. For with *Pythagoras* he concludeth, that all foreshewes and auguries are the voices and words of God, by the which he foretelleth man the good or evill that shall beetide.

Averroes. 12. *metaphysic.*

Trismegistus affirmeth, that all augurificall things are mooved by divels; *Porphyrie* saith by gods, or rather good angels: according to the opinion of *Plotinus* and *Iamblichus*. Some other affirme they are mooved by the moone wandering through the twelve signes of the Zodiake: bicause the moone hath dominion in all sudden matters. The *Aegyptian* astronomers hold, that the moone ordereth not those portentous matters, but *Stella errans*, a wandering starre, &c.

<hr>

Chapter xvii.

How ridiculous an art augurie is, how Cato mocked it, Aristotles reason against it, fond collections of augurors, who allowed, and who disallowed it.

The fond art of augurie convinced.
Acts. 1, 7

VERELIE all these observations being neither grounded on Gods word, nor physicall or philosophicall reason, are vanities, superstitions, lies, and meere witchcraft; as whereby the world hath long time beene, and is still abused and cousened. It is written; *Non est vestrum scire tempora & momenta*, &c: It is not for you to knowe the times and seasons, which the father hath put in his owne power. The most godlie men and the wisest philosophers have given no credit hereunto. S. *Augustine* saith; *Qui his divinationibus credit, sciat se fidem christianam & baptismum prævaricasse, & paganum Deiq; inimicum esse.* One told *Cato*, that a rat had carried awaie and eaten his hose, which the partie said was a woonderfull signe. Naie (said *Cato*) I thinke not so; but if the hose had eaten the rat, that had beene a wonderfull token indeed. When *Nonius* told *Cicero* that they should have good successe in battell, bicause seven eagles were taken in *Pompeies* campe, he answereth thus; No doubt it will be even so, if that we chance to fight with pies. In the like case also he answered *Labienus*, who prophesied like successe by such divinations, saieng, that through the hope of such toies, *Pompeie* lost all his pavillions not long before.

Arist. de somno.

What wiseman would thinke, that God would commit his counsell to a dawe, an owle, a swine, or a tode; or that he would hide his secret purposes in the doong and bowels of beasts? *Aristotle* thus reasoneth; Augurie or divinations are neither the causes nor effects of things to come; *Ergo*, they doo not thereby foretell things trulie, but by chance. As if I dreame that my freend will come to my house, and he commeth indeed: yet neither dreame nor imagination is more the cause of my freends comming, than the chattering of a pie.

August. lib. de doct. chri. 2. cap. 2. Psal. 4, 2.

When *Hanibal* overthrew *Marcus Marcellus*, the beast sacrificed wanted a peece of his hart; therefore forsooth *Marius*, when he sacrificed at Utica, and the beast lacked his liver, he must needs have the like successe. These are their collections, and as vaine, as if they said that the building of *Tenderden* steeple was the cause of *Goodwine sands*, or the decaie of *Sandwich* haven. S. *Augustine* saith, that these observations are most superstitious. But we read in the fourth psalme, a sentence which might dissuade anie christian from this follie and impietie; O ye sonnes of men, how long will you turne my glorie into shame, loving vanitie, and seeking lies? The like is read in manie other places of scripture.

Plin. lib. natural. hist. 28. cap. 2. Tho. Aquin. lib. de sortib.

Of such as allow this follie, I can commend *Plinie* best, who saith, that the operation of these auguries is as we take them. For if we take them in good part, they are signes of good lucke; if we take them in ill part, ill lucke followeth; if we neglect them, and wey them not, they doo neither good nor harme. *Thomas* of *Aquine* reasoneth in this wise; The starres, whose course is certeine, have greater affinitie and communitie with mans actions, than auguries; and yet our dooings are neither directed nor proceed from the starres. Which thing also *Ptolome* witnesseth, saieng; *Sapiens dominabitur astris*, A wiseman overruleth the starres.

CHAPTER XVIII.

Fond distinctions of the heathen writers, concerning augurie.

THE heathen made a distinction betweene divine, naturall, and casuall auguries. Divine auguries were such, as men were made beleeve were done miraculouslie, as when dogs spake; as at the expulsion of *Tarquinius* out of his kingdome; or when trees spake, as before the death of *Cæsar;* or when horsses spake, as did a horsse, whose name was *Zanthus*. Manie learned christians confesse, that such things as may indeed have divine cause, may be called divine auguries; or rather forewarnings of God, and tokens either of his blessings or discontentation: as the starre was a token of a safe passage to the magicians that sought Christ; so was the cockcrowing an augurie to *Peter* for his conversion. And manie such other divinations or auguries (if it be lawfull so to terme them) are in the scriptures to be found.

C. Epidius.
Homer.
Iliad. 19.

CHAPTER XIX.

Of naturall and casuall augurie, the one allowed, and the other disallowed.

NATURALL augurie is a physicall or philosophicall observation; bicause humane and naturall reason may be yeelded for such events: as if one heare the cocke crow manie times together, a man may ghesse that raine will followe shortlie; as by the crieng of rooks, and by their extraordinarie using of their wings in their flight, bicause through a naturall instinct, provoked by the impression of the heavenlie bodies, they are mooved to know the times, according to the disposition of the weather, as it is necessarie for their natures. And therefore *Jeremie* saith; *Milvus in cœlo cognovit tempus suum*. The physician may argue a strength towards in his patient, when he heareth him neeze twise, which is a naturall cause to judge by, and conjecture upon. But sure it is meere casuall, and also verie foolish and incredible, that by two neezings, a man should be sure of good lucke or successe in his businesse; or by meeting of a tode, a man should escape a danger, or atchieve an enterprise, &c.

CHAPTER XX.

A confutation of casuall augurie which is meere witchcraft, and upon what uncertaintie those divinations are grounded.

WHAT imagination worketh in man or woman, many leaves would not comprehend; for as the qualities thereof are strange, and almost incredible, so would the discourse thereof be long and tedious, wherof I had occasion to speake elsewhere. But the power of our imagination extendeth not to beasts, nor reacheth to birds, and therefore perteineth not hereunto. Neither can the chance for the right or left side be good or bad lucke in it selfe. Why should any occurrent or augurie be good? Bicause it commeth out of that part of the heavens, where the good or beneficiall stars are placed? By that reason, all things should be good and happie that live on that side; but we see the contrarie experience, and as commonlie as that.

The like absurditie and error is in them that credit those divinations; bicause the starres, over the ninth house have dominion at the time of augurie. If it should betoken good lucke, joy or gladnesse, to heare a noise in the house, when the moone is in *Aries:* and contrariwise, if it be a signe of ill lucke, sorrowe, or greefe for a beast to come into the house, the moone being in the same signe: here might be found a fowle error and contrarietie. And forsomuch as both may happen at once, the rule must needs be false and ridiculous. And if there were any certeine rules or notes to be gathered in these divinations; the abuse therein is such, as the word of God must needs be verefied therein; to wit, I will destroie the tokens of soothsaiers, and make them that conjecture, fooles.

The vanitie of casual augurie.

Isai. 44, 25.

CHAPTER XXI.

That figure-casters are witches, the uncerteintie of their art, and of their contradictions, Cornelius Agrippas sentence against judiciall astrologie.

THESE casters of figures may bee numbred among the cousening witches, whose practise is above their reach, their purpose to gaine, their knowledge stolne from poets, their art uncerteine & full of vanitie, more plainly derided in the scriptures, than any other follie. And thereupon many other trifling vanities are rooted and grounded; as physiognomie, palmestrie, interpreting of dreames, monsters, auguries, &c: the professors whereof confesse this to be the necessarie key to open the knowledge of all their secrets. For these fellowes erect a figure of the heavens, by the exposition whereof (togither with the conjectures of similitudes and signes) they seeke to find out the meaning of the significators, attributing to them the ends of all things, contrarie to truth, reason, and divinitie: their rules being so inconstant, that few writers agree in the verie principles therof. For the *Rabbins*, the old and new writers, and the verie best philosophers dissent in the cheefe grounds thereof, differing in the proprietie of the houses, whereout they wring the foretelling of things to come, contending even about the number of spheres, being not yet resolved how to erect the beginnings and endes of the houses: for *Ptolomie* maketh them after one sort, *Campanus* after another, &c.

The vaine and trifling trickes of figure-casters.

And as *Alpetragus* thinketh, that there be in the heavens diverse movings as yet to men unknowne, so doo others affirme (not without probabilitie) that there maie be starres and bodies, to whome these movings maie accord, which cannot be seene, either through their exceeding highnes, or that hitherto are not tried with anie observation of the art. The true motion of *Mars* is not yet perceived, neither is it possible to find out the true entring of the sunne into the equinoctiall points. It is not denied, that the astronomers themselves have received their light, and their verie art from poets, without whose fables the twelve signes and the northerlie and southerlie figures had never ascended into heaven. And yet (as *C. Agrippa* saith) astrologers doo live, cousen men, and gaine by these fables; whiles the poets, which are the inventors of them, doo live in beggerie.

Johan. Montiregius in epistola ad Blanchimē: & Gulielmus de sancto Clodoald. Rabbi Levi. C. Agrip. in lib. de vanit. scient. Archelaus. Cassander. Eudoxus, &c.

The verie skilfullest mathematicians confesse, that it is unpossible to find out anie certeine thing concerning the knowledge of judgements, as well for the innumerable causes which worke togither with the heavens, being all togither, and one with the other to be considered: as also bicause influencies doo not constraine but incline. For manie ordinarie and extraordinarie occasions doo interrupt them; as education, custome, place, honestie, birth, bloud, sicknesse, health, strength, weakenes, meate, drinke, libertie of mind, learning, &c. And they that have written the rules of judgement, and agree neerest therein, being of equall authoritie and learning, publish so contrarie opinions upon one thing, that it is unpossible for an astrologian to pronounce a certeintie upon so variable opinions; & otherwise, upon so uncerteine reports no man is able to judge herein. So as (according to *Ptolomie*) the foreknowledge of things to come by the starres, dependeth as well upon the affections of the mind, as upon the observation of the planets, proceeding rather from chance than art, as whereby they deceive others, and are deceived themselves also.

CHAPTER XXII.

The subtiltie of astrologers to mainteine the credit of their art, why they remaine in credit,
certeine impieties conteined in astrologers assertions.

IF you marke the cunning ones, you shall see them speake darkelie of things to come, devising by artificiall subtiltie, doubtfull prognostications, easilie to be applied to everie thing, time, prince, and nation: and if anie thing come to passe according to their divinations, they fortifie their old prognostications with new reasons. Nevertheles, in the multitude and varietie of starres, yea even in the verie middest of them, they find out some places in a good aspect, and some in an ill; and take occasion hereupon to saie what they list, promising unto some men honor, long life, wealth, victorie, children, marriage, freends, offices; & finallie everlasting felicitie. But if with anie they be discontent, they saie the starres be not favourable to them, and threaten them with hanging, drowning, beggerie, sickenes, misfortune, &c. And if one of these prognostications fall out right, then they triumph above measure. If the prognosticators be found to forge and lie alwaies (without such fortune as the blind man had in killing the crow) they will excuse the matter, saieng, that *Sapiens dominatur astris*, wheras (according to *Agrippas* words) neither the wiseman ruleth the starres, nor the starres the wiseman, but God ruleth them both. *Corn. Tacitus* saith, that they are a people disloiall to princes, deceiving them that beleeve them. And *Varro* saith, that the vanitie of all superstitions floweth out of the bosome of astrologie. And if our life & fortune depend not on the starres, then it is to be granted, that the astrologers seeke where nothing is to be found. But we are so fond, mistrustfull & credulous, that we feare more the fables of Robin good fellow; astrologers, & witches, & beleeve more the things that are not, than the things that are. And the more unpossible a thing is, the more we stand in feare thereof; and the lesse likelie to be true, the more we beleeve it. And if we were not such, I thinke with *Cornelius Agrippa*, that these divinors, astrologers, conjurors, and cousenors would die for hunger.

And our foolish light beleefe, forgetting things past, neglecting things present, and verie hastie to know things to come, doth so comfort and mainteine these cousenors; that whereas in other men, for making one lie, the faith of him that speaketh is so much mistrusted, that all the residue being true is not regarded. Contrariwise, in these cousenages among our divinors, one truth spoken by hap giveth such credit to all their lies, that ever after we beleeve whatsoever they saie; how incredible, impossible or false soever it be. Sir *Thomas Moore* saith, they know not who are in their owne chambers, neither who maketh themselves cuckoldes that take upon them all this cunning, knowledge, and great foresight. But to enlarge their credit, or rather to manifest their impudencie, they saie the gift of prophesie, the force of religion, the secrets of conscience, the power of divels, the vertue of miracles, the efficacie of praiers, the state of the life to come, &c: doth onlie depend upon the starres, and is given and knowne by them alone. For they saie, that when the signe of *Gemini* is ascended, and

Astrologers prognostications are like the answers of oracles.

S. Thomas Moores frumpe at judiciall astrologers.

Saturne and *Mercurie* be joined in *Aquarie*, in the ninth house of the heavens, there is a prophet borne : and therefore that Christ had so manie vertues, bicause he had in that place *Saturne* and *Gemini*. Yea these Astrologers doo not sticke to saie, that the starres distribute all sortes of religions : wherein *Jupiter* is the especiall patrone, who being joined with *Saturne*, maketh the religion of the Jewes; with *Mercurie*, of the Christians; with the Moone, of Antichristianitie. Yea they affirme that the faith of everie man maie be knowne to them as well as to God. And that Christe himselfe did use the election of houres in his miracles; so as the Jewes could not hurt him whilest he went to *Jerusalem*, and therefore

that he said to his disciples that forbad him to go; Are there not twelve houres in the daie?

CHAPTER XXIII.

Who have power to drive awaie divels with their onelie presence, who shall receive of God
whatsoever they aske in praier, who shall obteine everlasting life by meanes of constella-
tions, as nativitie-casters affirme.

THEY saie also, that he which hath *Mars* happilie placed in the ninth house of the heavens, shall have power to drive awaie divels with his onelie presence from them that be possessed. And he that shall praie to God, when he findeth the Moone and *Jupiter* joined with the dragons head in the middest of the heavens, shall obteine whatsoever he asketh : and that *Jupiter* and *Saturne* doo give blessednes of the life to come. But if anie in his nativitie shall have *Saturne* happilie placed in *Leone*, his soule shall have everlasting life. And

hereunto subscribe *Peter de Appona*, *Roger Bacon*, *Guido Bonatus*, *Arnold de villa nova*, and the Cardinall of *Alia*. Furthermore, the providence of God is denied, and the miracles of Christ are diminished, when these powers of the heavens and their influencies are in such sort advanced. *Moses*, *Esaie*, *Job* and *Jeremie*, seeme to dislike and reject it : and at *Rome* in times past it was banished, and by *Justinian* condemmed under paine of death. Finallie, *Seneca* derideth these

soothsaieng witches in this sort; Amongst the *Cleones* (saith he) there was a custome, that the χαλαζοφύλακες (which were gazers in the aier, watching when a storme of hail should fall) when they sawe by anie cloud that the shower was imminent and at hand; the use was (I saie) bicause of the hurt which it might doo to their vines, &c : diligentlie to warne the people thereof; who used not to provide clokes or anie such defense against it, but provided sacri-fices; the rich, cockes and white lambes; the poore would spoile themselves by cutting their thombes; as though (saith he) that little bloud could ascend up to the cloudes, and doo anie good there for their releefe in this matter.

And here by the waie, I will impart unto you a *Venetian* superstition, of great antiquitie, and at this daie (for ought I can read to the contrarie) in use. It is written, that everie yeere ordinarilie upon ascension daie, the Duke of *Venice*, accompanied with the States, goeth with great solemnitie unto the sea, and after certeine ceremonies ended, casteth thereinto a gold ring of great value and estimation for a pacificatorie oblation : wherewithall their predecessors supposed that the wrath of the sea was asswaged. By this action, as a late writer saith,

Joannes Gar-
ropius in
Venet. &
Hyperb.
Zach. 10. 1.
verse 2.

they doo *Desponsare sibi mare*, that is, espouse the sea unto themselves, &c.
Let us therefore, according to the prophets advise, aske raine of the Lord in the houres of the latter time, and he shall send white cloudes, and give us raine &c : for surelie, the idols (as the same prophet saith) have spoken vanitie, the soothsaiers have seene a lie, and the dreamers have told a vaine thing. They comfort in vaine, and therefore they went awaie like sheepe, &c. If anie sheepe-biter or witchmonger will follow them, they shall go alone for me.

BOOKE XII.

CHAPTER I.

*The Hebrue word Habar expounded, where also the supposed secret force of charmes and
inchantments is shewed, and the efficacie of words is diverse waies declared.*

THIS Hebrue word *Habar*, being in Greeke *Epathin*, and in Latine *Incantare*, is in English, To inchant, or (if you had rather have it so) to bewitch.
In these inchantments, certeine wordes, verses, or charmes, &c: are
secretlie uttered, wherein there is thought to be miraculous efficacie. There is
great varietie hereof: but whether it be by charmes, voices, images, characters,
stones, plants, metals, herbes, &c: there must herewithall a speciall forme of
words be alwaies used, either divine, diabolicall, insensible, or papisticall,
whereupon all the vertue of the worke is supposed to depend. This word is
speciallie used in the 58. psalme, which place though it be taken up for mine   *Psal. 58.*
adversaries strongest argument against me; yet me thinkes it maketh so with
me, as they can never be able to answer it. For there it plainelie appeareth,   *Psal. 58. 4. 5.*
that the adder heareth not the voice of the charmer, charme he never so cunninglie: contrarie to the poets fabling,

> *Frigidus in pratis contando rumpitur anguis.*   *Virgil. in*
> *Damone.*
>> *The coldish snake in medowes greene,*   *By Ab.*
>> *With charmes is burst in peeces cleene,*   *Fleming.*

But hereof more shall be said hereafter in due place.
I grant that words sometimes have singular vertue and efficacie, either in
persuasion or disuasion, as also diverse other waies; so as thereby some are
converted from the waie of perdition, to the estate of salvation: and so con-   *Prover. 18.*
trariwise, according to the saieng of *Solomon*; Death and life are in the instru-   *Chron. 30.*
ment of the toong: but even therein God worketh all in all, as well in framing   *Psal. 10.*
the heart of the one, as in directing the toong of the other: as appeareth in   *Psal. 51.*
manie places of the holie scriptures.   *Psal. 139.*
Jerem. 32.
Isai. 6.
Isai. 50.
Exod. 7, 8. 9.
Prov. 16.

CHAPTER II.

*What is forbidden in scriptures concerning witchcraft, of the operation of words, the superstition of the Cabalists and papists, who createth substances, to imitate God in some
cases is presumption, words of sanctification.*

THAT which is forbidden in the scriptures touching inchantment or
witch craft, is not the wonderfull working with words. For where words
have had miraculous operation, there hath beene alwaies the speciall providence, power and grace of God uttered to the strengthening of the faith of
Gods people, and to the furtherance of the gospell: as when the apostle with a   *Acts. 5.*
word slue *Ananias* and *Saphira*. But the prophanation of Gods name, the seducing, abusing, and cousening of the people, and mans presumption is hereby

prohibited, as whereby manie take upon them after the recitall of such names, as God in the scripture seemeth to appropriate to himselfe, to foreshew things to come, to worke miracles, to detect fellonies, &c: as the Cabalists in times past tooke upon them, by the ten names of God, and his angels, expressed in the scriptures, to worke woonders: and as the papists at this daie by the like names, by crosses, by gospels hanged about their necks, by masses, by exorcismes, by holie water, and a thousand consecrated or rather execrated things, promise unto themselves and others, both health of bodie and soule.

Jonas. 1.

But as herein we are not to imitate the papists, so in such things, as are the peculiar actions of God, we ought not to take upon us to conterfet, or resemble him, which with his word created all things. For we, neither all the conjurors, Cabalists, papists, soothsaiers, inchanters, witches, nor charmers in the world, neither anie other humane or yet diabolicall cunning can adde anie such strength to Gods workmanship, as to make anie thing anew, or else to exchange one thing into another. New qualities may be added by humane art, but no new substance can be made or created by man. And seeing that art faileth herein, doubtles neither the illusions of divels, nor the cunning of witches, can bring anie such thing truelie to passe. For by the sound of the words nothing commeth, nothing goeth, otherwise than God in nature hath ordeined to be doone by ordinarie speech, or else by his speciall ordinance. Indeed words of sanctification are necessarie and commendable, according to S. *Paules* rule; Let your meat be sanctified with the word of God, and by praier. But sanctification dooth not here signifie either change of substance of the meate, or the adding of anie new strength thereunto; but it is sanctified, in that it is received with thanksgiving and praier; that our bodies may be refreshed, and our soule thereby made the apter to glorifie God.

Words of sanctification, and wherein they consist.

CHAPTER III.

What effect and offense witches charmes bring, how unapt witches are, and how unlikelie to worke those things which they are thought to doo, what would followe if those things were true which are laid to their charge.

THE words and other the illusions of witches, charmers, and conjurors, though they be not such in operation and effect, as they are commonlie taken to be: yet they are offensive to the majestie and name of God, obscuring the truth of divinitie, & also of philosophie. For if God onlie give life & being to all creatures, who can put any such vertue or livelie feeling into a body of gold, silver, bread, or wax, as is imagined? If either preests, divels, or witches could so doo, the divine power shuld be checked & outfaced by magicall cunning, & Gods creatures made servile to a witches pleasure. What is not to be brought to passe by these incantations, if that be true which is attributed to witches? & yet they are women that never went to schoole in their lives, nor had any teachers: and therefore without art or learning; poore, and therefore not able to make any provision of metal or stones, &c: whereby to bring to passe strange matters, by naturall magicke; old and stiffe, and therefore not nimble handed to deceive your eie with legierdemaine; heavie, and commonlie lame, and therefore unapt to flie in the aire, or to danse with the fairies; sad, melancholike, sullen, and miserable, and therefore it should be unto them (*Invita Minerva*) to banket or danse with *Minerva;* or yet with *Herodias,* as the common opinion of all writers heerein is. On the other side, we see they are so malicious and spitefull, that if they by themselves, or by their divels, could trouble the elements, we should never have faire weather. If they could kill men, children, or cattell, they would spare none; but would destroy and kill

An ample description of women commonlie called witches.

124

whole countries and housholds. If they could transfer corne (as is affirmed) from their neighbors field into their owne, none of them would be poore, none other should be rich. If they could transforme themselves and others (as it is most constantlie affirmed) oh what a number of apes and owles should there be of us! If *Incubus* could beget *Merlins* among us, we should have a jollie manie of cold prophets.

Chapter iv.

Why God forbad the practise of witchcraft, the absurditie of the lawe of the twelve tables, whereupon their estimation in miraculous actions is grounded, of their woonderous works.

THOUGH it be apparent, that the Holie-ghost forbiddeth this art, bicause of the abuse of the name of God, and the cousenage comprehended therein: yet I confesse, the customes and lawes almost of all nations doo declare, that all these miraculous works, before by me cited, and many other things more woonderfull, were attributed to the power of witches. The which lawes, with the executions and judicials thereupon, and the witches confessions, have beguiled almost the whole world. What absurdities concerning witchcraft, are written in the law of the twelve tables, which was the highest and most ancient law of the *Romans?* Whereupon the strongest argument of witches omnipotent power is framed; as that the wisedome of such lawgivers could not be abused. Whereof (me thinks) might be made a more strong argument on our side; to wit, If the cheefe and principall lawes of the world be in this case ridiculous, vaine, false, incredible, yea and contrarie to Gods lawe; the residue of the lawes and arguments to that effect, are to be suspected. If that argument should hold, it might proove all the popish lawes against protestants, & the heathenish princes lawes against christians, to be good and in force: for it is like they would not have made them, except they had beene good. Were it not (thinke you) a strange proclamation, that no man (upon paine of death) should pull the moone out of heaven? And yet verie many of the most learned witchmongers make their arguments upon weaker grounds; as namelie in this forme and maner; We find in poets, that witches wrought such and such miracles; *Ergo* they can accomplish and doo this or that wonder. The words of the lawe are these; *Qui fruges incantasset pœnas dato, Néve alienam segetem pellexeris excantando, néq; incantando, Ne agrum defruganto:* the sense wherof in English is this; Let him be executed that bewitcheth corne, Transferre not other mens corne into thy ground by inchantment, Take heede thou inchant not at all neither make thy neighbors field barren: he that dooth these things shall die, &c.

A common and universall error.

J. Bodinus.
Danæus.
Hyperius.
Heming.
Bar. Spineus.
Mal. Malef.
Spinæus.

Chapter v.

An instance of one arreigned upon the lawe of the twelve tables, whereby the said lawe is proved ridiculous, of two witches that could doo woonders.

ALTHOUGH among us, we thinke them bewitched that wax suddenlie poore, and not them that growe hastilie rich; yet at *Rome* you shall understand, that (as *Plinie* reporteth) upon these articles one *C. Furius Cressus* was convented before *Spurius Albinus;* for that he being but a little while free, and delivered from bondage, occupieng onelie tillage; grew rich on the sudden, as

A notable purgation of C. F. C. convented for a witch.

having good crops: so as it was suspected that he transferred his neighbors corne into his fields. None intercession, no delaie, none excuse, no deniall would serve, neither in jest nor derision, nor yet through sober or honest meanes; but he was assigned a peremptorie daie, to answer for life. And therefore fearing the sentence of condemnation, which was to be given there, by the voice and verdict of three men (as we heere are tried by twelve) made his appearance at the daie assigned, and brought with him his ploughs and harrowes, spades and shovels, and other instruments of husbandrie, his oxen, horsses, and working bullocks, his servants, and also his daughter, which was a sturdie wench and a good huswife, and also (as *Piso* reporteth) well trimmed up in apparell, and said to the whole bench in this wise; Lo heere my lords I make mine appearance, according to my promise and your pleasures, presenting unto you my charmes and witchcrafts, which have so inriched me. As for the labour, sweat, watching, care, and diligence, which I have used in this behalfe, I cannot shew you them at this time. And by this meanes he was dismissed by the consent of that court, who otherwise (as it was thought) should hardly have escaped the sentence of condemnation, and punishment of death.

Mal. malef.
par. 2, quæ. 1.
cap. 5. It is constantlie affirmed in *M. Mal.* that *Stafus* used alwaies to hide himselfe in a monshoall, and had a disciple called *Hoppo*, who made *Stadlin* a maister witch, and could all when they list invisiblie transferre the third part of their neighbours doong, hay, corne, &c: into theire owne ground, make haile, tempests, and flouds, with thunder and lightning; and kill children, cattell, &c: reveale things hidden, and many other tricks, when and where they list. But these two shifted not so well with the inquisitors, as the other with the *Romane* and heathen judges. Howbeit, *Stafus* was too hard for them all: for none of all the lawiers nor inquisitors could bring him to appeere before them, if it be true that witchmongers write in these matters.

CHAPTER VI.

Lawes provided for the punishment of such witches as worke miracles, whereof some are mentioned, and of certeine popish lawes published against them.

Punishmēt
of impossi-
bilities. THERE are other lawes of other nations made to this incredible effect: as *Lex Salicarum* provideth punishment for them that flie in the aire from place to place, and meete at their nightlie assemblies, and brave bankets, carrieng with them plate, and such stuffe, &c: even as we should make a lawe to hang him that should take a church in his hand at *Dover*, and throwe it to *Callice*. And bicause in this case also popish lawes shall be seene to be as foolish and lewd as any other whatsoever, and speciallie as tyrannous as that which is most cruell: you shall heare what trim new lawes the church of *Rome* hath latelie devised. These are therefore the words of pope *Innocent* the eight to the inquisitors of *Almanie*, and of pope *Julius* the second, sent to the inquisitors of *Bergomen*. A wise lawe
of pope In-
nocent and
Julie, were
it not that
they wan-
ted wit
when they
made it. It is come to our eares, that manie lewd persons, of both kinds, as well male as female, using the companie of the divels *Incubus* and *Succubus*, with incantations, charmes, conjurations, &c: doo destroie, &c: the births of women with child, the yoong of all cattell, the corne of the feeld, the grapes of the vines, the frute of the trees: Item, men, women, and all kind of cattell and beats of the feeld: and with their said inchantments, &c: doo utterlie extinguish, suffocate, and spoile all vineyards, ortchards, medowes, pastures, grasse, greene corne, and ripe corne, and all other podware: yea men and women themselves are by their imprecations so afflicted with externall and inward paines and diseases, that men cannot beeget, nor women bring foorth anie children, nor yet accomplish the dutie of wedlocke, denieng the faith which they in baptisme professed, to the

destruction of their owne soules, *&c.* Our pleasure therefore is, that all impediments that maie hinder the inquisitors office, be utterlie removed from among
the people, least this blot of heresie proceed to poison and defile them that be
yet innocent. And therefore we doo ordeine, by vertue of the apostolicall
authoritie, that our inquisitors of high *Almanie*, maie execute the office of inquisition by all tortures and afflictions, in all places, and upon all persons, what and
wheresoever, as well in everie place and diocesse, as upon anie person; and that
as freelie, as though they were named, expressed, or cited in this our commission.

CHAPTER VII.

*Poetical authorities commonlie alleaged by witchmongers, for the proofe of witches miracu-
lous actions, and for confirmation of their supernaturall power.*

HERE have I place and oportunitie, to discover the whole art of witchcraft; even all their charmes, periapts, characters, amulets, praiers, blessings, curssings, hurtings, helpings, knaveries, cousenages, *&c.* But first I
will shew what authorities are produced to defend and mainteine the same, and
that in serious sort, by *Bodin, Spinæus, Hemingius, Vairus, Danæus, Hyperius: M.
Mal.* and the rest.

> *Carmina vel cœlo possunt deducere lunam,*
> *Carminibus Circe socios mutavit Ulyssis,*
> *Frigidus in pratis cantando rumpitur anguis:*   *Virg. eclog. 8.*

>> *Inchantments plucke out of the skie,*
>> *The moone, though she be plaste on hie:*
>> *Dame Circes with hir charmes so fine,*
>> *Ulysses mates did turne to swine:*
>> *The snake with charmes is burst in twaine,*
>> *In medowes, where she dooth remaine.*

Againe out of the same poet they cite further matter.

> *Has herbas, atq; hæc Ponto mihi lecta venena,*   *Virg. eclog. 8.*
> *Ipsa dedit Mæris: nascuntur plurima Ponto.*
> *His ego sæpè lupam fieri, & se condere sylvis,*
> *Mærim sæepe animas imis exire sepulchris,*
> *Atq; satas aliò vidi traducere messes.*

>> *These herbs did Meris give to me,*
>> *And poisons pluckt at Pontus,*
>> *For there they growe and multiplie,*
>> *And doo not so amongst us.*
>> *With these she made hir selfe become,*
>> *A wolfe, and hid hir in the wood,*
>> *She fetcht up soules out of their toome,*
>> *Remooving corne from where it stood.*

Furthermore out of Ovid they alledge these folowing.

> *Nocte volant, puerósq; petunt nutricis egentes,*   *Ovid. fast. 6.*
> *Et vitiant cunis corpora capta suis:*
> *Carpere dicuntur lactentia viscera rostris,*
> *Et plenumpotu sanguine gutur habent:*

>> *To children they doo flie by night,*
>> *And catch them while their nursses sleepe,*
>> *And spoile their little bodies quite,*
>> *And home they beare them in their beake.*

Againe out of Virgill in forme following.

Virg. Aene. 4.

Hinc mihi Massylæ gentis monstrata sacerdos,
Hesperidum templi custos, epulásq; draconi
Quæ dabat, & sacros servabat in arbore ramos,
Spargens humida mella, soporiferúmq; papaver.
Hæc se carminibus promittit solvere mentes,
Quas velit, ast aliis dur as immittere curas,
Sistere aquam fluviis, & vertere sidera retrò,
Nocturnósq; ciet manes, mugire videbis
Sub pedibus terram, & descendere montibus ornos:

Tho. Phaiers
translation of
the former
words of
Virg.

From thence a virgine preest is come,
　　from out Massyla land,
Sometimes the temple there she kept,
　　and from hir heavenlie hand
The dragon meate did take: she kept
　　also the frute divine,
With herbes and liquors sweete that still
　　to sleepe did men incline.
The minds of men (she saith) from love
　　with charmes she can unbind,
In whom she list: but others can
　　she cast to cares unkind.
The running streames doo stand, and from
　　their course the starres doo wreath,
And soules she conjure can: thou shalt
　　see sister underneath
The ground with roring gape, and trees
　　and mountaines turne upright, &c.

Ovid. meta-
mor. 7.

Moreover out of Ovid they alledge as followeth.

Cùm volui ripis ipsis mirantibus amnes
Infontes rediere suos, concússaq; sisto,
Stantia concutio, cantu freta nubila pello,
Nubiláq; induco, ventos abigóq; vocóq;,
Vipereas rumpo verbis & carmine fauces,
Viváque saxa, sua convulsáque robora terra,
Et sylvas moveo, jubeóque tremescere montes,
Et mugire solum, manésque exire sepulchris,
Téque luna traho, &c:

The rivers I can make retire,
Into the fountaines whence they flo,
(Whereat the banks themselves admire)
I can make standing waters go,
With charmes I drive both sea and clowd,
I make it calme and blowe alowd.
The vipers jawes, the rockie stone,
With words and charmes I breake in twaine
The force of earth congeald in one,
I moove and shake both woods and plaine;
I make the soules of men arise,
I pull the moone out of the skies.

Also out of the same poet.

Ovid. de
Media.

Virbáque ter dixit placidos facientia somnos,
Quæ mare turbatum, quæ flumina concita sistant:

And thrise she spake the words that causd
Sweete sleepe and quiet rest,
She staid the raging of the sea,
And mightie flouds supprest.

Et miserum tenues in jecur urget acus,

Ovid. de
Medea.
epistola, 4.

She sticketh also needels fine
In livers, whereby men doo pine.

Also out of other poets.

3. Amor.
Eclog. 6.

Carmine læsa Ceres, sterilem vanescit in herbam,
Deficiunt læsi carmine fontis aquæ,
Illicibus glandes, cantatáque vitibus uva
Decidit, & nullo poma movente fluunt:

With charmes the corne is spoiled so,
As that it vades to barren gras,
With charmes the springs are dried lowe,
That none can see where water was,
The grapes from vines, the mast from okes,
And beats downe frute with charming strokes

Quæ sidera excantata voce Thessala
Lunámque cœlo diripit:

Horac.
epod. 5.

She plucks downe moone and starres from skie,
With chaunting voice of Thessalie.

Hanc ego de cœlo ducentem sidera vidi,
Fluminis ac rapidi carmine vertit iter,
Hæc cantu findítque solum, manésque sepulchris
Elicit, & tepido devorat ossa rogo:
Cùm lubet hæc tristi depellit lumina cœlo,
Cùm lubet æstivo convocat orbe nives:

Tibul. de
fascinatrice,
lib. 1. Eleg. 2.

She plucks each star out of his throne,
And turneth backe the raging waves,
With charmes she makes the earth to cone,
And raiseth soules out of their graves:
She burnes mens bones as with a fire,
And pulleth downe the lights from heaven,
And makes it snowe at hir desire
Even in the midst of summer season.

Mens hausti nulla sanie polluta veneni,
Incantata perit:

Lucan. lib. de
bello civili. 6.

A man inchanted runneth mad,
That never anie poison had.

Cessavere vices rerum, dilatáque longa
Hæsit nocte dies, legi non paruit æther,
Torpuit & præceps audito carmine mundus:

Idem. Ibid.

The course of nature ceased quite,
The aire obeied not his lawe,
The daie delaid by length of night,
Which made both daie and night to yawe;
And all was through that charming geare,
Which causd the world to quake for feare.

Idem. Ibid.

Carmine Thessalidum dura in præcordia fluxit,
Non fatis adductus amor, flammísque severi
Illicitis arsere ignes:

> With Thessall charmes, and not by fate
> Hot love is forced for to flowe,
> Even where before hath beene debate,
> They cause affection for to growe.

Idem. Ibid.

Gens invisa diis maculandi callida cœli,
Quos genuit terra, mali qui sidera mundi
Juráque fixarum possunt pervertere rerum:
Nam nunc stare polos, & flumina mittere norunt,
Aethera sub terras adigunt, montésque revellunt:

> These witches hatefull unto God,
> And cunning to defile the aire,
> Which can disorder with a nod
> The course of nature everie where,
> Doo cause the wandring starres to staie
> And drive the winds beelow the ground,
> They send the streames another waie,
> And throwe downe hilles where they abound.

C. Manilius
astronom.
suæ. lib. 1.

——————linguis dixere volucrum,
Consultare fibras, & rumpere vocibus angues,
Solicitare umbras, ipsúmque Acheronta movere,
In noctémque dies, in lucem vertere noctes,
Omnia conando docilis solertia vincit:

> They talked with the toongs of birds,
> Consulting with the salt sea coasts,
> They burst the snakes with witching words,
> Solliciting the spirituall ghosts,
> They turne the night into the daie,
> And also drive the light awaie:
> And what ist that cannot be made
> By them that doo applie this trade?

CHAPTER VIII.

Poetrie and poperie compared in inchantments, popish witchmongers have more advantage herein than protestants.

YOU see in these verses, the poets (whether in earnest or in jest I know not) ascribe unto witches & to their charmes, more than is to be found in humane or diabolicall power. I doubt not but the most part of the readers hereof will admit them to be fabulous; although the most learned of mine adversaries (for lacke of scripture) are faine to produce these poetries for proofes, and for lacke of judgement I am sure doo thinke, that *Actæons* transformation was true. And why not? As well as the metamorphosis or transubstantiation of *Ulysses* his companions into swine: which S. *Augustine*, and so manie great clarkes credit and report.

Ovid. Meta-
morph. lib. 3.
fab. 2.
Ovid. Meta-
morph. 14.
fab. 5, 6.

Neverthelesse, popish writers (I confesse) have advantage herein of our protestants: for (besides these poeticall proofes) they have (for advantage) the word and authoritie of the pope himselfe, and others of that holie crue; whose charmes, conjurations, blessings, curssings, &c: I meane in part (for a tast) to set downe; giving you to understand, that poets are not altogither so impudent as papists herein, neither seeme they so ignorant, prophane, or impious. And therefore I will shew you how lowd also they lie, and what they on the other side ascribe to their charmes and conjurations; and togither will set downe with them all maner of witches charmes, as convenientlie as I maie.

The authors transition to his purposed scope.

CHAPTER IX

Popish periapts, amulets and charmes, agnus Dei, a wastcote of proofe, a charme for the falling evill, a writing brought to S. Leo from heaven by an angell, the vertues of S. Saviors epistle, a charme against theeves, a writing found in Christs wounds, of the crosse, &c.

THESE vertues under these verses (written by pope *Urbane* the fift to the emperour of the *Græcians*) are conteined in a periapt or tablet, to be continuallie worne about one, called *Agnus Dei*, which is a little cake, having the picture of a lambe carrieng of a flag on the one side; and Christs head on the other side, and is hollow: so as the gospell of S. *John*, written in fine paper, is placed in the concavitie thereof: and it is thus compounded or made, even as they themselves report.

> *Balsamus & munda cera, cum chrismatis unda*
> *Conficiunt agnum, quod munus do tibi magnum,*
> *Fonte velut natum, per mystica sanctificatum:*
> *Fulgura desursum depellit, & omne malignum,*
> *Peccatum frangit, ut Christi sanguis, & angit,*
> *Prægnans servatur, simul & partus liberatur,*
> *Dona refert dignis, virtutem destruit ignis,*
> *Portatus mundè de fluctibus eripit undæ:*

> > *Balme, virgine wax, and holie water,*
> > *an Agnus Dei make:*
> > *A gift than which none can be greater,*
> > *I send thee for to take.*
> > *From founteine cleere the same hath issue,*
> > *in secret sanctifide:*
> > *Gainst lightning it hath soveraigne vertue,*
> > *and thunder crackes beside.*
> > *Ech hainous sinne it weares and wasteth,*
> > *even as Christs precious blood,*
> > *And women, whiles their travell lasteth,*
> > *it saves, it is so good.*
> > *It doth bestow great gifts and graces,*
> > *on such as well deserve:*
> > *And borne about in noisome places,*
> > *from perill doth preserve.*
> > *The force of fire, whose heat destroieth,*
> > *it breaks and bringeth downe:*
> > *And he or she that this enjoieth,*
> > *no water shall them drowne.*

Englished by Abraham Fleming. Looke in the Beehive of the Romish church. Lib. 4. cap. 1. fol. 243.

¶ *A charme against shot, or a wastcote of proofe.*

Before the comming up of these *Agnus Deis*, a holie garment called a wastcote for necessitie was much used of our forefathers, as a holy relike, &c: as given by

131

the pope, or some such archconjuror, who promised thereby all manner of immunitie to the wearer thereof; in somuch as he could not be hurt with anie shot or other violence. And otherwise, that woman that would weare it, should have quicke deliverance: the composition thereof was in this order following.

The maner of making a waste-cote of proofe.

On Christmas daie at night, a threed must be sponne of flax, by a little virgine girle, in the name of the divell: and it must be by hir woven, and also wrought with the needle. In the brest or forepart thereof must be made with needle worke two heads; on the head at the right side must be a hat, and a long beard; the left head must have on a crowne, and it must be so horrible, that it maie resemble Belzebub, and on each side of the wastcote must de made a crosse.

¶ *Against the falling evill.*

Moreover, this insuing is another counterfet charme of theirs, whereby the falling evill is presentlie remedied.

Gaspar fert myrrham, thus Melchior, Balthasar aurum,
Hæc tria qui secum portabit nomina regum,
Solvitur à morbo Christi pietate caduco.

Gasper with his myrh beganne
    these presents to unfold,
Then Melchior brought in frankincense,
    and Balthasar brought in gold.
Now he that of these holie kings
    the names about shall beare,
The falling yll by grace of Christ
    shall never need to feare.

These effects are too good to be true in such a patched peece of poperie.

This is as true a copie of the holie writing, that was brought downe from heaven by an angell to S. *Leo* pope of *Rome; &* he did bid him take it to king *Charles*, when he went to the battell at *Roncevall*. And the angell said, that what man or woman beareth this writing about them with good devotion, and saith everie daie three *Pater nosters*, three *Aves*, and one *Creede*, shall not that daie be overcome of his enimies, either bodilie or ghostlie; neither shalbe robbed or slaine of theeves, pestilence, thunder, or lightening; neither shall be hurt with fier or water, nor combred with spirits, neither shall have displeasure of lords or ladies: he shall not be condemned with false witnesse, nor taken with fairies, or anie maner of axes, nor yet with the falling evill. Also, if a woman be in travell, laie this writing upō hir bellie, she shall have easie deliverance, and the child right shape and christendome, and the mother purification of holy church, and all through vertue of these holie names of Jesus Christ following:

✠ *Jesus* ✠ *Christus* ✠ *Messias* ✠ *Soter* ✠ *Emmanuel* ✠ *Sabbaoth* ✠ *Adonai* ✠ *Unigenitus* ✠ *Majestas* ✠ *Paracletus* ✠ *Salvator noster* ✠ *Agiros iskiros* ✠ *Agios* ✠ *Adanatos* ✠ *Gasper* ✠ *Melchior* ✠ *& Balthasar* ✠ *Matthæus* ✠ *Marcus* ✠ *Lucas* ✠ *Johannes.*

The epistle of S. *Savior*, which pope *Leo* went to king *Charles*, saieng, that whosoever carrieth the same about him, or in what daie so ever he shall read it, or shall see it, he shall not be killed with anie iron toole, nor be burned with fier, nor be drowned with water, neither anie evill man or other creature maie hurt him. The crosse of Christ is a woonderfull defense ✠ the crosse of Christ be alwaies with me ✠ the crosse is it which I doo alwaies worship ✠ the crosse of Christ is true health ✠ the crosse of Christ dooth lose the bands of death ✠ the crosse of Christ is the truth and the waie ✠ I take my journie upon the crosse of the Lord ✠ the crosse of Christ beateth downe everie evill ✠ the crosse of Christ giveth all good things ✠ the crosse of Christ taketh awaie paines everlasting ✠ the crosse of Christ save me ✠ O crosse of Christ be upon me, before me, and behind me ✠ bicause the ancient enimie cannot abide the sight of thee ✠ the crosse of Christ save me, keepe me, governe me, and direct me ✠ Thomas bearing this note of thy divine majestie ✠ Alpha ✠ Omega ✠ first ✠ and last ✠ middest ✠ and end ✠ beginning ✠ and first begotten ✠ wisedome ✠ vertue ✠.

¶ *A popish periapt or charme, which must never be said, but carried about one, against theeves.*

I doo go, and I doo come unto you with the love of God, with the humilitie of Christ, with the holines of our blessed ladie, with the faith of *Abraham*, with the justice of *Isaac*, with the vertue of *David*, with the might of *Peter*, with the constancie of *Paule*, with the word of God, with the authoritie of *Gregorie*, with the praier of *Clement*, with the floud of *Jordan*, *-p -p p c g e g a q q est p t 1 ka b g l k 2 a x t g t b am g 2 4 2 1 q; p x c g k q a 9 9 p o q q r*. Oh onelie Father ✠ oh onlie lord ✠ And Jesus ✠ passing through the middest of them ✠ went ✠ In the name of the Father ✠ and of the Sonne ✠ and of the Holie-ghost ✠.

¶ *Another amulet.*

Joseph of *Arimathea* did find this writing upon the wounds of the side of Jesus Christ, written with Gods finger, when the bodie was taken away frō the crosse. Whosoever shall carrie this writing about him, shall not die anie evill death, if he beleeve in Christ, and in all perplexities he shall soone be delivered, neither let him feare any danger at all. *Fons* ✠ *alpha & omega* ✠ *figa* ✠ *figalis* ✠ *Sabbaoth* ✠ *Emmanuel* ✠ *Adonai* ✠ *o* ✠ *Neray* ✠ *Elay* ✠ *Ihe* ✠ *Rentone* ✠ *Neger* ✠ *Sahe* ✠ *Pangeton* ✠ *Commen* ✠ *a* ✠ *g* ✠ *l* ✠ *a* ✠ *Matthæus* ✠ *Marcus* ✠ *Lucas* ✠ *Johannes* ✠ ✠ ✠ *titulus triumphalis* ✠ *Jesus Nasærenus rex Judæorum* ✠ *ecce dominicæ crucis signum* ✠ *fugite partes adversæ, vicit leo de tribu Judæ, radix, David, aleluijah, Kyrie eleeson, Christe eleeson, pater noster, ave Maria, & ne nos, & veniat super nos salutare tuum: Oremus, &c.*

I find in a Primer intituled The houres of our Ladie, after the use of the church of *Yorke*, printed anno 1516. a charme with this titling in red letters; To all them that afore this image of pitie devoutlie shall saie five *Pater nosters*, five *Aves*, and one *Credo*, pitiouslie beholding these armes of Christs passion, are granted thirtie two thousand seven hundred fiftie five yeares of pardon. It is to be thought that this pardon was granted in the time of pope *Boniface* the ninth; for *Platina* saith that the pardons were sold so cheape, that the apostolicall authoritie grew into contempt.

If the party faile in the number, he may go whistle for a pardon.

¶ *A papisticall charme.*

Signum sanctæ crucis defendat me à malis præsentibus, præteritis, & futuris, interioribus & exterioribus: that is, The signe of the crosse defend me from evils present, past, and to come, inward and outward.

¶ *A charme found in the canon of the masse.*

Also this charme is found in the canon of the masse, *Hæc sacrosancta commixtio corporis & sanguinis domini nostri Jesu Christi fiat mihi, omnibúsque sumentibus, salus mentis & corporis, & ad vitam promerendam, & capessendam, præparatio salutaris:* that is, Let this holie mixture of the bodie and bloud of our Lord Jesus Christ, be unto me, and unto all receivers thereof, health of mind and bodie, and to the deserving and receiving of life an healthfull preparative.

¶ *Other papisticall charmes.*

Aqua benedicta, sit mihi salus & vita:

> *Let holie water be, both health and life to me.*

Adque nomen Martini omnis hæreticus fugiat pallidus,

> *When Martins name is soong or said,*
> *Let heretikes flie as men dismaid.*

By Ab. Fleming.

But the papists have a harder charme than that; to wit, Fier and fagot, Fier and fagot.

¶ *A charme of the holie crosse.*

Nulla salus est in domo,
Nisi cruce munit homo
  Superliminaria.
Neque sentit gladium,
Nec amisit filium,
  Quisquis egit talia.

No health within the house dooth dwell,
Except a man doo crosse him well,
  at everie doore or frame,
He never feeleth the swords point,
Nor his sonne shall loose a joint,
  that dooth performe the same.

Furthermore as followeth.

Sancta crux æquiparatur salutifero Christo. O blasphæmiam inenarrabilem !

  Ista suos fortiores
    Semper facit, & victores,
  Morbos sanat & languores,
    Reprimit dæmonia.
  Dat captivis libertatem,
  Vitæ confert novitatem,
  Ad antiquam dignitatem,
    Crux reduxit omnia.
  O Crux lignum triumphale,
  Mundi vera salus vale,
  Inter ligna nullum tale,
    Fronde, flore, germine.
  Medicina Christiana,
  Salva sanos, ægros sana,
  Quod non valet vis humana,
    Fit in tuo nomine, &c.

Englished by Abraham Fleming. Looke in the Bee-hive of the Romish church. lib. 4. cap. 3. fol. 251, 252.

It makes hir souldiers excellent,
  and crowneth them with victorie,
Restores the lame and impotent,
  and healeth everie maladie.
The divels of hell it conquereth,
  releaseth from imprisonment,
Newnesse of life it offereth,
  it hath all at commandement.
O crosse of wood incomparable,
  to all the world most holsome:
No wood is halfe so honourable,
  in branch, in bud, or blossome.
O medcine which Christ did ordaine,
  the sound save everie hower,
The sicke and sore make whole againe,
  by vertue of thy power.
And that which mans unablenesse,
  hath never comprehended,
Grant by thy name of holinesse,
  it may be fullie ended, &c.

¶ *A charme taken out of the Primer.*

This charme following is taken out of the Primer aforesaid. *Omnipotens* ✠ *Dominus* ✠ *Christus* ✠ *Messias* ✠ with 34. names more, & as many crosses, &

then proceeds in this wise; *Ista nomina me protegant ab omni adversitate, plaga, & infirmitate corporis & animæ, plenè liberent, & assistent in auxilium ista nomina regum, Gasper, &c: & 12 apostoli (videlicet) Petrus, &c: & 4 evangelistæ (videlicet) Matthæus, &c: mihi assistent in omnibus necessitatibus meis, ac me defendant & liberent ab omnibus ericulis & corporis & animæ, & omnibus malis præteritis, præsentibus, & futuris, &c.*

CHAPTER X.

How to make holie water, and the vertues therof. S. Rufins charme, of the wearing and bearing of the name of Jesus, that the sacrament of confession and the eucharist is of as much efficacie as other charmes, & magnified by L. Vairus.

IF I did well, I should shew you the confection of all their stuffe, and how they prepare it; but it would be too long. And therefore you shall onlie have in this place a few notes for the composition of certeine receipts, which in stead of an Apothecarie if you deliver to any morrowmasse preest, he will make them as well as the pope himselfe. Marie now they wax everie parlement deerer and deerer; although therewithall, they utter many stale drugs of their owne.

If you looke in the popish pontificall, you shall see how they make their holie water; to wit, in this sort: I conjure thee thou creature of water, in the name of the father, and of the sonne, & of the Holie-ghost, that thou drive the divell out of everie corner and hole of this church, and altar; so as he remaine not within our precincts that are just and righteous. And water thus used (as *Durandus* saith) hath power of his owne nature to drive away divels. If you will learne to make any more of this popish stuffe, you may go to the verie masse booke, and find manie good receipts: marrie if you search *Durandus*, &c: you shall find abundance. *In ecclesiæ dedicatione.*   *In rationali divinorum officiorum.*

I know that all these charmes, and all these palterie confections (though they were farre more impious and foolish) will be mainteined and defended by massemongers, even as the residue will be by witchmongers; and therefore I will in this place insert a charme, the authoritie wherof is equall with the rest, desiring to have their opinions herein. I find in a booke called *Pomœrium sermonum quadragesimalium,* that S. *Francis* seeing *Rufinus* provoked of the divell to thinke himselfe damned, charged Rufinus to saie this charme, when he next met with the divell; *Aperi os, & ibi imponam stircus,* which is as much to saie in English as, Open thy mouth and I will put in a plumme: a verie ruffinlie charme. *Pom. sermon. 32.*

Leonard Vairus writeth, De veris, piis, ac sanctis amuletis fascinum atq̃; omnia veneficia destruentibus; wherein he speciallie commendeth the name of Jesus to be worne. But the sacrament of confession he extolleth above all things, saieng, that whereas Christ with his power did but throwe divels out of mens bodies, the preest driveth the divell out of mans soule by confession. For (saith he) these words of the preest, when he saith, *Ego te absolvo,* are as effectuall to drive awaie the princes of darknes, through the mightie power of that saieng, as was the voice of God to drive awaie the darknes of the world, when at the beginning he said, *Fiat lux.* He commendeth also, as holesome things to drive awaie divels, the sacrament of the eucharist, and solitarines, and silence. Finallie he saith, that if there be added hereunto an *Agnus Dei,* and the same be worne about ones necke by one void of sinne, nothing is wanting that is good and holesome for this purpose. But he concludeth, that you must weare and make dints in your forhead, with crossing your selfe when you put on your shooes, and at everie other action, & : and that is also a present remedie to drive awaie divels, for they cannot abide it. *L. Vairus. lib de fascin. 3. cap. 10. Idem, ibid.*   *Idem, ibid.*

Chapter XI.

Of the noble balme used by Moses, apishlie counterfeited in the church of Rome.

THE noble balme that *Moses* made, having indeed manie excellent vertues, besides the pleasant and comfortable savour thereof; wherewithall *Moses* in his politike lawes enjoined kings, queenes, and princes to be annointed in their true and lawfull elections and coronations, untill the everlasting king had put on man upon him, is apishlie counterfeited in the Romish church, with diverse terrible conjurations, three breathings, crossewise, (able to make a quezie stomach spue) nine mumblings, and three curtsies, saieng thereunto, *Ave sanctum oleum, ter ave sanctum balsamum.* And so the divell is thrust out, and the Holie-ghost let into his place. But as for *Moses* his balme, it is now not to be found either in *Rome* or elsewhere that I can learne. And according to this papisticall order, witches, and other superstitious people follow on, with charmes and conjurations made in forme; which manie bad physicians also practise, when their learning faileth, as maie appeare by example in the sequele.

Chapter XII.

The opinion of Ferrarius touching charmes, periapts, appensions, amulets, &c. Of Homericall medicines, of constant opinion, and the effects thereof.

Arg. Fer. lib. de medendi methodo. 2. cap. 11. De Homerica medicatione.

ARGERIUS FERRARIUS, a physician in these daies of great account, doth saie, that for somuch as by no diet nor physicke anie disease can be so taken awaie or extinguished, but that certeine dregs and relikes will remaine: therefore physicians use physicall alligations, appensions, periapts, amulets, charmes, characters, &c, which he supposeth maie doo good; but harme he is sure they can doo none: urging that it is necessarie and expedient for a physician to leave nothing undone that may be devised for his patients recoverie; and that by such meanes manie great cures are done. He citeth a great number of experiments out of *Alexander Trallianus, Aetius, Octavianus, Marcellus, Philodotus, Archigines, Philostratus, Plinie,* and *Dioscorides;* and would make men beleeve that *Galen* (who in truth despised and derided all those vanities) recanted in his latter daies his former opinion, and all his invectives tending against these magicall cures: writing also a booke intituled *De Homerica medicatione,* which no man could ever see, but one *Alexander Trallianus,* who saith he saw it: and further affirmeth, that it is an honest mans part to cure the sicke, by hooke or by crooke, or by anie meanes whatsoever. Yea he saith that *Galen* (who indeed wrote and taught that *Incantamenta sunt muliercularum figmenta,* and be the onlie clokes of bad physicians) affirmeth, that there is vertue and great force in incantations. As for example (saith *Trallian*) *Galen* being now reconciled to this opinion, holdeth and writeth, that the bones which sticke in ones throte, are avoided and cast out with the violence of charmes and inchanting words; yea and that thereby the stone, the chollicke, the falling sicknes, and all fevers, gowts, fluxes, fistulas, issues of bloud, and finallie whatsoever cure (even beyond the skill of himselfe or anie other foolish physician) is crude and perfectlie healed by words of inchantment. Marie M. *Ferrarius* (although he allowed and practised this kind of physicke) yet he protesteth that he thinketh it none otherwise effectuall, than by the waie of constant opinion: so as he affirmeth that neither the character, nor the charme, nor the witch, nor the devill accomplish the

This would be examined, to see if Galen be not slandered.

136

cure; as (saith he) the experiment of the toothach will manifestlie declare, wherein the cure is wrought by the confidence or diffidence as well of the patient, as of the agent; according to the poets saieng:

> *Nos habitat non tartara, sed nec sidera cœli*
> *Spiritus in nobis qui viget illa facit.*

> *Not hellish furies dwell in us,*
> *Nor starres with influence heavenlie;*
> *The spirit that lives and rules in us,*
> *Doth every thing ingeniouslie,*

Englished by Abraham Fleming.

This (saith he) commeth to the unlearned, through the opinion which they conceive of the characters and holie words: but the learned that know the force of the mind and imagination, worke miracles by meanes thereof; so as the unlearned must have externall helps, to doo that which the learned can doo with a word onelie. He saith that this is called *Homerica medicatio*, bicause *Homer* discovered the bloud of the word suppressed, and the infections healed by or in mysteries.

CHAPTER XIII.

Of the effects of amulets, the drift of Argerius Ferrarius in the commendation of charmes, &c: foure sorts of Homericall medicines, & the choice thereof; of imagination.

AS touching mine opinion of these amulets, characters, and such other bables, I have sufficientlie uttered it elsewhere: and I will bewraie the vanitie of these superstitious trifles more largelie hereafter. And therefore at this time I onelie saie, that those amulets, which are to be hanged or carried about one, if they consist of hearbs, rootes, stones, or some other metall, they maie have diverse medicinable operations; and by the vertue given to them by God in their creation, maie worke strange effects and cures: and to impute this vertue to anie other matter is witchcraft. And whereas *A. Ferrarius* commendeth certeine amulets, that have no shew of physicall operation; as a naile taken from a crosse, holie water, and the verie signe of the crosse, with such like popish stuffe: I thinke he laboureth thereby rather to draw men to poperie, than to teach or persuade them in the truth of physicke or philosophie. And I thinke thus the rather, for that he himselfe seeth the fraud hereof; confessing that where these magicall physicians applie three seeds of three leaved grasse to a tertian ague, and foure to a quartane, that the number is not materiall.

But of these Homericall medicines he saith there are foure sorts, whereof amulets, characters, & charmes are three: howbeit he commendeth and preferreth the fourth above the rest; and that he saith consisteth in illusions, which he more properlie calleth startagems. Of which sort of conclusions he alledgeth for example, how *Philodotus* did put a cap of lead upon ones head, who imagined he was headlesse, whereby the partie was delivered from his disease or conceipt. Item another cured a woman that imagined, that a serpent or snake did continuallie gnaw and teare hir entrailes; and that was done onelie by giving hir a vomit, and by foisting into the matter vomited a little serpent or snake, like unto that which she imagined was in hir bellie.

Foure sorts of Homericall medicines, and which is the principall.

Item, another imagined that he alwaies burned in the fier, under whose bed a fier was privilie conveied, which being raked out before his face, his fancie was satisfied, and his heate allaied. Hereunto perteineth, that the hickot is cured with sudden feare or strange newes: yea by that meanes agues and manie other strange and extreame diseases have beene healed. And some that

The force of fixed fansie, opinion, or strong conceipt.

have lien so sicke and sore of the gowt, that they could not remove a joint, through sudden feare of fier, or ruine of houses, have forgotten their infirmities and greefes, and have runne awaie. But in my tract upon melancholie, and the effects of imagination, and in the discorse of naturall magicke, you shall see these matters largelie touched.

CHAPTER XIV.

Choice of Charmes against the falling evill, the biting of a mad dog, the stinging of a scorpion, the toothach, for a woman in travell, for the Kings evill, to get a thorne out of any member, or a bone out of ones throte, charmes to be said fasting, or at the gathering of hearbs, for sore eies, to open locks, against spirits, for the bots in a horsse, and speciallie for the Duke of Albas horsse, for sowre wines, &c.

THERE be innumerable charmes of conjurers, bad physicians, lewd surgians, melancholike witches, and couseners, for all diseases and greefes; speciallie for such as bad physicians and surgions knowe not how to cure, and in truth are good stuffe to shadow their ignorance, whereof I will repeate some.

For the falling evill.

Take the sicke man by the hand, and whisper these wordes softlie in his eare, I conjure thee by the sunne and moone, and by the gospell of this daie delivered by God to *Hubert, Giles, Cornelius,* and *John,* that thou rise and fall no more. ☆ Otherwise: Drinke in the night at a spring water out of a skull of one that hath beene slaine. ☆ Otherwise: Eate a pig killed with a knife that slew a man. ☆ Otherwise as followeth.

Ananizapta ferit mortem, dum lædere quærit,
Est mala mors capta, dum dicitur Ananizapta,
Ananizapta Dei nunc miserere mei.

Englished by
Abraham
Fleming.

Ananizapta smiteth death,
* whiles harme intendeth he,*
This word Ananizapta say,
* and death shall captive be,*
Ananizapta ô of God,
* have mercie now on me.*

¶ *Against the biting of a mad dog.*

J. Bodinus.
lib. de dæmon
3. cap. 5.

Put a silver ring on the finger, within the which these words are graven ✠ *Habay* ✠ *habar* ✠ *hebar* ✠ & saie to the person bitten with a mad dog, I am thy saviour, loose not thy life: and then pricke him in the nose thrise, that at each time he bleed. ☆ Otherwise: Take pilles made of the skull of one that is hanged. ☆ Otherwise: Write upon a peece of bread, *Irioni, khiriora, esser, khuder, feres;* and let it be eaten by the partie bitten. ☆ Otherwise: *O rex gloriæ Jesu Christe, veni cum pace: In nomine patris max, in nomine filii max, in nomine spiritus sancti prax: Gasper, Melchior, Balthasar* ✠ *prax* ✠ *max* ✠ *Deus I max* ✠

But in troth this is verie dangerous; insomuch as if it be not speedilie and cunninglie prevented, either death or frensie insueth, through infection of the humor left in the wound bitten by a mad dog: which bicause bad surgions cannot cure, they have therfore used foolish cousening charmes. But *Dodonæus* in his herball saith, that the hearbe Alysson cureth it: which experiment, I doubt

138

not, will proove more true than all the charms in the world. But where he saith, that the same hanged at a mans gate or entrie, preserveth him and his cattell from inchantment or bewitching, he is overtaken with follie.

¶ *Against the biting of a scorpion.*

Saie to an asse secretlie, and as it were whispering in his eare; I am bitten with a Scorpion.

¶ *Against the toothach.*

Scarifie the gums in the greefe, with the tooth of one that hath beene slaine. ☆ Otherwise: *Galbes galbat, galdes galdat.* ☆ Otherwise: *A ab hur hus,* &c. ☆ Otherwise: At saccaring of masse hold your teeth togither, and say *Os non comminuetis ex eo.* ☆ Otherwise: *strigiles falcesq; dentatæ, dentium dolorem persanate;* O horssecombs and sickles that have so many teeth, come heale me now of my toothach.

That is,
You shall
not breake
or diminish
a bone of
him.

¶ *A charme to release a woman in travell.*

Throwe over the top of the house, where a woman in travell lieth, a stone, or any other thing that hath killed three living creatures; namelie, a man, a wild bore, and a she beare.

¶ *To heale the Kings or Queenes evill, or any other sorenesse in the throte.*

Remedies to cure the Kings or Queenes evill, is first to touch the place with the hand of one that died an untimelie death. ☆ Otherwise: Let a virgine fasting laie hir hand on the sore, and saie; *Apollo* denieth that the heate of the plague can increase, where a naked virgine quencheth it: and spet three times upon it.

¶ *A charme read in the Romish church, upon saint Blazes daie, that will fetch a thorne out of anie place of ones bodie, a bone out of the throte, &c: Lect. 3.*

For the fetching of a thorne out of any place of ones bodie, or a bone out of the throte, you shall read a charme in the Romish church upon S. *Blazes* daie; to wit, Call upon God, and remember S. *Blaze.* This S. *Blaze* could also heale all wild beasts that were sicke or lame, with laieng on of his hands: as appeareth in the lesson red on his daie, where you shall see the matter at large.

¶ *A charme for the headach.*

Tie a halter about your head, wherewith one hath beene hanged.

¶ *A charme to be said each morning by a witch fasting, or at least before she go abroad.*

The fier bites, the fier bites, the fier bites; Hogs turd over it, hogs turd over it, hogs turd over it; The father with thee, the sonne with me, the holie-ghost betweene us both to be: ter. Then spit over one shoulder, and then over the other, and then three times right forward.

¶ *Another charme that witches use at the gathering of their medicinable hearbs.*

> *Haile be thou holie hearbe*
> *growing on the ground*
> *All in the mount Calvarie*
> *first wert thou found,*
> *Thou art good for manie a sore,*
> *And healest manie a wound,*
> *In the name of sweete Jesus*
> *I take thee from the ground.*

Though
neither the
hearbe nor
the witch
never came
there.

¶ *An old womans charme, wherewith she did much good in the countrie, and grew famous thereby.*

An old woman that healed all diseases of cattell (for the which she never tooke any reward but a penie and a loafe) being seriouslie examined by what words she brought these things to passe, confessed that after she had touched the sicke creature, she alwaies departed immediatelie; saieng:

> *My loafe in my lap,*
> *my penie in my pursse;*
> *Thou are never the better,*
> *and I am never the wursse.*

Another like charme.

A Gentlewoman having sore eies, made hir mone to one, that promised hir helpe, if she would follow his advise: which was onelie to weare about hir necke a scroll sealed up, whereinto she might not looke. And she conceiving hope of cure thereby, received it under the condition, and left hir weeping and teares, wherewith she was woont to bewaile the miserable darknesse, which she doubted to indure: whereby in short time hir eies were well amended. But alas! she lost soone after that pretious jewell, and thereby returned to hir woonted weeping, and by consequence to hir sore eies. Howbeit, hir jewell or scroll being found againe, was looked into by hir deere friends, and this onelie posie was conteined therein:

> *The divell pull out both thine eies,*
> *And etish in the holes likewise.*

Whereby partlie you may see what constant opinion can doo, according to the saieng of *Plato;* If a mans fansie or mind give him assurance that a hurtfull thing shall doo him good, it may doo so, &c.

Note the force of constant opinion, or fixed fancy.

A charme to open locks.

Spell the word backward, and you shall soone see this slovenlie charme or appension.

Theevish charmes.

As the hearbes called *Aethiopides* will open all locks (if all be true that inchanters saie) with the help of certeine words: so be there charmes also and periapts, which without any hearbs can doo as much: as for example. Take a peece of wax crossed in baptisme, and doo but print certeine floures therein, and tie them in the hinder skirt of your shirt; and when you would undoo the locke, blow thrise therin, saieng: *Arato hoc partiko hoc maratarykin.* I open this doore in thy name that I am forced to breake, as thou brakest hell gates, *In nomine patris, & filii, & spiritus sancti, Amen.*

¶ A charme to drive awaie spirits that haunt anie house.

This is called and counted the Paracelsian charme.
Psal. 150.
Luk. 16.
Psa. 64.

Hang in everie of the foure corners of your house this sentence written upon virgine parchment; *Omnis spiritus laudet Dominum: Mosen habent & prophetas: Exurgat Deus et dissipentur inimici ejus.*

¶ A prettie charme or conclusion for one possessed.

The possessed bodie must go upon his or hir knees to the church, how farre so ever it be off from their lodging; and so must creepe without going out of the waie, being the common high waie, in that sort, how fowle and durtie soever the same be; or whatsoever lie in the waie, not shunning anie thing whatsoever, untill he come to the church, where he must heare masse devoutlie, and then followeth recoverie.

Memo·
randum
that hear-
ing of
masse be
in no case
omitted,
quoth Nota.

¶ *Another for the same purpose.*

There must be commended to some poore begger the saieng of five *Pater nosters*, and five *Aves;* the first to be said in the name of the partie possessed, or bewitched: for that Christ was led into the garden; secondlie, for that Christ did sweat both water and bloud; thirdlie, for that Christ was condemned; fourthlie, for that he was crucified guiltlesse; and fiftlie, for that he suffered to take awaie our sinnes. Then must the sicke bodie heare masse eight daies together, standing in the place where the gospell is said, and must mingle holie water with his meate and his drinke, and holie salt also must be a portion of the mixture.

¶ *Another to the same effect.*

The sicke man must fast three daies, and then he with his parents must come to church, upon an embering fridaie, and must heare the masse for that daie appointed, and so likewise the saturdaie and sundaie following. And the preest must read upon the sicke mans head, that gospell which is read in September, and in grape harvest, after the feast of holie crosse *In diebus quatuor temporum,* in ember daies: then let him write it and carrie it aboute his necke, and he shall be cured.

*Johannes
Anglicus ex
Constantino,
Gualtero,
Bernardo,
Gilberto, &c.*

¶ *Another charme or witch-craft for the same.*

This office or conjuration following was first authorised and printed at *Rome,* and afterwards at *Avenion, Anno.* 1515. And least that the divell should lie hid in some secret part of the bodie, everie part thereof is named: *Obsecro te Jesu Christe, &c:* that is: I beseech thee O Lord Jesus Christ, that thou pull out of everie member of this man all infirmities, from his head, from his haire, from his braine, from his forhead, from his eies, from his nose, from his eares, from his mouth, from his toong, from his teeth, from his jawes, from his throte, from his necke, from his backe, from his brest, from his paps, from his heart, from his stomach, from his sides, from his flesh, from his bloud, from his bones, from his legs, from his feete, from his fingers, from the soles of his feete, from his marrowe, from his sinewes, from his skin, and from everie joint of his members, &c.

Doubtles Jesus Christ could have no starting hole, but was hereby everie waie prevented and pursued; so as he was forced to doo the cure: for it appeareth hereby, that it had beene insufficient for him to have said; Depart out of this man thou uncleane spirit, and that when he so said he did not performe it. I doo not thinke that there will be found among all the heathens superstitious fables, or among the witches, conjurors, couseners, poets, knaves, fooles, &c: that ever wrote, so impudent and impious a lie or charme as is read in *Barnardine de bustis;* where, to cure a sicke man, Christs bodie, to wit: a wafer cake, was outwardlie applied to his side, and entred into his heart, in the sight of all the standers by. Now, if grave authors report such lies, what credit in these cases shall we attribute unto the old wives tales, that *Sprenger, Institor, Bodine,* and others write? Even as much as to *Ovids Metamorphosis, Aesops fables, Moores Utopia,* and diverse other fansies; which have as much truth in them, as a blind man hath sight in his eie.

*Barnard. de
bustis in Ro-
sar. serm.
serm.* 15.

¶ *A charme for the bots in a horsse.*

You must both saie and doo thus upon the diseased horsse three daies together, before the sunne rising: *In nomine pa ✠ tris & fi ✠ lii & spiritus ✠ sancti; Exorcizo te vermem per Deum pa ✠ trem, & fi ✠ lium & spiritum ✠ sanctum:* that is, In the name of God the Father, the Sonne, & the Holy-ghost, I conjure thee O worme by God the Father, the Sonne, & the Holy-ghost; that thou neither eat nor drinke the flesh bloud or bones of this horsse; and that thou hereby maist be made as patient as *Job,* and as good as S. *John Baptist,* when he baptised

Christ in *Jordan*, *In nomine pa✠tris* & *fi✠lii* & *spiritus* ✠ *sancti*. And then saie three *Pater nosters*, and three *Aves*, in the right eare of the horsse, to the glorie of the holie trinitie. *Do✠minus fili✠us spiri✠tus Mari✠a*.

There are also divers bookes imprinted, as it should appeare with the authoritie of the church of *Rome*, wherein are conteined manie medicinall praiers, not onelie against all diseases of horsses, but also for everie impediment and fault in a horsse: in so much as if a shoo fall off in the middest of his journie, there is a praier to warrant your horsses hoofe, so as it shall not breake, how far so ever he be from the Smithes forge.

Item, the Duke of *Alba* his horsse was consecrated, or canonized, in the lowe countries, at the solemne masse; wherein the popes bull, and also his charme was published (which I will hereafter recite) he in the meane time sitting as Vice-roy with his consecrated standard in his hand, till masse was done.

¶ *A charme against vineager.*

That wine wax not eager, write on the vessell,* *Gustate* & *videte, quoniam suavis est Dominus.*

CHAPTER XV.

The inchanting of serpents and snakes, objections aunswered concerning the same; fond reasons whie charmes take effect therin, Mahomets pigeon, miracles wrought by an Asse at Memphis in Aegypt, popish charmes against serpents, of miracle workers, the tameing of snakes, Bodins lie of snakes.

CONCERNING the charming of serpents and snakes, mine adversaries (as I have said) thinke they have great advantage by the words of *David* in the fiftie eight psalme; and by *Jeremie*, chapter eight, expounding the one prophet by *Virgil*, the other by *Ovid*. For the words of *David* are these;

Their poison is like the poison of a serpent, and like a deafe adder, that stoppeth his eare, and heareth not the voice of the charmer, charme he never so cunninglie. The words of *Virgil* are these, *Frigidus in pratis cantando rumpitur anguis.*

As he might saie, *David* thou liest; for the cold natured snake is by the charmes of the inchanters broken all to peeces in the field where he lieth. Then commeth

Ovid, and he taketh his countriemans part, saieng in the name and person of a witch; *Vipereas rumpo verbis* & *carmine fauces;* that is, I with my words and charmes can breake in sunder the vipers jawes. Marrie *Jeremie* on the other side encountereth this poeticall witch, and he not onelie defendeth, but expoundeth his fellowe prophets words, and that not in his owne name, but in the name of almightie God; saieng, I will send serpents and cockatrices among you, which cannot be charmed.

Now let anie indifferent man (christian or heathen) judge, whether the words and minds of the prophets doo not directlie oppugne these poets words (I will nor saie minds); for that I am sure they did therein but jest and trifle, according to the common fabling of lieng poets. And certeinlie, I can encounter them two with other two poets; namelie *Propertius* and *Horace*, the one merriliederiding, the other seriouslie impugning their fantasticall poetries, concerning the power and omnipotencie of witches. For where *Virgil*, *Ovid*, &c: write that witches with their charmes fetch downe the moone and starres from heaven, etc.; *Propertius* mocketh them in these words following:

142

At vos deductæ quibus est fallacia Lunæ,
  Et labor in magicis sacra piare focis,
En agedum dominæ mentem convertite nostræ,
  Et facite illa meo palleat ore magis,
Tunc ego crediderim vobis & sidera & amnes
Posse Circeis ducere carminibus:

But you that have the subtill slight,
  Of fetching downe the moone from skies;
And with inchanting fier bright,
  Attempt to purge your sacrifies:
Lo now, go to, turne (if you can)
  Our madams mind and sturdie hart,
And make hir face more pale and wan,
  Than mine: which if by magicke art
You doo, then will I soone beleeve,
  That by your witching charmes you can
From skies aloft the starres remeeve,
  And rivers turne from whence they ran.

*Englished by
Abraham
Fleming.*

And that you may see more certeinlie, that these poets did but jest and deride the credulous and timerous sort of people, I thought good to shew you what *Ovid* saith against himselfe, and such as have written so incredible and ridiculouslie of witches omnipotencie:

Nec mediæ magicis finduntur cantibus angues,
Nec redit in fontes unda supina suos:

Snakes in the middle are not riven
  with charmes of witches cunning,
Nor waters to their fountaines driven
  by force of backward running.

*Englished by
Abraham
Fleming.*

As for *Horace* his verses I omit them, bicause I have cited them in another place. And concerning this matter *Cardanus* saith, that at everie eclipse they were woont to thinke, that witches pulled downe the sunne and moone from heaven. And doubtles, hence came the opinion of that matter, which spred so farre, and continued so long in the common peoples mouthes, that in the end learned men grew to beleeve it, and to affirme it in writing.

Card. lib. 15.
*de var. rer.
cap.* 80.

But here it will be objected, that bicause it is said (in the places by me alledged) that snakes or vipers cannot be charmed; *Ergo* other things may: To answer this argument, I would aske the witchmonger this question, to wit; Whether it be expedient, that to satisfie his follie, the Holie-ghost must of necessitie make mention of everie particular thing that he imagineth may be bewitched? I would also aske of him, what privilege a snake hath more than other creatures, that he onelie may not, and all other creatures may be bewitched? I hope they will not saie, that either their faith or infidelitie is the cause thereof; neither doo I admit the answer of such divines as saie, that he cannot be bewitched: for that he seduced *Eve;* by meanes whereof God himselfe curssed him; and thereby he is so privileged, as that no witches charme can take hold of him. But more shall be said hereof in the sequele.

An objection answered.

Danæus saith, that witches charmes take soonest hold upon snakes and adders; bicause of their conference and familiaritie with the divell, whereby the rather mankind through them was seduced. Let us seeke then an answer for this cavill; although in truth it needeth not: for the phrase of speach is absolute, & importes not a speciall qualitie proper to the nature of a viper anie more, than when I saie; A connie cannot flie: you should gather & conclude thereupon, that I ment that all other beasts could flie. But you shall understand, that the cause why these vipers can rather withstand the voice & practise of inchanters and sorcerers, than other creatures, is: for that they being in bodie and nature venomous, cannot so soone or properlie receive their destruction by

Dan. in dialog. cap. 3.

venome, wherby the witches in other creatures bring their mischeefous practises more easilie to passe, according to *Virgils* saieng

Virg. geo. 4.

Corrupítque lacus, infecit pabula tabo,

*Englished by
Abraham
Fleming.*

> *She did infect with poison strong*
> *Both ponds and pastures all along.*

And thereupon the prophet alludeth unto their corrupt and inflexible nature,
with that comparison: and not (as *Tremelius* is faine to shift it) with stopping one
eare with his taile, and laieng the other close to the ground; bicause he would
not heare the charmers voice. For the snake hath neither such reason; nor the
words such effect: otherwise the snake must know our thoughts. It is also to be
considered, how untame by nature these vipers (for the most part) are; in so
much as they be not by mans industrie or cunning to be made familiar, or traind
Feates his
dog, and
Mahomets
pigeon.
to doo anie thing, whereby admiration maie be procured; as *Bomelio Feates* his
dog could doo; or *Mahomets* pigeon, which would resort unto him, being in the
middest of his campe, and picke a pease out of his eare; in such sort that manie
of the people thought that the Holie-ghost came and told him a tale in his eare:
the same pigeon also brought him a scroll, wherein was written, *Rex esto*, and
laid the same in his necke. And bicause I have spoken of the docilitie of a dog
and a pigeon, though I could cite an infinite number of like tales, I will be bold
to trouble you but with one more.
A storie
declaring
the great
docilitie of
an asse.
At *Memphis* in *Aegypt*, among other juggling knacks, which were there usuallie
shewed, there was one that tooke such paines with an asse, that he had taught
him all these qualities following. And for gaine he caused a stage to be made,
and an assemblie of people to meete; which being done, in the maner of a plaie,
he came in with his asse, and said; The *Sultane* hath great need of asses to helpe
to carrie stones and other stuffe, towards his great building which he hath in
hand. The asse immediatlie fell downe to the ground, and by all signes shewed
himselfe to be sicke, and at length to give up the ghost: so as the juggler begged
of the assemblie monie towards his losse. And having gotten all that he could,
he said; Now my maisters, you shall see mine asse is yet alive, and dooth but
counterfet; bicause he would have some monie to buie him provender, knowing
that I was poore, and in some need of releefe. Hereupon he would needs laie a
wager, that his asse was alive, who to everie mans seeming was starke dead.
And when one had laid monie with him thereabout, he commanded the asse to
rise, but he laie still as though he were dead: then did he beate him with a cudgell, but that would not serve the turne, untill he addressed this speech to the
asse, saieng (as before) in open audience; The *Sultane* hath commanded, that all
the people shall ride out to morrow, and see the triumph, and that the faire
ladies will then ride upon the fairest asses, and will give notable provender unto
them, and everie asse shall drinke of the sweete water of *Nilus:* and then lo the
asse did presentlie start up, and advance himselfe exceedinglie. Lo (quoth his
maister) now I have wonne: but in troth the Maior hath borrowed mine asse,
for the use of the old ilfavoured witch his wife: and thereupon immediatlie he
hoong downe his eares, and halted downe right, as though he had beene starke
lame. Then said his maister; I perceive you love yoong prettie wenches: at
which words he looked up, as it were with joifull cheere. And then his maister
did bid him go choose one that should ride upon him; and he ran to a verie
handsome woman, and touched hir with his head, *&c:* A snake will never be
*J. Bod. lib.
de dæm.* 2.
cap. 6.
brought to such familiaritie, *&c*. *Bodin* saith, that this was a man in the likenesse if an asse: but I maie rather thinke that he is an asse in the likenesse of a
man. Well, to returne to our serpents, I will tell you a storie concerning the
charming of them, and the event of the same.
*Mal. malef.
part* 2. *qu.* 2.
cap. 9.
John. Bodin.
In the citie of *Salisborogh* there was an inchanter, that before all the people
tooke upon him to conjure all the serpents and snakes within one mile compasse
into a great pit or dike, and there to kill them. When all the serpents were
gathered togither, as he stood upon the brinke of the pit, there came at the
last a great and a horrible serpent, which would not be gotten downe with all

the force of his incantations: so as (all the rest being dead) he flew upon the inchanter, and clasped him in the middest, and drew him downe into the said dike, and there killed him. You must thinke that this was a divell in a serpents likenesse, which for the love he bare to the poore snakes, killed the sorcerer; to teach all other witches to beware of the like wicked practise. And surelie, if this be not true, there be a great number of lies conteined in *M. Mal.* and in *J. Bodin.* And if this be well weighed, and conceived, it beateth downe to the ground all those witchmongers arguments, that contend to wring witching miracles out of this place. For they disagree notablie, some denieng and some affirming that serpents maie be bewitched. Neverthelesse, bicause in everie point you shall see how poperie agreeth with paganisme, I will recite certeine charmes against vipers, allowed for the most part in and by the church of *Rome:* as followeth.

I conjure thee O serpent in this houre, by the five holie woonds of our Lord, that thou remove not out of this place, but here staie, as certeinelie as God was borne of a pure virgine. ✫ Otherwise: I conjure thee serpent *In nomine patris,* & *filii,* & *spiritus sancti:* I command thee serpent by our ladie S. *Marie,* that thou obeie me, as wax obeieth the fier, and a fier obeieth water; that thou neither hurt me, nor anie other christian, as certeinelie as God was borne of an immaculate virgine, in which respect I take thee up, *In nomine patris* & *filii,* & *spiritus sancti: Ely lash eiter, ely lash eiter, ely lash eiter.* ✫ Otherwise: O vermine, thou must come as God came unto the Jewes. ✫ Otherwise: *L. Vairus* saith, that *Serpens quernis frondibus contacta,* that a serpent touched with oke leaves dieth, and staieth even in the beginning of his going, if a feather of the bird *Ibis* be cast or throwne upon him: and that a viper smitten or hot with a reed is astonied, and touched with a beechen branch is presentlie numme and stiffe.

Exorcismes or conjura-tiõs against serpents.

L. Vair. lib. de fascinat. 1. *cap.* 4.

Here is to be remembred, that manie use to boast that they are of S. *Paules* race and kinred, shewing upon their bodies the prints of serpents: which (as the papists affirme) was incident to all them of S. *Paules* stocke. Marie they saie herewithall, that all his kinsfolks can handle serpents, or anie poison without danger. Others likewise have (as they brag) a *Katharine* wheele upon their bodies, and they saie they are kin to S. *Katharine,* and that they can carrie burning coles in their bare hands, and dip their said hands in hot skalding liquor, and also go into hot ovens. Whereof though the last be but a bare jest, and to be doone by anie that will prove (as a bad fellow in *London* had used to doo, making no tariance at all therein): yet there is a shew made of the other, as though it were certeine and undoubted; by annointing the hands with the juice of mallowes, mercurie, urine, &c: which for a little time are defensatives against these scalding liquors, and scortching fiers.

Usurpers of kinred with blessed Paule and S. Katharine.

But they that take upon them to worke these mysteries and miracles, doo indeed (after rehearsall of these and such like words and charmes) take up even in their bare hands, those snakes and vipers, and sometimes put them about their necks, without receiving anie hurt thereby, to the terror and astonishment of the beholders, which naturallie both feare and abhorre all serpents. But these charmers (upon my word) dare not trust to their charmes, but use such an inchantment, as everie man maie lawfullie use, and in the lawfull use thereof maie bring to passe that they shalbe in securitie, and take no harme, how much soever they handle them: marie with a woollen rag they pull out their teeth before hand, as some men saie; but as truth is, they wearie them, and that is of certeintie. And surelie this is a kind of witchcraft, which I terme private confederacie. *Bodin* saith, that all the snakes in one countrie were by charmes and verses driven into another region: perhaps he meaneth *Ireland,* where S. *Patrike* is said to have doone it with his holinesse, &c.

J. Bodin. lib. de dæm. 1. *cap.* 3.

James Sprenger, and *Henrie Institor* affirme, that serpents and snakes, and their skins exceed all other creatures for witchcraft: in so much as witches doo use to burie them under mens thresholds, either of the house or stalles, whereby barrennes is procured both to woman and beast: yea and that the verie earth and ashes of them continue to have force of fascination. In respect whereof they wish all men now and then to dig awaie the earth under their threshholds, and to sprinkle holie water in the place, & also to hang boughes (hallowed on mid-summer daie) at the stall doore where the cattell stand : & produce examples thereupon, of witches lies, or else their owne, which I omit ; bicause I see my booke groweth to be greater than I meant it should be.

Chapter xvi.

Charmes to carrie water in a sive, to know what is spoken of us behind our backs, for bleare eies, to make seeds to growe well, of images made of wax, to be rid of a witch, to hang hir up, notable authorities against waxen images, a storie bewraieng the knaverie of waxen images.

L. Vairus lib. fascin. 1. ca. 5. Oratio Tus-cæ vestalis.

LEONARDUS VAIRUS saith, that there was a praier extant, whereby might be carried in a sive, water, or other liquor : I thinke it was Clam claie ; which a crow taught a maid, that was promised a cake of so great quantitie, as might be kneded of so much floure as she could wet with the water that she brought in a sive, and by that meanes she clamd it with claie, & brought in so much water, as whereby she had a great cake, and so beguiled hir sisters, &c. And this tale I heard among my grandams maides, whereby I can decipher this witchcraft. Item, by the tingling of the eare, men heretofore could tell what was spoken of them. If anie see a scorpion, and saie this word (*Bud*) he

Of the word (*Bud*) and the Greeke letters *Π* & *A*.

shall not be stoong or bitten therewith. These two Greeke letters *Π* and *A* written in a paper, and hoong about ones necke, preserve the partie from bleereiednesse. Cummin or hempseed sowne with curssing and opprobrious words grow the faster and the better. *Berosus Anianus* maketh witchcraft of great antiquitie : for he saith, that *Cham* touching his fathers naked member uttered a charme, wherby his father became emasculated or deprived of the powers generative.

¶ A charme teaching how to hurt whom you list with images of wax, &c.

Make an image in his name, whom you would hurt or kill, of new virgine wax ; under the right arme poke whereof place a swallowes hart, and the liver under the left ; then hang about the necke thereof a new thred in a new needle pricked into the member which you would have hurt, with the rehearsall of cer-teine words, which for the avoiding of foolish superstition and credulitie in this behalfe is to be omitted. And if they were inserted, I dare undertake they would doo no harme, were it not to make fooles, and catch gudgins. ☆ Other-wise : Sometimes these images are made of brasse, and then the hand is placed where the foote should be, and the foote where the hand, and the face downe-ward. ☆ Otherwise : For a greater mischeefe, the like image is made in the forme of a man or woman, upon whose head is written the certeine name of the

The practi-ser of these charmes must have skill in the planetarie motions, or else he may go shoo the goose.

partie : and on his or hir ribs these words, *Ailif, casyl, zaze, hit mel meltat:* then the same must be buried. ☆ Otherwise : In the dominion of *Mars*, two images must be prepared, one of wax, the other of the earth of a dead man ; each image must have in his hand a sword wherwith a man hath beene slaine, & he that must be slaine may have his head thrust through with a foine. In both must be written certeine peculiar characters, and then must they be hid in a certeine place. ☆ Otherwise : To obteine a womans love, an image must be made in the houre of *Venus*, of virgine wax, in the name of the beloved, wherupon a character is written, & is warmed at a fier, and in dooing therof the name of some angell must be mentioned. To be utterlie rid of the witch, and to hang hir up by the haire, you must prepare an image of the earth of a dead man to be baptised in another mans name, whereon the name, with a character, must be written : then must it be perfumed with a rotten bone, and then these psalmes read backward: *Domine Dominus noster, Dominus illuminatio mea, Domine exaudi orationem meam, Deus laudem meam ne tacueris:* and then burie it, first in one place, and afterwards in another. Howbeit, it is written in the 21 article of the determination of *Paris*, that to affirme that images of brasse, lead, gold, of white or red wax, or of any other stuffe (conjured, baptised, consecrated, or rather execrated through these magicall arts at certeine days) have woonderfull vertues, or such as are avowed in their bookes or assertions, is error in faith, naturall philosophie, and true astronomie: yea it is concluded in the 22 article of that councell, that it is as great an error to beleeve those things, as to doo them.

But concerning these images, it is certeine that they are much feared among the people, and much used among cousening witches, as partlie appeereth in this discourse of mine else-where, & as partlie you may see by the contents of this storie following. Not long sithence, a yoong maiden (dwelling at new *Romnie* heere in Kent) being the daughter of one M. *L. Stuppenie* (late Jurat of the same towne but dead before the execution hereof) and afterwards the wife of *Thomas Eps*, who is at this instant Maior of *Romnie*) was visited with sicknesse, whose mother and father in lawe being abused with credulitie concerning witches supernaturall power, repaired to a famous witch called mother *Baker*, dwelling not far from thence at a place called *Stonstreet*, who (according to witches cousening custome) asked whether they mistrusted not some bad neighbour, to whom they answered that indeed they doubted a woman neere unto them (and yet the same woman was, of the honester & wiser sort of hir neighbors, reputed a good creature.) Nevertheles the witch told them that there was great cause of their suspicion: for the same (said she) is the verie partie that wrought the maidens destruction, by making a hart of wax, and pricking the same with pins and needels; affirming also that the same neighbor of hirs had bestowed the same in some secret corner of the house. This being beleeved, the house was searched by credible persons, but nothing could be found. The witch or wise woman being certified hereof, continued hir assertion, and would needs go to the house where she hir selfe (as she affirmed) would certeinlie find it. When she came thither, she used hir cunning (as it chanced) to hir owne confusion, or at least wise to hir detection: for heerein she did, as some of the wiser sort mistrusted that she woulde doo, laieng downe privilie such an image (as she had before described) in a corner, which by others had beene most diligentlie searched & looked into, & by that means hir cousenage was notablie bewraied. And I would wish that all witchmongers might paie for their lewd repaire to inchantors, and consultation with witches, and such as have familiar spirits, as some of these did, and that by the order of the high commissioners, which partlie for respect of neighborhood, and partlie for other considerations, I leave unspoken of.

A proved storie concerning the premisses.

CHAPTER XVII.

Sundrie sorts of charmes tending to diverse purposes, and first, certeine charmes to make taciturnitie in tortures.

IMPARIBUS meritis tria
pendent corpora ramis,
Dismas & Gestas,
in medio est divina potestas,
Dismas damnatur,
Gestas ad astra levatur:

This charm seemeth to allude to Christ crucified betweene the two theevs.

> *Three bodies on a bough doo hang,*
>   *for merits of inequalitie,*
> *Dismas and Gestas, in the midst*
>   *the power of the divinitie.*
> *Dismas is damned, but Gestas lif-*
>   *ted up above the starres on hie.*

Psal. 44.

Also this: *Eructavit cor meum verbum bonum veritatem nunquam dicam regi.* ☆ Otherwise: As the milke of our ladie was lussious to our Lord Jesus Christ; so let this

Luk. 4.
John. 19.

torture or rope be pleasant to mine armes and members. ☆ Otherwise: *Jesus
autem transiens per medium illorum ibat.* ☆ Otherwise: You shall not break a bone
of him.

¶ *Counter charmes against these and all other witchcrafts, in the saieng also wherof witches
are vexed, &c.*

Psal. 44.
Scripture
properlie
applied.

Eructavit cor meum verbum bonum, dicam cuncta opera mea regi. ☆ Otherwise:
Domine labia mea aperies, & os meum annunciabit veritatem. ☆ Otherwise: *Contere
brachia iniqui rei, & lingua maligna subvertetur.*

¶ *A charme for the choine cough.*

Take three sips of a chalice, when the preest hath said masse, and swallow it
downe with good devotion, *&c.*

¶ *For corporall or spirituall rest.*

In nomine patris, up and downe,
Et filii & spiritus sancti upon my crowne,
Crux Christi upon my brest,
Sweete ladie send me eternall rest!

¶ *Charmes to find out a theefe.*

O most
woonder-
full vertue
hidden in
the letters
of S. He-
lens holie
name!

The meanes how to find out a theefe, is thus: Turne your face to the east, and
make a crosse upon christall with oile olive, and under the crosse write these two
words [*Saint Helen*]. Then a child that is innocent, and a chast virgine borne
in true wedlocke, and not base begotten, of the age of ten yeares, must take the
christall in his hand, and behind his backe, kneeling on thy knees, thou must
devoutlie and reverentlie saie over this praier thrise: I beseech thee my ladie
S. *Helen*, mother of king *Constantine*, which diddest find the crosse whereupon
Christ died: by that thy holie devotion, and invention of the crosse, and by the
same crosse, and by the joy which thou conceivedst at the finding thereof and by
the love which thou barest to thy sonne *Constantine*, and by the great goodnes
which thou dooest alwaies use, that thou shew me in this christall, whatsoever
I aske or desire to knowe; Amen. And when the child seeth the angell in the
christall, demand what you will, and the angell will make answer thereunto.
Memorandum, that this be doone just at the sunne rising, when the wether is
faire and cleere.

Card. lib. 16.
*de var. rer.
cap.* 93.

Cardanus derideth these and such like fables, and setteth downe his judgement
therein accordinglie, in the sixteenth booke *De rerum var.* These conjurors and
couseners forsooth will shew you in a glasse the theefe that hath stolne anie
thing from you, and this is their order. They take a glasse viall full of holie
water, and set it upon a linnen cloth, which hath beene purified, not onelie by
washing, but by sacrifice, *&c.* On the mouth of the viall or urinall, two olive
leaves must be laid acrosse, with a litle conjuration said over it, by a child; to
wit thus: *Angele bone, angele candide, per tuam sanctitatem, meámq; virginitatem,
ostende mihi furem:* with three *Pater nosters,* three *Aves,* and betwixt either of them

a crosse made with the naile of the thumbe upon the mouth of the viall; and then shall be seene angels ascending and descending as it were motes in the sunne beames. The theefe all this while shall suffer great torments, and his face shall be seene plainlie, even as plainlie I beleeve as the man in the moone. For in truth, there are toies artificiallie conveied into the glasse, which will make the water bubble, and devises to make images appeare in the bubbles: as also there be artificiall glasses, which will shew unto you that shall looke thereinto, manie images of diverse formes, and some so small and curious, as they shall in favour resemble whom so ever you thinke upon. Looke in *John Bap. Neap.* for the confection of such glasses. The subtilties hereof are so detected, and the mysteries of the glasses so common now, and their cousenage so well knowne, &c: that I need not stand upon the particular confutation hereof. *Cardanus* in the place before cited reporteth, how he tried with children these and diverse circumstances the whole illusion, and found it to be plaine knaverie and cousenage.

For if the crosse be forgotten all is not woorth a pudding.

¶ *Another waie to find out a theefe that hath stolne anie thing from you.*

Go to the sea side, and gather as manie pebles as you suspect persons and that matter; carrie them home, and throwe them into the fier, and burie them under the threshhold, where the parties are like to come over. There let them lie three daies, and then before sunne rising take them awaie. Then set a porrenger full of water in a circle, wherein must be made crosses everie waie, as manie as can stand in it; upon the which must be written: Christ overcommeth, Christ reigneth, Christ commandeth. The porrenger also must be signed with a crosse, and a forme of conjuration must be pronounced. Then each stone must be throwne into the water, in the name of the suspected. And when you put in the stone of him that is guiltie, the stone will make the water boile, as though glowing iron were put thereinto. Which is a meere knacke of legier de maine, and to be accomplished diverse waies.

¶ *To put out the theeves eie.*

Read the seven psalmes with the Letanie, and then must be said a horrible praier to Christ, and God the father, with a cursse against the theefe. Then in the middest of the step of your foote, on the ground where you stand, make a circle like an eie, and write thereabout certeine barbarous names, and drive with a coopers hammar, or addes into the middest thereof a brasen naile consecrated, saieng: *Justus es Domine, & justa judicia tua.* Then the theefe shall be bewraied by his crieng out.

¶ *Another waie to find out a theefe.*

Sticke a paire of sheeres in the rind of a sive, and let two persons set the top of each of their forefingers upon the upper part of the sheeres, holding it with the sive up from the ground steddilie, and aske *Peter* and *Paule* whether A. B. or C. hath stolne the thing lost, and at the nomination of the guiltie person, the sive will turne round. This is a great practise in all countries, and indeed a verie bable. For with the beating of the pulse some cause of that motion ariseth, some other cause by slight of the fingers, some other by the wind gathered in the sive to be staid, &c: at the pleasure of the holders. Some cause may be the imagination, which upon conceipt at the naming of the partie altereth the common course of the pulse. As may well be conceived by a ring held steddilie by a thred betwixt the finger and the thumbe, over or rather in a goblet or glasse; which within short space will strike against the side therof so manie strokes as the holder thinketh it a clocke, and then will staie: the which who so prooveth shall find true.

These be meere toies to mocke apes, and have in them no commendable devise

¶ *A charme to find out or spoile a theefe.*

Of this matter, concerning the apprehension of theeves by words, I will cite one charme, called S. *Adelberts* cursse, being both for length of words sufficient

to wearie the reader, and for substantiall stuffe comprehending all that apperteineth unto blasphemous speech or curssing, allowed in the church of *Rome*, as
an excommunication and inchantment.

¶ *Saint Adelberts cursse or charme against theeves.*

By the authoritie of the omnipotent Father, the Sonne, and the Holie-ghost,
and by the holie virgine *Marie* mother of our Lord Jesu Christ, and the holie
angels and archangels, and S. *Michaell*, and S. *John Baptist*, and in the behalfe of
S. *Peter* the apostle, and the residue of the apostles, and of S. *Steeven*, and of all
the martyrs, of S. *Sylvester*, and of S. *Adelbert*, and all the confessors, and S.
Alegand, and all the holie virgins, and of all the saints in heaven and earth, unto
whom there is given power to bind and loose: we doo excommunicate, damne,
cursse, and bind with the knots and bands of excommunication, and we doo
segregate from the bounds and lists of our holie mother the church, all those
theeves, sacrilegious persons, ravenous catchers, dooers, counsellers, coadjutors,
male or female, that have committed this theft or mischeefe, or have usurped

any part therof to their owne use. Let their share be with *Dathan* and *Abiran*,
whome the earth swallowed up for their sinnes and pride, and let them have
part with *Judas* that betraied Christ, Amen: and with *Pontius Pilat*, and with
them that said to the Lord, Depart from us, we will not understand thy waies;
let their children be made orphanes. Curssed be they in the field, in the grove,
in the woods, in their houses, barnes, chambers, and beds; and curssed be they
in the court, in the waie, in the towne, in the castell, in the water, in the church,
in the churchyard, in the tribunall place, in battell, in their abode, in the market
place, in their talke, in silence, in eating, in watching, in sleeping, in drinking in
feeling, in sitting, in kneeling, in standing in lieng, in idlenes, in all their
worke, in their bodie and soule, in their five wits, and in everie place. Curssed
be the fruit of their wombs, and curssed be the fruit of their lands, and curssed
be all that they have. Curssed be their heads, their mouthes, their nostrels, their
noses, their lips, their jawes, their teeth, their eies and eielids, their braines, the
roofe of their mouthes, their toongs, their throtes, their breasts, their harts, their
bellies, their livers, all their bowels, and their stomach.

Curssed be their navels, their spleenes, their bladder. Curssed be their thighs,
their legs, their feete, their toes, their necks, their shoulders. Curssed be their
backs, curssed be their armes, curssed be their elbowes, curssed be their hands,
and their fingers, curssed be both the nails of their hands and feete; curssed be
their ribbes and their genitals, and their knees, curssed be their flesh, curssed be
their bones, curssed be their bloud, curssed be the skin of their bodies, curssed
be the marrowe in their bones, curssed be they from the crowne of the head, to
the sole of the foote: and whatsoever is betwixt the same, be it accurssed, that
is to saie, their five senses; to wit, their seeing, their hearing, their smelling,
their tasting, and their feeling. Curssed be they in the holie crosse, in the passion
of Christ, with his five wounds, with the effusion of his bloud, and by the milke

of the virgine *Marie*. I conjure thee *Lucifer*, with all thy soldiers, by the father,
the son, and the Holie-ghost, with the humanitie and nativitie of Christ, with
the vertue of all saints, that thou rest not day nor night, till thou bringest them
to destruction, either by drowning or hanging, or that they be devoured by wild
beasts, or burnt, or slaine by their enimies, or hated of all men living. And as
our Lord hath given authoritie to *Peter* the apostle, and his successors, whose
place we occupie, and to us (though unworthie) that whatsoever we bind on
earth, shall be bound in heaven, and whatsoever we loose on earth, shall be
loosed in heaven: so we accordinglie, if they will not amend, doo shut from
them the gates of heaven, and denie unto them christian buriall, so as they shall
be buried in asses leaze. Furthermore, curssed be the ground wherein they are
buried, let them be confounded in the last daie of judgement, let them have no
conversation among christians, nor be houseled at the houre of death; let them
be made as dust before the face of the wind: and as *Lucifer* was expelled out of
heaven, and *Adam* and *Eve* our of paradise; so let them be expelled from the daie

light. Also let them be joined with those, to whome the Lord saith at the judge-   Matth. 15.
ment; Go ye curssed into everlasting fier, which is prepared for the divell and
his angels, where the worme shall not die, nor the fier be quenched. And as the
candle, which is throwne out of my hand here, is put out: so let their works and
their soule be quenched in the stench of hell fier, except they restore that which
they have stolne, by such a daie: and let everie one saie, Amen. After this must   That is, In
be soong *In media vita in morte sumus*, &c.   the midst of
life we are

in death,
This terrible cursse with bell, booke, and candell added thereunto, must   &c.
needs worke woonders: howbeit among theeves it is not much weighed, among
wise and true men it is not well liked, to them that are robbed it bringeth small
releefe: the preests stomach may well be eased, but the goods stolne will never
the sooner be restored. Hereby is bewraied both the malice and follie of popish
doctrine, whose uncharitable impietie is so impudentlie published, and in
such order uttered, as everie sentence (if oportunitie served) might be prooved
both hereticall and diabolicall. But I will answer this cruell cursse with another
cursse farre more mild and civill, performed by as honest a man (I dare saie) as
he that made the other, whereof mention was latelie made.

So it was, that a certeine sir *John*, with some of his companie, once went   [i.e. a
abroad a jetting, and in a moone light evening robbed a millers weire, and stole   priest.]
all his eeles. The poore miller made his mone to sir *John* himselfe, who willed
him to be quiet; for he would so cursse the theefe, and all his confederates, with
bell, booke, and candell, that they should have small joy of their fish. And therefore the next sundaie, sir *John* got him to the pulpit, with his surplisse on his
backe, and his stole about his necke, and pronounced these words following in
the audience of the people.

> *All you that have stolne the millers eeles,*
> *Laudate Dominum de cœlis,*   A cursse
> *And all they that have consented thereto.*   for theft.
> *Benedicamus Domino.*

Lo (saith he) there is sauce for your eeles my maisters.

¶ *Another inchantment.*

Certeine preests use the hundred and eight psalme as an inchantment or
charme, or at the leastwise saieng, that against whome soever they pronounce it,
they cannot live one whole yeere at the uttermost.

CHAPTER XVIII.

¶ *A charme or experiment to find out a witch.*

*I*N *die dominico sotularia juvenum axungia seu pinguedine porci, ut moris est, pro
restauratione fieri perungunt: and when she is once come into the church, the
witch can never get out, untill the seachers for hir give hir expresse leave
to depart.

But now it is necessarie to shew you how to prevent and cure all mischeefes
wrought by these charmes & witchcrafts, according to the opinion of *M. Mal.*   Preserva-
and others. One principall waie is to naile a horsse shoo at the inside of the   tives from
witchcraft
outmost threshhold of your house, and so you shall be sure no witch shall have   according
power to enter thereinto. And if you marke it, you shall find that rule observed in   to M. Mal.
manie countrie houses. ☆ Otherwise: Item the triumphant title to be written crosse-   L, Vairus
wise, in everie corner of the house, thus: *Jesus* ✠ *Nazarenus* ✠ *rex* ✠ *Judæorum* ✠   & others.
Memorandum you may joine heerewithall, the name of the virgine *Marie*, or of

the foure evangelists, or *Verbum caro factum est.* ☆ Otherwise: Item in some countries they naile a woolves head on the doore. ☆ Otherwise: Item they hang *Scilla* (which is either a roote, or rather in this place garlike) in the roofe of the house, for to keepe awaie witches and spirits: and so they doo Alicium also. ☆ Otherwise: Item perfume made of the gall of a blake dog, and his bloud besmeered on the posts and walles of the house, driveth out of the doores both devils and witches. ☆ Otherwise: The house where *Herba betonica* is sowne, is free from all mischeefes. ☆ Otherwise: It is not unknowne that the Romish church allowed and used the smoke of sulphur, to drive spirits out of their houses; as they did frankincense and water hallowed. ☆ Otherwise: *Apuleius* saith, that *Mercurie* gave to *Ulysses*, when he came neere to the inchantresse *Circe*, an hearbe called *Verbascum*, which in English is called Pullein, or *Tapsus barbatus*, or Longwoort; and that preserved him from the inchantments. ☆ Otherwise: Item *Plinie* and *Homer* both doo saie, that the herbe called Molie is an excellent herbe against inchantments; and saie all that thereby *Ulysses* escaped *Circes* hir sorceries, and inchantments. ☆ Otherwise also diverse waies they went to worke in this case, and some used this defensative, some that preservative against incantations.

And heerein you shall see, not onelie how the religion of papists, and infidels agree; but also how their ceremonies and their opinions are all one concerning witches and spirits.

For thus writeth Ovid touching that matter:

Ovid. de Medea.
Englished by Abraham Fleming.

Térque senem flamma, ter aqua, ter sulphure lustrat:

> *She purifies with fier thrise*
> *old horie headed Aeson,*
> *With water thrise, and sulphur thrise,*
> *as she thought meet in reason.*

Againe, the same Ovid commeth in as before:

Adveniat, quæ lustret anus, lectúmque locúmque,
Deferat & tremula sulphur & ova manu.

By Ab. Fleming.

> *Let some old woman hither come,*
> *and purge both bed and place,*
> *And bring in trembling hand new egs*
> *and sulphur in like case.*

Virg. in Bucolicis.

And Virgil also harpeth upon the like string:

————————baccare frontem
Cingite, ne vati noceat mala lingua futuro:

Englished by Abraham Fleming.

> *Of berrie bearing baccar bowze*
> *a wreath or garland knit,*
> *And round about his head and browze*
> *see decentlie it sit;*
> *That of an evill talking tung*
> *Our future poet be not stung.*

Futhermore, was it not in times of tempests the papists use, or superstition, to ring their belles against divels; trusting rather to the tonging of their belles, than to their owne crie unto God with fasting and praier, assigned by him in all adversities and dangers: according to the order of the *Thracian* preests, which would

Olaus Goth. lib. de gentib. Septentriona-lib. 3. cap. 8.

rore and crie, with all the noise they could make, in those tempests. *Olaus Gothus* saith, that his countriemen would shoot in the aire, to assist their gods, whome they thought to be then togither by the eares with others, and had consecrated arrowes, called *Sagittæ Joviales*, even as our papists had. Also in steed of belles, they had great hammers, called *Mallei Joviales*, to make a noise in time of thunder. In some countries they runne out of the doores in time of tempest, blessing themselves with a cheese, whereupon there was a crosse made with a ropes end upon ascension daie. Also three hailestones to be throwne into the fier in a tempest, and thereupon to be said three *Pater nosters*, and three *Aves*, S. *Johns* gospell, and *in fine fugiat tempestas*, is a present remedie. Item, to hang an eg laid on ascension daie in the roofe of the house, preserveth the same from all hurts. Item, I conjure you haile and wind by the five wounds of Christ, by the three nailes which pearsed his hands and his feete, and by the foure evangelists, *Matthew, Marke, Luke,* and *John,* that thou come downe dissolved into water. Item, it hath beene a usuall matter, to carrie out in tempests the sacraments and relikes, &c. Item, against stormes, and manie dumme creatures, the popish church useth excommunication as a principall charme. And now to be delivered from witches themselves, they hang in their entries an hearbe called pentaphyllon, cinquefole, also an olive branch, also frankincense, myrrh, valerian, verven, palme, antirchmon, &c.: also haythorne, otherwise white[t]horne gathered on Maie daie: also the smoke of a lappoints fethers driveth spirits awaie. There be innumerable popish exorcismes, and conjurations for hearbs and other things, to be thereby made wholsome both for the bodies and soules of men and beasts, and also for contagion of weather. *Memorandum,* that at the gathering of these magicall herbs, the *Credo* is necessarie to be said, as *Vairus* affirmeth; and also the *Pater noster,* for that is not superstitious. Also *Sprenger* saith, that to throw up a blacke chicken in the aire, will make all tempests to cease: so it be done with the hand of a witch. If a soule wander in the likenesse of a man or woman by night, molesting men, with bewailing their torments in purgatorie, by reason of tithes forgotten, &c: and neither masses not conjurations can helpe; the exorcist in his ceremoniall apparell must go to the toome of that bodie, and spurne thereat, with his foote, saieng; *Vade ad gehennam,* Get thee packing to hell: and by and by the soule goeth thither, and there remaineth for ever. ☆ Otherwise: There be masses of purpose for this matter, to unbewitch the bewitched. ☆ Otherwise: You must spet into the pissepot, where you have made water. ☆ Otherwise: Spet into the shoo of your right foote, before you put it on: and that *Vairus* saith is good and holsome to doo, before you go into anie dangerous place. ☆ Otherwise: That neither hunters nor their dogs maie be bewitched, they cleave an oken branch, and both they and their dogs passe over it. ☆ Otherwise: *S. Augustine* saith, that to pacifie the god *Liber,* whereby women might have fruite of the seeds they sowe, and that their gardens and feelds should not be betwitched; some cheefe grave matrone used to put a crowne upon his genitall member, and that must be publikelie done.

A witches conjuration to make haile cease and be dissolved.

L. Vair. lib. de fascin. 2. cap. 11. Mal. Malef. par. 2. quæ. 1. cap. 15. Note that you read never of anie spirit that walked by daie, quoth Nato.

Aug. de civit. Dei. lib. 7. cap. 12.

To spoile a theefe, a witch, or anie other enimie, and to be delivered from the evill.

Upon the Sabboth daie before sunrising, cut a hazell wand, saieng: I cut thee O bough of this summers growth, in the name of him whome I meane to beate or maime. Then cover the table, and saie ✠ *In nomine patris* ✠ & *filii* ✠ & *spiritus sancti* ✠ *ter.* And striking thereon saie as followeth (english it he that can) *Drochs myroch, esenaroth,* ✠ *betu* ✠ *baroch* ✠ *ass* ✠ *maaroth* ✠: and then saie; Holie trinitie punish him that hath wrought this mischiefe, & take it away by thy great justice, *Eson* ✠ *elion* ✠ *emaris, ales, age;* and strike the carpet with your wand.

¶ *A notable charme or medicine to pull out an arrowhead, or anie such thing that sticketh in the flesh or bones, and cannot otherwise be had out.*

Saie three severall times kneeling; *Oremus, præceptis salutaribus moniti, Pater noster, ave Maria.* Then make a crosse saieng: The Hebrew knight strake our Lord Jesu Christ, and I beseech thee, O Lord Jesu Christ ✠ by the same iron, speare, bloud and water, to pull out this iron: *In nomine patris* ✠ & *filii* ✠ *spiritus sancti* ✠.

The Hebrue knight was canonized a saint to wit, S. Longinus.

¶ *Charmes against a quotidian ague.*

Cut an apple in three peeces, and write upon one; The father is uncreated: upon the other; The father is incomprehensible: upon the third; The father is eternall. ☆ Otherwise: Write upon a massecake cut in three peeces; O ague to be worshipped: on the second; O sicknesse to be ascribed to health and joies: on the third; *Pax* ✠ *max* ✠ *fax* ✠ and let it be eaten fasting. ☆ Otherwise: Paint upon three like peeces of a massecake, *Pater pax* ✠ *Adonai* ✠ *filius vita* ✠ *sabbaoth* ✠ *spiritus sanctus* ✠ *Tetragrammaton* ✠ and eate it, as is afore said.

¶ *For all maner of agues intermittant.*

A crossed appension, with other appensions.

Joine two little stickes together in the middest, being of one length, and hang it about your necke in the forme of a crosse. ☆ Otherwise: For this disease the *Turkes* put within their doublet a ball of wood, with an other peece of wood, and strike the same speaking certeine frivolous words. ☆ Otherwise: Certeine monks hanged scrolles about the necks of such as were sicke, willing them to saie certeine praiers at each fit, and at the third fit to hope well: and made them beleeve that they should thereby receive cure.

Periapts, characters, &c: for agues, and to cure all diseases, and to deliver from all evill.

For bodie and soule.

The first chapter of S. *Johns* gospell in small letters consecrated at a masse, and hanged about ones necke, is an incomparable amulet or tablet, which delivereth from all witchcrafts and divelish practises. But me thinkes, if one should hang a whole testament, or rather a bible, he might beguile the divell terriblie. For indeed so would S. *Barnard* have done, whom the divell told, that he could shew him seven verses in the psalter, which being dailie repeated, would of themselves bring anie man to heaven, and preserve him from hell. But when S. *Barnard* desired the divell to tell him which they were, he refused, saieng, he might then thinke him a foole so to prejudice himselfe. Well (quoth S. *Barnard*) I will doo well enough for that, for J will dailie saie over the whole psalter. The divell hearing him saie so, told him which were the verses, least in reading over the whole psalter dailie, he should merit too much for others. But if the hanging of S. *Johns* gospell about the necke be so beneficiall; how if one should eate up the same?

S. Barnard overmatcheth the divell for all his subtiltie.

¶ *More charmes for agues.*

Pretious restorities.

Take the partie by the hand, and saie; *Aequè facilis sit tibi hæc febris, atque Mariæ virgini Christi partus.* ☆ Otherwise: Wash with the partie, and privilie saie this psalme, *Exaltabo te Deus meus, rex &c.* ☆ Otherwise: Weare about your necke, a peece of a naile taken from a crosse, and wrapped in wooll. ☆ Otherwise: Drinke wine, wherein a sworde hath beene drowned that hath cut off ones head. ☆ Otherwise: Take three consecrated massecakes, and write upon the first: *Qualis est pater talis est vita:* on the second; *Qualis est filius, talis est sanctus:* on the third; *Qualis est spiritus tale est remedium.* Then give them to the sicke man, enjoining him to eate none other thing that daie wherein he eateth anie of them, nor yet drinke: and let him saie fifteene *Pater nosters*, and as manie *Aves*, in the honour and praise of the Trinitie. ☆ Otherwise: Lead the sicke man on a fridaie before sunne rising towards the east, and let him hold up his hands towards the sunne, and saie: This is the daie, wherein the Lord God came to the crosse. But as the crosse shall never more come to him: so let never the hot or cold fit of this ague come anie more unto this man, *In nomine patris* ✠ *& fi* ✠ *lii, & spiritus* ✠ *sancti* ✠. Then saie seven and twentie *Pater nosters*, and as manie *Aves*, and use this three daies togither. ☆ Otherwise:

This is too mysticall to be englished quoth Nota.

Fécana, cagéti, daphnes, gebáre, gedáco,
Gébali stant, sed non stant phebas, hecas, & hedas.

Everie one of these words must be written upon a peece of bread, and be given in order one daie after another to the sicke bodie, and so must he be cured. This saith *Nicholas Hemingius* he chanced to read in the schooles in jest; so as one noting the words, practised the medicine in earnest; and was not onelie cured himselfe, but also cured manie others thereby. And therefore he concludeth, that this is a kind of a miraculous cure, wrought by the illusion of the divell: whereas in truth, it will fall out most commonlie, that a tertian ague will not hold anie man longer than so, though no medicine be given, nor anie words spoken. ☆ Otherwise: This word, *Abra cadabra* written on a paper, with a certeine figure joined therewith, and hanged about ones necke, helpeth the ague. ☆ Otherwise: Let the urine of the sicke bodie made earlie in the morning, be softlie heated nine daies togither continuallie, untill all be consumed into vapour. ☆ Otherwise: A crosse made of two litle twigs joined togither, wherewith when the partie is touched, he will be whole; speciallie if he weare it about his necke. ☆ Otherwise: Take a little quantitie of water out of three ponds of equall bignesse, and tast thereof in a new earthen vessell, and drinke of it when the fit commeth.

In the yeare of our lord 1568. the *Spaniards* and *Italians* received from the pope, this incantation following; whereby they were promised both remission of sinnes, and good successe in their warres in the lowe countries. Which whether it be not as prophane and impious, as anie witches charme, I report me to the indifferent reader. ✠ *Crucem pro nobis subiit* ✠ & *stans in illa sitiit* ✠ *Jesus sacratis manibus, clavis ferreis, pedibus perfossis, Jesus, Jesus, Jesus: Domine libera nos ab hoc malo, & ab hac peste:* then three *Pater nosters*, and three *ave Maries.* Also the same yeere their ensignes were by the authoritie aforesaid conjured with certeine ceremonies, & consecrated against their enimies. And if you read the histories of these warres, you maie see what victorie they gained hereby. Item, they baptised their cheefe standard, and gave it to name S. *Margaret*, who overthrew the divell. And bicause you shall understand the mysterie hereof, I have the rather set it downe elsewhere, being indeed worth the reading.

Fernelius.

Notable follies of the Spaniards & Italians.

¶ *For a bloudie flux, or rather an issue of bloud.*

Take a cup of cold water, and let fall thereinto three drops of the same bloud, and betweene each drop saie a *Pater noster*, and an *Ave*, then drinke to the patient, and saie; Who shall helpe you? The patient must answer *S. Marie.* Then saie you; *S. Marie* stop the issue of bloud. ☆ Otherwise: Write upon the patients forhead with the same bloud: *Consummatum est.* ☆ Otherwise: Saie to the patient; *Sanguis mane in te, sicut fecit Christus in se; Sanguis mane in tua vena, sicut Christus in sua pœna; Sanguis mane fixus, sicut Christus quando fuit crucifixus: ter.* ☆ Otherwise, as followeth.

He must answer by none other, for she perhaps hath the curing thereof by patent.

> In the bloud of Adam death was taken ✠
> In the bloud of Christ it was all too shaken ✠
> And by the same bloud I doo thee charge,
> That thou doo runne no longer at large.   ☆ Otherwise.

Christ was borne at *Bethelem*, and suffered at *Jerusalem*, where his bloud was troubled. I command thee by the vertue of God, and through the helpe of all saincts, to staie even as *Jordan* did, when *John* baptised Christ Jesus; *In nomine patris* ✠ & *filii* ✠ & *spiritus sancti* ✠ ☆ Otherwise: Put thy nameles finger in the wound, and make therwith three crosses upon the wound, and saie five *Pater nosters*, five *Aves*, and one *Credo*, in the honour of the five wounds. ☆ Otherwise: Touch that part and saie, *De latere ejus exivit sanguis & aqua.* ☆ Otherwise: *In nomine patris* ✠ & *filii* ✠ & *spiritus sancti* ✠ &c. *Chimrat, chara, sarite, confirma, consona, Imohalite.* ☆ Otherwise: *Sepa* ✠ *sepaga* ✠ *sepagoga* ✠ *sta sanguis in nomine patris* ✠ *podendi* ✠ & *filii* ✠ *podera* ✠ & *spiritus sancti* ✠ *pandorica* ✠ *pax tecum, Amen.*

See J. Wier. cap. 11. conf

¶ *Cures commensed and finished by witchcraft.*

There was a jollie fellowe that tooke upon him to be a notable surgion, in the dutchie of *Mentz*, 1567. to whom there resorted a Gentleman that had beene vexed with sicknesse, named *Elibert*, having a kerchiefe on his head, according to the guise of sicke folke. But the surgion made him pull off his kerchiefe, and willed him to drinke with him freelie. The sickeman said he durst not; for he was forbidden by physicke so to doo. Tush (said this cunning man) they know not your disease: be ruled by me, and take in your drinke lustilie. For he thought that when he was well tippled, he might the more easilie beguile him in his bargaine, and make his reward the greater, which he was to receive in part aforehand. When they had well droonke, he called the sicke man aside, and told him the greatnes and danger of his disease, and how that it grew by meanes of witchcraft, and that it would be universallie spread in his house, and among all his cattell, if it were not prevented: and impudentlie persuaded the sicke man to receive cure of him. And after bargaine made, he demanded of the sicke man, whether he had not anie at home, whom he might assuredlie trust. The sicke man answered, that he had a daughter and a servant. The consener asked how old his daughter was? The patient said, twentie. Well (said the cousener) that is fit for our turne. Then he made the mother and father to kneele on their knees to their daughter, and to desire hir in all things to obey the physician, and that she would doo in everie thing as he commanded hir; otherwise hir father could not be restored to his health. In which respect hir parents humblie besought hir on their knees so to doo. Then he assigned hir to bring him into his lodging hir fathers haire, and hir mothers, and of all those which he kept in his house, as well of men and women, as also of his cattell. When she came therewith unto him, according to the match made, and hir parents commandement, he lead hir downe into a lowe parlor, where having made a long speech, he opened a booke that laie on the boord, and laieth thereon two knives acrosse, with much circumstance of words. Then conjureth he, and maketh strange characters, and at length he maketh a circle on the ground, wherein he causeth hir to sticke one of those conjured knives; and after manie more strange words, he maketh hir sticke the other knife beside it. Then fell downe the maid in a swoone for feare; so as he was faine to frote hir and put a sop into hir mouth, after the receipt whereof she was sore troubled and amazed. Then he made hir brests to be uncovered, so as when they were bare, he dallied with them, diverslie and long together. Then he made hir lie right upward, all uncovered and bare belowe hir pappes. Wherein the maid being loth to obeie him, resisted, and in shame forbad that villanie. Then said the knave; Your fathers destruction is at hand: for except you will be ruled, he and all his familie shall susteine greater greefe and inconvenience, than is yet happened unto him. And no remedie, except you will seeke his utter overthrowe, I must have carnall copulation with you, and therewithall fell into hir bosome, and overthrew hir and his virginitie. So did he the second daie, and attempted the like on the third daie. But he failed then of his purpose, as the wench confessed afterwards. In the meane time he ministred so cruell medicines to the sicke man, that through the torments thereof he feared present death, and was faine to keepe his bed, whereas he walked about before verie well and lustilie. The patient in his torments called unto him for remedie, who being slacke and negligent in that behalfe, made roome for the daughter to accompanie hir father, who asked hir what she thought of the cure, and what hope she had of his recoverie. Who with teares remained silent, as being oppressed with greefe; till at the last in abundance of sorrowe she uttered the whole matter to hir father. This dooth *Johannes Wierus* report, saieng, that it came unto him by the lamentable relation of the father himselfe. And this is here at this time for none other purpose rehearsed, but that men may hereby learne to take heed of such cousening merchants, and knowe what they be that take upon them to be so cunning in witchcraft; least they be bewitched: as maister *Elibert* and his daughter were.

The surgion here most impudentlie setteth his knaverie abroch.

A pretended conjuration.

Ad vada tot vadid urna quòd ipsa cadit.

¶ *Another witchcraft or knaverie, practised by the same surgion.*

This surgeon ministred to a noble man, that laie sicke of an ague, offering unto him three peeces of a roote to be eaten at three morsels; saieng to the first: I would Christ had not beene borne; unto the second; I would he had not suffered; unto the third: I would he had not risen againe. And then putting them about the sicke mans necke, said; Be of good cheere. And if he lost them, whatsoever

Three morsels, the first charmed with christs birth, the

tooke them up, should therewithall take awaie his ague. ☆ Otherwise: Jesus Christ, which was borne, deliver thee from this infirmitie ✠ Jesus Christ which died ✠ deliver thee from this infirmitie ✠ Jesus Christ which rose againe ✠ deliver thee from this infirmitie. Then dailie must be said five *Pater nosters*, and five *Aves*.

second
with his
passion, the
third with
his resur-
rection.

¶ *Another experiment for one bewitched,*

Another such cousening physician persuaded one which had a timpanie, that it was one old viper, and twoo young mainteined in his bellie by witchcraft. But being watched, so as he could not conveie vipers into his ordure or excrements, after his purgations: at length he told the partie, that he should suffer the paines of childbirth, if it were not prevented; and therefore he must put his hand into his breech, and rake out those wormes there. But the mother of the sicke partie having warning thereof, said she could doo that hir selfe. So the cousener was prevented, and the partie died onelie of a timpanie, and the knave ran awaie out of the countrie.

A couse-
ning phy-
sician, and
a foolish
patient.

¶ *Otherwise.*

Monsieur Bodin telleth of a witch, who undertaking to cure a woman bewitched, caused a masse to be soong at mid-night in our ladies chapell. And when she had overlien the sicke partie, and breathed certeine words upon hir, she was healed. Wherein *Bodin* saith, she followed the example of *Elias* the prophet, who raised the *Sunamitie*. And this storie must need be true: for goodman *Hardivin Blesensis* his host at the signe of the lion told him the storie.

John. Bodin.

Kakozelia.

¶ *A knacke to know whether you be bewitched, or no, &c.*

It is also expedient to learne how to know whether a sicke man be bewitched or no: this is the practise thereof. You must hold molten lead over the sicke bodie, and powre it into a porrenger full of water; and then, if there appeare upon the lead, anie image, you may then knowe the partie is bewitched.

Mal. malef.
pa. 1. *quæ.* 17.
Barth. Spin.
in novo
Mal. malef.

CHAPTER XIX.

That one witchcraft maie lawfullie meete with another.

SCOTUS, *Hostiensis, Gofridus*, and all the old canonists agree, that it is lawfull to take awaie witchcraft by witchcraft, *Et vana vanis contundere.* And *Scotus* saith, It were follie to forbeare to encounter witchcraft by witchcraft; for (saith he) there can be none inconvenience therein; bicause the overthrower of witchcraft assenteth not to the works of the divell. And therefore he saith further, that it is meritorious so to extinguish and overthrow the divels workes. As though he should saie; It maketh no matter, though S. *Paule* saie; *Non facies malum, ut indè veniat bonum*, Thou shalt not doo evill, that good maie come thereof. *Humbertus* saith, that witchcraft maie be taken awaie by that meanes whereby it was brought. But *Gofredus* inveieth sore against the oppugners thereof. Pope *Nicholas* the fift gave indulgence and leave to bishop *Miraties* (who was so bewitched in his privities, that he could not use the gift of venerie) to seeke remedie at witches hands. And this was the clause of his dispensation, *Ut ex duobus malis fugiatur majus*, that of two evils, the greater should be avoided. And so a witch, by taking his doublet, cured him, and killed the other witch: as the storie saith, which is to be seene in *M. Mal.* and diverse other writers.

Scotus in 4.
distinct. 34.
de imperio.

Dist. 4.
Gofred. in
summa sua.

CHAPTER XX.

Who are privileged from witches, what bodies are aptest to be bewitched, or to be witches, why women are rather witches than men, and what they are.

Mal. malef.
par. 2. *quæ.* 1.
cap. 1.
Whereof
looke more
in a little
booke set
foorth in
print.

NOW if you will know who and what persons are privileged from witches, you must understand, that they be even such as cannot be bewitched. In the number of whome first be the inquisitors, and such as exercise publike justice upon them. Howbeit, a justice in *Essex*, whome for diverse respects I have left unnamed, not long since thought he was bewitched, in the verie instant whiles he examined the witch; so as his leg was broken therby, &c: which either was false, or else this rule untrue, or both rather injurious unto Gods providence. Secondlie, such as observe dulie the rites and ceremonies of holie church, and worship them with reverence, through the sprinkling of holie water, and receiving consecrated salt, by the lawfull use of candles hallowed on Candelmas daie, and greene leaves consecrated on Palme sundaie (which things they saie the church useth for the qualifieng of the divels power) are preserved from witchcraft. Thirdlie, some are preserved by their good angels, which attend and wait upon them.

But I maie not omit here the reasons, which they bring, to prove what bodies are the more apt and effectuall to execute the art of fascination. And that is, first they saie the force of celestiall bodies, which indifferentlie communicate their vertues unto men, beasts, trees, stones, &c. But this gift and naturall influence of fascination maie be increased in man, according to his affections and perturbations; as thorough anger, feare, love, hate, &c. For by hate (saith *Vairus*) entereth a fierie inflammation into the eie of man, which being violentlie sent out by beams and streames, &c: infect and bewitch those bodies against whome they are opposed. And therefore he saith (in the favour of women) that that is the cause why women are oftener found to be witches than men. For (saith he) they have such an unbrideled force of furie and concupiscence naturallie, that by no means it is possible for them to temper or moderate the same. So as upon everie trifling occasion, they (like brute beasts) fix their furious eies upon the partie whom they bewitch. Hereby it commeth to passe, that whereas women having a mervellous fickle nature, what greefe so ever happeneth unto them, immediatlie all peceablenes of mind departeth; and they are so troubled with evill humors, that out go their venomous exhalations, ingendred thorough their ilfavoured diet, and increased by meanes of their pernicious excrements, which they expell. Women are also (saith he) monethlie filled full of superfluous humors, and with them the melancholike bloud boileth; whereof spring vapors, and are carried up, and conveied through the nosethrels and mouth, &c.; to the bewitching of whatsoever it meeteth. For they belch up a certeine breath, wherewith they bewitch whomsoever they list. And of all other women, leane, hollow eied, old, beetlebrowed women (saith he) are the most infectious. Marie he saith, that hot, subtill, and thin bodies are most subject to be bewitched, if they be moist, and all they generallie, whose veines, pipes, and passages of their bodies are open. And finallie he saith, that all beautifull things whatsoever, are soone subject to be bewitched; as namelie goodlie yoongmen, faire women, such as are naturallie borne to be rich, goodlie beasts, faire horsses, ranke corne, beautifull trees, &c. Yea a freend of his told him, that he saw one with his eie breake a pretious stone in peeces. And all this he telleth as soberlie, as though it were true. And if it were true, honest women maie be witches, in despight of all inquisitors: neither can anie avoid being a witch, except shee locke hir selfe up in a chamber.

L. Vair. lib.
de fascin.
1. *c.* 12.

Much like
the eiebiting
witches, of
whom we
have els-
where
spoken.

Who are
most likelie
to bewitch,
and to be
bewitched.

CHAPTER XXI.

What miracles witchmongers report to have beene done by witches words, &c: contradictions of witchmongers among themselves, how beasts are cured herby, of bewitched butter, a charme against witches, and a counter charme, the effect of charmes and words proved by L. Vairus to be woonderfull.

IF I should go about to recite all charmes, I should take an infinite worke in hand. For the witching writers hold opinion, that anie thing almost maie be therby brought to passe; & that whether the words of the charme be understandable or not, it skilleth not: so the charmer have a steddie intention to bring his desire about. And then what is it that cannot be done by words? For *L. Vairus* saith, that old women have infeebled and killed children with words, and have made women with child miscarrie; they have made men pine awaie to death, they have killed horsses, deprived sheepe of their milke, transformed men into beasts, flowne in the aire, tamed and staied wild beasts, driven all noisome cattell and vermine from corne, vines and hearbs, staied serpents, *&c*: and all with words. In so much as he saith, that with certeine words spoken in a bulles eare by a witch, the bull hath fallen downe to the ground as dead. Yea some by vertue of words have gone upon a sharpe sword, and walked upon hot glowing coles, without hurt; with words (saith he) verie heavie weights and burthens have beene lifted up; and with words wild horsses and wild bulles have beene tamed, and also mad dogs; with words they have killed wormes, and other vermine, and staied all maner of bleedings and fluxes: with words all diseases in mans bodie are healed, and wounds cured; arowes are with wonderfull strangenesse and cunning plucked out of mens bones. Yea (saith he) there be manie that can heale all bitings of dogs, or stingings of serpents, or anie other poison: and all with nothing but words spoken. And that which is most strange, he saith, that they can remedie anie stranger, and him that is absent, with that verie sword wherewith they are wounded. Yea and that which is beyond all admiration, if they stroke the sword upwards with their fingers, the partie shall feele no paine: whereas if they drawe their finger downewards thereupon, the partie wounded shall feele intollerable paine. With a number of other cures, done altogither by the vertue and force of words uttered and spoken.

    Where, by the waie, I maie not omit this speciall note, given by *M. Mal.* to wit, that holie water maie not be sprinkled upon bewitched beasts, but must be powred into their mouthes. And yet he, and also *Nider*, saie, that It is lawfull to blesse and sanctifie beasts, as well as men; both by charmes written, and also by holie words spoken. For (saith *Nider*) if your cow be bewitched, three crosses, three *Pater nosters*, and three *Aves* will certeinlie cure hir; and likewise all other ceremonies ecclesiasticall. And this is a sure *Maxime*, that they which are delivered from witchcraft by shrift, are ever after in the night much molested (I beleeve by their ghostlie fathers.) Also they loose their monie out of their pursses and caskets: as *M. Mal.* saith he knoweth by experience. Also one generall rule is given by *M. Mal.* to all butter wives, and dairie maides, that they neither give nor lend anie butter, milke, or cheese, to anie witches, which alwaies use to beg thereof, when they meane to worke mischeefe to their kine or whitmeats. Whereas indeed there are in milke three substances commixted; to wit, butter, cheese, and whaie: if the same be kept too long, or in an evill place, or be sluttishlie used, so as it be stale and sower, which happeneth sometimes in winter, but oftener in summer, when it is set over the fier, the cheese and butter runneth togither, and congealeth, so as it will rope like birdlime, that you maie wind it about a sticke, and in short space it will be so drie, as you maie beate it to powder. Which alteration being strange, is woondered at, and imputed to witches. And herehence sometimes proceedeth the cause, why butter commeth not, which the countrie people see that it commeth not, then get they out of the

L. Vair. lib. de fascin. 1. *ca.* 5.

According to *Ovids* saieng of *Proteus & Medea*, which he indeed alledgeth therefore *Nunc aqua, nunc ales, modò bos, modò cervus abibat.*

Mal. Malef. par. 2. *quæ.* 2. *cap.* 7. *Nider in præceptorio, præcept.* 1. *ca.* 11. *Nider in fornicario. Mal. Malef. part.* 2. *cap.* 8.

A good devise to starve up poore women. *Mal. Malef. part.* 2. *quæ,* 2, *cap.* 7.

suspected witches house, a little butter, whereof must be made three balles, in the name of the holie trinitie; and so if they be put into the cherne, the butter will presentlie come, and the witchcraft will cease; *Sic ars deluditur arte.* But if you put a little sugar or sope into the cherne, among the creame, the butter will never come: which is plaine witchcraft, if it be closelie, cleanlie, and privilie handled. There be twentie severall waies to make your butter come, which for brevitie I omit; as to bind your cherne with a rope, to thrust thereinto a red hot spit, &c: but your best remedie and surest waie is, to looke well to your dairie maid or wife, that she neither eat up the creame, nor sell awaie your butter.

¶ *A charme to find hir that bewitched your kine.*

A ridiculous charme.

Put a paire of breeches upon the cowes head, and beate hir out of the pasture with a good cudgell upon a fridaie, and she will runne right to the witches doore, and strike thereat with hir hornes.

¶ *Another, for all that have bewitched anie kind of cattell.*

When anie of your cattell are killed with witchcraft, hast you to the place where the carcase lieth, and traile the bowels of the beast unto your house, and drawe them not in at the doore, but under the threshhold of the house into the kitchen; and there make a fier, and set over the same a grediron, and thereupon laie the inwards or bowels; and as they wax hot, so shall the witches entrailes be molested with extreame heate and paine. But then must you make fast your doores, least the witch come and fetch awaie a cole of your fier: for then ceaseth hir torments. And we have knowne saith *M. Mal.* when the witch could not come in, that the whole house hath beene so darkened, and the aire round about the same so troubled, with such horrible noise and earthquakes; that except the doore had beene opened, we had thought the house would have fallen on our heads. *Thomas Aquinas*, a principall treator herein, alloweth conjurations against the changelings, and in diverse other cases: whereof I will saie more in the word *Iidoni.*

¶ *A speciall charme to preserve all cattell from witchcraft.*

In anie case observe the festivall time, or else you marre all.

At Easter you must take certeine drops, that lie uppermost of the holie paschall candle, and make a little waxe candle thereof: and upon some sundaie morning rath, light it, and hold it, so as it maie drop upon and betweene the hornes and eares of the beast, saieng: *In nomine patris, & filii, et duplex s s:* and burne the beast a little betweene the hornes on the eares with the same wax: and that which is left thereof, sticke it in crossewise about the stable or stall, or upon the threshold, or over the doore, where the cattell use to go in and out, and for all that yeare your cattell shall never be bewitched. ☆ Otherwise: *Jacobus de Chusa Carthusianus* sheweth, how bread, water, and salt is conjured, and saith, that if either man or beast receive holie bread and holie water nine daies together, with three *Pater nosters*, and three *Aves*, in the honour of the trinitie, and of *S. Hubert*, it preserveth that man or beast from all diseases, and defendeth them against all assaults of witchcraft, of satan, or of a mad dog, &c.

Lo this is their stuffe, mainteined to be at the least effectuall, if not wholsome, by all papists and witchmongers, and speciallie of the last and proudest writers. But to proove these things to be effectuall, God knoweth their reasons are base and absurd. For they write so, as they take the matter in question as granted, and by that meanes go awaie therewith. For *L. Vairus* saith in the beginning of his booke, that there is no doubt of this supernaturall matter, bicause a number of writers agree herein, and a number of stories confirme it, and manie poets handle the same argument, and in the twelve tables there is a lawe against it, and bicause the consent of the common people is fullie with it, and bicause immoderate praise is to be approved a kind of witchcraft, and bicause old women have such charmes and superstitious meanes as preserve themselves

L. Vair. lib. de fascin. 1. cap. 1.

from it, and bicause they are mocked that take awaie the credit of such miracles, and bicause *Salomon* saith; *Fascinatio malignitatis obscurat bona*, and bicause the apostle saith; *O insensati Galatæ, quis vos fascinavit?* And bicause it is written, *Qui timent te, videbunt me.* And finallie he saith, least you should seeme to distrust and detract anie thing from the credit of so manie grave men, from histories, and common opinion of all men: he meaneth in no wise to proove that there is miraculous working by witchcraft and fascination; and proceedeth so, according to his promise.

Sapi. 4.
Gali. 3.
Psal. 119.

CHAPTER XXII.

Lawfull charmes, or rather medicinable cures for diseased cattell. The charme of charmes, and the power thereof.

BUT if you desire to learne true and lawfull charmes, to cure diseased cattell, even such as seeme to have extraordinarie sicknesse, or to be bewitched, or (as they saie) strangelie taken: looke in *B. Googe* his third booke, treating cattell, and happilie you shall find some good medicine or cure for them: or if you list to see more ancient stuffe, read *Vegetius* his foure bookes thereupon: or, if you be unlearned, seeke some cunning bullocke leech. If all this will not serve, then set *Jobs* patience before your eies. And never thinke that a poore old woman can alter supernaturallie the notable course, which God hath appointed among his creatures. If it had beene Gods pleasure to have permitted such a course, he would no doubt have both given notice in his word, that he had given such power unto them, and also would have taught remedies to have prevented them.

Furthermore, if you will knowe assured meanes, and infallible charmes, yeelding indeed undoubted remedies, and preventing all maner of witchcrafts, and also the assaults of wicked spirits; then despise first all cousening knaverie of priests, witches, and couseners: and with true faith read the sixt chapter of S. *Paule* to the *Ephesians*, and followe his counsell, which is ministered unto you in the words following, deserving worthilie to be called by the name insuing:

Direct and lawfull meanes of curing cattell, &c.

The charme of charmes.

Finallie my brethren, be strong in the Lord, and in the power of his might. Put on the whole armour of God, that you may stand against the assaults of the divell. For we wrestle not against flesh and bloud, but against principalities and powers, & against worldlie governors the princes of the darknes of this world, against spirituall wickednes, which are in the high places. For this cause take unto you the armour of God, that you may be able to resist the evill daie; and having finished all things, stand fast. Stand therefore, and your loines girded about with veritie, and having on the brestplate of righteousnes, &c: as followeth in that chapter, verses 15. 16. 17. 18. 1 *Thes.* 5. 1 *Pet.* 5, verse. 8. *Ephes.* 1. and elsewhere in the holie scripture.

A charme of charmes taken out of the sixt chapter of S. Paule to the Ephesians.

¶ Otherwise.

If you be unlearned, and want the comfort of freends, repaire to some learned, godlie, and discreet preacher. If otherwise need require, go to a learned physician, who by learning and experience knoweth and can discerne the difference, signes, and causes of such diseases, as faithlesse men and unskilfull physicians impute to witchcraft.

CHAPTER XXIII.

A confutation of the force and vertue falselie ascribed to charmes and amulets, by the authorities of ancient writers, both divines and physicians.

MY meaning is not, that these words, in the bare letter, can doo anie thing towards your ease or comfort in this behalfe; or that it were wholesome for your bodie or soule to weare them about your necke: for then would I wish you to weare the whole Bible, which must needs be more effectual than anie one parcell thereof. But I find not that the apostles, or anie of them in the primitive church, either carried S. *Johns* gospell, or anie *Agnus Dei* about them, to the end they might be preserved from bugges: neither that they looked into the foure corners of the house, or else in the roofe, or under the threshold, to find matter of witchcraft, and so to burne it, to be freed from the same; according to the popish rules. Neither did they by such and such verses or praiers made unto saints, at such or such houres, seeke to obtaine grace: neither spake they of anie old women that used such trades. Neither did Christ at anie time use or command holie water, or crosses, &c: to be used as terrors against the divell, who was not affraid to assault himselfe, when he was on earth. And therefore a verie thing it is to thinke that he feareth these trifles, or anie externall matter. Let us then cast awaie these prophane and odd wives fables. For (as *Origen* saith) *Incantationes sunt dæmonū irrisiones idololatriæ fœx, animarum infatuatio,* &c.

Chrysostome saith; There be some that carrie about their necks a peece of a gospell. But is it not dailie read (saith he) and heard of all men? But if they be never the better for it, being put into their eares, how shall they be saved, by carrieng it about their necks? And further he saith; Where is the vertue of the gospell? In the figure of the letter, or in the understanding of the sense? If in the figure, thou dooest well too weare it about thy necke; but if in the understanding, then thou shouldest laie it up in thine heart. *Augustine* saith; Let the faithfull ministers admonish and tell their people, that these magicall arts and incantations doo bring no remedie to the infirmities either of men or cattell, &c.

The heathen philosophers shall at the last daie confound the infidelitie and barbarous foolishnes of our christian or rather anti-christian and prophane witchmongers. For as *Aristotle* saith, that *Incantamenta sunt muliercularum figmenta:* so dooth *Socrates* (who was said to be cunning herein) affirme, that *Incantationes sunt verba animas decipientia humanas.* Others saie; *Inscitiæ pallium sunt carmina, maleficium, & incantatio. Galen* also saith, that such as impute the falling evill, and such like diseases to divine matter, and not rather to naturall causes, are witches, conjurers, &c. *Hippocrates* calleth them arrogant; and in another place affirming that in his time there were manie deceivers and couseners, that would undertake to cure the falling evill, &c: by the power and helpe of divels, by burieng some lots or inchantments in the ground, or casting them into the sea, concludeth thus in their credit, that they are all knaves and couseners: for God is our onlie defender and deliverer. O notable sentence of a heathen philosopher!

Mal. Malef. part. 2. qu. 2. cap. 6.

1. Tim. 4, 7. Origin. lib. 3. in Job. J. Chrysost. in Matth. Marke that here was no latine service. *Idem. Ibid. August. 26. quæ. ultim.*

Galen. in lib. de comitiali morbo. Hippocrat. lib. de morbo sacro.

BOOKE XIII.

Chapter i.

The signification of the Hebrue word Hartumim, where it is found written in the scriptures, and how it is diverslie translated: whereby the objection of Pharaos magicians is afterward answered in this booke; also of naturall magicke not evill in it selfe.

HARTUMIM is no naturall Hebrue word, but is borrowed of some other nation: howbeit, it is used of the Hebrues in these places; to wit, *Gen.* 4. 1. 8. 24. *Exod.* 7. 13. 24. & 8. 7. 18. & 9. 11. *Dan.* 1, 20. & 2. 2. *Hierome* sometimes translateth it *Conjectores*, sometimes *Malefici*, sometimes *Hieronymus. in Gen.* 41. 8, & 24. *In Exod.* 7, 13. *In Dan.* 1, 20. *Arioli:* which we for the most part translate by this word witches. But the right signification heereof may be conceived, in that the inchanters of *Pharao*, being conceived, in that the inchanters of *Pharao*, being magicians of *Aegypt*, were called *Hartumim.* And yet in *Exodus* they are named in some Latine translations *Venefici. Rabbi Levi* saith, it betokeneth such as doo strange and woonderfull things, naturallie, artificiallie, and deceitfullie. *Rabbi Isaac Natar* affirmeth, that such were so termed, as amongst the Gentiles professed singular wisedome. *Aben Ezra* expoundeth it, to signifie such as knowe the secrets of nature, and the qualitie of stones and hearbs, &c.; which is atteined unto by art, and speciallie by naturall magicke. But we, either for want of speech, or knowledge, call them all by the name and terme of witches.

Certeinlie, God indueth bodies with woonderfull graces, the perfect knowledge whereof man hath not reached unto: and on the one side, there is amongst them such mutuall love, societie, and consent; and on the other side, such naturall discord, and secret enimitie, that therein manie things are wrought to the astonishment of mans capacitie. But when deceit and diabolicall words are coupled therewith, then extendeth it to witchcraft and conjuration; as whereunto those naturall effects are falselie imputed. So as heere I shall have some occasion to The authors intention touching the matter hereafter to be discoursed upon. say somewhat of naturall magicke; bicause under it lieth hidden the venome of this word *Hartumim.* This art is said by some to be the profoundnesse, and the verie absolute perfection of naturall philosophie, and shewing foorth the active part thereof, & through the aid of naturall vertues, by the convenient applieng of them, works are published, exceeding all capacitie and admiration; and yet not so much by art, as by nature. This art of it selfe is not evill; for it consisteth in searching foorth the nature, causes, and effects of things. As farre as I can conceive, it hath beene more corrupted and prophaned by us Christians, than either by Jewes or Gentiles.

Chapter ii.

How the philosophers in times past travelled for the knowledge of naturall magicke, of Salomons knowledge therein, who is to be called a naturall magician, a distinction thereof, and why it is condemned for witchcraft.

MANIE philosophers; as namely, *Plato, Pythagoras, Empedocles, Democritus,* &c.: travelled over all the world to find out & learne the knowlege of this art; & at their returne they preached and taught, professed and published it. Yea, it should appeere by the magicians that came to adore

Christ, that the knowledge and reputation thereof was greater, than we conceive or make account of. But of all other, *Salomon* was the greatest traveller in this art, as may appeere throughout the booke of *Ecclesiastes*: and speciallie in the booke of *Wisedome*, where hee saith God hath given me the true science of things, so as I knowe how the world was made, and the power of the elements, the beginning and the end, and the middest of times, how times alter, and the change of seasons, the course of the yeare, and the situation of the starres, the nature of living things, and the furiousnesse of beasts, the power of the wind, and the imaginations of men, the diversities of plants, and the vertues of roots, and all things both secret and knowne, &c. Finallie, he was so cunning in this art, that he is said to have bene a conjurer or witch, and is so reputed in the Romish church at this daie. Whereby you may see, how fooles and papists are inclined to credit false accusations in matters of witchcraft and conjuration. The lesse knowledge we have in this art, the more we have it in contempt: in which respect *Plato* saith trulie to *Dionysius*; They make philosophie a mockerie, that deliver it to prophane and rude people. Certeinlie, the witchcraft, conjuration, and inchantment that is imputed to *Salomon*, is gathered out of these his words following: I applied my mind to knowledge, and to search and seeke out science, wisedome and understanding, to knowe the foolishnesse of the ungodlie, and the error of doting fooles. In this art of naturall magike (without great heed be taken) a student shall soone be abused. For manie (writing by report, without experience) mistake their authors, and set downe one thing for another. Then the conclusions being found false, the experiment groweth into contempt, and in the end seemeth ridiculous, though never so true. *Plinie* and *Albert* being curious writers heerein, are often deceived; insomuch as *Plinie* is called a noble lier, and *Albert* a rusticall lier; the one lieng by heeresaie, the other by authoritie.

A magician is indeed that which the Latines call a wise man, as *Numa Pompilius* was among the Romans; The Greeks, a philosopher, as *Socrates* was among them; the *Aegyptians* a preest, as *Hermes* was; the Cabalists called them prophets. But although these distinguished this art, accounting the one part thereof infamous, as being too much given unto wicked, vaine, and impious curiositie, as unto moovings, numbers, figures, sounds, voices, tunes, lights, affections of the mind, and words; and the other part commendable, as teaching manie good and necessarie things, as times and seasons to sowe, plant, till, cut, &c: and diverse other things, which I will make manifest unto you heereafter: yet we generallie condemne the whole art, without distinction, as a part of witchcraft; having learned to hate it, before we knowe it; affirming all to be witchcraft, which our grosse heads are not able to conceive, and yet can thinke that an old doting woman seeth through it, &c. Wherein we consider not how God bestoweth his gifts, and hath established an order in his works, graffing in them sundrie vertues to the comfort of his severall creatures; and speciallie to the use and behoofe of man: neither doo we therein weigh that art is servant unto nature, and waiteth upon hir as his handmaiden.

CHAPTER III.

What secrets do lie hidden, and what is taught in naturall magicke, how Gods glorie is magnified therein, and that it is nothing but the worke of nature.

IN this art of naturall magicke, God almightie hath hidden manie secret mysteries; as wherein a man may learne the properties, qualities, and knowledge of all nature. For it teacheth to accomplish maters in such sort and oportunitie, as the common people thinketh the same to be miraculous; and to be compassed none other waie, but onelie by witchcraft. And yet in

164

Margin notes:

Sap. 7, 17.
18.
19.
20.

21.
See *Iidioni.*

Eccle. 1. & 1.

A magician described and the art distinguished.

Read Plinie in natural. hist. Cardan de rerum variet. Albertus de occulta rerum proprietate.

truth, naturall magicke is nothing else, but the worke of nature. For in tillage, as nature produceth corne and hearbs; so art, being natures minister, prepareth it. Wherein times and seasons are greatlie to be respected: for *Annus non arvus producit aristas.*

But as manie necessarie and sober things are heerein taught; so dooth it partlie (I saie) consist in such experiments and conclusions as are but toies, but neverthelesse lie hid in nature, and being unknowne, doo seeme miraculous, speciallie when they are intermedled and corrupted with cunning illusion, or legierdemaine, from whence is derived the estimation of witchcraft. But being learned and knowne, they are contemned, and appeere ridiculous: for that onelie is woonderfull to the beholder, whereof he can conceive no cause nor reason, according to the saieng of *Ephesius, Miraculum solvitur unde videtur esse miraculum.* And therefore a man shall take great paines heerein, and bestow great cost to learne that which is of no value, and a meere jugling knacke. Whereupon it is said, that a man may not learne philosophie to be rich; but must get riches to learne philosophie: for to sluggards, niggards, & dizzards, the secrets of nature are never opened. And doubtlesse a man may gather out of this art, that which being published, shall set foorth the glorie of God, and be many waies beneficiall to the commonwealth: the first is doone by the manifestation of his works; the second, by skilfullie applieng them to our use and service.

Barthol. Neap. in natural. magia, & many others.

Naturall magicke hath a double end, which proveth ye excellencie of the same.

CHAPTER IV.

What strange things are brought to passe by naturall magicke.

THE dailie use and practise of medicine taketh awaie all admiration of the woonderfull effects of the same. Manie other things of lesse weight, being more secret and rare, seeme more miraculous. As for example (if it be true that *J. Bap. Neap.* and many other writers doo constantlie affirme.) Tie a wild bull to a figtree, and he will be presentlie tame; or hang an old cocke thereupon, and he will immediatlie be tender; as also the feathers of an eagle consume all other feathers, if they be intermedled together. Wherein it may not be denied, but nature sheweth hir selfe a proper workwoman. But it seemeth unpossible, that a little fish being but halfe a foot long, called *Remora* or *Remiligo,* or of some *Echeneis,* staieth a mightie ship with all hir loade and tackling, and being also under saile. And yet it is affirmed by so manie and so grave authors, that I dare not denie it; speciallie, bicause I see as strange effects of nature otherwise: as the propertie of the loadstone, which is so beneficiall to the mariner; and of Rheubarb, which onelie medleth with choler, and purgeth neither flegme nor melancholie, & is as beneficiall to the physician, as the other to the mariner.

Pompanatius. lib. de incant. cap. 3. J. Wierus de lamiis. Jasp. Peucer H. Cardan. &c.

CHAPTER V.

The incredible operation of waters, both standing and running; of wels, lakes, rivers, and of their woonderfull effects.

THE operation of waters, and their sundrie vertues are also incredible, I meane not of waters compounded and distilled: for it were endlesse to treat of their forces, speciallie concerning medicines. But we have heere even in *England* naturall springs, wels, and waters, both standing and running, of excellent vertues, even such as we had seene, and had experiment of, we would not beleeve to be *In rerum natura.* And to let the physicall nature of them passe (for the which we cannot be so thankefull to God, as they are wholesome for our bodies) is it not miraculous, that wood is by the qualitie of divers waters heere in *England* transubstantiated into a stone? The which vertue is also found to be in a lake besides the citie *Masaca* in *Cappadocia,* there is a river called *Scarmandrus,* that maketh yellow sheepe. Yea, there be manie waters, as in *Pontus & Thessalia,* and in the land of *Assyrides,* in a river of *Thracia* (as *Aristotle* saith) that if a white sheepe being with lambe drinke thereof, the lambe will be blacke. *Strabo* writeth of the river called *Crantes,* in the borders of *Italie,* running towards *Tarentum,* where mens haire is made white and yellow being washed therein. *Plinie* dooth write that of what colour the veines are under the rammes toong, of the same colour or colours will the lambs be. There is a lake in a field called *Cornetus,* in the bottome whereof manifestlie appeareth to the eie, the carcases of snakes, ewts, and other serpents : whereas if you put in your hand, to pull them out, you shall find nothing there. There droppeth water out of a rocke in *Arcadia,* the which neither a silverne nor a brasen boll can conteine, but it leapeth out, and sprinkleth awaie ; and yet will it remaine without motion in the hoofe of a mule. Such conclusions (I warrant you) were not unknowne to *Jannes* and *Jambres.*

Of late experience neere Coventrie, &c.
Aristot. in lib. de hist. animalium.

Plin. de lanicii colore.

CHAPTER VI.

The vertues and qualities of sundrie pretious stones, of cousening Lapidaries, &c.

THE excellent vertues and qualities of stones, found, conceived and tried by this art, is woonderfull. Howbeit many things most false and fabulous are added unto their true effects, wherewith I thought good in part to trie the reader's patience and cunning withall. An Aggat (they saie) hath vertue against the biting of scorpions or serpents. It is written (but I will not stand to it) that it maketh a man eloquent, and procureth the favour of princes ; yea that the fume thereof dooth turne awaie tempests. Alectorius is a stone about the bignesse of a beane, as cleere as the christall, taken out of a cocks bellie which hath beene gelt or made a capon foure yeares. If it be held in ones mouth, it asswageth thirst, it maketh the husband to love the wife, and the bearer invincible : for heereby *Milo* was said to overcome his enemies. A crawpocke delivereth from prison. Chelidonius is a stone taken out of a swallowe, which cureth melancholie : howbeit, some authors saie, it is the hearbe wherby the swallowes recover the sight of their yoong, even if their eies be picked out with an instrument. Geranites is taken out of a crane, and Draconites out of a dragon. But it is to be noted, that such stones must be taken out of the bellies of the serpents, beasts, or birds, (wherein they are) whiles they live : otherwise, they vanish awaie with the life, and so they reteine the vertues of those starres under which they are. Amethysus maketh a droonken man sober, and refresheth the wit. The corrall preserveth such as beare it from fascination or bewitching, and in this respect they are hanged about childrens necks. But from whence that superstition is derived, and who invented the lie, I knowe not : but I see how readie the people are to give credit thereunto, by the multitude of corrals that waie emploied. I find in good authors, that while it remaineth in the sea, it is an hearbe ; and when it is brought thence, into the aire, it hardeneth, and becommeth a stone.

Ludovicus Cælius. Rhodo. lib. antiq. lect. 11. ca. 70. Barthol. Anglicus, lib. 16.

Avicenna cano. 2. tract. 2. cap. 124. Serapio agg. cap. 100. Dioscor. lib. 5. cap. 93.

Heliotropius stancheth bloud, driveth awaie poisons, preserveth health : yea, and some write that it provoketh raine, and darkeneth the sunne, suffering not him that beareth it to be abused. Hyacinthus dooth all that the other dooth, and also preserveth from lightening. Dinothera hanged about the necke, collar, or yoke of any creature, tameth it presentlie. A Topase healeth the lunatike person of his passion of lunacie. Aitites, if it be shaken, soundeth as if there were a little stone in the bellie thereof: it is good for the falling sicknesse, and to prevent untimelie birth. Amethysus aforesaid resisteth droonkenesse, so as the bearers shall be able to drinke freelie, and recover themselves soone being droonke as apes: the same maketh a man wise. Chalcedonius maketh the bearer luckie in lawe, quickeneth the power of the bodie, and is of force also against the illusions of the divell, and phantasticall cogitations arising of melancholie. Corneolus mitigateth the heate of the mind, and qualifieth malice, it stancheth bloudie fluxes, speciallie of women that are troubled with their flowers. Heliotropius aforesaid darkeneth the sunne, raiseth shewers, stancheth bloud, procureth good fame, keepeth the bearer in health, and suffereth him not to be deceived. If this were true, one of them would be deerer than a thousand diamonds.

Plin. lib. 37. *cap.* 10. *Albert. lib.* 2. *cap.* 7. *Solin. cap.* 32.

Hyacinthus delivereth one from the danger of lightening, driveth awaie poison and pestilent infection, and hath manie other vertues. Iris helpeth a woman to speedie deliverance, and maketh rainebowes to appeere. A Saphire preserveth the members, and maketh them livelie, and helpeth agues and gowts, and suffereth not the bearer to be afraid: it hath vertue against venome, and staieth bleeding at the nose being often put thereto. A Smarag is good for the eiesight, and suffereth not carnall copulation, it maketh one rich and eloquent. A Topase increaseth riches, healeth the lunatike passion, and stancheth bloud. Mephis (as *Aaron* and *Hermes* report out of *Albertus Magnus*) being broken into powder, and droonke with water, maketh insensibilitie of torture. Heereby you may understand, that as God hath bestowed upon these stones, and such other like bodies, most excellent and woonderfull vertues; so according to the abundance of humane superstitions and follies, manie ascribe unto them either more vertues, or others than they have: other boast that they are able to adde new qualities unto them. And herein consisteth a part of witchcraft and common cousenage used sometimes of the Lapidaries for gaines; sometimes of others for cousening purposes. Some part of the vanitie heereof I will heere describe, bicause the place serveth well therefore. And it is not to be forgotten or omitted, that *Pharos* magicians were like enough to be cunning therein.

Rabbi Moses aphorism. partic. 22. *Isidor. lib.* 14. *cap.* 3. *Savanorola.*

Neverthelesse, I will first give you the opinion of one, who professed himselfe a verie skilfull and well experimented Lapidarie, as appeereth by a booke of his owne penning, published under this title of *Dactylotheca*, and (as I thinke) to be had among the booksellers. And thus followeth his assertion:

Evax rex Arabum fertur scripsisse Neroni,
(Qui post Augustum regnavit in orbe secundus)
Quot species lapidis, quæ nomina, quíve colores,
Quæq́; sit his regio, vel quanta potentia cuiq́;,
Ocult as etenim lapidum cognoscere vires,
Quorum causa latens effectus dat manifestos,
Egregium quiddam volumus rarúmque videri.
Scilicet hinc solers medicorum cura juvatur
Auxilio lapidum morbos expellere docta.
Nec minùs inde dari cunctarum commoda rerum
Autores perhibent, quibus hæc perspecta feruntur.
Nec dubium cuiquam debet falsúmque videri,
Quin sua sit gemmis divinitùs insita virtus:

Marbodeus Gallus in sua dactylotheca, pag. 5, 6.

> *Evax an old Arabian king*
> *is named to have writ*
> *A treatise, and on Neros Grace*
> *to have bestowed it,*
> *(Who in the world did second reigne*
> *after Augustus time)*
> *Of pretious stones the sundrie sorts,*
> *their names, and in what clime*

Englished by Abraham Fleming.

> *And countrie they were to be found,*
>   *their colours and their hue,*
> *Their private power and secret force,*
>   *the which with knowledge true*
> *To understand, their hidden cause*
>   *most plaine effects declare:*
> *And this will we a noble thing*
>   *have counted be and rare.*
> *The skilfull care of leeches learnd*
>   *is aided in this case,*
> *And hereby holpen, and are taught*
>   *with aid of stones to chase*
> *Awaie from men such sicknesses*
>   *as have in them a place.*
> *No less precise commodities*
>   *of althings else therebie*
> *Are ministred and given to men,*
>   *if authors doo not lie,*
> *To whome these things are said to bee*
>   *most manifestlie knowne.*
> *It shall no false or doubtfull case*
>   *appeare to anie one,*
> *But that by heavenlie influence*
>   *each pretious pearle and stone,*
> *Hath in his substance fixed force*
>   *and vertue largelie sowne.*

Vis gemmarum & lapillorum pretiosorum negatur, quia occulta est, rarissiméque sub sensum cadit.

Whereby it is to be concluded, that stones have in them certeine proper vertues, which are given them of a speciall influence of the planets, and a due proportion of the elements, their substance being a verie fine and pure compound, consisting of well tempered matter wherein is no grosse mixture; as appeareth by plaine proofe of *India* and *Aethopia*, where the sunne being orient and meridionall, dooth more effectuallie shew his operation, procuring more pretious stones there to be ingendred, than in the countries that are occident and septentrionall. Unto this opinion doo diverse ancients accord; namelie, *Alexander Peripateticus, Hermes, Evax, Bocchus Zoroastes, Isaac Judæus, Zacharias Balylonicus*, and manie more beside.

Manie mo authors may be named of no lesse antiquitie and learning.

CHAPTER VII.

Whence the pretious stones receive their operations, how curious Magicians use them, and of their seales.

CURIOUS Magicians affirme, that these stones receive their vertues altogether of the planets and heavenlie bodies, and have not onelie the verie operation of the planets, but sometimes the verie images and impressions of the starres naturallie ingraffed in them, and otherwise ought alwaies to have graven upon them, the similitudes of such monsters, beasts, and other devises, as they imagine to be both internallie in operation, and externallie in view, expressed in the planets. As for example, upon the Achate are graven serpents or venomous beasts; and sometimes a man riding on a serpent: which they know to be *Aesculapius*, which is the celestiall serpent, whereby are cured (they saie) poisons and stingings of serpents and scorpions. These grow in the river of *Achates*, where the greatest scorpions are ingendred, and their noisomnes

Plin. lib. 37. cap. 10. Albert. miner. li. 2. ca. 1.

is thereby qualified, and by the force of the scorpions the stones vertue is quick-
ened and increased. Also, if they would induce love for the accomplishment of
venerie, they inscribe and expresse in the stones, amiable embracings and
lovelie countenances and gestures, words and kissings in apt figures. For the
desires of the mind are consonant with the nature of the stones, which must also
be set in rings, and upon foiles of such metals as have affinitie with those stones,
thorough the operation of the planets whereunto they are addicted, whereby
they may gather the greater force of their working.

As for example, They make the images of *Saturne* in lead, of *Sol* in gold, of
Luna in silver. Marrie there is no small regard to be had for the certeine and
due times to be observed in the graving of them: for so are they made with more
life, and the influences and configurations of the planets are made thereby the
more to abound in them. As if you will procure love, you must wòrke in apt,
proper, and freendlie aspects, as in the house of *Venus*, &c: to make debate, the
direct contrarie order is to be taken. If you determine to make the image of
Venus, you must expect to be under *Aquarius* or *Capricornus*: for *Saturne*, *Taurus*,
and *Libra* must be taken heed of. Manie other observations there be, as to avoid
the infortunate seate and place of the planets, when you would bring a happie
thing to passe, and speciallie that it be not doone in the end, declination, or
heele (as they terme it) of the course thereof: for then the planet moorneth and
is dull.

Such signes as ascend in the daie, must be taken in the daie; if in the night
they increase, then must you go to worke by night, &c. For in *Aries*, *Leo*, and
Sagittarie is a certeine triplicitie, wherein the sunne hath dominion by daie,
Jupiter by night, and in the twielight the cold star of *Saturne*. But bicause there
shall be no excuse wanting for the faults espied herein, they saie that the vertues
of all stones decaie through tract of time: so as such things are not now to be
looked for in all respects as are written. Howbeit *Jannes* and *Jambres* were living
in that time, and in no inconvenient place; and therefore not unlike to have that
helpe towards the abusing of *Pharao*. *Cardane* saith, that although men attribute
no small force unto such seales; as to the seale of the sunne, authorities, honors,
and favors of princes; of *Jupiter*, riches and freends; of *Venus*, pleasures; of
Mars, boldnes; of *Mercurie*, diligence; of *Saturne*, patience and induring of labour;
of *Luna*, favour of people: I am not ignorant (saith he) that stones doo good, and
yet I knowe the seales or figures doo none at all. And when *Cardane* had shewed
fullie that art, and the follie thereof, and the maner of those terrible, prodigious,
& deceitfull figures of the planets with their characters, &c.: he saith that those
were deceitfull inventions devised by couseners, and had no vertue indeed nor
truth in them. But bicause we spake somewhat even now of signets and seales, I
will shew you what I read reported by *Vincentius in suo speculo*, where making
mention of the Jasper stone, whose nature and propertie *Marbodeus Gallus*
describeth in the verses following:

> *Jaspidis esse decem species septémque feruntur,*
> *Hic & multorum cognoscitur esse colorum,*
> *Et multis nasci perhibetur partibus orbis,*
> *Optimus in viridi translucentíque colore,*
> *Et qui plus soleat virtutis habere probatur,*
> *Castè gestatus febrem fugat, arcet hydropem,*
> *Adpositúsque juvat mulierem parturientem,*
> *Et tutamentum portanti creditur esse.*
> *Nam consecratus gratum facit atque potentem,*
> *Et, sicut perhibent, phantasmata noxia pellit,*
> *Cujus in argento vis fortior esse putatur,*

> Seven kinds and ten of Jasper stones
> reported are to be,
> Of manie colours this is knowne
> which noted is by mè,

Solin. cap. 11.
Diurius in
scrin. cap. de
complexioni-
bus & com-
plexatis.

Geor. Picto-
rius. Villang.
doct. medici
in scholiis
super Mar-
bod. dactyl.

H. Card. lib.
de subtil. 10.

H. Card. lib.
de var. rer.
16. cap. 90.

Marbodeus
in sua dacty-
lotheca, pag.
41, 52.

Englished by
Abraham
Fleming.

And said in manie places of
  the world for to be seene,
Where it is bred; but yet the best
  is thorough shining greene,
And that which prooved is to have
  in it more virtue plaste:

Memoran-
dum the
authors
meaning
is, that this
stone be set
in silver, &
worne on
the finger
for a ring:
as you shall
see after-
wards.

For being borne about of such
  as are of living chaste,
It drives awaie their ague fits,
  the dropsie thirsting drie,
And put unto a woman weake
  in travell which dooth lie
It helps, assists, and comforts hir
  in pangs when she dooth crie.
Againe, it is beleevd to be
  A safegard franke and free,
To such as weare and beare the same;
  and if it hallowed bee
It makes the parties gratious,
  and mightie too that have it,
And noysome fansies (as they write
  that ment not to deprave it)
It dooth displace out of the mind:
  the force thereof is stronger,
In silver if the same be set,
  and will endure the longer.

Vincent. lib.
9. cap. 77.
Dioscor. lib.
5. cap. 100.
Aristot. in
Lapidario.

But (as I said) *Vincentius* making mention of the Jasper stone, touching which (by the waie of a parenthesis) I have inferred *Marbodeus* his verses, he saith that some Jasper stones are found having in them the livelie image of a naturall man, with a sheeld at his necke and a speare in his hand, and under his feete a serpent: which stones so marked and signed, he preferreth before all the rest, bicause they are antidotaries or remedies notablie resisting poison. Othersome also are found figured and marked with the forme of a man bearing on his necke a bundle of hearbs and flowres, with the estimation and value of them noted, that they have in them a facultie or power restrictive, and will in an instant or moment of time stanch bloud. Such a kind of stone (as it is reported) *Galen* wore on his finger. Othersome are marked with a crosse, as the same author writeth, and these be right excellent against inundations or overflowings of waters. I could hold you long occupied in declarations like unto these, wherein I laie before you what other men have published and set foorth to the world, choosing rather to be an academicall discourser, than an universall determiner: but I am desirous of brevitie.

CHAPTER VIII.

The sympathie and antipathie of naturall and elementarie bodies declared by diverse examples of beasts, birds, plants, &c.

Agreement
& disagree-
ment in suf-
ferance.

IF I should write of the strange effects of Sympathia and Antipathia, I should take great paines to make you woonder, and yet you would scarse beleeve me. And if I should publish such conclusions as are common and knowne, you would not regard them. And yet *Empedocles* thought all things were wrought hereby. It is almost incredible, that the grunting or rather the wheeking of a little pig, or the sight of a simple sheepe should terrifie a mightie elephant: and yet by that meanes the *Romans* did put to flight *Pyrhus* and all his hoast. A man would hardlie beleeve, that a cocks combe or his crowing should abash a puissant lion: but the experience herof hath satisfied the whole world. Who would thinke that a serpent should abandon the shadow of an ash, *&c*? But it seemeth not strange, bicause it is common, that some man otherwise hardie and stout enough, should not dare to abide or endure the sight of a cat. Or that a draught of drinke should so overthrow a man, that never a part or member of his bodie should be able to performe his dutie and office; and should also so corrupt and alter his senses, understanding, memorie, and judgement, that he should in everie thing, saving in shape, beecome a verie beast. And herein the poets experiment of liquor is verified, in these words following:

> ──────────*sunt qui non corpora tantùm,*
> *Verùm animas etiam valeant mutare liquores:*

> Some waters have so powerfull ben,
> As could not onelie bodies change,
> But even the verie minds of men,
> Their operation is so strange.

Englished by Abraham Fleming.

The freendlie societie betwixt a fox and a serpent is almost incredible: how loving the lizzard is to a man, we maie read, though we cannot see. Yet some affirme that our newt is not onlie like to the lizzard in shape, but also in condition. From the which affection towards a man, a spaniell doth not much differ, whereof I could cite incredible stories. The amitie betwixt a castrell and a pigeon is much noted among writers; and speciallie how the castrell defendeth hir from hir enimie the sparowhawke: whereof they saie the doove is not ignorant. Besides, the woonderfull operation and vertue of hearbs, which to repeat were infinite: and therefore I will onlie referre you to *Mattheolus* his herball, or to *Dodonæus*. There is among them such naturall accord and discord, as some prosper much the better for the others companie, and some wither awaie being planted neere unto the other. The lillie and the rose rejoise in ech others neighborhood. The flag and the fernebush abhorre each other so much, that the one can hardlie live besides the other. The cowcumber loveth water, and hateth oile to the death. And bicause you shall not saie that hearbs have no vertue, for that in this place I cite none, I am content to discover two or three small qualities and vertues, which are affirmed to be in hearbs: marie as simple as they be, *Jannes* and *Jambres* might have done much with them, if they had had them. If you pricke out a yoong swallowes eies, the old swallow restoreth againe their sight, with the application (they saie) of a little Celondine. *Xanthus* the author of histories reporteth, that a yoong dragon being dead, was revived by hir dam, with an hearbe called Balim. And *Juba* saith, that a man in *Arabia* being dead was revived by the vertue of another hearbe.

Read a litle tract of Erasmus intituled De amicitia, where enough is said touching this point.

Xanthus in hist. prima.

Jub. lib. 25. cap. 2.

Chapter ix.

The former matter prooved by manie examples of the living and the dead.

AND as we see in stones, herbs, *&c*: strange operation and naturall love and dissention: so doo we read, that in the bodie of a man, there be as strange properties and vertues naturall. I have heard by credible report, and I have read many grave authors constantlie affirme, that the wound of a man murthered reneweth bleeding; at the presence of a deere freend, or of a mortall enimie. Diverse also write, that if one passe by a murthered bodie

This common experience can justifie.

(though unknowne) he shalbe striken with feare, and feele in him selfe some alteration by nature. Also that a woman, above the age of fiftie yeares, being bound hand and foote, hir clothes being upon hir, and laid downe softlie into the water, sinketh not in a long time; some saie, not at all. By which experiment they were woont to trie witches, as well as by *Ferrum candens:* which was, to hold hot iron in their hands, and by not burning to be tried. Howbeit, *Plutarch* saith that *Pyrhus* his great toe had in it such naturall or rather divine vertue, that no fier could burne it.

And *Albertus* saith, and manie other also repeat the same storie, saieng, that there were two such children borne in *Germanie*, as if that one of them had beene carried by anie house, all the doores right against one of his sides would flie open: and that vertue which the one had in the left side, the other brother had in the right side. He saith further, that manie sawe it, and that it could be referred to nothing, but to the proprietie of their bodies. *Pompanatius* writeth that the kings of *France* doo cure the disease called now the kings evill, or queenes evill; which hath beene alwaies thought, and to this daie is supposed to be a miraculous and a peculiar gift, & a speciall grace given to the kings and queenes of *England.* Which some referre to the proprietie of their persons, some to the peculiar gift of God, and some to the efficacie of words. But if the French king use it no woorsse than our Princesse doth, God will not be offended thereat: for hir maiestie onelie useth godlie and divine praier, with some almes, and referreth the cure to God and to the physician. *Plutarch* writeth that there be certeine men called *Psilli*, which with their mouthes heale the bitings of serpents. And *J. Bap. Neap.* saith, that an olive being planted by the hand of a virgine, prospereth; which if a harlot doo, it withereth awaie. Also, if a serpent or viper lie in a hole, it maie easilie be pulled out with the left hand, wheras with the right hand it cannot be remooved. Although this experiment, and such like, are like enough to be false; yet are they not altogether so impious as the miracles said to be done by characters, charmes, &c. For manie strange properties remaine in sundrie partes of a living creature, which is not universallie dispersed, and indifferentlie spred through the whole bodie: as the eie smelleth not, the nose seeth not, the eare tasteth not, &c.

J. Wierus.

Plutarch. in vita Pyrhi.

Albert. lib. de mor. animal. cap. 3.

Pompan. lib. de incant. cap. 4.

Plutar. in vita Catonis.

J. Bap. Neap. in lib. de natur. magia. 1.

Chapter x.

The bewitching venome conteined in the bodie of an harlot, how hir eie, hir toong, hir beautie and behavior bewitcheth some men: of bones and hornes yeelding great vertue.

The venom or poison of an harlot.

THE vertue conteined within the bodie of an harlot, or rather the venome proceeding out of the same maie be beheld with great admiration. For hir eie infecteth, entiseth, and (if I maie so saie) bewitcheth them manie times, which thinke themselves well armed against such maner of people. Hir toong, hir gesture, hir behaviour, hir beautie, and other allurements poison and intoxicate the mind: yea, hir companie induceth impudencie, corrupteth virginitie, confoundeth and consumeth the bodies, goods, and the verie soules of men. And finallie hir bodie destroieth and rotteth the verie flesh and bones of mans bodie. And this is common, that we woonder not at all thereat, naie we have not the course of the sunne, the moone, or the starres in so great admiration, as the globe, counterfeting their order: which is in respect but a bable made by an artificer. So as (I thinke) if Christ himselfe had continued long in the execution of miracles, and had left that power permanent and common in the church; they would have growne into contempt, and not have beene esteemed, according to his owne saieng: A prophet is not regarded in his owne countrie. I might recite infinite properties, wherewith God hath indued the bodie of man, worthie of admiration, and fit for this place. As touching other living creatures,

Matth. 13.
Marke. 6.
Luke. 4.
John. 4.

God hath likewise (for his glorie, and our behoofe) bestowed most excellent and miraculous gifts and vertues upon their bodies and members, and that in severall and woonderfull wise. We see that a bone taken out of a carps head, stancheth bloud, and so doth none other part besides of that fish. The bone also in a hares foot mitigateth the crampe, as none other bone nor part else of the hare doth. How pretious is the bone growing out of the forehead of a unicorne; if the horne, which we see, growe there, which is doubted: and of how small accompt are the residue of all his bones? At the excellencie whereof, as also at the noble and innumerable vertues of herbs we muse not at all; bicause it hath pleased God to make them common unto us. Which perchance might in some part assist *Jannes* and *Jambres*, towards the hardning of *Pharaos* heart. But of such secret and strange operations read *Albert De mineral. cap.* 1. 11. 17. Also *Marsilius Ficinus, cap.* 1. *lib.* 4. *Cardan de rerum varietate. J. Bap. Neap. de magia naturali.* Peucer, *Wier,* Pompanacius, *Fernelius,* and others.

Wonder-
full natu-
rall effects
in bones
of fishes,
beasts, &c.

CHAPTER XI.

Two notorious woonders and yet not marvelled at.

I THOUGHT good here to insert two most miraculous matters, of the one I am *Testis oculatus,* an eie witnesse; of the other I am so crediblie and certeinelie informed, that I dare and doo beleeve it to be verie true When Maister *T. Randolph* returned out of *Russia,* after his ambassage dispatched, a gentleman of his traine brought home a monument of great accompt, in nature and in propertie very wonderfull. And biause I am loath to be long in the description of circumstances, I will first describe the thing it selfe: which was a peece of earth of a good quantitie, and most excellentlie proportioned in nature, having these qualities and vertues following. If one had taken a peece of perfect steele, forked and sharpened at the end, and heated it red hot, offering therewith to have touched it; it would have fled with great celeritie: and on the other side, it would have pursued gold, either in coine or bulloine, with as great violence and speed as it shunned the other. No bird in the aire durst approch neere it; no beast of the field but feared it, and naturallie fled from the sight thereof. It would be here to daie, and to morrowe twentie miles off, and the next daie after in the verie place it was the first daie, and that without the helpe of anie other creature.

Strange
properties
in a peece
of earth.

Johannes Fernelius writeth of a strange stone latelie brought out of *India,* which hath in it such a marvellous brightnes, puritie, and shining, that therewith the aire round about is so lightned and cleared, that one may see to read thereby in the darknes of night. It will not be conteined in a close roome, but requireth an open and free place. It would not willinglie rest or staie here belowe on the earth, but alwaies laboureth to ascend up into the aire. If one presse it downe with his hand, it resisteth, and striketh verie, sharpelie. It is beautifull to behold, without either spot or blemish, and yet verie unplesant to taste or feele. If anie part thereof be taken awaie, it is never a whit diminished, the forme thereof being inconstant, and at everie moment mutable. These two things last rehearsed are strange, and so long woondered at, as the mysterie and moralitie thereof remaineth undiscovered: but when I have disclosed the matter, and told you that by the lumpe of earth a man is ment, and some of his qualities described; and that that which was conteined in the farre fetcht stone, was fier, or rather flame: the doubt is resolved, and the miracle ended. And yet (I confesse) there is in these two creatures conteined more miraculous matter, than in all the loadstones and diamonds in the world. And hereby is to be noted, that even a part of this art, which is called naturall or witching magicke, consisteth as well in the

Strange
properties
in a stone:
the like
qualities in
other stons:
See pag.
110–113, 170.

deceipt of words, as in the sleight of hand : wherein plaine lieng is avoided with a figurative speech, in the which, either the words themselves, or their interpretation have a double or doubtfull meaning, according to that which hath beene said before in the title *Ob* or *Pytho :* and shall be more at large hereafter in this treatise manifested.

Being the 7 booke of this disco-verie: *See pag.* 75–78, 91. Where dis-course is made of oracles, &c.

CHAPTER XII.

Of illusions, confederacies, and legierdemaine, and how they may be well or ill used.

MANIE writers have beene abused as well by untrue reports, as by illusion, and practises of confederacie and legierdemaine, &c: sometimes imputing unto words that which resteth in the nature of the thing; and sometimes to the nature of the thing, that which proceedeth of fraud and deception of sight. But when these experiments growe to superstition or impietie, they are either to be forsaken as vaine, or denied as false. Howbeit, if these things be doone for mirth and recreation, and not to the hurt of our neighbour, nor to the abusing or prophaning of Gods name, in mine opinion they are neither impious nor altogether unlawfull : though herein or hereby a naturall thing be made to seeme supernaturall. Such are the miracles wrought by jugglers, consisting in fine and nimble conveiance, called legierdemaine : as when they seeme to cast awaie, or to deliver to another that which they reteine still in their owne hands ; or conveie otherwise : or seeme to eate a knife, or some such other thing, when indeed they bestowe the same secretlie into their bosoms or laps. Another point of juggling is, when they thrust a knife through the braines and head of a chicken or pullet, and seeme to cure the same with words : which would live and doo well, though never a word were spoken. Some of these toies also consist in arythmeticall devises, partlie in experiments of naturall magike, and partlie in private as also in publike confederacie.

Look here-after in this booke for divers con-ceits of juggling set foorth at large. beginning at *pag.* 182.

CHAPTER XIII.

Of private confederacie, and of Brandons pigeon.

PRIVATE confederacie I meane, when one (by a speciall plot laid by himselfe, without anie compact made with others) persuadeth the beholders, that he will suddenlie and in their presence doo some miraculous feat, which he hath alredie accomplished privilie. As for example, he will shew you a card, or anie other like thing : and will saie further unto you ; Behold and see what a marke it hath, and then burneth it ; and nevertheles fetcheth another like card so marked out of some bodies pocket, or out of some corner where he himselfe before had placed it ; to the woonder and astonishment of simple beholders, which conceive not that kind of illusion, but expect miracles and strange works.

Example of a ridicu-lous woon-der.

What woondering and admiration was there at *Brandon* the juggler, who painted on a wall the picture of a dove, and seeing a pigeon sitting on the top of a house, said to the king ; Lo now your Grace shall see what a juggler can doo, if he be his craftes maister ; and then pricked the picture with a knife so hard and so often, and with so effectuall words, as the pigeon fell downe from the top of

174

the house starke dead. I need not write anie further circumstance to shew how the matter was taken, what woondering was thereat, how he was prohibited to use that feat anie further, least he should emploie it in anie other kind of murther; as though he, whose picture so ever he had pricked, must needs have died, and so the life of all men in the hands of a juggler: as is now supposed to be in the hands and willes of witches. This storie is, untill the daie of the writing hereof, in fresh remembrance, & of the most part beleeved as canonicall, as are all the fables of witches: but when you are taught the feate or sleight (the secrecie and sorcerie of the matter being bewraied, and discovered) you will thinke it a mockerie, and a simple illusion. To interpret unto you the revelation of this mysterie; so it is, that the poore pigeon was before in the hands of the juggler, into whome he had thrust a dramme of *Nux vomica*, or some other such poison which to the nature of the bird was so extreame a venome, as after the receipt thereof it could not live above the space of halfe an houre, and being let lose after the medicine ministred, she alwaies resorted to the top of the next house: which she will the rather doo, if there be anie pigeons alreadie sitting there, and (as it is alreadie said) after a short space falleth downe, either starke dead, or greatlie astonnied. But in the meane time the juggler useth words of art, partlie to protract the time, and partlie to gaine credit and admiration of the beholders. If this or the like feate should be done by an old woman, everie bodie would crie out for fier and faggot to burne the witch.

This I have prooved upon crows and pies.

This might be done by a confederate, who standing at some window in a church steeple, or other fit place, and holding the pigeon by the leg in a string, after a signe given by his fellowe, pulleth downe the pigeon, and so the woonder is wrought.

CHAPTER XIV.

Of publike confederacie, and whereof it consisteth.

PUBLIKE confederacie is, when there is before hand a compact made betwixt diverse persons; the one to be principall, the rest to be assistants in working of miracles, or rather in cousening and abusing the beholders. As when I tell you in the presence of a multitude what you have thought or doone, or shall doo or thinke, when you and I were thereupon agreed before. And if this be cunninglie and closelie handled, it will induce great admiration to the beholders; speciallie when they are before amazed and abused by some experiments of naturall magike, arythmeticall conclusions, or legierdemaine. Such were, for the most part, the conclusions and devises of *Feates*: wherein doubt you not, but *Jannes* and *Jambres* were expert, active, and readie.

CHAPTER XV.

How men have beene abused with words of equivocation, with sundrie examples thereof.

SOME have taught, and others have written certeine experiments; in the expressing whereof they have used such words of equivocation, as wherby manie have beene overtaken and abused through rash credulitie: so as sometimes (I saie) they have reported, taught, and written that which their capacitie tooke hold upon, contrarie to the truth and sincere meaning of the author. It is a common jest among the water men of the Thames, to shew the parish church of *Stone* to the passengers, calling the same by the name of the lanterne of *Kent;* affirming, and that not untrulie, that the said church is as light

A jest among watermen touching Stone

church in
Kent as
light at
midnight
as at mid-
daie.

(meaning in weight and not in brightnes) at midnight, as at noonedaie. Where-upon some credulous person is made beleeve, and will not sticke to affirme and sweare, that in the same church is such continuall light, that anie man may see to read there at all times of the night without a candle.

An excellent philosopher, whome (for reverence unto his fame and learning) I will forbeare to name, was overtaken by his hostesse at *Dover;* who merrilie told him, that if he could reteine and keepe in his mouth certeine pibbles (lieng at the shore side) he should not perbreake untill he came to *Calice,* how rough and tempestuous so ever the seas were. Which when he had tried, and being not forced by sicknes to vomit, nor to lose his stones, as by vomiting he must needs doo, he thought his hostesse had discovered unto him an excellent secret, nothing doubting of hir amphibologicall speech : and therefore thought it a worthie note to be recorded among miraculous and medicinable stones; and inserted it accordinglie into his booke, among other experiments collected with great·industrie, learning, travell, and judgement. All these toies helpe a subtill cousener to gaine credit with the multitude. Yea, to further their estimation, manie will whisper prophesies of their owne invention into the eares of such as are not of quickest capacitie; as to tell what weather, &c: shall followe. Which if it fall out true, then boast they and triumph, as though they had gotten some notable conquest; if not, they denie the matter, forget it, excuse it, or shift it off; as that they told another the contrarie in earnest, and spake that but in jest. All these helps might *Pharaos* jugglers have, to mainteine their cousenages and illusions, towards the hardening of *Pharaos* hart.

Hereunto belong all maner of charmes, periapts, amulets, characters, and such other superstitions, both popish and prophane : whereby (if that were true, which either papists, conjurors, or witches undertake to doo) we might dailie see the verie miracles wrought indeed, which *Pharaos* magicians seemed to performe. Howbeit, bicause by all those devises or cousenages, there cannot be made so much as a nit, so as *Jannes* and *Jambres* could have no helpe that waie, I will speake thereof in place more convenient.

CHAPTER XVI.

How some are abused with naturall magike, and sundrie examples thereof when illusion is added thereunto, of Jacobs pied sheepe, and of a blacke Moore.

BUT as these notable and wonderfull experiments and conclusions that are found out in nature it selfe (through wisedome, learning, and industrie) doo greatlie oppose and astonnish the capacitie of man : so (I saie) when deceipt and illusion is annexed thereunto, then is the wit, the faith, & constancie of man searched and tried. For if we shall yeeld that to be divine, supernaturall, and miraculous, which we cannot comprehend; a witch, a papist, a conjuror, a cousener, and a juggler may make us beleeve they are gods : or else with more impietie we shall ascribe such power and omnipotencie unto them, or unto the divell, as onelie and properlie apperteineth to God. As for example. By con-federacie or cousenage (as before I have said) I may seeme to manifest the secret thoughts of the hart, which (as we learne in Gods booke) none knoweth or searcheth, but God himselfe alone. And therfore, whosoever beleeveth that I can doo as I may seeme to doo, maketh a god of me, and is an idolater. In which respect, whensoever we heare papist, witch, conjuror, or cousener, take upon him more than lieth in humane power to performe, we may know & boldlie saie it if a knacke of knaverie ; and no miracle at all. And further we may know, that when we understand it, it will not be woorth the knowing. And at the discoverie of these miraculous toies, we shall leave to wonder at them, and beginne to

The incon-
venience
of holding
opinion,
that what-
soever pas-
seth our ca-
pacitie, is
divine, su-
pernaturall,
&c.

wonder at our selves, that could be so abused with bables. Howbeit, such things as God hath laid up secretlie in nature are to be weighed with great admiration, and to be searched out with such industrie, as may become a christian man : I meane, so as neither God, nor our neighbour be offended thereby, which respect doubtlesse *Jannes* and *Jambres* never had. We find in the scriptures diverse naturall and secret experiments practised; as namelie that of *Jacob*, for pied sheepe : which are confirmed by prophane authors, and not onelie verified in lambs and sheepe, but in horsses, pecocks, connies, &c. We read also of a wo-man that brought foorth a yoong blacke Moore, by meanes of an old blacke Moore who was in hir house at the time of her conception, whome she beheld in phantasie, as is supposed : howbeit, a gelous husband will not be satisfied with such phantasticall imaginations. For in truth a blacke Moore never faileth to beget blacke children, of what colour soever the other be : *Et sic è contra.*

J. Bap. Nea-pol. in natu-ral. mag.

CHAPTER XVII.

The opinion of witchmongers, that divels can create bodies, and of Pharaos magicians.

IT is affirmed by *James Sprenger* and *Henrie Institor*, in *M. Mal.* who cite *Albert In lib. de animalib.* for their purpose, that divels and witches also can truelie make living creatures as well as God; though not at an instant, yet verie suddenlie. Howbeit, all such as are rightlie informed in Gods word, shall mani-festlie perceive and confesse the contrarie, as hath beene by scriptures alreadie prooved, and may be confirmed by places infinite. And therefore I saie *Jannes* and *Jambres*, though sathan and also *Belzebub* had assisted them, could never have made the serpent or the frogs of nothing, nor yet have changed the waters with words. Neverthelesse, all the learned expositors of that place affirme, that they made a shew of creation, &c: exhibiting by cunning a resemblance of some of those miracles, which GOD wrought by the hand of *Moses.* Yea S. *Augustine* and manie other hold, that they made by art (and that trulie) the serpents, &c. But that they may by art approch somewhat neerer to those actions, than hath beene yet declared, shall and may appeere by these and manie other conclusions, if they be true.

M. Malef. p. 1. q. 10.

John. 1, 3.
Coloss. 1, 16.

CHAPTER XVIII.

How to produce or make monsters by art magike, and why Pharaos magicians could not make lice.

STRATO, *Democritus, Empedocles,* and of late, *Jo. Bap. Neap.* teach by what meanes monsters may be produced, both from beast and also from fowle. *Aristotle* himselfe teacheth to make a chicken have foure legs, and as manie wings, onlie by a doubled yolked eg : whereby also a serpent may be made to have manie legs. Or any thing that produceth egs, may likewise be made double membred, or dismembred : & the viler creature the sooner brought to monstrous deformitie, which in more noble creatures is more hardlie brought to passe. There are also prettie experiments of an eg, to produce anie fowle, with-out the naturall helpe of the hen : the which is brought to passe, if the eg be laid in the powder of the hens doong, dried and mingled with some of the hens

Naturall conclusiõs.

To produce anie fowle out of an eg, without the

naturall
helpe of
the hen.

The
mother of
marvels.

Two kind
of todes,
naturall &
temporall.

Maggotts
ingendred
of the in-
wards of a
beast are
good for
angling.

Giles. Alley :
See the
poore mans
librarie.

fethers, & stirred everie fourth houre. You may also produce (as they saie) the
most venomous, noisome, and dangerous serpent, called a cockatrice, by melting
a little arsenicke, and the poison of serpents, or some other strong venome, and
drowning an eg therein, which there must remaine certeine daies; and if the eg
be set upright, the operation will be the better. This may also be doone, if the
eg be laid in doong, which of all other things giveth the most singular and
naturall heate: and as *J. Bap. Neap.* saith is *Mirabilium rerum parens;* who also
writeth, that *Crines fœminæ menstruosæ* are turned into serpents within short space:
and he further saith, that basill being beaten, and set out in a moist place, betwixt a couple of tiles, dooth ingender scorpions. The ashes of a ducke, being
put betweene two dishes, and set in a moist place, dooth ingender a huge tode:
Quod etiam efficit sanguis menstruosus. Manie writers conclude, that there be two
maner of todes, the one bred by naturall course and order of generation, the
other growing of themselves, which are called temporarie, being onlie ingendred of shewers and dust: and (as *J. Bap. Neap.* saith) they are easie to be
made. *Plutarch* and *Heraclides* doo saie, that they have seene these to descend in
raine, so as they have lien and cralled on the tops of houses, &c. Also *Aelianus*
dooth saie, that he sawe frogs and todes, whereof the heads & shoulders were
alive, & became flesh; the hinder parts being but earth, & so cralled on two
feete, the other being not yet fashioned or fullie framed. And *Macrobius* reporteth, that in *Aegypt*, mice growe of earth and shewers; as also frogs, todes, and
serpents in other places. They saie that *Danmatus Hispanus* could make them
when & as manie as he listed. He is no good angler, that knoweth not how
soone the entrales of a beast, when they are buried, will engender maggots
(which in a civiler terme are called gentles) a good bait for small fishes. Whosoever knoweth the order of preserving silkewormes, may perceive a like conclusion: bicause in the winter, that is a dead seed, which in the summer is a
livelie creature. Such and greater experiments might be knowne to *Jannes* and
Jambres, and serve well to their purpose, especiallie with such excuses, delaies,
and cunning, as they could joine therewithall. But to proceed, and come a little
neerer to their feats, and to shew you a knacke beyond their cunning; I can assure
you that of the fat of a man or a woman, lice are in verie short space ingendered:
and yet I saie, *Pharaos* magicians could not make them, with all the cunning
they had. Whereby you may perceive, that God indeed performed the other
actions, to indurate *Pharao*, though he thought his magicians did with no lesse
dexteritie than *Moses* worke miracles and woonders. But some of the interpretors
of that place excuse their ignorance in that matter, thus; The divell (saie they)
can make no creature under the quantitie of a barlie corne, and lice being so
little cannot therefore be created by them. As though he that can make the
greater, could not make the lesse. A verie grosse absurditie. And as though that
he which hath power over great, had not the like over small.

<hr>

CHAPTER XIX.

*That great matters may be wrought by this art, when princes esteeme and mainteine it: of
divers woonderfull experiments, and of strange conclusions in glasses, of the art perspective, &c.*

HOWBEIT, these are but trifles in respect of other experiments to this
effect; speciallie when great princes mainteine & give countenance to
students in those magicall arts, which in these countries and in this age is
rather prohibited than allowed, by reason of the abuse commonlie coupled
therewith; which in truth is it that mooveth admiration and estimation of
miraculous workings. As for example. If I affirme, that with certeine charmes

and popish praiers I can set an horsse or an asses head upon a mans shoulders, I shall not be beleeved; or if I doo it, I shall be thought a witch. And yet if *J. Bap. Neap.* experiments be true, it is no difficult matter to make it seeme so: and the charme of a witch or papist joined with the experiment, will also make the woonder seeme to proceed thereof. The words used in such case are uncerteine, and to be recited at the pleasure of the witch or cousener. But the conclusion is this: Cut off the head of a horsse or an asse (before they be dead) otherwise the vertue or strength thereof will be the lesse effectuall, and make an earthern vessell of fit capacitie to conteine the same, and let it be filled with the oile and fat thereof; cover it close, and dawbe it over with lome: let it boile over a soft fier three daies continuallie, that the flesh boiled may run into oile, so as the bare bones may be seene: beate the haire into powder, and mingle the same with the oile; and annoint the heads of the standers by, and they shall seeme to have horsses or asses heads. If beasts heads be annointed with the like oile made of a mans head, they shall seeme to have mens faces, as diverse authors soberlie affirme. If a lampe be annointed heerewith, everie thing shall seeme most monstrous. It is also written, that if that which is called *Sperma* in anie beast be burned, and anie bodies face therewithall annointed, he shall seeme to have the like face as the beast had. But if you beate arsenicke verie fine, and boile it with a little sulphur in a covered pot, and kindle it with a new candle, the standers by will seeme to be hedlesse. Aqua composita and salt being fiered in the night, and all other lights extinguished, make the standers by seeme as dead. All these things might be verie well perceived and knowne, and also practised by *Jannes* and *Jambres.* But the woonderous devises, and miraculous sights and conceipts made and conteined in glasse, doo farre exceed all other; whereto the art perspective is verie necessarie. For it sheweth the illusions of them, whose experiments be seene in diverse sorts of glasses; as in the hallowe, the plaine, the embossed, the columnarie, the pyramidate or piked, the turbinall, the bounched, the round, the cornerd, the inversed, the eversed, the massie, the regular, the irregular, the coloured and cleare glasses: for you may have glasses so made, as what image or favour soever you print in your imagination, you shall thinke you see the same therein. Others are so framed, as therein one may see what others doo in places far distant; others, wherby you shall see men hanging in the aire; others, whereby you may perceive men flieng in the aire; others, wherin you may see one comming, & another going; others, where one image shall seeme to be one hundred, &c. There be glasses also, wherein one man may see another mans image, and not his owne; others, to make manie similitudes; others, to make none at all. Others, contrarie to the use of all glasses, make the right side turne to the right, and the left side to the left; others, that burne before and behind; others, that represent not the images received within them, but cast them farre off in the aire, appearing like aierie images, and by the collection of sunne beames, with great force setteth fier (verie farre off) in everie thing that may be burned. There be cleare glasses, that make great things seeme little, things farre off to be at hand; and that which is neere, to be far off; such things as are over us, to seeme under us; and those that are under us, to be above us. There are some glasses also, that represent things in diverse colours, & them most gorgeous, speciallie any white thing. Finally, the thing most worthie of admiration concerning these glasses, is, that the lesser glass dooth lessen the shape: but how big so ever it be, it maketh the shape no bigger than it is. And therfore *Augustine* thinketh some hidden mysterie to be therein. *Vitellius,* and *J. Bap. Neap.* write largelie thereof. These I have for the most part seene, and have the receipt how to make them: which, if desire of brevitie had not forbidden me, I would here have set downe. But I thinke not but *Pharaos* magicians had better experience than I for those and such like devises. And (as *Pompanacius* saith) it is most true, that some for these feats have been accounted saints, some other witches. And therefore I saie, that the pope maketh rich witches, saints; and burneth the poore witches.

Wonderfull experiments.

To set an horsses or an asses head on a mans neck and shoulders.

Strange things to be doone by perspective glasses.

Cocerning these glasses remember that the eiesight is deceived: for *Non est in speculo res quæ speculatur in eo.*

Rash opinion can never judge soundlie.

CHAPTER XX.

A comparison betwixt Pharaos magicians and our witches, and how their cunning consisted in juggling knacks.

THUS you see that it hath pleased GOD to shew unto men that seeke for knowledge, such cunning in finding out, compounding, and framing of strange and secret things, as thereby he seemeth to have bestowed upon man, some part of his divinitie. Howbeit, God (of nothing, with his word) hath created all things, and dooth at his will, beyond the power and also the reach of man, accomplish whatsoever he list. And such miracles in times past he wrought by the hands of his prophets, as here he did by *Moses* in the presence of *Pharao,* which *Jannes* and *Jambres* apishlie followed. But to affirme that they by themselves, or by all the divels in hell, could doo indeed as *Moses* did by the power of the Holie-ghost, is woorsse than infidelitie. If anie object and saie, that our witches can doo such feats with words and charms, as *Pharaos* magicians did by their art, I denie it; and all the world will never be able to shew it. That which they did, was openlie done; as our witches and conjurors never doo anie thing: so as these cannot doo as they did. And yet (as *Calvine* saith of them) they were but jugglers. Neither could they doo, as manie suppose. For as *Clemens* saith; These magicians did rather seeme to doo these woonders, than worke them indeed. And if they made but prestigious shewes of things, I saie it was more than our witches can doo. For witchcrafts (as *Erastus* himselfe confesseth in drift of argument) are but old wives fables. If the magicians serpent had beene a verie serpent, it must needs have beene transformed out of the rod. And therein had beene a double worke of God; to wit, the qualifieng and extinguishment of one substance, and the creation of another. Which are actions beyond the divels power, for he can neither make a bodie to be no bodie, nor yet no bodie to be a bodie; as to make something nothing, and nothing something; and contrarie things, one: naie, they cannot make one haire either white or blacke. If *Pharaos* magicians had made verie frogs upon a sudden, whie could they not drive them awaie againe? It they could not hurt the frogs, whie should we thinke that they could make them? Or that our witches, which cannot doo so much as counterfet them, can kill cattell and other creatures with words or wishes? And therefore I saie with *Jamblichus, Quæ fascinati imaginamur, præter imaginamenta nullā habent actionis & essentiæ veritatem;* Such things as we being bewitched doo imagine, have no truth at all either of action or essence, beside the bare imagination.

An apish imitation in Jannes and Jambres of working woonders.
Jo. Calvine, lib. institut. 1. cap. 8.
Cle. recog. 3.

Erast. in disputat. de lamiis.

Actions unpossible to divels: Ergo to witches, conjurors, &c.

Jamb. de mysteriis.

CHAPTER XXI.

That the serpents and frogs were trulie presented, and the water poisoned indeed by Jannes and Jambres, of false prophets, and of their miracles, of Balams asse.

TRUELIE I think there were no inconvenience granted, though I should admit that the serpent and frogs were trulie presented, and the water truelie poisoned by *Jannes* and *Jambres;* not that they could execute such miracles of themselves, or by their familiars or divels: but that God, by the hands of those counterfet couseners, contrarie to their owne expectations, overtooke them, and compelled them in their ridiculous wickednes to be instruments of his will and vengeance, upon their maister *Pharao:* so as by their hands God shewed some miracles, which he himselfe wrought: as appeareth in *Exodus.* For

Pharaos magicians were not maisters of their owne actions.
Exod. 10.

God did put the spirit of truth into *Baalams* mouth, who was hiered to cursse his people. And although he were a corrupt and false prophet, and went about a mischeevous enterprise; yet God made him an instrument (against his will) to the confusion of the wicked. Which if it pleased God to doo here, as a speciall worke, whereby to shew his omnipotencie, to the confirmation of his peoples faith, in the doctrine of their Messias delivered unto them by the prophet *Moses*, then was it miraculous and extraordinarie, and not to be looked for now. And (as some suppose) there were then a consort or crew of false prophets, which could also foretell things to come, and worke miracles. I answer, it was extraordinarie and miraculous, & that it pleased God so to trie his people; but he worketh not so in these daies: for the working of miracles is ceased. Likewise in this case it might well stand with Gods glorie, to use the hands of *Pharaos* magicians, towards the hardening of their maisters hart; and to make their illusions and ridiculous conceipts to become effectuall. For God had promised and determined to harden the heart of *Pharao*. As for the miracles which *Moses* did, they mollified it so, as he alwaies relented upon the sight of the same. For unto the greatnesse of his miracles were added such modestie and patience, as might have mooved even a heart of steele or flint. But *Pharaos* frowardnes alwaies grew upon the magicians actions: the like example, or the resemblance whereof, we find not againe in the scriptures. And though there were such people in those daies suffered and used by God, for the accomplishment of his will and secret purpose: yet it followeth not, that now, when Gods will is wholie revealed unto us in his word, and his sonne exhibited (for whome, or rather for the manifestation of whose comming all those things were suffered or wrought) such things and such people should yet continue. So as I conclude, the cause being taken awaie, the thing proceeding thence remaineth not. And to assigne our witches and conjurors their roome, is to mocke and contemne Gods woonderfull works; and to oppose against them cousenages, juggling knacks, and things of nought. And therefore, as they must confesse, that none in these daies can doo as *Moses* did: so it may be answered, that none in these daies can doo as *Jannes* and *Jambres* did: who, if they had beene false prophets, as they were jugglers, had yet beene more privileged to exceed our old women or conjurors, in the accomplishing of miracles, or in prophesieng, &c. For who may be compared with *Balaam?* Naie, I dare saie, that *Balaams* asse wrought a greater miracle, and more supernaturall, than either the pope or all the conjurors and witches in the world can doo at this daie.

To conclude, it is to be avouched (and there be proofes manifest enough) that our jugglers approch much neerer to resemble *Pharaos* magicians, than either witches or conjurors, & can make a more livelie shew of working miracles than anie inchantors can doo: for these practise to shew that in action, which witches doo in words and termes. But that you may thinke I have reason for the maintenance of mine opinion in this behalfe, I will surcease by multitude of words to amplifie this place, referring you to the tract following of the art of juggling, where you shall read strange practises and cunning conveiances; which bicause they cannot so convenientlie be described by phrase of speech, as that they should presentlie sinke into the capacitie of you that would be practitioners of the same; I have caused them to be set foorth in forme and figure, that your understanding might be somewhat helped by instrumentall demonstrations. And when you have perused that whole discoverie of juggling, compare the wonders thereof with the woonders imputed to conjurors and witches, (not omitting *Pharaos* sorcerers at anie hand in this comparison) and I beleeve you will be resolved, that the miracles doone in *Pharaos* sight by them, and the miracles ascribed unto witches, conjurors, &c: may be well taken for false miracles, meere delusions, &c; and for such cations as are commonlie practised by cunning jugglers; be it either by legierdemaine, confederacie, or otherwise.

[marginal notes]

God useth the wicked as instruments to execute his counsels & judgments.

The contrarie effects that the miracles of Moses and the miracles of the Aegyptian magiciäs wroght in the hart of Pharao.

That the art of juggling is more, or at least no les strange in working miracles than conjuring, witchcraft, &c.

CHAPTER XXII.

The art of juggling discovered, and in what points it dooth principallie consist.

NOW because such occasion is ministred, and the matter so pertinent to my purpose, and also the life of witchcraft and cousenage so manifestlie delivered in the art of juggling; I thought good to discover it, together with the rest of the other deceiptfull arts; being sorie that it falleth out to my lot, to laie open the secrets of this mysterie, to the hinderance of such poore men as live thereby: whose dooings herein are not onlie tollerable, but greatlie commendable, so they abuse not the name of God, nor make the people attribute unto them his power; but alwaies acknowledge wherein the art consisteth, so as thereby the other unlawfull and impious arts may be by them the rather detected and bewraied.

The true art therefore of juggling consisteth in legierdemaine; to wit, the nimble conveiance of the hand, which is especiallie performed three waies. The first and principall consisteth in hiding and conveieng of balles, the second in the alteration of monie, the third in the shuffeling of the cards. He that is expert in these may shew much pleasure, and manie feats, and hath more cunning than all other witches or magicians. All other parts of this art are taught when they are discovered: but this part cannot be taught by any description or instruction, without great exercise and expense of time. And for as much as I professe rather to discover than teach these mysteries, it shall suffice to signifie unto you, that the endevor and drift of jugglers is onelie to abuse mens eies and judgements. Now therefore my meaning is, in words as plaine as I can, to rip up certeine proper tricks of that art; whereof some are pleasant and delectable, other some dreadfull and desperate, and all but meere delusions, or counterfet actions, as you shall soone see by due observation of everie knacke by me heereafter deciphered.

In what respects juggling is tollerable and also commendable.

The three principall points wherein legierdemaine or nimblenes of hand dooth consist.

CHAPTER XXIII.

Of the ball, and the manner of legierdemaine therewith, also notable feats with one or diverse balles.

CONCERNING the ball, the plaies & devises thereof are infinite, in somuch as if you can by use handle them well, you may shewe therewith a hundreth feats. But whether you seeme to throw the ball into your left hand, or into your mouth, or into a pot, or up into the aier, &c: it is to be kept still in your right hand. If you practise first with a leaden bullet, you shall the sooner and better doo it with balles of corke. The first place at your first learning, where you are to bestow a great ball, is in the palme of your hand, with your ringfinger: but a small ball is to be placed with your thombe, betwixt your ringfinger and midlefinger, then are you to practise to doo it, betwixt the other fingers, then betwixt the forefinger and the thombe, with the forefinger and midlefinger jointlie, and therein is the greatest and strangest cunning shewed. Lastlie the same small ball is to be practised in the palme of the hand, and by use you shall not onelie seeme to put anie one ball from you, and yet reteine it in your hand; but you shall keepe foure or five as cleanelie and certeinelie as one. This being atteined unto, you shall worke woonderfull feats: as for example.

Laie three or foure balles before you, and as manie small candle-sticks, bolles, saltsellers, or saltseller covers, which is the best. Then first seeme to put one ball into your left hand, and therwithall seeme to hold the same fast: then take one

Great varietie of plaie with the balles, &c.

These feats are nimbly, cleanly, & swiftly to be conveied; so as the eies of the beholders may not piscerne or derceive the drift.

182

of the candlesticks, or anie other thing (having a hollow foot, & not being too great) and seeme to put the ball which is thought to be in your left hand, underneath the same, and so under the other candlesticks seeme to bestow the other balles: and all this while the beholders will suppose each ball to be under each candlesticke: this doone, some charme or forme of words is commonlie used. Then take up one candlesticke with one hand, and blow, saieng; Lo, you see that is gone: & so likewise looke under ech candlesticke with like grace and words, & the beholders will woonder where they are become. But if you, in lifting up the candlesticks with your right hand, leave all those three or foure balles under one of them (as by use you may easilie doo, having turned them all downe into your hand, and holding them fast with your little and ringfingers) and take the candlesticke with your other fingers, and cast the balles up into the hollownes thereof (for so they will not roll so soone awaie) the standers by will be much astonied. But it will seeme woonderfull strange, if also in shewing how there remaineth nothing under an other of those candlesticks, taken up with your left hand, you leave behind you a great ball, or anie other thing, the miracle will be the greater. For first they thinke you have pulled awaie all the balles by miracle; then, that you have brought them all togither againe by like meanes, and they neither thinke nor looke that anie other thing remaineth behind under anie of them. And therefore, after manie other feats doone, returne to your candlesticks, remembering where you left the great ball, and in no wise touch the same; but having an other like ball about you, seeme to bestow the same in maner and forme aforesaid, under a candlesticke which standeth furthest frō that where the ball lieth. And when you shall with words or charmes seeme to conveie the same ball from under the same candlesticke, and afterward bring it under the candlesticke which you touched not, it will (I saie) seeme woonderfull strange.

Memorandum that the juggler must set a good grace on the matter: for that is verie requisite.

As, Hey, fortuna furie, nunquam credo, passe, passe, when come you sirra: See pag. 83.

To make a little ball swell in your hand till it be verie great.

Take a verie great ball in your left hand, or three indifferent big balles; and shewing one or three little balles, seeme to put them into your said left hand, concealing (as you may well doo) the other balles which were there in before: then use words, and make them seeme to swell, and open your hand, &c. This plaie is to be varied a hundreth waies: for as you find them all under one candlesticke, so may you go to a stander by, and take off his hat or cap, and shew the balles to be there, by conveieng them thereinto, as you turne the bottome upward.

To consume (or rather to conveie) one or manie balles into nothing.

If you take one ball, or more, & seeme to put it into your other hand, and whilest you use charming words, you conveie them out of your right hand into your lap; it will seeme strange. For when you open your left hand immediatlie, the sharpest lookers on will saie it is in your other hand, which also then you may open; & when they see nothing there, they are greatlie overtaken.

How to rap a wag upon the knuckles.

But I will leave to speake anie more of the ball, for herein I might hold you all daie, and yet shall I not be able to teach you to use it, nor scarslie to understand what I meane or write concerning it: but certeinelie manie are persuaded that it is a spirit or a flie, &c. *Memorandum*, that alwaies the right hand be kept open and streight, onlie keepe the palme from view. And therefore you may end with this miracle. ¶ Laie one ball upon your shoulder, an other on your arme, and the third on the table: which because it is round, and will not easilie lie upon the point of your knife, you must bid a stander by laie it thereon, saieng that you meane to throwe all those three balles into your mouth at once: and holding a knife as a pen in your hand, when he is laieng in upon the point of your knife, you may easilie with the haft rap him on the fingers, for the other matter wilbe hard to doo.

This feate tendeth cheefelie to the mooving of laughter and mirth.

CHAPTER XXIV.

Of conveiance of monie.

THE conveieng of monie is not much inferior to the ball, but much easier to doo. The principall place to keepe a peece of monie is the palme of your hand, the best peece to keepe is a testor; but with exercise all will be alike, except the mony be verie small, and then it is to be kept betwixt the fingers, almost at the fingers end, whereas the ball is to be kept beelowe neere to the palme.

To conveie monie out of one of your hands into the other by legierdemaine.

First you must hold open your right hand, & lay therin a testor, or some big peece of monie: then laie thereupon the top of your long left finger, and use words, and upon the sudden slip your right hand from your finger wherwith you held downe the testor, and bending your hand a verie little, you shall reteine the testor still therein: and suddenlie (I saie) drawing your right hand through your left, you shall seeme to have left the testor there speciallie when you shut in due time your left hand. Which that it may more plainelie appeare to be trulie doone, you may take a knife, and seeme to knocke against it, so as it shall make a great sound: but in stead of knocking the peece in the left hand (where none is) you shall hold the point of the knife fast with the left hand, and knocke against the testor held in the other hand, and it will be thought to hit against the mony in the left hand. Then use words, and open your hand, and when nothing is seene, it will be woondered at how the testor was remooved.

To convert or transubstantiate monie into counters, or counters into monie.

Another waie to deceive the lookers on, is to doo as before, with a testor; and keeping a counter in the palme of the left hand secretlie to seeme to put the testor thereinto; which being reteined still in the right hand, when the left hand is opened, the testor will seeme to be transubstantiated into a counter.

To put one testor into one hand, and an other into the other hand, and with words to bring them togither.

He that hath once atteined to the facilitie of reteining one peece of monie in his right hand, may shew a hundreth pleasant conceipts by that meanes, and may reserve two or three as well as one. And lo then may you seeme to put one peece into your left hand, and reteining it still in your right hand, you may to- gither therewith take up another like peece, and so with words seeme to bring both peeces togither.

To put one testor into a strangers hand, and another into your owne, and to conveie both into the strangers hand with words.

Also you may take two testors evenlie set togither, and put the same in stead of one testor, into a strangers hand, and then making as though you did put one testor into your left hand, with words you shall make it seeme that you conveie the testor in your hand, into the strangers hand: for when you open your said left hand, there shall be nothing seene; and he opening his hand shall find two, where he thought was but one. By this devise (I saie) a hundreth conceipts may be shewed.

How to doo the same or the like feate otherwise.

To keepe a testor, &c: betwixt your finger, serveth speciallie for this and such like purposes. Hold out your hand, and cause one to laie a testor upon the palme

184

thereof, then shake the same up almost to your fingers ends, and putting your thombe upon it; you shall easilie, with a little practise, conveie the edge betwixt the middle and forefinger, whilest you proffer to put it into your other hand (provided alwaies that the edge appeere not through the fingers on the backside) which being doone, take up another testor (which you may cause a stander by to laie downe) and put them both together, either closelie instead of one into a strangers hand, or keepe them still in your owne: & (after words spoken) open your hands, and there being nothing in one, and both peeces in the other, the beholders will woonder how they came togither.

You must take heed that you be close and slie: or else you discredit the art.

To throwe a peece of monie awaie, and to find it againe where you list.

You may, with the middle or ringfinger of the right hand, conveie a testor into the palme of the same hand, & seeming to cast it awaie, keepe it still: which with confederacie will seeme strange; to wit, when you find it againe, where another hath bestowed the verie like peece. But these things without exercise cannot be doone, and therefore I will proceed to shew things to be brought to passe by monie, with lesse difficultie; & yet as strange as the rest: which being unknowne are marvellouslie commended, but being knowne, are derided, & nothing at all regarded.

Use and exercise maketh men readie and practive.

With words to make a groat or a testor to leape out of a pot, or to run alongst upon a table.

You shall see a juggler take a groat or a testor, and throwe it into a pot, or laie it in the midst of a table, & with inchanting words cause the same to leape out of the pot, or run towards him, or from him ward alongst the table. Which will seeme miraculous, untill you knowe that it is doone with a long blacke haire of a womans head, fastened to the brim of a groat, by meanes of a little hole driven through the same with a Spanish needle. In like sort you may use a knife, or anie other small thing: but if you would have it go from you, you must have a confederate, by which meanes all juggling is graced and amended.

This feat is the stranger if it be doone by night; a candle placed betweene the lookers on & the juggler: for by that means their eiesight is hindered from discerning the conceit.

To make a groat or a testor to sinke through a table, and to vanish out of a handkercher verie strangelie.

A juggler also sometimes will borrow a groat or a testor, &c: and marke it before you, and seeme to put the same into the middest of a handkercher, and wind it so, as you may the better see and feele it. Then will he take you the handkercher, and bid you feele whether the groat be there or naie; and he will also require you to put the same under a candlesticke, or some such thing. Then will he send for a bason, and holding the same under the boord right against the candlesticke, will use certeine words of inchantments; and in short space you shall heare the groat fall into the bason. This doone, one takes off the candlesticke, and the juggler taketh the handkercher by a tassell, and shaketh it; but the monie is gone: which seemeth as strange as anie feate whatsoever, but being knowne, the miracle is turned to a bable. For it is nothing else, but to sowe a groat into the corner of a handkercher, finelie covered with a peece of linnen, little bigger than your groat: which corner you must conveie in steed of the groat delivered to you, into the middle of your handkercher; leaving the other either in your hand or lap, which afterwards you must seeme to pull through the boord, letting it fall into a bason, &c.

A discoverie of this juggling knacke.

A notable tricke to transforme a counter to a groat.

Take a groat, or some lesse peece of monie, and grind it verie thin at the one side; and take two counters, and grind them, the one at the one side, the other on the other side: glew the smooth side of the groat to the smooth side of one of the counters, joining them so close together as may be, speciallie at the edges, which may be so filed, as they shall seeme to be but one peece; to wit, one side

185

The jug-
gler must
have none
of his trin-
kets wan-
ting: besides
that, it be-
hooveth
him to be
mindfull,
least he
mistake his
trickes.
a counter, and the other side a groat. Then take a verie little greene waxe (for that is softest and therefore best) and laie it so upon the smooth side of the other counter, as it doo not much discolour the groat: and so will that counter with the groat cleave togither, as though they were glewed; and being filed even with the groat and the other counter, it will seeme so like a perfect entire counter, that though a stranger handle it, he shall not bewraie it; then having a little touched your forefinger, and the thombe of your right hand with soft waxe, take therewith this counterfet counter, and laie it downe openlie upon the palme of your left hand, in such sort as an auditor laieth downe his counters, wringing the same hard, so as you may leave the glewed counter with the groat apparentlie in the palme of your left hand; and the smooth side of the waxed counter will sticke fast upon your thombe, by reason of the wax wherwith it is smeered, and so may you hide it at your pleasure. Provided alwaies, that you laie the waxed side downeward, and the glewed side upward: then close your hand, and in or after the closing thereof turne the peece, & so in stead of a counter (which they suppose to be in your hand) you shall seeme to have a groat, to the astonishment of the beholders, if it be well handled.

CHAPTER XXV.

An excellent feat, to make a two penie peece lie plaine in the palme of your hand, and to be passed from thence when you list.

As, Ailif,
casyl, zaze,
hit mel
meltat: Sa-
turnus, Ju-
piter, Mars,
Sol, Venus,
Mercurie,
Luna: or
such like.
PUT a little red wax (not too thin) upon the naile of your longest finger, then let a stranger put a two penie peece into the palme of your hand, and shut your fist suddenlie, and conveie the two penie peece upon the wax, which with use you may so accomplish, as no man shall perceive it. Then and in the meane time use words of course, and suddenlie open your hand, holding the tippes of your fingers rather lower than higher than the palme of your hand, and the beholders will woonder where it is become. Then shut your hand suddenlie again, & laie a wager whether it be there or no; and you may either leave it there, or take it awaie with you at your pleasure. This (if it be will handled) hath more admiration than any other feat of the hand. *Memorandum* this may be best handled, by putting the wax upon the two penie peece, but then must you laie it in your hand your selfe.

To conveie a testor out of ones hand that holdeth it fast.

Sticke a little wax upon your thombe, and take a stander by by the finger, shewing him the testor, and telling him you will put the same into his hand: then wring it downe hard with your waxed thombe, and using many words looke him in the face, & as soone as you perceive him to looke in your face, or frō your hand, suddenlie take awaie your thombe, & close his hand, and so will it seeme to him that the testor remaineth: even as if you wring a testor upon ones forehead, it will seeme to sticke, when it is taken awaie, especiallie if it be wet. Then cause him to hold his hand still, and with speed put into another mans hand (or into your owne) two testors in stead of one, and use words of course, wherby you shall make not onelie the beholders, but the holders, beleeve, when they open their hands, that by inchantment you have brought both togither.

To throwe a peece of monie into a deepe pond, and to fetch it againe from whence you list.

There be a marvellous number of feats to be doone with monie, but if you will worke by private confederacie, as to marke a shilling, or anie other thing, and throwe the same into a river or deepe pond, and having hid a shilling before with like marks in some other secret place; bid some go presentlie & fetch it, making them beleeve, that it is the verie same which you threw into the river: the beholders will marvell much at it. And of such feats there may be doone a marvellous number; but manie more by publike confederacie, whereby one may tell another how much monie he hath in his pursse, and a hundreth like toies, and all with monie.

cie Feats had the name, whilest he lived.

To conveie one shilling being in one hand into another, holding your armes abroad like a rood.

Evermore it is necessarie to mingle some merie toies among your grave miracles, as in this case of monie, to take a shilling in each hand, and holding your armes abroad, to laie a wager that you will put them both into one hand, without bringing them anie whit neerer togither. The wager being made, hold your armes abroad like a rood, and turning about with your bodie, laie the shilling out of one of your hands upon the table, and turning to the other side take it up with the other hand: and so you shall win your wager.

A knacke more merrie than marvellous.

How to rap a wag on the knuckles.

Deliver one peece of monie with the left hand to one, and to a second person another, and offer him that you would rap on the fingers the third; for he (though he be ungratious and subtill) seeing the other receive monie, will not lightlie refuse it: and when he offereth to take it, you may rap him on the fingers with a knife, or somewhat else held in the right hand, saieng that you knew by your familiar, that he ment to have kept it from you.

Another to the same purpose read in pag. 183.

CHAPTER XXVI.

To transforme anie one small thing into anie other forme by folding of paper.

TAKE a sheete of paper, or a handkercher, and fold or double the same, so as one side be a little longer than an other: then put a counter betweene the two sides or leaves of the paper or handkercher, up to the middle of the top of the fold, holding the same so as it be not perceived, and laie a groat on the outside thereof, right against the counter, and fold it downe to the end of the longer side: and when you unfold it againe, the groat will be where the counter was, and the counter where the groat was; so as some will suppose that you have transubstantiated the monie into a counter, and with this manie feats may be doone.

The like or rather stranger than it may be done, with two papers three inches square a peece, divided by two folds into three equall parts at either side, so as each folded paper remaine one inch square: then glew the backsides of the two papers together as they are folded, & not as they are open, & so shall both papers seeme to be but one; & which side soever you open, it shall appeare to be the same, if you hide handsomelie the bottome, as you may well doo with your middle finger, so as if you have a groat in the one and a counter in the other, you (having shewed but one) may by turning the paper seeme to transubstantiate it. This may be best performed, by putting it under a candlesticke, or a hat, &c: and with words seeme to doo the feat.

Such as you shall find in pag. 185 in the marginal notes or some strange terms of your owne devising.

CHAPTER XXVII.

Of cards, with good cautions how to avoid cousenage therein : speciall rules to conveie and handle the cards, and the maner and order how to accomplish all difficult and strange things wrought with cards.

HAVING now bestowed some waste monie among you, I will set you to cards; by which kind of witchcraft a great number of people have juggled awaie not onelie their monie, but also their lands, their health, their time, and their honestie. I dare not (as I could) shew the lewd juggling that chetors practise, least it minister some offense to the well disposed, to the simple hurt and losses, and to the wicked occasion of evill dooing. But I would wish all gamesters to beware, not onlie with what cards and dice they plaie, but speciallie with whome & where they exercise gaming. And to let dice passe (as whereby a man maie be inevitablie cousened) one that is skilful to make and use Bumcards, may undoo a hundreth wealthie men that are given to gaming : but if he have a confederate present, either of the plaiers or standers by, the mischiefe cannot be avoided. If you plaie among strangers, beware of him that seemes simple or drunken; for under their habit the most speciall couseners are presented, & while you thinke by their simplicitie and imperfections to beguile them (and therof perchance are persuaded by their confederats, your verie freends as you thinke) you your selfe will be most of all overtaken. Beware also of bettors by, and lookers on, and namelie of them that bet on your side; for whilest they looke in your game without suspicion, they discover it by signs to your adversaries, with whome they bet, and yet are their confederates.

But in shewing feats, and juggling with cards, the principall point consisteth in shuffling them nimblie, and alwaies keeping one certeine card either in the bottome, or in some knowne place of the stocke, foure or five cards from it. Hereby you shall seeme to worke woonders; for it will be easie for you to see or spie one card, which though you be perceived to doo, it will not be suspected, if you shuffle them well afterwards. And this note I must give you, that in reserv- ing the bottome card, you must alwaies (whilest you shuffle) keepe him a little before or a little behind all the cards lieng underneath him, bestowing him (I saie) either a little beyond his fellowes before, right over the forefinger, or else behind the rest, so as the little finger of the left hand may meete with it : which is the easier, the readier, and the better waie. In the beginning of your shuffling, shuffle as thicke as you can; and in the end throw upon the stocke the nether card (with so manie mo at the least as you would have preserved for anie pur- pose) a little before or behind the rest. Provided alwaies, that your forefinger, if the packe be laied before, or the little finger, if the packe lie behind, creepe up to meete with the bottome card, and not lie betwixt the cards : and when you feele it, you may there hold it, untill you have shuffled over the cards againe, still leaving your kept card below. Being perfect herein, you may doo almost what you list with the cards. By this meanes, what packe soever you make, though it consist of eight, twelve, or twentie cards, you may keepe them still together un- severed next to the nether card, and yet shuffle them often to satisfie the curious beholders. As for example, and for brevities sake, to shew you diverse feats under one.

How to deliver out foure aces, and to convert them into foure knaves.

Make a packe of these eight cards ; to wit, foure knaves and foure aces : and al- though all the eight cards must lie immediatlie together, yet must ech knave and ace be evenlie severed, and the same eight cards must lie also in the lowest place of the bunch. Then shuffle them so, as alwaies at the second shuffling, or at least wise at the end of your shuffling the said packe, and of the packe one ace may lie nethermost, or so as you may know where he goeth and lieth : and alwaies (I saie) let your foresaid packe with three or foure cards more lie unseparablie together immediatlie upon and with that ace. Then using some speech or other devise, and putting your hands with the cards to the edge of the table to hide the action, let out privilie a peece of the second card, which is one of the knaves, holding foorth the stocke in both your hands, and shewing to the standers by the nether card (which is the ace or kept card) covering also the head or peece of the knave (which is the next card) with your foure fingers, draw out the same knave, laieing it downe on the table : then shuffle againe, keeping your packe whole, and so have you two aces lieng together in the bottome. And therfore, to reforme that disordered card, as also for a grace and countenance to that action, take off the uppermost card of the bunch, and thrust it into the middest of the cards : and then take awaie the nethermost card, which is one of your said aces, and bestow him likewise. Then may you begin as before, shewing an other ace, and in steed thereof, laie downe an other knave : and so foorth, untill in steed of foure aces you have laied downe foure knaves. The beholders all this while thinking that there lie foure aces on the table, are greatlie abused, and will marvell at the transformation.

shuffling of the bunch, least you overshoot your selfe.

How to tell one what card he seeth in the bottome, when the same card is shuffled into the stocke.

When you have seene a card privilie, or as though you marked it not, laie the same undermost, and shuffle the cards as before you are taught, till your card lie againe below in the bottome. Then shew the same to the beholders, willing them to remember it : then shuffle the cards, or let anie other shuffle them ; for you know the card alreadie, and therefore may at anie time tell them what card they saw : which neverthelesse would be done with great circumstance and shew of difficultie.

For that will drawe the action into the greater admiration.

An other waie to doo the same, having your selfe indeed never seene the card.

If you can see no card, or be suspected to have seene that which you meane to shew, then let a stander by first shuffle, and afterwards take you the cards into your hands, and (having shewed and not seene the bottome card) shuffle againe, and keepe the same card, as before you are taught ; and either make shift then to see it when their suspicion is past, which maie be done by letting some cards fall, or else laie downe all the cards in heaps, remembring where you laid your bottome card. Then spie how manie cards lie in some one heape, and laie the heape where your bottome card is upon that heape, and all the other heapes upon the same : and so, if there were five cards in the heape wheron you laied your card, then the same must be the sixt card, which you now may throw out, or looke upon without suspicion : and tell them the card they saw.

To tell one without confederacie what card he thinketh.

Laie three cards on a table, a little waie distant, and bid a stander by be true and not waver, but thinke one of them three, and by his eie you shall assuredlie perceive which he both seeth and thinketh. And you shall doo the like, if you cast downe a whole paire of cards with the faces upward, whereof there will be few or none plainlie perceived, and they also coate cards. But as you cast them downe suddenlie, so must you take them up presentlie, marking both his eie and the card whereon he looketh.

The eie bewraieth the thought.

CHAPTER XXVIII.

How to tell what card anie man thinketh, how to conveie the same into a kernell of a nut or cheristone, &c: and the same againe into ones pocket: how to make one drawe the same or anie card you list, and all under one devise.

Tricks with
cards, &c.:
which must
be doone
with confe-
deracie.

TAKE a nut, or a cheristone, & burne a hole through the side of the top of the shell, and also through the kernell (if you will) with a hot bodkin, or boare it with a nall; and with the eie of a needle pull out some of the kernell, so as the same may be as wide as the hole of the shell. Then write the number or name of a card in a peece of fine paper one inch or halfe an inch in length, and halfe so much in bredth, and roll it up hard: then put it into a nut, or cheristone, and close the hole with a little red waxe, and rub the same with a litle dust, and it will not be perceived, if the nut or cheristone be browne or old. Then let your confederate thinke that card which you have in your nut, &c: and either con-veie the same nut or cheristone into some bodies pocket, or laie it in some strange place: then make one drawe the same out of the stocke held in your hand, which by use you may well doo. But saie not: I will make you perforce draw such a card: but require some stander by to draw a card, saieing that it skils not what card he draw. And if your hand serve you to use the cards well, you shall prefer unto him, and he shall receive (even though he snatch at an other) the verie card which you kept, and your confederate thought, and is written in the nut, and hidden in the pocket, &c. You must (while you hold the stocke in your hands, tossing the cards to and fro) remember alwaies to keepe your card in your eie, and not to loose the sight thereof. Which feate, till you be perfect in, you may have the same privilie marked; and when you perceive his hand readie to draw, put it a little out towards his hand, nimblie turning over the cards, as though you numbred them, holding the same more loose and open than the rest, in no wise suffering him to draw anie other: which if he should doo, you must let three or foure fall, that you may beginne againe. ¶ This will seeme most strange, if your said paper be inclosed in a button, and by confederacie sowed upon the doublet or cote of anie bodie. This tricke they commonlie end with a

A merrie
conceipt,
the like
whereof
you shall
find in pag.
183 & 186.

nut full of inke, in which case some wag or unhappie boie is to be required to thinke a card: and having so doone, let the nut be delivered him to crake, which he will not refuse to doo, if he have seene the other feate plaied before.

CHAPTER XXIX.

Of fast or loose, how to knit a hard knot upon a handkercher, and to undo the same with words.

Fast and
loose with
a hand-
kercher.

THE *Aegyptians* juggling witchcraft or sortilegie standeth much in fast or loose, wherof though I have written somwhat generallie alreadie, yet hav-ing such opportunitie I will here shew some of their particular feats; not treating of their common tricks which is so tedious, nor of their fortune telling which is so impious; and yet both of them meere cousenages. ¶ Make one plaine loose knot, with the two corner ends of a handkercher, and seeming to draw the same verie hard, hold fast the bodie of the said handkercher (neere to the knot) with your right hand, pulling the contrarie end with the left hand, which is the corner of that which you hold. Then close up handsomlie the knot, which will be yet somewhat loose, and pull the handkercher so with your right hand, as the left hand may be neere to the knot: then will it seeme a true and a firme knot. And to make it appeare more assuredlie to be so indeed, let a stranger pull at the end which you hold in your left hand, whilest you hold fast the other in your right hand: and then holding the knot with your forefinger & thombe, & the nether part of your handkercher with your other fingers, as you hold a bridle when you would with one hand slip up the knot and lengthen your reines. This doone, turne your handkercher over the knot with the left hand, in dooing whereof you must suddenlie slip out the end or corner, putting up the knot of your handkercher with your forefinger and thombe, as you would put up the foresaid knot of your bridle. Then deliver the same (covered and wrapt in the middest of your handkercher) to one, to hold fast, and so after some words used, and wagers laied, take the handkercher and shake it, and it will be loose.

A notable feate of fast or loose; namelie, to pull three beadstones from off a cord, while you hold fast the ends thereof, without removing of your hand.

Take two little whipcords of two foote long a peece, double them equallie, so as there may appeare foure ends. Then take three great beadstones, the hole of one of them beeing bigger than the rest; and put one beadstone upon the eie or bowt of the one cord, and an other on the other cord. Then take the stone with the greatest hole, and let both the bowts be hidden therein: which may be the better doone, if you put the eie of the one into the eie or bowt of the other. Then pull the middle bead upon the same, being doubled over his fellow, and so will the beads seeme to be put over the two cords without partition. For holding fast in each hand the two ends of the two cords, you may tosse them as you list, and make it seeme manifest to the beholders, which may not see how you have doone it, that the beadstons are put upon the two cords without anie fraud. Then must you seeme to adde more effectuall binding of those beadstones to the string, and make one halfe of a knot with one of the ends of each side; which is for no other purpose, but that when the beadstones be taken awaie, the cords may be seene in the case which the beholders suppose them to be in before. For when you have made your halfe knot (which in anie wise you may not double to make a perfect knot) you must deliver into the hands of some stander by those two cords; namelie, two ends evenlie set in one hand, and two in the other, and then with a wager, &c.: beginne to pull off your beadstones, &c: which if you handle nimblie, and in the end cause him to pull his two ends, the two cords will shew to be placed plainelie, and the beadstones to have come through the cords. But these things are so hard and long to be described, that I will leave them; whereas I could shew great varietie.

Margin notes:
Fast or lose with whip-cords and beades.

This conveiance must be closelie doone: *Ergo* it must be no bunglers worke.

Juggling knacks by confederacie, and how to know whether one cast crosse or pile by the ringing.

LAIE a wager with your confederate (who must seeme simple, or obstinatlie opposed against you) that standing behind a doore, you will (by the sound or ringing of the monie) tell him whether he cast crosse or pile: so as when you are gone, and he hath fillipped the monie before the witnesses who are to be cousened, he must saie; What is it, if it be crosse; or What ist, if it be pile: or some other such signe, as you are agreed upon, and so you need not faile to gesse rightlie. By this meanes (if you have aine invention), you may seeme to doo a hundreth miracles, and to discover the secrets of a mans thoughts, or words spoken a far off.

Margin notes:
What is it? What ist? signes of confederacie.

To make a shoale of goslings drawe a timber log.

To make a shoale of goslings, or (as they saie) a gaggle of geese to seeme to drawe a timber log, is doone by that verie meanes that is used, when a cat dooth drawe a foole through a pond or river: but handled somewhat further off from the beholders.

To make a pot or anie such thing standing fast on the cupboard, to fall downe thense by vertue of words.

Let a cupboard be so placed, as your confederate may hold a blacke thred without in the court, behind some window of that roome; and at a certeine lowd word spoken by you, he may pull the same thred, being woond about the pot, &c. And this was the feate of *Eleazar*, which *Josephus* reporteth to be such a miracle.

Eleazers feate of cō-federacie,

To make one danse naked.

Make a poore boie confederate with you, so as after charmes, &c: spoken by you, he uncloth himselfe, and stand naked, seeming (whilst he undresseth him) to shake, stampe, and crie, still hastening to be unclothed, till he be starke naked: or if you can procure none to go so far, let him onelie beginne to stapem and shake, &c: and to uncloth him, and then you may (for the reverence of the companie) seeme to release him.

To transforme or alter the colour of ones cap or hat.

As, Droch myroch, & senaroth betu ba-roch assma-aroth, roū-see faroun-see, hey passe passe, &c.: or such like strange words.
Pope and Tailor cō-federates.

Take a confederates hat, and use certeine words over it, and deliver it to him againe, and let him seeme to be wroth, and cast it backe to you againe, affirming that his was a good new blacke hat, but this is an old blew hat, &c: and then you may seeme to countercharme it, and redeliver it, to his satisfaction.

How to tell where a stollen horsse is become.

By meanes of confederacie, *Steeven Tailor* and one *Pope* abused divers countrie people. For *Steeven Tailor* would hide awaie his neighbours horsses, &c: and send them to *Pope*, (whom he before had told where they were) promising to send the parties unto him, whome he described and made knowne by divers signes: so as this *Pope* would tell them at their first entrance unto the doore. Wherefore they came, and would saie that their horsses were stollen, but the theefe should be forced to bring backe the horsses, &c: and leave them within one mile south and bywest, &c: of his house, even as the plot was laid, and the packe made before by *Steeven* and him. This *Pope* is said of some to be a witch, of others he is accompted a conjuror; but commonlie called a wise man, which is all one with a soothsaier or witch.

CHAPTER XXXI.

Boxes to alter one graine into another, or to consume the graine or corne to nothing.

Note the maner of this conveiance.

THERE be divers juggling boxes with false bottoms, wherein manie false feates are wrought. First they have a box covered or rather footed alike at each end, the bottome of the one end being no deeper than as it may con-teine one lane of corne or pepper glewed thereupon. Then use they to put into the hollow end thereof some other kind of graine, ground or unground; then doo they cover it, and put it under a hat or candlesticke: and either in putting it therinto, or pulling it thence, they turne the box, and open the contrarie end, wherein is shewed a contrarie graine: or else they shew the glewed end first (which end they suddenlie thrust into a boll or bag of such graine as is glewed alreadie thereupon) and secondlie the emptie box.

How to conveie (with words or charmes) the corne conteined in one box into an other.

There is another box fashioned like a bell, wherinto they doo put so much, and such corne or spice as the foresaid hollow box can conteine. Then they stop or cover the same with a peece of lether, as broad as a testor, which being thrust up hard towards the midle part or waste of the said bell, will sticke fast, & beare up the corne. And if the edge of the leather be wet, it will hold the better. Then take they the other box dipped (as is aforesaid) in corne, and set downe the same upon the table, the emptie end upward, saieng that they will conveie the graine therein into the other box or bell: which being set downe somewhat hard upon the table, the leather and the corne therein will fall downe, so as the said bell being taken up from the table, you shall see the corne lieng thereon, and the stopple will be hidden therwith, & covered: & when you uncover the other box, nothing shall remaine therein. But presentlie the corne must be swept downe with one hand into the other, or into your lap or hat. Manie feats maie be done with this box, as to put therein a tode, affirming the same to have beene so turned from corne, &c: and then manie beholders will suppose the same to be the jugglers divell, whereby his feats and miracles are wrought. But in truth, there is more cunning witchcraft used in transferring of corne after this sort, than is in the transferring of one mans corne in the grasse into an other mans feeld: which the lawe of the twelve tables dooth so forceablie condemne: for the one is a cousening slight, the other is a false lie.

You must take heed that when the corne commeth out it cover & hide the leather, &c.

See the 12 booke of this discoverie, in the title Habar, cap. 4. pag. 125.

Of an other boxe to convert wheat into flower with words, &c.

There is an other boxe usuall among jugglers, with a bottome in the middle thereof, made for the like purposes. One other also like a tun, wherin is shewed great varietie of stuffe, as well of liquors as spices, and all by means of an other little tun within the same, wherein and whereon liquors and spices are shewed. But this would aske too long a time of description.

Of diverse petie juggling knacks.

There are manie other beggerlie feats able to beguile the simple, as to make an ote stir by spetting thereon, as though it came to passe by words. Item to deliver meale, pepper, ginger, or anie powder out of the mouth after the eating of bread, &c: which is doone by reteining anie of those things stuffed in a little paper or bladder conveied into your mouth, and grinding the same with your teeth. ¶ Item, a rish through a peece of a trencher, having three holes, and at the one side the rish appearing out in the second, at the other side in the third hole, by reason of a hollow place made betwixt, them both so as the slight consisteth in turning the peece of trencher.

These are such sleights that even a bungler may doo them: and yet prettie, &c.

CHAPTER XXXII.

To burne a thred, and to make it whole againe with the ashes thereof.

IT is not one of the woorst feats to burne a thred handsomelie, and to make it whole againe: the order whereof is this. Take two threds, or small laces, of one foote in length a peece: roll up one of them round, which will be then of the quantitie of a pease, bestow the same betweene your left forefinger and

Marke the maner of this conceit and devise.

That is, neatlie and deintilie.

your thombe. Then take the other thred, and hold it foorth at length, betwixt the forefinger and thombe of each hand, holding all your fingers deintilie, as yong gentlewomen are taught to take up a morsell of meate. Then let one cut asunder the same thred in the middle. When that is doone, put the tops of your two thombes together, and so shall you with lesse suspicion receive the peece of thred which you hold in your right hand into your left, without opening of your left finger and thombe: then holding these two peeces as you did the same before it was cut, let those two be cut also asunder in the middest, and they conveied againe as before, untill they be cut verie short, and then roll all those ends together, and keepe that ball of short threds before the other in your left hand, and with a knife thrust out the same into a candle, where you may hold it untill the said ball of short threds be burnt to ashes. Then pull backe the knife with your right hand, and leave the ashes with the other ball betwixt the forefinger and thombe of your left hand, and with the two thombs & two forefingers together seeme to take paines to frot and rub the ashes, untill your thred be renewed, and drawe out that thred at length which you kept all this while betwixt your left finger and thombe. This is not inferior to anie jugglers feate if it be well handled, for if you have legierdemaine to bestowe the same ball of thred, and to change it from place to place betwixt your other fingers (as may easilie be doone) then will it seeme verie strange.

A thred cut in manie peeces and burned to ashes made whole againe.

To cut a lace asunder in the middest, and to make it whole againe.

By a devise not much unlike to this, you may seeme to cut asunder any lace that hangeth about ones necke, or any point, girdle, or garter, &c: and with witchcraft or conjuration to make it whole and closed together againe. For the accomplishment whereof, provide (if you can) a peece of the lace, &c: which you meane to cut, or at the least a patterne like the same, one inch and a halfe long, & (keeping it double privilie in your left hand, betwixt some of your fingers neere to the tips thereof) take the other lace which you meane to cut, still hanging about ones necke, and drawe downe your said left hand to the bought thereof: and putting your owne peece a little before the other (the end or rather middle whereof you must hide betwixt your forefinger and thombe) making the eie or bought, which shall be seene, of your owne patterne, let some stander by cut the same asunder, and it will be surelie thought that the other lace is cut; which with words and froting, &c: you shall seeme to renew & make whole againe. This, if it be well handled, will seeme miraculous.

The means discovered.

How to pull laces innumerable out of your mouth, of what colour or length you list, and never anie thing seene to be therein.

As for pulling laces out of the mouth, it is somewhat a stale jest, whereby jugglers gaine monie among maides, selling lace by the yard, putting into their mouths one round bottome as fast as they pull out an other, and at the just end of everie yard they tie a knot, so as the same resteth upon their teeth: then cut they off the same, and so the beholders are double and treble deceived, seeing as much lace as will be conteined in a hat, and the same of what colour you list to name, to be drawne by so even yards out of his mouth, and yet the juggler to talke as though there were nothing at all in his mouth.

A common juggling knacke of flat cousenage plaied among the simple, &c.

Chapter XXXIII.

How to make a booke, wherein you shall shew everie leafe therein to be white, blacke, blew, red, yellow, greene, &c.

THERE are a thousand jugglings, which I am loth to spend time to describe, whereof some be common, and some rare, and yet nothing else but deceipt, cousenage, or confederacie: whereby you may plainelie see the art to be a kind of witchcraft. I will end therfore with one devise, which is not common, but was speciallie used by *Clarvis*, whome though I never saw to exercise the feat, yet am I sure I conceive aright of that invention. He had (they saie) a booke, whereof he would make you thinke first, that everie leafe was cleane white paper: then by vertue of words he would shew you everie leafe to be painted with birds, then with beasts, then with serpents, then with angels, &c: the devise thereof is this. ¶ Make a booke seven inches long, and five inches broad, or according to that proportion; and let there be xlix, leaves; to wit, seven times seven conteined therin, so as you may cut upon the edge of each leafe six notches, each notch in depth halfe a quarter of an inch, and one inch distant. Paint everie fourteenth and fifteenth page (which is the end of everie sixt leafe, & the beginning of everie seventh) with like colour, or one kind of picture. Cut off with a paire of sheares everie notch of the first leafe, leaving onlie one inch of paper in the uppermost place uncut, which will remaine almost halfe a quarter of an inch higher than anie part of that leafe. Leave an other like inch in the second place of the second leafe, clipping away one inch of paper in the highest place immediatlie above it, and all the notches below the same, and so orderlie to the third, fourth, &c: so as there shall rest upon each leafe one onlie inch of paper above the rest. One high uncut inch of paper must answer to the first, directlie in everie seventh leafe of the booke: so as when you have cut the first seven leaves, in such sort as I first described, you are to begin in the selfe same order at the eight leafe, descending in such wise in the cutting of seven other leaves, and so againe at the fifteenth, to xxi, &c: untill you have passed through everie leafe, all the thicknes of your booke.

Now you shall understand, that after the first seven leaves, everie seventh leafe in the booke is to be painted, saving one seven leaves, which must remaine white. Howbeit you must observe, that at each Bumleafe or high inch of paper, seven leaves distant, opposite one directlie and lineallie against the other, through the thicknesse of the booke, the same page with the page precedent so to be painted with the like colour or picture; and so must you passe through the booke with seven severall sorts of colours or pictures: so as, when you shall rest your thombe upon anie of those Bumleaves, or high inches, and open the booke, you shall see in each page one colour or picture through out the booke; in an other rowe, an other colour, &c. To make that matter more plaine unto you, let this be the description hereof. Hold the booke with your left hand, and (betwixt your forefinger and thombe of your right hand) slip over the booke in what place you list, and your thombe will alwaies rest at the seventh leafe; to wit, at the Bumleafe or high inch of paper from whence when your booke is streined, it will fall or slip to the next, &c. Which when you hold fast, & open the booke, the beholders seeing each leafe to have one colour or picture with so manie varieties, all passing continuallie & directlie thrugh the whole booke, will suppose that with words you can discolour the leaves at your pleasure. But because perhaps you will hardlie conceive herof by this description, you shall (if you be disposed) see or buie for a small value the like booke, at the shop of *W. Brome* in Powles churchyard, for your further instruction. ¶ There are certaine feats of activitie, which beautifie this art exceedinglie: howbeit even in these, some are true, and some are counterfet; to wit, some done by practise, and some by confederacie. ¶ There are likewise divers feats arythmeticall & geometricall:

Juggling a kind of witchcraft. The invention of Clarvis.

This knack is sooner learned by demonstrative means, than taught by words of instruction.

This will seeme rare to the beholders.

Wher such bookes may be gotten.

195

for them read *Gemma Phrysius*, and *Record*, &c. which being exercised by jugglers add credit to their art. ¶ There are also (besides them which I have set downe in this title of *Hartumim*) sundrie strange experiments reported by *Plinie*, *Albert*, *Joh. Bap. Port. Neap.* and *Thomas Lupton*, wherof some are true, and some false: which being knowne to *Jannes* and *Jambres*, or else to our jugglers, their occupation is the more magnified, and they thereby more reverenced. ¶ Here is place to discover the particular knaveries of casting of lots, and drawing of cuts (as they terme it) whereby manie cousenages are wrought: so as I dare not teach the sundrie devises thereof, least the ungodlie make a practise of it in the commonwealth, where manie things are decided by those meanes, which being honestlie meant may be lawfullie used. But I have said alreadie somewhat hereof in generall, and therefore also the rather have suppressed the particularities, which (in truth) are meere juggling knackes: whereof I could discover a great number.

See more hereof in the 11. book of this discoverie, in the title. Nahas, cap. 10, pag. 113.

CHAPTER XXXIV.

Desperate or dangerous juggling knacks, wherein the simple are made to thinke, that a seelie juggler with words can hurt and helpe, kill and revive anie creature at his pleasure: and first too kill anie kind of pullen, and to give it life againe.

TAKE a hen, a chicke, or a capon, and thrust a nall or a fine sharpe pointed knife through the midst of the head thereof, the edge towards the bill, so as it may seeme impossible for hir to scape death: then use words, and pulling out the knife, laie otes before hir, &c: and she will eate and live, being nothing at all greeved or hurt with the wound; bicause the braine lieth so far behind in the head as it is not touched, though you thrust your knife betweene the combe and it: and after you have doone this, you may convert your speach and actions to the greevous wounding and present recovering of your owne selfe.

The naturall cause why a hen thrust thorough the head with a bodkin dooth live notwithstanding.

To eate a knife, and to fetch it out of anie other place.

Take a knife, and conteine the same within your two hands, so as no part be seene thereof but a little of the point, which you must so bite at the first, as noise may be made therewith. Then seeme to put a great part thereof into your mouth, and letting your hand slip downe, there will appeare to have beene more in your mouth than is possible to be conteined therein. Then send for drinke, or use some other delaie, untill you have let the said knife slip into your lap, holding both your fists close together as before, and then raise them so from the edge of the table where you sit (for from thence the knife may most privilie slip downe into your lap) and in steed of biting the knife, knable a little upon your naile, and then seeme to thrust the knife into your mouth, opening the hand next unto it, and thrust up the other, so as it may appeare to the standers by, that you have delivered your hands therof, and thrust it into your mouth: then call for drinke, after countenance made of pricking and danger, &c. Lastlie, put your hand into your lap, and taking that knife in your hand, you may seeme to bring it out from behind you, or from whence you list. ¶ But if you have another like knife and a confederate, you may doo twentie notable woonders hereby: as to send a stander by into some garden or orchard, describing to him some tree or herbe, under which it sticketh; or else some strangers sheath or pocket, &c.

It must be cleanelie conveied in any case.

To thrust a bodkin into your head without hurt.

Take a bodkin so made, as the haft being hollowe, the blade thereof may slip thereinto as soone as you hold the point upward: and set the same to your fore-

The maner & meanes of this action.

196

head, and seeme to thrust it into your head, and so (with a little sponge in your hand) you may wring out bloud or wine, making the beholders thinke the bloud or the wine (whereof you may saie you have drunke verie much) runneth out of your forehead. Then, after countenance of paine and greefe, pull awaie your hand suddenlie, holding the point downeward; and it will fall so out, as it will seeme never to have beene thrust into the haft: but immediatlie thrust that bodkin into your lap or pocket, and pull out an other plaine bodkin like the same, saving in that conceipt.

To thrust a bodkin through your toong, and a knife through your arme: a pittifull sight, without hurt or danger.

Make a bodkin the blade therof being sundred in the middle, so as the one part be not neere to the other almost by three quarters of an inch, each part being kept a sunder with one small bought or crooked piece of iron, of the fashion described hereafter in place convenient. Then thrust your toong betwixt the foresaid space; to wit, into the bought left it the bodkin blade, thrusting the said bought behind your teeth, and biting the same: and then shall it seeme to sticke so fast in and through your toong, as that one can hardlie pull it out. ¶ Also the verie like may be doone with a knife so made, and put upon your arme: and the wound will appeare the more terrible, if a little bloud be powred thereupon.

A forme or patterne of this bodkin and knife you shal see described if you turne over a few leaves forward.

To thrust a peece of lead into one eie, and to drive it about (with a sticke) betweene the skin and flesh of the forehead, untill it be brought to the other eie, and there thrust out.

Put a peece of lead into one of the nether lids of your eie, as big as a tag of a point, but not so long (which you may doo without danger) and with a little juggling sticke (one end therof being hollow) seeme to thrust the like peece of lead under the other eie lid; but conveie the same in deed into the hollownes of the sticke, the stopple or peg whereof may be privilie kept in your hand untill this feate be doone. Then seeme to drive the said peece of lead, with the hollow end of the said sticke, from the same eie: and so with the end of the said sticke, being brought along upon your forhead to the other eie, you maie thrust out the peece of lead, which before you had put thereinto; to the admiration of the beholders. ¶ Some eat the lead, and then shoove it out at the eie: and some put it into both, but the first is best.

To cut halfe your nose asunder, and to heale it againe presentlie without anie salve.

Take a knife having a round hollow gap in the middle, and laie it upon your nose, and so shall you seeme to have cut your nose halfe asunder. Provided alwaies, that in all these you have an other like knife without a gap, to be shewed upon the pulling out of the same, and words of inchantment to speake, bloud also to beeraie the wound, and nimble conveiance.

This is easilie doone, howbeit being clenlie handled it will deceive the sight of the beholders.

To put a ring through your cheeke.

There is an other old knacke, which seemeth dangerous to the cheeke. For the accomplishing whereof you must have two rings, of like colour and quantitie; the one filed asunder, so as you may thrust it upon your cheeke; the other must be whole, and conveied upon a sticke, holding your hand thereupon in the middle of the sticke, delivering each end of the same sticke to be holden fast by a stander by. Then conveieng the same cleanlie into your hand, or (for lacke of good conveiance) into your lap or pocket, pull awaie your hand from the sticke: and in pulling it awaie, whirle about the ring, and so will it be thought that you have put thereon the ring which was in your cheeke.

To cut off ones head, and to laie it in a platter, &c: which the jugglers call the decollation of John Baptist.

This was doone by one Kingsfield of London, at a Bartholomewtide, An. 1582. in the sight of diverse that came to view this spectacle.

To shew a most notable execution by this art, you must cause a boord, a cloth, and a platter to be purposelie made, and in each of them holes fit for a boies necke. The boord must be made of two planks, the longer and broader the better: there must be left within halfe a yard of the end of each planke halfe a hole; so as both planks being thrust togither, there may remaine two holes, like to the holes in a paire of stocks: there must be made likewise a hole in the table-cloth or carpet. A platter also must be set directlie over or upon one of them, having a hole in the midle thereof, of the like quantitie, and also a peece cut out of the same, so big as his necke, through which his head may be conveied into the middest of the platter: and then sitting or kneeling under the boord, let the head onlie remaine upon the boord in the same. Then (to make the sight more dredfull) put a little brimstone into a chafing dish of coles, setting it before the head of the boie, who must gaspe two or three times, so as the smoke enter a little into his nostrils and mouth (which is not unholsome) and the head present-lie will appeare starke dead; if the boie set his countenance accordinglie: and if a little bloud be sprinkled on his face, the sight will be the stranger.

Necessarie observations to astonish the beholders.

This is commonlie practised with a boie instructed for that purpose, who being familiar and conversant with the companie, may be knowne as well by his face, as by his apparell. In the other end of the table, where the like hole is made, an other boie of the bignesse of the knowne boie must be placed, having upon him his usuall apparell: he must leane or lie upon the boord, and must put his head under the boord through the said hole, so as his bodie shall seeme to lie on the one end of the boord, and his head shall lie in a platter on the other end. ¶ There are other things which might be performed in this action, the more to astonish the beholders, which because they offer long descriptions, I omit: as to put about his necke a little dough kneded with bullocks bloud, which being cold will appeare like dead flesh; & being pricked with a sharpe round hollow quill, will bleed, and seeme verie strange, &c. ¶ Manie rules are to be observed herein, as to have the table cloth so long and wide as it may almost touch the ground. ¶ Not to suffer the companie to staie too long in the place, &c.

To thrust a dagger or bodkin into your guts verie strangelie, and to recover immediatlie.

Of a juggler that failing in the feats of his art lost his life.

An other miracle may be shewed touching counterfeit executions; namelie, that with a bodkin or a dagger you shall seeme to kill your selfe, or at the least make an unrecoverable wound in your bellie: as (in truth) not long since a juggler caused himself to be killed at a taverne in cheapside, from whence he presentlie went into Powles churchyard and died. Which misfortune fell upon him through his owne follie, as being then drunken, and having forgotten his plate, which he should have had for his defense. The devise is this. ¶ You must prepare a paste boord, to be made according to the fashion of your bellie and brest: the same must by a painter be coloured cunninglie, not onelie like to your flesh, but with pappes, navill, haire, &c: so as the same (being handsomelie trussed unto you) may shew to be your naturall bellie. Then next to your true bellie you may put a linnen cloth, and thereupon a double plate (which the juggler that killed himselfe forgot, or wilfullie omitted) over and upon the which you may place the false bellie. Provided alwaies, that betwixt the plate & the false bellie you place a gut or bladder of bloud, which bloud must be of a calfe or of a sheepe; but in no wise of an oxe or a cow, for that will be too thicke. Then thrust, or cause to be thrust into your brest a round bodkin, or the point of a dagger, so far as it may pearse through your gut or bladder: which being pulled out againe, the said bloud will spin or spirt out a good distance from you,

But herein see you be circumspect.

especiallie if you straine your bodie to swell, and thrust therewith against the plate. You must ever remember to use (with words, countenance, and gesture) such a grace, as may give a grace to the action, and moove admiration in the beholders.

To drawe a cord through your nose, mouth or hand, so sensiblie as is woonderful to see.

There is an other juggling knacke, which they call the bridle, being made of two elder sticks, through the hollownes therof is placed a cord, the same being put on the nose like a paire of tongs or pinsars; and the cord, which goeth round about the same, being drawne to and fro, the beholders will thinke the cord to go through your nose verie dangerouslie. The knots at the end of the cord, which doo staie the same from being drawne out of the sticke, may not be put out at the verie top (for that must be stopped up) but halfe an inch beneath each end: and so I saie, when it is pulled, it will seeme to passe through the nose; and then may you take a knife, and seeme to cut the cord asunder, and pull the bridle from your nose.

A forme of patterne of this bridle you shall see descri-bed if you turne over a few leaues.

The conclusion, wherin the reader is referred to certeine patterns of instruments wherewith diverse feats heere specified are to be executed.

Herein I might wade infinitelie, but I hope it sufficeth, that I have delivered unto you the principles, and also the principall feats belonging to this art of juggling; so as any man conceiving throughlie hereof may not onlie doo all these things, but also may devise other as strange, & varie everie of these devises into other formes as he can best conceive. And so long as the power of almightie God is not transposed to the juggler, nor offense ministred by his uncomlie speach and behaviour, but the action performed in pastime, to the delight of the beholders, so as alwaies the juggler confesse in the end that these are no supernaturall actions, but devises of men, and nimble conveiances, let all such curious conceipted men as cannot affoord their neighbors anie comfort or com-moditie, but such as pleaseth their melancholike dispositions say what they list, for this will not onelie be found among indifferent actions, but such as greatlie advance the power and glorie of God, discovering their pride and falshood that take upon them to worke miracles, and to be the mightie power of God, as *Jannes* and *Jambres* and also *Simon Magus* did.

Among what actions jug-gling is to be counted.

If anie man doubt of these things, as whether they be not as strange to behold as I have reported, or thinke with *Bodin* that these matters are performed by familiars or divels; let him go into S. Martins, and inquire for one *John Cautares* (a Frenchman by birth, in conversation an honest man) and he will shew as much and as strange actions as these, who getteth not his living hereby, but laboureth for the same with the sweat of his browes, and neverthelesse hath the best hand and conveiance (I thinke) of anie man that liveth this daie.

A matchles fellowe for legierde-maine.

Neither doo I speake (as they saie) without booke herein. For if time, place, and occasion serve, I can shew so much herein, as I am sure *Bodin, Spinæus,* and *Vairus,* would sweare I were a witch, and had a familiar divell at commande-ment. But truelie my studie and travell herein hath onelie beene emploied to the end I might proove them fooles, and find out the fraud of them that make them fooles, as whereby they may become wiser, and God may have that which to him belongeth.

And bicause the maner of these juggling conveiances are not easilie conceived by discourse of words; I have caused to be set downe diverse formes of instru-ments used in this art; which may serve for patterns to them that would throughlie see the secrets thereof, and make them for their owne private prac-tises, to trie the event of such devises, as in this tract of legierdemaine are shewed. Where note, that you shall find everie instrument that is most neces-sarilie occupied in the working of these strange feats, to beare the just and true number of the page, where the use thereof is in ample words declared.

Touching the pat-ternes of diverse jug-gling in-struments.

Now will I proceed with another cousening point of witchcraft, apt for the place, necessarie for the time, and in mine opinion meet to be discovered, or at the least to be defaced among deceitfull arts. And bicause manie are abused heereby to their utter undooing, for that it hath had passage under the protec-tion of learning, wherby they pretend to accomplish their works, it hath gone freelie without generall controlment through all ages, nations & people.

199

*Heere follow patternes of certeine instruments to be used in the former
juggling knacks.*

To pull
three bead-
stones from
off a cord,
while you
hold fast
the ends
thereof,
without
remooving
of your
hand.

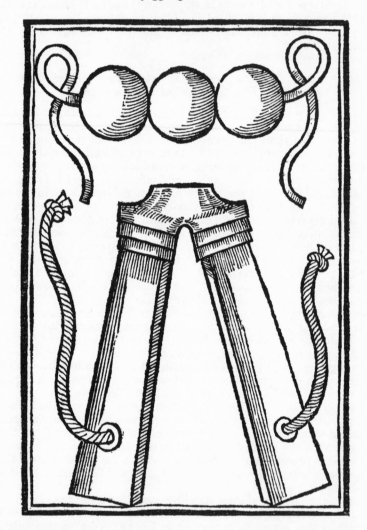

To draw a
cord tho-
rough your
nose, mouth
or hand,
which is
called the
bridle.

To be instructed in the right use of the said beadstones, read page 191. As
for the bridle, read page 199.

To thrust a bodkin into your head, and through your toong, &c.

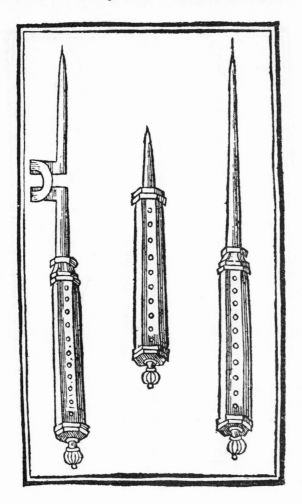

The hethermost is the bodkin wᵗ the bowt: yᵉ midlemost is the bodkin with the holow haft: the furthermost is the plaine bodkin serving for shew.

To be instructed and taught in the right use and readie practise of these bodkins, read pag. 196.

To thrust a knife through your arme, and to cut halfe your nose asunder, &c.

The middle most knife is to serve for shew; the other two be the knives of device.

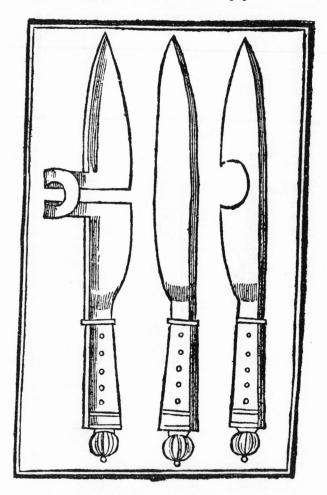

To be readie in the use and perfect in the practise of these knives here portraied, see page 196. and 197.

To cut off ones head, and to laie it in a platter, which the jugglers call the decollation of
John Baptist.

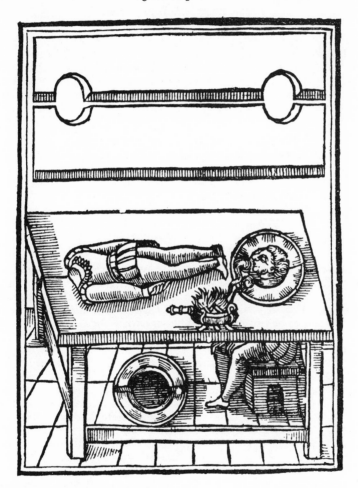

The forme
of yᵉ planks,
&c.

The order
of the acti-
on, as it is
to be shewed.

What order is to be observed for the practising heereof with great admiration,
read page 198.

BOOKE XIV.

CHAPTER I.

Of the art of Alcumystrie, of their woords of art and devises to bleare mens eies, and to procure credit to their profession.

Alcumy-strie a craft. not an art.

HERE I thought it not impertinent to saie somewhat of the art or rather the craft of Alcumystrie, otherwise called Multiplication; which *Chaucer*, of all other men, most livelie deciphereth. In the bowels herof dooth both witchcraft and conjuration lie hidden, as whereby some cousen others, and some are cousened themselves. For by this mysterie (as it is said in the chanons mans prolog)

G. Chaucer in the Chanons mans prolog.

> *They take upon them to turne upside downe,*
> *All the earth betwixt Southwarke & Canturburie towne,*
> *And to pave it all of silver and gold, &c.*
> *But ever they lacke of their conclusion,*
> *And to much folke they doo illusion.*
> *For their stuffe slides awaie so fast,*
> *That it makes them beggers at the last,*
> *And by this craft they doo never win,*
> *But make their pursse emptie, and their wits thin.*

And bicause the practisers heereof would be thought wise, learned, cunning, and their crafts maisters, they have devised words of art, sentences and epithets obscure, and confectious so innumerable (which are also compounded of strange and rare simples) as confound the capacities of them that are either set on worke heerein, or be brought to behold or expect their conclusions. For what plaine man would not beleeve, that they are learned and jollie fellowes, that have in such readinesse so many mysticall termes of art: as (for a tast) their subliming, amalgaming, engluting, imbibing, incorporating, cementing, ritrination, terminations, mollifications, and indurations of bodies, matters combust and coagulat, ingots, tests, &c. Or who is able to conceive (by reason of the abrupt confusion, contrarietie, and multitude of drugs, simples, and confections) the operation and mysterie of their stuffe and workemanship. For these things and many more, are of necessitie to be prepared and used in the execution of this indevor; namelie orpiment, sublimed *Mercurie*, iron squames, *Mercurie* crude, groundlie large, bole armoniake, verdegrece, borace, boles, gall, arsenicke, sal armoniake, brimstone, salt, paper, burnt bones, unsliked lime, claie, saltpeter, vitriall, saltartre, alcalie, sal preparat, claie made with horsse doong, mans haire, oile of tartre, allum, glasse, woort, yest, argoll, resagor, gleir of an eie, powders, ashes, doong, pisse, &c. Then have they waters corosive and lincall, waters of albification, and waters rubifieng, &c. Also oiles, ablutions, and metals fusible. Also their lamps, their urinalles, discensories, sublimatories, alembecks, viols, croslets, cucurbits, stillatories, and their fornace of calcination: also their soft and subtill fiers, some of wood, some of cole, composed specialle of beech, &c. And bicause they will not seeme to want anie point of cousenage to astonish the simple, or to moove admiration to their enterprises, they have (as they affirme) foure spirits to worke withall, whereof the first is, orpiment; the second, quicksilver; the third, sal armoniake; the fourth, brimstone. Then have they seven celestiall bodies; namelie, *Sol, Luna, Mars, Mercurie, Saturne, Jupiter*, and *Venus*; to whome they applie seven

The termes of the art alcumystical devised of purpose to bring credit to cousenage.

204

terrestriall bodies; to wit, gold, silver, iron, quickesilver, lead, tinne, and copper, attributing unto these the operation of the other; speciallie if the terrestriall bodies be qualified, tempered, and wrought in the houre and daie according to the feats of the celestiall bodies: with more like vanitie.

CHAPTER II.

The Alcumysters drift, the Chanons yeomans tale, of alcumysticall stones and waters.

NOW you must understand that the end and drift of all their worke, is, to atteine unto the composition of the philosophers stone, called Alixer, and to the stone called Titanus; and to Magnatia, which is a water made of the foure elements, which (they saie) the philosophers are sworne neither to discover, nor to write of. And by these they mortifie quicke silver, and make it malleable, and to hold touch: heereby also they convert any other mettall (but speciallie copper) into gold. This science (forsooth) is the secret of secrets; even as *Salomons* conjuration is said among the conjurors to be so likewise. And thus, when they chance to meete with yong men, or simple people, they boast and brag, and saie with *Simon Magus*, that they can worke miracles, and bring mightie things to passe. In which respect *Chaucer* trulie heereof saith:

Each man is as wise as Salomon,
When they are togither everichone:
But that seemes wisest, is most foole in preefe,
And he that is truest, is a verie theefe.
They seeme friendlie to them that knowe nought,
But they are feendlie both in word and thought,
Yet many men ride and seeke their acquaintance,
Not knowing of their false governance.

Acts. 8.

G. Chaucer in the Chanons mans tale. [Prologue.]

He also saith, and experience verifieth his assertion, that they looke ill favouredlie, & are alwaies beggerlie attired: his words are these:

These fellowes looke ill favouredlie,
And are alwaies tired beggerlie,
So as by smelling and thredbare araie,
These folke are knowne and discerned alwaie.
But so long as they have a sheet to wrap them in by night,
Or a rag to hang about them in the day light,
They will it spend in this craft,
They cannot stint till nothing be laft.
Here one may learne if he have ought,
To multiplie and bring his good to naught,
But if a man aske them privilie,
Whie they are clothed so unthriftilie,
They will round him in the eare and saie,
If they espied were, men would them slaie,
And all bicause of this noble science:
Lo thus these folke beetraien innocence.

Idem, ibid.

The tale of the chanons yeoman published by *Chaucer*, dooth make (by waie of example) a perfect demonstration of the art of Alcumystrie or multiplication: the effect whereof is this. A chanon being an Alcumyster or cousenor, espied a covetous preest, whose pursse he knew to be well lined, whome is assaulted with flatterie and subtill speach, two principall points belonging to this art. At the

The points or parts of the art Alcumysticall

which may
be called
the mystie
or smokie
science.

length he borrowed monie of the preest, which is the third part of the art, without the which the professors can doo no good, nor indure in good estate. Then he at his daie repaied the monie, which is the most difficult point in this art, and a rare experiment. Finallie, to requite the preests courtesie, he promised unto him such instructions, as wherby with expedition he should become infinitelie rich, and all through this art of multiplication. And this is the most common point in this science; for herein they must be skilfull before they can be famous, or atteine to anie credit. The preest disliked not his proffer; speciallie bicause it tended to his profit, and embraced his courtesie. Then the chanon willed him foorthwith to send for three ownces of quicke silver, which he said he would transubstantiate (by his art) into perfect silver. The preest thought that a man of his profession could not dissemble, and therefore with great joy and hope accomplished his request.

　　And now (forsooth) goeth this jollie Alcumyst about his busines and worke of multiplication, and causeth the preest to make a fier of coles, in the bottome whereof he placeth a croslet; and pretending onelie to helpe the preest to laie the coles handsomelie, he foisteth into the middle ward or lane of coles, a beechen cole, within the which was conveied an ingot of perfect silver, which (when the cole was consumed) slipt downe into the croslet, that was (I saie) directlie under

The Alcu-
mysts bait
to catch a
foole.

it. The preest perceived not the fraud, but received the ingot of silver, and was not a little joyfull to see such certeine successe proceed from his owne handie worke wherein could be no fraud (as he surelie conceived) and therefore verie willinglie gave the cannon fortie pounds for the receipt of this experiment, who for that summe of monie taught him a lesson in Alcumystrie, but he never returned to heare repetitions, or to see how he profited.

<hr/>

Chapter iii.

Of a yeoman of the countrie cousened by an Alcumyst.

I COULD cite manie Alcumysticall cousenages wrought by Doctor *Burcot*, *Feates*, and such other; but I will passe them over and onelie repeate three experiments of that art; the one practised upon an honest yeoman in the countie of *Kent*, the other upon a mightie prince, the third upon a covetous preest. And first touching the yeoman, he was overtaken and used in maner and forme following, by a notable cousening varlot, who professed Alcumystrie, juggling, witchcraft, and conjuration: and by meanes of his companions and confederats discussed the simplicitie and abilitie of the said yeoman, and found out his estate and humor to be convenient for his purpose; and finallie came a wooing (as they saie) to his daughter, to whome he made love cunninglie in words, though his purpose tended to another matter. And among other illusions and tales, concerning his owne commendation, for welth, parentage, inheritance, alliance, activitie, learning, pregnancie, and cunning, he boasted of his knowledge and experience in Alcumystrie; making the simple man beleeve that he could multiplie, and of one angell make two or three. Which seemed strange to the poore man, in so much as he became willing enough to see that conclusion: whereby the Alcumyster had more hope and comfort to atteine his desire, than if his daughter had yeelded to have maried him. To be short, he in the presence

Note the
cousening
conveiance
of this al-
cumystical
practitioner.

of the said yeoman, did include within a little ball of virgine wax, a couple of angels; and after certeine ceremonies and conjuring words he seemed to deliver the same unto him: but in truth (through legierdemaine) he conveied into the yeomans hand another ball of the same scantling, wherein were inclosed manie more angels than were in the ball which he thought he had received. Now (forsooth) the Alcumyster bad him laie up the same ball of wax, and also use certeine ceremonies (which I thought good heere to omit). And after certeine daies, houres, and minuts they returned together, according to the appointment and found great gaines by the multiplication of the angels. Insomuch as he, being a plaine man, was heereby persuaded, that he should not onelie have a rare and notable good sonne in lawe; but a companion that might helpe to adde unto his welth much treasure, and to his estate great fortune and felicitie. And to increase this opinion in him, as also to winne his further favour; but speciallie to bring his cunning Alcumystrie, or rather his lewd purpose to passe; he told him that it were follie to multiplie a pound of gold, when as easilie they might multiplie a millian: and therefore counselled him to produce all the monie he had, or could borrowe of his neighbours and freends; and did put him out of doubt, that he would multiplie the same, and redouble it exceedinglie, even as he sawe by experience how he delt with the small summe before his face. This yeoman, in hope of gaines and preferment, &c: consented to this sweete motion, and brought out and laid before his feete, not the one halfe of his goods, but all that he had, or could make or borrowe anie maner of waie. Then this juggling Alcumyster, having obteined his purpose, folded the same in a ball, in quantitie farre bigger than the other, and conveieng the same into his bosome or pocket, delivered another ball (as before) of the like quantitie unto the yeoman, to be reserved and safelie kept in his chest; whereof (bicause the matter was of importance) either of them must have a key, and a severall locke, that no interruption might be made to the ceremonie, nor abuse by either of them, in defrauding ech other. Now (forsooth) these circumstances and ceremonies being ended, and the Alcumysters purpose therby performed; he told the yeoman that (untill a certeine daie and houre limitted to returne) either of them might emploie themselves about their busines, and necessarie affaires; the yeoman to the plough, and he to the citie of *London*, and in the meane time the gold shuld multiplie, &c. But the Alcumyster (belike) having other matters of more importance came not just at the houre appointed, nor yet at the daie, nor within the yeare: so as, although it were somewhat against the yeomans conscience to violate his promise, or breake the league; yet partlie by the longing he had to see, and partlie the desire he had to enjoie the fruit of that excellent experiment, having (for his owne securitie) and the others satisfaction, some testimonie at the opening thereof, to witnesse his sincere dealing, he brake up the coffer, and lo he soone espied the ball of wax, which he himselfe had laid up there with his owne hand. So as he thought (if the hardest should fall) he should find his principall: and whie not as good increase hereof now, as of the other before. But alas! when the wax was broken, and the metall discovered, the gold was much abased, and became perfect lead.

Now who so list to utter his follie,
Let him come foorth, and learne to multiplie;
And everie man that hath ought in his cofer,
Let him appeare, and waxe a philosopher,
In learning of this elvish nice lore,
All is in vaine, and pardee much more
Is to learne a lewd man this sutteltee,
Fie, speake not thereof it woll not bee:
For he that hath learning, and he that hath none,
Conclude alike in multiplicatione.

Margin notes:

A notable foole.

A cousening devise by running awaie to save the credit of the art.

G. Chaucer in the tale of the chanone yeoman. [Prologue.]

Chapter iv.

A certeine king abused by an Alcumyst, and of the kings foole a pretie jest.

A king cou-
sened by
Alcumy-
strie.

THE second example is of another Alcumyst that came to a certeine king, promising to worke by his art manie great things, as well in compounding and transubstantiating of mettals, as in executing of other exploites of no lesse admiration. But before he beganne, he found the meanes to receive by vertue of the kings warrant, a great summe of monie in prest, assuring the king and his councell, that he would shortlie returne, and accomplish his promise, &c. Soone after, the kings foole, among other jestes, fell into a discourse and discoverie of fooles, and handled that common place so pleasantlie, that the king began to take delight therein, & to like his merrie veine. Whereupon he would needes have the foole deliver unto him a schedull or scroll, conteining the names of all the most excellent fooles in the land.

So he caused the kings name to be first set downe, and next him all the names of the lords of his privie councell. The king seeing him so sawcie and malepert, ment to have had him punished: but some of his councell, knowing him to be a fellow pleasantlie conceipted, besought his majestie rather to demand of him a

A wise
foole.

reason of his libell, &c: than to proceed in extremitie against him. Then the foole being asked why he so sawcilie accused the king and his councell of principall follie, answered; Bicause he sawe one foolish knave beguile them all, and to cousen them of so great a masse of monie, and finallie to be gone out of their reach. Why (said one of the councell) he maie returne and performe his promise, &c. Then (quoth the foole) I can helpe all the matter easilie. How (said the king) canst thou doo that? Marie sir (said he) then I will blotte out your name, and put in his, as the most foole in the world. Manie other practises of the like nature might be hereunto annexed, for the detection of their knaverie and deceipts whereupon this art dependeth, whereby the readers maie be more delighted in reading, than the practisers benefited in simplie using the same. For it is an art consisting wholie of subtiltie and deceipt, whereby the ignorant and plaine minded man through his too much credulitie is circumvented, and the humor of the other slie cousener satisfied.

Chapter v.

A notable storie written by Erasmus of two Alcumysts, also of longation and curtation.

Eras. in col-
loq. de arte
alcumystica.

THE third example is reported by *Erasmus*, whose excellent learning and wit is had to this daie in admiration. He in a certeine dialog intituled *Alcu-mystica* doth finelie bewraie the knaverie of this craftie art; wherein he proposeth one *Balbine*, a verie wise, learned, and devout preest, howbeit such a one as was bewitched, and mad upon the art of Alcumystrie. Which thing another cousening preest perceived, and dealt with him in maner and forme following.

A flattering
& clawing
preamble.

M. Doctor *Balbine* (said he) I being a stranger unto you maie seeme verie saucie to trouble your worship with my bold sute, who alwaies are busied in great and divine studies. To whome *Balbine*, being a man of few words, gave a nodde: which was more than he used to everie man. But the preest knowing his humor, said; I am sure sir, if you knew my sute, you would pardon mine importunitie. I praise thee good sir *John* (said *Balbine*) shew me thy mind, and

208

be breefe. That shall I doo sir (said he) with a good will. You know M. Doctor, through your skill in philosophie, that everie mans destinie is not alike; and I for my part am at this point, that I cannot tell whether I maie be counted happie or infortunate. For when I weigh mine owne case, or rather my state, in part I seeme fortunate, and in part miserable. But *Balbine* being a man of some surlinesse, alwaies willed him to draw his matter to a more compendious forme: which thing the preest said he would doo, and could the better performe; bicause *Balbine* himselfe was so learned and expert in the verie matter he had to repeat, and thus he began.

I have had, even from my childhood, a great felicitie in the art of Alcumystrie, which is the verie marrow of all philosophie. *Balbine* at the naming of the word Alcumystrie, inclined and yeelded himselfe more attentivelie to hearken unto him: marie it was onelie in gesture of bodie; for he was spare of speech, and yet he bad him proceed with his tale. Then said the preest, Wretch that I am, it was not my lucke to light on the best waie: for you M. *Balbine* know (being so universallie learned) that in this art there are two waies, the one called longation, the other curtation; and it was mine ill hap to fall upon longation. When *Balbine* asked him the difference of those two waies; Oh sir said the preest, you might count me impudent, to take upon me to tell you, that of all other are best learned in this art, to whome I come, most humblie to beseech you to teach me that luckie waie of curtation. The cunninger you are, the more easilie you maie teach it me: and therefore hide not the gift that God hath given you, from your brother, who maie perish for want of his desire in this behalfe; and doubtlesse Jesus Christ will inrich you with greater blessings and endowments. *Longation and curtation in Alcumystrie.*

Balbine being abashed partlie with his importunitie, and partlie with the strange circumstance, told him that (in truth) he neither knew what longation or curtation meant; and therefore required him to expound the nature of those words. Well (quoth the preest) since it is your pleasure, I will doo it, though I shall thereby take upon me to teach him that is indeed much cunninger than my selfe. And thus he began: Oh sir, they that have spent all the daies of their life in this divine facultie, doo turne one nature and forme into another, two waies, the one is verie breefe, but somewhat dangerous; the other much longer, marie verie safe, sure, and commodious. Howbeit, I thinke my selfe most unhappie that have spent my time and travell in that waie which utterlie misliketh me, and never could get one to shew me the other that I so earnestlie desire. And now I come to your worship, whom I know to be wholie learned and expert herein, hoping that you will (for charities sake) comfort your brother, whose felicitie and well doing now resteth onelie in your hands; and therefore I beseech you releeve me with your counsell. *Note how the couse- ner circum- venteth Balbine.*

By these and such other words when this cousening varlot had avoided suspicion of guile, and assured *Balbine* that he was perfect and cunning in the other waie: *Balbine* his fingers itched, and his hart tickled; so as he could hold no longer, but burst out with these words: Let this curtation go to the divell, whose name I did never so much as once heare of before, and therefore doo much lesse understand it. But tell me in good faith, doo you exactlie understand longation? Yea said the preest, doubt you not hereof: but I have no fansie to that waie, it is so tedious. Why (quoth *Balbine*) what time is required in the accomplishment of this worke by waie of longation? Too too much said the Alcumyster, even almost a whole yeere: but this is the best, the surest, and the safest waie, though it be for so manie moneths prolonged, before it yeeld advantage for cost and charges expended thereabouts. Set your hart at rest (said *Balbine*) it is no matter, though it were two yearees, so as you be well assured to bring it then to passe. *Faire words make fooles faine, and large offers blind the wise.*

Finallie, at was there and then concluded, that presentlie the preest should go in hand with the worke, and the other should beare the charge, the gaines to be indifferentlie divided betwixt them both, and the worke to be doone privilie in *Balbins* house. And after the mutuall oth was taken for silence, which is usuall and requisite alwaies in the beginning of this mysterie; *Balbine* delivered monie to the Alcumyster for bellowes, glasses, coles, &c: which should serve for the erection and furniture of the forge. Which monie the Alcumyster had no sooner fingered, but he ran merilie to the dice, to the alehouse, & to the stewes, and who there so lustie as cousening sir *John:* who indeed this waie made a kind of alcumysticall transformation of monie. Now *Balbine* urged him to go about his businesse, but the other told him, that if the matter were once begun, it were halfe ended: for therein consisted the greatest difficultie.

Well, at length he began to furnish the fornace, but now forsooth a new supplie of gold must be made, as the seed and spawne of that which must be ingendred and grow out of this worke of Alcumystrie. For even as a fish is not caught without a bait, no more is gold multiplied without some parcels of gold: and therfore gold must be the foundation and groundworke of that art, or else all the fat is in the fier. But all this while *Balbine* was occupied in calculating, and musing upon his accompt; casting by arythmetike, how that if one ownce yeelded fifteene, then now much gaines two thousand ownces might yeeld: for so much he determined to emploie that waie.

When the Alcumyst had also consumed this monie, shewing great travell a moneth or twaine, in placing the bellowes, the coles, and such other stuffe, and no whit of profit proceeding or comming thereof: *Balbine* demanded how the world went, our Alcumyst was as a man amazed. Howbeit he said at length; Forsooth even as such matters of importance commonlie doo go forward, wherunto there is alwaies verie difficult accesse. There was (saith he) a fault (which I have now found out (in the choice of the coles, which were of oke, and should have beene of beech. One hundredth duckets were spent that waie, so as the dising house and the stewes were partakers of *Balbines* charges. But after a new supplie of monie, better coles were provided, and matters more circumspectlie handled. Howbeit, when the forge had travelled long, and brought foorth nothing, there was another excuse found out; to wit, that the glasses were not temperered as they ought to have beene. But the more monie was disbursed hereabouts, the woorsse willing was *Balbine* to give over, according to the disers veine, whome frutelesse hope bringeth into a fooles paradise.

Balbine was bewitched with desire of gold, &c.

The Alcumyst, to cast a good colour upon his knaverie, tooke on like a man moonesicke, and protested with great words full of forgerie and lies, that he never had such lucke before. But having found the error, he would be sure enough never hereafter to fall into the like oversight, and that henceforward all should be safe and sure, and throughlie recompensed in the end with large increase. Hereupon the workehouse is now the third time repaired, and a new supplie yet once againe put into the Alcumysts hand; so as the glasses were changed. And now at length the Alcumyst uttered another point of his art and cunning to *Balbine:* to wit, that those matters would proceed much better, if he sent our Ladie a few French crownes in reward; for the art being holie, the matter cannot prosperouslie proceed, without the favour of the saints. Which counsell exceedinglie pleased *Balbine*, who was so devout and religious, that no daie escaped him but he said our Ladie mattens.

Notable cousenage.

Now our Alcumyster having received the offering of monie, goeth on his holie pilgrimage, even to the next village, & there consumeth it everie penie, among bawds and knaves. And at his returne, he told *Balbine* that he had great hope of good lucke in his businesse; the holie virgine gave such favourable countenance, and such attentive eare unto his praiers and vowes. But after this, when there had beene great travell bestowed, and not a dream of gold yeelded nor levied from the forge; *Balbine* began to expostulate and reason somewhat roundlie with the cousening fellowe; who still said he never had such filthie lucke in all his life before, and could not devise by what meanes it came to passe, that things went so overthwartlie. But after much debating betwixt them upon the matter, at length it came into *Balbines* head to aske him if he had not foreslowed to heare masse, or to saie his houres: which if he had doone, nothing could prosper under his hand. Without doubt (said the cousener) you have hit the naile on the head. Wretch that I am! I remember once or twice being at a long feast, I omitted to saie mine *Ave Marie* after dinner. So so (said *Balbine*) no marvell then that a matter of such importance hath had so evill successe. The Alcumyster promised to doo penance; as to heare twelve masses for two that he

The Alcumyster bringeth Balbin into a fooles paradise.

had foreslowed; and for everie *Ave* overslipped, to render and repeate twelve to our Ladie.

Soone after this, when all our Alcumysters monie was spent, & also his shifts failed how to come by any more, he came home with this devise, as a man woonderfullie fraied and amazed, pitiouslie crieng and lamenting his misfortune. Whereat *Balbine* being astonished, desired to knowe the cause of his complaint. Oh (said the Alcumyster) the courtiers have spied our enterprise; so as I for my part looke for nothing but present imprisonment. Whereat *Balbine* was abashed, bicause it was flat fellonie to go about that matter, without speciall licence. But (quoth the Alcumyster) I feare not to be put to death, I would it would fall out so: marrie I feare least I shall be shut up in some castell or towre, and there shall be forced to tug about this worke and broile in this businesse all the daies of my life.

Here the Alcumyster uttereth a notorious point of cousening knaverie.

Now the matter being brought to consultation, *Balbine*, bicause he was cunning in the art of rhetorike, and not altogither ignorant in lawe, beat his braines in devising how the accusation might be answered, and the danger avoided. Alas (said the Alcumyster) you trouble your selfe all in vaine, for you see the crime is not to be denied, it is so generallie bruted in court: neither can the fact be defended, bicause of the manifest lawe published against it. To be short, when manie waies were devised, and divers excuses alledged by *Balbine*, and no sure ground to stand on for their securitie; at length the Alcumyster having present want and need of monie, framed his speech in this sort; Sir said he to *Balbine*, we use slowe counsell, and yet the matter requireth hast. For I thinke they are comming for me yer this time to hale me awaie to prison; and I see no remedie but to die valiantlie in the cause. In good faith (said *Balbine*) I knowe not what to saie to the matter. No more do I said the Alcumyster, but that I see these courtiers are hungrie for monie, and so much the readier to be corrupted & framed to silence. And though it be a hard matter, to give those rakehels till they be satisfied: yet I see no better counsell or advise at this time. No more could *Balbine*, who gave him thirtie ducats of gold to stop their mouthes, who in an honest cause would rather have given so manie teeth out of his head, than one of those peeces out of his pouch. This coine had the Alcumyster, who for all his pretenses & gaie gloses was in no danger, other than for lacke of monie to lesse his leman or concubine, whose acquaintance he would not give over, nor forbeare hir companie, for all the goods that he was able to get, were it by never such indirect dealing and unlawfull meanes.

Marke how this Alcumyster goeth frō one degree of cousenage to another.

Well, yet now once againe dooth *Balbine* newlie furnish the forge, a praier being made before to our Ladie to blesse the enterprise. And all things being provided and made readie according to the Alcumysters owne asking, & all necessaries largelie ministred after his owne liking; a whole yeare being likewise now consumed about this bootlesse businesse, and nothing brought to passe; there fell out a strange chance, and that by this meanes insuing, as you shall heare.

Our Alcumyster forsooth used a little extraordinarie lewd cōpanie with a courtiers wife, whiles he was from home, who suspecting the matter, came to the doore unlooked for, and called to come in, threatning them that he would breake open the doores upon them. Some present devise (you see) was now requisite, and there was none other to be had, but such as the oportunitie offered; to wit, to leape out at a backe window: which he did, not without great hazard, and some hurt. But this was soone blazed abroad, so as it came to *Balbines* eare, who shewed in countenance that he had heard heereof, though he said nothing. But the Alcumyster knew him to be devout, & somewhat superstitious: and such men are easie to be intreated to forgive, how great soever the fault be, and devised to open the matter in maner and forme following.

The mildest and softest nature is cōmonlie soonest abused.

O Lord (saith he before *Balbine*) how infortunatlie goeth our businesse forward! I marvell what should be the cause. Whereat *Balbine*, being one otherwise that seemed to have vowed silence, tooke occasion to speake, saieng; It is not hard to knowe the impediment and stop heereof: for it is sinne that hindereth this matter; which is not to be dealt in but with pure hands. Whereat the

Alcumyster fell upon his knees, beating his breast, & lamentablie cried, saieng; Oh maister *Balbine*, you saie most trulie, it is sinne that hath doone us all this displeasure; not your sinne sir, but mine owne, good maister *Balbine*. Neither will I be ashamed to discover my filthinesse unto you, as unto a most holy and ghostlie father. The infirmitie of the flesh had overcome me, and the divell had caught me in his snare. Oh wretch that I am! Of a preest I am become an adulterer. Howbeit, the monie that erstwhile was sent to our Ladie, was not utterlie lost: for if she had not beene, I had certeinlie beene slaine. For the good man of the house brake open the doore, and the windowe was lesse than I could get out thereat. And in that extremitie of danger it came into my mind to fall downe prostrate to the virgine; beseeching hir (if our gift were acceptable in hir sight) that she would, in consideration thereof, assist me with hir helpe. And to be short, I ran to the windowe, and found it bigge enough to leape out at. Which thing *Balbine* did not onelie beleeve to be true, but in respect therof forgave him, religiouslie admonishing him to shew himselfe thankfull to that pitifull and blessed Ladie.

En immensa cavi spirant mendacia folles.

Now once againe more is made a new supplie of monie, and mutuall promise made to handle this divine matter hence forward purelie and holilie. To be short, after a great number of such parts plaied by the Alcumyster; one of *Balbins* acquaintance espied him, that knew him from his childhood to be but a cousening merchant; and told *Balbine* what he was, and that he would handle him in the end, even as he had used manie others; for a knave he ever was, and so he would proove. But what did *Balbine*, thinke you? Did he complaine of this counterfet, or cause him to be punished? No, but he gave him monie in his pursse, and sent him awaie; desiring him, of all courtesie, not to blab abroad how he had cousened him. And as for the knave Alcumyster, he needed not care who knew it, or what came of it: for he had nothing in goods or fame to be lost. And as for his cunning in Alcumystrie, he had as much as an asse. By this discourse *Erasmus* would give us to note, that under the golden name of Alcumystrie there lieth lurking no small calamitie; wherein there be such severall shifts and sutes of rare subtilties and deceipts, as that not onelie welthie men are thereby manie times impoverished, and that with the sweete allurement of this art, through their owne covetousnesse; as also by the flattering baits of hoped gaine: but even wise and learned men hereby are shamefullie overshot, partlie for want of due experience in the wiles and subtilties of the world, and partlie through the softenesse and pliablenesse of their good nature, which cousening knaves doo commonlie abuse to their owne lust and commoditie, and to the others utter undooing.

Balbine is ashamed that he should be overshot and over-seene in a case of flat cousenage.

CHAPTER VI.

The opinion of diverse learned men touching the follie of Alcumystrie.

The sub-stances of things are not trans-mutable.

ALBERT in his booke of minerals reporteth, that *Avicenna* treating of Alcumystrie, saith; Let the dealers in Alcumystrie understand, that the verie nature and kind of things cannot be changed, but rather made by art to resemble the same in shew and likenesse: so that they are not the verie things indeed, but seeme so to be in appearance: as castels and towers doo seeme to be built in the clouds, whereas the representations there shewed, are nothing else but the resemblance of certeine objects beelow, caused in some bright and cleere cloud, when the aire is void of thicknes and grossenes. A sufficient proofe hereof maie be the looking glasse. And we see (saith he) that yellow or orrenge colour laid upon red, seemeth to be gold. *Francis Petrarch* treating of the same matter in forme of a dialogue, introduceth a disciple of his, who fansied the foresaid fond profession and practise, saieng; I hope for prosperous successe in

Franc. Pe-trarch. lib. de remed. utr. fort. 1. *cap.* 10.

Alcumystrie. *Petrarch* answereth him; It is a woonder from whence that hope should spring, sith the frute thereof did never yet fall to thy lot, nor yet at anie time chance to anie other; as the report commonlie goeth, that manie rich men, by this vanitie and madnes have beene brought to beggerie, whiles they have wearied themselves therewith, weakened their bodies, and wasted their wealth in trieng the means to make gold ingender gold. I hope for gold according to the workemans promise, saith the disciple. He that hath promised thee gold, will runne awaie with thy gold, and thou never the wiser, saith *Petrarch*. He promiseth mee great good, saith the disciple. He will first serve his owne turne, and releeve his private povertie, saith *Petrarch;* for Alcumysters are a beggerlie kind of people, who though they confesse themselves bare and needie, yet will they make others rich and welthie; as though others povertie did more molest and pitie them than their owne. These be the words of *Petrarch*, a man of great learning and no lesse experience; who as in his time he sawe the fraudulent fetches of this compassing craft: so hath there beene no age, since the same hath beene broched, wherein some few wisemen have not smelt out the evill meaning of these shifting merchants, and bewraied them to the world.

An ancient writer of a religious order, who lived above a thousand yeares since, discovering the diversities of theftes, after a long enumeration, bringeth in Alcumysters, whom he calleth *Falsificantes metallorum* & *mineralium*, witches and counterfetters of metals and minerals; and setteth them as deepe in the degree of theeves, as anie of the rest, whose injurious dealings are brought to open arreignment. It is demanded (saith he) why the art of Alcumystrie doth never prove that in effect, which it pretendeth in precept and promise. The answer is readie; that if by art gold might be made, then were it behoovefull to know the maner and proceeding of nature in generation; sith art is said to imitate and counterfet nature. Againe, it is bicause of the lamenesse and unperfectnesse of philosophie, speciallie concerning minerals: no such manner of proceeding being set downe by consent and agreement of philosophers in writing, touching the true and undoubted effect of the same. Where upon one supposeth that gold is made of one kind of stuffe this waie, others of another kind of stuffe that waie. And therefore it is a chance if anie atteine to the artificiall applieng of the actives and passives of gold and silver. Moreover, it is certeine, that quicke silver and sulphur are the materials (as they terme them) of mettals, and the agent is heate, which directeth: howbeit it is verie hard to know the due proportion of the mixture of the materials; which proportion the generation of gold doth require. And admit that by chance they atteine to such proportion; yet can they not readilie resume or doo it againe in another worke, bicause of the hidden diversities of materials, and the uncerteintie of applieng the actives and passives.

The same ancient author concluding against this vaine art, saith, that of all christian lawmakers it is forbidden, and in no case tollerable in anie common-welth: first bicause it presumeth to forge idols for covetousnes, which are gold and silver; whereupon saith the apostle, Covetousenesse is idolworship: secondlie, for that (as *Aristotle* saith) coine should be skant and rare, that it might be deere; but the same would waxe vile, and of small estimation, if by the art of Alcumystrie gold and silver might be multiplied: thirdlie, bicause (as experience prooveth) wisemen are thereby bewitched, couseners increased, princes abused, the rich impoverished, the poore beggered, the multitude made fooles, and yet the craft and craftesmaisters (oh madnes!) credited. Thus far he. Whereby in few words he discountenanceth that profession, not by the imaginations of his owne braine, but by manifold circumstances of manifest proofe. Touching the which practise I thinke inough hath beene spoken, and more a great deale than needed; sith so plaine and demonstrable a matter requireth the lesse travell in confutation.

Goschalcus Boll. ordinis S. August. in suo præcepto-rio, fol. 244. col. b. c. d. & 1.

No certein ground in the art Al-cumystical.

Idem. ibid.

Avaritia idolorum cultus.

CHAPTER VII.

That vaine and deceitfull hope is a great cause why men are seduced by this alluring art,
and that there labours therein are bootelesse, &c.

HITHERTO somewhat at large I have detected the knaverie of the art
Alcumysticall, partlie by reasons, and partlie by examples: so that the
thing it selfe maie no lesse appeare to the judiciall eie of the considerers;
than the bones and sinewes of a bodie anatomized, to the corporall eie of the
beholders. Now it shall not be amisse nor impertinent, to treate somewhat of the
nature of that vaine and frutelesse hope, which induceth and draweth men forward as it were with chordes, not onelie to the admiration, but also to the appro-
bation of the same: in such sort that some are compelled rufullie to sing (as one
in old time did, whether in token of good or ill lucke, I doo not now well remember) *Spes & fortuna valete;* Hope and good hap adieu.

No mervell then though Alcumystrie allure men so sweetlie, and intangle
them in snares of follie; sith the baits which it useth is the hope of gold, the
hunger wherof is by the poet termed *Sacra,* which some doo English, Holie; not
understanding that it is rather to be interpreted, Curssed or detestable, by the
figure *Acyron,* when a word of an unproper signification is cast in a clause as it
were a cloud: or by the figure *Antiphrasis,* when a word importeth a contrarie
meaning to that which it commonlie hath. For what reason can there be, that
the hunger of gold should be counted holie, the same having (as depending upon
it) so manie milians of mischeefes and miseries: as treasons, theftes, adulteries,
manslaughters, trucebreakings, perjuries, cousenages, and a great troope of
other enormities, which were here too long to rehearse. And if the nature of
everie action be determinable by the end thereof, then cannot this hunger be
holie, but rather accurssed, which pulleth after it as it were with iron chaines
such a band of outrages and enormities, as of all their labor, charge, care and
cost, &c: they have nothing else left them in lieu of lucre, but onlie some few
burned brickes of a ruinous fornace, a pecke or two of ashes, and such light
stuffe, which they are forced peradventure in fine to sell, when beggerie hath
arrested and laid his mace on their shoulders. As for all their gold, it is resolved
In primam materiam, or rather *In levem quendam fumulum,* into a light smoke or
fumigation of vapors, than the which nothing is more light, nothing lesse substantiall, spirits onelie excepted, out of whose nature and number these are not
to be exempted.

Of vaine
hope.

J. Cal. in
Comment.
upon Deut.
serm. 127.
pa. 781. *col.* 1.
number. 40.

A maxime.

CHAPTER VIII.

A continuation of the former matter, with a conclusion of the same.

THAT which I have declared before, by reasons, examples, and authorities,
I will now prosecute and conclude by one other example; to the end that
we, as others in former ages, maie judge of vaine hope accordinglie, and
be no lesse circumspect to avoid the inconveniences therof, than *Ulysses* was
warie to escape the incantations of *Circes* that old transforming witch. Which
example of mine is drawne from *Lewes* the French king, the eleventh of that
name, who being on a time at *Burgundie,* fell acquainted by occasion of hunting
with one *Conon,* a clownish but yet an honest and hartie good fellow. For
princes and great men delight much in such plaine clubhutchens. The king

Erasmus in
colloq. cui ti-
tulus Convi-
vium fabu-
losum.

oftentimes, by meanes of his game, used the countrimans house for his refreshing; and as noble men sometimes take pleasure in homelie and course things, so the king did not refuse to eate turnips and rape rootes in *Conons* cotage. Shortlie after king *Lewes* being at his pallace, void of troubles and disquietnesse, *Conons* wife wild him to repaire to the court, to shew himselfe to the king, to put him in mind of the old intertainement which he had at his house, and to present him with some of the fairest and choisest rape rootes that she had in store. *Conon* seemed loth, alledging that he should but lose his labour: for princes (saith he) have other matters in hand, than to intend to thinke of such trifeling courtesies. But *Conons* wife overcame him, and persuaded him in the end, choosing a certeine number of the best and goodliest rape rootes that she had: which when she had given hir husband to carrie to the court, he set forward on his journie a good trudging pase. But *Conon* being tempted by the waie, partlie with desire of eating, and partlie with the toothsomnes of the meate which he bare, that by little and little he devoured up all the roots saving one, which was a verie faire and a goodlie great one indeed. Now when *Conon* was come to the court, it was his lucke to stand in such a place, as the king passing by, and spieng the man, did well remember him, and commanded that he should be brought in. *Conon* verie cheerelie followed his guide hard at the heeles, and no sooner sawe the king, but bluntlie comming to him, reached out his hand, and presented the gift to his maiestie. The king received it with more cheerefulnes than it was offered, and bad one of those that stood next him, to take it, and laie it up among those things which he esteemed most, & had in greatest accompt. Then he had *Conon* to dine with him, and after dinner gave the countriman great thanks for his rape roote; who made no bones of the matter, but boldlie made challenge and claime to the kings promised courtesie. Whereupon the king commanded, that a thousand crownes should be given him in recompense for his roote.

A hungrie bellie will not be brideled.

A princelie largesse.

The report of this bountifulnes was spred in short space over all the kings houshold: in so much as one of his courtiers, in hope of the like or a larger reward gave the king a verie proper ginnet. Whose drift the king perceiving, and judging that his former liberalitie to the clowne, provoked the courtier to this covetous attempt, tooke the ginnet verie thankefullie: and calling some of his noble men about him, began to consult with them, what mends he might make his servant for his horsse. Whiles this was a dooing, the courtier conceived passing good hope of some princelie largesse, calculating and casting his cards in this maner; If his maiestie rewarded a sillie clowne so bountifullie for a simple rape roote, what will he doo to a jollie courtier for a gallent gennet? Whiles the king was debating the matter, and one said this, another that, and the courtier travelled all the while in vaine hope, at last saith the king, even upon the sudden; I have now bethought me what to bestowe upon him: and calling one of his nobles to him, whispered him in the eare, and willed him to fetch a thing, which he should find in his chamber wrapped up in silke. The roote is brought wrapped in silke, which the king with his owne hands gave to the courtier, using these words therewithall, that he sped well, in so much as it was his good hap to have for his horsse a jewell that cost him a thousand crownes. The courtier was a glad man, and at his departing longed to be looking what it was, and his hart dansed for joy. In due time therefore he unwrapped the silke (a sort of his fellow courtiers flocking about him to testifie his good lucke) and having unfolded it, he found therein a drie and withered rape roote. Which spectacle though it set the standers about in a lowd laughter, yet it qualied the courtiers courage, and cast him into a shrewd fit of pensifenes. Thus was the confidence of this courtier turned to vanitie, who upon hope of good speed was willing to part from his horsse for had I wist.

Sic ars deluditur arte.

This storie dooth teach us into what follie and madnes vaine hope may drive undiscreete and unexpert men. And therefore no mervell though Alcumysters dreame and dote after double advantage, faring like *Aesops* dog, who greedilie coveting to catch and snatch at the shadowe of the flesh which he carried in his mouth over the water, lost both the one and the other: as they doo their increase and their principall. But to breake off abruptlie from this matter, and to leave

The morall of the præmisses.

215

these hypocrits (for whie may they not be so named, who as *Homer*, speaking in detestation of such rakehelles, saith verie divinelie and trulie;

Homer.

> *Odi etenim seu claustra Erebi, quicúnque loquuntur*
> *Ore aliud, tacitóque aliud sub pectore claudunt:*

Englished by Abraham Fleming.

> *I hate even as the gates of hell,*
> *Those that one thing with toong doo tell,*
> *And notwithstanding closelie keepe,*
> *Another thing in hart full deepe)*

To leave these hypocrits (I saie) in the dregs of their dishonestie, I will conclude against them peremptorilie, that they, with the rable above rehearsed, and the rowt hereafter to be mentioned, are ranke couseners, and consuming cankers to the common wealth, and therefore to be rejected and excommunicated from the fellowship of all honest men. For now their art, which turneth all kind of metals that they can come by into mist and smoke, is no lesse apparent to the world, than the cleere sunnie raies at noone sted; in so much that I may saie with the poet,

Aul. Persius, satyr. 3.

> *Hos populus ridet, multúmque torosa juventus*
> *Ingeminat tremulos naso crispante cachinnos:*

Englished by Abraham Fleming.

> *All people laugh them now to scorne,*
> *each strong and lustie blood*
> *Redoubleth quavering laughters lowd*
> *with wrinkled nose a good.*

So that, if anie be so addicted unto the vanitie of the art Alcumysticall (as everie foole will have his fansie) and that (beside so manie experimented examples of divers, whose wealth hath vanished like a vapor, whiles they have beene over rash in the practise hereof) this discourse will not moove to desist from such extreame dotage, I saie to him or them and that aptlie.

Idem, ibid.

> ————————*dictíque facítque quod ipse*
> *Non sani esse hominis non sanus juret Orestes:*

By Ab. Fleming.

> *He saith and dooth that verie thing,*
> *which mad Orestes might*
> *With oth averre beecame a man*
> *beereft of reason right.*

BOOKE XV.

CHAPTER I.

The exposition of Iidoni, and where it is found, whereby the whole art of conjuration is deciphered.

THIS word *Iidoni* is derived of *Iada*, which properlie signifieth to knowe: it is sometimes translated, *Divinus*, which is a divinor or soothsaier, as in *Deut.* 18. *Levit.* 20: sometimes *Ariolus*, which is one that also taketh upon him to foretell things to come, and is found *Levit.* 19, 2 *Kings.* 23. *Esai.* 19. To be short, the opinion of them that are most skilfull in the toongs, is, that it comprehendeth all them, which take upon them to knowe all things past and to come, and to give answers accordinglie. It alwaies followeth the word *Ob*, and in the scriptures is not named severallie from it, and differeth little from the same in sense, and doo both concerne oracles uttered by spirits, possessed people, or couseners. What will not couseners or witches take upon them to doo? Wherein will they professe ignorance? Aske them anie question, they will undertake to resolve you, even of that which none but God knoweth. And to bring their purposes the better to passe, as also to winne further credit unto the counterfet art which they professe, they procure confederates, whereby they worke wonders. And when they have either learning, eloquence, or nimblenesse of hands to accompanie their confederacie, or rather knaverie, then (forsooth) they passe the degree of witches, and intitle themselves to the name of conjurors. And these deale with no inferiour causes: these fetch divels out of hell, and angels out of heaven; these raise up what bodies they list, though they were dead, buried, and rotten long before; and fetch soules out of heaven or hell with much more expedition than the pope bringeth them out of purgatorie. These I saie (among the simple, and where they feare no law nor accusation) take upon them also the raising of tempests, and earthquakes, and to doo as much as God himselfe can doo. These are no small fooles, they go not to worke with a baggage tode, or a cat, as witches doo; but with a kind of majestie, and with authoritie they call up by name, and have at their commandement seventie and nine principall and princelie divels, who have under them, as their ministers, a great multitude of legions of pettie divels; as for example.

The large signification of the word Iidoni.

Vide Philast Brix. episc. hæreseôn catal. de phitonissa.

J. Wierus in Pseudomonarchia dæmonum.

CHAPTER II.

An inventarie of the names, shapes, powers, governement, and effects of divels and spirits, of their severall segniories and degrees: a strange discourse woorth the reading.

THEIR first and principall king (which is of the power of the east) is called *Baëll;* who when he is conjured up, appeareth with three heads; the first, like a tode; the second, like a man; the third, like a cat. He speaketh with a hoarse voice, he maketh a man go invisible, he hath under his obedience and rule sixtie and six legions of divels.

Salomons notes of conjuration. Baell.

The first duke under the power of the east, is named *Agares*, he commeth up

Agares.

217

mildlie in the likenes of a faire old man, riding upon a crocodile, and carrieng a hawke on his fist; hee teacheth presentlie all maner of toongs, he fetcheth backe all such as runne awaie, and maketh them runne that stand still; he over-throweth all dignities supernaturall and temporall, hee maketh earthquakes, and is of the order of vertues, having under his regiment thirtie one legions.

Marbas.

Marbas, alias Barbas is a great president, and appeareth in the forme of a mightie lion; but at the commandement of a conjuror commeth up in the like-nes of a man, and answereth fullie as touching anie thing which is hidden or secret: he bringeth diseases, and cureth them, he promoteth wisedome, and the knowledge of mechanicall arts, or handicrafts; he changeth men into other shapes, and under his presidencie or gouvernement are thirtie six legions of divels conteined.

Amon.

Amon, or *Aamon*, is a great and mightie marques, and commeth abroad in the likenes of a woolfe, having a serpents taile, spetting out and breathing flames of fier; when he putteth on the shape of a man, he sheweth out dogs teeth, and a great head like to a mightie raven; he is the strongest prince of all other, and understandeth of all things past and to come, he procureth favor, and recon-cileth both freends and foes, and ruleth fourtie legions of divels.

Barbatos.

Barbatos, a great countie or earle, and also a duke, he appeareth in *Signo sagit-tarii sylvestris*, with foure kings, which bring companies and great troopes. He understandeth the singing of birds, the barking of dogs, the lowings of bullocks, and the voice of all living creatures. He detecteth treasures hidden by magicians and inchanters, and is of the order of vertues, which in part beare rule: he knoweth all things past, and to come, and reconcileth freends and powers; and governeth thirtie legions of divels by his authoritie.

Buer.

Buer is a great president, and is seene in this signe; he absolutelie teacheth philosophie morall and naturall, and also logicke, and the vertue of herbes: he giveth the best familiars, he can heale all diseases, speciallie of men, and reigneth over fiftie legions.

Gusoin.

Gusoin is a great duke, and a strong, appearing in the forme of a *Xenophilus*, he answereth all things, present, past, and to come, expounding all questions. He reconcileth freendship, and distributeth honours and dignities, and ruleth over fourtie legions of divels.

Botis.

Botis, otherwise *Otis*, a great president and an earle he commeth foorth in the shape of an ouglie viper, and if he put on humane shape, he sheweth great teeth, and two hornes, carrieng a sharpe sword in his hand: he giveth answers of things present, past, and to come, and reconcileth friends, and foes, ruling sixtie legions.

Bathin.

Bathin, sometimes called *Mathim*, a great duke and a strong, he is seene in the shape of a verie strong man, with a serpents taile, sitting on a pale horsse, under-standing the vertues of hearbs and pretious stones, transferring men suddenlie from countrie to countrie, and ruleth thirtie legions of divels.

Purson.

Purson, alias Curson, a great king, he commeth foorth like a man with a lions face, carrieng a most cruell viper, and riding on a beare; and before him go alwaies trumpets, he knoweth things hidden, and can tell all things present, past, and to come: he bewraieth treasure, he can take a bodie either humane or aierie; he answereth truelie of all things earthlie and secret, of the divinitie and creation of the world, and bringeth foorth the best familiars; and there obeie him two and twentie legions of divels, partlie of the order of vertues, & partlie of the order of thrones.

Eligor.

Eligor, alias Abigor, is a great duke, and appeereth as a goodlie knight, carrieng a lance, an ensigne, and a scepter: he answereth fullie of things hid-den, and of warres, and how souldiers should meete: he knoweth things to come, and procureth the favour of lords and knights, governing sixtie legions of divels.

Leraie.

Leraie, alias Oray, a great marquesse, shewing himselfe in the likenesse of a galant archer, carrieng a bowe and a quiver, he is author of all battels, he dooth putrifie all such wounds as are made with arrowes by archers, *Quos optimos objicit tribus diebus*, and he hath regiment over thirtie legions.

Valefar, alias Malephar, is a strong duke, comming foorth in the shape of a lion, and the head of a theefe, he is verie familiar with them to whom he maketh himself acquainted, till he hath brought them to the gallowes, and ruleth ten legions.

Valefar.

Morax, alias Foraii, a great earle and a president, he is seene like a bull, and if he take unto him a mans face, he maketh men wonderfull cunning in astronomie, & in all the liberall sciences: he giveth good familiars and wise, knowing the power & vertue of hearbs and stones which are pretious, and ruleth thirtie six legions.

Morax.

Ipos, alias Ayporos, is a great earle and a prince, appeering in the shape of an angell, and yet indeed more obscure and filthie than a lion, with a lions head, a gooses feet, and a hares taile: he knoweth things to come and past, he maketh a man wittie, and bold, and hath under his jurisdiction thirtie six legions.

Ipos.

Naberius, alias Cerberus, is a valiant marquesse, shewing himselfe in the forme of a crowe, when he speaketh with a hoarse voice: he maketh a man amiable and cunning in all arts, and speciallie in rhetorike, he procureth the losse of prelacies and dignities: nineteene legions heare and obeie him.

Naberius.

Glasya Labolas, alias Caacrinolaas, or *Caassimolar*, is a great president, who commeth foorth like a dog, and hath wings like a griffen, he giveth the knowledge of arts, and is the captaine of all mansleiers: he understandeth things present and to come, he gaineth the minds and love of freends and foes, he maketh a man go invisible, and hath the rule of six and thirtie legions.

Glasya Labolas.

Zepar is a great duke, appearing as a souldier, inflaming women with the loove of men, and when he is bidden he changeth their shape, untill they maie enjoie their beloved, he also maketh them barren, and six and twentie legions are at his obeie and commandement.

Zepar.

Bileth is a great king and a terrible, riding on a pale horsse, before whome go trumpets, and all kind of melodious musicke. When he is called up by an exorcist, he appeareth rough and furious, to deceive him. Then let the exorcist or conjuror take heed to himself, and to allaie his courage, let him hold a hazell bat in his hand, wherewithall he must reach out toward the east and south, and make a triangle without besides the circle; but if he hold not out his hand unto him, and he bid him come in, and he still refuse the bond or chaine of spirits; let the conjuror proceed to reading, and by and by he will submit himselfe, and come in, and doo whatsoever the exorcist commandeth him, and he shalbe safe. If *Bileth* the king be more stubborne, and refuse to enter into the circle at the first call, and the conjuror shew himselfe fearfull, or if he have not the chaine of spirits, certeinelie he will never feare nor regard him after. Also, if the place he unapt for a triangle to be made without the circle, then set there a boll of wine, and the exorcist shall certeinlie knowe when he commeth out of his house, with his fellowes, and that the foresaid *Bileth* will be his helper, his friend, and obedient unto him when he commeth foorth. And when he commeth, let the exorcist receive him courteouslie, and glorifie him in his pride, and therfore he shall adore him as other kings doo, bicause he saith nothing without other princes. Also, if he be cited by an exorcist, alwaies a silver ring of the middle finger of the left hand must be held against the exorcists face, as they doo for *Amaimon*. And the dominion and power of so great a prince is not to be pretermitted; for there is none under the power & dominion of the conjuror, but he that deteineth both men and women in doting love, till the exorcist hath had his pleasure. He is of the orders of powers, hoping to returne to the seaventh throne, which is not altogether credible, and he ruleth eightie five legions.

Bileth.

Vide Amaimon.

Stiri, alias Bitru, is a great prince, appeering with the face of a leopard, and having wings as a griffen: when he taketh humane shape, he is verie beautiful, he inflameth a man with a womans love, and also stirreth up women to love men, being commanded he willinglie deteineth secrets of women, laughing at them and mocking them, to make them luxuriouslie naked, and there obeie him sixtie legions.

Stiri a bawdie divell.

Paimon is more obedient in *Lucifer* than other kings are. *Lucifer* is heere to be understood he that was drowned in the depth of his knowledge: he would needs

Paimon.

Ezech. 88.

be like God, and for his arrogancie was throwne out into destruction, of whome it is said; Everie pretious stone is thy covering. *Paimon* is constrained by divine vertue to stand before the exorcist; where he putteth on the likenesse of a man: he sitteth on a beast called a dromedarie, which is a swift runner, and weareth a glorious crowne, and hath an effeminate countenance. There goeth before him an host of men with trumpets and well sounding cymbals, and all musicall instruments. At the first he appeereth with a great crie and roring, as in *Circulo Salomonis*, and in the art is declared. And if this *Paimon* speake sometime that the conjuror understand him not, let him not therefore be dismaied. But when he hath delivered him the first obligation, to observe his desire, he must bid him also answer him distinctlie and plainelie to the questions he shall aske you, of all philosophie, wisedome, and science, and of all other secret things. And if you will knowe the disposition of the world, and what the earth is, or what holdeth it up in the water, or any other thing, or what is *Abyssus*, or where the wind is, or from whence it commeth, he will teach you aboundantlie. Consecrations also as well of sacrifices as otherwise may be reckoned. He giveth dignities and confirmations; he bindeth them that resist him in his owne chaines, and subjecteth them to the conjuror; he prepareth good familiars, and hath the understanding of all arts. Note, that at the calling up of him, the exorcist must looke towards the northwest, bicause there is his house. When he is called up, let the exorcist receive him constantlie without feare, let him aske what questions or demands he list, and no doubt he shall obteine the same of him. And the exorcist must beware he forget not the creator, for those things, which have beene rehearsed before of *Paimon*, some saie he is of the order of dominations; others saie, of the order of cherubim. There follow him two hundred legions, partlie of the order of angels, and partlie of potestates. Note that if *Paimon* be cited alone by an offering or sacrifice, two kings followe him; to wit, *Beball* & *Abalam*, & other potentates: in his host are twentie five legions, bicause the spirits subject to them are not alwaies with them, except they be compelled to appeere by divine vertue.

Cautions for the Exorcist or conjuror.

The fall of Beliall.

Some saie that the king *Beliall* was created immediatlie after *Lucifer*, and therefore they thinke that he was father and seducer of them which fell being of the orders. For he fell first among the worthier and wiser sort, which went before *Michael* and other heavenlie angels, which were lacking. Although *Beliall* went before all them that were throwne downe to the earth, yet he went not before them that tarried in heaven. This *Beliall* is constrained by divine vertue, when he taketh sacrifices, gifts, and offerings, that he againe may give unto the offerers true answers. But he tarrieth not one houre in the truth, except he be constrained by the divine power, as is said. He taketh the forme of a beautifull angell, sitting in a firie chariot; he speaketh faire, he distributeth preferments of senatorship, and the favour of friends, and excellent familiars: he hath rule over eightie legions, partlie of the order of vertues, partlie of angels; he is found in the forme of an exorcist in the bonds of spirits. The exorcist must consider, that this *Beliall* doth in everie thing assist his subjects. If he will not submit himselfe, let the bond of spirits be read: the spirits chaine is sent for him, wherewith wise *Salomon* gathered them togither with their legions in a brasen vessell, where were inclosed among all the legions seventie two kings, of whome the cheefe was *Bileth*, the second was *Beliall*, the third *Asmoday*, and above a thousand thousand legions. Without doubt (I must confesse) I learned this of my maister *Salomon;* but he told me not why he gathered them together, and shut them up so: but I beleeve it was for the pride of this *Beliall*. Certeine nigromancers doo saie, that *Salomon*, being on a certeine daie seduced by the craft of a certeine woman, inclined himselfe to praie before the same idoll, *Beliall* by name: which is not credible. And therefore we must rather thinke (as it is said) that they were gathered together in that great brasen vessell for pride and arrogancie, and throwne into a deepe lake or hole in *Babylon*. For wise *Salomon* did accomplish his workes by the divine power, which never forsooke him. And therefore we must thinke he worshipped not the image *Beliall;* for then he could not have constrained the spirits by divine vertue: for this *Beliall*, with three

Salomon gathered al the divels togither in a brasen vessell.

kings were in the lake. But the *Babylonians* woondering at the matter, supposed   The Baby-
that they should find therein a great quantitie of treasure, and therefore with   lonians dis-
one consent went downe into the lake, and uncovered and brake the vessell, out   of their
of the which immediatlie flew the capteine divels, and were delivered to their   hope.
former and proper places. But this *Beliall* entred into a certeine image, and there
gave answer to them that offered and sacrificed unto him: as *Tocz.* in his sentences reporteth, and the *Babylonians* did worship and sacrifice thereunto.

    Bune is a great and a strong Duke, he appeareth as a dragon with three heads,   *Bune.*
the third whereof is like to a man; he speaketh with a divine voice, he maketh
the dead to change their place, and divels to assemble upon the sepulchers of the
dead: he greatlie inricheth a man, and maketh him eloquent and wise, answering trulie to all demands, and thirtie legions obeie him.

    Forneus is a great marquesse, like unto a monster of the sea, he maketh men   *Forneus.*
woonderfull in rhetorike, he adorneth a man with a good name, and the knowledge of toongs, and maketh one beloved as well of foes as freends: there are
under him nine and twentie legions, of the order partlie of thrones, and partlie
of angels.

    Ronove a marquesse and an earle, he is resembled to a monster, he bringeth   *Ronove.*
singular understanding in rhetorike, faithfull servants, knowledge of toongs,
favour of freends and foes; and nineteene legions obeie him.

    Berith is a great and a terrible duke, and hath three names. Of some he is called   *Berith* a
Beall; of the Jewes *Berithi;* of Nigromancers *Bolfry:* he commeth foorth as a red   golden
souldier, with red clothing, and upon a horsse of that colour, and a crowne on his   divell.
head. He answereth trulie of things present, past, and to come. He is compelled
at a certeine houre, through divine vertue, by a ring of art magicke. He is also
a lier, he turneth all mettals into gold, he adorneth a man with dignities, and
confirmeth them, he speaketh with a cleare and a subtill voice, and six and
twentie legions are under him.

    Astaroth is a great and a strong duke, comming foorth in the shape of a fowle   *Astaroth.*
angell, sitting upon an infernall dragon, and carrieng on his right hand a viper:
he answereth trulie to matters present, past, and to come, and also of all secrets.
He talketh willinglie of the creator of spirits, and of their fall, and how they
sinned and fell: he saith he fell not of his owne accord. He maketh a man
woonderfull learned in the liberall sciences, he ruleth fourtie legions. Let everie
exorcist take heed, that he admit him not too neere him, bicause of his stinking
breath. And therefore let the conjuror hold neere to his face a magicall ring, and
that shall defend him.

    Foras, alias Forcas is a great president, and is seene in the forme of a strong   *Foras.*
man, and in humane shape, he understandeth the vertue of hearbs and pretious
stones: he teacheth fullie logicke, ethicke, and their parts: he maketh a man
invisible, wittie, eloquent, and to live long; he recovereth things lost, and discovereth treasures, and is lord over nine and twentie legions.

    Furfur is a great earle, appearing as an hart, with a firie taile, he lieth in everie   *Furfur.*
thing, except he be brought up within a triangle; being bidden, he taketh
angelicall forme, he speaketh with a hoarse voice, and willinglie maketh love
betweene man and wife; he raiseth thunders and lightnings, and blasts. Where
he is commanded, he answereth well, both of secret and also of divine things,
and hath rule and dominion over six and twentie legions.

    Marchosias is a great marquesse, he sheweth himselfe in the shape of a cruell   *Marchosias.*
shee woolfe, with a griphens wings, with a serpents taile, and spetting I cannot
tell what out of his mouth. When he is in a mans shape, he is an excellent fighter,
he answereth all questions trulie, he is faithfull in all the conjurors businesse, he
was of the order of dominations, under him are thirtie legions: he hopeth after
1200. yeares to returne to the seventh throne, but he is deceived in that
hope.

    Malphas is a great president, he is seene like a crowe, but being cloathed   *Malphas.*
with humane image, speaketh with a hoarse voice, he buildeth houses and high
towres wonderfullie, and quicklie bringeth artificers togither, he throweth
downe also the enimies edifications, he helpeth to good familiars, he receiveth

sacrifices willinglie, but he deceiveth all the sacrificers, there obeie him fourtie legions.

Vepar.

Vepar, alias Separ, a great duke and a strong, he is like a mermaid, he is the guide of the waters, and of ships laden with armour; he bringeth to passe (at the commandement of his master) that the sea shalbe rough and stormie, and shall appeare full of shippes; he killeth men in three daies, with putrifieng their wounds, and producing maggots into them; howbeit, they maie be all healed with diligence, he ruleth nine and twentie legions.

Sabnacke.

Sabnacke, alias Salmac, is a great marquesse and a strong, he commeth foorth as an armed soldier with a lions head, sitting on a pale horsse, he dooth marvelouslie change mans forme and favor, he buildeth high towres full of weapons, and also castels and cities; he inflicteth men thirtie daies with wounds both rotten and full of maggots, at the exorcists commandement, he provideth good familiars, and hath dominion over fiftie legions.

Sidonay.

Sidonay, alias Asmoday, a great king, strong and mightie, he is seene with three heads, whereof the first is like a bull, the second like a man, the third like a ram, he hath a serpents taile, he belcheth flames out of his mouth, he hath feete like a goose, he sitteth on an infernall dragon, he carrieth a lance and a flag in his hand, he goeth before others, which are under the power of *Amaymon.* When the conjuror exerciseth this office, let him be abroad, let him be warie and standing on his feete; if his cap be on his head, he will cause all his dooings to be bewraied, which if he doo not, the exorcist shalbe deceived by *Amaymon* in everie thing. But so soone as he seeth him in the forme aforesaid, he shall call him by his name, saieng; Thou art *Asmoday;* he will not denie it, and by and by he boweth downe to the ground; he giveth the ring of vertues, he absolutelie teacheth geometrie, arythmetike, astronomie, and handicrafts. To all demands he answereth fullie and trulie, he maketh a man invisible, he sheweth the places where treasure lieth, and gardeth it, if it be among the legions of *Amaymon,* he hath under his power seventie two legions.

Gaap.

Gaap, alias Tap, a great president and a prince, he appeareth in a meridionall signe, and when he taketh humane shape he is the guide of the foure principall kings, as mightie as *Bileth.* There were certeine necromancers that offered sacrifices and burnt offerings unto him; and to call him up, they exercised an art, saieng that *Salomon* the wise made it. Which is false: for it was rather *Cham,* the sonne of *Noah,* who after the floud began first to invocate wicked spirits. He invocated *Bileth,* and made an art in his name, and a booke which is knowne to manie mathematicians. There were burnt offerings and sacrifices made, and gifts given, and much wickednes wrought by the exorcists, who mingled therewithall the holie names of God, the which in that art are everie where expressed. Marie there is an epistle of those names written by *Salomon,* as also write *Helias Hierosolymitanus* and *Helisæus.* It is to be noted, that if anie exorcist have the art of *Bileth,* and cannot make him stand before him, nor see him, I may not bewraie how and declare the meanes to conteine him, bicause it is abhomination, and for that I have learned nothing from *Salomon* of his dignitie and office. But yet I will not hide this; to wit, that he maketh a man woonderfull in philosophie and all the liberall sciences: he maketh love, hatred, insensibilitie, invisibilitie, consecration, and consecration of those things that are belonging unto the domination of *Amaymon,* and delivereth familiars out of the possession of other conjurors, answering truly and perfectly of things present, past, & to come, & transferreth men most speedilie into other nations, he ruleth sixtie six legions, & was of the order of potestats.

Who was the first necromancer.

Shax.

Shax, alias Scox, is a darke and a great marquesse, like unto a storke, with a hoarse and subtill voice: he dooth marvellouslie take awaie the sight, hearing and understanding of anie man, at the commandement of the conjuror: he taketh awaie monie out of everie kings house, and carrieth it backe after 1200. yeares, if he be commanded, he is a horssestealer, he is thought to be faithfull in all commandements: and although he promise to be obedient to the conjuror in all things; yet is he not so, he is a lier, except he be brought into a triangle, and there he speaketh divinelie, and telleth of things which are hidden, and not kept of wicked spirits, he promiseth good familiars, which are accepted if they be not deceivers, he hath thirtie legions.

Procell is a great and a strong duke, appearing in the shape of an angell, but speaketh verie darklie of things hidden, he teacheth geometrie and all the liberall arts, he maketh great noises, and causeth the waters to rore, where are none, he warmeth waters, and distempereth bathes at certeine times, as the exorcist appointeth him, he was of the order of potestats, and hath fourtie eight legions under his power. *Procell.*

Furcas is a knight and commeth foorth in the similitude of a cruell man, with a long beard and a hoarie head, he sitteth on a pale horsse, carrieng in his hand a sharpe weapon, he perfectlie teacheth practike philosophie, rhetorike, logike, astronomie, chiromancie, pyromancie, and their parts: there obeie him twentie legions. *Furcas.*

Murmur is a great duke and an earle, appearing in the shape of a souldier, riding on a griphen, with a dukes crowne on his head; there go before him two of his ministers, with great trumpets, he teacheth philosophie absolutelie, he constraineth soules to come before the exorcist, to answer what he shall aske them, he was of the order partlie of thrones, and partlie of angels, and ruleth thirtie legions. *Murmur.*

Caim is a great president, taking the forme of a thrush, but when he putteth on man's shape, he answereth in burning ashes, carrieng in his hand a most sharpe swoord, he maketh the best disputers, he giveth men the understanding of all birds, of the lowing of bullocks, and barking of dogs, and also of the sound and noise of waters, he answereth best of things to come, he was of the order of angels, and ruleth thirtie legions of divels. *Caim.*

Raum, or *Raim* is a great earle, he is seene as a crowe, but when he putteth on humane shape, at the commandement of the exorcist, he stealeth woonderfullie out of the kings house, and carrieth it whether he is assigned, he destroieth cities, and hath great despite unto dignities, he knoweth things present, past, and to come, and reconcileth freends and foes, he was of the order of thrones, and governeth thirtie legions. *Raum.*

Halphas is a great earle, and commeth abroad like a storke, with a hoarse voice, he notablie buildeth up townes full of munition and weapons, he sendeth men of warre to places appointed, and hath under him six and twentie legions. *Halphas.*

Focalor is a great duke comming foorth as a man, with wings like a griphen, he killeth men, and drowneth them in the waters, and overturneth ships of warre, commanding and ruling both winds and seas. And let the conjuror note, that if he bid him hurt no man, he willinglie consenteth thereto: he hopeth after 1000. yeares to returne to the seventh throne, but he is deceived, he hath three legions. *Focalor.*

Vine is a great king and an earle, he showeth himselfe as a lion, riding on a blacke horsse, and carrieth a viper in his hand, he gladlie buildeth large towres, he throweth downe stone walles, and maketh waters rough. At the commandement of the exorcist he answereth of things hidden, of witches, and of things present, past, and to come. *Vine.*

Bifrons is seene in the similitude of a monster, when he taketh the image of a man, he maketh one woonderfull cunning in astrologie, absolutelie declaring the mansions of the planets, he dooth the like in geometrie, and other admesurements, he perfectlie understandeth the strength and vertue of hearbs, pretious stones, and woods, he changeth dead bodies from place to place, he seemeth to light candles upon the sepulchres of the dead, and hath under him six and twentie legions. *Bifrons.*

Gamigin is a great marquesse, and is seene in the forme of a little horsse, when he taketh humane shape he speaketh with a hoarse voice, disputing of all liberall sciences; he bringeth also to passe, that the soules, which are drowned in the sea, or which dwell in purgatorie (which is called *Cartagra*, that is, affliction of soules) shall take aierie bodies, and evidentlie appeare and answer to interrogatories at the conjurors commandement; he tarrieth with *Gamigin.*

223

the exorcist, untill he have accomplished his desire, and hath thirtie legions under him.

Zagan.

Zagan is a great king and a president, he commeth abroad like a bull, with griphens wings, but when he taketh humane shape, he maketh men wittie, he turneth all mettals into the coine of that dominion, and turneth water into wine, and wine into water, he also turneth bloud into wine, & wine into bloud, & a foole into a wise man, he is head of thirtie and three legions.

Orias.

Orias is a great marquesse, and is seene as a lion riding on a strong horsse, with a serpents taile, and carrieth in his right hand two great serpents hissing, he knoweth the mansion of planets and perfectlie teacheth the vertues of the starres, he transformeth men, he giveth dignities, prelacies, and confirmations, and also the favour of freends and foes, and hath under him thirtie legions.

Valac.

Valac is a great president, and commeth abroad with angels wings like a boie, riding on a twoheaded dragon, he perfectlie answereth of treasure hidden, and where serpents may be seene, which he delivereth into the conjurors hands, void of anie force or strength, and hath dominion over thirtie legions of divels.

Gomory.

Gomory a strong and a mightie duke, he appeareth like a faire woman, with a duchesse crownet about hir midle, riding on a camell, he answereth well and truelie of things present, past, and to come, and of treasure hid, and where it lieth: he procureth the love of women, especiallie of maids, and hath six and twentie legions.

Decarabia.

Decarabia or *Carabia*, he commeth like a * and knoweth the force of herbes and pretious stones, and maketh all birds flie before the exorcist, and to tarrie with him, as though they were tame, and that they shall drinke and sing, as their maner is, and hath thirtie legions.

Amduscias.

Amduscias a great and a strong duke, he commeth foorth as an unicorne, when he standeth before his maister in humane shape, being commanded, he easilie bringeth to passe, that trumpets and all musicall instruments may be heard and not seene, and also that trees shall bend and incline, according to the conjurors will, he is excellent among familiars, and hath nine and twentie legions.

Andras.

Andras is a great marquesse, and is seene in an angels shape with a head like a blacke night raven, riding upon a blacke and a verie strong woolfe, flourishing with a sharpe sword in his hand, he can kill the maister, the servant, and all assistants, he is author of discords, and ruleth thirtie legions.

Andrealphus.

Andrealphus is a great marquesse, appearing as a pecocke, he raiseth great noises, and in humane shape perfectlie teacheth geometrie, and all things belonging to admeasurements, he maketh a man to be a subtill disputer, and cunning in astronomie, and transformeth a man into the likenes of a bird, and there are under him thirtie legions.

Ose.

Ose is a great president, and commeth foorth like a leopard, and counterfeting to be a man, he maketh one cunning in the liberall sciences, he answereth truelie of divine and secret things, he transformeth a mans shape, and bringeth a man to that madnes, that he thinketh himselfe to be that which he is not; as that he is a king or a pope, or that he weareth a crowne on his head, *Durátque id regnum ad horam.*

Aym.

Aym or *Haborim* is a great duke and a strong, he commeth foorth with three heads, the first like a serpent, the second like a man having two * the third like a cat, he rideth on a viper, carrieng in his hand a light fier brand, with the flame whereof castels and cities are fiered, he maketh one wittie everie kind of waie, he answereth truelie of privie matters, and reigneth over twentie six legions.

Orobas.

Orobas is a great prince, he commeth foorth like a horsse, but when he putteth on him a mans idol, he talketh of divine vertue, he giveth true answers of things present, past, and to come, and of the divinitie, and of the creation, he deceiveth none, nor suffereth anie to be tempted, he giveth dignities and prelacies, and the favour of freends and foes, and hath rule over twentie legions.

Vapula is a great duke and a strong, he is seene like a lion with griphens   *Vapula.*
wings, he maketh a man subtill and wonderfull in handicrafts, philosophie, and
in sciences conteined in bookes, and is ruler over thirtie six legions.

Cimeries is a great marquesse and a strong, ruling in the parts of *Aphrica;* he   *Cimeries.*
teacheth perfectlie grammar, logicke, and rhetorike, he discovereth treasures
and things hidden, he bringeth to passe, that a man shall seeme with expedition
to be turned into a soldier, he rideth upon a great blacke horsse, and ruleth
twentie legions.

Amy is a great president, and appeareth in a flame of fier, but having taken   *Amy.*
mans shape, he maketh one marvelous in astrologie, and in all the liberall
sciences, he procureth excellent familiars, he bewraieth treasures preserved by
spirits, he hath the governement of thirtie six legions, he is partlie of the order
of angels, partlie of potestats, he hopeth after a thousand two hundreth yeares to
returne to the seventh throne: which is not credible.

Flauros a strong duke, is seene in the forme of a terrible strong leopard, in   *Flauros.*
humane shape, he sheweth a terrible countenance, and fierie eies, he answereth
trulie and fullie of things present, past, and to come; if he be in a triangle, he lieth
in all things and deceiveth in other things, and beguileth in other busines, he
gladlie talketh of the divinitie, and of the creation of the world, and of the fall;
he is constrained by divine vertue, and so are all divels or spirits, to burne and
destroie all the conjurors adversaries. And if he be commanded, he suffereth the
conjuror not to be tempted, and he hath twentie legions under him.

Balam is a great and a terrible king, he commeth foorth with three heads, the   *Balam.*
first of a bull, the second of a man, the third of a ram, he hath a serpents taile,
and flaming eies, riding upon a furious beare, and carrieng a hawke on his fist,
he speaketh with a hoarse voice, answering perfectlie of things present, past, and
to come, hee maketh a man invisible and wise, hee governeth fourtie legions, and
was of the order of dominations.

Allocer is a strong duke and a great, he commeth foorth like a soldier, riding   *Allocer.*
on a great horsse, he hath a lions face, verie red, and with flaming eies, he
speaketh with a big voice, he maketh a man woonderfull in astronomie, and in
all the liberall sciences, he bringeth good familiars, and ruleth thirtie six
legions.

Saleos is a great earle, he appeareth as a gallant soldier, riding on a crocodile,   *Saleos.*
and weareth a dukes crowne, peaceable, &c.

Vuall is a great duke and a strong, he is seene as a great and terrible drome-   *Vuall.*
darie, but in humane forme, he soundeth out in a base voice the *Ægyptian* toong.
This man above all other procureth the especiall love of women, and knoweth
things present, past, and to come, procuring the love of freends and foes, he was
of the order of potestats, and governeth thirtie seven legions.

Haagenti is a great president, appearing like a great bull, having the wings of a   *Haagenti.*
griphen, but when he taketh humane shape, he maketh a man wise in everie
thing, he changeth all mettals into gold, and changeth wine and water the one
into the other, and commandeth as manie legions as *Zagan.*

Phœnix is a great marquesse, appearing like the bird *Phœnix*, having a childs   *Phœnix.*
voice: but before he standeth still before the conjuror, he singeth manie sweet
notes. Then the exorcist with his companions must beware he give no eare to
the melodie, but must by and by bid him put on humane shape; then will he
speake marvellouslie of all woonderfull sciences. He is an excellent poet, and
obedient, he hopeth to returne to the seventh throne after a thousand two
hundreth yeares, and governeth twentie legions.

Stolas is a great prince, appearing in the forme of a nightraven, before the   *Stolas.*
exorcist, he taketh the image and shape of a man, and teacheth astronomie,
absolutelie understanding the vertues of herbes and pretious stones; there are
under him twentie six legions.

¶ *Note that a legion is 6 6 6 6, and now by multiplication count how manie legions doo
arise out of everie particular.*

This was
the work of
one T. R.
written in
faire letters
of red &
blacke upō
parchment,
and made
by him, Ann.
1570. to the
maintenance
of his living,
the edifieng
of the poore,
and the
glorie of
gods holie
name: as he
himselfe
saith.

✠*Secretum secretorum,*
  The secret of secrets;
Tu operans sis secretus horum,
  Thou that workst them, be secret in them.

CHAPTER III.

The houres wherin principall divels may be bound, to wit, raised and restrained from dooing of hurt.

AMAYMON king of the east, *Gorson* king of the south, *Zimimar* king of the north, *Goap* king and prince of the west, may be bound from the third houre, till noone, and from the ninth houre till evening. Marquesses may be bound from the ninth houre till compline, and from compline till the end of the daie. Dukes may be bound from the first houre till noone; and cleare wether is to be observed. Prelates may be bound in anie houre of the daie. Knights from daie dawning, till sunne rising; or from evensong, till the sunne set. A President may not be bound in anie houre of the daie, except the king, whome he obeieth, be invocated; nor in the shutting of the evening. Counties or erles may be bound at anie houre of the daie, so it be in the woods or feelds, where men resort not.

CHAPTER IV.

The forme of adjuring or citing of the spirits aforesaid to arise and appeare.

WHEN you will have anie spirit, you must know his name and office; you must also fast, and be cleane from all pollution, three or foure daies before; so will the spirit be the more obedient unto you. Then make a circle, and call up the spirit with great intention, and holding a ring in your hand, rehearse in your owne name, and your companions (for one must alwaies be with you) this praier following, and so no spirit shall annoie you, and your purpose shall take effect. And note how this agreeth with popish charmes and conjurations.

In the name of our Lord Jesus Christ the ✠ father ✠ and the sonne ✠ and the Hollie-ghost ✠ holie trinitie and unseparable unitie, I call upon thee, that thou maiest be my salvation and defense, and the protection of my bodie and soule, and of all my goods through the vertue of thy holie crosse, and through the vertue of thy passion, I beseech thee O Lord Jesus Christ, by the merits of thy blessed mother S. *Marie,* and of all thy saints, that thou give me grace and divine power over all the wicked spirits, so as which of them soever I doo call by name, they may come by and by from everie coast, and accomplish my will, that they neither be hurtfull or fearefull unto me, but rather obedient and diligent about me. And through thy vertue streightlie commanding them, let them fulfill my commandements, Amen. Holie, holie, Lord God of sabboth, which wilt come to judge the quicke and the dead, thou which art A and Ω, first and last, King of kings and Lord of lords, *Ioth, Aglanabrath, El, Abiel, Anathiel, Amazim, Sedomel, Gayes, Heli, Messias, Tolimi, Elias, Ischiros, Athanatos, Imas.* By these thy holie names, and by all other I doo call upon thee, and beseech

Note what
names are
attributed
unto Christ
by the con-

226

juror in this his exorcising exercise.

thee O Lord Jesus Christ, by thy nativitie and baptisme, by thy crosse and passion, by thine ascension, and by the comming of the Holie-ghost, by the bitternesse of thy soule when it departed from thy bodie, by thy five wounds, by the bloud and water which went out of thy bodie, by thy vertue, by the sacrament which thou gavest thy disciples the daie before thou sufferedst, by the holie trinitie, and by the inseparable unitie, by blessed *Marie* thy mother, by thine angels, archangels, prophets, patriarchs, and by all thy saints, and by all the sacraments which are made in thine honour, I doo worship and beseech thee, I blesse and desire thee, to accept these praiers, conjurations, and words of my mouth, which I will use. I require thee O Lord Jesus Christ, that thou give me thy vertue & power over all thine angels (which were throwne downe from heaven to deceive mankind) to drawe them to me, to tie and bind them, & also to loose them, to gather them togither before me, & to command them to doo all that they can, and that by no meanes they contemne my voice, or the words of my mouth; but that they obeie me and my saiengs, and feare me. I beseech thee by thine humanitie, mercie and grace, and I require thee *Adonay, Amay, Horta, Vege dora, Mitai, Hel, Suranat, Ysion, Ysesy,* and by all thy holie names, and by all thine holie he saints and she saints, by all thine angels and archangels, powers, dominations, and vertues, and by that name that *Salomon* did bind the divels, and shut them up, *Elhrach, Ebanher, Agle, Goth, Ioth, Othie, Venoch, Nabrat,* and by all thine holie names which are written in this booke, and by the vertue of them all, that thou enable me to congregate all thy spirits throwne downe from heaven, that they may give me a true answer of all my demands, and that they satisfie all my requests, without the hurt of my bodie or soule, or any thing else that is mine, through our Lord Jesus Christ thy sonne, which liveth and reigneth with thee in the unitie of the Holie-ghost, one God world without end.

What wonderfull force conjurors doo beleeve cõsisteth in these forged names of Christ.

Oh father omnipotent, oh wise sonne, oh Holie-ghost, the searcher of harts, oh you three in persons, one true godhead in substance, which didst spare *Adam* and *Eve* in their sins; and oh thou sonne, which diedst for their sinnes a most filthie death, susteining it upon the holie crosse; oh thou most mercifull, when I flie unto thy mercie, and beseech thee by all the means I can, by these the holie names of thy sonne; to wit, *A* and *Ω,* and all other his names, grant me thy vertue and power, that I may be able to cite before me, thy spirits which were throwne downe from heaven, & that they may speake with me, & dispatch by & by without delaie, & with a good will, & without the hurt of my bodie, soule, or goods, &c: as is conteined in the booke called *Annulus Salomonis.*

Oh great and eternall vertue of the highest, which through disposition, these being called to judgement, *Vaicheon, Stimulamaton, Esphares, Tetragrammaton, Olioram, Cryon, Esytion, Existion, Eriona, Onela, Brasim, Noym, Messias, Soter, Emanuel, Sabboth, Adonay,* I worship thee, I invocate thee, I imploie thee with all the strength of my mind, that by thee, my present praiers, consecrations, and conjurations be hallowed: and whersoever wicked spirits are called, in the vertue of thy names, they may come togither from everie coast, and diligentlie fulfill the will of me the exorcist. *Fiat, fiat, fiat, Amen.*

CHAPTER V.

A confutation of the manifold vanities conteined in the precedent chapters, speciallie of commanding of divels.

HE that can be persuaded that these things are true, or wrought indeed according to the assertion of couseners, or according to the supposition of witchmongers & papists, may soone be brought to beleeve that the moone is made of greene cheese. You see in this which is called *Salomons* conjuration, there is a perfect inventarie registred of the number of divels, of their names, of their offices, of their personages, of their qualities, of their powers, of their properties, of their kingdomes, of their governments, of their orders, of their dispositions, of their subjection, of their submission, and of the waies to bind or loose them; with a note what wealth, learning, office, commoditie, pleasure, &c: they can give, and may be forced to yeeld in spight of their harts, to such (forsooth) as are cunning in this art: of whome yet was never seene any rich man, or at least that gained any thing that waie; or any unlearned man, that became learned by that meanes; or any happie man, that could with the helpe of this art either deliver himselfe, or his freends, from adversitie, or adde unto his estate any point of felicitie: yet these men, in all worldlie happinesse, must needs exceed all others; if such things could be by them accomplished, according as it is presupposed. For if they may learne of *Marbas*, all secrets, and to cure all diseases; and of *Furcas*, wisdome, and to be cunning in all mechanicall arts; and to change anie mans shape, of *Zepar:* if *Bune* can make them rich and eloquent, if *Beroth* can tell them of all things, present, past, and to come; if *Asmodaie* can make them go invisible and shew them all hidden treasure; if *Salmacke* will afflict whom they list, & *Allocer* can procure them the love of any woman; if *Amy* can provide them excellent familiars, if *Caym* can make them understand the voice of all birds and beasts, and *Buer* and *Bifrons* can make them live long; and finallie, if *Orias* could procure unto them great friends, and reconcile their enimies, & they in the end had all these at commandement; should they not live in all worldlie honor and felicitie? whereas contrariwise they lead their lives in all obloquie, miserie, and beggerie, and in fine come to the gallowes; as though they had chosen unto themselves the spirit *Valefer*, who they saie bringeth all them with whom he entreth into familiaritie, to no better end than the gibet or gallowes. But before I proceed further to the confutation of this stuffe, I will shew other conjurations, devised more latelie, and of more authoritie; wherein you shall see how fooles are trained to beleeve these absurdities, being woone by little and little to such credulitie. For the author heereof beginneth, as though all the cunning of conjurors were derived and fetcht from the planetarie motions, and true course of the stars, celestiall bodies, &c.

This is contrarie to the scripture, which saith that everie good gift commeth from the father of light, &c.

A breviarie of the inventarie of spirits.

The authors further purpose in the detection of cōjuring.

CHAPTER VI.

The names of the planets, their characters, togither with the twelve signes of the zodiake, their dispositions, aspects, and government, with other observations.

The Characters of the Planets.

♄	♃	♂	☉	♀	☿	☾
Saturn.	*Jupiter.*	*Mars.*	*Sol.*	*Venus.*	*Mercury.*	*Luna.*

The five Planetary Aspects.

☌	⚹	□	△	☍
Conjunction.	*Sextile.*	*Quadrat.*	*Trine.*	*Opposition.*

The twelve signs of the Zodiake, their Characters and Denominations, &c.

♈	♉	♊	♋	♌	♍
Aries.	*Taurus.*	*Gemini.*	*Cancer.*	*Leo.*	*Virgo.*
♎	♏	♐	♑	♒	♓
Libra.	*Scorpio.*	*Sagittarius.*	*Capricornus.*	*Aquarius.*	*Pisces.*

Their Disposition or Inclinations.

♈ ♋ ♉ ♓ ♐ Good signes. ♎ ♏ ♑ ♒ ♊ Evil signes. ♒ ♏ ♋ ♓ ♍ Signes indifferent.

♈ ♎ ♐ Very good signes. ♑ ♊ ♌ ♉ Very evil signes.

The disposition of the planets.

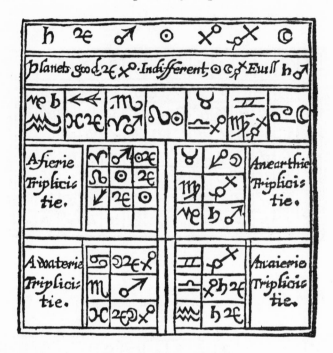

The aspects of the planets.

☌ Is the best aspect, with good planets, and woorst with evill.
✳ Is a meane aspect in goodnesse or badnesse.
△ Is verie good in aspect to good planets, & hurteth not in evill.
▢ This aspect is of enimitie not full perfect.
☍ This aspect is of enimitie most perfect.

The five
planetarie
aspects:
Conjunct.
Sextil.
Trine.
Quartil.
Opposit.

How the daie is divided or distinguished.

A daie naturall is the space of foure and twentie houres, accounting the night withall, and beginneth at one of the clocke after midnight.

An artificiall daie is that space of time, which is betwixt the rising and falling of the ⊙ &c. All the rest is night, & beginneth at the ⊙ rising.

Hereafter followeth a table, showing how the daie and the night is divided by houres, and reduced to the regiment of the planets.

The division of the daie, and the planetarie regiment.

The division of the night, and the planetarie regiment.

CHAPTER VII.

The characters of the angels of the seaven daies, with their names: of figures, seales and periapts.

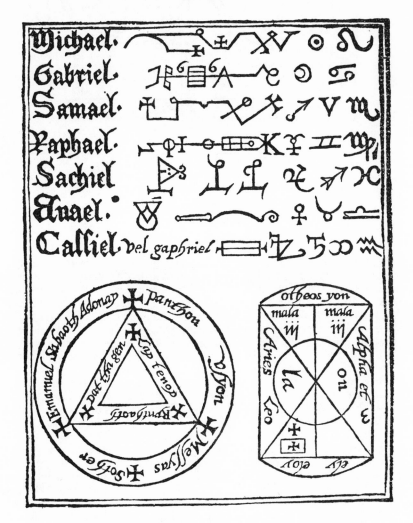

{ *These figures are called the seales of the earth, without the* }
{ *which no spirit will appeere, except thou have them with thee.* }

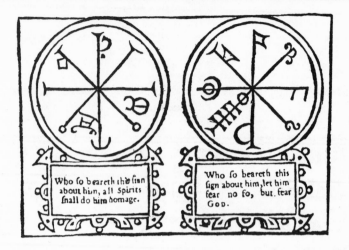

Who so beareth this sign about him, all Spirits shall do him homage.

Who so beareth this sign about him, let him fear no fo, but fear God.

CHAPTER VIII.

An experiment of the dead.

Conjuring for a dead spirit.

FIRST fast and praie three daies, and absteine thee from all filthinesse; go to one that is new buried, such a one as killed himselfe or destroied himselfe wilfullie: or else get thee promise of one that shalbe hanged, and let him sweare an oth to thee, after his bodie is dead, that his spirit shall come to thee, and doo thee true service, at thy commandements, in all daies, houres, and minuts. And let no persons see thy doings, but thy fellow. And about eleven a clocke in the night, go to the place where he was buried, and saie with a bold faith & hartie desire, to have the spirit come that thou doost call for, thy fellow having a candle in his left hand, and in his right hand a christall stone, and saie these words following, the maister having a hazell wand in his right hand, and these names of God written thereupon, *Tetragrammaton* ✠ *Adonay* ✠ *Agla* ✠ *Craton* ✠ Then strike three strokes on the ground, and saie; Arise *N.* Arise *N.* Arise *N.* I conjure thee spirit *N.* by the resurrection of our Lord Jesu Christ, that thou doo obey to my words, and come unto me this night verelie and trulie, as thou beleevest to be saved at the daie of judgement. And I will sweare to thee on oth, by the perill of my soule, that if thou wilt come to me, and appeare to me this night, and shew me true visions in this christall stone, and fetch me the fairie *Sibylia*, that I may talke with hir visiblie, and she may come before me, as the conjuration leadeth: and in so doing, I will give thee an almesse deed, and praie for thee *N.* to my Lord God, wherby thou maiest be restored to thy salvation at the resurrection daie, to be received as one of the elect of God, to the everlasting glorie, Amen.

The maister standing at the head of the grave, his fellow having in his hands the candle and the stone, must begin the conjuration as followeth, and the spirit will appeare to you in the christall stone, in a faire forme of a child of twelve yeares of age. And when he is in, feele the stone, and it will be hot; and feare nothing, for he or shee will shew manie delusions, to drive you from your worke. Feare God, but feare him not. This is to constraine him, as followeth.

I conjure thee spirit *N.* by the living God, the true God, and by the holie God, and by their vertues and powers which have created both thee and me, and all the world. I conjure thee *N.* by these holie names of God, *Tetragrammaton* ✠ *Adonay* ✠ *Algramay* ✠ *Saday* ✠ *Sabaoth* ✠ *Planaboth* ✠ *Panthon* ✠ *Craton* ✠

<aside>For the cousenor (the conjuror I should saie) can do nothing to any purpose without his côfederate. Note that numerous ternarius, which is counted mysticall, be observed. *Ex inferno nulla redemptio*, saith the scripture: *Ergo* you lie quoth Nota.</aside>

232

Neupmaton ✠ Deus ✠ Homo ✠ Omnipotens ✠ Sempiturnus ✠ Ysus ✠ Terra ✠ Unigenitus ✠ Salvator ✠ Via ✠ Vita ✠ Manus ✠ Fons ✠ Origo ✠ Filius ✠ And by their vertues and powers, and by all their names, by the which God gave power to man, both to speake or thinke; so by their vertues and powers I conjure thee spirit *N.* that now immediatlie thou doo appeare in this christall stone, visiblie to me and to my fellow, without anie tarrieng or deceipt. I conjure thee N. by the excellent name of Jesus Christ *A* and *Ω*, the first and the last. For this holie name of Jesus is above all names: for in this name of Jesus everie knee dooth bow and obeie, both of heavenlie things, earthlie things, and infernall. And everie toong doth confesse, that our Lord Jesus Christ is in the glorie of the father: neither is there anie other name given to man, whereby he must be saved. Therefore in the name of Jesus of Nazareth, and by his nativitie, resurrection, and ascension, and by all that apperteineth unto his passion, and by their vertues and powers I conjure thee spirit *N.* that thou doo appeare visiblie in this christall stone to me, and to my fellow, without anie dissimulation. I conjure thee *N.* by the bloud of the innocent lambe Jesus Christ, which was shed for us upon the crosse: for all those that doo beleeve in the vertue of his bloud, shalbe saved. I conjure thee *N.* by the vertues and powers of all the riall names and words of the living God of me pronounced, that thou be obedient unto me and to my words rehearsed. If thou refuse this to doo, I by the holie trinitie, and their vertues and powers doo condemne thee thou spirit *N.* into the place where there is no hope of remedie or rest, but everlasting horror and paine there dwelling, and a place where is paine upon paine, dailie, horriblie, and lementablie, thy paine to be there augmented as the starres in the heaven, and as the gravell or sand in the sea: except thou spirit *N.* doo appeare to me and to my fellow visiblie, immediatlie in this christall stone, and in a faire forme and shape of a child of twelve yeares of age, and that thou alter not thy shape, I charge thee upon paine of everlasting condemnation. I conjure thee spirit *N.* by the golden girdle, which girded the loines of our Lord Jesus Christ: so thou spirit *N.* be thou bound into the perpetuall paines of hell fier, for thy disobedience and unreverent regard, that thou hast to the holie names and words, and his precepts. I conjure thee *N.* by the two edged sword, which *John* sawe proceed out of the mouth of the almightie; and so thou spirit *N.* be torne and cut in peeces with that sword, and to be condemned into everlasting paine, where the fier goeth not out, and where the worme dieth not. I conjure thee *N.* by the heavens, and by the celestiall citie of *Jerusalem*, and by the earth and the sea, and by all things conteined in them, and by their vertues & powers. I conjure thee spirit *N.* by the obedience that thou doost owe unto the principall prince. And except thou spirit *N.* doo come and appeare in this christall stone visiblie in my presence, here immediatlie as it is aforesaid. Let the great cursse of God, the anger of God, the shadowe and darknesse of death, and of eternall condemnation be upon thee spirit *N.* for ever and ever; bicause thou hast denied thy faith, thy health, & salvation. For thy great disobedience, thou art worthie to be condemned. Therefore let the divine trinitie, thrones, dominions, principats, potestats, virtutes, cherubim and seraphim, and all the soules of saints, both of men and women, condemne thee for ever, and be a witnesse against thee at the daie of judgement, bicause of thy disobedience. And let all creatures of our Lord Jesus Christ, saie thereunto; *Fiat, fiat, fiat:* Amen.

And when he is appeared in the christall stone, as is said before, bind him with this bond as followeth; to wit, I conjure thee spirit *N.* that art appeared to me in this christall stone, to me and to my fellow; I conjure thee by all the riall words aforesaid, the which did constraine thee to appeare therein, and their vertues; I charge thee spirit by them all, that thou shalt not depart out of this christall stone, untill my will being fulfilled, thou be licenced to depart. I conjure and bind thee spirit *N.* by that omnipotent God, which commanded the angell S. *Michael* to drive *Lucifer* out of the heavens with a sword of vengeance, and to fall from joy to paine; and for dread of such paine as he is in, I charge thee spirit *N.* that thou shalt not go out of the christall stone; nor yet to alter thy shape at this time, except I command thee otherwise; but to come unto me at

Dæmones credendo contremiscunt.

A heavie sentence denounced of the conjuror against the spirit in case of disobedience, contempt, or negligence.

How can that be, when a spirit hath neither flesh, bloud, nor bones?

The conjuror imputeth the appearing of a spirit by constraint unto words quoth Nota.

all places, and in all houres and minuts, when and wheresoever I shall call thee, by the vertue of our Lord Jesus Christ, or by anie conjuration of words that is written in this booke, and to shew me and my freends true visions in this christall stone, of anie thing or things that we would see, at anie time or times: and also to go and to fetch me the fairie *Sibylia*, that I may talke with hir in all kind of talke, as I shall call hir by anie conjuration of words conteined in this booke. I conjure thee spirit *N.* by the great wisedome and divinitie of his godhead, my will to fulfill, as is aforesaid: I charge thee upon paine of condemnation, both in this world, and in the world to come, *Fiat, fiat, fiat:* Amen.

This done, go to a place fast by, and in a faire parlor or chamber, make a circle with chalke, as hereafter followeth: and make another circle for the fairie *Sibylia* to appeare in, foure foote from the circle thou art in, & make no names therein, nor cast anie holie thing therein, but make a circle round with chalke; & let the maister and his fellowe sit downe in the first circle, the maister having the booke in his hand, his fellow having the christall stone in his right hand, looking in the stone when the fairie dooth appeare. The maister also must have

upon his brest this figure here written in parchment, and beginne to worke in the new of the ☽ and in the houre of ♃ the ☉ and the ☽ to be in one of inhabiters signes, as ♋ ♐ ♓. This bond as followeth, is to cause the spirit in the christall stone, to fetch unto thee the fairie *Sibylia*. All things fulfilled, beginne this bond as followeth, and be bold, for doubles they will come before thee, before the conjuration be read seven times.

I conjure thee spirit *N.* in this christall stone, by God the father, by God the sonne Jesus Christ, and by God the Holie-ghost, three persons and one God, and by their vertues. I conjure thee spirit, that thou doo go in peace, and also to come againe to me quicklie, and to bring with thee into that circle appointed, *Sibylia* fairie, that I may talke with hir in those matters that shall be to hir honour and glorie; and so I charge thee declare unto hir. I conjure thee spirit *N.* by the bloud of the innocent lambe, the which redeemed all the world; by the vertue thereof I charge thee thou spirit in the christall stone, that thou doo declare unto hir this message. Also I conjure thee spirit *N.* by all angels and archangels, thrones, dominations, principats, potestates, virtutes, cherubim and seraphim, and by their vertues and powers. I conjure the *N.* that thou doo depart with speed, and also to come againe with speed, and to bring with thee the fairie *Sibylia*, to appeare in that circle, before I doo read the conjuration in this booke seven times. Thus I charge thee my will to be fulfilled, upon paine of ever-lasting condemnation: *Fiat, fiat, fiat;* Amen.

Then the figure aforesaid pinned on thy brest, rehearse the words therein, and saie, ✠ *Sorthie* ✠ *Sorthia* ✠ *Sorthios* ✠ then beginne your conjuration as followeth here, and saie; I conjure thee *Sibylia*, O gentle virgine of fairies, by the mercie of the Holie-ghost, and by the dreadfull daie of doome, and by their vertues and powers; I conjure thee *Sibylia*, O gentle virgine of fairies, and by all the angels of ♃ and their characters and vertues, and by all the spirits of ♃ and ♀ and their characters and vertues, and by all the characters that be in the firmament, and by the king and queene of fairies, and their vertues, and by the faith and obedience that thou bearest unto them. I conjure thee *Sibylia* by the bloud that ranne out of the side of our Lord Jesus Christ crucified, and by the opening of heaven, and by the renting of the temple, and by the darkenes of the sunne in the time of his death, and by the rising up of the dead in the time of his resurrection, and by the virgine *Marie* mother of our Lord Jesus Christ, and by the unspeakable name of God, *Tetragrammaton*. I conjure thee O *Sibylia*, O blessed and beautifull virgine, by all the riall words aforesaid; I conjure thee *Sibylia* by all their vertues to appeare in that circle before me visible, in the forme and shape of a beautifull

✠ ✠ ✠
Sorthie, Sorthia,
Sorthios.

And whie might not he doo it himselfe, as well as madam *Sibylia*.

The faire Sibylia conjured to appeare, &c.

woman in a bright and vesture white, adorned and garnished most faire, and to appeare to me quicklie without deceipt or tarrieng, and that thou faile not to fulfill my will & desire effectuallie. For I will choose thee to be my blessed virgine, & will have common copulation with thee. Therfore make hast & speed to come unto me, and to appeare as I said before: to whome be honour and glorie for ever and ever, Amen.

The which doone and ended, if shee come not, repeate the conjuration till they doo come: for doubtles they will come. And when she is appeared, take your censers, and incense hir with frankincense, then bind hir with the bond as followeth. ¶ I doo conjure thee *Sibylia*, by God the Father, God the sonne, and God the Holie-ghost, three persons and one God, and by the blessed virgine *Marie* mother of our Lord Jesus Christ, and by all the whole and holie companie of heaven, and by the dreadfull daie of doome, and by all angels and archangels, thrones, dominations, principates, potestates, virtutes, cherubim and seraphim, and their vertues and powers. I conjure thee, and bind thee *Sibylia*, that thou shalt not depart out of the circle wherein thou art appeared, nor yet to alter thy shape, except I give thee licence to depart. I conjure thee *Sibylia* by the bloud that ranne out of the side of our Lord Jesus Christ crucified, and by the vertue hereof I conjure thee *Sibylia* to come to me, and to appeare to me at all times visiblie, as the conjuration of words leadeth, written in this booke, I conjure thee *Sibylia*, O blessed virgine of fairies, by the opening of heaven, and by the renting of the temple, and by the darknes of the sunne at the time of his death, and by the rising of the dead in the time of his glorious resurrection, and by the unspeakable name of God ✠ *Tetragrammaton* ✠ and by the king and queene of fairies, & by their vertues I conjure thee *Sibylia* to appeare, before the conjuration be read over foure times, and that visiblie to appeare, as the conjuration leadeth written in this booke, and to give me good counsell at all times, and to come by treasures hidden in the earth, and all other things that is to doo me pleasure, and to fulfill my will, without anie deceipt or tarrieng; nor yet that thou shalt have anie power of my bodie or soule, earthlie or ghostlie, nor yet to perish so much of my bodie as one haire of my head. I conjure thee *Sibylia* by all the riall words aforesaid, and by their vertues and powers, I charge and bind thee by the vertue thereof, to be obedient unto me, and to all the words aforesaid, and this bond to stand betweene thee and me, upon paine of everlasting condemnation, *Fiat, fiat, fiat*, Amen.

The maner of binding the fairie Sibylia at hir appearing.

If all this will not fetch hir up the divell is a knave.

CHAPTER IX.

A licence for Sibylia to go and come by at all times.

I CONJURE thee *Sibylia*, which art come hither before me, by the commandement of thy Lord and mine, that thou shalt have no powers, in thy going or comming unto me, imagining anie evill in anie maner of waies, in the earth or under the earth, of evill dooings, to anie person or persons. I conjure and command thee *Sibylia* by all the riall words and vertues that be written in this booke, that thou shalt not go to the place from whence thou camest, but shalt remaine peaceablie invisiblie, and looke thou be readie to come unto me, when thou art called by anie conjuration of words that be written in this booke, to come (I saie) at my commandement, and to answer unto me truelie and duelie of all things, my will quicklie to be fulfilled. *Vade in pace, in nomine patris, & filii, & spiritus sancti.* And the holie ✠ crosse ✠ be betweene thee and me, or betweene us and you, and the lion of *Juda*, the roote of *Jesse*, the kindred of *David*, be betweene thee & me ✠ Christ commeth ✠ Christ commandeth ✠ Christ giveth power ✠ Christ defend me ✠ and his innocent bloud ✠ from all perils of bodie and soule, sleeping or waking: *Fiat, fiat*, Amen.

CHAPTER X.

To know of treasure hidden in the earth.

This would
be much
practised if
it were not
a cousening
knacke.

W RITE in paper these characters following, on the saturdaie, in the houre of ☽, and laie it where thou thinkest treasure to be: if there be anie, the paper will burne, else not. And these be the characters.

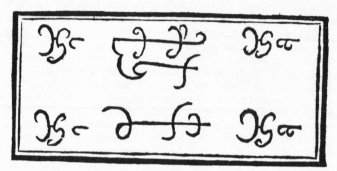

This is the waie to go invisible by these three sisters of fairies.

In the name of the Father, and of the Sonne, and of the Holie-ghost. First go to a faire parlor or chamber, & an even ground, and in no loft, and from people nine daies; for it is the better: and let all thy clothing be cleane and sweete. Then make a candle of virgine waxe, and light it, and make a faire fier of charcoles, in a faire place, in the middle of the parlor or chamber. Then take faire cleane water, that runneth against the east, and set it upon the fier: and yer thou washest thy selfe, saie these words, going about the fier, three times, holding the candle in the right hand ✠ *Panthon* ✠ *Craton* ✠ *Muriton* ✠ *Bisecog-naton* ✠ *Siston* ✠ *Diaton* ✠ *Maton* ✠ *Tetragrammaton* ✠ *Agla* ✠ *Agarion* ✠ *Tegra* ✠ *Pentessaron* ✠ *Tendicata* ✠ Then reherse these names ✠ *Sorthie* ✠ *Sorthia* ✠ *Sorthios* ✠ *Milia* ✠ *Achilia* ✠ *Sibylia* ✠ *in nomine patris*, & *filii*, & *spiritus sancti*, Amen. I conjure you three sisters of fairies, *Milia, Achilia, Sibylia*, by the father,

The three
sisters of
the fairies,
Milia,
Achilia, and
Sibylia.

by the sonne, and by the Holie-ghost, and by their vertues and powers, and by the most mercifull and living God, that will command his angell to blowe the trumpe at the daie of judgement; and he shall saie, Come, come, come to judgement; and by all angels, archangels, thrones, dominations, principats, potestates, virtutes, cherubim and seraphim, and by their vertues and powers. I conjure you three sisters, by the vertue of all the riall words aforesaid: I charge you that you doo appeare before me visiblie, in forme and shape of faire women, in white vestures, and to bring with you to me, the ring of invisibilitie, by the which I may go invisible at mine owne will and pleasure, and that in all houres, and minuts: *in nomine patris*, & *filii*, & *spiritus sancti*, Amen. ☆ Being appeared, saie this bond following.

O blessed virgins ✠ *Milia* ✠ *Achilia* ✠ I conjure you in the name of the father, in the name of the sonne, and in the name of the Holie-ghost, and by their vertues I charge you to depart from me in peace, for a time. And *Sibylia*, I conjure thee, by the vertue of our Lord Jesus Christ, and by the vertue of his flesh and pretious bloud, that he tooke of our blessed ladie the virgine, and by all the holie companie in heaven: I charge thee *Sibylia*, by all the vertues aforesaid, that thou be obedient unto me, in the name of God; that when, and at what time and place I shall call thee by this foresaid conjuration written in this booke, looke thou be readie to come unto me, at all houres and minuts, and to bring

The ring of
invisibilitie.

unto me the ring of invisibilitie, whereby I may go invisible at my will and pleasure, and that at all houres and minuts; *Fiat, fiat*, Amen.

And if they come not the first night, then doo the same the second night, and so the third night, untill they doo come: for doubtles they will come, and lie thou in thy bed, in the same parlor or chamber. And laie thy right hand out of the bed, and looke thou have a faire silken kercher bound about thy head, and be not afraid, they will doo thee no harme. For there will come before thee three faire women, and all in white clothing; and one of them will put a ring upon thy finger, wherwith thou shalt go invisible. Then with speed bind them with the bond aforesaid. When thou hast this ring on thy finger, looke in a glasse, and thou shalt not see thy selfe. And when thou wilt go invisible, put it on thy finger, the same finger that they did put it on, and everie new ☽ renew it againe. For after the first time thou shalt ever have it, and ever beginne this worke in the new of the ☽ and in the houre of ♃ and the ☽ in ♋ ♐ ♓.

Such a ring it was that advanced Giges to the kingdome of Lydia: Plato. lib. 2 de justo.

CHAPTER XI.

An experiment following, of Citrael, &c: angeli diei dominici.

¶ *Saie first the praiers of the angels everie daie, for the space of seaven daies.*

Michael.	☉
Gabriel.	☽
Samael.	♂
Raphael.	☿
Sachiel.	♃
Anael.	♀
Cassiel.	♄

O Ye glorious angels written in this square, be you my coadjutors, & helpers in all questions and demands, in all my busines, and other causes, by him which shall come to judge the quicke and the dead, and the world by fier. *O angeli gloriosi in hac quadra scripti, estote coadjutores & auxiliatores in omnibus quæstionibus & interrogationibus, in omnibus negotiis, cæterísque causis, per eum qui venturus est judicare vivos & mortuos, & mundum per ignem.*

¶ *Saie this praier fasting, called Regina linguæ.*

O queene or governesse of the toong.

✠ *Lemaac* ✠ *solmaac* ✠ *elmay* ✠ *gezagra* ✠ *raamaasin* ✠ *ezierego* ✠ *mial* ✠ *egziephiaz* ✠ *Josamin* ✠ *sabach* ✠ *ha* ✠ *aem* ✠ *re* ✠ *b* ✠ *e* ✠ *sepha* ✠ *sephar* ✠ *ramar* ✠ *semoit* ✠ *lemaio* ✠ *pheralon* ✠ *amic* ✠ *phin* ✠ *gergoin* ✠ *letos* ✠ *Amin* ✠ *amin* ✠.

In the name of the most pitifullest and mercifullest God of Israel and of paradise, of heaven and of earth, of the seas and of the infernalles, by thine omnipotent helpe may performe this worke, which livest and reignest ever one God world without end, Amen.

O most strongest and mightiest God, without beginning or ending, by thy clemencie and knowledge I desire, that my questions, worke, and labour may be fullie and trulie accomplished, through thy worthines, good Lord, which livest and reignest, ever one God, world without end, Amen.

O holie, patient, and mercifull great God, and to be worshipped, the Lord of all wisedome, cleare and just; I most hartilie desire thy holines and clemencie, to fulfill, performe and accomplish this my whole worke, thorough thy worthines, and blessed power: which livest and reignest, ever one God, *Per omnia sæcula sæculorum*, Amen.

Chapter xii.

How to enclose a spirit in a christall stone.

THIS operation following, is to have a spirit inclosed into a christall stone or berill glasse, or into anie other like instrument, &c. ¶ First thou in the new of the ☽ being clothed with all new, and fresh, & cleane araie, and shaven, and that day to fast with bread and water, and being cleane confessed, saie the seaven psalmes, and the letanie, for the space of two daies, with this praier following.

I desire thee O Lord God, my mercifull and most loving God, the giver of all graces, the giver of all sciences, grant that I thy welbeloved *N.* (although unworthie) may knowe thy grace and power, against all the deceipts and craftines of divels. And grant to me thy power, good Lord, to constraine them by this art: for thou art the true, and livelie, and eternall GOD, which livest and reignest ever one GOD through all worlds, Amen.

Thou must doo this five daies, and the sixt daie have in a redines, five bright swords: and in some secret place make one circle, with one of the said swords. And then write this name, *Sitrael:* which doone, standing in the circle, thrust in thy sword into that name. And write againe *Malanthon,* with another sword; and *Thamaor,* with another; and *Falaur,* with another; and *Sitrami,* with another; and doo as ye did with the first. All this done, turne thee to *Sitrael,* and kneeling saie thus, having the christall stone in thine hands.

O *Sitrael, Malantha, Thamaor, Falaur,* and *Sitrami,* written in these circles, appointed to this worke, I doo conjure and I doo exorcise you, by the father, by the sonne, and by the Holy-ghost, by him which did cast you out of paradise, and by him which spake the word and it was done, and by him which shall come to judge the quicke and the dead, and the world by fier, that all you five infernall maisters and princes doo come unto me, to accomplish and to fulfill all my

desire and request, which I shall command you. Also I conjure you divels, and command you, I bid you, and appoint you, by the Lord Jesus Christ, the sonne of the most highest God, and by the blessed and glorious virgine *Marie,* and by all the saints, both of men and women of God, and by all the angels, archangels, patriarches, and prophets, apostles, evangelists, martyrs, and confessors, virgins, and widowes, and all the elect of God. Also I conjure you, and everie of you, ye infernall kings, by heaven, by the starres, by the ☉ and by the ☽ and by all the planets, by the earth, fier, aier, and water, and by the terrestriall paradise, and by all things in them conteined, and by your hell, and by all the divels in it, and dwelling about it, and by your vertue and power, and by all whatsoever, and with whatsoever it be, which maie constreine and bind you. Therefore by all these foresaid vertues and powers, I doo bind you and constreine you into my will and power; that you being thus bound, may come unto me in great humilitie, and to appeare in your circles before me visiblie, in faire forme and shape of mankind kings, and to obeie unto me in all things, whatsoever

I shall desire, and that you may not depart from me without my licence. And if you doo against my precepts, I will promise unto you that you shall descend into the profound deepenesse of the sea, except that you doo obeie unto me, in the part of the living sonne of God, which liveth and reigneth in the unitie of the Holie-ghost, by all world of worlds, Amen.

Saie this true conjuration five courses, and then shalt thou see come out of the northpart five kings, with a marvelous companie: which when they are come to the circle, they will allight downe off from their horsses, and will kneele downe before thee, saieng: Maister, command us what thou wilt, and we will out of hand be obedient unto thee. Unto whome thou shall saie; See that ye depart not from me, without my licence; and that which I will command you to doo, let it be done trulie, surelie, faithfullie and essentiallie. And then they all will

238

sweare unto thee to doo all thy will. And after they have sworne, saie the conjuration immediatlie following.

I conjure, charge, and command you, and everie of you, *Sirrael, Malanthan, Thamaor, Falaur,* and *Sitrami,* you infernall kings, to put into this christall stone one spirit learned and expert in all arts and sciences, by the vertue of this name of God *Tetragrammaton,* and by the crosse of our Lord Jesu Christ, and by the bloud of the innocent lambe, which redeemed all the world, and by all their vertues & powers I charge you, ye noble kings, that the said spirit may teach, shew, and declare unto me, and to my freends, at all houres and minuts, both night and daie, the truth of all things, both bodilie and ghostlie, in this world, whatsoever I shall request or desire, declaring also to me my verie name. And this I command in your part to doo, and to obeie thereunto, as unto your owne lord and maister. That done, they will call a certeine spirit, whom they will command to enter into the centre of the circled or round christall. Then put the christall betweene the two circles, and thou shalt see the christall made blacke.

Then command them to command the spirit in the christall, not to depart out of the stone, till thou give him licence, & to fulfill thy will for ever. That done, thou shalt see them go upon the christall, both to answer your requests, & to tarrie your licence. That doone, the spirits will crave licence: and say; Go ye to your place appointed of almightie God, in the name of the father, &c. And then take up thy christall, and looke therein, asking what thou wilt, and it will shew it unto thee. Let all your circles be nine foote everie waie, & made as followeth. Worke this worke in ♋ ♏ or ♓ in the houre of the ☽ or ♃. And when the spirit is inclosed, if thou feare him, bind him with some bond, in such sort as is elsewhere expressed alreadie in this our treatise.

The five spirits of the north: as you shall see in the type expressed in pag. 414. next folowing. [A third variation]

A figure or type proportionall, shewing what forme must be observed and kept, in making the figure whereby the former secret of inclosing a spirit in christall is to be accomplished, &c.

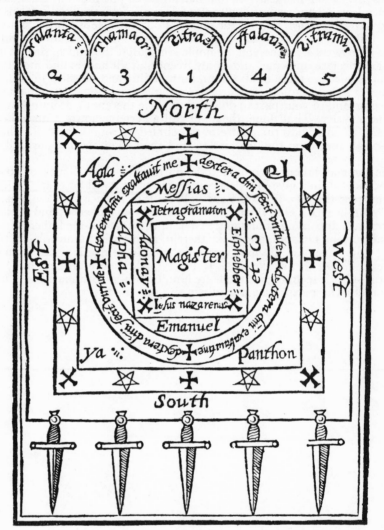

The names written within the five circles doo signifie the five infernall kings: *See* pag. 233. 234.

CHAPTER XIII.

An experiment of Bealphares.

THIS is proved the noblest carrier that ever did serve anie man upon the earth, & here beginneth the inclosing of the said spirit, & how to have a true answer of him, without anie craft or harme; and he will appeare unto thee in the likenesse of a faire man, or faire woman, the which spirit will come to thee at all times. And if thou wilt command him to tell thee of hidden treasures that be in anie place, he will tell it thee: or if thou wilt command him to bring to thee gold or silver, he will bring it thee: or if thou wilt go from one countrie to another, he will beare thee without anie harme of bodie or soule. Therefore he that will doo this worke, shall absteine from lecherousnes and dronkennesse, and from false swearing, and doo all the abstinence that he may doo; and namelie three daies before he go to worke, and in the third daie, when the night is come, and when the starres doo shine, and the element faire and cleare, he shall bath himselfe and his fellowes (if he have anie) all together in a quicke welspring. Then he must be cloathed in cleane white cloathes, and he must have another privie place, and beare with him inke and pen, wherewith he shall write this holy name of God almightie in his right hand ✠ *Agla* ✠ & in his left hand this name ✠ ∐ ℞ ⚥ ℞ ✠ And he must have a drie thong of a lions or of a harts skin, and make thereof a girdle, and write the holie names of God all about, and in the end ✠ *A* and *Ω* ✠ And upon his brest

Memorandum with what vices the cousenor (the conjuror I should saie) must not be polluted: therfore he must be no knave, &c.

he must have this present figure or marke written in virgine parchment, as it is here shewed. And it must be sowed upon a peece of new linnen, and so made fast upon thy brest. And if thou wilt have a fellow to worke with thee, he must be appointed in the same maner. You must have also a bright knife that was never occupied, and he must write on the one side of the blade of the knife ✠ *Agla* ✠ and on the other side of the knifes blade ✠ ∐ ℞ ⚥ ℞ ✠ And with the same knife he must make a circle, as hereafter followeth: the which is called *Salomons* circle. When that he is made, go into the circle, and close againe the place, there where thou wentest in, with the same knife, and saie; *Per crucis hoc signum* ✠ *fugiat procul omne malignum; Et per idem signum* ✠ *salvetur quodque benignum*, and make suffumigations to thy selfe, and to thy fellow or fellowes, with frankincense, mastike, *lignum aloes:* then put it in wine, and saie with good devotion, in the worship of the high God almightie, all together, that he may defend you from all evils. And when he that is maister will close the spirit, he shall saie towards the east, with meeke and devout devotion, these psalmes and praiers as followeth here in order.

The conjurors brestplate.

✠ ✠ ✠
*Homo sacarus,
museo lomeas,
cherubozca.*
✠

Salomons circle.

¶ *The two and twentieth psalme.*

O My God my God, looke upon me, whie hast thou forsaken me, and art so farre from my health, and from the words of my complaint? ¶ And so foorth to the end of the same psalme, as it is to be founde in the booke.

This psalme also following, being the fiftie one psalme, must be said three times over, &c.

Memorandum that you must read the 22. and 51. psalms. all over: or else rehearse them by hart: for these are counted necessarie, &c.

Have mercie upon me, O God, after thy great goodnes, according to the multitude of thy mercies, doo awaie mine offenses. ¶ And so foorth to the end of the same psalme, concluding it with, Glorie to the Father and to the Sonne, and to the Holie-ghost, As it was in the beginning, is now, and ever shall be, world without end, Amen. Then saie this verse: O Lord leave not my soule with the wicked; nor my life with the bloudthirstie. Then saie a *Pater noster* an *Ave Maria*, and a *Credo*, & *ne nos inducas*. O Lord shew us thy mercie, and we shall be saved. Lord heare our praier, and let our crie come unto thee. Let us praie.

O Lord God almightie, as thou warnedst by thine angell, the three kings of *Cullen, Jasper, Melchior*, and *Balthasar*, when they came with worshipfull presents towards *Bethleem: Jasper* brought myrrh; *Melchior*, incense; *Balthasar*, gold; worshipping the high king of all the world, Jesus Gods sonne of heaven, the second person in trinitie, being borne of the holie and cleane virgine S. *Marie*, queene of heaven, empresse of hell, and ladie of all the world: at that time the holie angell *Gabriel* warned and bad the foresaid three kings, that they should take another waie, for dread of perill, that *Herod* the king by his ordi-

Gaspar,
Balthsar
and Mel-
chior, who
followed
the starre,
wherin was
yᵉ image of
a litle babe
bearing a
crosse: if
*Longa legē-
da Coloniæ*
lie not.

nance would have destroied these three noble kings, that meekelie sought out our Lord and saviour. As wittilie and truelie as these three kings turned for dread, and tooke another waie: so wiselie and so truelie, O Lord GOD, of thy mightifull mercie, blesse us now at this time, for thy blessed passion save us, and keepe us all together from all evill; and thy holie angell defend us. Let us praie.

O Lord, king of all kings, which conteinest the throne of heavens, and beholdest all deepes, weighest the hilles, and shuttest up with thy hand the earth; heare us, most meekest GOD, and grant unto us (being unworthie) according to thy great mercie, to have the veritie and vertue of knowledge of hidden treasures by this spirit invocated, through thy helpe O Lord Jesus Christ, to whome be all honour and glorie, from worlds to worlds everlastinglie, Amen. Then saie these names ✠ *Helie* ✠ *helyon* ✠ *esseiere* ✠ *Deus æternus* ✠ *eloy* ✠ *clemens* ✠ *heloye* ✠ *Deus sanctus* ✠ *sabaoth* ✠ *Deus exercituum* ✠ *adonay* ✠ *Deus mirabilis* ✠ *iao* ✠ *verax* ✠ *anepheneton* ✠ *Deus ineffabilis* ✠ *sodoy* ✠ *dominator dominus* ✠ *ôn fortissimus* ✠ *Deus* ✠ *qui*, the which wouldest be praied unto of sinners: receive (we beseech thee) these sacrifices of praise, and our meeke praiers, which we unworthie doo offer unto thy divine majestie. Deliver us, and have mercie upon us, and prevent with thy holie spirit this worke, and with thy blessed helpe to followe after; that this our worke begunne of thee, may be ended by thy mightie power, Amen. Then saie this anon after ✠ *Homo* ✠ *sacarus* ✠ *museolameas* ✠ *cherubozca* ✠ being the figure upon thy brest aforesaid, the girdle about thee, the circle made, blesse the circle with holie water, and sit downe in the middest, and read this conjuration as followeth, sitting backe to backe at the first time.

I exorcise and conjure Bealphares, the practiser and preceptor of this art, by the maker of heavens and of earth, and by his vertue, and by his unspeakable name *Tetragrammaton*, and by all the holie sacraments, and by the holie majestie and deitie of the living God. I conjure and exorcise thee *Bealphares* by the vertue of all angels, archangels, thrones, dominations, principats, potestats, virtutes, cherubim and seraphim, and by their vertues, and by the most truest and speciallest name of your maister, that you doo come unto us, in faire forme of man or womankind, here visiblie, before this circle, and not terrible by anie manner of waies. This circle being our tuition and protection, by the mercifull goodnes of our Lord and Saviour Jesus Christ, and that you doo make answer truelie, without craft or deceipt, unto all my demands and questions, by the vertue and power of our Lord Jesus Christ, Amen.

Which must
be environed
with a
goodlie
companie
of crosses.

CHAPTER XIV.

To bind the spirit Bealphares, and to lose him againe.

NOW when he is appeared, bind him with these words which followe. ¶ I conjure thee *Bealphares*, by God the father, by God the sonne, and by God the Holie-ghost, and by all the holie companie in heaven; and by their vertues and powers I charge thee *Bealphares*, that thou shalt not depart out of my sight, nor yet to alter thy bodilie shape, that thou art appeared in, nor anie power shalt thou have of our bodies or soules, earthlie or ghostlie, but to be obedient to me, and to the words of my conjuration, that be written in this booke. I conjure thee *Bealphares*, by all angels and archangels, thrones, dominations, principats, potestats, virtutes, cherubim and seraphim, and by their vertues and powers. I conjure and charge, bind and constreine thee *Bealphares*, by all the riall words aforesaid, and by their vertues, that thou be obedient unto me, and to come and appeare visiblie unto me, and that in all daies, houres, and

242

minuts, whersoever I be, being called by the vertue of our Lord Jesu Christ, the which words are written in this booke. Looke readie thou be to appeare unto me, and to give me good counsell, how to come by treasures hidden in the earth, or in the water, and how to come to dignitie and knowledge of all things, that is to saie, of the magike art, and of grammar, dialectike, rhetorike, arythmetike, musike, geometrie, and of astronomie, and in all other things my will quicklie to be fulfilled : I charge thee upon paine of everlasting condemnation, *Fiat, fiat, fiat,* Amen.

On sundaies, festivall daies, and holie daies, none excepted.

When he is thus bound, aske him what thing thou wilt, and he will tell thee, and give thee all things that thou wilt request of him, without anie sacrifice dooing to him, and without forsaking thy God, that is, thy maker. And when the spirit hath fulfilled thy will and intent, give him licence to depart as followeth.

He dares doo no other being so conjured I trowe.

A licence for the spirit to depart.

Go unto the place predestinated and appointed for thee, where thy Lord GOD hath appointed thee, untill I shall call thee againe. Be thou readie unto me and to my call, as often as I shall call thee, upon paine of everlasting damnation. And if thou wilt, thou maiest recite, two or three times, the last conjuration, untill thou doo come to this tearme, *In throno.* If he will not depart, and then say *In throno,* that thou depart from this place, without hurt or damage of anie bodie, or of anie deed to be doone; that all creatures may knowe, that our Lord is of all power, most mightiest, and that there is none other God but he, which is three, and one, living for ever and ever. And the malediction of God the father omnipotent, the sonne and the holie ghost, descend upon thee, and dwell alwaies with thee, except thou doo depart without damage of us, or of any creature, or anie other evill deed to be doone: & thou to go to the place predestinated. And by our Lord Jesus Christ I doo else send thee to the great pit of hell, except (I saie) that thou depart to the place, whereas thy Lord God hath appointed thee. And see thou be readie to me and to my call, at all times and places, at mine owne will and pleasure, daie or night, without damage or hurt of me, or of anie creature; upon paine of everlasting damnation : *Fiat, fiat, fiat;* Amen, Amen. ¶ The peace of Jesus Christ bee betweene us and you; in the name of the father, and of the sonne, and of the Holie-ghost; Amen. *Per crucis hoc* ✠ *signum, &c.* Saie *In principio erat verbum, & verbum erat apud Deum;* In the beginning was the word, and the word was with God, and God was the word: and so forward, as followeth in the first chapter of saint *Johns* Gospell, staieng at these words, Full of grace and truth: to whom be all honour and glorie world without end, Amen.

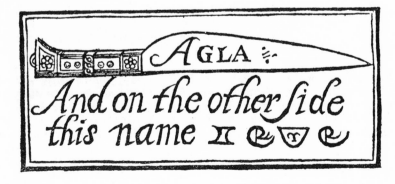

The fashion or forme of the conjuring knife, with the names theron to bee graven or written.

A type or figure of the circle for the maister and his fellowes to sit in, shewing how and after what fashion it should be made.

This is the circle for the maister to sit in, and his fellowe or fellowes, at the first calling, sit backe to backe, when he calleth the spirit; and for the fairies make this circle with chalke on the ground, as is said before. This spirit *Bealphares* being once called and found, shall never have power to hurt thee. Call him in the houre of ♃ or ♀ the ☽ increasing.

CHAPTER XV.

The making of the holie water.

Absque exorcismo sal non sit sanctus.

EXORCISO *te creaturam salis, per Deum vivum* ✠ *per Deum* ✠ *verum* ✠ *per Deum sanctum* ✠ *per Deum qui te per Elizæum prophetam in aquam mitti jussit, ut sanaretur sterilitas aquæ, ut efficiaris sal exorcisatus in salutem credentium; ut sis omnibus te sumentibus sanitas animæ & corporis, & effugiat atque discedat ab eo loco, qui aspersus fuerit omnis phantasia & nequitia, vel versutia diabolicæ fraudis, omnisq; spiritus immundus, adjuratus per eum, qui venturus est judicare vivos & mortuos, & sæculum per ignem, Amen. Oremus:*

Immensam clementiam tuam, omnipotens ceterne Deus, humiliter imploramus, ut hanc creaturam salis, quam in usum generis humani tribuisti, bene ✠ *dicere & sancti* ✠ *ficare tua pietate digneris, ut sit omnibus sumentibus salus mentis & corporis, ut quicquid ex eo tactum fuerit, vel respersum, careat omni immundicia, omniq; impugnatione spiritualis nequitiæ, per Dominum nostrum Jesum Christum filium tuum, qui tecum vivit & regnat in unitate spiritus sancti, Deus per omnia sæcula sæculorum, Amen.*

To the water saie also as followeth.

Exorciso te creaturam aquæ in nomine ✠ patris ✠ & Jesu Christi filii ejus Domini nostri, & in virtute spiritus ✠ sancti ✠ ut fias aqua exorcisata, ad effugandam omnem potestatem inimici, & ipsum inimicum eradicare & explantare valeas, cum angelis suis apostatis, per virtutem ejusdem Domini nostri Jesu Christi, qui venturus est judicare vivos & mortuos, & sæculum per ignem, Amen. Oremus:

Deus, qui ad salutem humani generis maxima quæque sacramenta in aquarum substantia condidisti, adesto propitius invocationibus nostris, & elemento huic multimodis purificationibus præparato, virtutem tuæ bene✠dictionis infunde, ut creatura tua mysteriis tuis serviens, ad abigendos dæmones, morbosq; pellendos, divinæ gratiæ sumat effectum, ut quicquid in domibus, vel in locis fidelium hæc unda resperserit, careat omni immundicia, liberetur à noxa, non illic resideat spiritus pestilens, non aura corrumpens, discedant omnes insidiæ latentis inimici, & si quid est, quod aut incolumitati habitantium invidet aut quieti, aspersione hujus aquæ effugiat, ut salubritas per invocationem sancti tui nominis expetita ab omnibus sit impugnationibus defensa, per Dominum nostrum Jesum Christum filium tuum, qui tecum vivit & regnat, in unitate spiritus sancti Deus per omnia sæcula sæculorum, Amen.

Then take the salt in thy hand, and saie putting it into the water, making in the maner of a crosse.

Commixtio salis & aquæ pariter fiat, in nomine patris, & filii, & spiritus sancti, Amen. Dominus vobiscum, Et cum spiritu tuo, Oremus: ¶ Deus invictæ virtutis author, & insuperabilis imperii rex, ac semper magnificus triumphator, qui adversæ dominationis vires reprimis, qui inimici rugientis sævitiam superas, qui hostiles nequitias potens expugnas; te Domine trementes & supplices deprecamur ac petimus, ut hanc creaturam salis & aquæ aspicias, benignus illustres, pietatis tuæ rore sancti fices, ubicunq; fuerit aspersa, per invocationem sancti tui nominis, omnis infestatio immundi spiritus abjiciatur, terrórq; venenosi serpentis procul pellatur, & præsentia sancti spiritus nobis misericordiam tuam poscentibus ubiq; adesse dignetur, per Dominum nostrum Jesum Christum filium tuum, qui tecum vivit & regnat in unitate spiritus sancti Deus per omnia sæcula sæculorum, Amen.

Oratio ad Deum ut sali exorcisato vires addat.

Then sprinkle upon anie thing, and saie as followeth.

Asperges me Domine hyssopo, & mundabor, lavabis me, & supra nivem dealbabor. Miserere mei Deus, secundum magnam misericordiam tuam, & supra nivem dealbabor. Gloria patri, & filio, & spiritui sancto: Sicut erat in principio, & nunc, & semper, & in sæcula sæculorum, Amen. Et supra nivem dealbabor, asperges me, &c. Ostende nobis Domine misericordiam tuam, & salutare tuum da nobis; exaudi nos Domine sancte, pater omnipotens, æterne Deus, & mittere dignare sanctum angelum tuum de cælis, qui custodiat, foveat, visitet, & defendat omnes habitantes in hoc habitaculo, per Christum Dominum nostrum, Amen, Amen.

Oratio, in qua dicenda, exorcista sese sacri laticis aspergine debes perrorare.

CHAPTER XVI.

To make a spirit to appeare in a christall.

I DOO conjure thee *N.* by the father, and the sonne, and the Holie-ghost, the which is the beginning and the ending, the first and the last, and by the latter daie of judgement, that thou *N.* doo appeare, in this christall stone, or anie other instrument, at my pleasure, to mee and to my felow, gentlie and beautifullie, in faire forme of a boy of twelve yeares of age, without hurt or damage of anie of our bodies or soules; and certeinlie to informe and to shew me, without anie guile or craft, all that we doo desire or demand of thee to know, by the vertue of him, which shall come to judge the quicke and the dead, and the world by fier, Amen.

Marke how
consonant
this is with
poperie, &c.

Also I conjure and exorcise thee *N.* by the sacrament of the altar, and by the substance therof, by the wisedome of Christ, by the sea, and by his vertue, by the earth, & by all things that are above the earth, and by their vertues, by the ☉ and the ☽ by ♄ ♃ ♂ and ♀ and by their vertues, by the apostles, martyrs, confessors, and the virgins and widowes, and the chast, and by all saints of men or of women, and innocents, and by their vertues, by all the angels and archangels, thrones, dominations, principats, potestats, virtutes, cherubim, and seraphim, and by their vertues, & by the holie names of God, *Tetragrammaton, El, Ousion, Agla,* and by all the other holie names of God, and by their vertues, by the circumcision, passion, and resurrection of our Lord Jesus Christ, by the heavines of our ladie the virgine, and by the joy which she had when she sawe hir sonne rise from death to life, that thou *N.* doo appeare in this christall stone, or in anie other instrument, at my pleasure, to me and to my felow, gentlie, and beautifullie, and visiblie, in faire forme of a child of twelve yeares of age, without hurt or damage of anie of our bodies or soules, and trulie to informe and shew unto me & to my felow, without fraud or guile, all things according to thine oth and promise to me, whatsoever I shall demand or desire of thee, without anie hinderance or tarrieng, and this conjuration be read of me three times, upon paine of eternall condemnation, to the last daie of judgement : *Fiat, fiat, fiat,* Amen.

For hidden
treasure.

And when he is appeared, bind him with the bond of the dead above written : then saie as followeth. ¶ I charge thee *N.* by the father, to shew me true visions in this christall stone, if there be anie treasure hidden in such a place *N.* & wherin it lieth, and how manie foot from this peece of earth, east, west, north, or south.

CHAPTER XVII.

An experiment of the dead.

FIRST go and get of some person that shalbe put to death, a promise, and sweare an oth unto him, that if he will come to thee, after his death, his spirit to be with thee, and to remaine with thee all the daies of thy life, and will doo thee true service, as it is conteined in the oth and promise following.

Promises &
oths inter-
changeablie
made be-
tweene the
conjuror &
the spirit.

Then laie thy hand on thy booke, and sweare this oth unto him. I *N.* doo sweare and promise to thee *N.* to give for thee an almesse everie moneth, and also to praie for thee once in everie weeke, to saie the Lords praier for thee, and so to continue all the daies of my life, as God me helpe and holie doome, and by the contents of this booke. Amen.

Then let him make his oth to thee as followeth, and let him saie after thee, laieng his hand upon the booke. ¶ I *N.* doo sweare this oth to thee *N.* by God the father omnipotent, by God the son Jesus Christ, and by his pretious bloud which hath redeemed all the world, by the which bloud I doo trust to be saved at the generall daie of judgment, and by the vertues therof, I *N.* doo sweare this oth to thee *N.* that my spirit that is within my bodie now, shall not ascend, nor descend, nor go to anie place of rest, but shall come to thee *N.* and be verie well pleased to remaine with thee *N.* all the daies of thy life, and so to be bound to thee *N.* and to appeare to thee *N.* in anie christall stone, glasse, or other mirror, and so to take it for my resting place. And that, so soone as my spirit is departed out of my bodie, streightwaie to be at your commandements, and that in and at all daies, nights, houres, and minutes, to be obedient unto thee *N.* being called of thee by the vertue of our Lord Jesu Christ, & out of hand to have common talke with thee at all times, and in all houres & minuts, to open and declare to thee *N.* the truth of all things present, past, and to come, and how to worke the magike art, and all other noble sciences, under the throne of

246

God. If I doo not performe this oth and promise to thee *N.* but doo flie from anie part thereof, then to be condemned for ever and ever. Amen.

Note the penaltie of breaking promise with the spirit.

Also I *N.* doo sweare to thee by God the Holie-ghost, and by the great wisedome that is in the divine Godhead, and by their vertues, and by all the holie angels, archangels, thrones, dominations, principats, potestats, virtutes, cherubim and seraphim, and by all their vertues doo I *N.* sweare, and promise thee to be obedient as is rehearsed. And heere, for a witnesse, doo I *N.* give thee *N.* my right hand, and doo plight thee my faith and troth, as God me helpe and holiedoome. And by the holie contents in this booke doo I *N.* sweare, that my spirit shall be thy true servant, all the daies of thy life, as is before rehearsed. And here for a witnesse, that my spirit shall be obedient to thee *N.* and to those bonds of words that be written in this *N.* before the bonds of words shall be rehearsed thrise; else to be damned for ever: and thereto saie all faithfull soules and spirits, Amen, Amen.

Then let him sweare this oth three times, and at everie time kisse the booke, and at everie time make marks to the bond. Then perceiving the time that he will depart, get awaie the people from you, and get or take your stone or glasse, or other thing in your hand, and saie the *Pater noster, Ave,* and *Credo,* and this praier as followeth. And in all the time of his departing, rehearse the bonds of words; and in the end of everie bond, saie oftentimes; Remember thine oth and promise. And bind him stronglie to thee, and to thy stone, and suffer him not to depart, reading thy bond 24 times. And everie daie when you doo call him by your other bond, bind him stronglie by the first bond: by the space of 24 daies applie it, & thou shalt be made a man for ever.

Three times, in reverence (peradventure) of the Trinitie, P. F. S S.

Now the Pater noster, Ave, and Credo must be said, and then the praier immediatlie following.

O God of *Abraham,* God of *Isaac,* God of *Jacob,* God of *Tobias;* the which diddest deliver the three children from the hot burning oven, *Sidrac, Misac* and *Abdenago,* and *Susanna* from the false crime, and *Daniel* from the lions power: even so O Lord omnipotent, I beseech thee, for thy great mercie sake, to helpe me in these my works, and to deliver me this spirit of *N.* that he may be a true subject to me *N.* all the daies of my life, and to remaine with me, and with this *N.* all the daies of my life. O glorious God, Father, Sonne, and Holie-ghost, I beseech thee to help me at this time, and to give me power by thine holie name, merits and vertues, wherby I may conjure & constreine this spirit of *N.* that he may be obedient unto me, and may fulfill his oth and promise, at all times, by the power of all thine holines. This grant O Lord God of hosts, as thou art righteous and holy, and as thou art the word, and the word God, the beginning and the end, sitting in the thrones of thine everlasting kingdoms, & in the divinitie of thine everlasting Godhead, to whom be all honour and glorie, now and for ever and ever, Amen, Amen.

CHAPTER XVIII.

A bond to bind him to thee, and to thy N. as followeth.

I *N.* conjure and constreine the spirit of *N.* by the living God, by the true God, and by the holie God, and by their vertues and powers I conjure and constreine the spirit of thee *N.* that thou shalt not ascend nor descend out of thy bodie, to no place of rest, but onelie to take thy resting place with *N.* and with this *N.* all the daies of my life, according to thine oth and promise. I conjure and constreine the spirit of *N.* by these holie names of God ✠ *Tetragram-*

Note the summe of this obligation or bond.

maton ✠ *Adonay* ✠ *Agla* ✠ *Saday* ✠ *Sabaoth* ✠ *planabothe* ✠ *panthon* ✠ *craton* ✠ *neupmaton* ✠ *Deus* ✠ *homo* ✠ *omnipotens* ✠ *sempiternus* ✠ *ysus* ✠ *terra* ✠ *unigenitus* ✠ *salvator* ✠ *via* ✠ *vita* ✠ *manus* ✠ *fons* ✠ *origo* ✠ *filius* ✠ and by their vertues and powers I conjure and constreine the spirit of *N.* that thou shalt not rest nor remaine in the fier, nor in the water, in the aier, nor in anie privie place of the earth, but onelie with me *N.* and with this *N.* all the daies of my life. I charge the spirit of *N.* upon paine of everlasting condemnation, remember thine oth and promise. Also I conjure the spirit of *N.* and constreine thee by the excellent name of Jesus Christ, *A* and *Ω*, the first and the last; for this holie name of Jesus is above all names, for unto it all knees doo bow and obey, both of heavenlie things, earthlie things, and infernalles. Nor is there anie other name given to man, whereby we have anie salvation, but by the name of Jesus. Therefore by the name, and in the name of Jesus of *Nazareth,* and by his nativitie, resurrection and ascension, and by all that apperteineth to his passion, and by their vertues and powers, I doo conjure and constreine the spirit of *N.* that thou shalt not take anie resting place in the ☉ nor in the ☽ nor in ♄ nor in ♃ nor in ♂ nor in ♀ nor in ☿ nor in anie of the twelve signes, nor in the concavitie of the clouds, nor in anie other privie place, to rest or staie in, but onelie with me *N.* or with this *N.* all the daies of my life. If thou be not obedient unto me, according to thine oth and promise, I *N.* doo condemne the spirit of *N.* into the pit of hell for ever, Amen.

I conjure and constreine the spirit of *N.* by the bloud of the innocent lambe Jesus Christ, the which was shed upon the crosse, for all those that doo obeie unto it, and beleeve in it, shall be saved and by the vertue thereof, and by all the aforesaid riall names and words of the living God by mee pronounced, I doo conjure and constreine the spirit of *N.* that thou be obedient unto me, according to thine oth and promise. If thou doo refuse to doo as is aforesaid, I *N.* by the holie trinitie, and by his vertue and power doo comdemne the spirit of *N.* into the place whereas there is no hope of remedie, but everlasting condemnation, and horror, and paine upon paine, dailie, horriblie, & lamentablie the paines there to be augmented, so thicke as the stars in the firmament, and as the gravell sand in the sea : except thou spirit of *N.* obeie me *N.* as is afore rehearsed ; else I *N.* doo condemne the spirit of *N.* into the pit of everlasting condemnation ; *Fiat, fiat,* Amen. Also I conjure thee, and constreine the spirit of *N.* by all angels, archangels, thrones, dominations, principats, potestats, virtutes, cherubim & seraphim, & by the foure evangelists, *Matthew, Marke, Luke,* and *John,* and by all things conteined in the old lawe and the new, and by their vertues, and by the twelve apostles, and by all patriarchs, prophets, martyrs, confessors, virgins, innocents, and by all the elect and chosen, is, and shall be, which followeth the lambe of God ; and by their vertues and powers I conjure and constreine the spirit of *N.* stronglie, to have common talke with me, at all times, and in all daies, nights, houres, and minuts, and to talke in my mother toong plainelie, that I may heare it, and understand it, declaring the truth unto me of all things, according to thine oth and promise ; else to be condemned for ever ; *Fiat, fiat,* Amen.

Also I conjure and constreine the spirit of *N.* by the golden girdle, which girded the loines of our Lord Jesus Christ, so thou spirit of *N.* be thou bound, and cast into the pit of everlasting condemnation, for thy great disobedience and unreverent regard that thou hast to the holie names and words of God almightie, by me pronounced : *Fiat,* Amen.

Also I conjure, constreine, command, and bind the spirit of *N.* by the two edged sword, which *John* saw proceed out of the mouth of God almightie : except thou be obedient as is aforesaid, the sword cut thee in peeces, and condemne thee into the pit of everlasting paines, where the fier goeth not out, and where the worme dieth not ; *Fiat, fiat, fiat,* Amen.

Also I conjure and constreine the spirit of *N.* by the throne of the Godhead, and by all the heavens under him, and by the celestiall citie new *Jerusalem,* and by the earth, by the sea, and by all things created and conteined therein, and by their vertues and powers, and by all the infernalles, and by their vertues and powers, and all things conteined therein, and by their vertues and powers, I

Marginal notes:

Scripture as well applied of the conjuror, as that of satan in tempting Christ, Matth. 4, 6.

Note what sore penalties the spirit is injoined to suffer for disobedience.

There is no mention made in the gospels that Christ was woorth a golden girdle. Bugs words.

conjure and constreine the spirit of *N.* that now immediatlie thou be obedient unto me, at all times hereafter, and to those words of me pronounced, according to thine oth and promise: else let the great cursse of God, the anger of God, the shadowe and darknesse of everlasting condemnation be upon thee thou spirit of *N.* for ever and ever, bicause thou hast denied thine health, thy faith, and salvation, for thy great disobedience thou are worthie to be condemned. Therefore let the divine trinitie, angels, and archangels, thrones, dominations, principats, potestates, virtues, cherubim and seraphim, and all the soules of the saints, that shall stand on the right hand of our Lord Jesus Christ, at the generall daie of judgement, condemne the spirit of *N.* for ever and ever, and be a witnesse against thee, bicause of thy great disobedience, in and against thy promises, *Fiat, fiat,* Amen.

Being thus bound, he must needs be obedient unto thee, whether he will or no: proove this. And here followeth a bond to call him to your *N.* and to shew you true visions at all times, as in the houre of ♄ to bind or inchant anie thing, and in the houre of ♃ for peace and concord, in the houre of ♂ to marre, to destroie, and to make sicke, in the houre of the ☉ to bind toongs and other bonds of men, in the houre of ♀ to increase love, joy, and good will, in the houre of ☿ to put awaie enimitie or hatred, to know of theft, in the houre of the ☽ for love, goodwill and concord, ♄ lead ♃ tinne ♂ iron ☉ gold ♀ coppar ☿ quicksilver ☽ silver, &c.

Is it possible to be greater than S. Adelberts cursse? *See in Habar. lib.* 12. *ca.* 17: *pag.* 149. 150.

CHAPTER XIX.

This bond as followeth, is to call him into your christall stone, or glasse, &c.

ALSO I doo conjure thee spirit *N.* by God the father, by God the sonne, and by God the holie-ghost, *A* and *Ω*, the first and the last, and by the latter daie of judgement, of them which shall come to judge the quicke and the dead, and the world by fier, and by their vertues and powers I constreine thee spirit *N.* to come to him that holdeth the christall stone in his hand, & to appeare visiblie, as hereafter foloweth. Also I conjure thee spirit *N.* by these holie names of God ✠ *Tetragrammaton* ✠ *Adonay* ✠ *El* ✠ *Ousion* ✠ *Agla* ✠ *Jesus* ✠ *of Nazareth* ✠ and by the vertues thereof, and by his nativitie, death, buriall, resurrection, and ascension, and by all other things apperteining unto his passion, and by the blessed virgine Marie mother of our Lord Jesu Christ, and by all the joy which shee had when shee saw hir sonne rise from death to life, and by the vertues and powers therof I constreine thee spirit *N.* to come into the christall stone, & to appeare visiblie, as herafter shalbe declared. Also I conjure thee *N.* thou spirit, by all angels, archangels, thrones, dominations, principats, potestats, virtues, cherubim and seraphim, and by the ☉ ☽ ♄ ♃ ♂ ♀ ☿, and by the twelve signes, and by their vertues and powers, and by all things created and confirmed in the firmament, and by their vertues & powers I constreine thee spirit *N.* to appeare visiblie in that christall stone, in faire forme and shape of a white angell, a greene angell, a blacke angell, a man, a woman, a boie, a maiden virgine, a white grehound, a divell with great hornes, without anie hurt or danger of our bodies or soules, and trulie to informe and shew unto us, true visions of all things in that christall stone, according to thine oth and promise, and that without anie hinderance or tarrieng, to appeare visiblie, by this bond of words read over by mee three times, upon paine of everlasting condemnation; *Fiat, fiat,* Amen.

A popish supplement.

Belike he had the gift to appeare in sundrie shapes, as it is said of *Proteus* in *Ovid lib. metamor.* 8. *fab.* 10: and of *Vertumnus ; lib. metamor.* 14. *fab.* 16.

Then being appeared, saie these words following.

I conjure thee spirit, by God the father, that thou shew true visions in that christall stone, where there be anie *N.* in such a place or no, upon paine of everlasting condemnation, *Fiat*, Amen. Also I conjure thee spirit *N.* by God the sonne Jesus Christ, that thou doo shew true visions unto us, whether it be gold or silver, or anie other metals, or whether there were anie or no, upon paine of condemnation, *Fiat*, Amen. Also I conjure thee spirit *N.* by God the Holie-ghost, the which dooth sanctifie all faithfull soules and spirits, and by their vertues and powers I constreine thee spirit *N.* to speake, open, and to declare, the true waie, how we may come by these treasures hidden in *N.* and how to have it in our custodie, & who are the keepers thereof, and how manie there be, and what be their names, and by whom it was laid there, and to shew me true visions of what sort and similitude they be, and how long they have kept it, and to knowe in what daies and houres we shall call such a spirit, *N.* to bring unto us these treasures, into such a place *N.* upon paine of everlasting condemnation ✠ Also I constreine thee spirit *N.* by all angels, archangels, thrones, dominations, principats, potestats, virtutes, cherubim & seraphim, that you doo shew a true vision in this christall stone, who did conveie or steale away such a *N.* and where it is, & who hath it, and how farre off, and what is his or hir name, and how and when to come unto it, upon paine of eternall condemnation, *Fiat*, Amen. Also I conjure thee spirit *N.* by the ☉ ☽ ♄ ♃ ♂ ♀ ☿ and by all the characters in the firmament, that thou doo shew unto me a true vision in this christall stone, where such *N.* and in what state he is, and how long he hath beene there, and what time he will be in such a place, what daie and houre: and this and all other things to declare plainelie, in paine of hell fier; *Fiat*, Amen.

Note that the spirit is tied to obediēce under paine of condemnation and hell fier.

A licence to depart.

Depart out of the sight of this christall stone in peace for a time, and readie to appeare therein againe at anie time or times I shall call thee, by the vertue of our Lord Jesus Christ, and by the bonds of words which are written in this booke, and to appeere visiblie, as the words be rehersed. I constreine thee spirit *N.* by the divinitie of the Godhead, to be obedient unto these words rehearsed, upon paine of everlasting condemnation, both in this world, and in the world to come; *Fiat, fiat, fiat*, Amen.

CHAPTER XX.

When to talke with spirits, and to have true answers to find out a theefe.

THE daies and houres of ♄ ♂ ☿ and the ☽ is best to doo all crafts of necromancie, & for to speake with spirits, and for to find theft, and to have true answer thereof, or of anie other such like. ¶ And in the daies and houres of ☉ ♃ ♀ is best to doo all experiments of love, and to purchase grace, and for to be invisible, and to doo anie operation, whatsoever it be, for anie thing, the ☽ being in a convenient signe. ¶ As when thou laborest for theft, see the moone be in an earthie signe, as ♉ ♍ ♑, or of the aier, as ♊ ♎ ♒. ¶ And if it be for love, favor or grace, let the ☽ be in a signe of the fier, as ♈ ♌ ♐, and for hatred, in a signe of the water, as ♋ ♏ ♓. For anie other experiment, let the ☽ be in ♈. ¶ And if thou findest the ☉ & the ☽ in one signe that is called in even number, then thou maiest write, consecrate, conjure, and make readie all maner of things that thou wilt doo, &c.

This is condemned for ranke follie by the doctors: as by *Chrysos. sup. Matth. Gregor. in homil. sup. Epiphan. Domini ;* and others.

To speake with spirits.

Call these names, *Orimoth, Belimoth, Lymocke,* and say thus: I conjure you up by the names of the angels *Satur* and *Azimor,* that you intend to me in this houre, and send unto me a spirit called *Sagrigrit,* that hee doo fulfill my commandement and desire, and that also can understand my words for one or two yeares, or as long as I will, *&c.*

CHAPTER XXI.

A confutation of conjuration, especiallie of the raising, binding and dismissing of the divell, of going invisible, and other lewd practises.

THUS farre have we waded in shewing at large the vanitie of necromancers, conjurors, and such as pretend to have reall conference and consultation with spirits and divels: wherein (I trust) you see what notorious blasphemie is committed, besides other blind superstitious ceremonies, a disordered heap, which are so far from building up the endevors of these blacke art practitioners, that they doo altogether ruinate & overthrow them, making them in their follies and falshoods as bare and naked as an anatomie. As for these ridiculous conjurations, last rehearsed, being of no small reputation among the ignorant, they are for the most part made by *T. R.* (for so much of his name he bewraieth) and *John Cokars,* invented and devised for the augmentation and maintenance of their living, for the edifieng of the poore, and for the propagating and inlarging of Gods glorie, as in the beginning of their booke of conjurations they protest; which in this place, for the further manifestation of their impietie, and of the witchmongers follie and credulitie, I thought good to insert, whereby the residue of their proceedings may be judged, or rather detected. For if we seriouslie behold the matter of conjuration, and the drift of conjurors, we shall find them, in mine opinion, more faultie than such as take upon them to be witches, as manifest offenders against the majestie of God, and his holie lawe, and as apparent violators of the lawes and quietnesse of this realme: although indeed they bring no such thing to passe, as is surmised and urged by credulous persons, couseners, liers, and witchmongers. For these are alwaies learned, and rather abusers of others, than they themselves by others abused.

    But let us see what appearance of truth or possibilitie is wrapped within these mysteries, and let us unfold the deceipt. They have made choice of certeine words, whereby they saie they can worke miracles, &c. And first of all, that they call divels & soules out of hell (though we find in the scriptures manifest proofes that all passages are stopped concerning the egresse out of hell) so as they may go thither, but they shall never get out, for *Ab inferno nulla est redemptio,* out of hell there is no redemption. Well, when they have gotten them up, they shut them in a circle made with chalke, which is so stronglie beset and invironed with crosses and names, that they cannot for their lives get out; which is a verie probable matter. Then can they bind them, and lose them at their pleasures, and make them that have beene liers from the beginning, to tell the truth: yea, they can compell them to doo anie thing. And the divels are forced to be obedient unto them, and yet cannot be brought to due obedience unto God their creator. This done (I saie) they can worke all maner of miracles (saving blew miracles) and this is beleeved of manie to be true:

    Tam credula mens hominis, & arrectæ fabulis aures,

      So light of beleefe is the mind of man,
      And attentive to tales his eares now and than.

Marginal notes:

All the former practises breeflie confuted.

See the title of the booke, with the authors intent, in a marginall note, pag. 224.

Luk. 16. &c.

An ironicall confutation.

Englished by Abraham Fleming.

251

But if Christ (onelie for a time) left the power of working miracles among his apostles and disciples for the confirmation of his gospell, and the faith of his elect: yet I denie altogether, that he left that power with these knaves, which hide their cousening purposes under those lewd and foolish words, according to that which *Peter* saith; With feined words they make merchandize of you. And therfore the counsell is good that *Paule* giveth us, when he biddeth us take heed that no man deceive us with vaine words. For it is the Lord only that worketh great woonders, and bringeth mightie things to passe. It is also written, that Gods word, and not the words of conjurors, or the charmes of witches, healeth all things, maketh tempests, and stilleth them.

But put case the divell could be fetched up and fettered, and loosed againe at their pleasure, &c: I marvell yet, that anie can be so bewitched, as to be made to beleeve, that by vertue of their words, anie earthlie creature can be made invisible. We thinke it a lie, to saie that white is blacke, and blacke white: but it is a more shamelesse assertion to affirme, that white is not, or blacke is not at all; and yet more impudencie to hold that a man is a horsse; but most apparent impudencie to saie, that a man is no man, or to be extenuated into such a quantitie, as therby he may be invisible, and yet remaine in life and health, &c: and that in the cleare light of the daie, even in the presence of them that are not blind. But surelie, he that cannot make one haire white or blacke, whereof (on the other side) not one falleth from the head without Gods speciall providence, can never bring to passe, that the visible creature of God shall become nothing, or lose the vertue and grace powred therinto by God the creator of all things.

If they saie that the divell covereth them with a cloud or veile, as *M. Mal.* *Bodin*, & manie other doo affirme; yet (me thinkes) we should either see the cover, or the thing covered. And though perchance they saie in their harts; Tush, the Lord seeth not, who indeed hath blinded them, so as seeing, they see not: yet they shall never be able to persuade the wise, but that both God and man dooth see both them and their knaverie in this behalfe. I have heard of a foole, who was made beleeve that he should go invisible, and naked; while he was well whipped by them, who (as he thought) could not see him. Into which fooles paradise they saie he was brought, that enterprised to kill the prince of Orenge.

Anastro both Spaniards. Ann. Dom. 1582. March 18. after dinner upon a sundaie this mischeefe was done. Read the whole discourse hereof printed at London for Tho: Chard and Will: Brome booksellers.

2. Pet. 2.
Ephes. 5.
Ps. 72, & 78.

Sap. 16.
Ecclus. 43.

To denie the subsistence or naturall being of a thing mater-iall and visible is impudēcie.

Ezec. 8. & 9.
Isai. 6, & 26 and 30.

John Jaure-gui servant to Gasper

CHAPTER XXII.

A comparison betweene popish exorcists and other conjurors, a popish conjuration published by a great doctor of the Romish church, his rules and cautions.

I SEE no difference betweene these and popish conjurations; for they agree in order, words, and matter, differing in no circumstance, but that the papists doo it without shame openlie, the other doo it in hugger mugger secretlie. The papists (I saie) have officers in this behalfe, which are called exorcists or conjurors, and they looke narrowlie to other cousenors, as having gotten the upper hand over them. And bicause the papists shall be without excuse in this behalfe, and that the world may see their cousenage, impietie, and follie to be as great as the others, I will cite one conjuration (of which sort I might cite a hundred) published by *Jacobus de Chusa*, a great doctor of the Romish church, which serveth to find out the cause of noise and spirituall rumbling in houses, churches, or chappels, and to conjure walking spirits: which evermore is knaverie and cousenage in the highest degree. Marke the cousening devise hereof, and conferre the impietie with the others.

Jac. de Chusæ in lib. de ap-paritionib. quorundam spirituum.

252

First (forsooth) he saith it is expedient to fast three daies, and to celebrate a certeine number of masses, and to repeate the seven psalmes penitentiall: then foure or five preests must be called to the place where the haunt or noise is, then a candle hallowed on candlemas daie must be lighted, and in the lighting thereof also must the seven psalmes be said, and the gospell of S. *John.* Then there must be a crosse and a censer with frankincense, and therewithall the place must be censed or perfumed, holie water must be sprinkled, and a holie stoale must be used, and (after diverse other ceremonies) a praier to God must be made, in maner and forme following:

Observations for the exorcising preest.

O Lord Jesus Christ, the knower of all secrets, which alwaies revealest all hoalsome and profitable things to thy faithfull children, and which sufferest a spirit to shew himselfe in this place, we beseech thee for thy bitter passion, *&c*: vouchsafe to command this spirit, to reveale and signifie unto us thy servants, without our terror or hurt, what he is, to thine honour, and to his comfort; *In nomine patris,* &c. And then proceed in these words: We beseech thee, for Christs sake, O thou spirit, that if there be anie of us, or among us, whom thou wouldest answer, name him, or else manifest him by some signe. Is it frier *P.* or doctor *D.* or doctor *Burc.* or sir *Feats,* or sir *John,* or sir *Robert*: *Et sic de cæteris circunstantibus.* For it is well tried (saith the glosse) he will not answer everie one. If the spirit make anie sound of voice, or knocking, at the naming of anie one, he is the cousener (the conjuror I would saie) that must have the charge of this conjuration or examination. And these forsooth must be the interrogatories, to wit: Whose soule art thou? Wherefore camest thou? What wouldest thou have? Wantest thou any suffrages, masses, or almes? How manie masses will serve thy turne, three, six, ten, twentie, thirtie, *&c*? By what preest? Must he be religious or secular? Wilt thou have anie fasts? What? How manie? How great? And by what persons? Among hospitalles? Lepres? Or beggars? What shall be the signe of thy perfect deliverance? Wherefore liest thou in purgatorie? And such like. This must be doone in the night.

Memorandum that he must be the veriest knave or foole in all the companie.

If there appeare no signe at this houre, it must be deferred untill another houre. Holie water must be left in the place. There is no feare (they saie) that such a spirit will hurt the conjuror: for he can sinne no more, as being in the meane state betweene good and evill, and as yet in the state of satisfaction. If the spirit doo hurt, then it is a damned soule, and not an elect. Everie man may not be present hereat, speciallie such as be weake of complexion. They appeare in diverse maners, not alwaies in bodie, or bodilie shape (as it is read in the life of S. *Martine,* that the divell did) but sometimes invisible, as onelie by sound, voice, or noise. Thus farre *Jacobus de Chusa.*

These spirits are not so cunning by daie as by night. For so they might be bewraied. For so the cousenage may be best handled.

But bicause you shall see that these be not emptie words, nor slanders; but that in truth such things are commonlie put in practise in the Romish church, I will here set downe an instance, latelie and truelie, though lewdlie performed: and the same in effect as followeth.

CHAPTER XXIII.

A late experiment, or cousening conjuration practised at Orleance by the Franciscane Friers, how it was detected, and the judgement against the authors of that comedie.

IN the yeare of our Lord 1534. at *Orleance* in *France,* the Maiors wife died, willing and desiring to be buried without anie pompe or noise, *&c*. Hir husband, who reverenced the memoriall of hir, did even as she had willed him. And bicause she was buried in the church of the *Franciscans,* besides her father and grandfather, and gave them in reward onelie six crownes, whereas they hoped for a greater preie; shortlie after it chanced, that as he felled certeine

A cousening conjuration.

Of this order read noble stuffe in a booke printed at *Frankeford* under the title of *Alcoran. Franciscanorum*. Note how the Franciscans cannot conjure without a confederate.

woods and sold them, they desired him to give them some part thereof freelie without monie: which he flatlie denied. This they tooke verie greevouslie. And whereas before they misliked him, now they conceived such displeasure as they devised this meanes to be revenged; to wit, that his wife was damned for ever. The cheefe workemen and framers of this tragedie were *Colimannus*, and *Stephanus Aterbatensis*, both doctors of divinitie; this *Coliman.* was a great conjuror, & had all his implements in a readines, which he was woont to use in such busines. And thus they handled the matter. They place over the arches of the church, a yoong novice; who about midnight, when they came to mumble their praiers, as they were woont to do, maketh a great rumbling, and noise. Out of hand the moonks beganne to conjure and to charme, but he answered nothing. Then being required to give a signe, whether he were a dumme spirit or no, he beganne to rumble againe: which thing they tooke as a certeine signe. Having laid this foundation, they go unto certeine citizens, cheefe men, and such as favoured them, declaring that a heavie chance had happened at home in their monasterie; not shewing what the matter was, but desiring them to

O notorius impudencie! with such shamelesse faces to abuse so worshipfull a companie.

come to their mattens at midnight. When these citizens were come, and that praiers were begunne, the counterfet spirit beginneth to make a marvellous noise in the top of the church. And being asked what he meant, and who he was, gave signes that it was not lawfull for him to speake. Therefore they commanded him to make answer by tokens and signes to certeine things they would demand of him. Now was there a hole made in the vawt, through the which he might heare and understand the voice of the conjuror. And then had he in his hand a litle boord, which at everie question, he strake, in such sort as he might easilie be heard beneath. First they asked him, whether he were one of them that had beene buried in the same place. Afterwards they reckoning manie by name, which had been buried there; at the last also they name the Maiors wife: and there by and by the spirit gave a signe that he was hir soule. He was further asked, whether he were damned or no; and if he were, for what cause, for what desert, or fault; whether for covetousnes, or wanton lust, for pride or want of charitie; or whether it were for heresie, or for the sect of *Luther* newlie sproong up: also what he meant by that noise and stirre he kept there; whether it were to have the bodie now buried in holie ground to be digged up againe, and laid in some other place. To all which points he answered by signes, as he was commanded, by the which he affirmed or denied anie thing, according as he strake the boord twise or thrise together. And when he had thus given them

The confederate spirit was taught that lesson before.

to understand, that the verie cause of his damnation was *Luthers* heresie, and that the bodie must needs be digged up againe: the moonks requested the citizens, whose presence they had used or rather abused, that they would beare witnesse of those things which they had seene with their eies; and that they would subscribe to such things as were doone a few days before. The citizens taking good advise on the matter, least they should offend the Maior, or bring themselves in trouble, refused so to doo. But the moonks notwithstanding take from thence the sweete bread, which they called the host and bodie of our Lord, with all the relikes of saintes, and carrie them to another place, and there saie their masse. The bishops substitute judge (whome they called Officiall) understanding that matter, commeth thither, accompanied with certeine honest men, to the intent he might knowe the whole circumstance more exactlie: and therefore he commandeth them to make conjuration in his presence; and also he requireth certeine to be chosen to go up into the top of the vawt, and there to

For so might the confederate be found.

see whether any ghost appeered or not. *Stephanus Aterbatensis* stiffelie denied that to be lawfull, and marvellouslie persuading the contrarie, affirmed that the spirit in no wise ought to be troubled. And albeit the Official urged them verie much, that there might be some conjuring of the spirit; yet could he nothing prevaile.

Whilest these things were dooing, the Maior, when he had shewed the other Justices of the citie, what he would have them to doo, tooke his journie to the king, and opened the whole matter unto him. And bicause the moonks refused judgement upon plea of their owne lawes and liberties, the king choosing out certeine of the aldermen of *Paris*, giveth them absolute and full authoritie to make inquirie of the matter. The like dooth the Chancelor maister *Anthonius Pratensis* cardinall and legat for the pope throughout *France*. Therefore, when they had no exception to alledge, they were conveied unto *Paris*, and there constrained to make their answer. But yet could nothing be wroong out of them by confession, whereupon they were put apart into divers prisons: the novice being kept in the house of maister *Fumanus*, one of the aldermen, was oftentimes examined, and earnestlie requested to utter the truth, but would notwithstanding confesse nothing; bicause he feared that the moonks would afterwards put him to death for staining their order, and putting it to open shame. But when the judges had made him sure promise that he should escape punishment, and that he should never come into their handling, he opened unto them the whole matter as it was doone: and being brought before his fellowes, avouched the same to their faces. The moonks, albeit they were convicted, and by these meanes almost taken tarde with the deed doing; yet did they refuse the judges, bragging and vaunting themselves on their priviledges, but all in vaine. For sentence passed upon them, and they were condemned to be carried backe againe to *Orleance*, and there to be cast in prison, and so should finallie be brought foorth into the cheefe church of the citie openlie, and from thence to the place of execution, where they should make open confession of their trespasses.

    Surelie this was most common among moonks and friers, who mainteined their religion, their lust, their liberties, their pompe, their wealth, their estimation and knaverie by such cousening practises. Now I will shew you more speciall orders of popish conjurations, that are so shameleslie admitted into the church of *Rome*, that they are not onelie suffered, but commanded to be used, not by night secretlie, but by daie impudentlie. And these forsooth concerne the curing of bewitched persons, and such as are possessed; to wit, such as have a divell put into them by witches inchantments. And herewithall I will set downe certeine rules delivered unto us by such popish doctors, as are of greatest reputation.

An obstinate and wilfull persisting in the denieng or not confessing of a fault committed.

A parecuasis or transition of the author to matter further purposed.

<hr>

CHAPTER XXIV.

Who may be conjurors in the Romish church besides priests, a ridiculous definition of superstition, what words are to be used and not used in exorcismes, rebaptisme allowed, it is lawfull to conjure any thing, differences betweene holie water and coniuration.

THOMAS AQUINAS saith, that anie bodie, though he be of an inferior or superior order, yea though of none order at all (and as *Gulielmus Durandus glossator Raimundi* affirmeth, a woman so she blesse not the girdle or the garment, but the person of the bewitched) hath power to exercise the order of an exorcist or conjuror, even as well as any preest may saie masse in a house unconsecrated. But that is (saith *M. Mal.*) rather through the goodnesse and licence of the pope, than through the grace of the sacrament. Naie, there are examples set downe, where some being bewitched were cured (as *M. Mal.* taketh it) without any conjuration at all. Marrie there were certeine *Pater nosters*, *Aves*, and *Credos* said, and crosses made, but they are charmes, they saie, and no conjurations. For they saie that such charmes are lawfull, bicause there is no superstition in them, *&c.*

    And it is woorth my labour, to shew you how papists define superstition, and how they expound the definition thereof. Superstition (saie they) is a religion observed beyond measure, a religion practised with evill and unperfect circumstances. Also, whatsoever usurpeth the name of religion, through humane tradition, without the popes authoritie, is superstitious: as to adde to joine

In 4 dist. 23. sent.

Et glos. super illo ad coll. 2.

anie hymnes to the masse, to interrupt anie diriges, to abridge anie part of the creed in the singing thereof, or to sing when the organs go, and not when the quier singeth, not to have one to helpe the priest to masse : and such like, &c.

Mendaces debent esse memores, multò magis astuti exorcistæ.

These popish exorcists doo manie times forget their owne rules. For they should not directlie in their conjurations call upon the divell (as they doo) with intreatie, but with authoritie and commandement. Neither should they have in their charmes and conjurations anie unknowne names. Neither should there be (as alwaies there is) anie falshood conteined in the matter of the charme of conjuration, as (saie they) old women have in theirs, when they saie; The blessed virgine passed over *Jordan*, and then S. *Steven* met hir, and asked hir, &c. Neither should they have anie other vaine characters, but the crosse (for those are the words :) and manie other such cautions have they, which they observe not, for they have made it lawfull elsewhere.

Tho. Aquin. super. Marc. ultim. Mark, 16, 17.

But *Thomas* their cheefe piller prooveth their conjuring and charmes lawfull by S. *Marke*, who saith; *Signa eos qui crediderunt;* And, *In nomine meo dæmonia ejicient,* &c; whereby he also prooveth that they maie conjure serpents. And there he taketh paines to proove, that the words of God are of as great holinesse as relikes of saints, whereas (in such respect as they meane) they are both alike, and indeed nothing woorth. And I can tell them further, that so they maie be carried, as either of them maie doo a man much harme either in bodie or soule.

A trimme consequent.

But they proove this by S. *Augustine*, saieng; *Non est minus verbum Dei, quàm corpus Christi:* whereupon they conclude thus; By all mens opinions it is lawfull to carrie about reverentlie the relikes of saints; *Ergo* it is lawfull against evill spirits, to invocate the name of God everie waie; by the *Pater noster*, the *Ave*, the nativitie, the passion, the five wounds, the title triumphant, by the seven words spoken on the crosse, by the nailes, &c : and there maie be hope reposed in them.

Mal. malef. par. 2. quæ. 2.

Yea, they saie it is lawfull to conjure all things, bicause the divell maie have power in all things. And first, alwaies the person or thing, wherein the divell is, must be exorcised, and then the divell must be conjured. Also they affirme, that it is as expedient to consecrate and conjure porrage and meate, as water and salt, or such like things.

Rites, ceremonies, and relikes of exorcisme in rebaptising of the possessed or bewitched.

The right order of exorcisme in rebaptisme of a person possessed or bewitched, requireth that exsufflation and abrenunciation be doone toward the west. Item, there must be erection of hands, confession, profession, oration, benediction, imposition of hands, denudation and unction, with holie oile after baptisme, communion, and induition of the surplis. But they saie that this needeth not, where the bewitched is exorcised : but that the bewitched be first confessed, and then to hold a candle in his hand, and in steed of a surplise to tie about his bare bodie a holie candle of the length of Christ, or of the crosse whereupon he died, which for monie maie be had at *Rome*. *Ergo* (saith *M. Mal.*) this maie be said ; I conjure thee *Peter* or *Barbara* being sicke, but regenerate in the holie water of baptisme, by the living God, by the true God, by the holie God, by the God which redeemed thee with his pretious bloud, that thou maiest be made a conjured man, that everie fantasie and wickednesse of diabolicall deceipt doo avoid and depart from thee, and that everie uncleane spirit be conjured through him that shall come to judge the quicke and the dead, and the world by fier, Amen : *Oremus*, &c. And this conjuration, with *Oremus*, and a praier, must be thrise repeated, and at the end alwaies must be said; *Ergo maledicte diabole recognosce sententiam tuam*, &c. And this order must alwaies be followed. And

Memorandum that this is for one bewitched.

finallie, there must be diligent search made, in everie corner, and under everie coverlet and pallet, and under everie threshhold of the doores, for instruments of witchcraft. And if anie be found, they must streightwaie be throwne into the fier. Also they must change all their bedding, their clothing, and their habitation. And if nothing be found, the partie that is to be exorcised or conjured, must come to the church rath in the morning : and the holier the daie is, the better, speciallie our Ladie daie. And the preest, if he be shriven himselfe and in perfect state, shall doo the better therein. And let him that is exorcised hold a holie candle in his hand, &c. Alwaies provided, that the holie water be throwne upon him, and a stoale put about his necke, with *Deus in adjutorium*, and the Letanie, with invocation of saints. And this order maie continue thrise a

Note the proviso.

weeke, so as (saie they) through multiplication of intercessors, or rather intercessions, grace maie be obteined, and favor procured.

There is also some question in the Romish church, whether the sacrament of the altar is to be received before or after the exorcisme. Item in shrift, the confessor must learne whether the partie be not excommunicate, and so for want of absolution, endure this vexation. *Thomas* sheweth the difference betwixt holie water and conjuration, saieng that holie water driveth the divell awaie from the externall and outward parts; but conjurations from the internall and inward parts; and therefore unto the bewitched partie both are to be applied.

Tho. Aquin.
supr. dist. 6.

CHAPTER XXV.

The seven reasons why some are not rid of the divell with all their popish conjurations, why there were no conjurors in the primitive church, and why the divell is not so soone cast out of the bewitched as of the possessed.

THE reason why some are not remedied for all their conjurations, the papists say is for seven causes. First, for that the faith of the standers by is naught; secondlie, for that theirs that present the partie is no better; thirdlie, bicause of the sinnes of the bewitched; fourthlie, for the neglecting of meete remedies; fiftlie, for the reverence of vertues going out into others; sixtlie, for the purgation; seventhlie, for the merit of the partie bewitched. And lo, the first foure are proved by *Matthew* the 7. and *Marke* the 4. when one presented his sonne, and the multitude wanted faith, & the father said, Lord help mine incredulitie or unbeleefe. Wherupon was said, Oh faithlesse and perverse generation, how long shall I be with you? And where these words are written; And Jesus rebuked him, &c. That is to saie, saie they, the possessed or bewitched for his sinnes. For by the neglect of due remedies it appeereth, that there were not with Christ good and perfect men: for the pillers of the faith; to wit, *Peter, James,* and *John* were absent. Neither was there fasting and praier, without the which that kind of divels could not be cast out. For the fourth point; to wit, the fault of the exorcist in faith maie appeare; for that afterwards the disciples asked the cause of their impotencie therin. And Jesus answered, it was for their incredulitie; saieng that if they had as much faith as a graine of mustard seed, they should move mountaines, &c. The fift is prooved by *Vitas patrum,* the lives of the fathers, where it appeereth that S. *Anthonie* could not doo that cure, when his scholar *Paule* could doo it, and did it. For the proofe of the sixt excuse it is said, that though the fault be taken awaie therby; yet it followeth not that alwaies the punishment is released. Last of all it is said, that it is possible that the divell was not conjured out of the partie before baptisme by the exorcist, or the midwife hath not baptised him well, but omitted some part of the sacrament. If any object that there were no exorcists in the primitive church, it is answered, that the church cannot now erre. And saint *Gregorie* would never have instituted it in vaine. And it is a generall rule, that who or whatsoever is newlie exorcised must be rebaptised: as also such as walke or talke in their sleepe; for (saie they) call them by their names, and presentlie they wake, or fall if they clime: whereby it is gathered, that they are not trulie named in baptisme. Item they saie, it is somewhat more difficult to conjure the divell out of one bewitched, than out of one possessed: bicause in the bewitched, he is double; in the other single. They have a hundred such beggerlie, foolish, and frivolous notes in this behalfe.

1
2
3, 4
5
6, 7

Proper proofes of the former seven reasons

Why there were no conjurors in ye primitive church with other subtill points.

CHAPTER XXVI.

Other grosse absurdities of witchmongers in this matter of conjurations.

SURELIE I cannot see what difference or distinction the witchmongers doo put betweene the knowledge and power of God and the divell; but that they think, if they praie, or rather talke to God, till their hearts ake, he never heareth them; but that the divell dooth knowe everie thought and imagination of their minds, and both can and also will doo any thing for them. For if anie that meaneth good faith with the divell read certeine conjurations, he commeth up (they saie) at a trice. Marrie if another that hath none intent to raise him, read or pronounce the words, he will not stirre. And yet *J. Bodin* confesseth, that he is afraid to read such conjurations as *John Wierus* reciteth; least (belike) the divell would come up, and scratch him with his fowle long nailes. In which sort I woonder that the divell dealeth with none other, than witches and conjurors. I for my part have read a number of their conjurations, but never could see anie divels of theirs, except it were in a plaie. But the divell (belike) knoweth my mind; to wit, that I would be loth to come within the compasse of his clawes. But lo what reason such people have. *Bodin, Bartholomeus Spineus, Sprenger,* and *Institor,* &c: doo constantlie affirme, that witches are to be punished with more extremitie than conjurors; and sometimes with death, when the other are to be pardoned doing the same offense: bicause (say they) the witches make a league with the divell, & so doo not conjurors. Now if conjurors make no league by their owne confession, and divels indeed know not our cogitations (as I have sufficientlie prooved) then would I weet of our witchmongers the reason, (if I read the conjuration and performe the ceremonie) why the divell will not come at my call? But oh absurd credulitie! Even in this point manie wise & learned men have beene & are abused: wheras, if they would make experience, or dulie expend the cause, they might be soone resolved; specially when the whole art and circumstance is so contrarie to Gods word, as it must be false, if the other be true. So as you may understand, that the papists do not onlie by their doctrine, in bookes & sermons teach & publish conjurations, & the order thereof, whereby they may induce men to bestowe, or rather cast awaie their monie upon masses and suffrages for their soules; but they make it also a parcell of their sacrament of orders (of the which number a conjuror is one) and insert manie formes of conjurations into their divine service, and not onelie into their pontificals, but into their masse bookes; yea into the verie canon of the masse.

A conjuror then belike must not be timerous or fearefull.

Where a witch cureth by incantation, and the conjuror by conjuration.

CHAPTER XXVII.

Certaine conjurations taken out of the pontificall and out of the missall.

BUT see yet a little more of popish conjurations, and conferre them with the other. In the pontificall you shall find this conjuration, which the other conjurors use as solemnelie as they: I conjure thee thou creature of water in the name of the fa✠ther, of the so✠nne, and of the Holie✠ghost, that thou drive awaie the divell from the bounds of the just, that he remaine not in the darke corners of this church and altar. ☆ You shall find in the same title, these words following, to be used at the hallowing of the churches. There must a crosse of ashes be made upon the pavement, from one end of the church to the other, one handfull broad: and one of the priests must write on the one side

Tit. de ecclesiæ dedicatione.

Ibidem, fol. 108.

258

thereof the Greeke alphabet, and on the otherside the Latin alphabet. *Durandus* yeeldeth this reason thereof; to wit, It representeth the union in faith of the Jewes and Gentiles. And yet well agreeing to himselfe he saith even there, that the crosse reaching from the one end to the other, signifieth that the people, which were in the head, shalbe made the taile.

Durand. de ecclesiæ dedicatione lib. 1. fol. 12.

¶ *A conjuration written in the masse booke. Fol. 1.*

I conjure thee O creature of salt by God, by the God ✠ that liveth, by the true ✠ God, by the holie ✠ God, which by *Elizæus* the prophet commanded, that thou shouldest be throwne into the water, that it thereby might be made whole and sound, that thou salt [here let the preest looke upon the salt] maist be conjured for the health of all beleevers, and that thou be to all that take thee, health both of bodie and soule; and let all phantasies and wickednesse, or diabolicall craft or deceipt, depart from the place whereon it is sprinkled; as also everie uncleane spirit, being conjured by him that judgeth both the quicke and the dead by fier. *Resp:* Amen. Then followeth a praier to be said, without *Dominus vobiscum;* but yet with *Oremus;* as followeth :

In Missali. fol. 1. The maner of conjuring salt.

¶ *Oremus.*

Almightie and everlasting God, we humblie desire thy clemency [here let the preest looke upon the salt] that thou wouldest vouchsafe, through thy pietie, to bl✠esse and sanc✠tifie this creature of salt, which thou hast given for the use of mankind, that it may be to all that receive it, health of mind and bodie; so as whatsoever shall be touched thereby, or sprinkled therewith, may be void of all uncleannesse, and all resistance of spirituall iniquitie, through our Lord, Amen.

A praier to be applied to the former exorcisme.

What can be made but a conjuration of these words also, which are written in the canon, or rather in the saccaring of masse? This holie commixtion of the bodie and·bloud of our Lord Jesus Christ, let it be made to me, and to all the receivers thereof, health of mind and bodie, and a wholesome preparative for the deserving and receiving of everlasting life, through our Lord Jesus, Amen.

Chapter XXVIII.

That popish priests leave nothing unconjured, a forme of exorcisme for incense.

ALTHOUGH the papists have manie conjurations, so as neither water, nor fier, nor bread, nor wine, nor wax, nor tallowe, nor church, nor churchyard, nor altar, nor altar cloath, nor ashes, nor coles, nor belles, nor bell ropes, nor copes, nor vestments, nor oile, nor salt, nor candle, nor candle-sticke, nor beds, nor bedstaves, &c; are without their forme of conjuration: yet I will for brevitie let all passe, and end here with incense, which they doo conjure in this sort ✠. I conjure thee most filthy and horrible spirit, and everie vision of our enimie, &c: that thou go and depart from out of this creature of frankincense, with all thy deceipt and wickednes, that this creature may be sanctified, and in the name of our Lord ✠ Jesus ✠ Christ ✠ that all they that taste, touch, or smell the same, may receive the virtue and assistance of the Holie-ghost; so as wheresoever this incense or frankincense shall remaine, that there thou in no wise be so bold as to approch or once presume or attempt to hurt: but what uncleane spirit so ever thou be, that thou with all thy craft and subtiltie avoid and depart, being conjured by the name of God the father almightie, &c. And that wheresoever the fume or smoke thereof shall come, everie kind and sort of divels may be driven awaie, and expelled; as they were at the increase of the liver of fish, which the archangell *Raphaell* made, &c.

A conjuration of frankincense set foorth in forme.

CHAPTER XXIX.

The rules and lawes of popish Exorcists and other conjurors all one, with a confutation of their whole power, how S. Martine conjured the divell

Papists and conjurors cousening compeers.

THE papists you see, have their certeine generall rules and lawes, as to absteine from sinne, and to fast, as also otherwise to be cleane from all pollutions, &c: and even so likewise have the other conjurors. Some will saie that papists use divine service, and praiers; even so doo common conjurors (as you see) even in the same papisticall forme, no whit swarving from theirs in faith and doctrine, nor yet in ungodlie and unreasonable kinds of petitions. Me

I. Sam. 16, 7.
I. Reg. 8, 39.
Jere. 17, 10.
Psal. 44, 21.
Psal. 72, 18.

thinks it may be a sufficient argument, to overthrow the calling up and miraculous works of spirits, that it is written; God onelie knoweth and searcheth the harts, and onelie worketh great woonders. The which argument being prosecuted to the end, can never be answered: insomuch as that divine power is required in that action.

And if it be said, that in this conjuration we speake to the spirits, and they heare us, & therefore need not know our thoughts and imaginations: I first aske them whether king *Baell*, or *Amoimon*, which are spirits reigning in the furthest regions of the east (as they saie) may heare a conjurors voice, which calleth for them, being in the extreamest parts of the west, there being such noises interposed, where perhaps also they may be busie, and set to worke on the like affaires. Secondlie, whether those spirits be of the same power that God is, who is everiewhere, filling all places, and able to heare all men at one instant, &c. Thirdlie, whence commeth the force of such words as raise the dead, and command divels. If sound doo it, then may it be doone by a taber and a pipe, or any other instrument that hath no life. If the voice doo it, then may it be doone by any beasts or birds. If words, then a parret may doo it. If in mans words onlie, where is the force, in the first, second, or third syllable? If in syllables, then not in words. If in imaginations, then the divell knoweth our thoughts. But all this stuffe is vaine and fabulous.

Sap. 1. 14.
Ecclesi. 9.
Gen. 1.

Act. 19.

It is written; All the generations of the earth were healthfull and there is no poison of destruction in them. Why then doo they conjure holsome creatures; as salt, water, &c: where no divels are? God looked upon all his works, and sawe they were all good. What effect (I praie you) had the 7. sonnes of *Sceva;* which is the great objection of witchmongers? They would needs take upon them to conjure divels out of the possessed. But what brought they to passe? Yet that was in the time, whilest God suffered miracles commonlie to be wrought. By that you may see what conjurors can doo.

Mark 16. 17.

Where is such a promise to conjurors or witches, as is made in the Gospell to the faithfull? where it is written; In my name they shall cast out divels, speake with new toongs: if they shall drinke any deadlie thing, it shall not hurt them; they shall take awaie serpents, they shall laie hands on the sicke, and they shall recover. According to the promise, this grant of miraculous working was performed in the primitive church, for the confirmation of Christs doctrine, and the establishing of the Gospell.

Isai. 43. 11.
verse. 13.
cap. 44.
verse. 7.
verse. 25.

But as in another place I have prooved, the gift thereof was but for a time, and is now ceased; neither was it ever made to papist, witch, or conjuror. They take upon them to call up and cast out divels; and to undoo with one divell, that which another divell hath doone. If one divell could cast out another, it were a kingdome divided, and could not stand. Which argument Christ himselfe maketh: and therfore I maie the more boldlie saie even with Christ, that they have no such power. For besides him, there is no saviour, none can deliver out of his hand. Who but hee can declare, set in order, appoint, and tell what is to come? He destroieth the tokens of soothsaiers, and maketh the conjecturers fooles, &c. He declareth things to come, and so cannot witches.

There is no helpe in inchanters and soothsaiers, and other such vaine sciences. For divels are cast out by the finger of God, which *Matthew* calleth the spirit of God, which is the mightie power of God, and not by the vertue of the bare name onelie, being spoken or pronounced: for then might everie wicked man doo it. And *Simon Magus* needed not then to have proffered monie to have bought the power to doo miracles and woonders: for he could speake and pronounce the name of God, as well as the apostles. Indeed they maie soone throwe out all the divels that are in frankincense, and such like creatures, wherein no divels are: but neither they, nor all their holie water can indeed cure a man possessed with a divell, either in bodie or mind; as Christ did. Naie, why doo they not cast out the divell that possesseth their owne soules? *Isai. 46. 10. cap. 47. vers. 12. 13, &c. Luke. 11. 20. Matt. 12. 28. Acts, 8. 19.*

Let me heare anie of them all speake with new toongs, let them drinke but one dramme of a potion which I will prepare for them, let them cure the sicke by laieng on of hands (though witches take it upon them, and witchmongers beleeve it) and then I will subscribe unto them. But if they, which repose such certeintie in the actions of witches and conjurors, would diligentlie note their deceipt, and how the scope whereat they shoote is monie (I meane not such witches as are falselie accused, but such as take upon them to give answers, &c: as mother *Bungie* did) they should apparentlie see the cousenage. For they are abused, as are manie beholders of jugglers, which suppose they doo miraculouslie, that which is doone by slight and subtiltie. *Monie is the marke whereat al witches & conjurors doo aime.*

But in this matter of witchcrafts and conjurations, if men would rather trust their owne eies, than old wives tales and lies, I dare undertake this matter would soone be at a perfect point; as being easier to be perceived than juggling. But I must needs confesse, that it is no great marvell, though the simple be abused therein, when such lies concerning those matters are mainteined by such persons of account, and thrust into their divine service. As for example: It is written that S. *Martine* thrust his fingers into ones mouth that had a divell within him, and used to bite folke; and then did bid him devoure them if he could. And bicause the divell could not get out at his mouth, being stopt with S. *Martins* fingers, he was faine to run out at his fundament. O stinking lie! *S. Martins cōjuration: In die sancti Martini. lect. 1.*

That it is a shame for papists to beleeve other conjurors dooings, their owne being of so litle force, Hipocrates his opinion herein.

AND still me thinks papists (of all others) which indeed are most credulous, and doo most mainteine the force of witches charmes, and of conjurors cousenages, should perceive and judge conjurors dooings to be void of effect. For when they see their owne stuffe, as holie water, salt, candles, &c: conjured by their holie bishop and preests; & that in the words of consecration or conjuration (for so their owne doctors terme them) they adjure the water, &c: to heale, not onelie the soules infirmitie, but also everie maladie, hurt, or ach of the bodie; and doo also command the candles, with the force of all their authoritie and power, and by the effect of all their holie words, not to consume: and yet neither soule nor bodie anie thing recover, nor the candles last one minute the longer: with what face can they defend the others miraculous workes; as though the witches and conjurors actions were more effectuall than their owne? *Hippocrates* being but a heathen, and not having the perfect knowledge of God, could see and perceive their cousenage and knaverie well enough, who saith; They which boast so, that they can remoove or helpe the infections of diseases, with sacrifices, conjurations, or other magicall instruments or meanes, are but needie fellowes, wanting living; and therefore referre their words to the *To wit, Vincent. dominica in albis : in octa. pasch. sermone. 15. Durand. de exorcist.*

divell: bicause they would seeme to know somewhat more than the common people. It is marvell that papists doo affirme, that their holie water, crosses, or bugges words have such vertue and violence, as to drive awaie divels: so as they dare not approch to anie place or person besmeered with such stuffe; when as it appeareth in the gospell, that the divell presumed to assault and tempt Christ himselfe. For the divell indeed most ernestlie busieth himselfe to seduce the godlie: as for the wicked, he maketh reckoning and just accompt of them, as of his owne alreadie. But let us go forward in our refutation.

CHAPTER XXXI.

How conjurors have beguiled witches, what bookes they carie about to procure credit to their art, wicked assertions against Moses and Joseph.

THUS you see that conjurors are no small fooles. For whereas witches being poore and needie, go from doore to doore for releefe, have they never so manie todes or cats at home, or never so much hogs doong and charvill about them, or never so manie charmes in store: these conjurors (I saie) have gotten them offices in the church of *Rome*, wherby they have ob-

A fowle of-
fense to
backbite
ye absent,
& to beelie
the dead.

teined authoritie & great estimation. And further, to adde credit to that art, these conjurors carrie about at this daie, bookes intituled under the names of *Adam, Abel, Tobie, & Enoch;* which *Enoch* they repute the most divine fellow in such matters. They have also among them bookes that they saie *Abraham, Aaron* and *Salomon* made. Item they have bookes of *Zacharie, Paule, Honorius, Cyprian, Jerome, Jeremie, Albert,* and *Thomas:* also of the angels, *Riziel, Razael,* and *Raphael;* and these doubtlesse were such bookes as were said to have beene

Acts. 19.

burnt in the lesser *Asia.* And for their further credit they boast, that they must be and are skilfull and learned in these arts; to wit, *Ars Almadell, ars Notoria, ars Bulaphiæ, ars Arthephii, ars Pomena, ars Revelationis, &c.* Yea, these conjurors

Just. lib. 16.

in corners sticke not (with *Justine*) to report and affirme, that *Joseph*, who was a true figure of Christ that delivered and redeemed us, was learned in these arts, and thereby prophesied and expounded dreames: and that those arts came from

Plin. lib. 30.
cap. 2.
Strab. lib. 16.

him to *Moses*, and finallie from *Moses* to them: which thing both *Plinie* and *Tacitus* affirme of *Moses.* Also *Strabo* in his cosmographie maketh the verie like blasphemous report. And likewise *Apollonius, Molon, Possidonius, Lisimachus,* and *Appian* terme *Moses* both a magician and a conjuror: whom *Eusebius* confuteth with manie notable arguments. For *Moses* differed as much from a magician, as truth from falshood, and pietie from vanitie: for in truth, he confounded all magicke, and made the world see, and the cunningest magicians of the earth confesse, that their owne dooings were but illusions, and that his miracles were wrought by the finger of God. But that the poore old witches knowledge

Dan. in dia-
log. de sorti-
ariis.

reacheth thus farre (as *Danæus* affirmeth it dooth) is untrue: for their furthest fetches that I can comprehend, are but to fetch a pot of milke, &c: from their neighbors house, halfe a mile distant from them.

CHAPTER XXXII.

All magicall arts confuted by an argument concerning Nero, what Cornelius Agrippa and Carolus Gallus have left written thereof, and prooved by experience.

SURELIE *Nero* prooved all these magicall arts to be vaine and fabulous lies, and nothing but cousenage and knaverie. He was a notable prince, having gifts of nature enow to have conceived such matters, treasure enough to have emploied in the search thereof, he made no conscience therein, he had singular conferences thereabout; he offered, and would have given halfe his kingdome to have learned those things, which he heard might be wrought by magicians; he procured all the cunning magicians in the world to come to *Rome*, he searched for bookes also, and all other things necessarie for a magician; and never could find anie thing in it, but cousenage and legierdemaine. At length he met with one *Tiridates*, the great magician, who having with him all his companions, and fellowe magicians, witches, conjurors, and couseners, invited *Nero* to certeine magicall bankets and exercises. Which when *Nero* required to learne, he (to hide his cousenage) answered that he would not, nor could not teach him, though he would have given him his kingdome. The matter of his refusall (I saie) was, least *Nero* should espie the cousening devises thereof. Which when *Nero* conceived, and sawe the same, and all the residue of that art to be vaine, lieng and ridiculous, having onelie shadowes of truth, and that their arts were onelie veneficall; he prohibited the same utterlie, and made good and strong lawes against the use and the practisers thereof: as *Plinie* and others doo report. It is marvell that anie man can be so much abused, as to suppose that sathan may be commanded, compelled, or tied by the power of man: as though the divell would yeeld to man, beyond nature; that will not yeeld to God his creator, according to the rules of nature. And in so much as there be (as they confesse) good angels as well as bad; I would know whie they call up the angels of hell, and not call downe the angels of heaven. But this they answer (as *Agrippa* saith.) Good angels (forsooth) doo hardlie appeare, and the other are readie at hand. Here I may not omit to tell you how *Cor. Agrippa* bewraieth, detecteth, and defaceth this art of conjuration, who in his youth travelled into the bottome of all these magicall sciences, and was not onelie a great conjuror and practiser thereof, but also wrote cunninglie *De occulta philosophia*. Howbeit, afterwards in his wiser age, he recanteth his opinions, and lamenteth his follies in that behalfe, and discovereth the impietie and vanities of magicians, and inchanters, which boast they can doo miracles: which action is now ceased (saith he) and assigneth them a place with *Jannes* and *Jambres*, affirming that this art teacheth nothing but vaine toies for a shew. *Carolus Gallus* also saith; I have tried oftentimes, by the witches and conjurors themselves, that their arts (especiallie those which doo consist of charmes, impossibilities, conjurations, and witchcrafts, whereof they were woont to boast) to be meere foolishnes, doting lies, and dreames. I for my part can saie as much, but that I delight not to alledge mine owne proofes and authorities; for that mine adversaries will saie they are parciall, and not indifferent.

Tiridates the great magician biddeth the emperor Nero to a banket, &c.

Nero made lawes against conjurers and conjurations.

C. Agrip. lib. de vanitat. scient.

Chapter XXXIII.

Of Salomons conjurations, and of the opinion conceived of his cunning and practise therein.

IT is affirmed by sundrie authors, that *Salomon* was the first inventor of those conjurations; and thereof *Josephus* is the first reporter, who in his fift booke *De Judæorum antiquitatibus*, cap. 22. rehearseth soberlie this storie following; which *Polydore Virgil*, and manie other repeat verbatim, in this wise, and seeme to credit the fable, whereof there is skant a true word.

Salomon was the greatest philosopher, and did philosophie about all things, and had the full and perfect knowlege of all their proprieties: but he had that gift given from above to him, for the profit and health of mankind: which is effectuall against divels. He made also inchantments, wherewith diseases are driven awaie; and left diverse maners of conjurations written, whereunto the divels giving place are so driven awaie, that they never returne. And this kind of healing is very common among my countrimen: for I sawe a neighbour of mine, one *Eleazer*, that in the presence of *Vespasian* and his sonnes, and the rest of the souldiers, cured many that were possessed with spirits. The maner and order of his cure was this. He did put unto the nose of the possessed a ring, under the seale wherof was inclosed a kind of roote, whose verture *Salomon* declared, and the savour thereof drewe the divell out at his nose; so as downe fell the man, and then *Eleazer* conjured the divell to depart, & to return no more to him. In the meane time he made mention of *Salomon*, reciting incantations of *Salomons* owne making. And then *Eleazer* being willing to shew to standers by his cunning, and the wonderfull efficacie of his art, did set not farre from thence, a pot or basen full of water, & commanded the divell that went out of the man, that by the overthrowing thereof, he would give a signe to the beholders, that he had utterlie forsaken and leaft the man. Which thing being doone, none there doubted how great *Salomons* knowledge and wisedome was. Wherin a jugling knacke was produced, to confirme a cogging cast of knaverie or cousenage.

Another storie of *Salomons* conjuration I find cited in the sixt lesson, read in the church of *Rome* upon S. *Margarets* daie, far more ridiculous than this. Also *Peter Lombard* maister of the sentences, and *Gratian* his brother, the compiler of the golden decrees; and *Durandus* in his *Rationale divinorum*, doo all soberlie affirme *Salomons* cunning in this behalfe; and speciallie this tale; to wit, that *Salomon* inclosed certeine thousand divels in a brasen bowle, and left it in a deepe hole or lake, so as afterwards the *Babylonians* found it, and supposing there had beene gold or silver therein, brake it, and out flew all the divels, &c. And that this fable is of credit, you shall perceive, in that it is thought woorthie to be read in the Romish church as parcell of their divine service. Looke in the lessons of S. *Margarets* daie the virgine, and you shall find these words verbatim: which I the rather recite, bicause it serveth me for divers turnes; to wit, for *Salomons* conjurations, for the tale of the brasen vessell, and for the popes conjurations, which extended both to faith and doctrine, and to shew of what credit their religion is, that so shamefullie is stained with lies and fables.

Probatum est upon a patient before witnes: *Ergo* no lie.

Lib. 4 *dist.* 14. *Decret. aureum. dist.* 21. *Rub. de exorcist.*

Lect. 5. & 6.

CHAPTER XXXIV.

Lessons read in all churches, where the pope hath authoritie, on S. Margarets daie, translated into English word for word.

HOLIE *Margaret* required of GOD, that she might have a conflict face to face with hir secret enimie the divell; and rising from praier, she sawe a terrible dragon, that would have devoured hir, but she made the signe of the crosse, and the dragon burst in the middest.

Afterwards, she sawe another man sitting like a Niger, having his hands bound fast to his knees, she taking him by the haire of the head, threw him to the ground, and set hir foote on his head; and hir praiers being made, a light shined from heaven into the prison where she was, and the crosse of Christ was seene in heaven, with a doove sitting thereon, who said; Blessed art thou O *Margaret*, the gates of paradise attend thy comming. Then she giving thanks to God, said to the divell, Declare to me thy name. The divell said; Take awaie thy foote from my head, that I may be able to speake, and tell thee: which being done, the divell said, I am *Veltis*, one of them whome *Salomon* shut in the brasen vessell, and the *Babylonians* comming, and supposing there had beene gold therein, brake the vessell, and then we flew out: ever since lieng in wait to annoie the just. But seeing I have recited a part of hir storie, you shall also have the end therof: for at the time of hir execution this was hir praier following.

Grant therefore O father, that whosoever writeth, readeth, or heareth my passion, or maketh memoriall of me, may deserve pardon for all his sinnes: whosoever calleth on me, being at the point of death, deliver him out of the hands of his adversaries. And I also require, O Lord, that whosoever shall build a church in the honor of me, or ministreth unto me anie candles of his just labour, let him obteine whatsoever he asketh for his health. Deliver all women in travell that call upon me, from the danger thereof.

Hir praier ended, there were manie great thunderclaps, and a doove came downe from heaven, saieng; Blessed art thou O *Margaret* the spouse of Christ. Such things as thou hast asked, are granted unto thee; therefore come thou into everlasting rest, &c. Then the hangman (though she did bid him) refused to cut off hir head: to whome she said; Except thou doo it, thou canst have no part with me, and then lo he did it, &c. But sithens I have beene, and must be tedious, I thought good to refresh my reader with a lamentable storie, depending upon the matter precedent, reported by manie grave authors, word for word, in maner and forme following.

Lect. in die sanctissimæ Marg. vir. 5.

Lect. 6.

Looke in the word Iidoni, pag. 218.

For the preests profit, I warrant you. This is cõmon (they saie) when a witch or conjuror dieth.

CHAPTER XXXV.

A delicate storie of a Lombard, who by S. Margarets example would needs fight with a reall divell.

THERE was (after a sermon made, wherein this storie of S. *Margaret* was recited, for in such stuffe consisted not onelie their service, but also their sermons in the blind time of poperie:) there was (I saie) a certeine yoong man, being a *Lombard*, whose simplicitie was such, as he had no respect unto the commoditie of worldlie things, but did altogither affect the salvation of his soule, who hearing how great S. *Margarets* triumph was, began to consider with himselfe, how full of slights the divell was. And among other things thus he

Kakozelia.

265

said; Oh that God would suffer, that the divell might fight with me hand to hand in visible forme! I would then surelie in like maner overthrow him, and would fight with him till I had the victorie. And therefore about the twelfe houre he went out of the towne, and finding a convenient place where to praie, secretlie kneeling on his knees, he praied among other things, that God would suffer the divell to appeare unto him in visible forme, that according to the example of S. *Margaret*, he might overcome him in battell. And as he was in the middest of his praiers, there came into that place a woman with a hooke in hir hand, to gather certeine hearbs which grew there, who was dumme borne. And when she came into the place, and saw the yoong man among the hearbs on his knees, she was afraid, and waxed pale, and going backe, she rored in such sort, as hir voice could not be understood, and with hir head and fists made threatning signes unto him. The yoong man seeing such an ilfavoured fowle queane, that was for age decrepit and full of wrinkles, with a long bodie, leane of face, pale of colour, with ragged cloathes, crieng verie lowd, and having a voice not understandable, threatning him with the hooke which she carried in hir hand, he thought surelie she had beene no woman, but a divell appearing unto him in the shape of a woman, and thought God had heard his praiers. For the which causes he fell upon hir lustilie, and at length threw hir downe to the ground, saieng; Art thou come thou curssed divell, art thou come? No no, thou shalt not overthrow me in visible fight, whome thou hast often overcome in invisible temptation.

And as he spake these words, he caught hir by the haire, and drew hir about, beating hir sometimes with his hands, sometimes with his heeles, and sometimes with the hooke so long, and wounded hir so sore, that he left hir a dieng. At the noise whereof manie people came running unto them, and seeing what was doone, they apprehended the yoong man, and thrust him into a vile prison. S. *Vincent* by vertue of his holines understanding all this matter, caused the bodie that seemed dead to be brought unto him, and thereupon (according to his maner) he laid his hand upon hir, who immediatlie revived, and he called one of his chaplines to heare hir confession. But they that were present said to the man of God, that it were altogether in vaine so to doo, for that she had beene from hir nativitie dumbe, and could neither heare nor understand the priest; neither could in words confesse hir sinnes. Notwithstanding, S. *Vincent* bad the priest heare hir confession, affirming that she should verie distinctlie speake all things unto him. And therfore, whatsoever the man of God commanded, the priest did confidentlie accomplish and obeie: and as soone as the priest approched unto hir, to heare hir confession, she, whome all *Cathalonia* knew to be dumbe borne, spake, and confessed hir selfe, pronouncing everie word as distinctlie, as though she had never beene dumbe. After hir confession she required the eucharist and extreame unction to be ministred unto hir; and at length she commended hir selfe to God; and in the presence of all that came to see that miracle, she spake as long as she had anie breath in hir bodie. The yoong man that killed hir being saved from the gallowes by S. *Vincents* meanes, and at his intercession, departed home into *Italie*. This storie last rehearsed is found in *Speculo exemplorum*, and repeated also by *Robert Carocul*: bishop of *Aquinas*, and manie others, and preached publikelie in the church of *Rome*.

Mutuall error by meanes of sudden sight.

S. Vincent raiseth the dead woman to life.

S. Vincent maketh the dumbe to speake.

Dist. 8. exempl. 17. serm. 59. cap. 20.

CHAPTER XXXVI.

The storie of Saint Margaret prooved to be both ridiculous and impious in everie point.

FIRST, that the storie of S. *Margaret* is a fable, may be prooved by the incredible, impossible, foolish, impious, and blasphemous matters conteined therein, and by the ridiculous circumstance thereof. Though it were cruellie doone of hir to beat the divell, when his hands were bound; yet it was courteouslie doone of hir, to pull awaie hir foot at his desire. He could not speake so long as she troad on his head, and yet he said; Tread off, that I may tell you what I am. She sawe the heavens open, and yet she was in a close prison. But hir sight was verie cleare, that could see a little dove sitting upon a crosse so farre off. For heaven is higher than the sunne; and the sunne, when it is neerest to us, is 3966000. miles from us. And she had a good paire of eares, that could heare a dove speake so farre off. And she had good lucke, that S. *Peter*, who (they saie) is porter, or else the pope, who hath more dooings than Peter, had such leisure as to staie the gates so long for hir. *Salomon* provided no good place, neither tooke good order with his brasen bowle. I marvell how they escaped that let out the divels. It is marvell also they melted it not with their breath long before: for the divels carrie hell and hell fier about with them alwaies; in so much as (they saie) they leave ashes evermore where they stand. Surelie she made in hir praier an unreasonable request. But the date of hir patent is out: for I beleeve that whosoever at this daie shall burne a pound of good candle before hir, shall be never the better, but three pence the worsse. But now we may find in S. *Margarets* life, who it is that is Christes wife: whereby we are so much wiser than we were before. But looke in the life of S. *Katharine*, in the golden legend, and you shall find that he was also married to S. *Katharine*, and that our ladie made the marriage, &c. An excellent authoritie for bigamie. Here I will also cite other of their notable stories, or miracles of authoritie, and so leave shaming of them, or rather troubling you the readers thereof. Neither would I have written these fables, but that they are authentike among the papists, and that we that are protestants may be satisfied, as well of conjurors and witches miracles, as of the others: for the one is as grosse as the other.

Secundùm Bordinum Corrigens. Quæsit. Math. tract. I. sect. 77.

Psellus de operatione dæmonum.

CHAPTER XXXVII.

A pleasant miracle wrought by a popish preest.

WHAT time the *Waldenses* heresies beganne to spring, certeine wicked men, being upheld and mainteined by diabolicall vertue, shewed certeine signes and woonders, wherby they strengthened and confirmed their heresies, and perverted in faith many faithfull men; for they walked on the water and were not drowned. But a certeine catholike preest seeing the same, and knowing that true signes could not be joined with false doctrine, brought the bodie of our Lord, with the pix, to the water, where they shewed their power and vertue to the people, and said in the hearing of all that were present: I conjure thee O divell, by him, whom I carrie in my hands, that thou exercise not these great visions and phantasies by these men, to the drowning of this people. Notwithstanding these words, when they walked still on the water, as they did before, the preest in a rage threw the bodie of our Lord, with the pix into the river, and by and by, so soone as the sacrament touched the element, the phantasie gave place to the veritie; and they being prooved and made false, did sinke like lead to the bottome, and were drowned; the pix with the sacrament immediatlie was taken awaie by an angell. The preest seeing all these things, was verie glad of the miracle, but for the losse of the sacrament he was verie pensive, passing awaie the whole night in teares and moorning: in the morning he found the pix with the sacrament upon the altar.

In speculo exemplorum, dist. 6. ex lib. exemplorum, Cæsariis, exempl. 69.

Memorandum, it is confessed in poperie that true miracles cannot be joined with false doctrine: *Ergo* neither papist, witch, nor conjuror can worke miracles.

CHAPTER XXXVIII.

The former miracle confuted, with a strange storie of saint Lucie.

HOW glad Sir John was now it were follie for me to saie. How would he have plagued the divell, that threw his god in the river to be drowned? But if other had had no more power to destroie the *Waldenses* with sword and fier, than this preest had to drowne them with his conjuring boxe & cousening sacraments, there should have beene many a life saved. But I may not omit one fable, which is of authoritie, wherein though there be no conjuration expressed, yet I warrant you there was cousenage both in the dooing and telling thereof. ☞ You shall read in the lesson on saint *Lucies* daie, that she being condemned, could not be remooved from the place with a teeme of oxen, neither could any fier burne hir, insomuch as one was faine to cut off hir head with a sword, and yet she could speake afterwards as long as she list. And this passeth all other miracles, except it be that which *Bodin* and *M. Mal.* recite out of *Nider*, of a witch that could not be burned, till a scroll was taken awaie from where she hid it, betwixt hir skin and flesh.

Lect. in die sanctæ Luciæ 7 & 8.

CHAPTER XXXIX.

Of visions, noises, apparitions, and imagined sounds, and of other illusions, of wandering soules: with a confutation thereof.

MANIE thorough melancholie doo imagine, that they see or heare visions, spirits, ghosts, strange noises, &c: as I have alreadie prooved before, at large. Manie againe thorough feare proceeding from a cowardlie nature and complexion, or from an effeminate and fond bringing up, are timerous and afraid of spirits, and bugs, &c. Some through imperfection of sight also are afraid of their owne shadowes, and (as *Aristotle* saith) see themselves sometimes as it were in a glasse. And some through weakenesse of bodie have such unperfect imaginations. Droonken men also sometimes suppose they see trees walke, &c: according to that which *Salomon* saith to the droonkards; Thine eies shall see strange visions, and mervellous appearances.

In all ages moonks and preests have abused and bewitched the world with counterfet visions; which proceeded through idlenes, and restraint of marriage, wherby they grew hot and lecherous, and therefore devised such meanes to compasse and obteine their loves. And the simple people being then so superstitious, would never seeme to mistrust, that such holie men would make them cuckholds, but forsooke their beds in that case, and gave roome to the cleargie. Item, little children have beene so scared with their mothers maids, that they could never after endure to be in the darke alone, for feare of bugs. Manie are deceived by glasses through art perspective. Manie hearkening unto false reports, conceive and beleeve that which is nothing so. Manie give credit to that which they read in authors. But how manie stories and bookes are written of walking spirits and soules of men, contrarie to the word of God; a reasonable volume cannot conteine. How common an opinion was it among the papists, that all soules walked on the earth, after they departed from their bodies? In so much as it was in the time of poperie a usuall matter, to desire sicke people in their death beds, to appeare to them after their death, and to reveale their estate. The fathers and ancient doctors of the church were too credulous herein,

see the storie of Simõ Davie and Ade his wife, lib. 3. cap. 10. pag. 31, 32.

Against the counterfet visions of popish preests, & other cousening devises.

268

&c. Therefore no mervell, though the common simple sort of men, and least of all, that women be deceived herein. God in times past did send downe visible angels and appearances to men; but now he dooth not so. Through ignorance of late in religion, it was thought, that everie churchyard swarmed with soules and spirits: but now the word of God being more free, open, and knowne, those conceipts and illusions are made more manifest and apparent, &c.

The doctors, councels, and popes, which (they saie) cannot erre, have confirmed the walking, appearing, & raising of soules. But where find they in the scriptures anie such doctrine? And who certified them, that those appearances were true? Trulie all they cannot bring to passe, that the lies which have beene spread abroad herein, should now beginne to be true, though the pope himselfe subscribe, seale, and sweare thereunto never so much. Where are the soules that swarmed in times past? Where are the spirits? Who heareth their noises? Who seeth their visions? Where are the soules that made such mone for trentals, whereby to be eased of the paines in purgatorie? Are they all gone into *Italie*, bicause masses are growne deere here in *England?* Marke well this illusion, and see how contrarie it is unto the word of God. Consider how all papists beleeve this illusion to be true, and how all protestants are driven to saie it is and was popish illusion. Where be the spirits that wandered to have buriall for their bodies? For manie of those walking soules went about that busines. Doo you not thinke, that the papists shew not themselves godlie divines, to preach and teach the people such doctrine; and to insert into their divine service such fables as are read in the Romish church, all scripture giving place thereto for the time? You shall see in the lessons read there upon S. *Stevens* daie, that *Gamaliel Nichodemus* his kinsman, and *Abdias* his sonne, with his freend S. *Steven*, appeared to a certeine preest, called Sir *Lucian*, requesting him to remove their bodies, and to burie them in some better place (for they had lien from the time of their death, untill then, being in the reigne of *Honorius* the emperor; to wit, foure hundred yeeres buried in the field of *Gamaliel*, who in that respect said to Sir *Lucian; Non mei solummodo causa solicitus sum, sed potiùs pro illis qui mecum sunt;* that is, I am not onlie carefull for my selfe, but cheefelie for those my friends that are with me. Whereby the whole course may be perceived to be a false practise, and a counterfet vision, or rather a lewd invention. For in heaven mens soules remaine not in sorow and care; neither studie they there how to compasse and get a worshipfull buriall here in earth. If they did, they would not have foreslowed it so long. Now therefore let us not suffer our selves to be abused anie longer, either with conjuring preests, or melancholicall witches; but be thankfull to God that hath delivered us from such blindness and error.

This doctrine was not onlie preached, but also prooved; note the particular instãces following.

CHAPTER XL

Cardanus opinion of strange noises, how counterfet visions grow to be credited, of popish appeerances, of pope Boniface.

CARDANUS speaking of noises, among other things, saith thus; A noise is heard in your house; it may be a mouse, a cat, or a dog among dishes; it may be a counterfet or a theefe indeed, or the fault may be in your eares. I could recite a great number of tales, how men have even forsaken their houses, bicause of such apparitions and noises: and all hath beene by meere and ranke knaverie. And wheresoever you shall heare, that there is in the night season such rumbling and fearefull noises, be you well assured that it is flat knaverie, performed by some that seemeth most to complaine, and is least mistrusted. And hereof there is a verie art, which for some respects I will not discover. The divell seeketh dailie as well as nightlie whome he may devoure,

H. Card. lib. de var. rer. 15. ca. 92.

and can doo his feats as well by daie as by night, or else he is a yoong divell, and a verie bungler. But of all other couseners, these conjurors are in the highest degree, and are most worthie of death for their blasphemous impietie. But that these popish visions and conjurations used as well by papists, as by the popes themselves, were meere cousenages; and that the tales of the popes recited by *Bruno* and *Platina,* of their magicall devises, were but plaine cousenages and knaveries, may appeare by the historie of *Bonifacius* the eight, who used this kind of inchantment, to get away the popedome from his predecessor *Cælestinus.* He counterfetted a voice through a cane reed, as though it had come from heaven, persuading him to yeeld up his authoritie of popeship, and to institute therein one *Bonifacius,* a worthier man: otherwise he threatened him with damnation. And therfore the foole yeelded it up accordinglie, to the said *Bonifacius, An.* 1264. of whom it was said; He came in like a fox, lived like a woolfe, and died like a dog.

Pope *Cæle-stinus* couse-ned of his popedome by pope *Boniface.*

There be innumerable examples of such visions, which when they are not detected, go for true stories: and therefore when it is answered that some are true tales and some are false, untill they be able to shew foorth before your eies one matter of truth, you may replie upon them with this distinction; to wit: visions tried are false visions, undecided and untried are true.

Visions dis-tinguished.

CHAPTER XLI.

Of the noise or sound of eccho, of one that narrowlie escaped drowning thereby, &c.

ALAS! how manie naturall things are there so strange, as to manie seeme miraculous; and how manie counterfet matters are there, that to the simple seeme yet more wonderfull? *Cardane* telleth of one *Comensis,* who comming late to a rivers side, not knowing where to passe over, cried out alowd for some bodie to shew him the foord: who hearing an eccho to answer according to his last word, supposing it to be a man that answered him and informed him of the waie, he passed through the river, even there where was a deepe whirlepoole, so as he hardlie escaped with his life; and told his freends, that the divell had almost persuaded him to drowne himselfe. And in some places these noises of eccho are farre more strange than other, speciallie at *Ticinum* in *Italie,* in the great hall, where it rendereth sundrie and manifold noises or voices, which seeme to end so lamentablie, as it were a man that laie a dieng; so as few can be persuaded that it is the eccho, but a spirit that answereth.

H. Card. lib. de subtili-tat. 18.

Idem, ibid.

The noise at *Winchester* was said to be a verie miracle, and much wondering was there at it, about the yeare 1569. though indeed a meere naturall noise ingendered of the wind, the concavitie of the place, and other instrumentall matters helping the sound to seeme strange to the hearers; speciallie to such as would adde new reports to the augmentation of the woonder.

Of Win-chester noise.

CHAPTER XLII.

Of Theurgie, with a confutation thereof, a letter sent to me concerning these matters.

THERE is yet another art professed by these cousening conjurors, which some fond divines affirme to be more honest and lawfull than necromancie, which is called Theurgie; wherein they worke by good angels. Howbeit, their ceremonies are altogether papisticall and superstitious, consisting in clean-

270

lines partlie of the mind, partlie of the bodie, and partlie of things about and belonging to the bodie; as in the skinne, in the apparell, in the house, in the vessell and houshold stuffe, in oblations and sacrifices; the cleanlines whereof, they saie, dooth dispose men to the contemplation of heavenlie things. They cite these words of *Esaie* for their authoritie; to wit: Wash your selves and be cleane, &c. In so much as I have knowne diverse superstitious persons of good account, which usuallie washed all their apparell upon conceits ridiculouslie. For uncleanlinesse (they say) corrupteth the aire, infecteth man, and chaseth awaie cleane spirits. Hereunto belongeth the art of *Almadel*, the art of *Paule*, the art of Revelations, and the art Notarie. But (as *Agrippa* saith) the more divine these arts seeme to the ignorant, the more damnable they be. But their false assertions, their presumptions to worke miracles, their characters, their strange names, their diffuse phrases, their counterfet holines, their popish ceremonies, their foolish words mingled with impietie, their barbarous and unlearned order of construction, their shameles practises, their paltrie stuffe, their secret dealing, their beggerlie life, their bargaining with fooles, their cousening of the simple, their scope and drift for monie dooth bewraie all their art to be counterfet cousenage. And the more throughlie to satisfie you herein, I thought good in this place to insert a letter, upon occasion sent unto me, by one which at this present time lieth as a prisoner condemned for this verie matter in the kings bench, and reprived by hir majesties mercie, through the good mediation of a most noble and vertuous personage, whose honorable and godlie disposition at this time I will forbeare to commend as I ought. The person truelie that wrote this letter seemeth unto me a good bodie, well reformed, and penitent, not expecting anie gaines at my hands, but rather fearing to speake that which he knoweth further in this matter, least displeasure might ensue and follow.

Appendents unto the supposed divine art of Theurgie.

The copie of a letter sent unto me R. S. by T. E.

Maister of art, and practiser both of physicke, and also in times past, of certeine vaine sciences; now condemned to die for the same: wherein he openeth the truth touching these deceits.

MAISTER R. SCOT, according to your request, I have drawne out certeine abuses worth the noting, touching the worke you have in hand; things which I my selfe have seene within these xxvi. yeares, among those which were counted famous and skilfull in those sciences. And bicause the whole discourse cannot be set downe, without nominating certeine persons, of whom some are dead & some living, whose freends remaine yet of great credit: in respect therof, I knowing that mine enimies doo alreadie in number exceed my freends; I have considered with my selfe, that it is better for me to staie my hand, than to commit that to the world, which may increase my miserie more than releeve the same. Notwithstanding, bicause I am noted above a great manie others to have had some dealings in those vaine arts and wicked practises; I am therefore to signifie unto you, and I speake it in the presence of God, that among all those famous and noted practisers, that I have beene conversant withall these xxvi. yeares, I could never see anie matter of truth to be doone in those wicked sciences, but onelie meere cousenings and illusions. And they, whome I thought to be most skilfull therein, sought to see some things at my hands, who had spent my time a dozen or fourteen years, to my great losse and hinderance, and could never at anie time see anie one truth, or sparkle of truth therein. Yet at this present I stand worthilie condemned for the same; for that, contrarie to my princes lawes, and the lawe of God, and also to mine owne conscience, I did spend my time in such vaine and wicked studies and practises: being made and remaining a spectacle for all others to receive warning by. The Lord grant I may be the last (I speake it from my hart) and I wish it, not onlie in my native coûtrie, but also through the whole face of the earth, speciallie among Christians. For mine owne part I lament my time lost, & have repented me five years past: at which time I sawe a booke,

Marke the summe and scope of this letter.

written in the old Saxon toong, by one Sir John Malborne a divine of Oxenford, three hundred yeares past; wherein he openeth all the illusions & inventions of those arts and sciences: a thing most worthie the noting. I left the booke with the parson of Slangham in Sussex, where if you send for it in my name, you may have it. You shall thinke your labour well bestowed, and it shall greatlie further the good enterprise you have in hand: and there shall you see the whole science throughlie discussed, and all their illusions and cousenages deciphered at large. Thus craving pardon at your hands for that I promised you, being verie fearefull, doubtfull, and loth to set my hand or name under any thing that may be offensive to the world, or hurtfull to my selfe, considering my case, except I had the better warrant from my L. of Leicester, who is my verie good Lord, and by whome next under God (hir Majestie onelie excepted) I have beene preserved; and therefore loth to doo any thing that may offend his Lordships eares. And so I leave your Worship to the Lords keeping, who bring you and all your actions to good end and purpose, to Gods glorie, and to the profit of all Christians. From the bench this 8. of March, 1582. Your Worships poore and desolate friend and servant, T. E.

I sent for this booke of purpose, to the parson of *Slangham*, and procured his best friends, men of great worship and credit, to deale with him, that I might borrowe it for a time. But such is his follie and superstition, that although he confessed he had it; yet he would not lend it: albeit a friend of mine, being knight of the shire would have given his word for the restitution of the same safe and sound.

The conclusion therefore shall be this, whatsoever heeretofore hath gone for currant, touching all these fallible arts, whereof hitherto I have written in ample sort, he now counted counterfet, and therefore not to be allowed no not by common sense, much lesse by reason, which should sift such cloked and pretended practises, turning them out of their rags and patched clowts, that they may appeere discovered, and shew themselves in their nakednesse. Which will be the end of everie secret intent, privie purpose, hidden practise, and close devise, have they never such shrowds and shelters for the time: and be they with never so much cautelousnesse and subtill circumspection clouded and shadowed, yet will they at length be manifestlie detected by the light, according to that old rimed verse:

Quicquid nix celat, solis calor omne revelat:

> What thing soever snowe dooth hide,
> Heat of the sunne dooth make it spide.

And according to the verdict of Christ, the true Nazarite, who never told untruth, but who is the substance and groundworke of truth it selfe, saieng; *Nihil est tam occultum quod non sit detegendum,* Nothing is so secret, but it shall be knowne and revealed.

BOOKE XVI.

Chapter I.

A conclusion, in maner of an epilog, repeating manie of the former absurdities of witch-mongers conceipts, confutations thereof, and of the authoritie of James Sprenger and Henrie Institor inquisitors and compilers of M. Mal.

HITHERTO you have had delivered unto you, that which I have conceived and gathered of this matter. In the substance and principall parts wherof I can see no difference among the writers heereupon; of what countrie, condition, estate, or religion so ever they be; but I find almost all of them to agree in unconstancie, fables, and impossibilities; scratching out of *M. Mal.* the substance of all their arguments: so as their authors being disapproved, they must coine new stuffe, or go to their grandams maids to learne more old wives tales, whereof this art of witchcraft is contrived. But you must know that *James Sprenger*, and *Henrie Institor*, whome I have had occasion to alledge manie times, were coparteners in the composition of that profound & learned booke called *Malleus Maleficarum*, & were the greatest doctors of that art: out of whom I have gathered matter and absurditie enough, to confound the opinions conceived of witchcraft; although they were allowed inquisitors and assigned by the pope, with the authoritie and commendation of all the doctors of the universitie of *Collen*, &c: to call before them, to imprison, to condemne, and to execute witches; and finallie to seaze and confiscate their goods.

The compilers or makers of the booke called A Mallet to braine witches.

These two doctors, to mainteine their their credit, and to cover their injuries, have published those same monsterous lies, which have abused all Christendome, being spread abroad with such authoritie, as it will be hard to suppresse the credit of their writings, be they never so ridiculous and false. Which although they mainteine and stirre up with their owne praises; yet men are so bewitched, as to give credit unto them. For proofe whereof I remember they write in one place of their said booke, that by reason of their severe proceedings against witches, they suffered intollerable assaults, speciallie in the night, many times finding needdels sticking in their biggens, which were thither conveied by witches charmes: and through their innocencie and holinesse (they saie) they were ever miraculouslie preserved from hurt. Howbeit they affirme that they will not tell all that might make to the manifestation of their holines: for then should their owne praise stinke in their owne mouthes. And yet God knoweth their whole booke conteineth nothing but stinking lies and poperie. Which groundworke and foundation how weake and wavering it is, how unlike to continue, and how slenderlie laid, a child may soone discerne and perceive.

No marvel that they were so opinionative herein, for God gave them over into strong delusions.

CHAPTER II.

By what meanes the common people have beene made beleeve in the miraculous works of witches, a definition of witchcraft, and a description thereof.

THE common people have beene so assotted and bewitched, with whatsoever poets have feigned of witchcraft, either in earnest, in jest, or else in derision; and with whatsoever lowd liers and couseners for their pleasures heerein have invented, and with whatsoever tales they have heard from old doting women, or from their mothers maids, and with whatsoever the grandfoole their ghostlie father, or anie other morrow masse preest had informed them; and finallie with whatsoever they have swallowed up through tract of time, or through their owne timerous nature or ignorant conceipt, concerning these matters of hagges and witches: as they have so settled their opinion and credit thereupon, that they thinke it heresie to doubt in anie part of the matter; speciallie bicause they find this word witchcraft expressed in the scriptures; which is as to defend praieng to saincts, bicause *Sanctus, Sanctus, Sanctus* is written in *Te Deum.*

The definition or description of witchcraft.

And now to come to the definition of witchcraft, which hitherto I did deferre and put off purposelie: that you might perceive the true nature thereof, by the circumstances, and therefore the rather to allow of the same, seeing the varietie of other writers. Witchcraft is in truth a cousening art, wherin the name of God is abused, prophaned and blasphemed, and his power attributed to a vile creature. In estimation of the vulgar people, it is a supernaturall worke, contrived betweene a corporall old woman, and a spirituall divell. The maner thereof is so secret, mysticall, and strange, that to this daie there hath never beene any credible witnes therof. It is incomprehensible to the wise, learned or faithfull; a probable matter to children, fooles, melancholike persons and papists. The trade is thought to be impious. The effect and end thereof to be sometimes evill, as when thereby man or beast, grasse, trees, or corne, &c; is hurt: sometimes good, as whereby sicke folkes are healed, theeves bewraied, and true men come to their goods, &c. The matter and instruments, wherewith it is accomplished, are words, charmes, signes, images, characters, &c: the which words although any other creature doo pronounce, in maner and forme as they doo, leaving out no circumstance requisite or usuall for that action: yet none is said to have the grace or gift to performe the matter, except she be a witch, and so taken, either by hir owne consent, or by others imputation.

The formal cause.

The finall cause.

The materiall cause.

CHAPTER III.

Reasons to proove that words and characters are but bables, & that witches cannot doo such things as the multitude supposeth they can, their greatest woonders prooved trifles, of a yoong gentleman cousened.

THAT words, characters, images, and such other trinkets, which are thought so necessarie instruments for witchcraft (as without the which no such thing can be accomplished) are but bables, devised by couseners, to abuse the people withall; I trust I have sufficientlie prooved. And the same maie be further and more plainelie perceived by these short and compendious reasons following.

First, in that the *Turkes* and infidels, in their witchcraft, use both other words, and other characters than our witches doo, and also such as are most contrarie. In so much as, if ours be bad, in reason theirs should be good. If their witches can doo anie thing, ours can doo nothing. For as our witches are said to renounce Christ, and despise his sacraments: so doo the other forsake *Mahomet*, and his lawes, which is one large step to christianitie.

A necessarie sequele.

It is also to be thought, that all witches arc couseners; when mother *Bungie*, a principall witch, so reputed, tried, and condemned of all men, and continuing in that exercise and estimation manie yeeres (having cousened & abused the whole realme, in so much as there came to hir, witchmongers from all the furthest parts of the land, she being in diverse bookes set out with authoritie, registred and chronicled by the name of the great witch of *Rochester*, and reputed among all men for the cheefe ringleader of all other witches) by good proofe is found to be a meere cousener; confessing in hir death bed freelie, without compulsion or inforcement, that hir cunning consisted onlie in deluding and deceiving the people: saving that she had (towards the maintenance of hir credit in that cousening trade) some sight in physicke and surgerie, and the assistance of a freend of hirs, called *Heron*, a professor thereof. And this I know, partlie of mine owne knowledge, and partlie by the testimonie of hir husband, and others of credit, to whome (I saie) in hir death bed, and at sundrie other times she protested these things; and also that she never had indeed anie materiall spirit or divell (as the voice went) nor yet knew how to worke anie supernaturall matter, as she in hir life time made men beleeve she had and could doo.

Probatum est, by mother Bungies confessiō that al witches are couseners.

The like may be said of one *T.* of *Canturburie*, whose name I will not litterallie discover, who wonderfullie abused manie in these parts, making them thinke he could tell where anie thing lost became: with diverse other such practises, whereby his fame was farre beyond the others. And yet on his death bed he confessed, that he knew nothing more than anie other, but by slight and devises, without the assistance of anie divell or spirit, saving the spirit of cousenage: and this did he (I saie) protest before manie of great honestie, credit, & wisedome, who can witnesse the same, and also gave him good commendations for his godlie and honest end.

Againe, who will mainteine, that common witchcrafts are not cousenages, when the great and famous witchcrafts, which had stolne credit not onlie from all the common people, but from men of great wisdome and authoritie, are discovered to be beggerlie slights of cousening varlots? Which otherwise might and would have remained a perpetuall objection against me. Were there not three images of late yeeres found in a doonghill, to the terror & astonishment of manie thousands? In so much as great matters were thought to have beene pretended to be doone by witchcraft. But if the Lord preserve those persons (whose destruction was doubted to have beene intended therby) from all other the lewd practises and attempts of their enimies; I feare not, but they shall easilie withstand these and such like devises, although they should indeed be practised against them. But no doubt, if such bables could have brought those matters of mischeefe to passe, by the hands of traitors, witches, or papists; we should long since have beene deprived of the most excellent jewell and comfort that we enjoy in this world. Howbeit, I confesse, that the feare, conceipt, and doubt of such mischeefous pretenses may breed inconvenience to them that stand in awe of the same. And I wish, that even for such practises, though they never can or doo take effect, the practisers be punished with all extremitie: bicause therein is manifested a traiterous heart to the Queene, and a presumption against God.

J. Bodin in the preface before his booke of *Dæmonomania* reporteth this by a conjuring preest late Curat of Islington: hee also sheweth to what end: read the place you that understād Latine.

But to returne to the discoverie of the aforesaid knaverie and witchcraft. So it was that one old cousener, wanting monie, devised or rather practised (for it is a stale devise) to supplie his want, by promising a yoong Gentleman, whose humor he thought would make that waie be well served, that for the summe of fourtie pounds, he would not faile by his cunning in that art of witchcraft, to procure unto him the love of anie three women whome he would name, and of whome he should make choise at his pleasure. The yoong Gentleman being abused

Note this devise of the waxen images found of late neere London.

with his cunning devises, and too hastilie yeelding to that motion, satisfied this cunning mans demand of monie. Which, bicause he had it not presentlie to disbursse, provided it for him at the hands of a freend of his. Finallie, this cunning man made the three puppets of wax, &c: leaving nothing undone that appertained to the cousenage, untill he had buried them, as you have heard. But I omit to tell what a doo was made herof, and also what reports and lies were bruted; as what white dogs and blacke dogs there were seene in the night season passing through the watch, mawgre all their force and preparation against them, &c. But the yoong Gentleman, who for a litle space remained in hope mixed with joy and love, now through tract of time hath those his felicities powdered with doubt and despaire. For in steed of atchieving his love, he would gladlie have obteined his monie. But bicause he could by no meanes get either the one or the other (his monie being in huckster's handling, and his sute in no better forwardnes) he revealed the whole matter, hoping by that meanes to recover his monie; which he neither can yet get againe, nor hath paied it where he borrowed. But till triall was had of his simplicitie or rather follie herein, he received some trouble himselfe hereabouts, though now dismissed.

CHAPTER IV.

Of one that was so bewitched that he could read no scriptures but canonicall, of a divel that could speake no Latine, a proofe that witchcraft is flat cousenage.

A strange miracle, if it were true.

HERE I may aptlie insert another miracle of importance, that happened within the compasse of a childes remembrance, which may induce anie resonable bodie to conceive, that these supernaturall actions are but fables & cousenages. There was one, whom for some respects I name not, that was taken blind, deafe, & dumbe; so as no physician could helpe him. That man (forsooth) though he was (as is said) both blind, dumbe & deafe, yet could he read anie canonicall scriptures; but as for apocrypha, he could read none:

There the hypocrite was over-matcht for all his dissembled gravitie.

wherein a Gods name consisted the miracle. But a leafe of apocrypha being extraordinarilie inserted among the canonicall scriptures, he read the same as authentike: wherein his knaverie was bewraied. Another had a divell, that answered men to all questions, marie hir divell could understand no Latine, and so was she (and by such meanes all the rest may be) bewraied. Indeed our witching writers saie, that certeine divels speake onelie the language of that countrie where they are resiant, as French, or English, &c.

Furthermore, in my conceipt, nothing prooveth more apparentlie that witchcraft is cousenage, and that witches instruments are but ridiculous bables, and altogither void of effect; than when learned and godlie divines, in their serious writings, produce experiments as wrought by witches, and by divels at witches commandements: which they expound by miracles, although indeed meere trifles. Whereof they conceive amisse, being overtaken with credulitie.

CHAPTER V.

Of the divination by the sive and sheeres, and by the booke and key, Hemingius his opinion thereof confuted, a bable to know what is a clocke, of certeine jugling knacks, manifold reasons for the overthrowe of witches and conjurors, and their cousenages, of the divels transformations, of Ferrum candens, &c.

TO passe over all the fables, which are vouched by the popish doctors, you shall heare the words of *N. Hemingius*, whose zeale & learning otherwise I might justlie commend: howbeit I am sorie and ashamed to see his ignorance and follie in this behalfe. Neither would I have bewraied it, but that he himselfe, among other absurdities concerning the maintenance of witches omnipotencie, hath published it to his great discredit. Popish preests (saith he) as the *Chaldæans* used the divination by sive and sheeres for the detection of theft, doo practice with a psalter and a keie fastned upon the 49. psalme, to discover a theefe. And when the names of the suspected persons are orderlie put into the pipe of the keie, at the reading of these words of the psalme [If thou sawest a theefe thou diddest consent unto him] the booke will wagge, and fall out of the fingers of them that hold it, and he whose name remaineth in the keie must be the theefe. Hereupon *Hemingius* inferreth, that although conjuring preests and witches bring not this to passe by the absolute words of the psalme, which tend to a farre other scope; yet sathan dooth nimblie, with his invisible hand, give such a twitch to the booke, as also in the other case to the sive and the sheeres, that downe falles the booke and keie, sive and sheeres, up starts the theefe, and awaie runneth the divell laughing, &c.

But alas, *Hemingius* is deceived, as not perceiving the conceipt, or rather the deceipt hereof. For where he supposeth those actions to be miraculous, and done by a divell; they are in truth meere bables, wherein consisteth not so much as legierdemaine. For everie carter may conceive the slight hereof: bicause the booke and keie, sive and sheeres, being staied up in that order, by naturall course, of necessitie must within that space (by means of the aire, and the pulse beating at the fingers end) turne and fall downe. Which experience being knowne to the witch or conjuror, she or he doo forme and frame their prophesie accordinglie: as whosoever maketh proofe thereof shall manifestlie perceive it. By this art, practise, or experience, you shall knowe what it is a clocke, if you hold betweene your finger and your thumbe a thred of six or seven inches long, unto the other end whereof is tied a gold ring, or some such like thing: in such sort as upon the beating of your pulse, and the mooving of the ring, the same may strike upon either side of a goblet or glasse. These things are (I confesse) witchcraft, bicause the effect or event proceedeth not of that cause which such couseners saie, and others beleeve they doo. As when they laie a medicine for the ague, &c: to a childs wrists, they also pronounce certeine words or charmes, by vertue whereof (they saie) the child is healed: whereas indeed the medicine onelie dooth the feate. And this is also a sillie jugglers knacke, which wanteth legierdemaine, whom you shall see to thrust a pinne, or a small knife, through the head and braine of a chicken or pullet, and with certeine mysticall words seeme to cure him: whereas, though no such words were spoken, the chicken would live, and doo well enough; as experience teacheth and declareth.

Againe, when such as have mainteined the art and profession of conjuring, and have written thereupon most cunninglie, have published recantations, and confessed the deceipts thereof, as *Cornelius Agrippa* did, whie should we defend it? Also, when heathen princes, of great renowne, authoritie, & learning, have searched, with much industrie and charge, the knowledge & secrecie of conjuration and witchcraft, & finallie found by experience all to be false and vaine

Heming. in lib. de superst. magicis.

[p. 149]

The greatest clarkes are not the wisest men.

A naturall reason of the former knacke.

[p. 196.]

C. Agripp. in lib. de vanit. scient. & in epistola ante librum de occulta philosophia.

Plin. lib.
natural. hist.
30. cap. 1.
Pet. Mart.
in locis com-
munibus.

that is reported of them, as *Nero*, *Julianus apostata*, and *Valence* did; whie should we seeke for further triall, to proove witchcraft and conjuration to be cousenage?

Also, when the miracles imputed unto them, exceed in quantitie, qualitie and number, all the miracles that Christ wrought here upon earth, for the establishing of his gospell, for the confirmation of our faith, and for the advancement of his glorious name; what good christian will beleeve them to be true? And when Christ himselfe saith; The works that I doo, no man else can accomplish; whie should we thinke that a foolish old woman can doo them all, and manie more?

Also, when Christ knew not these witches, nor spake one word of them in all the time of his being here upon earth, having such necessarie occasion (if at leastwise they with their familiars could doo as he did by the spirit of God, as is constantlie affirmed) whie should we suppose that they can doo as they saie, but rather that they are deceivers[?] When they are faine to saie, that witches wrought not in that art, all those thirtie three yeares that Christ lived, and that there were none in *Jobs* time, and that the cousening oracles are now ceased; who seeth not that they are witlesse, and madde fooles that mainteine it? When all the mischeefes are accomplished by poisons and naturall meanes, which they affirme to be brought to passe by words, it manifesteth to the world their cousenage. When all the places of scripture, which witchmongers allowe for the proofe of such witches, are prooved to make nothing for their purpose, their own fables and lies deserve small credit. When one of the cheefe points in controversie; to wit, execution of witches, is grounded upon a false translation; namelie, You shall not suffer a witch to live (which is in Latine, *Veneficam non retinebitis in vita*) where the word in everie mans eare soundeth to be a poisoner, rather than a worker of miracles, and so interpreted by the seventie interpretors, *Josephus*, and almost of all the *Rabbins*, which were *Hebrues* borne: whie should anie of their interpretations or allegations be trusted, or well accounted of? When working of miracles is ceased, and the gift of prophesie also; so as the godlie, through invocation of the holie spirit, cannot performe such wonderful things, as these witches and conjurors by the invocation of divels and wicked spirits undertake, and are said to doo; what man that knoweth and honoureth God will be so infatuate as to beleeve these lies, and so preferre the power of witches and divels before the godlie endued with Gods holie spirit? When manie printed bookes are published, even with authoritie, in confirmation of such miracles wrought by those couseners, for the detection of witchcraft; and in fine all is not onelie found false, and to have beene accomplished by cousenage, but that there hath beene therein a set purpose to defame honest matrones, as to make them be thought to be witches: whie should we beleeve *Bodin*, *M. Mal.* &c: in their cousening tales and fables? When they saie that witches can flie in the aire, and come in at a little coane, or a hole in a glasse windowe, and steale awaie sucking children, and hurt their mothers; and yet when they are brought into prison, they cannot escape out of the grate, which is farre bigger: who will not condemne such accusations or confessions to be frivolous, &c? When (if their assertions were true) concerning the divels usuall taking of shapes, and walking, talking, conferring, hurting, and all maner of dealing with mortall creatures, Christs argument to *Thomas* had beene weake and easilie answered; yea the one halfe, or all the whole world might be inhabited by divels, everie poore mans house might be hired over his head by a divell, he might take the shape and favor of an honest woman, and plaie the witch; or of an honest man, and plaie the theefe, and so bring them both, or whome he list to the gallowes: who seeth not the vanitie of such assertions? For then the divell might in the likenes of an honest man commit anie criminal offense; as *Lavater* in his nineteenth chapter *De spectris* reporteth of a grave wise magistrate in the territorie of *Tigurie*, who affirmed, that as he and his servant went through certeine pastures, he espied in a morning, the divell in likenes of one whome he knew verie well, wickedlie dealing with a mare. Upon the sight whereof he immediatlie went to that fellowes house, and certeinlie learned

Note that
during all
Christs time
upon earth,
which was
33. yeares,
witches
were put
to silence,
&c.

But Christs
argument
was un-
doubted:
Ergo, &c.

I marvell
for what
purpose the

there, that the same person went not out of his chamber that daie. And if he
had not wiselie boolted out the matter, the good honest man (saith he) had
surelie beene cast into prison, and put on the racke, &c.

    The like storie we read of one *Cunegunda*, wife to *Henrie* the second emperor
of that name, in whose chamber the divell (in the likenes of a yoongman, with
whome she was suspected to be too familiar in court) was often seene comming
in and out. How beit, she was purged by the triall *Candentis ferri*, and prooved
innocent: for she went upon glowing iron unhurt, &c. And yet *Salomon* saith;
Maie a man carrie fier in his bosome and his clothes not be burned? Or can a
man go upon coles, & his feete not scortched? And thus might the divell get
him up into everie pulpit, and spred heresies, as I doubt not but he dooth in the
mouth of wicked preachers, though not so grosselie as is imagined and reported
by the papists and witchmongers. And because it shall not be said that I beelie
them, I will cite a storie crediblie reported by their cheefest doctors; namelie
James Sprenger, and *Henrie Institor*, who saie as followeth, even word for word.

magistrate
went to that
fellowes
house.

*Albertus
Crantzius in
lib.* 4. *metro-
polis. cap.* 4.

Prov. 6.

*Mal. malef.
par.* 2. *quæ.* 1.
cap. 9.

Chapter VI.

*How the divell preached good doctrine in the shape of a preest, how he was discovered, and
that it is a shame (after confutation of the greater witchcrafts) for anie man to give
credit to the lesser points thereof.*

ON a time the divell went up into a pulpit, and there made a verie catholike
sermon: but a holie preest comming to the good speed, by his holinesse
perceived that it was the divell. So he gave good eare unto him, but could
find no fault with his doctrine. And therefore so soone as the sermon was doone,
he called the divell unto him, demanding the cause of his sincere preaching;
who answered: Behold I speake the truth, knowing that while men be hearers of
the word, and not followers, God is the more offended, and my kingdome the
more inlarged. And this was the strangest devise (I thinke) that ever anie divell
used: for the apostles themselves could have done no more. Againe, when with
all their familiars, their ointments, &c: whereby they ride invisiblie, nor with
all their charmes, they can neither conveie themselves from the hands of such
as laie wait for them; nor can get out of prison, that otherwise can go in and out
at a mouse hole; nor finallie can save themselves from the gallowes, that can
transubstantiate their own and others bodies into flies or fleas, &c: who seeth not,
that either they lie, or are beelied in their miracles? When they are said to transfer their neighbors corne into their owne ground, and yet are perpetuall beggers,
and cannot inrich themselves, either with monie or otherwise: who is so foolish
as to remaine longer in doubt of their supernaturall power? When never any
yet from the beginning of the world till this daie, hath openlie shewed any other
tricke, conceipt, or cunning point of witchcraft, than legierdemaine or cousenage: who will tarrie any longer for further triall? When both the common law
and also the injunctions doo condemne prophesieng, & likewise false miracles,
and such as beleeve them in these daies: who will not be afraid to give credit
to those knaveries? When heereby they make the divell to be a god that heareth
the praiers, and understandeth the minds of men: who will not be ashamed,
being a christian, to be so abused by them? When they that doo write most
franklie of these matters, except lieng *Sprenger* & *Institor*, have never seene any
thing heerin; insomuch as the most credible proofe that *Bodin* bringeth of his
woonderfull tales of witchcraft, is the report of his host at an alehouse where he
baited: who will give further eare unto these incredible fables? When in all the
new testament, we are not warned of these bodilie appearances of divels, as we
are of his other subtilties, &c: who will be afraid of their bugs? When no such

He should
rather have
asked who
gave him
orders and
licence to
preach.

[pp. 52, 126.]

John. Bodin.

bargaine is mentioned in the scriptures, why should we beleeve so incredible and impossible covenants, being the ground of all witchmongers religion, without the which they have no probabilitie in the rest of their foolish assertions? When as, if any honest mans conscience be appealed unto, he must confesse he never saw triall of such witchcraft or conjuration to take effect, as is now so certeinlie affirmed: what conscience can condemne poore soules that are accused wrong-fullie, or beleeve them that take upon them impiouslie to doo or worke those impossible things? When the whole course of the scripture is utterlie repugnant to these impossible opinions, saving a few sentences, which neverthelesse rightlie understood, releeve them nothing at all: who will be seduced by their fond arguments? When as now that men have spied the knaverie of oracles, & such pelfe, and that there is not one oracle in the world remaining: who cannot perceive that all the residue heeretofore of those devises, have beene cousenages, knaveries, and lies? When the power of God is so impudentlie transferred to a base creature, what good christian can abide to yeeld unto such miracles wrought by fooles? When the old women accused of witchcraft, are utterlie insensible, and unable to saie for themselves; and much lesse to bring such matters to passe, as they are accused of: who will not lament to see the extremitie used against them? When the foolisher sort of people are alwaies most mistrustfull of hurt by witchcraft, and the simplest and dotingest people mistrusted to doo the hurt: what wise man will not conceive all to be but follie? When it were an easie matter for the divell, if he can doo as they affirme, to give them great store of monie, and make them rich, and dooth it not; being a thing which would procure him more disciples than any other thing in the world: the wise must needs condemne the divell of follie, and the witches of peevish-nesse, that take such paines, and give their soules to the divell to be tormented in hell fier, and their bodies to the hangman to be trussed on the gallowes, for nichels in a bag.

CHAPTER VII.

A conclusion against witchcraft, in maner and forme of an Induction.

B Y this time all kentishmen know (a few fooles excepted) that Robin good-fellowe is a knave. All wisemen understand that witches miraculous enter-prises, being contrarie to nature, probabilitie and reason, are void of truth or possibilitie. All protestants perceive, that popish charmes, conjurations, execrations, and benedictions are not effectuall, but be toies and devises onelie to keepe the people blind, and to inrich the cleargie. All christians see, that to confesse witches can doo as they saie, were to attribute to a creature the power of the Creator. All children well brought up conceive and spie, or at the least are taught, that juglers miracles doo consist of legierdemaine and confederacie. The verie heathen people are driven to confesse, that there can be no such con-ference betweene a spirituall divell and a corporall witch, as is supposed. For no doubt, all the heathen would then have everie one his familiar divell; for they would make no conscience to acquaint themselves with a divell that are not acquainted with God.

I have dealt, and conferred with manie (marrie I must confesse papists for the most part) that mainteine every point of these absurdities. And surelie I allow better of their judgements, than of others, unto whome some part of these cousenages are discovered and seene: and yet concerning the residue, they remaine as wise as they were before; speciallie being satisfied in the highest and greatest parts of conjuring and cousening; to wit, in poperie, and yet will be abused with beggerlie jugling, and witchcraft.

CHAPTER VIII.

Of naturall witchcraft or fascination.

BUT bicause I am loth to oppose my selfe against all the writers heerin, or altogither to discredit their stories, or wholie to deface their reports, touching the effects of fascination or witchcraft; I will now set downe certeine parts thereof, which although I my selfe cannot admit, without some doubts, difficulties and exceptions, yet will I give free libertie to others to beleeve them, if they list; for that they doo not directlie oppugne my purpose.

Manie great and grave authors write, and manie fond writers also affirme, that there are certeine families in *Aphrica* which with their voices bewitch whatsoever they praise. Insomuch as, if they commend either plant, corne, infant, horsse, or anie other beasts, the same presentlie withereth, decaieth and dieth. This mysterie of witchcraft is not unknowne or neglected of our witchmongers, and superstitious fooles heere in *Europa.* But to shew you examples neere home heere in *England,* as though our voice had the like operation: you shall not heare a butcher or horssecourser cheapen a bullocke or a jade, but if he buie him not, he saith, God save him; if he doo forget it, and the horsse or bullocke chance to die, the fault is imputed to the chapman. Certeinelie the sentence is godlie, if it doo proceed from a faithfull and a godlie mind: but if it be spoken as a superstitious charme, by those words and syllables to compound with the fascination and misadventure of infortunate words, the phrase is wicked and superstitious, though there were farre greater shew of godlinesse than appeereth therein.

Isigonus.
Memphra-
dorus.
Solon, &c.
Vairus.
J. Bodinus.
Mal. malef.

CHAPTER IX.

Of inchanting or bewitching eies.

MANIE writers agree with *Virgil* and *Theocritus* in the effect of witching eies, affirming that in *Scythia,* there are women called *Bithiæ,* having two balles or rather blacks in the apple of their eies. And as *Didymus* reporteth, some have in the one eie two such balles, and in the other the image of a horsse. These (forsooth) with their angrie lookes doo bewitch and hurt not onelie yoong lambs, but yoong children. There be other that reteine such venome in their eies, and send it foorth by beames and streames so violentlie, that therewith they annoie not onlie them with whom they are conversant continuallie; but also all other, whose companie they frequent, of what age, strength, or complexion soever they be: as *Cicero, Plutarch, Philarchus,* and manie others give out in their writings.

This fascination (saith *John Baptista Porta Neapolitanus*) though it begin by touching or breathing, is alwaies accomplished and finished by the eie, as an extermination or expulsion of the spirits through the eies, approching to the hart of the bewitched, and infecting the same, &c. Wherby it commeth to passe, that a child, or a yoong man endued with a cleare, whole, subtill and sweet bloud, yeeldeth the like spirits, breath, and vapors springing from the purer bloud of the hart. And the lightest and finest spirits, ascending into the highest parts of the head, doo fall into the eies, and so are from thence sent foorth, as being of all other parts of the bodie the most cleare, and fullest of

With the like propertie were the old Illyrian people: if we will credit the words of Sabinus grounded upon the report of Aul. Gell.
J. Bap. Neapol. in lib. de naturali magia.

This is held
of some for
truth.

veines and pores, and with the verie spirit or vapor proceeding thence, is conveied out as it were by beames and streames a certeine fierie force; whereof he that beholdeth sore eies shall have good experience. For the poison and disease in the eie infecteth the aire next unto it, and the same proceedeth further, carrieng with it the vapor and infection of the corrupted bloud: with the contagion whereof, the eies of the beholders are most apt to be infected. By this same meanes it is thought that the cockatrice depriveth the life, and a woolfe taketh awaie the voice of such as they suddenlie meete withall and behold.

*Non est in
speculo res
quæ specu-
latur in eo.*

Old women, in whome the ordinarie course of nature faileth in the office of purging their naturall monethlie humors, shew also some proofe hereof. For (as the said *J.B.P.N.* reporteth, alledging *Aristotle* for his author) they leave in a looking glasse a certeine froth, by meanes of the grosse vapors proceeding out of their eies. Which commeth so to passe, bicause those vapors or spirits, which so abundantlie come from their eies, cannot pearse and enter into the glasse, which is hard, and without pores, and therefore resisteth: but the beames which are carried in the chariot or conveiance of the spirits, from the eies of one bodie to another, doo pearse to the inward parts, and there breed infection, whilest they search and seeke for their proper region. And as these beames & vapors doo proceed from the hart of the one, so are they turned into bloud about the hart of the other: which bloud disagreeing with the nature of the bewitched partie, infeebleth the rest of his bodie, and maketh him sicke: the contagion wherof so long continueth, as the distempered bloud hath force in the members. And bicause the infection is of bloud, the fever or sicknes will be continuall; whereas if it were of choler, or flegme, it would be intermittent or alterable.

CHAPTER X.

Of naturall witchcraft for love, &c.

*Nescio quis
oculus tene-
ros mihi
fascinat ag-
nos,* saith
Virgil : and
thus Engli-
shed by
*Abraham
Fleming.*
I wote not I
What witching
eie
Doth use to
hant
My tender
lams
Sucking their
dams
And them
inchant,

BUT as there is fascination and witchcraft by malicious and angrie eies unto displeasure: so are there witching aspects, tending contrariwise to love, or at the least, to the procuring of good will and liking. For if the fascination or witchcraft be brought to passe or provoked by the desire, by the wishing and coveting of anie beautifull shape or favor, the venome is strained through the eies, though it be from a far, and the imagination of a beautifull forme resteth in the hart of the lover, and kindleth the fier wherewith it is afflicted. And bicause the most delicate, sweete, and tender bloud of the belooved doth there wander, his countenance is there represented shining in his owne bloud, and cannot there be quiet; and is so haled from thence, that the bloud of him that is wounded, reboundeth and slippeth into the wounder, according to the saieng of *Lucretius* the poet to the like purpose and meaning in these verses:

*Englished by
Abraham
Fleming.*

Idque petit corpus, mens unde est saucia amore,
Námque omnes plerúnque cadunt in vulnus, & illam
Emicat in partem sanguis, unde icimur ictu;
Et si cominùs est, os tum ruber occupat humor:

And to that bodie tis rebounded,
From whence the mind by love is wounded,
For in a maner all and some,
Into that wound of love doo come,

And to that part the bloud doth flee
From whence with stroke we striken bee,
If hard at hand, and neere in place,
Then ruddie colour filles the face.

Thus much may seeme sufficient touching this matter of naturall magicke; whereunto though much more may be annexed, yet for the avoiding of tediousnes, and for speedier passage to that which remaineth; I will breake off this present treatise. And now somewhat shall be said concerning divels and spirits in the discourse following.